W9-CMR-397

PAINTING
THE DARKNESS

ROBERT GODDARD

POSEIDON PRESS
NEW YORK · LONDON · TORONTO · SYDNEY · TOKYO

Poseidon Press
Simon & Schuster Building
Rockefeller Center
1230 Avenue of the Americas
New York, New York 10020

Originally published in Great Britain by Transworld Publishers Ltd.

POSEIDON PRESS is a registered trademark
of Simon & Schuster Inc.

POSEIDON‑PRESS colophon is a trademark
of Simon & Schuster Inc.

Manufactured in the United States of America

Quality Printing and Binding by:
Orange Graphics
P.O. Box 791
Orange, VA 22960 U.S.A.

To my mother

ACKNOWLEDGEMENT

I am grateful to the management of Ticehurst House Hospital, East Sussex, for access to the archives and grounds of the institution; and to my good friend Jeffrey Davis for information on the history of psychiatry drawn from his incomplete doctoral thesis on the subject.

THE DAVENALL FAMILY
(as at 1st October 1882)

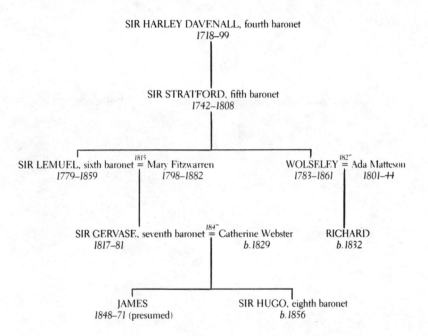

SIR HARLEY DAVENALL, fourth baronet
1718–99

SIR STRATFORD, fifth baronet
1742–1808

SIR LEMUEL, sixth baronet ¹⁸¹⁵= Mary Fitzwarren   WOLSELEY ^{182–}= Ada Matteson
1779–1859   *1798–1882*   *1783–1861*   *1801–44*

SIR GERVASE, seventh baronet ^{184–}= Catherine Webster   RICHARD
1817–81   *b.1829*   *b.1832*

JAMES   SIR HUGO, eighth baronet
1848–71 (presumed)   *b.1856*

ONE

I

It was ten years since William Trenchard had first met Constance Sumner and helped her begin to forget the tragedy of her fiancé's suicide. Absorbed at the time in a grief dangerously close to martyrdom, she had at first supposed that no man could ever mean nearly as much to her as the forever absent James Davenall. But in that, as in much else, she was wrong.

It was seven years since the newly married Trenchards had moved into The Limes, a St John's Wood town house acquired for them by William's father, co-founder of the Trenchard & Leavis retailing chain. They had seemed, in doing so, to absorb into their lives the restraint of the pollarded trees lining Avenue Road and the rectitude implicitly bricked and wainscoted within their stolid household. They must each have thought then that the uncertainties of youth were gone for good and all. But in that, as in much else, they were wrong.

It was four years since the birth of his daughter, Patience, had seemed to confirm that William's greater commitment of late to the business of Trenchard & Leavis was no transitory phenomenon. His father began then to believe that, even if William could never rival the energy and acumen of his brother Ernest, he was at least safe from making of his life anything that was less than respectable. But in that, as in much else, he was wrong.

It was just over a year since Constance, making her way one afternoon towards Regent's Park, where she intended to surprise Patience and her nanny during their customary sojourn by the boating-lake, had seemed to recognize, amongst a smattering of spectators bustling away from Lord's cricket ground, a sombre middle-aged man whose suit was too heavy for the warmth of the day. Later, entering the park by Hanover Gate, she had remembered who he was:

9

Richard Davenall, an older member of the family she had so nearly married into. She had thought then, and smiled to herself as she did so, how odd it was that she would never know any more of the affairs of the Davenall family, in which she had once been so closely involved. But in that, as in much else, she was wrong.

It was only two days since William Trenchard, proceeding in the opposite direction across the park at the dusty mist-tinged close of an Indian summer's day, had turned at the sound of laughter from a tree-hung bank that ran down to the lake, and had seen, reclining on the sun-stippled grass, a startlingly beautiful young woman in a pink dress, taking amused issue with her male admirer, who was crouched at her feet, waving his bowler hat in demonstration of a trivial point. The gesture had struck Trenchard as ludicrous, and he had smiled, then grown suddenly sombre. From all the daring beauty and unexpected drama he had fleetingly perceived in the girl's face, he felt excluded by age and dress and station. It was, of course, merely the sensation of a moment. He was not dissatisfied with his life, did not crave change or any disruption to the pattern of his existence. He was thirty-four years old; complacent, yes, but unworthy never. He had made his way home reflecting, a touch wearily, that the pleasures of his particular world possessed at least the warmth of utter security. But in that, as in much else, he was wrong.

It was only an hour since William Trenchard, tiring of pushing Patience on the swing old Burrows had rigged up beneath the stoutest of the apple trees, had packed his daughter off to bother his wife in the conservatory while he took a quiet Sunday-afternoon pipe, sat on the croquet bench and admired, as he often did, the great knotted tangles of wistaria that swathed the southern gable of the house. It was the first day of October 1882, but there seemed no other beginnings to detect in the mild autumnal air, there or elsewhere, in the whole, braced, eventless inertia of a secure unchanging Empire. Not that William Trenchard bothered overmuch with philosophy, or even patriotism beyond the level of a decent instinct. Indeed, he might have been judged if viewed from a little way off – through the open side-gate, perhaps – to embody most of what was worst and best in the limited imaginings of the average upper-middle-class Victorian gentleman. But in that, as in much else, he would have been wrongly judged. For only an hour later William Trenchard's life, and that of every occupant of The Limes, St John's Wood, had changed utterly – and for ever. An hour was all it took for ten years to overtake them.

II

Burrows must have left the side-gate open. I remember noticing it from where I was seated on the croquet bench and thinking how careless he was growing. Not that I was surprised, in view of his age, or even irritated, thanks to the soothing effects of good pipe tobacco and a splash of evening sunshine, but it drew my attention by the view it afforded of the drive in front of the house curving towards the road. Any slight movement in the street – where generally there was none – would have tended to catch my eye, and that – as no more than a flicker on the very edge of my vision – is how I first saw him.

It was six weeks later, in circumstances he could never have foreseen, that William Trenchard commenced a written account of the events which were to be set in motion that seemingly innocent Sunday afternoon in St John's Wood. His reason for writing such an account was as compelling as its effect is revealing, for it removes at a stroke the need to speculate about why he reacted as he did to the circumstances which overtook him. His every action, his every statement, stands justified or condemned – in his own words.

A tall slim man, elegantly dressed in dark top-hat, frock-coat and fawn trousers, carrying a silver-topped cane, stopped as he passed the entrance to the house, with just the barest scrape of leather sole on paving stone, drew up like one who had just remembered a commitment of no great importance. The sun caught the silver on his cane as he tossed it from his right hand to his left, twitched back his coat with his free hand and reached into his waistcoat pocket. He drew out a scrap of paper and looked at it, then replaced it and turned slowly in my direction.

I have struggled to recollect my immediate impression of him, laboured to erase all that subsequently happened so that I can see him clearly for what he was then: a man of about my own age, darkly handsome, bearded, though not extravagantly so, perfectly attired, tie-pin and watch-chain glinting, the thumb of one kid-gloved hand resting in his waistcoat pocket whilst the other swung the malacca cane in slow silent arcs beside him. I was sure I did not know him, even as a local resident: he looked as if St James's were more his mark than St John's Wood. There was something scarcely suburban about the tilt of his hat, something vaguely disturbing about the private smile hovering on his mouth.

He began to walk slowly up the drive, rather too slowly merely for decorum's sake, as if deliberately delaying the moment of his arrival. My attention, at first so idly focused, was now clamped upon him. As he passed the side-gate, he saw me watching him and, as he looked towards me, I felt suddenly cold.

He stepped through the brick-arched gateway, stooping slightly to clear the crown of his hat, and stood there, ten yards from me, neither advancing nor retreating, neither speaking nor motioning; daring me, as it were, to break the silence.

I rose from the bench and moved towards him. 'Good afternoon,' I said. 'Can I help you?'

'I am so sorry to intrude,' he said as I drew closer. 'Do I have the pleasure of addressing Mr William Trenchard?' The voice was rich and low-pitched, cultured and correct, a little too correct one might have said, a little too mannered for comfort.

'I am William Trenchard, yes. As you see' – I gestured at my shabby attire – 'we were not expecting visitors.'

'Forgive me. The circumstances of my visit are somewhat . . . unusual. They must excuse this . . . unannounced arrival.' He extended his hand. 'The name I go under is Norton. James Norton.'

His grip was firm and unwavering, mine anything but. 'Have we met before, Mr Norton?'

'We have not.'

'Is it, then, a matter of business? If so, Trenchard and Leavis are—'

'The matter is entirely personal . . . and profoundly delicate. I hardly know where to begin.'

I bridled. This proclaimed uncertainty clashed utterly with what I had so far seen of him. It smacked of a prepared approach. 'I think, Mr Norton, it would be as well if you stated your business plainly.'

He timed a pause perfectly to allow me to begin to believe he could be swiftly disposed of, then resumed as courteously as before. 'Of course. You are quite right. I said that we had not met before, and that is true. It is with your wife that I am acquainted.'

What man, even one as contentedly married as me, could have heard his wife spoken of in this way by a stranger without some frisson of an unworthy suspicion? 'What is your meaning, sir? I am acquainted with all my wife's friends, and you are not among them.'

He smiled. 'Perhaps I should have made myself clearer. Your wife and I knew each other many years ago, before you married her. In point of fact, we were at one time engaged.'

I felt then that I knew he was lying; felt relieved, indeed, that the lie was as obvious as this. 'You are mistaken, Mr Norton. Perhaps you have called at the wrong house.'

He continued undaunted. 'Your wife's maiden name was Sumner. We were engaged to be married eleven years ago. I have come here today—'

'You have come here today either under a grotesque misapprehension or under false pretences.' He could see now that I was angry, but there was no change in his expression. Perhaps he sensed that my anger was directed at myself as much as at him. Somewhere, beyond the reach of logic, I had begun to question Constance's account of her life before we

12

met. That, as much as the softly spoken Mr Norton, is what I was trying to talk down. 'My wife was engaged to another man eleven years ago, it's true. But that man is dead.'

'No.' He shook his head slowly, as if he were truly sorry to disillusion me. 'I'm afraid not, Mr Trenchard. I am that man. Not James Norton, but James Davenall. And, as you can see, far from dead.'

I was about to respond – with a request for him to leave in short order – when I saw Constance coming towards us from the house. She must have seen us from the conservatory and wondered who our visitor was. Mercifully, Patience was not with her. As it was, with his back turned towards her, Norton could not have known she was there, but may have guessed it from the look on my face. At all events, he continued as if playing to a gallery of more than one.

'I have not come here to antagonize you, nor to shock Constance, merely to seek her support in establishing my identity. There are, you see, those who wish to deny that I am James Davenall.'

These last words Constance must have heard. She pulled up sharply and frowned towards me in anxious puzzlement. A moment before, she had been the placidly beautiful woman I had married. Now, at the audible mention of that name, there crossed her face that cast of grief I had not seen since the earliest days of our acquaintance.

'What does this mean?' she said.

I should have answered, should have prepared her, should have armed her against him. But I hesitated, and in the moment of my hesitation Norton turned and looked directly at her. I could not see his face, but I could see Constance's and could read there, as he must have done, the uncertainty that proclaimed louder than any words: it might be true.

'It's no ghost you see, Connie,' he said. 'It's me, true enough. I'm so sorry to have deceived you.'

She moved closer, eyeing him with rigid scrutiny, erasing from her features that initial eloquent moment of doubt. 'There is no need to apologize,' she said levelly. 'You have not deceived me. There has been a mistake. You are not James Davenall.'

He replied softly, with nerveless conviction. 'You know that I am.'

'James Davenall took his own life eleven years ago.'

'Until a moment ago, you could believe that. Now you know it isn't true.'

I decided it was time to intervene. I stepped forward and took Constance's arm. There we stood, together against him, we on the grass, he on the gravel, shadows lengthening about us. 'What do you want of us, Mr Norton?'

'I had hoped that Connie – that your wife – would be prepared to admit that she knows me. I have been turned away by my family and—'

13

'You have been to them?' said Constance.

'Yes. I have been to them – and they have set their faces against me.' He glanced at his feet, as if pained by the thought, then back at us or, rather, at Constance, for I had become a mere observer of their exchanges. 'Will you join them in their pretence – or listen to my explanation? There is much that I have to tell you.'

'Mr Norton,' she replied, 'I do not know what purpose you think will be served by this macabre fiction, but you may take it that I wish to hear no more of it.'

'If only it were as simple as that,' he said. 'I tried to pretend myself that James Davenall no longer existed – and I didn't succeed. Now others are making the same mistake.'

'Excuse me, Mr Norton. There is nothing more to be said.' She turned and walked back towards the house. As he watched her go, I scanned his face for the deceit or devilry I expected to find there, but found only a questing sadness. Absurdly, it made me feel almost callous in saying what I said next.

'Will you leave now? Or must I summon a constable?'

He seemed to ignore the question. 'I'm staying in the hotel at Paddington station. When Connie's had a chance to think about it . . .'

'We will not be thinking about you, Mr Norton. We will be doing our best to pretend you never came here, which is what I advise you to do as well. You have heard our last word on the matter.'

'I think not.'

Before I could say anything else, he turned and walked smartly back through the side-gate and away down the drive. As soon as he was out of sight, I headed for the house.

I found Constance in the drawing-room. She was standing before the wood-framed mirror that topped the mantelpiece, around which was arranged a selection of family photographs: her parents, mine, her late brother, Patience playing with a bauble at the age of three months. And our wedding: May Day 1875. An assortment of Trenchards and Sumners striking poses in the palm-fringed ballroom of a Wiltshire hotel. A perfect marriage of church and trade and the ghost at the feast still seven years in the future.

I put my arm round her shoulders. 'He's gone now. I'm sorry if he upset you.'

She shuddered. 'It's not that.'

'There's no possibility, is there, that he could be who he says he is? I know Davenall was supposed to have drowned, but . . .'

Her eyes met mine in the mirror. 'You saw it, too, then?'

'I saw nothing. It's for you to say. You knew him.'

She turned and looked at me directly. 'James died. We all know that. There was . . . a resemblance. But not enough. And yet . . .'

14

'You can't be absolutely certain?'

'Perhaps I should have listened to him.'

'It would have nailed the lie soon enough if you had. As it is, he can claim we didn't give him a fair chance to state his case.'

She fell silent, leaning against me and rocking slightly as she thought. I heard the clock ticking with exaggerated solemnity on the mantelpiece beside us. From above came the patter of Patience's feet in the nursery and a splash of water: it was bath-time for our daughter.

'He's just a fraudster, Connie. There's a baronetcy at stake – and an inheritance, too. Missing heirs are meat and drink to these fellows. Remember the Tichborne nonsense?'

She looked up at me as if she had not heard a word. 'I need to be sure. It is . . . just possible. We must speak to his family.'

'Very well,' I said. 'I'll see them – tonight if I can. That should settle it.'

III

A little after six o'clock that evening, William Trenchard picked up a cab in the Wellington Road and bade it take him to Bladeney House, Chester Square, the London residence of Sir Hugo Davenall. He sat well back in the cab and smoked a pipe to calm his nerves while the driver made good time through the sabbath-emptied streets.

Quite why he was so nervous he was not sure. Socially, he and the Davenalls were clearly worlds apart. Had Constance been their daughter, marriage to the son of a shopkeeper, which, making all due allowances for old Lionel Trenchard's success, William undoubtedly was, would have been out of the question. He had, as a matter of fact, never met any of them. His knowledge of them was entirely confined to what Constance had told him. Perhaps this, after all, was the root of his present insecurity. An unannounced visit on a Sunday evening was certain to be forgiven in view of the compelling circumstances, but the suddenly shifting sands of what had always seemed to him so firmly, if tragically, founded – his wife's past – were quite another matter. As the cab turned into Baker Street and slowed reverentially at sight of a Salvation Army parade in the Marylebone Road, Trenchard began to review in his mind what little he actually knew.

James Davenall and Constance's late brother, Roland Sumner, had been contemporaries at Oxford. James commenced paying suit to Constance shortly after coming down, and their engagement was announced in the autumn of 1870. Canon Sumner viewed this imminent connection with a titled family as a social triumph – which it was – and arranged for his daughter's wedding to take place in

15

Salisbury Cathedral. Barely a week before the ceremony was due, in June 1871, Davenall vanished utterly, the only clue to his intentions being a note left at his family's country residence near Bath, which seemed to allow no room for doubt that he meant to take his life. His movements were traced to London, where a cabby recalled dropping him near the riverside in Wapping. There, it was assumed, he had drowned himself, the Thames bearing his corpse out to sea. No reason for such an act was ever adduced, its total inexplicability serving only to deepen the tragedy.

When Trenchard first met Constance, she was still bowed down by the numb grief of Davenall's disappearance, followed as it was within five months by her brother Roland's death in a riding accident. Trenchard never wished to see her again as she was then: habituated to mourning with a pellucid, frozen beauty that only the long absence of happiness could have bred. Theirs had been a difficult but ultimately rewarding road from that day to this, and he had no intention of turning back. The thought stiffened his nerve as the cab passed down Park Lane. If he had his way, nothing from that time – least of all James Davenall – should ever reappear.

What, he wondered, had Sir Hugo Davenall made of Norton? He had inherited the baronetcy in the spring of 1881 – Trenchard remembered reading of it in the newspaper – and could not have welcomed this sudden threat to his position. But was it any real threat at all? No, Trenchard told himself. It was just a cool-nerved attempt at bare-faced fraud, doomed to failure from the outset. If so, his dash to Chester Square might seem to smack of panic. But that could not be helped.

The cab pulled up with a jolt. They were there, before the railed-off balconied frontage of a tall Regency house. Trenchard climbed out, paid off the driver and looked about him. Dusk was settling on the square, pigeons cooing on their nocturnal perches among the pediments and pillars. The cab clopped away and left him, feeling slightly foolish, at a lordly stranger's door.

IV

At Bladeney House, a stern-faced servant showed me into a tile-flagged hall. I remember light flooding down a curving staircase, silhouetting a figure in evening dress who was slowly descending to meet me. A tall, loose-limbed young man with dark tousled hair, and bloodshot, almost bruised eyes. He was smoking a cigar and did not remove it from his wide, full-lipped mouth as he said to his servant: 'Visitor, Greenwood?'

'A Mr Trenchard, sir. I have not yet established—'

16

'Sir Hugo?' I interrupted.

'The very same.' He paused on the bottom stair, removed the cigar and essayed a satirical, stiff-shouldered bow.

'Good evening, sir. I'm married to your late brother's former fiancée, Miss Constance Sumner as was. We've met a Mr Norton—'

'Norton?' He jerked his head upright at the word, scattering cigar ash on the stair-carpet. 'You've seen the blighter, too?'

'Yes. He claims—'

'I know what he damn well claims.' His lip quivered visibly. 'Man's a charlatan.'

'I realize that.'

'Mmm?' He looked at me. 'Yes, of course. You would.' A moment's thought, a puff on the cigar, then: 'Come through, Trenchard. I can't stop long, but long enough, eh?' He clapped me on the shoulder and ushered me towards a door, tossing back a dismissal to his servant as we went. 'We'll be in the music room, Greenwood.'

We passed through a richly furnished anteroom that looked out on to the square, then turned towards open double doors where, beyond, I could see french windows giving on to a garden. Somebody was playing an irreverent ballad on a finely tuned piano.

'Could have done without this nonsense,' Sir Hugo lisped on his cigar. 'Just a bloody nuisance as far as I'm concerned.'

We entered the music room. A young sandy-haired man turned from the piano and beamed in our direction. He, too, was in evening dress. The other occupant of the room, a middle-aged man seated in an armchair by the french windows, was not; he laid aside a newspaper and rose to meet us, smiling amiably.

'The appalling pianist is a friend of mine, Trenchard,' said Sir Hugo. 'Freddy Cleveland. If you follow the turf at all, you'll probably have lost money on one of his nags.'

For all his boyish good looks, Cleveland was not as young as I had at first thought; there were creases about his eyes when he smiled. I took him for the affected, dim-witted type a youthful baronet might be expected to befriend and felt, all at once, out of my depth amidst their West End quips.

'Mr Trenchard don't look the race-goin' type, Hugo,' Cleveland said as he shook my hand.

'Indeed I'm not.'

'But he is here', Sir Hugo put in, 'about the damned maverick that's cantered into our paddock.' He turned to the third man. 'My cousin, Richard Davenall, also my legal adviser.'

Richard Davenall was grey-haired and bearded, his face lined with the cares of his profession, sombrely suited and dejectedly slope-shouldered, a wearily tolerant look in his watery sea-blue eyes. He shook my hand with none of the gusto of the other two but with rather more conviction.

'Trenchard?' he said quizzically. 'Didn't you marry Constance Sumner?'

'I had that honour, sir, yes.'

'I was glad to hear she'd settled down . . . after what happened. Do I take it you've heard from Norton?'

'Yes. That's why I'm here.'

'How did your wife react?'

'She was horrified by his claim. When he said he'd already been to see his family, the real James's family that is—'

'You thought you'd better check the lie of the land,' said Sir Hugo. 'Don't blame you. Want a drink?'

'No, thank you.'

'Fetch me a Scotch and soda, Freddy, there's a good fellow. Sure you won't have one, Trenchard?'

'Quite, thank you.'

While Cleveland pattered off to the drinks-trolley, Sir Hugo slumped into an armchair and gestured for me to do the same. Richard Davenall resumed his place by the french windows. Cleveland returned with a large glass for Sir Hugo and one for himself, then went back to the piano stool, from where he surveyed us with a child-like grin.

'Freddy finds the situation amusing,' said Sir Hugo. 'I suppose I would myself in his shoes.'

'It does have a comical element,' said Cleveland. 'The man's a capital actor. He's got Jimmy's dress sense, and that soft voice of his, off to a T.'

Sir Hugo took a swig from his glass. 'An actor who's learned his lines. That's all.'

'You can't be sure, though, can you?' Cleveland continued. 'That's the beauty of it. Do you know, last winter, I bumped into old Cazabon on the Brighton train – or thought I did. Looked like Cazabon, talked like Cazabon, but denied it to my face. Said he was a dentist from Haywards Heath. Got off there, too, just to prove the point. Like peas in a pod, they were. Just goes to show, you see. Of course, Cazabon did owe me money, so maybe it was him after all.' He laughed hoarsely – and alone.

I decided to come to the point. 'Sir Hugo, I never met your brother, but my wife assures me there is no possibility that he and Norton could be one and the same. Is that the view of you and your family also?'

Sir Hugo was still gazing with restrained wrath at Cleveland. 'Of course it is.'

Then Richard Davenall came to my rescue. 'Perhaps I might elucidate the situation for you, Trenchard. This man Norton presented himself five days ago at Cleave Court in Somerset, where Hugo's

18

mother lives, claiming to be her dead son James. Lady Davenall saw through the imposture at once and sent him away. On Friday, he called on me at my offices in Holborn. Yesterday—'

'He turned up here,' said Sir Hugo with a scowl. 'I had the blighter thrown out.'

'And none of us', his cousin continued, 'entertained his claim for a moment. With his visit to you, I imagine he has run the gamut of those he hoped to deceive.'

'I thought his old nanny took him in her arms,' Cleveland put in, 'and called him Jamie?'

A snort from Sir Hugo. 'The woman's senile.'

'It is true', said Richard Davenall, 'that Nanny Pursglove acknowledged Norton as her former charge. She lives in a cottage on the estate, Trenchard, you understand, and Norton looked her up. But it is also true that she is over eighty, with poor eyesight and a touching wish to believe that James is still alive. Against James's own mother, and brother, not to mention his former fiancée, such support will count for nothing.'

'In that case, gentlemen,' I said, 'can we safely discount Mr Norton? My only concern is that he should cease to distress my wife.'

'I think so,' said Richard Davenall. 'As long as he lacks a single advocate within James's intimate circle, he can scarcely hope to be of more than nuisance value. Thanks to the amount of circumstantial information he has diligently amassed, however, that nuisance could be quite considerable.'

'I'll not buy him off,' said Sir Hugo with sudden violence. 'He'll not have a penny from me.'

'Then, he may go to the sensation-seeking end of the national press,' said his cousin, 'and plaster his claims over their front pages. Would it not be preferable—'

'No!' Sir Hugo slammed his glass down on a side-table to emphasize his point. 'Show him nothing but silent contempt – and he'll slink back to the crevice he came from.'

'As you please.'

'Yes, Richard, it is as I please. I'm head of this family now, as you'd do well to remember.' A silence fell, during which Cleveland continued to grin inanely while Sir Hugo appeared to realize that he might have gone too far. He resumed in a more conciliatory tone. 'Have you found out who this Norton really is yet?'

'These are early days, Hugo. If there's a real James Norton to be traced, we will trace him. But I imagine he's covered his tracks well.'

'Talking of tracks,' said Cleveland, 'shouldn't we be making 'em, Hugo? Gussie will be disappointed if we're not there by nine.'

I took the opportunity to make my excuses and depart. Superficially, they had reassured me, but I dared not stay to see the fragility of their

19

conviction grow ever more apparent. The Davenalls, of whom I had been so long in awe, seemed, on this showing, no better or worse than any family, no more proof than my own against a well-armed intruder.

As I made to leave, Richard Davenall volunteered to go out with me. We left Sir Hugo contemplating ruefully the dimples of his whisky-glass while Cleveland checked his bow-tie in a mirror above the piano. Greenwood was waiting in the hall to hand us our hats and gloves.

'Where do you live, Trenchard?' Davenall asked as we descended the front steps.

'St John's Wood.'

'I'm for Highgate. Shall we travel some of the way together? We can pick up a cab at the corner.'

I agreed readily; sensed, indeed, that he wanted an opportunity to share his thoughts with me away from his cousin's bellicose indignation. We walked slowly in the direction of Grosvenor Place, our footsteps echoing back from the tall and silent house-fronts of the square, where night had fallen with cool, aloof indifference.

'I must apologize for Sir Hugo,' Davenall said. 'Sometimes he seems younger even than his years.'

'It is not long since he inherited the baronetcy, I believe.'

'Indeed not. Barely eighteen months. Yes, the boy's had a good deal to cope with. Sir Gervase's final illness was a lengthy one – and then there was the business of having James legally pronounced dead.'

'Was that only done recently?'

'It could have been done as soon as seven years had elapsed, especially in view of the clear indications of suicide, but Sir Gervase would never hear of it.'

'Did he not believe his son was dead?'

'He claimed to doubt it, which was odd. He was not a man to entertain sentimental notions in any other connection. At all events, the necessary legal moves were not put in hand until Sir Gervase was non compos mentis, so that Hugo's title did not become clear until somewhat late in the day. What with that and taking on the running of the estate – Sir Gervase had rather let things slip, I'm afraid – Hugo can claim some excuse for displaying signs of strain. Nevertheless . . .'

'It's of no account, Mr Davenall. I'm glad to have had my mind put at rest.'

Of course, it was not truly at rest – as, I think, Richard Davenall perceived. After we had procured a cab and started north together, he volunteered some more of his family's troubles. For a solicitor, he was strangely forthcoming, as if finding in me the audience he sought for his own misgivings.

'It has, in all conscience, been a difficult year for my family, Trenchard. Hugo's grandmother was killed in February by intruders in her house. She was extremely old, and had lived, out of touch, in

20

Ireland for many years, but her death cast a distressing shadow of needless violence. Hugo inherits an estate in County Mayo through her. She was an eligible heiress when Hugo's grandfather, my uncle Lemuel, married her, oh, nearly seventy years ago, but she never took to life in England and went back to Ireland as soon as her son came of age. Sir Gervase — well, all of us — rather neglected her, I fear. I suppose a rambling old house, poorly staffed and containing what few signs of wealth are to be detected in that Godforsaken wilderness, must have attracted the wrong kind of attention.'

I thought I detected his drift. 'Not from these appalling Fenians?'

'I don't think so: Mary never ill-treated her tenants. I believe robbery was the intention and that Mary simply got in the way: she was a spirited old soul. Not that Hugo agrees with me. Since the Phoenix Park murders, he sees Fenians behind every lamp-post. He won't hear of going over there.'

'I can't say I blame him.'

'Nor I. But now Norton crawls out of the woodwork to make London uncomfortable for him as well. We seem not so much unlucky as . . . ill-fated.'

Fate. He had said the word which had swirled like November fog round my journey to and from Bladeney House. So now I had to ask him. 'Mr Davenall, there's a question I must put to you. I know what you said in Sir Hugo's presence, but this man Norton . . .'

'Could he be James?'

'Yes. That is what I cannot help wondering.'

'It is why you called tonight. Had your wife been absolutely certain, you would not have required a second opinion.'

'It is true. I cannot deny the man has me rattled. Constance and I would never have married, would never have met—'

'Had James lived — or not disappeared. Well, his own mother disowned him and his brother likewise. What more do you want?'

'Your unequivocal judgement, I suppose — as a man of the law.'

The cab lurched to a halt. We were at Gloucester Gate, where I had asked to be dropped. Davenall leaned out through the window and told the driver to do a circuit of the park. Clearly, whatever else his judgement was, it was not unequivocal. He eased himself back into the seat with a slight but audible sigh.

'You seem to hesitate, sir. As did my wife when I asked her the same.'

'And for the same reason, Trenchard. Hugo was only fifteen when James disappeared and, besides, must see Norton as a threat both to his title and to his wealth, all of which would revert to his brother if he were alive. So Hugo cannot be looked to for a rational judgement. His mother certainly appears to be in no doubt that the man is an imposter. I have not spoken to Catherine myself, but I gather she is quite adamant on the point. I, of course, had the advantage — which she did

21

not – of being forewarned. When Norton presented himself at my offices, I knew what to expect.'

'A fraudster?'

'Yes. That is what I expected. And that is what I still believe him to be. For what else, after all, could he be? It is inconceivable that James should have staged his disappearance and then, having done so, return eleven years later. Unaccountable though his suicide was, it cannot be gainsaid by a mere fortune-hunter, however accomplished.'

'If he claims to be James, he must have an explanation for his conduct.'

'He says he has one. But I refused to hear it. When – or if – it comes to that, I want witnesses, Trenchard, I want us to hear his story together, so that it cannot be twisted or tailored to suit our individual susceptibilities. I want there to be no room for doubt.'

'Is there, then . . . room for doubt?'

'I would have to admit that there is. To say Norton is not the James Davenall we knew is easy enough. But we knew a carefree young man. He was twenty-three when he vanished, about to be married, seemingly with everything to live for. Yet we know that was not the truth, that something – never to this day explained – was tragically wrong with his life. So, eleven years later, how would we expect him to be? Catherine's letter to Hugo prepared me for a blustering imposter trading on a vague physical resemblance and a good memory for the facts he had unearthed. But that is not how he was. Sad, lonely, refined, baffled but unsurprised by our denial of him. And, yes, I have to say it: a little like James might have been.'

Silence followed, but for the clop of the horse's hoofs and the creak of swaying leather, silence in the still and gentle night, enough for us each to contemplate the strange, dark, gaping possibility: Norton might be James Davenall after all. Somewhere, across the city, alone in his hotel room, he might be staring at the blank wall that was his family's reception of an unwelcome prodigal, leaving the Davenalls and me united in one unworthy wish: that he should stay dead. I wanted no ghost of my wife's lost love to cross our lives, far less proclaim himself no ghost at all. Though never expressed in words, I knew she had accepted me as second-best to a dead man, and that was good enough, good enough just so long as he was truly dead.

'I think I'll get out here,' I said. 'I think I'd like to walk the rest of the way home.'

Davenall leaned out and gave the order to the driver, then held the door open for me. 'I'm sorry I couldn't give you what you asked for, Trenchard.'

'Unequivocal judgement, you mean?' I said, looking back as I climbed out. 'Perhaps I asked for too much.'

'I am a lawyer,' he replied. 'My profession deals in opinion. What you seek is for judge and jury to decide.'

'Will it come to that?'

'If Norton continues to make no headway, or if Sir Hugo heeds my advice to buy him off – I don't think so. But if Norton thinks he can win, or, of course, if he is genuine, then it may do. It may very well do. Here's my card.' I took it from his extended hand. 'Keep in touch. We may need to talk again.' He slapped the side of the cab and was borne away.

V

Avenue Road was but a twenty-minute walk from where Trenchard left the cab, yet it took him nearly twice that time to cover the distance, walking slowly, head bowed, stirring with his feet the leaves that lay about the pavement, listening to the faint rustle of others falling, dislodged in the tender nocturnal breeze. An owl hooted in the woodland of the park, a distant hansom jingled its fare towards Marylebone. And Trenchard's mind voyaged backwards, to another mellow autumn ten years before, to Canon Sumner's drawing-room in Salisbury, where shafts of sunlight split the gloom of Constance Sumner's mournful vigil. If Davenall had come back then, he would have found her waiting.

'They tell me', she had said, 'that he is dead. Yet to believe that would seem a kind of betrayal.'

'Your refusal to believe it does you credit,' Trenchard had said. 'Yet surely he would not have wanted you to turn away from life simply because, for some reason, he has chosen to.'

At first, she had resisted. When, later, she had yielded to his healing charm, Canon Sumner had pronounced it a truly Christian act and Trenchard had basked in his gratitude. Now, already, Norton had forced him to reappraise that fine and patient courtship. It had always been more calculating than he would have cared to admit, for there had been a vulnerability in her bereavement and he had played upon it. Worse, there had been the pleasure, the secret satisfaction, of winning her from another, a hint of the adulterous in what had been so transparently correct. Without his insidious conquest of her affections, she might have remained loyal to a memory, might have gone on believing the incredible long enough to see it come true.

He turned into Avenue Road, still absorbed in the resentful flow of his unwelcome memories. He approached The Limes slowly, preparing in his mind the assurances he would give Constance, rehearsing the means by which he would conceal his doubts from her. It was not easy, as is so little that is not honest, and in its difficulty we may find the means to explain a greater error.

23

In the shadow cast by the last tree before the entrance to The Limes – a pool of inky black amidst the encircling moonlit grey – stood James Norton, watching Trenchard as he approached. He had taken shelter beneath the tree at sight of the other drawing near but might well have assumed, even so, that he could not escape being noticed. As it was, Trenchard walked straight and steadily by, looking neither to right nor to left, and turned up the drive to his home.

Norton remained motionless for several minutes, until he heard the distant click of a front door closing and the rattle of a bolt being slipped. Then he seemed to smile, or it may just have been that a shard of moonlight caught his mouth as he moved for the first time. Reaching into his coat pocket, he drew out a silver cigarette-case, on which – who knew? – had it been light enough, a tell-tale monogram might have been visible. A moment later came the brief yellow flare of a match, a faint sigh of pleasure at the first inhalation, then the sound of his footsteps as he moved away, a mobile shadow in the stationary night, leaving only a drift of smoke and an acrid scent among the moon-blanched leaves.

TWO

I

Constance Trenchard slept poorly that night. Having waited up for her husband to return from Bladeney House, she had found him first reassuring and then, upon being questioned, uncharacteristically testy. They had, at length, retired to bed in a mutually shocked silence born of dismay at how easily and swiftly an interloper could disturb their equilibrium.

Not that, Constance was ashamed to admit to herself over a solitary breakfast on the morrow, it was William's evident distress that had occupied her during so many sleepless hours. His was not the face she had seen whenever she had closed her eyes, his were not the words she had struggled, despite herself, to retrieve from the distant season of a last, remembered meeting. She watched the sunlight from the window wreath itself in the plumes of steam rising from her coffee, felt her mind drift to a Somerset meadow sown with rank grass and the casual splendour of a summer afternoon. Poppies splashed and scattered amid the yellow carpet of flowers, intentions suspended in the airless oven of sudden crisis. June 1871. So near and yet so very, very far. His face, carved like cool ivory as he looked at her, in his eyes a veiled and questioning sorrow that could have been contempt. He drew his hand away from her. 'This is how it begins,' he had said haltingly. 'And this is how it ends.'

'Second post, ma'am.' It was Hillier, with her dumpling grin, and a silver salver bearing a clutch of newly arrived letters.

Constance looked at them. All for William, save one. Addressed to her in a sloping, correct, reminiscent hand. The similarity was sufficient to make her wrench it open without reaching for the letter-knife.

25

Great Western Royal Hotel
Praed Street
LONDON W.

1st October 1882

Dear Constance,

I hope my handwriting has not also changed beyond recognition. Of course, I was never much of a letter-writer, was I?
Now it seems the only way I can communicate with you to any
purpose.

I am sorry to have shocked you by arriving unannounced
this afternoon. Yet how could it not have been a shock? I can
only say that I left eleven years ago for the best of reasons and
have returned now for the same. I would wish to explain all
that lies behind this statement, but I feel it must await an
occasion when we can talk freely, face to face. Will you grant
me that one favour – for old times' sake? You will find me here
waiting, should you feel able to call. Naturally, I shall not call
at The Limes again until I know it is with your approval.

Neither of us can forget, can we, what happened in that
meadow? Perhaps I should have explained then. I would like
to do so now, more than I can properly tell. Concede, I beg
you, the possibility that I may warrant your forgiveness – and
your recognition.

Ever yours,
James

Constance replaced the letter in its jaggedly torn envelope and rose
unsteadily from the table. She reminded herself that she was no longer
the slip of a girl who might have swooned at the prospect of her fiancé's
return. She asserted her mature level-headed womanhood by the calm
precision with which she slid her chair beneath the table, then turned
and walked slowly to the door.

In the hallway, Hillier was dusting energetically, humming in
rhythm to her work. She looked up at her mistress and smiled.

'Lovely morning, ma'am.'

'Yes, Hillier. Indeed it is. You may clear breakfast whenever you
wish. Where is Patience?'

'In the nursery, ma'am, learning 'er alphabet.'

Constance nodded. 'Did Mr Trenchard intimate whether he would
be returning here for luncheon?'

''E thought not, ma'am.'

'I see. Thank you. I will be in the drawing-room if you need me.'

'Very good, ma'am.'

The girl went back to her work with a will, but, just in case she

26

should be watching, Constance moved down the hall with measured, restrained treads. She turned into the drawing-room and closed the door behind her.

Against the wall facing the window stood a modest walnut bureau. Constance stood in front of it and lowered the lid, which was never locked, then reached into one of the pigeon-holes for the key to the small drawer which she was in the habit of securing. It opened at one turn.

This drawer housed Constance's few preserved personal letters; its sanctity was respected by William, who stored his papers and correspondence in a more substantial escritoire in the study. The bundle, fastened with pink legal tape rather than with any obviously feminine ribbon, was a slender one: Constance was no sentimental hoarder. But she had retained, long unread, one letter of James Davenall's and it was to this that she wished now to refer.

She slid it out without untying the tape and laid it beside Norton's letter on the blotter, scrutinizing and comparing the handwriting of each. One was in blue ink, the other in black. She could not say, with hand on heart, that they had been written by the same man, nor yet by different men. They were eleven years and who knew what experiences apart, and Constance was well aware that James's letter had been scribed with much less deliberation and in far greater haste than Norton's. She opened it to remind herself of the contents. It was as she recalled, a scrawled urgent message on the headed notepaper of his London club.

16th June 1871

Dearest Connie,
I must hurry if I am to catch the post and so ensure that this reaches you tomorrow morning. I will, by then, be heading in the same direction.
    The reason for my abrupt visit to London and the reason why I do not wish to return directly to Cleave Court are the same. Please – if you love me – be at the aqueduct at noon tomorrow. I will walk down from Bathampton and meet you there.

All my love,
James

Staying at Cleave Court for a few days prior to the wedding, Constance had become irritated by how little time she and James were able to spend together that was not shared by assorted members of the Davenall household. There had ensued James's sudden departure for London and this strange summons to a noon rendezvous just one week short of the day itself. She had not forgotten and nor, it seemed, had Norton.

She returned the letter to its envelope, then slid it and Norton's

27

communication into the bundle, dropped it back into the drawer and turned the key. Ordinarily, the key belonged in one of the pigeon-holes, but this time she slipped it into the small felt pouch that hung from the belt at her waist. Then she took out some notepaper and a pen, opened the inkstand and began to write a letter of her own.

Its composition was neither easy nor swift. Indeed, the clock showed nearly eleven when she sealed the envelope, affixed the stamp and pressed the address to the blotter. She took a deep breath, rose and left the room.

It was not Constance's custom – nor that of any lady – to post her own letters, but she decided that the fineness of the morning would seem an adequate excuse for doing so on this occasion. It was probable, indeed, that Hillier would not even know she had gone. Accordingly, donning only a boater to shade her eyes, she stepped out of the front door and walked smartly in the direction of the pillar box which lay but a hundred yards distant. She was surprised by how hot she felt and was grateful for the breeze that fanned her flushed cheeks.

On reaching the box, she glanced once more at the letter in her hand. It was odd, she thought, to have waited so long to address a letter thus. She pushed it into the box and heard it fall with the rest.

II

I was in the office above the Orchard Street branch on the Thursday following my visit to Bladeney House when I heard of Norton's next move. I had been standing by the window, listening inattentively to Parfitt, the manager, whilst he explained at length the aesthetic and commercial advantages of a new marbled mosaic design for the cold meats department and had ceased to wonder why the poor man could not see that it was my father, not me, who would have to be persuaded of the case for such expenditure. Instead, I had gazed into the street and watched the traffic's ceaseless bustle, had heard the rattle and rumble of the carts and the cry of a newspaper-vendor rising behind Parfitt's monotone and had asked myself, as I had lately found myself asking in any idle moment: Where is he now? What is he doing?

An answer, of a kind, came sooner than I might have expected. A familiar figure turned aside from the throng of Oxford Street and crossed the road, bound, it seemed, for our door. He looked up as he did so and, catching my eye, touched his hat in salutation. It was Richard Davenall.

Poor Parfitt was at once cut short and asked to ensure that my imminent guest was shown up promptly. Within a few minutes, Davenall was seated opposite me, breathing heavily and apologizing for having given no warning of his visit.

'I would have written, but I thought you might value some discussion of the point.'

'Have you heard from Norton again, then?'

'Mr Norton has engaged a solicitor to prosecute his claim. Warburton, of Warburton, Makepeace and Thrower. A respected man, though more so for his results than for his methods. The firm is noted for its occasional unorthodoxy and might therefore seem the natural choice. Yet, in my eyes, it weakens Norton's case.'

'In what way?'

'It is hard to believe that James, were he alive, would resort to such a man. And, besides, Warburton does not come cheap. Perhaps you have asked yourself where Norton's money comes from. He deigns to stay in a railway hotel, it is true, but he appears to contemplate expensive litigation. How is he funding all this?'

'Have you any ideas?'

'None. Mr Norton remains a blank. But we are shortly to be given the opportunity to determine just how blank, which is the subject of my visit. Warburton has proposed a formal examination of Norton's claim, a meeting between him and the interested parties, before witnesses. I had thought you might wish to attend.'

'Very much. Does this mean that Norton will have to substantiate his claim by providing satisfactory answers to detailed questions, or, failing that, admit the whole thing is a hoax?'

'Exactly so. Warburton's offices next Wednesday, the eleventh. I have suggested to Sir Hugo that those attending should meet at Bladeney House the previous evening to agree how matters should be handled. The examination could prove fraught, but, if it succeeds in crushing this imposture at the outset, it will certainly be worth while.'

'It seems too good to be true.'

Richard smiled. 'I fear you may be right, Trenchard. Sir Hugo thinks it will cook Norton's goose, but my impression is that he would not have agreed to this if he did not think he could emerge unscathed.'

I rose from my desk and returned to the window. I needed its distractions to lessen the sense in which I felt that Constance and I were undermining the Davenalls' case. 'It might reflect the confidence of one who knows he is right.'

Davenall swivelled in his chair and looked towards me. 'There is that, too. Yet it has to be faced, sooner or later.'

'Perhaps you should know, then, that my wife is not to be looked to for a categorical refutation of Norton's claim.'

Only a twitch of one eyebrow betrayed his reaction. 'I see.' A pause, then: 'I imagine that places you in a difficult, not to say delicate, position.'

I walked back across the room and settled my elbow on the mantelpiece beneath the oil painting of Ephraim Leavis. 'Yes. It does.

*However, I hope the difficulty will soon be resolved. Constance has
written to Lady Davenall, suggesting that they should meet to discuss
what has happened. And Lady Davenall has been kind enough to invite
us to visit her at Cleave Court on Saturday to do just that. I am
confident that she will convince Constance where I have so far failed.
Indeed, I thought you might have heard of the invitation and guessed its
purpose.'*

For the first time, Davenall's legal calm seemed ruffled. 'Catherine
retains her own solicitor in Bath, who will doubtless represent her at the
examination. She is not in the habit of communicating with me.
Generally, I only hear from her through Sir Hugo.'

'Forgive me. I did not mean to intrude.'

The smile reasserted itself. 'There is nothing to forgive. What you
propose is most desirable. Catherine and your wife were once very close,
I believe. They will be able to reassure each other. It is timely, most
timely.'

'You really think so?'

'I do, without doubt.' He rose from his chair, with something of an
effort: there was a touch of fatigue in his words and movements. 'But I
must be on my way. Time and tide, et cetera. We will meet at Bladeney
House next Tuesday – at eight o'clock?'

'I'll be there.'

'Good, good. Until then.' We shook hands and, as we did so, he must
have sensed my downcast mood. 'Does something worry you about this
visit to Cleave Court, Trenchard?'

I looked straight at him. 'What should there be to worry me?'

'I don't know.'

'Nor do I. And perhaps that is it. Perhaps what worries me is the
thought that I might not know my wife as well as I should.'

He grasped my forearm sympathetically. 'Steady, man. The probability is that, a week from now, it will all be over. Then you will be
able to smile at such thoughts. Trust me: Mr Norton is just a nine days'
wonder.'

III

James Norton had, as a matter of fact, already exceeded Richard
Davenall's estimate of his span by three days when, on Saturday, 7th
October 1882, William and Constance Trenchard entrained at
Paddington station for their visit to Cleave Court. They arrived late,
studiously eschewing mention of the possibility that Norton might,
even then, be breakfasting at his ease in the adjoining hotel, and
settled themselves hastily in a first-class compartment. After indulging

in some peripheral conversation concerning the arrangements made for Patience's entertainment during their absence and commenting briefly on the kindness of the weather as the sun emerged over the tree-dotted valley of the River Brent, each subsided into the safety of reading, in William's case that morning's issue of *The Times*, in Constance's a collection of sonnets by Charles Tennyson Turner.

Neither was, in truth, absorbed in such study, but each preferred it to reopening what had already proved a painful subject. Should Constance not have consulted William before writing to Lady Davenall? William felt, understandably, that she should; he would not have objected to the proposed visit, and she should have known that. Constance felt, also understandably, that she could not explain her impulsive dispatch of the letter without showing William another letter presently lodged in a locked drawer of her bureau; by virtue of its reference to something of which she believed no living soul other than she knew, such a revelation was not to be contemplated. So it was that William Trenchard's prophetic remarks to Richard Davenall seemed, in some measure, already to be borne out.

Not until the travellers had changed trains at Bath and boarded the local for Freshford did one of them attempt to break their silence. Sadly, the attempt was ill-timed. The train had wound down the Avon valley slowly, and was slowing still further for its scheduled stop at Limpley Stoke, when William Trenchard spoke. He could not have failed to notice the reverie into which his wife had fallen, gazing from the window at the fields and wooded slopes, but he had taken it for vague nostalgia rather than for any specific recollection tied to the Dundas Aqueduct beneath which they had passed but a few minutes before.

'This part of the world must be full of memories for you,' he said, exerting himself to inject some brightness into his voice.

She looked at him distantly – from within, as it were, the memories he had referred to – her expression blurred by intervening sunlight or the frontiers of her private world; he could not tell which. The violet dress she had not worn in years, the loosely draped lace shawl, the pearl ear-rings, the veil of gauze thrown back across the purple ribbons of her straw-brimmed hat: these were clues, these were tokens, but somehow, he knew, not meant for him.

He regretted the remark as soon as he had made it, regretted the panic that had inspired it, but knew it could not be otherwise: he was too weak not to try to bridge the growing gulf with words.

Suddenly, Constance smiled. 'I am glad we came together, William. Really I am.' But, if her words were meant to reassure him, they failed. They only served to convince him that she wished she had come alone.

He blundered on. 'When were you last here?'

31

'Not since that day.'

Which day? Trenchard had not the courage to ask, and Constance, in her distraction, did not realize the slip she had made.

At Freshford station Lady Davenall's carriage was awaiting them. A gloomy footman drove them up in silence through the mellow-stoned village and out, along winding high-hedged lanes to their destination.

They crossed the boundaries of Cleave Court long before they saw it, bowled down the curving drive through the deer park screened by a dark avenue of elms, stricken into unobservance by the knowledge that one had been that way before and the other had not. At length, emerging from the canopy of elms, they could no longer disregard it. Bathed in sunlight, flanked by hangers of birch, chorused by a squadron of rooks, Cleave Court declared itself with stony rectangularity: a classical façade of tall windows and Doric columns, of pediments and balustrades, of pilastered wealth and corniced tradition.

'The first baronet was Paymaster-General under Queen Anne,' Trenchard murmured, almost to himself. Then, catching sight of Constance's surprised look: 'I felt I ought to know a little more about the Davenalls.' His smile was not entirely warm. 'The house was completed in 1713, just in time for Sir Christopher to retire to. Since then, the family has really done very little, besides fight in the odd campaign.' Constance remained silent. 'They also have the good fortune to own a substantial portion of the Somerset coalfield.' The carriage pulled up in front of the house, and the footman jumped out to open the door and let down the step. 'Of course,' Trenchard continued, 'I don't suppose you can see any of the spoil-heaps from here.' He gazed up at the distant line of the roof, broken by the bulbous shapes of stone-draped urns. 'On the other hand, I don't suppose anybody tries. Their family motto is "In captia vitalitas". Loosely translated, "To live is to hunt . . . ".'

Constance glanced back from the open doorway of the house and finished the sentence for him. 'Or be hunted.'

IV

When Constance and I reached Cleave Court on the appointed day, Lady Davenall received us in the orangery, attached to the main part of the house as a single-storey wing. It was a strange place to choose, with its stone-flagged floor and scatter of oriental rugs, luxuriant potted plants brought in against an early frost and dotted amongst thick-cushioned wicker chairs. We had passed through several richly furnished apartments to reach it, and it came to me, when we arrived, and found

Lady Davenall reclining on a chaise-longue, crooking her finger at a peacock who strutted and pecked at a sprinkling of seed in the open french windows, that she might, in a sense, be in flight from all the wood-panelled opulence which marriage to a baronet had brought her.

Seated opposite Lady Davenall was a stout tweed-suited man, cradling a tea-cup and saucer in his arms as if fearful of dropping them and squeezed, with apparent discomfort, into a low-backed bamboo chair that creaked ominously at his every move. With a crescendo of such creaks, he rose to greet us as the servant announced our names.

'Baverstock, sir, solicitor,' he breathed. His handshake left a sheen of sweat on my palm. 'And commissioner for oaths,' he added superfluously.

Lady Davenall had, by now, also risen and welcomed Constance with an unhurried regal kiss. She shook my hand briefly, and I was at once dismayed by the iciness of her touch. It explained the alabaster paleness of her complexion, though not its smoothness, not its unnatural denial of the age I knew she must be. Her hair was grey, of course, as was her dress, no doubt still reflecting some diminished state of mourning for Sir Gervase, yet there were hints of pink somewhere in the fabric, implications of indifference, even to the object of our visit, about her reluctant formal smile. In other circumstances, I might have thought her bored with us before we began.

'It is enchanting to see you again, Constance,' she said. 'And to meet the man who brought you happiness at last. I am so sorry that my family should once again be the unwitting cause of your distress.'

Fresh China tea was brought and dispensed. Constance and I sat together on a wicker sofa and participated in the customary platitudes about the comfort of our journey. I found myself wondering, not for the first time, just what Constance had said in her letter. I could not let Lady Davenall know that she had kept it from me, of course, so I attempted to strike a confident note.

'We all hope that this unpleasantness will soon be at an end. We have only come here today to reassure ourselves that you are in no doubt as to the falsity of Norton's claim.'

Constance said nothing, though I felt her stiffen beside me. As for Lady Davenall, she gazed towards me with as much expression as she might have conferred on a pane of glass.

'I am in no doubt,' she said after a pause. 'He presented himself here last week, as you know. He was able to suborn the servants – none of whom has been here long enough to remember James – into admitting him. I could see how they might have been taken in. The man has what I believe is called charisma. But he is not my son. My son is dead.' Her words were delivered with flat unemotional authority.

'Perhaps I should add', said Baverstock, 'that Norton had the effrontery to visit Mr James's old doctor – Fiveash – whilst he was here. Dr Fiveash is prepared to swear that this man is not his former patient.'

33

'So you see', continued Lady Davenall, 'this is not merely the addled judgement of a confused old lady.' It seemed a patently absurd description to apply to herself, but it was Constance who took her meaning.

'Unlike, you mean, that of Nanny Pursglove?'

'Esme Pursglove', said Lady Davenall, with a thoughtful compression of the mouth, 'was as loyal and diligent a nanny as one could wish for. So far as a rational judgement is concerned, however, one might as well consult this bay tree.' She gestured vaguely at a leafy growth behind her.

'You saw in Norton, then,' I said, 'no resemblance, however slight, to your son?'

'None whatever.'

'He displayed no knowledge that tended to sway you?'

'Likewise, none.'

'That, of course,' put in Baverstock, 'is the purpose of the examination on the eleventh: to expose Norton's ignorance of all details of Mr James's life.'

'Ignorant or well-informed,' said Lady Davenall, 'it will make no difference to me. The man is an imposter, so transparent that he scarcely warrants the description.'

Then, prefacing her words only with a slightly jarred replacement of her cup in its saucer, Constance said what I had feared she might. 'I cannot agree with you, Lady Davenall.' If there was shock at her words, only Baverstock and I displayed it. The mistress of Cleave Court did not so much as glance in Constance's direction. When she did respond, it was not even to the point.

'Would you and your husband care to see a little of the grounds before luncheon? You may find the few changes made since you were last here of interest. Besides, we must leave Mr Baverstock to concentrate on the rent-book for a while.'

V

Later, Trenchard would remember the pace Lady Davenall set as she led him and Constance through the terraced gardens, discoursing as she did so, with no sign of breathlessness, on the seasonal beauties of the acer glade, on the difficulties of keeping the fallow deer out of that part of the grounds, on the tendency of the conduit serving the fountain to clog with fallen leaves. She carried a pannier basket under her arm and would stop periodically to remove dead leaves and twigs from favoured plants; her exchanges with a passing gardener were cold but knowledgeable.

34

Rather sooner, Trenchard would recall how little attention Constance paid to Lady Davenall's commentary; he had to reply several times on her behalf when invited to praise some modification of the landscaping. If Constance did see what was pointed out to her, it was, he felt sure, at another time, with a different companion. She and Trenchard were walking together, but moving apart.

When they entered the deer park by a wicket gate from the wooded hillside behind the house, Lady Davenall inclined the route back towards the orangery, where she felt, presumably, that Baverstock had been given long enough to reconcile the Michaelmas rent-rolls. It was then that Constance pulled up and spoke for the first time since setting off on their tour.

'Lady Davenall,' she said, 'surely we are not to return to the house without showing William the pride of Cleave Court?'

Lady Davenall turned and looked back at her coolly. 'What can you mean, my dear?'

'Why, the maze of course. Sir Harley's Maze.' Constance smiled at her husband with genuine pleasure. 'There is a yew-tree maze here which you really should see, William. It's on the other side of the deer park, beyond the walled garden.' She pointed in that direction. 'I often went there—' She broke off suddenly.

'The maze has been abandoned,' said Lady Davenall flatly. 'I found it impossible to justify the labour which its upkeep entailed. The hedges have been allowed to grow back for some years now, and the gates are kept locked.'

Constance seemed taken aback. 'Abandoned? I can hardly believe it. What of Sir Harley's bust in the centre? Why, there was a bench to rest on and—'

'Left to nature,' Lady Davenall replied. 'Bust and all. Quite overgrown. Impenetrable in fact.' She smiled. 'I suggest we go in now.'

She moved ahead, walking calmly and steadily towards the house. Constance lingered for a moment, her brow furrowed in bemusement, then slowly shook her head.

'What's wrong?' said Trenchard.

'The maze was clipped and swept and marvelled at for more than a hundred years,' she replied in an undertone. 'Sir Gervase loved to sit in the centre by his great-grandfather's bust; he knew nobody could find him there except . . . I'm astonished that Lady Davenall should not have maintained it.'

'Nor Sir Hugo?'

'He never was one for conundrums. No, he'd not care about it. But come, we'd better go in.'

They went on their way. They did not refer to the maze again, then or over luncheon. To Trenchard it was unimportant – and wholly irrelevant to the purpose of their visit. To Constance it was, however, merely another strand in her growing mystification. James had been fond of the maze, as had his father. Its abandonment seemed a curious way for Lady Davenall to remember them, positively disrespectful in fact. But the true significance of this did not come to her until near the end of the meal, when Baverstock, notwithstanding a mouthful of Stilton, attempted to reassure Lady Davenall that Norton posed no real threat to her family.

'His claim is wholly untenable,' the lawyer said, nodding sagely. 'You have absolutely nothing to fear from him.'

'Fear?' said Lady Davenall. 'You should know, Mr Baverstock, that I have never feared anything in my life.'

It was the use of the word 'fear' that made the connection. It was then that Constance remembered.

September 1870. She had visited Cleave Court before, but never as a weekend guest. Now its lavish society came as something of a shock after the sober comforts of Cathedral Close, Salisbury. Yet the shock was a splendid, head-turning, gorgeously intoxicating one for the twenty-year-old Constance. Her impulsive nature had long chafed at the disciplined piety of the Sumner household. Now she began to understand why her brother had befriended James Davenall. And now she also began to understand that the courtesy and consideration James showed her was not merely what he felt was due to the sister of a friend. The weekend, in fact, was to end in his proposal of marriage. And her initial dismayed reluctance was to end in acceptance.

Before that stage was reached, however, James showed himself neglectful of Roland to the extent of insisting that Constance allow him to show her the famous maze of his ancestor, Sir Harley Davenall. She was, in truth, glad to leave the house, where she had found herself increasingly ill at ease in the company of Sir Gervase and another guest, an immense and corpulent French nobleman who was introduced to her as the Count of Moncalieri and with whom, she was given to understand, Sir Gervase had seen service in the Crimea. That his presence in England was in some way connected with the recently concluded Franco-Prussian War was attested by an outburst of profanity when served with hock at luncheon, but his patriotic gloom did not prevent him casting several unpleasantly suggestive glances in Constance's direction. All in all, she was grateful to be out of his sight.

The maze was a series of concentrically circled yew hedges surrounded by a wooden palisade. Its design was unusually complex and produced, in the minds of those entering it, a curious sensation of movement, as if the hedges – and the yew-arched portals by which one passed from one circular path to the next – were always rotating in the opposite direction to the walker. The illusion was enhanced by the fact that each circle of hedges was slightly lower as one passed inwards and the ground seemed also to fall away towards the centre. The whole effect implied a manic obsession with topiary and geometry on the part of Sir Harley, and this James was happy to confirm.

'The old boy was totally mad, of course,' he said, as they came at last to the centre and found Sir Harley's grinning bust awaiting them atop a stone column. 'But perhaps he had to be mad to plan this. It's deceived many people who thought they knew its secret.'

Constance turned to him with an alarm that was rather more than mock. 'We can find our way out again, can't we?'

James smiled. 'With me to guide you, yes. But how would you feel if I weren't here?'

'A little frightened.'

'Only a little?'

She looked momentarily stern. 'I should be confident of finding the route eventually.'

'Hear that, old chap?' said James, grinning at Sir Harley. 'Not all the womenfolk are in fear and trembling of your wretched maze.'

'I should hope not,' said Constance.

'You should have asked my mother to bring you,' James replied. 'Then you'd have seen what I meant. She never sets foot here.'

'Never?'

'Not for as long as I can remember. I often tried to persuade her in when I was a boy, but I never succeeded. I think it truly frightens her.'

'Surely not. She seems—'

'To know no fear? I would have thought so. But the maze is an exception. She fears this place, though I can't imagine why.'

Twelve years later, Constance was in no doubt. Whatever fear the maze held for Lady Davenall, she had conquered it. She had locked the gates and let the paths grow over. With the maze abandoned, she could safely pretend that she knew no fear – nor ever had.

VI

When we left Cleave Court that afternoon, it was, in my case, with an acute sense of failure. The object of the visit – for Constance and Lady Davenall to reassure each other that Norton was a fraud – had been evaded by both of them. Just as Constance no longer seemed to want her suspicions that he might be genuine subjected to any kind of rational analysis, so Lady Davenall resisted all reasoned debate of her rejection of him. The result was an icily reticent duel between two women who harboured more unforgotten differences than merely their opinion of Norton. The past – theirs and others' – shrieked louder than the peacocks across the unwalked lawns. But of what that past held I still knew next to nothing. And when Lady Davenall bade me a wintry farewell that day I realized that was how she wanted it to remain.

Baverstock, who was returning to Bath at the same time, offered to convey us to the Spa station in his four-wheeler, and I readily agreed. On the way up the drive, whilst Constance gazed thoughtfully back at the dwindling view of the house, I asked him how long he had acted for the Davenalls.

'Not the Davenalls, Mr Trenchard,' he replied. 'Lady Davenall. Sir Gervase used a cousin of his. I was only taken on when Sir Gervase became incapacitated.'

'I see. You don't have any dealings with Sir Hugo, then?'

'None at all. Sir Hugo seldom comes down here.'

At this point, Constance showed herself to have been less preoccupied than I had supposed. 'You would not remember the maze, then, Mr Baverstock?'

Baverstock smiled back at her over his shoulder. 'Sir Harley's Maze? You'd not visit Cleave Court often without hearing mention of it, though not from Lady Davenall.'

'Then, from whom?'

'The staff. They all thought it a crying shame when she decided to abandon it straight after Sir Gervase was taken ill. I wouldn't know myself. Crowcroft, the head gardener, left on account of it, though, which says something. There were a good many changes then. Quinn, the butler, left, too, though not—'

'Did Lady Davenall give a reason for her decision?'

Baverstock chuckled. 'I should say not.'

'It seems a pity', Constance continued wistfully, 'that there aren't more staff left who remember James.'

'There is always', I put in sarcastically, 'Nanny Pursglove.'

'Yes, there is,' said Constance. 'Did I gather she still lives on the estate, Mr Baverstock?'

'On the dower portion beyond Limpley Stoke, Mrs Trenchard. A charming little cottage near the canal. I'm confident her tenure won't be prejudiced by this latest eccentricity.'

'If you wish,' I said, 'we could perhaps call on her. You and she do have something in common, after all.'

Constance looked at me sharply. 'Would that be possible, Mr Baverstock?'

'Simplicity itself, I should say. The dear old soul adores visitors.'

So it was agreed and, as Baverstock had implied, easily accomplished. We descended through Limpley Stoke to the flat valley bottom and there, in a sunny hollow overlooked by the railway line, found Miss Pursglove's grace-and-favour cottage, smoke curling from the chimney, the thatch well kept, hanging baskets still in blossom, the rush of the weir on the river behind us softening the silence. Miss Pursglove saw us *coming from the kitchen window and pushed it open to trill a greeting. She recognized Constance at once.*

'It's Miss Sumner, as I live and breathe. It's been too long, my dear, far too long.' Her wizened bright-eyed face was transported with delight. A moment later, she was at the door. 'Welcome one and welcome all. Mr Baverstock and . . .'

'My husband, Nanny,' Constance said. 'I am Mrs Trenchard now.'

Momentarily, Miss Pursglove looked crestfallen; I found myself guessing what she might have hoped. 'Do all come in and make yourselves at home. Will you take some tea? Lupin and I have baked some scones.'

Lupin, it transpired, was a cat, whom Miss Pursglove fussed over between filling pots and jugs and cups and passing plates and spoons and doilies. Baverstock lent an ineffectual hand in a way that suggested he was no stranger to the ritual. He and I were seldom called upon to speak. When Miss Pursglove was not talking – which was not often – Constance was. Their memories, it seemed, were of brighter, better days than Lady Davenall had ever known. And, borne in with their memories, there stood an invisible guest at our tea-party beside the river: James Davenall, the man both women wanted to believe was still alive.

'How I did cry when I saw my Jamie again,' Miss Pursglove said at length. 'How I did chide him for misleading us all.'

'Now, Nanny,' said Baverstock, 'you know Lady Davenall doesn't want this man Norton talked of as if—'

'Stuff and nonsense! If she can't tell her own son from Adam, let the woman who raised him do it for her. I never believed he was dead anyway. That's what you lawyers would have had us believe, but I knew better.'

There was no denying her conviction; Baverstock cast a defeatist glance in my direction. Constance, however, seemed eager that she should continue. 'How did you know for certain, Nanny?'

'He came in here with that shy-eyed bit of a stoop he used to put on when he'd misbehaved as a boy. I'd have known him anywhere. He's my Jamie and no mistake. I know Sir Hugo doesn't think so, but he wouldn't, would he? Always a difficult boy, that Hugo. Not sweet-tempered like Jamie.'

'Even so—' I began.

'Begging your pardon, Mr Trenchard, but, even so as even is, Mr James is back among us. Sir James, as I must learn to call him. Back as he promised he would be.'

'Promised?' said Constance.

'The last time I saw him. Eleven years ago. He came up to see me in my room over the nursery before he went on that trip to London. Said he was going away and might not be back for a long time. I never thought* *he meant this long. But I did make him promise to come back. And he said he would. "Don't worry, Nanny," he said. "You'll see me again."'*

'Perhaps', put in Baverstock, 'he meant when he returned from London.'

'Fiddlesticks! He meant what he said. And now he's kept his promise. "Well, Nanny," he said when he called on me here, "I'm back, just like I said I would be." Doesn't that prove he's the same man who said goodbye to me all those years ago?'

'I hardly—' Baverstock began. He was cut short by Constance rising from her chair.

'Would you all excuse me for a short while?' she said. 'I think I am in need of some air.' I made to rise, but she gestured me to remain. 'Do stay and finish your tea, William. I know you will have more questions for Nanny. I will be back long before you have asked them all.'

I looked at her nonplussed. 'Well, I—'

'Please,' she said. Suddenly, in her eyes, she was imploring me to let her go. She craved this time alone as water in a desert and, though I could not imagine why she should, I had not the heart to obstruct her.

'Very well,' I said. 'You'll not stray far?'

'No, William. Not far.'

'Bless me, Constance can't come to any harm round here,' said Miss Pursglove. 'Have another scone, Mr Trenchard, and settle your mind.'

I subsided into the armchair and consoled myself, as Constance went out, with the thought that she might have tired of Nanny's confident assertion that James had returned. I had myself, though not because the old lady had shown herself to be as feeble-minded as the Davenalls had portrayed her. Far indeed from that was this gimlet-eyed little figure in her pinafore dress, polishing her memories as bright as the copper kettle that stood on her range, defying us with the confidence her lost charge had given her eleven years before: he would return.

'Sixty-five years I've worked for the Davenalls,' she recalled, nodding proudly. 'Long enough, I think, to make me sure of some things. The year of grace 1817, it was, when I was just fifteen, the year Sir Gervase was born. Sir Lemuel was my first master, you see, though I was just a nurserymaid then. It wasn't until the first Lady Davenall took homesick for Ireland and went back there for good that I had to look after the young master single-handed. To think I remember him in his cradle and lived to see him in his grave. Well, well.' She nodded her head. 'He was a holy terror, was Sir Gervase, man and boy. Sir Lemuel banished him once to his mother's in Ireland, but I don't know as it did much good. He came back just as scapegrace as he went. Now, little Jamie, he was different. You could tell from the moment he came into the world that he would be a proper gentleman. . . .'

VII

Trenchard was whistling in the dark. Constance had not tired of Nanny Pursglove's recollections, nor yet of her recital of the ways by which she knew James Davenall. It was simply that she had returned in her mind to that last leavetaking in June 1871 and wished now, whilst she could engineer some time alone, to return to it in person.

Nanny Pursglove's home stood hard by the canal. Constance knew that she had only to walk up the steep lane to the lock-keeper's cottage and could there gain access to the towpath. She did so unhurriedly, glorying in the solitude of the gentle afternoon. For this, she knew well, was the way she had come before, walking up from Cleave Court in answer to her fiancé's summons. She knew no better now than then what it was that troubled him, but went obediently, sensing as she trod the path that this was to be no ordinary rendezvous.

The canal dappled sluggishly at the bank. On its other side bunched the greenery of Conkwell Wood, beyond whose slopes, then as now, stretched secret pastures where, if you knew the path, as they once had . . .

A narrowboat came into view, turning into the straight from the aqueduct ahead of her. Below, to her left, lay the river and the railway line. Behind, in cosy ignorance at Nanny Pursglove's cottage, her husband sat seeking ways to deny what, even now, she dared not quite admit herself.

On that day in 1871, she had reached the bend wondering if he would, as promised, be there waiting for her. She had hesitated in the shelter of the overhanging trees, felt heat and doubt grow momentarily, then had gone on, and found him, leaning against the parapet, gazing down at the river and smoking a cigarette, his hair a touch awry, his cheeks hollow, his eyes shifting and uncertain. He had looked up at the sound of her approach, had smiled without erasing that first impression of desperation in his pose, had stepped forward to kiss her and been the first to speak.

On this day in 1882, she reached the bend unnerved by her own presentiments. She hesitated in the shelter of the overhanging trees, recalling the words and expression of their rejected visitor, retracing in her mind the lines of his unexpected letter. 'Neither of us can forget, can we?' In that he had been right. How could he know? Unless . . .

She went on. She walked slowly, following the curve of the towpath as it rounded the right angle described by the canal. A little way ahead, the waterway narrowed as it crossed the aqueduct. The open valley loomed suddenly beneath her. A man was standing in her path, leaning against the parapet, smoking a cigarette. He was there, as she now knew she had foreseen he would be. He was there, awaiting her.

41

VIII

' . . . So I didn't believe them when they told me he was dead. No, you may be sure of that. I said to Mr Quinn, I said: "If Mr James tells me I'll see him again, then I know he'll be as good as his word." Quinn scoffed at that right enough, as he scoffed at much else. I wish he was here now to admit I was right. Not that he would. No, not him. It was odd, now I come to think of it, that Mr James didn't ask why Quinn had left. Not that I knew the ins and outs of his going, of course, but he was Mr James's valet, when all's said and done. Yet, when I mentioned him, Mr James said nothing at all, almost as if he already knew what—'

The clock on Miss Pursglove's crowded mantelpiece struck five. Baverstock started in his chair. 'Upon my soul,' he spluttered. 'Is that the time? I should have been in Bath half an hour since. Where's your wife, Mr Trenchard? We must be going.'

It was absurd. I had almost forgotten that Constance had left us. Now I grew suddenly anxious: she was long overdue. Leaving Baverstock with Miss Pursglove, I hurried out into the lane, but there was no sign of her. My anxiety increased. I tried the uphill route, thinking she might be out of sight at the top, but came only on the canal, and a bailiff in waders by the bank, cutting back the reeds. I asked him if he had seen a lady pass that way. He paused in his work to consider my description, then nodded slowly.

'Ar, more 'n 'alf-hour ago. She followed the towpath towards the aqueduct.'

'Aqueduct?'

'That way.' He gestured with his thumb. 'Just under the mile.'

I found myself running in the direction he had indicated. His words had struck a chord. During our courtship in Salisbury, Constance had occasionally referred to her last meeting with James Davenall 'by the aqueduct'. There could not be two. This had been no mere stroll for fresh air's sake. This had been the retracing of a route that led unerringly to a lost allegiance. I quickened my pace, fleeing as much as pursuing the suspicions already massing in my head.

IX

He had been the first to speak.

'When you told me in your letter that you were to visit Cleave Court, I knew it was not to seek my mother's reassurance as you said, but to seek reassurance of a different kind. So here I am. You knew I would be waiting for you, didn't you? Now as then.'

If you had happened to be standing on the river bank beneath the Dundas Aqueduct that October afternoon, if you had happened to look up and see two people standing by the parapet, one an elegant, modestly bearded man in a grey jacket and pinned cravat, bare-headed and gazing imploringly at the other, a woman in a violet dress, lace shawl and ribboned straw hat, one hand clutching the coping stone with an intensity mirrored in her face, what would you have thought? Would you have read the struggle of wonder with doubt in her expression as she looked towards him? Would you have guessed the question already forming on her lips?

'How did you know? Who told you these things? It isn't possible that—'

'Nobody told me, Connie. I lived it, like you, with you. There's no illusion, no trick. I met you here eleven years ago, when the leaves were green, not yellow.' He glanced back at the basin beyond the aqueduct. 'We crossed at the lock gate and walked up through the woods. Didn't we?'

He looked at her directly, seeming to compel her to recollect, with him, the events of that day. Her reply, when it came, was from the distance of eleven years. 'Yes.'

Now he was looking past her and speaking more loudly. 'We went as far as the bluebell meadow, didn't we?'

'Yes.'

'And there . . .'

Suddenly, Constance spun round. Her husband was standing twelve yards away, panting slightly, his face contorted not with exertion but with trust betrayed. She put her hand to her mouth. 'William—'

'Be silent!' Trenchard's voice was a stern travesty of its normal self. He strode past her and stopped beside Norton. 'You followed us here, didn't you? You staged this meeting to convince my wife—'

'I staged nothing!' Norton removed his elbow from the parapet and squared his shoulders, facing Trenchard without the slightest flinch. 'I came here for the same reason as Connie. Had you not intervened, I would have told her the truth about why I went away—'

'Easy to say!'

'—and why I have returned.' He smiled faintly. 'Now that must await another opportunity.' He looked at Constance and bowed stiffly. 'Until we meet again.' Then he turned and walked smartly away across the aqueduct.

Not until Norton had passed from view beyond the canal basin did Trenchard speak to Constance and then without looking at her. His words were addressed to her, but his gaze remained fixed in Norton's direction. 'You should not have come here, Constance. You should not have spoken to him. Don't you see what harm you're doing?'

Constance, too, was looking elsewhere. 'I hardly know what I see any more.'

Trenchard took her arm. 'Come back with me now. We will speak no more of this. Henceforth, you will leave me to handle this affair. You will not see him again. I forbid it. Should you do so by chance, you will not speak to him.' They began to move slowly back along the towpath, back towards where Baverstock would be waiting with his four-wheeler to hurry them to the station. 'Do you understand me, Connie?'

Her reply was meek enough to suggest compliance. 'I understand.'

Indeed she did. She understood that day, for the first time, where her duty lay.

THREE

I

Through the deceptive calm of the day after our visit to Somerset, I watched Constance as a gaoler would his charge. There were no bars, of course, no keys, no locked doors, just all the other barriers that Norton had succeeded in erecting between us. It was only a week since he had entered our lives and, already, the possibility that he might be James Davenall was worse than any certainty.

Patience played on the carpet after tea that Sunday afternoon, and Constance sat reading by the window. I slunk away to my study, where at least silence was normal, if no more bearable, and sought in vain to calm my anxieties. If only I could have talked to Constance, if only I could have asked her the vital question: if she believed him, what of her love for me? But I had placed an embargo on all such conversation, and she had abided by it. I had asserted my authority as head of the household, and she had respected it. I had insisted on being left to deal with the matter alone and now, pacing the room or peering uneasily from the window to check that the street was empty, I realized how helpless I was to do so.

My confused state of mind must explain the foolish course I took the following morning. Leaving home after an early breakfast, before Constance had risen, I diverged from my normal route to Orchard Street and proceeded to Paddington, harbouring the absurd notion that I might be able to take Norton unawares at his hotel and extract from him a withdrawal of his claim.

The clerk at the desk intimated that he was taking breakfast in the dining-room: I went straight in. There, sure enough, at a pillar table, Norton sat reading a newspaper and smoking a cigarette over the last of his coffee. The room was full but quiet in the way of such establishments at such an hour. A periodic rattle of cutlery and waiters' whispered enquiries were all that was to be heard.

Norton saw me approaching him, but displayed no reaction. He did not even lower his newspaper. Eventually, after standing awkwardly by his table for some moments, I said: 'I'd like to speak to you.'

Now he consented to fold the newspaper away. 'Then, sit down.'

I did so, eyeing him over the table through a curl of smoke rising from his cigarette, which he had propped in an ashtray. 'Preferably in private.'

'I haven't finished my coffee,' he said, ostentatiously refilling his cup. 'If you wish to speak to me, you must do so here. If not, I shan't object.'

I lowered my voice. 'Because you think you can work your mischief on my wife alone.'

His tone remained level, nonchalantly pitched, his eyebrows arched as if to imply disdainful surprise at my remarks. 'It is because we have nothing to say to each other. We both know what it is that you fear.'

I leant across the table. 'All I want of you is an undertaking that you will cease to harass my wife.'

'I am not harassing her. You are, by your clumsy attempts to prevent us meeting. I must tell you' – he smiled – 'as one who knows her, that you will only succeed in alienating her by such a course of action. Were I the fraudster you believe me to be, I would take greater pleasure than I do in your inclination to self-destruction.'

He had me, pinned and helpless, in this venue that I had chosen for him. 'After Wednesday, you will be obliged to do as I ask.'

'On the contrary. After Wednesday, I rather suspect you will lose what little authority over Connie you think you retain. Did she tell you that she had written to me?'

'You lie!'

'Ask her yourself – if you dare. I would show you the letter, but, as a gentleman, you will understand that I must respect its confidentiality.'

Again, he had perfectly exploited my weakness. If I did ask Constance, it would imply that I believed him. And, if I believed him, could I believe her answer? 'There is no such letter. You will not succeed by such ploys in sowing discord in my marriage.'

'I'm glad to hear it. Unhappily, there is no need to sow a crop when it is already sprouting. Has Connie ever given you a full account of what took place on the last occasion we met before my . . . time away?'

For answer, I could only stand on a crumbling dignity. 'There are no secrets between us.'

He drained his cup, then smiled across at me. 'But there are. In fact I rather think that may be all there is between you.'

I stood up abruptly, the legs of my chair scraping loudly on the floor. I wanted to be away from his cruel ironic stare, but could not *find a retreat that seemed other than headlong. 'You have said enough.'*

'You initiated this conversation. You are at liberty to end it.'

I did so. But, as I walked away across the dining-room with what decorum I could muster, I sensed his smile broadening. I sensed he knew now that he had me where he wanted me.

II

Tuesday, 10th October 1882 was a day of preparation for the principals in what would soon be known as the case of *Norton versus Davenall*. Norton himself spent the greater part of it closeted at the Staple Inn offices of Warburton, Makepeace & Thrower, rehearsing with Hector Warburton all that the following day's examination might hold for him.

It was a close grey day of incipient fog, perversely clammy enough for Warburton's office windows to stand open to the noise and smoke of the city. Warburton himself approached all legal business in the same way: would it pay and would he win? His entrée to the finest brains of the Bar was frequently attributed to his record of bringing them only the finest ingredients. And in the case laid before him by James Norton he detected ingredients calculated to appeal to the most demanding barrister.

Regarding his client with studied indifference across his desk, Warburton found himself unable to deny a considerable admiration for James Norton – whoever he really was. Had Norton been defending himself against criminal charges rather than proposing a civil action against the Davenall estate, Warburton might even have recommended him to represent himself. The man was so fluently plausible, so demonstrably honourable, that nobody ignorant of the facts could doubt his word for a moment. As for those not so ignorant, only time would tell whether Norton's confidence that he could win them over was justified. For the moment, Warburton listened with awe to the man's account of himself and his alleged predicament. He began to list in his mind those barristers whom he might approach to handle the case, for, unlike his client, he was sure it would come to court before the Davenalls would yield; it would require nothing less than a QC, he felt, but, with the right one, there would not be a dry eye in the jury-box. Already, his own grittily arid mind's eye saw how it was likely to be – and the prospect was inviting.

Less than half a mile away, though it might have seemed further through the fetid air of Holborn that morning, Richard Davenall was poring over precedents and regretting his earlier shortness of temper with the clerks. Sir Hugo had declined to discuss their tactics for the

47

examination, preferring to spend the day at the races with Freddy Cleveland, and there had been no opportunity to compare notes with Baverstock. He therefore had no one in whom he could confide his misgivings about the event. Sir Hugo seemed to see it as an opportunity to scupper Norton once and for all, but Norton had been under no obligation to agree to such a meeting, so why had he done so? And what, he could not help but wonder, what did Catherine Davenall really believe?

What indeed? There would have been no way of telling from her calm progress through the day at Cleave Court. A little estate management in the morning, a meeting in Bath of one of her beneficent committees in the afternoon. No troubled pilgrimage to the Davenall vault in the village church to commune with the soul of her late husband. No prolonged audience with Baverstock to clear his cluttered mind. No pause, no haste, no space for doubt to visit any part of her fixed and private mind.

Equal placidity might have been found at Esme Pursglove's cottage, where the only drama of the day was Lupin stabbing his paw with a cactus spine. As a matter of fact, Miss Pursglove had been told nothing of what was intended, but, even had she been, it would not have discomposed her. Her faith in her former charge was immaculately unquestioning. He could be trusted in any crisis, however pressing. Meanwhile, there were paws to be patched.

At The Limes, St John's Wood, Mavis Hillier was growing increasingly fretful at the unmistakable signs of domestic disharmony: the master testy and inclined to come and go at all hours, the mistress withdrawn, uncommunicative and manifestly out of sorts; even Burrows had complained that he could accomplish little in the garden if Mrs Trenchard was to be forever mooning about the flower borders. The contagion had spread to Patience, whose recent fits of temper were as uncharacteristic as they were unsettling, and Hillier had agreed with Cook that such an awkward atmosphere was not to be tolerated for long. Precisely what they would do if it did persist was not specified. Instead, they consoled each other by sharing the succulent game pie in which their employers had expressed such little interest at Monday dinner.

At Newbury racecourse, Freddy Cleveland's fancies were proving, as Sir Hugo Davenall often found, expensively fickle. Ordinarily, he would have laughed at another lost wager, cast the fragments of his betting-slip to the ground and proposed a gentle restorative in the bar. Today, however, he would have had to admit that a little honest long-odds luck would not have gone amiss. In its absence, he could not even vent his sarcasm at Cleveland's expense because of the presence of their distinguished guest: a tall, immensely stout French-man whose entirely proportional vanity had to be flattered in every particular if his hostility to Norton was to be relied upon. One of these particulars was the maintenance of his ludicrous alias as 'Monsieur le Comte de Moncalieri'. Not that Sir Hugo cared how he chose to register himself at Claridge's. What smattering of knowledge he had acquired in his short and pampered existence told him that all men had something to hide and some had more than most. That, indeed, was what he was relying on.

Back in Holborn, Norton's exegesis was at an end. As it concluded on a note of softly spoken conviction, Hector Warburton admitted to his mind for a fleeting moment the wholly rhetorical question: Could he really be James Davenall? Not that it was even of academic interest to him. The thought had only been inspired by Norton's consummate mastery of his role. Whether that mastery derived from truth or from theatrical excellence made no difference to Warburton. Indeed, it was imperative that he should not trammel his preparation of the case with any genuinely held belief. It was important, in other words, that he should not know the answer. For others, however – in fact for more than supposed it to be the case – it was all that mattered, all that mattered in the world.

III

I reached Chester Square that evening earlier than I had intended, despite lingering at Orchard Street longer than necessary, even allowing for my brother Ernest's visit to discuss the half-yearly accounts. I went so far as encouraging him to prolong his stay by taking a glass of sherry, which must have struck him as unusual. Perhaps I had hopes of enlisting his advice in my present predicament. If so, they were to be dashed. He made a reproachful face at the proffered decanter and took himself off into the dusk.

So, despite all my stratagems, I arrived at Bladeney House sooner than I would have wished. Greenwood informed me that none of the other visitors who were expected had arrived, but that I might find Mr Cleveland in the music room as usual. He, it seemed, was not classed as a visitor.

Cleveland was draped across a sofa, legs extravagantly akimbo, chuckling over a copy of Punch. *He looked up as I entered.*

'You here, Trenchard? For the council of war, I take it.'

'Yes. What about you?'

'Hugo insists. It seems I'm to fire questions at the blighter along with the rest of you – and be coached into the bargain.'

'Really?'

'Absolutely. What did he have for breakfast before the Boxing Day Hunt at Cleave Court in 1869? That sort of thing.'

49

I sat down opposite him. 'And what is the answer?'

'Blowed if I know. Whatever he says, I'm to contradict it.' He laughed, and I joined him. 'Bit desperate, what?'

'Perhaps it needs to be.'

Cleveland pulled himself into a more upright posture. 'Do you really think so? Surely not. James's doctor is being trooped out, you know. Not to mention the Great Panjandrum himself.'

'I beg your pardon?'

He leaned towards me and altered his voice to a stage whisper. 'Hugo's star witness. The so-called Count of Moncalieri. You may recognize him. If you do, say nothing: he's grown frightfully shy in his old age. Besides, I believe his identity is to be a test of Norton's, so to speak.'

'I'm not sure I—'

I broke off as the doors opened. It was Sir Hugo and a massively built, Gallic-faced man who could only be the anonymous Count. Sir Hugo looked surprised to see me, the Count dyspeptically unmoved. I rose to meet them.

'Trenchard,' said Sir Hugo. 'Glad you could be here.' We shook hands briefly. 'Count, this is the gentleman who married Miss Sumner: William Trenchard. Trenchard: Monsieur le Comte de Moncalieri.'

I extended my hand again, but the Count did not reciprocate. Instead, he bowed gravely. 'Bonsoir, monsieur.' His voice was rich and syrupy. As for his face, it meant nothing to me: set folds of patrician fat on an undeniably noble countenance, eyes bright and piercing beneath a hooded, somewhat brooding brow. I took him for some fleshy fragment of Second Empire nobility for whom the Third Republic was not an agreeable haven.

'I am honoured to make your acquaintance, Count.'

'You need not be, Monsieur Trenchard.' His English was suddenly perfect, as if the French accent were as contrived as the title. 'Mine is the honour: to meet such an embodiment of English virtues.'

'I'm sorry?'

'Hugo tells me that the Trenchards are très grands épiciers. Shop-keeping is, in this country, a noble calling. Thus am I honoured.' It was impossible to tell from his expression whether he was attempting to be humorous or insulting. I merely smiled weakly.

'Do I gather that you have met my wife, Count?'

'Many years ago. I doubt she would recall the occasion. Yet who knows? Recollection is suddenly in season, is it not, Hugo?'

Sir Hugo seemed equally uncertain as to his meaning. 'The Count is an old friend of my father, Trenchard, and hence well acquainted with my late brother. Whilst in London, he has generously agreed to—'

'Inspect your inconvenient pretender.' The Count bowed. 'That, too, will be an honour.'

50

Cleveland had struggled from his seat to join us. 'Seems only fitting, Count. After all, pretenders are rather your national speciality, what?'

Again, there was no flicker of the fixed sullen expression. 'Frédéric's sense of humour has always been an education to me, Monsieur Trenchard, as, no doubt, it is to you.'

'I must admit I didn't see this as a laughing matter.'

'No?' said Cleveland with a pained look. 'Then, I'd better take myself off to the dunce's corner.' He drifted away, but only to the piano, where he flopped down on the stool and commenced playing a Mozart concerto with disarming ease. Sir Hugo smiled in a show of tolerance, seated the Count, proffered drinks and bustled about the room, leaving me to meet Moncalieri's morbidly searching gaze from the sofa opposite.

'How did you come to be acquainted with Sir Gervase, Count?' I asked.

For a moment, he seemed disinclined to respond, toying with the watch-chain stretched across his silk-waistcoated midriff and twitching his mouth inconclusively. Then he suddenly decided the question warranted an answer. 'I was a guest at Cleave Court in the year 1846, when the world was young, and I with it, when one could take one's pleasure without fear of . . . the consequences.'

'Before James Davenall was born?'

He ignored the question. 'Sir Gervase and I later served together – in the Crimea.'

Sir Hugo intervened from the other side of the room, where he was pacing about beneath a Landseer hunting scene. 'The Count is a long-standing friend of the family, Trenchard. As such, he is well qualified to expose Norton as an imposter.'

'You have not yet met Mr Norton, Count?'

'No, monsieur. That treat is reserved for tomorrow.'

'Some treat!' said Sir Hugo. He was by the doorway now, where something caught his attention from the room beyond, the windows of which looked on to the street. 'Ah! Here's Richard. Excuse me.' He hurried out, giving me an opportunity to test the extent of Moncalieri's friendship with Sir Gervase.

'I gather Sir Gervase resisted the notion that his son was dead, Count. As his friend, did you comprehend his reasons?'

'Surely it is easy to understand a father's weakness. Gervase could not abandon his son whilst hope remained, however slender. But I am not to be swayed by such . . . faiblesse du coeur.'

'Nor, strangely enough, is Lady Davenall. I do understand a father's weakness. But what of a mother's?'

For the first time, Moncalieri's face betrayed a faint tremor of reaction. 'Too subtle, monsieur. Too subtle for your own good, I think.' His eyes fixed themselves upon me whilst the piano played on behind us and the sound of opening and closing doors elsewhere in the house

51

announced an arrival. 'Ask yourself only one question. Do you wish James Davenall to be alive – or dead? I suggest you think well before answering, because much may depend upon it.'

Cleveland stopped playing in the middle of a bar and swung round. 'If it comes to it, Count, I don't wish poor old Jimmy dead. He was my friend, dammit.'

'Is not Hugo your friend? Do you wish him to lose his title and his fortune?'

'Well . . . no.'

'Then, you do wish James dead, Frédéric, just as Monsieur Trenchard does.'

'Do I?'

'I believe so, monsieur. I believe each of us here this evening wishes the same. That is why we came.'

The Count was right, of course. Over dinner, Richard Davenall listed the questions he would put to Norton, the ways he hoped to catch him out, the traps he thought he might fall into, and we all nodded and consented to play our parts. Not for the first time, I could not keep from my mind the awful thought: How would it feel to return as Norton claimed he had and be denied by those who once had called him son and brother and friend? I can claim no credit for the sentiment, for it was as quickly swamped by the growing conviction that I must show him no quarter: in the contest about to open, it was every man for himself. Yet the worst of it was that I did not feel his equal. If only Richard Davenall could have announced that his investigations had uncovered a real, live, fraudulent James Norton. But he had learned nothing: Norton remained a total enigma. That, I think, is why the foreboding with which the journey to Somerset had left me remained as strong as ever, proof against our confident talk of crushing his claim once and for all. So long as I did not know our enemy, I could not truly believe that we had the beating of him.

IV

It had rained all morning in Holborn. The traffic had reduced the street to squelching lines of mud, whilst standing pools in sluggish gutters encroached on the crowded pavements. Awnings dripped and horses steamed; costermongers cursed and carts lurched; the louring clouds choked and smeared the business of the day. Every surface was clammy, every small silence invaded by the irregular percussion of the rain. Where did the river end and the city begin? No man, squinting and storm-collared, could be certain on such a day as this.

It was wanting but an hour to noon, yet, in confirmation of the conditions, the gas-lamps burned in the partners' room of Warburton, Makepeace & Thrower, the high gallery windows that looked up Gray's Inn Road doing little to relieve the gloom. Rain washed the mullioned glass and cast its mobile shadow on the plaster friezework; an unfastened stay rattled periodically at a lofty transom; coal sputtered and flared in a draughty grate; and Hector Warburton called the meeting to order.

'Gentlemen, now that introductions are concluded, may we begin?'

Warburton was seated at the head of the table, in the high-backed chair normally reserved for his father: the fire was behind him and so did nothing to light his pale and predatory features. Not so James Norton, who sat to his left, leaning slightly forward, with hands resting calmly on the table, his expression clear-browed and placidly expectant, firelight catching in his eyes a look bordering on the arrogantly confident. Opposite him, Warburton's clerk, Lechlade, stooped diligently over his papers, making a preliminary note of the proceedings. Next to Lechlade, Sir Hugo Davenall was all frenetic movement and gesture, his hands forever twitching at pockets and cuffs, his eyes darting around the table, seldom resting anywhere for long and never on Norton. His cousin, Richard, regarded him impassively from the other side of the table, exerting himself to display only level-headed legalistic concern for his client but wishing, more in the way of an anxious uncle, that he would sit still and stop smoking: the broken smouldering backs of three cigarettes already stood in an ashtray by Sir Hugo's elbow.

At Richard Davenall's shoulder was his fellow-lawyer, Arthur Baverstock, ill at ease in his present surroundings, and opposite Baverstock, combining this state with barely disguised impatience to be elsewhere, was Dr Duncan Fiveash. He had travelled from Bath under duress, knowing better than to antagonize such a wealthy client as Lady Davenall by declining to go but not troubling to hide his resentment from her lawyer. Now he chewed his beard, fiddled with an empty pipe in his breast pocket and consoled himself with the thought of being away by noon and visiting old Emery at St Thomas's. Fiveash was not a young man, nor any longer an ambitious one. These factors, whilst they did not liberate him from the necessity of attendance, at least relieved him of the obligation to pretend that it was an honour.

It was the strangely mixed company to which Fiveash took particular exception: sundry Davenalls, with all the many and excessive insights into their ways a medical man was bound to have after treating three generations of their ailments; a bevy of parsimonious lawyers eager to prolong proceedings in proportion to the growth of their fees, whereas there was nothing in this for him save a dubious quantity of goodwill; and a trio of family friends: one stout choleric French nobleman whom he vaguely recalled and who appeared to be suffering from indigestion, to judge by his frequent shiftings of weight in the chair; an unexceptional preoccupied fellow to his right named Trenchard; and, at the end of the table, lolling back in his seat and engaged in an effort to blow smoke rings which the current of air from the upper windows rendered pointless, a flippant idler introduced to him as Freddy Cleveland. Fiveash despaired of them all and turned his attention to the chairman.

'My client,' Warburton was explaining, 'insisted that this meeting should take place despite my advice to the contrary. I pointed out to him that he was under no obligation to give those who disputed his identity a second opportunity to do so short of the court hearing to which I felt he should have early recourse.'

'So you—' Sir Hugo began, but was at once cut short by his cousin.

'I would suggest Mr Warburton be allowed to finish,' Richard Davenall said emphatically. Sir Hugo snorted and subsided into silence.

'Thank you,' said Warburton, with a nod in Davenall's direction. 'As I say, I advised my client that, if he agreed to such a meeting, you on your side would, in all likelihood, ensure that only those whose hostility could be utterly relied upon would attend.' He looked slowly round the table. 'Such, indeed, appears to be the case, as I foresaw.' A faint smile. 'My client insisted, nevertheless, that we should go ahead. He believed – and I am sure you will agree that the sentiment does him only credit – that his family should be given every opportunity to acknowledge him before their refusal to do so became public. He believed that by this time, the initial shock of his reappearance having somewhat subsided, you might feel able to abandon your denial of his identity, with no residual ill will on either side. He has emphasized—'

Sir Hugo brought the flat of his hand down on the table in front of him with the force of renewed anger, shocking Warburton into silence. He glared across at Norton. 'I'll see you, and your case, and your lawyer—'

'Please! Hugo!' Richard Davenall had intervened once again. And, once again, Sir Hugo gave way, though with greater reluctance.

'Say your piece, Mr Warburton,' he concluded sarcastically.

'Thank you. It is simply this: Take this opportunity to forget the unfortunate course of recent events by accepting the self-evident truth of James Davenall's reappearance or proceed to a long and expensive court-case which will end in your defeat and, in all probability, the lasting division of your family. My client wishes to avert these consequences. He hopes that you will do the same.'

Sir Hugo this time said nothing. It was Richard Davenall who responded, in measured tones. 'I am bound to say on Sir Hugo's behalf that Mr Norton's proposal is both deeply offensive and completely unacceptable. No member of the late James Davenall's family has entertained Mr Norton's claim for a moment. The man is a stranger to them. His attempt to pass himself off as their deceased relative has occasioned them both anguish and outrage. If he swears in writing, here and now, to withdraw his claim, Sir Hugo will make no more of it. Failing that, Sir Hugo will seek an injunction against Mr Norton and will take out a private prosecution against him. Those are our terms, which I believe to be, if anything, over-generous. If Mr Norton had hopes of an *ex gratia* payment – what I believe is known as "nuisance money" – I must tell him that it will not be countenanced.' He turned to Baverstock. 'I believe that is also Lady Davenall's position?'

Baverstock cleared his throat. 'It is.'

Silence intruded, an interval of entrenchment in the irreconcilable positions so clearly stated. Cleveland's chair creaked as he swung back on it. Sir Hugo drummed his fingers. The fire spat. And Norton raised one eyebrow in a slight but unmistakable signal to Warburton that he was ready to speak.

His tone was low and mellow, his inflexion perfectly suited to the occasion: determination veined with sorrow. 'It is the deepest grief to me that my family will not acknowledge me. I know you feel wronged by my earlier deceit of you, but do not, I pray, let that stand now between us. Had my father lived, it would, I think, have been different—'

'Had my father lived,' Sir Hugo put in, 'you'd not have come fortune-hunting.'

Norton continued, as if uninterrupted. 'I believe he held out against my being legally pronounced dead. I conclude he had guessed the truth. Would that I could have found him living still. But that cannot be helped.' He grew thoughtful. 'I cannot call the dead as witnesses, save in one sense to which I will return later. Nor can I, on this occasion, call upon the two people who have acknowledged me and are conspicuous by their absence today: Miss Pursglove, whom you will say is too old to be relied upon; and Mrs Trenchard, whose husband is here to contradict all that has passed between us.' Trenchard said nothing and looked straight ahead. 'Very well. I understand why you wish I were really dead, Hugo. Believe me, I do. I even understand why you, Richard, should feel obliged to fall in with the prevailing view. As for you, Freddy, I dare say you are already running a book on the outcome.'

'I say, dammit—'

Norton held up his hand. 'Hear me out, please,' he said mildly. 'I understand why you, Trenchard, should not want your wife's former fiancé to return from the dead; why you, Dr Fiveash, should have been able to persuade yourself that I am not your former patient.'

'Young man—'

Again, the placatory gesture. 'So how can I begin to persuade you all that you are mistaken? There is only one way: the truth.'

'The truth', Moncalieri intervened in booming tones, 'is that you, monsieur, are not James Davenall. The truth—'

'Is that you are Prince Napoleon Joseph Charles Paul Bonaparte, official Bonapartist pretender to the Imperial throne of France,' said Norton with quiet conviction. 'The truth is that I often visited you in Paris with my father, in palmier days for your good self. I am surprised to see you here, Prince, and curious as to the reason. It cannot simply be to assist poor Hugo. That strikes me as altogether too altruistic a gesture.'

Trenchard looked from one to the other of them with amazement. There was no doubt that Norton was right: the shock of it was imprinted on Moncalieri's flushed and writhing countenance. He was no mere count at all, but a prince of the Bonaparte blood. Fiveash recognized him now, and was sure of it: there was even a Napoleonic cast to his features. He had met the man once at Cleave Court with Sir Gervase, many years before, when he had made no secret of his identity.

At last, the Prince spat out a response. 'I do not have to account to you for the name I choose to use.'

'Yet it would have been said later that I failed to recognize a former acquaintance by his proper name. I am sorry to have embarrassed you, but I thought it best to demonstrate that I will not be deflected by such tricks.'

'Not bad,' said Cleveland with jarring good cheer. 'How'd you twig him, old man?'

'My fame goes before me,' the Prince put in, seeming to have recovered his composure. 'Monsieur Norton's recognition of me proves nothing.'

'We last met in November 1870,' said Norton coolly. 'You dined at Bladeney House with your mistress. How is Cora these days?'

'*Mon Dieu*, this is too much! I will not—'

'Pretend any longer that I am not James Davenall?'

Prince Napoleon was angry. He might have been vaguely flattered to be recognized, but to be reminded of a discarded mistress was not at all what he had expected of this encounter. Hardly pausing to consider how Norton could have known the composition of a dinner-party twelve years before, he rose red-faced from the table. 'The Devil take you, Monsieur Norton – or whoever you are. I did not come here to be insulted. This is all . . . *la tromperie*. The misfortune of a public life is that it should attract lies . . . and gossip.' He advanced towards Norton, his features working malevolently, his towering frame hunched slightly at the shoulders, as if already wounded by the other man's words. 'You have proved nothing except that you cannot be James Davenall.'

Norton turned to look at the approaching figure. 'Sensitive because you've left poor Cora to starve? I'm sure there's no need to be. You have more to be sensitive about than a cast-off mistress. Far more, I'd have said.'

The Prince pulled up sharply. He was standing behind Richard Davenall now, one hand on his chair-back, as if in need of support. 'What do you mean?' he said slowly.

'You were a friend of the family before I was born. You were introduced to Cleave Court by your cousin, Prince Louis Napoleon, during his exile in Bath; he had befriended my grandfather, Sir Lemuel. That is how you first met my father, during a visit to your cousin in Bath in the autumn of 1846. I believe you were travelling then under the name Count of Montfort.'

'How did you—?'

'My father told me. How else should I know? Scrupulous research, perhaps? Even though I had no inkling that you would be here today? It is just possible, I suppose. Perhaps you would care for something a little more definitive.'

Prince Napoleon stooped over Norton, so that their faces were but inches apart. 'I care for nothing about you, monsieur – *rien!*'

'Had you known all that my father told me about Your Imperial Highness, I doubt you would have dared confront me. So cast your mind back. Thirty-six years ago. A long time, I grant you, but what is time to a prince? Sir Harley's Maze at Cleave Court: the twentieth of September 1846.'

A roar escaped from Prince Napoleon. He jerked himself upright, ran one hand round his quivering throat and looked down at Norton. 'Who *are* you?'

Norton ignored the question. 'My mother has abandoned the maze. Did they tell you? I expect you can guess why. She would not care for any reminders of that date. Shall I explain its significance to everyone else?'

Prince Napoleon glared across the table at Sir Hugo. 'I blame you for this!' His voice was rising to a raging pitch. 'Your mother should have warned me!'

'Calm yourself, Prince,' said Norton. 'My mother wasn't to know the extent to which my father confided in me.'

But there was no calming the Prince. With an oath, he turned on his heel and swept to the door. There he paused long enough to glower back at his tormentor. 'I will not tolerate this inquisition. Much good may you all have of it. Involve me no more.' Then he flung the door open and was gone.

V

During the interval that followed, Sir Hugo stared incredulously and for the first time at Norton, as if trying to read in those refined and reticent features the secret of his knowledge. Shock had silenced the rest of the party also; only the scratching of Lechlade's pen and the rattling of the door – left ajar by Prince Napoleon's attempt to slam it – sounded in the room above the insidious plash and patter of the rain. Nothing moved, save half a dozen sets of thoughts in vain pursuit of deductions that had already outpaced them.

Richard Davenall was perhaps best placed to assimilate what had occurred. He had long known of Sir Gervase's friendship with Prince Napoleon and had never thought it better than unfortunate. The Prince had always combined bad luck with bad manners in a way calculated to alienate those whom it did not amuse: into the amused category he had mentally pigeon-holed his cousin. Yet their friendship had survived longer than mere entertainment could possibly have justified; Sir Gervase had even written to *The Times* in 1854 defending the Prince against imputations of cowardice for leaving the Crimea at an early stage of the campaign (on grounds of a dubious illness), which had been as generously unlike him then as it was incipiently suggestive now. They had first met in 1846, true enough, but under what circumstances had their lifelong affinity been forged? How could Norton know of such things when Richard did not? Unless . . . His mind drifted to the late autumn of that year of 1854, when he, aged twenty-two and still not out of articles, had been entrusted with the stewardship of the Cleave Court estate in Sir Gervase's absence on Her Majesty's service. Catherine, having loyally accompanied her husband to the Crimea, had returned home, unannounced and in unexplained distress, in mid-December. Only later had she hinted at the reason: an encounter with Prince Napoleon in Constantinople, the Prince enraged at suggestions in the press that he was cutting and running, enraged enough to let slip something of which, until then, Catherine had had no inkling. To that, and all that followed, he reached now in his thoughts . . .

The door shut with the force and sound of a gunshot from a distant battle, and Richard Davenall was not the only one to start. Cleveland, who had walked across and pushed the door to with the toe of his shoe, apologized with a shamefaced smile. 'Sorry. Didn't mean it to slam.' He returned to his seat.

The noise seemed to have woken Sir Hugo from a trance. 'Who *are* you?' he said suddenly, still staring at Norton. 'That's what he asked. That's what I want to know.'

'You know who I am,' was the calm reply.

'You're not my brother.'

'Then answer your own question. I imagine you've had an army of private investigators trying to pin another identity on me. What have they found?'

'As yet', said Richard Davenall, 'we have reached no conclusion concerning your activities prior to visiting Cleave Court on the twenty-sixth of September.'

'Permit me to lighten your darkness. From the summer of 1871 until earlier this year I lived in North America. I only left in order to confirm a suspicion which had recently been growing in my mind. This I was able to do in France. Once that was done, the whole purpose of my disappearance eleven years ago stood vitiated. It required some months to adjust to my suddenly altered circumstances. Now that I have done so, I come before you as the man I am, whether you like it or no: James Davenall.'

'Gentlemen,' Warburton interposed, 'might I cut to the root of this matter? Does any of you dispute the facts which my client adduced in confutation of Prince Napoleon? I shall not comment on the ethics of introducing him here under an alias, Davenall' – he nodded to his fellow-lawyer – 'in view of the poverty of his showing. Plainly, however angry it made him, he was convinced.'

'I should have to reserve our position on that.'

'But are the facts disputed?'

'Not . . . as they stand.'

'Then, come, how could my client, if he were an imposter, know such things?'

'It is . . . hard to say.'

'It is, in fact, impossible, is it not? Will you not now give way?'

'Certainly not.'

'Then I must warn you that the further proofs my client may be compelled to put before you – perhaps to put before a court – will not redound to your family's credit.'

Davenall found himself clutching at straws. 'We should wish to examine photographs, to consult James's tailor, his shoemaker, anybody who could—'

'We've consulted his damned doctor!' cried Sir Hugo with sudden unhealthy energy. 'A sight more intimate than fuzzy photographs or a cobbler's last, I'd have said. Let's hear your verdict, Doctor.'

Fiveash pursed his lips in irritation at the young man's manner, but obliged in restrained tones. 'Mr Norton came to my surgery on the evening of the twenty-sixth of September. I conducted a rigorous examination—'

'At whose request?' put in Warburton.

'Since I could only express total disbelief of his claim to be my former patient, it seemed the best way to settle—'

'But at whose request?'

'It was agreed between us.'

'My client did not resist, then?'

'No.'

'Hardly the act of a guilty man. He could easily have refused.'

'Be that as it may, I examined him – by mutual consent.'

'What did you find?'

'A man in his mid-thirties who enjoys good health. More to the point, not James Davenall.'

'What makes you say so? Is he too tall, too thin, too muscular? Is there some conspicuous mole or birthmark in which he is lacking?'

'I keep no precise record of my patients' physical dimensions. He is about the same height, though somewhat more strongly built.'

'Could a change in his way of life account for that?'

'It could. As for distinguishing marks, I have no record or recollection of ones which might be significant for these purposes.'

'So on what do you base your conclusion?'

'I base it on the methods which I apply when recognizing myself in the mirror of a morning. I do not recognize this man.'

'These methods scarcely seem medical.'

'There were also medical considerations which confirmed my opinion.'

'What were they?'

'Considerations which are confidential between a doctor and his patient.'

'You allege your patient to be dead, Doctor. Does not confidentiality end there? Surely the Hippocratic Oath does not extend beyond the grave.'

'It may, in certain circumstances.'

Warburton turned to Richard Davenall. 'This is special pleading on an outrageous scale. Do you really think it will suffice?'

'I believe it will serve.'

'I fear not.' Norton had signalled once more to his solicitor that he would speak. 'I am grateful to Dr Fiveash for his misplaced loyalty, but his misapprehension cannot be allowed to continue. I must put before you squarely what may be as painful to him as it is to me. When he examined me last month, he looked for signs of an illness which he had originally diagnosed in 1871. He based his conclusion on the absence of any such signs.'

Fiveash was plainly astounded; Trenchard could read in his face less anger but more bafflement than he had in Prince Napoleon's. 'How did you—?' the doctor began.

'I fled eleven years ago because of that diagnosis. I have returned because I have learned that it was false. You were mistaken, Doctor, simply mistaken.'

Now Fiveash's professional pride had been hurt: anger welled

60

in him. 'How dare you? This is . . . this is insult piled upon guesswork.'

'No, Doctor. It is the simple truth. I came to you in April 1871 suffering from what I believed to be an optical disorder. You eventually diagnosed . . . syphilis.'

The attention he commanded was absolute. Lechlade had stopped writing. Even Cleveland sat hunched forward in his chair, cigarette abandoned, eyes fixed upon him. Trenchard was motionless, beating back from his ears the ghastly ring of truth. If James Davenall had been told he had syphilis, if James Davenall were an honourable man, what could he do a few weeks short of his wedding to an innocent woman? What could he do but . . .?

'I do not blame or condemn you: I believe the symptoms of syphilis are notoriously fickle, in my case demonstrably so. I even sought a second opinion from a Harley Street specialist. The verdict was the same, mistaken but the same. Clearly, I could not proceed with my marriage to Miss Sumner, but how could I explain why? I confess that I fled rather than admit to her the truth, rather than live some other fatuous lie. When I left the note at Cleave Court, suicide was in my mind, as it was when I reached London that night. But I had not the courage for it. The seventeenth of June 1871 was not, as you see, the day of my death, though sometimes I might almost agree that it should have been. I left the country in a steamer bound for Halifax, Nova Scotia, travelling under an assumed name. Not Norton, not then, for I have known several names. I wished only to erase myself from the world I had known. It was the one way to tolerate the shame I felt. And I succeeded – as you see.'

It fluttered then, in more heads than one, the thought that was either honour or folly: This man is in earnest – he is James Davenall. Trenchard struggled to face the realization of his worst fears and saw only something worse still: if he was to fight this man beyond this point, as he must if he was to keep Constance, he would be alone and, in all probability, in the wrong. It was not his wish, it was not his duty, yet he would do it. To prove his love was stronger than he sometimes sensed, he would fight this man to the end. He looked at Norton and steeled himself to the thought: This man I could have known as a friend is henceforth my enemy. He shuddered.

Fiveash's reaction had evidently been running along different lines. Old, set and complacently avuncular, he stood now condemned and confounded. He was not ready, it was not time, this was not the place. All the diligent, decent, seemly bedside manner of an entire career curdled in mockery of his fallibility. He cursed silently. There had been so much to mislead him. All that had gone before had unconsciously prepared him for James Davenall's illness. It had seemed almost just, almost appropriate. Could he have been so catastrophically wrong? He raged against the thought.

'No! It isn't possible. There was no room for doubt. James Davenall was incurably ill. I sent you to Emery, and he confirmed it.'

'You sent me. Yes, that's right. You did and now you've said it. You know it was me.'

'A slip. A slip of the tongue. I didn't mean . . . didn't mean . . . you.'

'You told me I was incurable, and I believed you. I crept away to die. But I didn't die. The symptoms slowly vanished. I thought they would return. But they didn't. I consulted an American doctor. He told me I was fully fit. There was no sign of syphilis. I consulted the eminent French venereologist, Fabius, in Paris. He said the same. You were mistaken, Doctor. You were all mistaken.'

Again, a hush fell. Then Trenchard spoke at last. 'One moment. Am I to take it that you are willing to admit in court that you believed you were suffering from syphilis?'

Norton's gaze was unflinching. 'If necessary, yes.'

'Then, you would also admit that, whether the diagnosis was correct or not, you had good reason at the time to believe that it might be correct.'

Norton's only reply was a smile.

Sir Hugo turned on Trenchard. 'What the devil are you doing, man? You're playing his game, assuming this isn't all a pack of lies.'

'Trenchard is looking to his own,' said Norton. 'He cannot be blamed for that. A man does not believe he has syphilis unless he knows he has been exposed to infection. Trenchard's point is that I must have been unfaithful to Constance during our engagement if that is the case.'

'What's that to me?' snapped Sir Hugo.

'Nothing, dear brother. It is nothing to you, but everything to Trenchard. Alas for him, it is also based upon a misconception. I had good cause to fear I had been infected with syphilis, but it involved no infidelity to Constance.'

'Then, how do you account for it?' said Trenchard.

'Dr Fiveash satisfied me on the point eleven years ago, and I will leave him to satisfy you in the same way now.'

'Good God,' said Fiveash slowly.

'Yes, Doctor?'

'It is not possible. Say what you like, practise what tricks you may, you cannot know what passed between us unless you are James Davenall. And I will never believe – never admit – that you are.'

'Because it would compromise your professional reputation?'

'Damnation, no. I will not admit it because it is not true.'

'You do not want to admit it because you do not want it to be true.'

'No.'

'Will you tell them what you told me then – or must I?'

'I will say nothing.'

Another pause, another wordless gulf. Then, suddenly and noiselessly, Norton rose from the table: 'Then I will say nothing, either.'

A desperate whoop from Sir Hugo. 'Because you don't know! Fiveash has called your bluff.'

If the man Norton looked down at was his brother, it was clear from his expression that there was precious little fraternal pity to lessen his contempt. 'No, Hugo, I refrain for the moment, but that is all. I will speak if I must, but, if I do, you will regret it. That is all I will say for the present.' A courteous bow to the gathering. 'Mr Warburton will explain my position. I hope to hear from you soon – for all our sakes. Now I will bid you good morning.' He walked slowly past them to the door and went out quietly. There was dignity and reserve in his retreat, just enough said and enough withheld to suggest the decency of one who would insist on his rights but never grasp at another's. The door clicked shut behind him and, as it did so, the Staple Inn clock began to strike. It was noon, only an hour since they had first assembled, yet far longer to judge by the lines that hour had scratched in their lives. Warburton looked from one to the other of them and waited for the clock to finish striking.

'Gentlemen,' he said at last, 'I trust the strength of our case is now clear to you. My client has instructed me to give you one further opportunity to consider your position. If we have not heard from you by this time two days hence – noon on Friday the thirteenth – we shall seek a hearing in Chancery at the earliest possible date of our application for the removal of the impediments being placed before Sir James Davenall in the assumption of his property and title. I doubt there is any more to be said at this stage.'

'There's everything to be said,' cried Sir Hugo. 'I've questions he won't be able to—'

'Hugo!' Richard Davenall interrupted, more sharply than before. 'Mr Warburton is right.' He glanced at the other man. 'I will see that word reaches you by the due time.'

'I'm obliged.'

'Now I think we should withdraw. Baverstock?'

The rural lawyer started in his chair. Dumbstruck throughout, he now found his voice with difficulty. 'Yes. Yes, of course. Absolutely.'

'One last point,' said Warburton. 'Lest you should pin any hopes on Sir Hugo's belief that my client is ignorant of what he currently declines to state openly, I should tell you that we have obtained a copy of Sir Gervase Davenall's death certificate. The implications of its contents will be used in court if there appears to be no alternative.'

Richard Davenall looked towards Fiveash. 'Is the import of this clear to you, Doctor?'

The reply was a husky whisper. 'Yes.'

VI

Sir Hugo Davenall sat like a man stunned in the corner of his cousin's office off High Holborn. His earlier anxiety had departed and had been replaced by a sullen lethargy: he had not even removed the sodden overcoat in which he had walked from Staple Inn. He stared straight ahead, breathing heavily, lower lip protruding, his chin cradled in his left hand whilst, with his right, he traced and retraced the embroidered relief of the pattern on the arm of his chair.

Cleveland stood by the window, clutching a glass of Scotch to his chest and smoking languidly, staring vacantly out at the street. Beside him, Trenchard was propped against the sill, back turned to the passing trams, apparently lost in thought. To one side of the window, behind a broad and disordered desk, Richard Davenall was immersed in whispered conference with Baverstock; both wore worried frowns. By the door, Dr Fiveash was pacing to and fro, sometimes pausing by the ceiling-high bookcase to squint at the spine of a legal tome – though never taking it down to read; sometimes pulling out his pocket-watch to check the time – though never commenting on its significance beyond a heavy sigh as he returned the watch to his waistcoat.

Only Trenchard looked up when the door opened and a clerk entered. He walked straight over to Richard Davenall's desk and craned across it.

'Yes, Benson?'

'A messenger from Claridge's Hotel delivered this note for you a few moments ago, sir. The sender's name is Moncalieri.'

Davenall had opened and read the note before the door had even closed behind its bearer, but a click of the tongue was his only immediate reaction.

'What does Bonny Prince Napoleon have to say for himself?' asked Cleveland.

Davenall smiled grimly. 'He is more than somewhat displeased. It seems he is to return to France . . . immediately.'

'Deserting the sinking ship?'

'He may see it that way. Certainly he has no taste for further encounters with Mr Norton. He found their discussion . . . disagreeable. Perhaps it is just as well. I fear Warburton would make considerable capital out of remarks like this: "Monsieur Norton's reference to a specific date in 1846 is pure moonshine. It has no significance. Moreover, it is inconceivable that Sir Gervase should have told him of such things."'

'What things?'

'Precisely. If the date is insignificant, there is nothing to tell. Yet he implies there is. No wonder the Bonapartist cause has not prospered under his leadership.' Davenall slowly tore the note in four and dropped the pieces into a wastepaper-basket. 'So much for our noble ally.'

'I've thought very carefully about everything that Norton said,' Trenchard interjected.

'I'm sure we all have,' Davenall snapped. Then: 'I do beg your pardon, Trenchard. Nerves a touch frayed. What do you conclude from his remarks?'

'That he spoke the truth. Something happened, involving Prince Napoleon and Sir Gervase, at Cleave Court in September 1846. Something discreditable, perhaps even disgraceful. And Norton knows about it. Who else would know?'

'Only Catherine. I have agreed with Baverstock' – a nod to his colleague – 'that he should broach the subject with her. But she may be unable to help us.'

'Surely she can – if Norton is right about her reasons for abandoning the maze.'

'I agree. Yet she may still deny all knowledge. Having met her, Trenchard, I'm sure you can imagine that.' A meaningful glance.

'Yes. I can.'

'Besides, what could it be? And does it really matter now that Prince Napoleon has withdrawn from the case? It cannot prove or disprove Norton's claim. James wasn't even born in 1846.'

'When was he born?'

'February 1848. Why do you ask?'

'I don't know, really. It's just . . .'

'You said you felt that everything Norton said was true. Does that extend to his claim to be James? We may as well know where we all stand.'

'It could be, you know,' Cleveland put in. 'I know it's tough on you fellows, but I find the chap awfully convincin.'

'But you, Trenchard,' said Davenall. 'What do you think?'

'I don't know your family well enough to say. I never met James. Was he . . . close to his father?'

'No. That's the strangest part of all this. Sir Gervase was the coolest, least forthcoming, least fatherly of men. I always felt he wouldn't have given James the time of day. But, then, how well can I claim to have known him? I was his solicitor first, his cousin . . . hardly ever. Dr

Fiveash' – he turned towards the pacing figure by the door – 'have you yet resolved your crisis of medical conscience?'

Fiveash glared across at them. 'It is not to be taken lightly.'

'I'm sorry. I didn't mean to imply that it was. At least you can clear up this business of the death certificate. I understood Sir Gervase to have died of the continuing effects of a stroke.' He looked back at Trenchard. 'Sir Gervase suffered a stroke . . . oh, three years ago. He spent the last eighteen months of his life in a nursing home in a perfectly helpless condition. Ironically, the stroke seemed to be brought on by a series of disagreements – and open arguments – stemming from his refusal to have James pronounced dead.' His gaze returned to Fiveash. 'Would you care to comment, Doctor?'

Fiveash pulled himself up with a great sigh. 'The certificate will show the cause of death as general paralysis of the insane.'

'Insane?'

'A mere form of words. The symptoms are not inconsistent with a stroke and, indeed, he did suffer a mild stroke.'

'Mild? I was told at the time that it was severe.'

'The illness was severe, the deterioration rapid, but the symptoms were of long standing. The point Norton was making is, however, a simple one. General paralysis of the insane is a common manifestation of tertiary syphilis. Put plainly, Sir Gervase died of syphilis.' He slumped down in a chair.

Richard Davenall glanced across at his cousin. 'Did you know of this, Hugo?'

'Mmm?' Sir Hugo stirred from his lethargy. 'Yes. The old boy had the pox. Did you expect me to announce it in *The Times*?'

'You might have told me.'

'I didn't consider it any of your business.'

'It is now. Does your mother know?'

'Not from me. And I don't think she guessed. She never visited him, not once. I trooped out there often enough, God knows, and he'd look at me, disappointment written on his face. It wasn't me he wanted to see. Sometimes, I didn't even think it was Mother.'

'But James?'

'Yes. My precious vanished brother James.' He suddenly grasped the tasseled fringe on the arm of his chair, twisting and grinding it in his hand. 'That man isn't James. He can't be. He's too . . . too damned impressive.'

'And he is not syphilitic,' Fiveash added mournfully.

Richard Davenall leaned across his desk, staring at the doctor intently. 'Will you now state plainly what you declined to disclose earlier?'

'Very well. James consulted me in April 1871 – just as Norton said. He complained of deteriorating vision, combined with watering of the

66

eyes, spasm of the lids and sensitivity to thc light. These symptoms were not then well developed, but they were clearly indicative of interstitial keratitis, the commonest cause of which is congenital syphilis.'

'Congenital?'

'He means, cousin,' said Sir Hugo, 'that James inherited the disease.'

'Good God. You knew this?'

It was Fiveash who replied. 'When I disclosed the true nature of his father's illness to Sir Hugo, I felt obliged to inform him of the slight risk to which he had been exposed. It was something which had always concerned me. Sir Gervase contracted syphilis more than thirty years ago. I hoped at the time that he had not infected Lady Davenall and hence James, but there was no guarantee of it. Lady Davenall has never displayed any signs of the disease. Unfortunately, it is possible for some carriers of syphilis to exhibit no symptoms but still pass it on to their offspring. When James asked me to examine him, my worst fears were confirmed. In Sir Hugo's case, the risk was substantially reduced. By the time he was born, the progress of the disease would, in all likelihood, have gone beyond the infectious stage.'

Nobody spoke for several minutes after Fiveash had finished. He himself sat hunched in his chair, lips pursed, plainly distressed at having had to reveal so many secrets of the consulting-room. Trenchard found himself struggling to suppress sympathy for the man who might have borne the yoke of his father's sins and realized then what Norton had meant: for one member at least of the Davenall family there was, in this disease, no dishonour.

'How much did you tell James?' said Richard Davenall at length.

Fiveash sighed. 'All that I could. The young man was in acute distress: he was entitled to know why. God knows there was little enough else I could do for him. Some palliative eye-drops . . . and some grim advice.'

'What advice?'

'That the disease was incurable, that the symptoms would worsen and multiply, that its end was a painful and lingering death compounded by mental disintegration. To tell a patient such things is the doctor's most unpleasant duty, gentlemen, the more so when that patient is a sweet-natured and otherwise healthy young man standing on the brink of matrimony. The last was the hardest part of all. I had to tell him that it was imperative he should not marry; that he should, in short, avoid all risk of infecting his fiancée.'

'Did you need to be . . . so explicit?'

'Surely you can see I had no choice.'

'Did it not occur to you subsequently that this might have driven him to suicide?'

'Of course it did. But would you – would any of your family – have thanked me for volunteering such information? Lady Davenall was and is ignorant of her husband's infidelity. Would you have wanted her disillusioned? I think not, sir.'

'Is it possible you were mistaken, Doctor?' said Trenchard. 'Is it possible that Norton is telling the truth?'

'I made exhaustive tests. I sent James to a specialist who confirmed my diagnosis. There was no possibility of error. The idea is preposterous.'

'Is, then, a spontaneous recovery conceivable?'

'Nothing is absolutely certain in medicine, but the irreversible nature of syphilis is as near it as makes no odds. Sir Gervase possessed an extremely robust constitution, but it availed him nought in the end. If James Davenall were alive today, he would not be the picture of health that James Norton is. I would expect him, for instance, to be blind.'

'So we have him,' said Sir Hugo, almost to himself. 'Hoist with his own petard.'

Fiveash looked at him in amazement. 'You cannot be thinking of making any of this public?'

'Why not?'

Richard Davenall stared across at his cousin. 'The Doctor is quite right, Hugo. None of this must go beyond these four walls. Your father exposed as syphilitic, your mother dishonoured, our family disgraced: such would be the consequences of using this information to defend any action Norton brings. He knows that as well as we do.'

'Then, let's call his bluff.'

'You cannot be serious. You have not thought this out.' The older man stared at the younger in vain search of understanding. 'Our family would be ruined.'

'You would prefer it if the ruin were reserved for me? You're the lawyer, Richard. What will happen if Norton wins?'

'I hardly think—'

'What will happen?'

'In that unlikely event, the baronetcy would revert to him and . . .'

'Yes?'

'And the whole of the estate,' he replied haltingly. 'Your father bequeathed all his property to James in the will set aside as a result of the presumption-of-death proceedings. Cleave Court, Bladeney House, all rental income: your entire legacy would revert to him.'

'Is that all?'

'There might even be a requirement for you to compensate him for any assets or proceeds of the estate you have disposed of since obtaining title, but this is all—'

'This is all I have gleaned from other sources less reticent than you. I

68

could wish you remembered more often, cousin, that it is *my* interests you should be protecting, not our family's. If the choice is between my being pauperized and the Davenall name taking a dent, then you should know that in my mind there is really no choice at all.'

'But your mother—'

'Would have her eyes opened concerning the man she married. I cannot help that. If you wish to avoid it, find a way for me to stop Norton. You have two full days, I believe. I suggest you put them to good use. Meanwhile, I've had my fill of the subject.' He rose from the chair. 'Coming, Freddy? I think a drink is in order.'

The two men departed with every outward show of unconcern, leaving the others to contemplate the stark course Sir Hugo had made it clear he was prepared to follow. For him, simplicity had concentrated the mind. He enjoyed wealth and the profligacy that went with it far above the esteem of respectable society. Now that wealth was threatened, all secondary considerations – including his mother's peace of mind – were to be set aside in its defence.

FOUR

I

The rain was still falling when I left Richard Davenall's offices that afternoon. If anything, it seemed more intense than before, moving in sheets across the prematurely dark skyline of drenched brick and dripping stone. Abandoning hope of a cab in such conditions, I turned west and trudged wearily in the direction of Orchard Street, feeling, in some respects, restored by the rain beating in my face; I was in need of it to wash away the memory of what the day had held. Unlike those who had known James Davenall, I had not even a conflicting recollection to cling to, nothing to reassure me in moments of solitary fear that Norton was not what he claimed. How could he know so much unless he spoke the truth? There was no answer save another taunting question: What would I tell Constance – what could I tell her?

As I waited to cross Southampton Row, a cab pulled up unbidden beside me and Dr Fiveash's large bearded face protruded from the window. 'You look soaked, man. Jump in!'

For a moment, I hesitated, uncertain whether I desired anybody's company, especially that of one who had been party to the day's bitter counsel. Then I relented and climbed aboard.

'It's good of you to have stopped for me,' I said.

'Least I could do. I'm returning to my hotel in Bayswater. Will that suit you?'

'I'll come halfway if I may. Are you going back to Bath tonight?'

'Tomorrow. I shan't be sorry at that.'

'I imagine not.'

He slapped his thigh in suppressed irritation. 'This is the very devil of a business! The very devil!'

I felt almost as sorry for Fiveash as I did for myself. Norton had called into question some hitherto utterly reliable aspects of both our lives: in

Fiveash's case his professional competence, in mine a happy marriage.
'*Perhaps you feel as I do: helpless.*'

'*It's worse than that. I've been in practice for more than forty years. I've ministered to the Davenall's aches and pains all that time without so much as complaining once how slow they've been to settle my bills. I nursed Sir Gervase through thirty years of self-inflicted ailments and never once told him what I thought of him. Now this happens – and that young wastrel Sir Hugo says he'll happily risk me being branded as incompetent for the sake of keeping himself in whisky and soda. I do feel helpless, yes, but I also feel betrayed.*'

'*By the Davenalls – or by fate?*'

He frowned. 'You don't think he is an impostor, do you?'

'*I'm in no position to say. But you are.*'

'*Then take my word for it. He is not James Davenall.*'

'*I'm happy to believe it; but, if he isn't, how can he know what passed between you and the real James Davenall in utter confidence eleven years ago?*'

The frown deepened. 'I have asked myself the same question. I spoke of it to nobody until this day. When I told Sir Hugo the true nature of his father's illness, he might have guessed, but—'

'*Would scarcely be likely to tell anybody if he had.*'

'*Quite so.' He stared out at the jolting view of the street and grew more thoughtful still. 'I referred James to a colleague of mine, Dr Emery, but his discretion is beyond question. Besides, I believe the poor fellow went to him under an alias.' He looked back at me. 'Is it possible Norton learned of it from James Davenall's own lips, do you suppose?*'

'*If they ever knew one another, Norton would have been recognized by the family. And why would he wait eleven years to come forward?*'

He nodded mournfully. 'As you say.'

'*Do you keep any kind of records to which Norton might have had access?*'

'*Naturally I keep records, but they are not left lying around for idle passers-by to read.' His professional pride, already bruised, had been hurt again. 'Forgive me. What I mean is that the records I keep on my patients are under lock and key. Besides, why should anyone think to consult them? How would they know what to look for?*'

I did not need to reply. Our theories were desperate enough to speak for themselves. We fell silent and stared from opposite windows of the cab, as it wound sluggishly through the waterlogged traffic of Oxford Street, at the same dismal prospect. We were as far as ever, if not further, from finding an answer.

71

II

Two miles away, beyond one of the exclusive Palladian façades of Pall Mall, lay the windowless refuge chosen by Sir Hugo Davenall to revive his battered spirits. There, in the subfuscous billiards-room of a club whose committee could be relied upon to blackball any shopkeeper's son who had the temerity to put up for membership, Sir Hugo and Freddy Cleveland sought to erase the disagreeable taste of the day's proceedings with regular infusions of whisky and soda and half a dozen frames of pyramids.

Sir Hugo was angry. That much was apparent to Cleveland from the accuracy and ferocity with which he played his shots, and that much he did not resent. The sullen silences interspersed with biting sarcasm were quite another matter, however. Cleveland expected his friends to be as consistently frivolous as he was himself. Sir Hugo having fallen far short of this for several days past, he was in danger of being classified a bore. And Cleveland did not choose to associate with bores.

'Why don't you strike some kind of bargain with the fellow?' he asked idly as Sir Hugo pocketed another ball with a violent thrust of the cue. 'There's surely room for both of you. He seems an accomodatin' sort.'

The only answer he received was a scowl as Sir Hugo took a swig from his glass before returning to the table.

'Otherwise, I can't see it goin' well for you. Even I can't swear any more that he's not Jimmy. There is somethin' about him, you know.' Another ball was slammed down. 'Somethin' – I don't know – uncanny.'

Sir Hugo's uncommunicative state was scarcely to be wondered at. It was not simply that he hated Norton, although he did – as, for that matter, he had hated his brother James. It was not even that he did not know how to defeat him, although, by arrogantly leaving his cousin to solve the problem, he had, in truth, merely revealed his own incapacity. There was more to it than either of these uncomfortable realities: there was Norton's ability to recall the past and use it as a weapon in the present. How potent a weapon it might prove Sir Hugo was only now coming to realize, as he stalked the table and listened to the faint hiss of the gasalier above his head, concentrating on it to shut out Cleveland's chatter.

It was, he remembered, in the autumn of 1879 that dear cousin Richard suggested a weekend at Cleave Court might suffice for him to persuade his inexplicably reluctant father that the time really had come to have James pronounced dead in law as well as in fact.

He did not want to go. He hated Cleave Court. Whether it was full of his father's hunting and shooting neighbours or empty and echoing

72

only with the unheard footfalls of his vanished brother, whether greyly assailed by its characteristic rains or fatuously alive with birdsong and dew-prinked flowers, he loathed its every draughty chimney and creaking board. A sickly child they had thought him, a truculent ingrate unappreciative and unworthy of the privileges and obligations of a landed title, mercifully the younger of Sir Gervase's two sons, to be consigned in due course to the Army and pulled into some kind of shape. It had gone otherwise, for them and for him, and he had found his element in the heady heedless whirl of London society, darling of every hostess, friend of all who were anybody, his worst indiscretions tolerated because, thanks be to James, he was the future baronet.

So he went to Cleave Court and was at once relieved to discover that he would be spared the tedious society of north Somerset gentry. Quinn, the butler, for whom Hugo felt a twinge of sympathy because the man never troubled to disguise his dislike of Lady Davenall, a dislike which Hugo often sensed he shared himself, reported that they had not 'entertained' since the previous Christmas and were not about to.

Lady Davenall herself exhibited maternal feelings in fits of startling unpredictability. She was in the midst of one such on this occasion. 'I can make no excuse for your father, Hugo. Such improvidence is insufferable. You must have it out with him – man to man.'

Hugo could not see why the matter was so urgent. His father was only sixty-two – good for another ten years at least, he supposed. But he had not seen him in more than six months and, when he did so, he realized that Sir Gervase had suddenly become a frail old man: haggard and forgetful, beset by a facial tremor, all faculties impaired save his temper, which was as fearsomely changeable as ever. Over dinner, he was positively maudlin in his pleasure at Hugo's company. Afterwards, when Hugo explained the purpose of his visit, his mood was in savage contrast.

'I gather it's a legal nicety, Papa. It simply removes any doubt over the succession.'

Sir Gervase seemed not to hear. He was slumped in a wing-back chair, staring at an oil painting of his great-grandfather, Sir Harley Davenall, and massaging his tremulous cheek with a bony hand.

'You really must bring yourself to accept that James is dead.'

Sir Gervase flashed a glare at him. 'Be damned!'

'Papa!'

Suddenly, the old man lurched from his chair and flung his brandyglass across the room. It smashed against the coping of the grate, the fragments showering across the hearth and the residue of spirit sizzling on the fire. Hugo was tense in every muscle. His father turned on him, eyes blazing, mouth working. 'You young fool! Don't you know why?' He gestured wildly towards the rooms his wife had withdrawn to. 'Don't you know why she wants this?'

73

'It's simply—'

Sir Gervase moved with the speed of a cat pouncing. He grasped Hugo by the collar and dragged him bodily from his chair. Hugo heard his collar-stud snap free and bounce against a tray on the table beside them. He stared into his father's face, a quivering mask of illegible emotion, and noticed, most alarming of all, that the old man was dribbling: his chin was bathed in saliva. 'I'll tell you why she wants this, the scheming bitch.'

'Papa! For God's sake—'

Suddenly, he was bouncing in his chair, released from Sir Gervase's grasp, let fall like a mouse from an eagle's beak. His father loomed above him, the great predatory outline of him carved in the shape he had feared all his life, his outstretched right hand frozen in the taloned hold he had so abruptly abandoned. Then he, too, was falling, tilting sideways and plunging floorwards with no attempt to break his descent. He crashed to the carpet, overturning the table and its trayload of decanters as he did so, then sagged on to his back and lay motionless amidst the scatter of wood and glass.

It took several days to establish that he would not recover. Hugo had already tired of visiting the shrunken speechless husk of his father that they propped up on pillows in his bed every morning when Lady Davenall announced that, on Dr Fiveash's advice, Sir Gervase would be removed to a nursing home in Bristol, whence he was not expected to return.

'I dare say it's for the best,' she remarked brightly over breakfast. 'And Dr Fiveash is prepared to state your father's no longer in control of his mental faculties, which means we can proceed to have you pronounced his heir.' It was difficult to tell what prevented her commenting how worth while Hugo's visit had been.

'I may as well return to London, then.'

'Yes, dear, you may as well. But I do have a couple of errands for you to run in Bath first. I've arranged for you to call on Baverstock this morning. You know, the solicitor in Cheap Street.'

'What on earth for?'

'Why, to put the probate proceedings in train, of course.'

'But surely you'll use Richard.'

She smiled blithely. 'No. I prefer a local man.'

Hugo was dismayed, but had not the energy to argue. 'Very well.'

'And Dr Fiveash wants to see you. He suggests his surgery at two o'clock this afternoon.'

'What does he want?'

'I can't imagine. I suggest you go along and find out.'

So he went, albeit reluctantly, to Fiveash's large comfortless house on the outskirts of Bath, perched precariously on the steepling slope of Claverton Down, and found the doctor awaiting him in his consulting-room. Always a bustling serious man, Fiveash seemed, on

74

this occasion, more preoccupied and anxious than ever. He walked up and down by the window, slapping his hands together and sucking his beard, till, in the end, Hugo felt obliged to broach the subject for him.

'Is it about my father, Doctor?'

'Yes, yes. It is. Indeed it is.'

'My mother has told me there's no prospect of a recovery.'

'None. No, none at all.'

'We have adjusted to the fact. A stroke was—'

'It was not a stroke.' Fiveash turned and regarded Hugo solemnly.

'Not a stroke? Then, what?'

The doctor took a deep breath. 'Your father has syphilis. Has had for many years. This is only the most distressing – and final – stage of the illness.'

'Good God.'

'I felt you ought to know. I imagined you might wish your mother to remain in ignorance of it.'

'Yes. That would be best.'

'It should not prove unduly difficult. The nursing home I have recommended can be relied upon to handle such matters delicately. A stroke may cover a multitude of sins – so to speak. There is, however, something else I feel you ought to know.'

'Well?'

'When I first diagnosed your father's illness, I had to tell him that, in the interests of his wife – and of any unborn offspring – he should, from that time on, refrain from all . . . conjugal relations.'

'When was this?'

'Before you were born.'

'You mean—'

'I mean that I have reason to believe your mother may have been infected by your father, although she has never displayed any symptoms. There exists, therefore, a slight risk that you have inherited the disease, although I would say that risk was very slight indeed. In any event, your father should never have allowed your mother to conceive again in view of what I had told him. It was . . . grossly irresponsible. More to the point, I feel obliged to acquaint you with the warning signs in case . . .'

Fiveash continued, but Hugo was not listening. Already, he was pondering something of which the doctor could have no inkling. A husband required to live in celibacy with his wife. A wife left to attribute that celibacy to the worst imaginable reasons. One son lost whom his father would not accept was dead. Another son whom he did not want for his heir and whom he was about to tell . . .

He had overstruck the shot. The cue ball cannoned over the red and bounced clear of the table, clattering away across the wooden floor.

'Bad luck!' said Cleveland.

75

Sir Hugo straightened up and looked towards him, imagining how easy his friend would find it to accept Norton as a Davenall and wondering if he could adjust as readily to the idea that Sir Hugo might not be one himself after all. 'It was bound to catch up with me,' he said musingly.

'What's that, old man?'

'My luck, Freddy. I'm surprised it's held this long.'

III

Some time after the train left Reading and began to track across the Vale of the White Horse towards Swindon, rain ceased to fling itself against the window of Arthur Baverstock's compartment and the provincial lawyer felt his resentment of London practices in general and Richard Davenall's in particular fall away, little by little, as the landscape grew more homely and his memory of the day's discomforts less acute. It had been agreed that he should return at once to Bath with a view to asking Lady Davenall what might have happened at Cleave Court in September 1846, and he was glad of the excuse to leave the other Davenalls to their own devices. Indeed, he would have been happy to dissociate himself from the whole affair but, just as Lady Davenall would answer questions or not (and probably not) as she pleased, so her wish to be separately represented was something Baverstock knew better than to challenge.

It was strange, he reflected, as he gazed from the window at the flooded fields flanking the line, that he probably already knew more about the significance of the date Norton had quoted than he was ever likely to glean from Lady Davenall. He was surprised, and secretly pleased, that Richard Davenall seemed to know nothing of it; but, then, he had been denied, if denial it was, Baverstock's advantage of lengthy conversation with Esme Pursglove, who had seen more and forgotten less in sixty-five years at Cleave Court than anybody else alive or dead. On more occasions in recent times than he cared to remember, he had been a captive guest for tea at Miss Pursglove's cottage, listening with half an ear to her interminable reminiscences of a lifetime in service to the Davenalls. If only he had been more attentive, it now transpired, he might hold something more coherent in his mind than a jumble of stray remarks scattered, months apart, across random tea-time monologues. But that, he did not doubt, could soon be set to rights. Meanwhile, he could not do better than recollect what had first prompted Miss Pursglove to call the event to mind. It was the maze, of course, the confounded maze in which he took so little interest. That is what had done it.

'Mr Crowcroft came to see me yesterday. First Quinn, now Crowcroft. Where will it end, eh? He was so dreadfully upset about the maze. Not allowed to maintain it any more. That's what he said . . . *Not allowed.* No wonder the poor man's going . . .

'Of course, there are some who say the maze is haunted by old Sir Harley, but that's plain nonsense. It's just an excuse: they're afraid of not being able to find the way out. As for Lady Davenall, I suppose it's that serious mind of hers. I've never known her go there, so she must think it's a waste keeping it up. I can't believe she's afraid of being lost in it. She's too sensible for that . . .

'Now I come to think back, she *did* use to go there, but that was a long, long time ago. I can see her now, twirling her parasol and asking Sir Gervase to show her the secret route. It must have been before they were married, when she was just a slip of a thing, no more than seventeen, because they were always accompanied by her governess, as was only proper . . .

'Miss Strang. That was her name. Lady Davenall was plain Miss Webster then, though not so plain in looks. But she was put in the shade by Miss Strang and no mistake. I only met her a couple of times. A close, grave Scottish piece, but she had the heather and the moors in her looks. There were those who said it was Miss Strang as Sir Gervase was really courting all along. It wouldn't surprise me. He was always one to want what he couldn't have. Perhaps Colonel Webster was put wise. At all events, she was suddenly gone. Dismissed, we heard.

'When would it have been, now? Sir Gervase and Lady Davenall were married in the spring of 1847, so it must have—'

'Ticket, please, sir.'

Baverstock pulled his mind back to the present and fumbled in his pocket. Not that the interruption troubled him unduly. He was sure of it now. By the time he had found the ticket and the inspector had left him alone again, he was certain in his own mind that that was what she had said.

' . . . . it must have been the previous September. September 1846.'

IV

In the event, I told Constance nothing. I clung to the convenient fiction that, if Norton's story were true, it was too appalling to be told and, if it were not, it was not worth telling. So the grudging silence which had prevailed between us since our return from Somerset held to the end of an agonized evening. We both sat reading whilst time ticked slowly away, our thoughts filled in neither case with what was before us on the page.

At length, though still self-consciously early, Constance rose and said

77

that she would retire for the night. Only then, when she had gone as far as the door and paused on the threshold, did she refer to what we both knew the day had held.

'You have said nothing about your visit to Mr Norton's solicitor, William.'

I closed my book and looked up at her. I might have responded by confessing then all the unworthy fears and dreadful notions which had driven me into this futile attempt to muzzle her hope along with my suspicion. Instead, I only fuelled its futility. 'We agreed not to speak of it again.' Even to myself, my words sounded harsh and foolish.

'We have spoken of nothing else.'

'That is your choice.'

'No, William. I would happily share all my thoughts with you. You must see—'

'I only see that Norton is an impostor. There is no need for you—'

'If you had proved that today, you would have said so.'

'Nothing was altered by today's exchanges.'

'And I see nothing will be altered now. Very well. Good night, William.' She turned and left the room.

I filled my pipe, then discarded it unlit. I drank some whisky and found I had no taste for it. There seemed, in fact, nothing to do but pace the floor and wrestle in my mind, as I had done countless times already, with the intimidating certainty of James Norton, the repellent truth that I feared him much more than I doubted him. It was not to be wondered at, for I had good reason to fear him and none at all, so far, to doubt him.

I found myself standing by the bureau which Constance used in her management of the household expenses. She kept her few personal papers there, as I kept mine in the study, in neither case under lock and key, for we had never felt the need of secrecy – until now. I tried the lid, which was, sure enough, unsecured, and lowered it slowly, taking care that it should not creak. There was a row of three small drawers within which represented the only places where anything of real value might be concealed. I tried the knob of each in turn and found the last to be locked. This was innocuous enough in itself, for the key to the drawers was kept in one of the pigeon-holes above. I sifted through their contents carefully in search of it. Then I did so again. It was not there. I tried the locked drawer again: it would not give. Silently, I cursed my own folly for making the attempt. It had only confirmed what I already knew: that I was driving Constance away from me. For the first time, there were secrets between us.

When I went upstairs, Constance was sitting by the dressing-table in her nightgown, brushing her hair – her long, lustrous chestnut hair. I watched its strands catch the light as they fell free of the brush, imagined myself walking across, as I might have done on any other occasion, taking the brush from her hand and running it through her hair, then stooping to kiss her neck above the lace collar of her gown. I paused behind her as the thought invaded my self-pity and, at that moment, her eyes met mine in the mirror. Perhaps she yearned for me to touch her, to stop the slide before it carried us both over the brink. But all she could have seen was the stern line of my mouth, the unyielding remoteness of my expression. I had remembered the locked drawer and the missing key and now walked quickly away to the bathroom.

V

Richard Davenall had inherited his tall, dark, oversized home in North Road, Highgate, from his father, Wolseley Davenall, whose austere unbending soul it so exactly suited. It lacked almost everything Richard required in terms of comfort and convenience, but he had lived alone there for more than twenty years now and he did not suppose he was about to leave it. He sat in the study that evening, listening to the wind howling in the chimney, watching the flame of the oil-lamp before him on the desk flutter periodically in North Road's perpetual draughts, and recalled standing once just beyond the same faltering circle of lamplight whilst his father sat where he sat now, on the evening of his abrupt return from Cleave Court in the summer of 1855.

He remembered shifting his weight awkwardly from one foot to another, remembered trying to look anywhere but into his father's grey-green flinty eyes and remembered, too, with a sudden flush of shame, the guilt that all his evasions must so amply have proclaimed. There had been no hint of remission in his father's gaze, no trace of gentleness in his voice, nor was there any now, as he recalled them.

'Your uncle' – by which he meant his brother, Sir Lemuel – 'has spoken to me. It was not an agreeable discussion.'

'I am sorry for that, sir.' Richard's voice cracked as he spoke.

His father nodded his lean grave head, and Richard reflected, for a crazy moment, how like a tortoise he looked with his thin wrinkled neck emerging from a stiff oversized collar. 'So you should be – and so you will be. Into the' – he curled his upper lip – 'particulars, I will not enquire. Suffice to say that I did not send you to Cleave Court to cause me this . . . vexation.' Vexation, in Wolseley Davenall's vocabulary, implied the wrath of his extreme displeasure.

'There is nothing I can say, sir.'

'From what I gather, you have already said – and done – too much. It is to your advantage, though not on your account, that I have

79

persuaded your uncle to ensure that his son knows nothing – absolutely nothing – of what has occurred.' So Wolseley had done no pleading on his son's behalf.

'May I ask—?'

'You may ask nothing!' Wolseley's eyes widened for a moment, sufficient to reveal the anger lurking behind his ingrained reserve. Was it only anger? Richard sometimes believed his father might harbour even less paternal sentiments towards him. An elderly bridegroom who had become a middle-aged widower, Wolseley Davenall had built a life – if you could call it that – on implied resentments and inferred regrets. For such a father, a son could only be a sounding-board for his misanthropy. At last, Richard understood. His father took pleasure in his disgrace: it was all he could have hoped for. 'I have decided to place you under Mr Chubb's supervision until your conduct suggests greater application and less – I should say *no* – self-indulgence.'

Richard closed his eyes. Gregory Chubb had never hidden his hatred of the senior partner's son. Now he would have dominion over him. It was a heavy price to pay for one young man's helpless lapse, a price he was to pay, as events fell out, for six long years.

'Perhaps not so heavy after all.'

He had addressed the remark to himself, had heard it fall amongst the inanimate stirrings of the room, had watched his twenty-seven-years-younger self turn from the lamplight and fuse with the crouched and threatening shadows of his father's house. For it was true. It had not been so bad, not nearly so bad, as for another – if Norton was that other and he did not lie.

From amongst the papers on his desk, Richard lifted one sheet and leaned forward in his chair to read it, not for the first time that night. It fitted, he could not deny, Norton's claims better than any of the elaborate constructions he and others had placed upon it, then and since. And rereading seemed only to make denial more precarious still.

17th June 1871

Dear Mother and Father,
This is the last you will ever hear from me. I am determined to end my life this day. I have no wish to ease your pain, for you will know how well-deserved it is. It is for Constance's sake that I must do this. God forgive me – and you. I leave you with love but no respect.

James

Found by Sir Gervase in his dressing-room early that evening, its bitter poignant farewell never, till this day, explained, it was a suicide note that had seemed also to murder a family. The Davenalls now lived in an armed camp of their own hostility, leading separate loveless lives. Only James's parents and Richard, their solicitor, had seen the note, but its message clung to the family still, dogged them across the distances they placed between themselves, defied them, now more than ever, to say it could be forgotten.

The note dropped from Richard's fingers. He sat still for some moments, staring ahead as if the mystery of James's disappearance were imprinted on the darkness, then moved his hand to another, flimsier sheet of paper and held it up to read.

In Confidence
Report to R. Davenall
Subject: James Norton

I have exhaustively monitored the movements of the above for one week. They have given me no clue as to his origins, means and associates, beyond what you already know, with the sole exception of the address of his banker, Hazlitt's in the Strand. He has left London on one occasion: Saturday, 7th October. He proceeded by train to Bathampton in Somerset, from where he walked south along the towpath of the Kennet & Avon Canal to a point where he met Mrs Trenchard. Their interview was of brief duration and appeared to conclude abruptly, consequent upon Mr Trenchard's arrival on the scene. The subject then returned to Bathampton on foot and by train to London.

On three occasions, he has left his hotel late at night, returning in the early hours of the morning. On each such occasion, he has proved impossible to follow. He appears well practised in the arts of evasion and elusion, so much so that I suspect he is aware he is followed and is presumably content for his movements to be known, save on these nocturnal expeditions, which generally lead towards the lowest and most squalid districts of the city, though whether the route is chosen to render pursuit the more difficult or for other reasons I cannot say.

The subject, though well dressed, has attracted little attention at his hotel, where he is noted as sober and correct, a reliable but not extravagant tipper, in all respects the model guest. He pays his bill every third day and is clearly not short of money.

T. ROFFEY
10th October 1882

Roffey was the best of his unsavoury kind, yet even Roffey had made no headway. Richard spoke aloud for a second time. 'Who *are* you?' he said quietly. 'Who *are* you?' He could not quite believe, nor yet disbelieve, the answer beckoning to him across the years.

VI

When I reached Orchard Street the following morning, I was in no mood to pay much attention to my surroundings, so spared scarcely a glance for the few passers-by in the region of Trenchard & Leavis. Accordingly, I was taken aback when one of them stepped into my path and held up his umbrella to make himself known: it was Dr Fiveash.

'Good Lord,' I said, pulling up sharply. 'You quite startled me, Doctor.'

'Forgive me, Trenchard. I thought it vital that I should speak to you before I returned to Bath.' He looked as if he meant it. Indeed, his red-rimmed eyes and disordered appearance suggested that he had passed a still more disturbed night than I had myself. His vitality was of a drained and desperate character.

I invited him up to my office, but he expressed a preference for the open air, so I led him back towards Marble Arch. Oxford Street was quiet and sparsely populated beneath a sky squeezed dry by the previous day's rain but still grey and sullen of aspect. Fiveash looked about him as we went with an air of tired confusion, as if returning to a former home to find it changed beyond recognition.

'There was a time', he said, as we neared the Arch, 'when I thought London the very Mecca of my ambitions. I dreamed of being a famous surgeon at one of the teaching hospitals. Now I visit this city only when compelled.'

'And leave it with relief?'

'Exactly so.'

We entered the park by Cumberland Gate and began a slow progress down one of the damp leaf-strewn paths. After thirty yards or so, Fiveash began to speak again.

'I came to you because neither of us wishes to be involved in this damnable business and because I do not trust the Davenalls. As victims of their manoeuvring, we must stick together. And I have thought much on what you said yesterday.'

'I only—'

'You only asked how anybody could know what I told James Davenall eleven years ago. Well, I have asked myself nothing else since and I called on you this morning because I can now say that there is a way.'

'What way?'

'You spoke of my records. It is true that if anybody were to read the notes I made when James Davenall consulted me they would know the nature of his illness and from that might construe the motive behind his suicide.'

'But you said they were kept under lock and key.'

'So they are. Nobody but my secretary and I have access to them, and

82

Miss Arrow has been with me for eighteen years: her loyalty is beyond question. It was only last night, when I was turning over in my mind the absurd possibility that she might have betrayed me, that I thought of it.

'In January of this year, Miss Arrow broke her leg in a cycling accident. Her bicycle brakes failed whilst descending Bathwick Hill, and she ran out of control. She was fortunate, indeed, not to be more seriously injured. My own plight – that of being deprived of her services for several months – was, typically, uppermost in her mind, and she recommended that I take on in her stead a witness to her accident who had subsequently visited her in hospital: a highly personable young lady named Miss Whitaker, who, as it happened, was waiting to take up a teaching appointment after Easter and was, in consequence, glad to step into the breach. Miss Whitaker proved both charming and efficient, swiftly mastering Miss Arrow's procedures and learning my ways without difficulty. She even volunteered to reorganize my anti-quated system of medical records and worked her way dutifully through the somewhat haphazard files we keep on each patient.'

'You mean—'

'I mean that, had Miss Whitaker been seeking information on James Davenall's medical history, she could not have been better placed to find it. I had no reason to suspect any such thing, of course. The acquisition of her services I regarded as fortunate in the extreme. But, in the middle of February, Miss Whitaker vanished. She simply failed to arrive one morning, and when I called at her lodgings I was told she had left unexpectedly, leaving no forwarding address. It was unac-countable.'

'What did you do?'

'I dismissed the matter from my mind. After all, I had lost nothing by it. Or so I thought.'

'Until now?'

'Precisely. What if Miss Arrow's accident were no accident at all? Brakes may be tampered with easily enough, and Miss Whitaker witnessed the incident, remember. Is that all she did? I wonder. It gave her the opportunity to wheedle her way into my employment, where her zeal and enthusiasm made delving into my records seem merely another example of her diligence. Then, once she had obtained what she wanted, she simply disappeared.'

We had come to the band-stand, deserted and bedraggled in the dull morning air, and, after one circuit, began to retrace our steps. 'How would you describe Miss Whitaker, Doctor?'

'How? She was young, pretty, vivacious. She brought a breath of spring to my wintry old surgery. Had I been thirty years younger, I might have set my cap at her. She had . . . winning ways. If I am right, she made a thorough fool of me, but I doubt I was the first she did that

83

to, nor yet the last. For such an easy conversationalist, she said very little about herself. She gave her age as twenty-two, though she could easily have been older – or younger. She was evidently well educated. She said that her family lived abroad, though I cannot recall her saying where. There was the hint of an accent in her voice – something faintly French, I often thought. And that is really all. It isn't much, is it?'

Fiveash was wrong. To me it was everything: it was something to cling to. 'Surely it is enough for our purposes. You can hardly believe it's a coincidence that Norton should come forward so soon afterwards. How can you explain Miss Whitaker's behaviour unless she was acting as his spy?'

'I cannot. But to go to such lengths . . . Miss Arrow might have been killed. It seems incredible—'

'If it enabled Norton to pass himself off as James Davenall, they might have thought it worth while. And think of the devilish cunning of it. They discover that James had syphilis, so make a virtue of necessity by claiming that your diagnosis was faulty. Presumably, Norton really was examined by a specialist. They obtain a copy of Sir Gervase's death certificate, which confirms what they know and gives them cause to hope that the family will knuckle under rather than have his immorality paraded in court.'

'But what of the rest? How was Norton able to bamboozle Prince Napoleon?'

'I don't pretend to have all the answers yet, Doctor. For the first time, though, I feel there's something to work on. For the first time, I feel absolutely certain: he isn't James Davenall.'

'Then, who? I return to my suspicion that he must already have been familiar with the affairs of the Davenalls before setting out on such a conspiracy. I can only believe that Miss Whitaker was his spy if I also believe that they knew there was something to spy on. It cannot have been mere supposition.'

But I was not to be deflected by Fiveash's reservations. He had brought me a gift more precious than any proof: confidence. I could see my enemy now. His name was Norton, his crime imposture, his weakness a woman called Whitaker. 'We'll nail him in the end, Doctor. You have my word on it.'

'I hope so, Trenchard. I truly hope so.'

'What will you do now?'

'Return to Bath. I will inform Baverstock of my suspicions, as I am bound to do. No doubt he will inform Richard Davenall. They must make what they can of it. Since my professional competence has been challenged, I rather think I may take legal advice on my own account. I fear, however, that it will all come to nothing unless a connection between Norton and Miss Whitaker can be established. She must be found – as soon as possible.'

'I think the Davenalls can be relied upon to devote all their resources to that end.'

'Yes. But it may not be enough, even then. I may still be deluding myself.'

I looked at him quizzically. 'I don't understand.' Indeed I did not. None of the comfort I had taken from his words seemed to have eased his own mind.

'I dined with Emery last night,' he replied after a pause. 'The specialist I sent James to eleven years ago. He saw him twice, on the second occasion only two days before his disappearance. Emery dug out his notes for me, and there it was, in his own hand: confirmation of my diagnosis.'

'Isn't that what you wanted?'

'Yes, but not all that I wanted. I wanted Emery to reassure me, I suppose, to say we could not have been mistaken, to say for that reason alone that Norton could not be James Davenall.' We went on for a few paces in silence, then he resumed. 'Instead he reminded me that syphilis is the most deceptive of diseases. It may hide behind other ailments. It may proclaim itself falsely. It is impossible to be certain. Sir Gervase's illness pre-disposed us to explain his son's illness in the same way. But we may have been mistaken. Miss Whitaker may have vanished for all manner of reasons. Norton may be telling the truth. If he is, think of the misery to which I needlessly condemned him. For I think of it, Trenchard. I think of it often.'

VII

'We're delighted to see you, Mr Baverstock, aren't we, Lupin? Delighted and no mistake. We've had rare society these past few weeks, when normally we're left so very much to ourselves. 'Tis either feast or famine: that's my experience. And Lupin's, too.

'The tea should have mashed by now, so here's your cup. Who did you say you wanted to know about? Miss Strang? Fancy you plucking that name from all the others I might have mentioned. Vivien Strang. Ah me. You wouldn't have called her pretty, Mr Baverstock. No, not pretty exactly. *Magnificent* was the word. A proud cold face and a bearing to match. Would you care for some shortbread? I know you've a sweet tooth.

'I've told you about Miss Strang before. September 1846. Yes, that would be right. An exact date? You lawyers expect an awful lot, I must say. It was a fine late summer, that I do remember. A happy summer, too. Sir Gervase and Lady Davenall were engaged, so we saw a good deal at Cleave Court of Miss Webster, as she was then, and Miss

Strang. Sir Lemuel was delighted. All Gervase's past scrapes were forgotten and forgiven, it seemed. Maybe that spell in Ireland did him some good, after all.

'Then that appalling Frenchman turned up. Plon-Plon, they called him. Prince Napoleon, that's right. You've met him? Well, I don't suppose the years have mellowed him. A more disagreeable, overbearing, foul-mouthed . . . I can't abide profanity, Mr Baverstock, you know that, and, come to think, I can't abide the French – those I've met anyway.

'The Prince took up with Gervase. Or perhaps it was the other way round. They were of an age and, if I had to swear to it, they were of a character, too. They led each other into bad habits. It caused some disagreements with Miss Webster, I won't deny. She was only seventeen then, but as wilful and strong-minded as I see you've found her to this day. She didn't take to the Prince, which was only sensible of her, so she must have been relieved when he took himself off so suddenly.

'It was towards the end of September, I think. The weather was still warm, I remember, so much warmer than these weak-as-water summers the good Lord sends us now. And that Plon-Plon was staying the weekend. Sir Lemuel gave a ball on the Saturday night. Miss Webster came, and Miss Strang, too, of course. And the Prince's cousin, as I think he was, who later became the French emperor. He was living in Bath then. It was a grand event and no mistake. Cleave Court was a far different place then, I can tell you. Sir Lemuel had lanterns hung in the trees in the park, with oranges and lemons fixed to the branches. Oh, they were such a picture.

'That's the last time I ever saw Vivien Strang, standing in a corner and looking down her nose at all the revelry, oh so disapproving, like only a sober Scot can be. Three days later, we heard that Colonel Webster had turned her out. Dismissed, without notice. Make of that what you will. Pilfering, it was suggested.

'Crowcroft had a different story, mind. He claimed he found her in the maze – the maze, mark you – on the Monday morning after the ball. He was no gossip, was Crowcroft. He'd not have made it up. He went up to the maze at dawn, seemingly, and there she was, coming out, coming out where she had no business going in, at dawn. Crowcroft said her hair was all awry, and her dress was torn. Well, it seems odd, doesn't it?

'What's odder still, the Prince left Cleave Court that same Monday. Went back to Bath to stay with his cousin. It wasn't expected, that I know. Still, you can never rely on a Frenchman to do what's expected, that's what I say.

'You keep asking about the date, and I keep telling you: I don't know. I've told you what happened – as much of it as I knew. Isn't that enough? Now, do you want another cup of tea or must Lupin and I finish the pot between us?'

VIII

Dr Fiveash returned home that afternoon. He dropped his bag in the hall and went straight into the surgery office, where Miss Arrow was in conference with his junior partner, the dishevelled and disorganized Dr Perry.

'Ah, Dr Fiveash,' said Perry. 'Good to see you back.'

Fiveash nodded and pulled out his watch. 'How are the rounds going?'

'Oh, just off. Right away.' Perry grasped his bulging bag and made for the door.

'London disagree with you, Doctor?' said Miss Arrow, after Perry had gone.

'More than usual.' He slumped heavily into a chair. 'Don't worry about young Perry. He's thick-skinned.'

'We do cope in your absence, you know.' Miss Arrow was stolid and unflappable, matronly by nature and former occupation, given to pawky remarks at her doctors' expense – above all, wholly indispensable.

'I've something on my mind, Miss Arrow. It concerns Miss Whitaker. You do remember her?'

Miss Arrow frowned. 'How could I forget the minx? You'd have thought she was Miss Nightingale herself the way she came to the rescue after my accident.'

'Brake failure, wasn't it?'

'Yes. A cable snapped. I've never forgiven Mr Westaway – he'd only just serviced it. As for Miss Whitaker, I'll never forgive her – or myself – for the way she deserted you. But there's no use—'

'What did you know of her background?'

She frowned again. 'Only what I told you, which was next to nothing. Why?'

'She said nothing to you during her visits to you in hospital? About friends, or relatives, or where—'

'Dr Fiveash, what is the point—?'

'Did she leave anything behind here? When you returned—'

'She left nothing at all, to speak of. She was very particular, I'll say that for her. Everything here was in perfect order. She'd reorganized the files really rather well, I have to admit. I dare say she was allowed more time for that side of her work than I am. It's only a pity she didn't finish.'

'And she left no possessions of any kind?'

Miss Arrow's brow furrowed in thought. 'One or two bits and pieces in her – my – desk drawer. That's all.'

'What did you do with them?'

'Dr Fiveash, it was months ago.'

He smiled. 'I know you.'

She smiled, too. 'I didn't throw them away, just in case . . . I'd have given her such a piece of my mind if she had returned for them. But they weren't worth returning for, in all conscience. I put them in an old shoe-box.' She rose and crossed to a tall cupboard in the corner; there was still a slight limp as she walked. The doors of the cupboard stood open on crooked stacks of jumbled papers, files and medical texts. From a lower shelf, Miss Arrow pulled out a battered cardboard box and stood it on the desk. Fiveash rose and peered in at the contents: a pen and some pencils, a bottle of ink, a needle and thread, a faded scrap of ribbon, a matchbox full of pins, a Bath omnibus timetable, a spiral-bound diary of the 1881–2 academic year. He leafed through its pages: they were blank. Beneath it, lining the base of the box, was a folded, yellowed old newspaper. He took it out and laid it flat on the desk. It was *The Times* for 12th July 1841.

'A forty-year-old newspaper, Miss Arrow. What do you make of this?'

'It's from your own archive, Doctor.'

'Really?' He had kept all copies of *The Times* over the years that contained medical reports and this, presumably, was one. 'What would she have wanted with this?'

'I've no idea.'

He turned the first page, then the next. And there, in the top corner of the facing page, was the jagged rim of a torn edge, a rough rectangle ripped from the sheet. Miss Whitaker had, he recalled, sorted all the medical reports into date order. Something had attracted her notice in this one, something she had decided to remove. He folded the newspaper and replaced it in the box. 'I'm just going out, Miss Arrow.'

'You've only just come in.'

'I shan't be gone long. I'll be back in plenty of time for evening surgery.'

IX

Even as Dr Fiveash was hastening down Bathwick Hill into the city, Arthur Baverstock was brooding at his desk in his first-floor office above the bustle of Cheap Street. Open before him on the blotter was a battered almanac. His interview of the morning with Lady Davenall had told him nothing. She had affected indifference to most of the proceedings he had described and had claimed total ignorance of the significance of any date in 1846. How she would have reacted to the suggestion that she might be a carrier of syphilis he had not been so unfortunate as to discover; that was something he would happily leave to Richard Davenall.

Tea with Esme Pursglove, however, had been a vastly different affair. She had been as cheerfully informative as Lady Davenall had been haughtily unenlightening. The almanac's perpetual calendar, indeed, had provided Baverstock with the one item of intelligence Miss Pursglove did not possess. Sir Lemuel Davenall had hosted a ball in honour of the Princes Bonaparte on a Saturday in September 1846. Crowcroft had encountered Miss Strang in the maze the following Monday at dawn, in a distressed condition. And 20th September 1846 had been a Sunday.

X

The librarian on duty was an occasional patient of Dr Fiveash and displayed unwonted celerity in fetching for him bound back copies of *The Times* for the third quarter of 1841. Ignoring a jocular enquiry as to the object of his researches, Fiveash retreated with the volume to an alcove table, perched his pince-nez on his nose and turned up the issue for Monday, 12th July.

The portion removed from his copy by Miss Whitaker was, he now saw, one of the editorial columns. Dotted through the piece, in distinctive capitals, was the name DAVENALL. Fiveash pressed the bulky tome flat with his elbows, bent low over the page, extended his tongue in a sign of concentration that Miss Arrow would at once have recognized, and began to read.

As if the indignities inflicted upon the reputation of British justice as a result of the trial, if it may be honoured with that description, of the EARL of CARDIGAN earlier this year were not a sufficient insult to public opinion, we now learn that the duelling, not to say murderous, inclinations of another Hussar officer have been the beneficiaries of selective blindness on the part of our magistracy.

It is difficult to know how else to characterize the entire want of legal proceedings against Lieutenant Gervase DAVENALL of the 27th Hussars, who, it is clearly established, fought with, and severely injured by pistol shot, Lieutenant Harvey THOMPSON of the same Hussar regiment, at Wimbledon Common on 22nd May this year.

As to the cause of the duel, *cherchez la femme?* As to the outcome, Lieut. THOMPSON is, we understand, still resident in the regimental infirmary at Colchester. As to the consequences, we must seek in vain. Generous spirits may argue that Lieut. THOMPSON has suffered sufficiently for his intemperate conduct, since it appears certain he will be unable to resume his commission by reason of his injuries; we do not concur but we shall not demur. What of Lieut. DAVENALL? Has he been cashiered and placed in police custody awaiting trial for attempted murder? He has not. Has he been arraigned before a court martial for assaulting a fellow-officer? He has not. And why not? We venture to suggest that the leniency of the authorities is not unconnected with the friendship known to exist between Lieut. DAVENALL's father, Sir Lemuel DAVENALL, and the Commander-in-Chief, LORD HILL.

Sir Lemuel is not an insensitive man. He has induced his son to relinquish his commission and retire, for a while, to manage the family property in Ireland. Sir Lemuel is not an unworthy man. His own military career is nothing less than a fine adornment to his family name; his conduct in the Peninsula and at Waterloo deserves ever to be remembered. But nor, we submit, is Sir Lemuel an entirely prudent man. He has demonstrated that which we all privately knew but publicly denied: that the severities of the law are not visited equally upon the son of a baronet and the son of a butcher. The one, having taken up arms illegally, is reduced to half pay and sent away to Ireland to suffer a little boredom. The other, were he to do the same, would now be labouring on the treadmill in one of our houses of correction.

Cui bono? Not, experience compels us to conclude, the unrepentant Lieut. DAVENALL, nor yet his indulgent father. Such latitude, once allowed, cannot be compressed, for such latitude, once enjoyed, is ever after expected. Who knows to what excesses Lieut. DAVENALL may now feel at liberty to proceed? If it be any consolation to those who rail at such collusions of the well-connected, we take leave to doubt that the family DAVENALL will ever have cause to do other than abundantly regret this unwholesome clemency.

XI

I walked up Avenue Road late that afternoon looking forward to telling Constance what I had learned from Fiveash. In my own mind, the information crushed Norton's claim outright, but there was something brutal as well as deluded in my eagerness to tell her. It was as if I wanted her to let me see that it was more a disappointment than a relief, as if I craved the endorsement of my suspicion more than the return of a lost harmony.

Only this state of mind can explain why, when Hillier greeted me in the hall and said that Constance was taking tea in the conservatory with a visitor, and that the visitor's name was Davenall, I thought at once of Norton. As I thrust my hat and coat at Hillier and blundered through, some part of me, I believe, wanted it to be Norton.

But it was Richard Davenall. He and Constance looked up, first in alarm, then with puzzled smiles, as I burst through the doors.

'Trenchard!' Davenall said. 'I thought you would be here already. Otherwise I would have called at Orchard Street. But your wife has made me very welcome.'

'Good,' I said, panting slightly.

Constance rose and kissed me lightly on the cheek. 'Now you've arrived, William, I'll leave you and Richard together. Shall I ask Hillier to bring more tea?'

'No. No, thank you.' She nodded and went out. Abruptly, I dismissed her from my mind: Davenall would do as well as any other audience. 'Have you heard from Fiveash?' I said as soon as the doors had closed on us.

'No.'

I sat down opposite him, sensing but not subduing the signs of straining eagerness in my face and voice. 'He believes somebody has spied on his medical records – in order to supply Norton with the details he made use of yesterday.'

'Tell me more.'

So I did, plunging on with all the constructions I had placed upon Fiveash's words, scarcely heeding the frown of disquiet on Davenall's face. Whether it was the frailty of the evidence that disturbed him or the excess of confidence I drew from it was impossible to tell; he was not a lawyer for nothing. When I had finished, some moments passed before he responded.

'No doubt I will receive a considered report of this from Baverstock.'

'Yes. But meanwhile—'

'Meanwhile it is suggestive but hardly conclusive. I can well understand Fiveash making much of it in the light of recent events, but, frankly, it is flimsy in the extreme.'

'You can't seriously be suggesting it's a coincidence?'

'I think it highly probable that it is. Even if it is not, where is the evidence that she is connected with Norton? For the present, I fear it takes us nowhere.'

'This is pure defeatism. I had—'

'It is pure realism, Trenchard. I have to give Warburton some kind of answer by noon tomorrow. Unsubstantiated accusations that Norton has set a spy on Fiveash will not help.'

I stood up and walked to the window. Through a screen of vine leaves, I could see Constance at the far end of the lawn, moving slowly amongst the herb borders. She had taken of late to wandering in the

91

garden whenever I was at home, dreamily picking posies of thyme and rosemary; Burrows had even gone so far as to complain about it. But Constance would not have explained her actions even had I asked her to. Past associations called from beyond these symbols of disenchantment, disenchantment with our life but enchantment with another. I turned back to Davenall with a sigh. 'What brought you here today?'

'The urgency of the position. And I am glad I came. I see now just how urgent it really is.'

'What do you mean?'

'Constance fended off my enquiries politely enough, Trenchard, but it is clear to me she believes in Norton, as it must be clear to you.'

'We have not discussed it.'

'Not discussed it?' He looked at me with frank incredulity. 'Have you told her how matters stand?'

'No.'

'Now I see why she was so apparently incurious. I appreciate syphilis is hardly a fitting—'

'I have told her nothing of what occurred yesterday and I will tell her nothing until such time as I can prove Norton a liar.'

Davenall rose and joined me by the window. He glanced towards the garden and must have seen Constance as a pale shape flitting distantly amongst the falling leaves, like a delicate petal afloat on a dank and swollen pond. When I looked at him, his expression was creased with a sharp suggestion of genuine pain.

'What's wrong?'

'You are playing with fire, man. Constance loved him once. If you try to shut her out—'

'Loved who once?'

Our eyes met and contended for a moment with the ambiguities that rippled in the humid air. Beyond the glass, Constance might have felt the moist breeze stir her hair, worn longer today in honour of some private memory, might have let the damp descending gloom wrap her in a spirit of luscious mourning; she looked back once in our direction.

'Even you're not sure. You sat there yesterday and gave nothing away, but you're not sure, are you?'

His gaze did not shift. 'No, Trenchard. I'm not sure. None of us is.'

'I am.'

'Then, perhaps I have chosen wisely.'

'Chosen?'

'I had lunch with Hugo. I think I succeeded in persuading him that confronting Norton in court would prove disastrous. At all events, he agreed that we should make one last effort to avoid it.'

'How?'

'By offering Norton enough money to persuade any impostor that he has more to gain by accepting it than by persisting with his claim. It is what I originally advocated, except that the sum involved has had to be increased.'

'How much?'

'Ten thousand pounds.' He must have noticed my eyes widen. 'Woundingly expensive, even given Hugo's means. His agreement is a measure of his desperation. It is not a king's ransom, but it is a baronet's. I suggested – and he concurred – that you should be the one to put it to Norton.'

'Why me?'

'Because you are not a Davenall, because it is not your money, because you want rid of him as badly as we do.'

'In short, I am to do Sir Hugo's dirty work for him?'

'If I made this offer through Warburton, it could be used against us. If Hugo went to Norton with it, I could not trust him to keep his head. Besides, you are sure he is an impostor. This is your chance to prove it.'

'How?'

'If he is an impostor, he will accept. It is easy money. It can be quickly done. A banker's draft for ten thousand pounds in exchange for a written undertaking to withdraw his claim. Throw in terms of your own if you wish. A contrite letter to Constance, perhaps?'

'When?'

'Before noon tomorrow. I have the draft with me. Will you act for us?'

'You called this "nuisance money" yesterday. You spoke of it with contempt.'

'As I would today. It is contemptible. Yet you heard what was said in that room. This is what it has driven us to.'

'What if he refuses?'

'Offer him more. Hugo is good for twice as much. Only the conditions are inflexible.'

'And if he cannot be bribed?'

'Every man has his price.'

'His may not be measured in pounds.'

'So you and I fear, Trenchard. I cannot read this man. I hope money is all he wants. I suggest you do the same.'

'Very well. I will see him.'

Perversely, I was already relishing the prospect. I did not mind acting as the Davenalls' messenger if it also gave me the opportunity to make Norton understand that I, at least, knew he would accept their offer – and why. I would wake Constance from her dream of James and banish Norton from my nightmares. In less than twenty-four hours, it would be done.

FIVE

I

Norton received me in the sitting-room of his second-floor suite at the Great Western. It was ten o'clock in the morning, but he was still clad in his dressing-gown, smoking a cigarette and standing by the window, which looked down on the busy side-exit of the station. He did not turn in my direction until the page-boy had closed the door behind me.

'I'm sorry I wasn't in when you called last night.'

'No matter. You're here now.'

'Yes, and only two short hours before Richard delivers his answer to my solicitor. I must say I thought he would be the breathless last-minute visitor. But I'm glad it's you instead. How is Connie?'

'I've not come here to discuss my wife.'

'Really? If you say so, of course.' He turned back to the window. 'The manager offered me rooms facing Praed Street, you know, but I prefer these. I can watch all the travellers scurrying to and fro from here.' He craned forward. 'All on their busy, busy errands.' I was standing beside him by now and found my gaze shifting, with his, to the crowded street below. 'And what is your errand, Trenchard, I wonder?' With a start, I realized he was looking straight at me. 'Mmm?'

'I've come here to say just two things to you.'

'And they are?' His composed ironical stare met my eyes. Silently, I damned the man for his infernal coolness, his air of bored fore-knowledge, the unspoken implication behind his every remark that nothing I could say or do would surprise him.

I surrendered to the goading indifference of his question. 'First, you may as well know I'm on to you. A woman calling herself Whitaker obtained the information you have on James Davenall's illness from Dr Fiveash's confidential records.'

His face, which I scanned for a reaction, betrayed not the slightest flicker; he did not even blink. *'I'm afraid I don't know the lady.'*

'I didn't expect you to admit it.'

'Then, you'll not be disappointed.'

'I told you so you'd understand: you don't fool me for a minute. You are not James Davenall.'

'I find it odd that my most vehement opponent is somebody whom I never knew. I know why, of course. You're afraid I'll take Connie away from you. She only married you because she believed me dead. Well, I can understand how you feel. You really are in a difficult position, aren't you?'

'It's no—'

'But not as difficult as my own position, eleven years ago. Has that occurred to you?'

'I told you: you are not that man.'

He smiled. *'You recite it, Trenchard, to make yourself believe it. It won't do, you know. It really won't do.'* I felt my anger threatening to run out of control. Before I could summon a reply, he spoke again. *'What was the second reason for your visit?'*

'The Davenalls are prepared to buy you off.'

'Hush money. So it has come to that. How much?'

'I have a banker's draft with me for ten thousand pounds.'

'As much as that?'

'I'm to say—'

'Don't trouble yourself to explain the conditions, Trenchard. The money is of no interest to me. It's mine anyway. Soon, very soon, Hugo will have to accept that. And so will you. Not that money is what worries you. It's property of a different kind, isn't it?'

Desperately, I clung to the offer I had come to make. *'They're prepared to pay you ten thousand pounds.'*

'Are you prepared to surrender your wife?'

'Damn you, Norton—'

'Not Norton!' His face was close to mine; for the first time, the mask of languid unconcern was lowered. *'Davenall is the name. James Davenall. Eleven years ago, I had to give up everything to preserve my family in happy ignorance of their own corruption. Do you know what I've discovered since then? That none of it meant a scrap to me, not even a scrap of paper with a row of noughts on it. Except Constance. Giving her up was the hardest, noblest thing I've ever done. Now I know I didn't need to, there's no nobility left to call on – and certainly no greed. All I've come to reclaim is what is rightfully mine – Constance most of all.'*

'She'll never—'

'She'll never forget our love for each other. When I told her I was leaving, I couldn't tell her why. You can't imagine how hard that was. I

cried for her as well as for myself. She tried to stop me. She offered herself to me that day, as a proof of her love, as a way of keeping me.'

'That's not true.'

'I had to turn my back on her and walk away. I won't do so again.'

I should have hit him then, should have forced him to take back what he had said. But his words had gone deeper than any blows could reach. I stared at him in dumb horror.

'Do you understand now, Trenchard? Forget my family. This is between us. For Connie's sake, I'm prepared to destroy you.'

I left the hotel a vanquished man. In my turmoil, I hardly knew which way I was going, only to pull up with a start on realizing that I was in the vicinity of Lancaster Gate. Retracing my steps towards Praed Street, I paused at the junction with Eastbourne Terrace to wait for a gap in the traffic.

Ahead of me, I could see figures moving in and out of the Great Western Hotel. Suddenly, I caught my breath. One of them was Norton, immaculately turned out in top-hat and grey overcoat, twirling his cane and pausing at the foot of the hotel steps to stub out a cigarette. He made no move to hail a cab, merely moved off smartly in the direction of Marylebone. Clearly, he had not seen me. And that is what planted the idea in my mind.

Abruptly, I was conscious of a crossing-sweeper twitching at my sleeve; he had mistaken my hesitation for custom. I flipped him a farthing, then hurried across before he could earn it. There was no time to lose: Norton was walking quickly, his tall figure easily distinguishable amongst the bobbing heads, but receding fast. The effort of keeping him in view was enough to stifle any examination of my motives.

Norton's pace did not slacken as he turned into the Edgware Road and headed south, but he did not once look back; following him became comparatively simple. He passed on into Park Lane, still heading resolutely south, and I began to hang back as the crowds thinned. Not that I needed to worry: whatever his thoughts were on, it was not the possibility of pursuit. Most of the way down Park Lane, he turned into Hyde Park; I followed.

There he was, ahead of me, nothing but trees and grass between us, no intervening throng, no bustle and noise in which to cloak my trailing steps. I began to fall back still further, fearing that at any moment he might look round. But he did not. Then another sensation, more withering than any fear, found its root in me. The steadily pacing figure, the straggling path between us, the invisible string by which he wound me in: suddenly, their meaning was clear. I nearly cried out at the certainty of it: he knew I was there; he wanted me to follow him.

The Achilles statue loomed ahead, a smattering of strangers taking their ease at its foot: Norton made straight for them. Then one figure *among the rest, standing with back turned and hands resting on the chain that skirted the base of the statue, emerged from the anonymity of the people and the place. I took one step closer, felt an intake of breath that could have been a clutch at the heart, and then I knew: it was Constance.*

I stood motionless in the shade of one of the trees flanking the path and watched, transfixed, as Norton moved to her elbow. At his touch, she turned and looked up at him. It was her face, glimpsed within the fringe of a familiar hood; her gaze, met by my own so many times before; her smile, which I had lately banished from her lips. There was no doubt, no question, no hope of error.

They began to circumnavigate the statue, moving slowly, following the line of the perimeter chain. In a moment, I knew, they would pass from view behind the plinth on which Achilles stood. I could not bear still to be watching when they reappeared. I turned and began to walk quickly back along the path.

II

'Clearly, I should have made my instructions more explicit, Mr Baverstock. Permit me to do so now. Cease these wasteful enquiries into the obscure and ancient history of my family affairs. It is not of the least interest to me whether or no this man Norton has some hold over Prince Napoleon. It would not surprise me. The Prince is a man of such monumental vices that I should guess he has a store of blackmailers to match. But their bearing on the present case is only to be compared to that of Nanny Pursglove's twitterings concerning Miss Strang. Both issues are irrelevant, and I do not take kindly to paying your fee when it is spent on such trifles.

'Twice in as many days you have dallied here when your time was better spent in London establishing Norton's true identity. The reason my father dispensed with Miss Strang's services was not disclosed to me at the time, but I can assure you that Nanny Pursglove's lurid imaginings – and Crowcroft's alleged sightings – are as wide of the mark as it is possible to be. I have neither knowledge nor curiosity where Miss Strang's subsequent career is concerned. I would surmise she went back to Scotland. And there, I must insist, you will leave the matter.

'Convey this message to my son. Norton is to be offered no money, shown no favour, allowed no advantage. Should he have either the temerity or the means – both of which I doubt – to pursue his preposterous claim in the courts, we will face him with contempt – and dignity. As to the means of defeating him, it is for you – and my cousin – to find them. Is that explicit enough?'

III

Richard Davenall was not at his offices, though he was expected back shortly. I did not wait. Indeed, I was glad, in a sense, to miss him. It enabled me to leave a hastily written note with Benson relating Norton's rejection of the offer and start back to St John's Wood straight away; I wanted to be there before Constance returned.

At The Limes, I found Hillier gossiping with the bread-boy in the drive; she looked surprised to see me.

'Where is your mistress?' I barked. The tone of my voice at once communicated itself to the bread-boy, who cycled off with shamefaced speed.

'Not in, sir.'

'Then where?'

Hillier was not easily cowed. Her reply was coolly factual. 'She didn't say where she was going, sir.'

'When are you expecting her back?'

'Cook's expecting 'er for luncheon, sir. Will you also be lunching at 'ome?'

She received no reply. I was already on my way into the house, hurrying lest any pause should allow my resolution to fail. I went straight to the drawing-room, opened the bureau and tried the locked drawer again: it was still locked. There was no point searching once more for the key; I knew it was not there. I picked up the letter-knife, slid its thin blade into the narrow gap between drawer-top and frame, and exerted more and more leverage until, with a sudden splintering wrench, the lock gave way.

There was a bundle of letters within, fastened with tape. I pulled them loose and sifted through them. Several were in my own hand, addressed to Constance in Salisbury and postmarked Blackheath: written, then, from my father's house in the days of our courtship. I felt suddenly sickened by the stark contrast between the tentative declarations of love such letters contained and the violence I had already done to their memory. There were other letters, some in what I was sure was James Davenall's hand, pre-dating his disappearance; one from Constance's brother, Roland, dated a few months before his death; several from a doting aunt in Broadstairs, since deceased; and, innocuously interleaved with the rest, two much more recent communications. Their handwriting was similar to Davenall's: they could only be from Norton. I sat down and read them.

He had written the first on the day of his visit to The Limes. I read it without surprise, either at the contents or at Constance's secretion of it. It was only what I had expected, after all, only what I had half-hoped to find. Then, towards its end, one sentence seized my attention. 'Neither of us can forget, can we, what happened in that meadow?' It had to be

*the same meadow he had been speaking of when I interrupted them on
the aqueduct. 'We went as far as the bluebell meadow, didn't we?'
What could it mean? I scrabbled up the second letter in search of an
answer.*

Great Western Royal Hotel
Praed Street
LONDON W.

11th October 1882

Dear Constance,
I have as little doubt as, I suspect, you have that what William
tells you of today's meeting at my solicitor's office – if he tells
you anything – is not to be relied upon. I cannot entirely blame
him for that, but nor can I accept that you should be kept in
ignorance.
  If you can face the truth, which is that my love for you is as
strong as the day I left eleven years ago, meet me at the Achilles
statue in Hyde Park at eleven o'clock on Friday morning. Then
we will have done with pretence – for good and all.

Ever yours,
JAMES

I left the letters, discarded and open on the blotter, and retreated
from the room. If only I had answered her questions, as she had
implored me to, his letter would have struck a false note. As it was, my
secrecy had paved the way for him. I was determined to condemn
Constance for agreeing to meet him but, in my heart, I no longer
blamed her.
  My aimless anxious steps took me to the front drive. I believe I had
some notion to see if a cab might be setting down its passenger at our
door: Constance, perhaps, back from a rendezvous about which I now
knew too much. All I found, though, was Burrows weeding sciatically
amongst the shrubbery. Seeing me approach, he broke off and lurched
out into my path.
  'A word, sir, begging your pardon.'
  Reluctantly, I halted. 'Yes?'
  'The mistress likes a splash of colour in these borders, and I do my best
to oblige.'
  'I'm sure—'
  'So I 'ope you'll not mind my saying: it don't 'elp if you go trampling
and emptying your pipe 'mongst my lobelias.' He propped his elbow on
the handle of his hoe and regarded me with defiant certainty.
  'I'm not in the habit—'
  'The marks are there to be seen.' He gestured with his thumb towards

99

a clump of flowers beneath a silver birch tree set back from the drive.
'Clear as the nose on your face. I'd 'ave said it might be little Patience
but for the ash.'

Irritated, I crossed the grass and looked down at the crushed lobelias.
Somebody certainly seemed to have stood on them. And there was the
scatter of ash Burrows had complained about. I stooped to examine it,
my irritation turning to curiosity.

'This isn't pipe dottle,' I said, half to myself. 'It's cigarette ash. And I
don't smoke cigarettes.'

'If you say so, sir.'

It was clear Burrows did not believe me, but his opinion was not
what concerned me. We were at a point quite close to the front gates
and, in my mind, I was imagining a man standing beneath the silver
birch where I now stood, but at night, so that he did not notice the
lobelias beneath his feet. He could have slipped through the gates,
which were never locked, and stood there in the darkness, watching the
house, smoking a cigarette as he calmly observed the lighted windows,
the movement of figures behind the shades, the agreed signals from the
one occupant who knew he was there. I shuddered.

IV

Hector Warburton permitted himself a smug glance at the clock,
which showed ten minutes past noon, when Lechlade showed Richard
Davenall into his office at Staple Inn. Davenall looked, as well he
might, sad and lined and weary. Warburton, however, who did not
envy him the task of constructing a defence against his client, felt no
grain of sympathy for his fellow-lawyer. He would not have attained
his current eminence by admitting such unprofessional thoughts to his
soul. This, after all, was a matter of business. If Davenall had lapsed so
far from his own professional standards as to entangle family sentiment
in the business of the law, so much the worse for him. Warburton, for
his part, would show him no mercy.

'You are somewhat overdue, Davenall,' he said, neutrally enough.
'Take a seat.'

'Thank you, but I'll stand.' Richard was well enough aware of his
own difficulty to sense that posture was one dignity he could retain –
and needed to.

'Has Sir Hugo changed his mind?'

'He has not.'

'I see. Then, I have no choice but to proceed.'

'If those are your instructions.'

'They are. As a matter of fact, the Chancery Office has offered me a place on their list for the sixth of November. I shall now confirm the date.'

Richard Davenall stroked his beard, then looked directly at Warburton. 'That is significantly earlier than I had anticipated. In the interests of all concerned—'

'No further delay can be countenanced. Sir James wishes to establish his title as soon as possible.'

Warburton had styled his client 'Sir James' deliberately; it would do no harm to goad Davenall, given his inclination to procrastinate. But Richard was not to be goaded. He was, in truth, more professionally motivated than Warburton knew. He was determined to do all he could to help Hugo and, to that end, was prepared to tolerate any humiliation – if it would do any good. 'Mr Norton', he said deliberately, 'did not seem to relish the prospect of a full-blown court action. I am simply—'

'It is being forced upon him – by your client.'

Richard lowered himself into the chair beside him in a gesture as significant as his earlier determination to stand. 'Warburton' – he leaned intently across the desk – 'I need time . . . to prepare Hugo's mind . . .'

Warburton maintained his distance; he wanted no hint of complicity. 'It is only a hearing. I doubt an early date will be set for the full suit.'

Nervously, Richard licked his lips. Ordinarily, he would never have demeaned himself by asking favours of Warburton; he had rebuked the dead Gervase often since Wednesday for leaving him no choice but to do so. With Warburton senior it might have been different: a nod, a wink and a helping hand. But what was there in this man's lean, hollow-cheeked, watery-eyed face to inspire hope? Nothing. Yet hope he did. 'As you say, it is only a hearing. May I take it therefore that no mention will be made at that stage of the . . . medical evidence?'

'You may not.'

'Surely you wouldn't—'

'I will do whatever is necessary to prosecute my client's claim. Henceforth there will be no . . . accommodations. Is that clear? If so, I believe there is no more to be said. We will serve the necessary papers as soon as possible.'

Richard sighed and rose to his feet. Warburton was right: there was no more to be said. With the barest nod, he turned and left the room. As he descended the stairs, he reached into his coat pocket and screwed into a ball the note he had carried with him from his office, the note Trenchard had left for him, with its three-word message imprinted on his mind: 'Norton says no.'

V

Constance came to me in the study, where I had half-drawn the shades and felt the desolation of my anger drain into a morbid contemplation of my own folly. I had seen her walk up the drive and, a few minutes later, she stood in the doorway of the room.

'Hillier said you wanted to see me as soon as I returned.' She spoke breathlessly, as if she had raced up the stairs.

I did not move from my chair, steeled myself to be the unyielding master, paused deliberately to steady my voice. 'I know where you've been.'

Quietly, she closed the door, then took a few steps towards me. I could see her face more clearly now, flushed, I fancied, from something more than running upstairs. She was wearing a dark-blue floral-patterned dress, high-necked, with a lace ruff, and lace also at the cuffs and hem – soft flattering fabric that moulded itself to her hips as she moved and showed the rapid rise and fall of her bosom. I was aware now, in the moment of our intimacy's imminent loss, of the mature beauty of this woman I called my wife, aware – with heightened sense – of the elements that fed my love for her and fed also her detachment from me. She did not speak, but, in her gaze, the message was clear enough: she was not ashamed.

'You met Norton in Hyde Park – by prior arrangement.' Still she did not speak. 'You have received letters from him – and kept them from me.' Her eyes said all she needed to say: my breach of trust preceded and exceeded hers. 'You have allowed him – or encouraged him – to persuade you that he is James Davenall.' And what, she silently replied, if he really is? 'You have disobeyed me at every turn.'

At last, she spoke. 'You should have told me the truth.'

'The truth?' I tried a weary gibe. 'What did he say the truth was?'

'I know why he went away and why he has returned.' Suddenly, her expression softened. 'Surely you can see that I cannot but be moved by his plight?'

Was it my hand that thumped the table before me? It seemed, rather, as if another man, whom I was watching, performed the gesture and fashioned my harsh reply. 'I see that you are prepared to imperil our marriage for the sake of a dalliance with a worthless imposter.'

'If that is what you really see, William, then you are blind. I had to meet him to learn the truth. I am not about to forget it.'

'You will do as I say.'

She walked past me to the window, raised the shade a touch and turned to look at me. 'You cannot command me in this. You know I would have married James had he lived. Now I can no longer doubt that he does live. Such a thing cannot be forgotten.'

The question that Norton had planted within me forced its way to the surface. 'Is that because of what happened when you last saw him?'

'What do you mean?'

'You were speaking of it when I found you on the aqueduct. All you've ever told me is that he left you there, eleven years ago. But that isn't true, is it? You went somewhere else, didn't you? A meadow nearby. What happened there?'

'Whatever happened can't alter—'

'You said I was blind. So enlighten me. What happened?'

Her gaze faltered, but not through weakness. She seemed drawn by my words towards the scene I had asked her to describe. 'Across that field,' she murmured. 'So far and fast. Running . . . and never stopping.'

'What?'

She drew herself up, looked at me once more, returned her mind to the present. 'This morning, James told me everything. Now I understand. He acted out of love for me.'

'Constance—'

'This morning, he offered to withdraw his claim.'

'He did what?'

'He said that, for my sake, he would halt all legal proceedings and give the world to understand that he was an impostor. He would resume his identity as James Norton. He would leave our lives for good. He would cease to come between us. He said that he would do all this – if I asked him to.'

This, then, was the final test he had constructed. Absorbed in self-pity, I did not pause to consider the torment such an offer must have caused Constance; I only demanded its result. 'Did you ask him?'

'No.'

'Why not?'

'Because he has suffered enough. Because I had no right to ask him to return to exile.'

'Or because you love him?'

'He told me you had offered him money – on Hugo's behalf. Is that true?'

'Yes.'

'But he refused it?'

'Yes. Because you had given him cause to hope he could gain still more . . . from . . .' My voice trailed into a silence that was truly mine. In Constance's eyes, there was an expression I had never seen before. Norton and I, between us, had finally succeeded. We had crushed her love for me.

She walked past me and moved decisively to the door. There she turned back. 'In fairness to us both, William, I must go away. I will take Patience and stay with my father. James said there was to be a hearing next month. After that, I will decide what to do.'

'You *will decide?*'

'*Yes; I will decide. Until then, I will see neither of you. That is a promise.*'

'Constance—'

'*No. Say nothing. It is for the best. I will leave in the morning. Please, for both our sakes, do not try to prevent me.*'

VI

Richard Davenall found Sir Hugo at his club in Pall Mall. A fruitless visit to Bladeney House had only exacerbated the symptoms of pent-up emotion with which he had left Staple Inn. Now this least clubbable of fellows was obliged to seek out his cousin in the mid-afternoon fug of a tastelessly decorated bar, where, in his view, there were too many mirrors and velvet-upholstered chairs and where, above all, a gentleman had no business idling away the daylight hours. Thus there was little of the legal manner about him as he ignored a waiter and dismissed, with eloquent glare, Hugo's corner-table drinking companion.

'Cleveland not with you?' he opened tartly.

'No.' Hugo gazed wistfully after his departing acquaintance. 'But Leighton's a good fellow. Get you a drink?'

Richard sat down, pointedly ignoring the question. Hugo was clearly drunk – more so than usual. Well, Richard could not entirely blame him for that. Without his years of training in the ways of sober respectability, he might have joined him. 'Norton's turned us down.'

'Has he, by Jove?' Hugo began tapping a cigarette on the low table before him. A waiter appeared silently at his elbow and lit a match for him. 'Another large one, Emmett, if you please,' drawled Hugo as he accepted the light.

'Don't you think you've had enough?' said Richard.

'The only thing I've had enough of, dear cousin, is friend Norton. Do you think we pitched the offer too low?'

'No. I think he believes he has us on the run.'

Hugo snorted. 'Maybe he has.'

'Warburton anticipates arranging a hearing for the sixth of November.'

'Can we stop him?'

'No. Nor do I think we can stop the case going to full trial. You should prepare yourself for the worst.'

Emmett returned with a recharged glass. Hugo took a large gulp from it. 'Prepare? When did my family ever prepare me for anything?'

'There's no question your father behaved badly, but—'

Hugo brought his glass down on the table with a crash. 'My father! What I wouldn't give to have him here now – to shake the truth from him. Tell me, Richard, why do you think my father never accepted that James was dead?'

'Fatherly weakness, I suppose.'

'Fatherly weakness be damned! He never showed me any . . . fatherly weakness. And you know why, don't you?'

'No, I don't.'

'You heard what Fiveash said.' For all his drunken state, Hugo lowered his voice. 'He told my father that he must not allow my mother to conceive for a second time. Yet she did, didn't she?'

'What are you suggesting?'

Suddenly, Hugo threw himself back in his chair, rubbed his eyes and sighed. 'I don't know. Has my mother said anything about this . . . this date Norton quoted?'

'I've not yet heard from Baverstock.'

'What do you know about it? Eighteen forty-six, wasn't it?'

'Nothing. It seems too far in the past to have any relevance—'

'The past?' Hugo took another drink and ran his fingers through his hair. 'Seems I've to thank the past for this whole damn mess.' His red-rimmed eyes cast an accusing look at his cousin. 'Well, you know more about the past than I do, Richard. So use it – to get me out.'

Richard Davenall did not leave the club straight away, though he left Hugo, set, it seemed, on drinking away the afternoon. Richard conceded one point to his cousin's mordant flailings: the past did have a good deal to answer for. And, since this warren of a building, whose rooms varied from the gloomy to the garish, had something of a stake, including two club presidents, in the Davenalls' past, he could not lightly leave it. Rather in the manner of a pilgrimage – for he had long allowed his own subscription to lapse – he ascended the wide staircase, lit by the mellow hues of a stained-glass window, to the cavernous and dust-laden library, where Hugo's generation seldom strayed, but where older, more eminent members were celebrated by gilt-framed portraits lodged in shadowy grottoes amongst the neglected bookstacks.

Not because it had been moved, but in confirmation of the length of his absence, Richard spent some time searching before he located the portrait he had in mind. The frame was heavier than he recalled, the oils darker: he had to light the lamp on the nearby table to make it out at all. But there it was, attested by the panel fixed to the base of the frame: Sir Lemuel Davenall, Bt (1779–1859), painted in the first year of his presidency, fifty years ago.

Sir Lemuel resembled his brother Wolseley, Richard's father, in the way a Bengal tiger resembles a domesticated English cat: the features were similar, but on an altogether grander scale. The face was lean –

leaner than Wolseley's, if anything, but fringed by defiant militaristic whiskers; the eyes had the same tinge of green, but they warmed his expression, where Wolseley's soured his; he held himself proudly, chest puffed beneath the medals he had won at Waterloo, while the only pride his brother knew was an obsessive pursuit of an independent reputation. Whilst Lemuel fought for his country, Wolseley studied the law of tort. Whilst Lemuel rode to hounds, Wolseley ran down leases. Whilst Lemuel owned all he surveyed and indulged his generosity, Wolseley grudged his prodigality and cultivated his resentments. Whose son would Richard rather have been? He had no doubt as he surveyed the weatherbeaten countenance of a grand old baronet in this bastion of his joyful self-esteem.

Richard's earliest memories of his uncle were as a welcome interloper in the tedium of a Highgate childhood, a white-haired old man who would toss him an india-rubber ball in the garden and make faces behind his hand whilst his father discussed rental income over a dinner of reluctant mutton. Later, Richard remembered an idyllic summer passed at Cleave Court after his first year at Shrewsbury: Gervase was away in Ireland, by implication in some measure of disgrace, though the scandal of a duel sounded wonderfully glamorous to young Richard. That, in so far as he could fix the moment in time, is when he first contemplated how much happier he might be as Lemuel's son than as his father's. He even thought that it might make Sir Lemuel happier as well; for, though the old man talked much and laughed often, the pain he had been caused by an absentee wife and a disobedient son was clear to see.

What was not clear to the superficial mind of the young Richard was how much pleasure his father derived from the contrast his own respectable marriage and respectful son presented with Sir Lemuel's disorderly arrangements: a wife who loved her homeland more than her husband, an heir who had disgraced the reputation of his regiment. All this was only brought home to him when he stood at his father's deathbed on a winter's day in 1861.

It was the first time Richard had ever seen his father surprised. Angry, yes, outraged often, severe always; but life had held, it seemed, no surprises for this far- if narrow-sighted man. Only death had the capacity to take him unawares. To die at seventy-seven, when his brother had lived, with infinitely less caution, to eighty, formed his final and least-expected grudge against the world.

'How are you, sir?' Richard said banally.

'Dying,' his father rasped. 'It is typical of you not to notice the obvious.'

'I hope—'

'Don't bother to. All my hopes for you came to nothing. Why should your own be any different?'

'I am sorry, Father.' (It represented a concession of a kind not to address him as 'sir'.)

'Sorrow is all I ever had from you.'

Richard leaned closer. 'Have I not lived some of it down? Any of it?'

'None. I sent you to Cleave Court to show your uncle how a gentleman's son should behave, what he should be. I trusted you. You betrayed me.'

'But since then—'

'Since then you have been a clerk like any other. All that matters is that you handed your uncle a victory over me . . . when I had been preparing his defeat for fifty years. Since then, you have been no son to me.'

'In time, I thought I might earn your forgiveness.'

'Impossible.' The old man moved, as if trying to raise himself on the pillow. But it was not that. He only wished to be certain that Richard could see him clearly. 'You have laboured in vain, boy – as I intended.' Then he grinned, his teeth showing between the thin stretched lips, a grin more horrible than any grimace, a grin of contempt that was his final offering to an unloved son.

'In vain.' Richard looked up at the paint-crusted smile of Sir Lemuel and found himself agreeing. It had been very largely in vain, his life to date, his fifty years of seeking to do what was expected, of striving to maintain a standard from which he was held to have lapsed. What did it amount to but a suspicion long suppressed, a disguise of moral cowardice beneath the cloak of what was right and proper?

July 1855 was a month of drought and heat at Cleave Court. Sir Lemuel seldom left the house, but sat reading and dozing in his ground-floor study, with the french windows open and the shades down. It was there that he summoned Richard on a mid-morning of windless brilliance for the last words that ever passed between them. There was a letter open on his lap, his magnifying glass resting on it; he had let his right hand fall beside his chair to scratch the muzzle of his faithful Labrador. When Richard entered the room, he thought Sir Lemuel might be asleep, but no: his immobility was the quietude of sadness.

'I believe you wanted to see me, sir.'

Sir Lemuel looked at him gravely. 'Gervase is being invalided home. Not wounded, but ill. Not seriously, but sufficiently. I have this letter from his commanding officer. By its date, I judge he will arrive any day. You might have thought he would have written himself. Perhaps he wished to arrive unexpectedly.'

'I can't imagine why.'

'Can you not? Nor could I – until young Jamie blurted out what he had seen. The young fellow is not to be blamed. It is only what I might have seen myself – had I wished to.'

'What do you mean, sir?'

'I mean that I have indulged my daughter-in-law's sensitivity too long – and my liking for you too much. You must leave us, Richard, at once. I want you gone by the time Gervase returns.'

'Why?'

'Because if he has cause to suspect anything amiss I would fear for your life. And if you remain he will have cause. You must leave.'

'If it is your wish, I have no choice.'

'No choice?' Sir Lemuel cast an eye towards the haze-shimmered view of the terraced garden. 'Of course you have a choice. You could disobey me – as my wife and my son have done often enough. But that would only compound the sadness. No, Richard. You are a better man than my son. That is why you must leave.'

Richard Davenall walked slowly down the curving staircase. He had left Cleave Court that day, clutching at Sir Lemuel's paltry tribute to warm the seeping chill of his shame. He had gone because his uncle had persuaded him that it was not too late to pull back from the brink of an irrevocable act. Now, as he emerged into the seemly grey light of Pall Mall and moved slowly eastwards, he began to question more than just the worth of a life led in constant propitiation of the tenets wished upon it by his mean-spirited father; he began to question the whole purpose of his flight from one summer's tempting passion twenty-seven years ago. His father's dying grin had done more than parody a lifelong denial of joy. It had opened a window on a world of lies.

There, looming to his left, stood the Crimea monument. He turned towards it and smiled, welcoming the end he sensed this man who called himself James Davenall would make of all their lies. He thought of Hugo – baffled, drunken, sulking Hugo – and laughed aloud, then clapped his hand to his face as his eyes smarted with tears. To pull back from the brink? To think he ever believed it possible. With an effort of will, he composed himself, summoned his failing dignity and walked steadily forward.

VII

Prince Napoleon Joseph Charles Paul Bonaparte, alias the Count of Moncalieri, alias Citizen Jerome-Napoleon, was born in wandering exile to the sometime King of Westphalia (a younger brother of the great Napoleon) and never seemed content in any other state. A handsome youth of charm and intellect, possessed of a patrician build and a striking facial resemblance to his celebrated uncle, he contrived to squander his life in ill-tempered buffoonery, to waste his assets – be they dynastic or intellectual, to heap upon his proud head – as if by design – the derision of all who knew him.

Such was the tall bare-headed figure who strode pensively along the Avenue des Champs Elysées in the failing light of a Parisian afternoon, haughty remnant of a lost Imperial cause, tolerated in his homeland only because so vastly ignored. Thirty-seven years before, he had been banished because the peasants had hailed him as the 'new Napoleon'. Now he stepped idly into a wayside *boulangerie*, bought a pastry and ate it in the street, letting the crumbs fall down the front of his coat whilst he watched a girl on the other side of the road, pacing sensuously to and fro before the scrubbed frontage of a restaurant not yet open for business.

A sweet tooth and a wandering eye. Often enough, he reflected, they had been his downfall. Now he was sixty years old, stout, balding and troubled by flights of stairs. He smiled. The girl's face reminded him of that minx in Stuttgart. She had been worth the thrashing he suffered at her father's hands. Well, he had had his chances and wasted all of them: that he could not deny. He had common tastes but lacked the common touch: a fatal combination. In 1848, they had passed him over in favour of his scheming cousin, who had – against all odds – left a son behind him to sustain the Bonapartist cause in exile. Since then, being passed over had become commonplace: opportunity had only flattered to deceive.

He finished his pastry, brushed off the remaining crumbs and walked on. It was Black Friday – suitably ill-omened for the step he was about to take into a seamy reach of his past. He knew it was a step better not taken, but his life had largely comprised imprudent acts and he was too old to change now. That man Norton – or Davenall, whoever he was – had pricked his conscience, or touched a nerve. Whichever it was, he could not leave it alone.

There was number twenty-three, on the other side of the road, closed gates at the side bearing the name G. PILON (CARROSSIER). He crossed over and tugged at the first-floor flat-bell. A thin-faced maid answered. She flashed him a look of unsmiling recognition.

'*Quelle surprise,*' she said coldly.

'*Pour moi aussi, Eugénie.*'

The maid's lip curled. '*Comme si de rien n'était.*'

He ignored the jibe. '*Votre maîtresse, est-elle à la maison?*'

'*Pour vous, sans doute. Suivez-moi, s'il vous plaît.*'

She led him upstairs to a sitting-room and left him there. He looked around, admiring the faded lavishness of the decorations – flock wallpaper, purple upholstery, an ormolu clock, a gilt-framed mirror he fancied he might once have owned himself. There was evidence of decline in the fortunes of his one-time mistress, but it was not yet overwhelming. She would be forty now, even if her own estimate was to be believed, which it was not. He had lately heard her name linked with a wealthy American. Perhaps there was more money in *parvenus* than in princes these days. Perhaps there always had been.

The door opened and she entered, smiling. Her face displayed with unmistakable starkness the eight years that had passed since their last meeting, though her hair was still dark and immaculately curled. He let his glance run over her body, wrapped in the clinging folds of a silk *peignoir*, and acknowledged that occasional privation had done her figure no harm at all.

'Bonjour, Cora. How is my English pearl?'

Cora, mistress of her native coolness, maintained her distance. 'I am Cora still, but minus any pearls.'

'You still have Eugénie.'

'Only because her arrears are so considerable.'

'Come, come. An apartment on the Champs Elysées? It cannot be that bad'

'How would you know? You have kept away for so long.'

'We have both had our troubles, Cora. We were never . . . friends in need.'

Cora smiled. 'That is true. No rebukes, Plon-Plon. We are too old for them, are we not?'

In the look they then exchanged there was the silent complicity of two who understood that bitterness at the changing times was pointless. The Second Empire had raised them both high – Prince Napoleon as the Emperor's honour-laden cousin, Cora as an English courtesan trading on the loose morals of an immature aristocracy. Now all that was gone, they could consider themselves lucky to survive, however precariously.

'How is your wife?' said Cora neutrally.

'As saintly as ever.'

'And your sons?'

'Surely you know, Cora? The Prince Imperial was good enough to die young but cunning enough to nominate my son Victor as his heir. I have been passed over once again.'

'Is that why you have come? For consolation?'

'Hah!' The Prince laughed his bellowing gale-like laugh, crossed the room and smacked a kiss on Cora's forehead. 'No, Cora. I am past consoling.' He ran one hand down over her shoulder towards the inviting curve of a silk-cradled breast, then broke away and crossed to a side-table, where he began to toy with a piece of china.

'Then, why?'

'Do you remember the Davenall family?'

'How could I forget? Your friend Sir Gervase was so very . . . insistent.'

'Dead now.'

'So many of my clients are. What of it?'

'He had a son – James.'

'I remember. He brought him to Meudon more than once. And we met him in Somerset – that last time. The young man who killed himself.'

'Supposedly. Now somebody has come forward claiming to be James Davenall, heir to the baronetcy. An impostor, we must assume – after the money.'

'What is this to me – or to you?'

'I agreed to help Sir Hugo in resisting the claim.'

'Why?'

'For friendship's sake.'

'You are incapable of friendship, Plon-Plon. I do not say it to hurt you. You have admitted it often enough.'

He put down the piece of china. '*C'est vrai*. Well, Cora, since you ask, Sir Hugo agreed to make a substantial contribution to my campaign fund.'

'Campaign? You still have—?'

'I still have hopes. But not of Sir Hugo. The claimant knew too much about me for me to be of any use. It was quite . . . disarming.'

'Perhaps he is not an impostor.'

'He is certainly not a fool. He knew a great deal about how I first met Gervase Davenall. Tell me, did I ever . . . gossip to you about my first visit to the Davenalls . . . in 1846?'

'Not that I remember. Your pillow talk usually revolved around how superior you were to the Emperor. Which you were, in all the ways that mattered.'

'I might have said something – at some time.'

'If you did, I have forgotten it.'

'I would not blame you if you had sold the information.'

'So that is it. No, Plon-Plon. I have not met this man. I have told him nothing.'

'He uses the name Norton.'

'Norton? Why didn't you say so?'

He swung round on her. 'You know him?'

'Norton? Yes. But he is not—'

Suddenly, he was in front of her, grasping her shoulders with no hint of a caress. 'Not who?'

'I met a man named Norton earlier this year. Plon-Plon, you're hurting me!'

He released her. '*Pardon*. Tell me quickly, Cora. How did you meet him?'

'I have good days and bad days. This is a good day. That was a bad day. It was February, with snow lying in the Bois de Boulogne. I had

111

gone there for a drive with . . . an admirer. We were both drunk. There was a time when I would have been . . . more selective. He took a fancy to a girl in the Pré Catalan and threw me out of his carriage. Can you imagine? The famous Cora Pearl, raddled and drunk, alone in the snow, with no fur stole to warm her. I sat on a bench and cried. Perhaps you find it hard to imagine.'

'No. I wish I did.'

'A young Englishman took pity on me. He gave me his overcoat and brought me home. He bought me dinner on the way. He was handsome . . . and generous. He said his name was Norton.'

'What was he doing in Paris?'

'Visiting a doctor, he said, though he scarcely looked as if he needed to.'

'Did he ask you about the Davenalls?'

'No.'

'Or me?'

'No. He said we had met before but doubted I would remember. I didn't believe him.'

'Nothing else?'

'No. He was a model of courtesy.'

'Damn his courtesy!' The Prince strode across the room and slumped down heavily in a chair. 'Do you have anything to drink, Cora? I feel in need of something.'

'For you, Plon-Plon, I will broach the finest brandy. Wait here.'

She slipped from the room, and Prince Napoleon, cracking his knuckles and chewing his lip, slipped, too, in his mind, through the curtain of years, to the time a persistent stranger seemed to recall better than he did himself.

They called him the Prince de Montfort then. He had come from Italy to visit his exiled cousin, Prince Louis Napoleon, in Bath. Confined at Pulteney's Hotel, the twenty-four-year-old Plon-Plon chafed at the recreational limitations of his escorts, Monsieur and Madame Cornu, until Louis Napoleon ingenuously introduced him to the household of Sir Lemuel Davenall at nearby Cleave Court.

Sir Lemuel's son, Gervase, was five years older than Plon-Plon. They shared nothing beyond a love of excess, but that they shared exuberantly. Behind the staid and gracious terraces of Bath, Gervase knew of bewitching routes into a warren of debased sensation. Down them he led an eager Plon-Plon; it was his initiation into a world he never abandoned, at once his ruin and his salvation. It explained why, thirty-six years later, he sat lost in thought in an ageing whore's apartment above the fading charms of the Champs Elysées, rejected and reviled by the world.

Gervase had a fiancée, a pretty, agreeable girl to be sure, but nothing more than a drawing-room ornament as far as he was concerned. The fiancée had a governess, Miss Strang, arch, graceful, entrancing Miss Strang, who lured Gervase hopelessly with her every forbidding glare. She represented the one indulgence he was absolutely denied: it gave her power over him. He watched her through all his dilatory courtship of her charge, watched and waited and never found his opportunity.

Until Plon-Plon came to Cleave Court, that is, for then Gervase, ever scanning Miss Strang for a single sign of weakness, noticed one at last and determined to exploit it. He explained it to his friend over a card game following the grand ball Sir Lemuel had held in honour of Louis Napoleon and his young guest. All the other revellers had departed. Only the two young men to whom it had been the tamest of entertainment drank still, and wagered and argued, as the small hours reached towards dawn on Sunday, 20th September 1846.

'Did you see the way she looked at you, Plon-Plon?'

'*Moi? Mais non, mon ami.* Mademoiselle Webster, she has the eyes for you.'

'I'm talking about the Scots bitch. Catherine's governess: Vivien Strang.'

'Mademoiselle Strang *encore*? Gervase, you are obsessed.'

'I've sworn to have her. And now I've seen a way. She couldn't take her eyes off you.'

'*Donc*, a lady of taste. For myself, *les écossaises* are . . . too cold.'

'It's what she thinks of you that's important.'

'We danced, we conversed: nothing more. *Mais c'est vrai*: I could have been having more if I had been wanting it. I think she found me . . . dazzling.'

'So what do you say? Write her a note suggesting a secret rendezvous . . . at midnight. I could deliver it when I go there for this Godawful tea-party.'

'What I say, Gervase, is that she would not come – and I would not want her to. She is too . . . *sévère*.'

'I would keep the rendezvous for you, Plon-Plon. And I'll wager you she would come.'

'Wager? This becomes interesting. Combien?'

'Aha! Now the dog sees the rabbit. Well, you've had the devil's own luck tonight, *mon ami*. So what do you say to all I owe you: double or quits?'

'*Alors*, I accept the wager. It is a noble wager. I will win, *sans aucun doute*. It will be a pleasure.'

'You will lose, Plon-Plon. And the pleasure . . . will all be mine.'

'Your brandy, Plon-Plon.'

Cora's return to the room had taken him unawares. He looked up

113

sharply – and caught his breath. She was standing by the door, holding a tray with a frosted bottle and two glasses on it. She was smiling, as she had been earlier, but now she had discarded the *peignoir*. She presented herself naked before him, walking slowly across to the low table beside his chair and leaning forward to place the tray by his elbow.

'You always said you liked me in anything – but most of all in nothing,' she said. 'Excuse my vanity, but all is still, as you see, in good order.'

Prince Napoleon breathed out slowly. There she stood, better than he remembered, because so long forgone, the flesh still unwrinkled, the curves still unresisting, his intact inviting Cora. *'Superbe,'* he murmured. *'Toujours superbe.'*

'Do you remember when I was served like this, on a giant silver platter, at the Café Anglais?'

'As the dish too good to eat.'

'You do remember.'

'Do you remember the card I sent you after our first meeting?'

'"Où? Quand? Combien?"'

'You remember also.' Suddenly, he closed his eyes, Cora's words drawing his mind to another distant bargain. He had accepted the wager. He had written the note. But he had not thought . . . She was close to him. He could smell her perfume. It was his favourite brand. She took his hand in hers.

'Chez moi. Ce soir. Pour rien.' She kissed his hand and pressed it to her breasts. 'Or are you really past consoling?'

He opened his eyes and smiled broadly. 'No, Cora,' he said. 'Not quite.'

SIX

I

Edgar Parfitt reached Orchard Street even earlier than normal that Saturday morning, 14th October. He did not believe in giving the staff any room for complaint about him, in order that he should have ample room for complaint about them. To arrive before them was therefore an article of faith. Today, however, he had surpassed himself. It was barely light as he approached the rear door. He rubbed his hands in eager anticipation of a quiet half-hour, to be spent putting the finishing touches to his marbling scheme. It would soon be ready for presentation to Mr Ernest, whom he had high hopes of winning over. After all, Mr Ernest . . .

What was this? The door was unlocked, and the first post had been removed from the cage. He had been forestalled! Who could it be? The adjoining offices were empty, their shutters drawn. There was no sign of the post. Then he heard a movement above. Mr William already in his office? It was unprecedented. He hung up his hat and coat grumpily, then climbed the stairs.

Unprecedented or not, there was Mr William, the least formidable of the Trenchards and the least respected, seated at his desk reading a letter from the post, his office door open.

'Good morning, sir,' said Parfitt.

Trenchard looked up. 'Oh. It's you.' He was haggard and unshaven, Parfitt noticed, his hair awry. He had not so much as fitted a collar to his shirt. As Parfitt stepped into the room, he was met by an odour of stale pipe-smoke and . . . yes, alcohol, quite definitely. 'What time is it?'

'A little after seven.'

Trenchard blinked, as if his eyes were sore, and reached forward to extinguish the lamp still burning on his desk. 'Do you always arrive this early?'

115

'Habitually, sir, yes.' Parfitt's eyes darted round the room. A smeared tumbler stood on the mantelpiece. Trenchard's jacket and overcoat were draped over a chair-back. Was it possible he had been there all night?

Trenchard coughed and rose from his chair. 'Well, I'll have to leave you to it, I'm afraid.' He picked up his jacket, shrugged it on and moved unsteadily to a mirror hanging on the opposite wall.

'Going out again, sir?'

From his jacket pocket, Trenchard had pulled a collar and tie. He squinted into the mirror and began to fasten them about his neck. 'Yes, Parfitt. Straight away.'

Parfitt shifted his gaze to the abandoned desk-top. There were tumbler-shaped rings on the blotter, flakes of tobacco amongst the scattered papers. And there was the letter Trenchard had been reading, restored now to its envelope. Parfitt could just make out the postmark: Bath, 13 October.

'So you'll have to excuse me.' Trenchard leaned past him, plucked the letter off the desk and moved to the door. 'Needs must . . .'

'When the devil drives,' Parfitt muttered to himself as he listened to Trenchard's footsteps descending the stairs. Well, Mrs Parfitt had always said that one would go to the bad. And she was seldom wrong.

II

Brotherton & Baverstock,
Commissioners for Oaths,
Albany Chambers,
Cheap Street,
BATH,
Somerset.

13th October 1882

Dear Davenall,

Excuse my addressing this letter to your home. I did not wish to run the risk of its lying unread at your office over the weekend.

Lady Davenall persists in maintaining that 20th September 1846 is a date of no significance. I know from Miss Pursglove, however, that Lady Davenall's governess at that time, a Scottish spinster named Strang, was dismissed in September 1846 following an unspecified incident at the Cleave Court maze. I also know, from the same source, that Prince Napoleon attended a ball at Cleave Court in September 1846,

116

probably on the 19th. Lady Davenall, however, has instructed me to leave the Strang question entirely alone, which I am, therefore, bound to do.

Lady Davenall has also instructed me to tell Sir Hugo – which I trust I may leave you to do on my behalf – that Mr Norton's claim is to be uncompromisingly resisted. She would oppose any monetary inducements being offered to him to withdraw. I might add that she has heard of none through me.

You will appreciate that I now enjoy little scope for movement in this matter. I should be obliged if you would let me know how and when Warburton intends to proceed.

> I remain,
> Yours truly,
> ARTHUR E. BAVERSTOCK

The cab drew to a halt, and Richard Davenall slid Baverstock's letter back into his pocket: here they were at The Limes. He climbed out and paid the man off, then took a lungful of St John's Wood air – somehow sweeter than ever frowsty Highgate – and marched up the drive. There was a spring in his step and a tilt to his hat, as if, from all the unpromising circumstances crowding around his head, he had drawn some unreasonable inspiration.

The front door was open. A trunk stood in the hall. At the foot of the stairs, a small girl, dressed in a travelling cape, her hair tied in pig-tails, sat on the bottom step, staring intently ahead and clutching a bonnet in her lap. Richard recognized her from his previous visit.

'Hello,' he said, stepping in. 'It's Patience, isn't it?' She did not reply. 'Going somewhere?'

The little girl's eyes clamped themselves on him, as only a little girl's can, but still she said nothing.

'Is your father in?' With the diffidence of a confirmed bachelor, he stooped to her level. 'Your daddy – do you know where he is?'

At last, she spoke, slowly, as if the words had been rehearsed. 'Daddy . . . isn't . . . coming.'

Richard frowned. What could she mean? Suddenly, the stairs before him vibrated with the descent of a flustered female figure. 'No time to sit there mooning, Patience!' she cried. 'We must be up and doing!' Richard looked up. It was the child's nanny, all calm efficiency last time, transformed now into an embodiment of bustling frenzy. 'Come along,' she said, plucking Patience from her seat. 'We'll soon be ready to go.' The pair vanished together into an adjoining room, Patience gazing back at him solemnly as they went.

Richard rose slowly and looked about him. At the end of the hall, in an open doorway, stood Constance, watching him with some of her daughter's solemnity. How long she had been there he could not tell.

'Good morning,' he said lamely.

'Hello, Richard,' she replied. 'Looking for William?'

'Yes.'

'He isn't here. Won't you come in?' She retreated into the room, and he followed. 'Please close the door.' He did so. 'I was just writing you a letter.'

'Really?'

'I thought you should know my course of action – and my reasons for it.' She took the letter, as yet unfolded, from the bureau and handed it to him. His gaze rested, despite himself, on the splintered wood showing above one sagging broken drawer of the bureau. 'Here you are.'

He carried the letter to the window and began to read. It did not take long.

'Well?' she said, when he had clearly finished.

He looked at her, the light from the window falling full on her face, and noticed, for the first time, how superficial her composure was. There was some tumult within her, some moving passion at which the letter only hinted. 'If you choose to live with your father rather than with your husband, Constance, it is no business of mine.'

'Yet the reason is.'

'Where is William?'

'At Orchard Street. He decided to spare us both this parting.'

'I've been there this morning. They told me he'd left. That's why I came here.'

'Oh?' Her lack of reaction shocked him. It was as if she was no longer interested in Trenchard's movements; as if, already, the ties of an earlier, unconsecrated union were stronger than any legal marriage.

'Do you intend to declare openly your support for Norton's claim?'

'I shall await the outcome of the hearing.'

'And then?'

Her gaze, which had hitherto drifted, gossamer-like, about the room, now fixed itself upon him. There was his answer, clear to see in the candour of her expression. 'Your refusal to accept James baffles me,' she said at last. 'William is jealous, Hugo avaricious. And Lady Davenall has always been a mystery to me. But you, Richard – how can *you* maintain the pretence?'

'The evidence is—'

She silenced him with one upraised hand. 'I ask you as his cousin and his friend – not as his solicitor.'

Something in her commanded him to be honest. 'Because I can't be sure who he really is. He knows enough to persuade anyone – I don't deny that. Yet, sometimes, he seems to know too much. More of James in some things, less in others. As if—'

'Yes?'

'As if he is the man James might have been – but wasn't.'

'He is James. I no longer doubt it.'

They were standing, side by side, before the window and the view it presented of the garden. All this hedge-trimmed order, all this inner domestic calm, was about to be ended – for the sake of . . . what? A falling leaf floated by, close against the glass, moved by the invisible breezes of the season; moved, as they were, by forces unseen yet irresistible.

'His story, which you all tried to keep from me, I had from his own lips.' Her voice dropped to a whisper. 'It seared my heart.'

Richard, too, spoke in an undertone. 'As if he holds within him all the false steps and treacherous turns we've taken. As if he's all our pasts demanding satisfaction, our consciences, which we can no longer stifle.'

A moment of silence followed. Then she seemed to hear what he had said. 'What?'

He turned and smiled at her. 'Nothing. I see you are not to be dissuaded. As Catherine is to you, so are you to me.'

'A mystery? But I have—'

'You have her will, her strength. Now, today, for the first time, I see the resemblance.' His gaze drifted back to the window and passed, to a different day, through the refracting surface of his memory.

For those eight months that served as the meagre season of passion in Richard Davenall's life, his cousin's wife, Catherine, was a person he had never known before and would never know again. Whatever had so struck at her complacent serenity in the Crimea, whatever Prince Napoleon had disclosed to her in a fit of rage in Constantinople, had ushered in the brief flowering of her true self. For Catherine, as he and she alone knew, was neither the pliant wallflower of her youth nor the forbidding recluse of her middle age. There was another, secret Catherine, who returned to Cleave Court in December 1854 and honoured Richard with her company during the months that followed.

She was twenty-five years old, at the peak of her physical beauty, suddenly restless and resentful at all she had been denied between a domineering father and a domineering husband. What had sparked this mood of convulsive emotion she never revealed, and Richard never asked. As a young and diffident man of twenty-two, ostensibly dedicated to learning the ways of estate management and earning the approbation of his demanding father, he ought to have resisted the slightest suggestion of something more than the respect he owed her. But he did not. Instead, he fanned the flame of a dangerous sensation.

The spring of 1855 set in early, as if Cleave Court were in Italy rather than in Somerset. April was a succession of numbingly perfect days, during which Richard found himself accompanying Catherine on endless walks and drives and languid excursions. As if bewitched, like Richard, by the eerie paradise the weather had made of his home, Sir Lemuel offered the two only encouragement, seeming to draw some sap of youth from their heedless ways. There was no work, no duty, no threatened end to their idyll. Gervase was far away and forgotten by those who claimed to love him. The world was compounded of Catherine's smile, and bouncing hair, and running feet on warm grass. And the world's end was not ordained.

The first time he kissed her, he held back, hesitating before the prospect of what he might be about to do. They were in the woods behind Cleave Court, in a realm of green-pillared sunlight set aside for their pleasure. Her hair hung loose to her shoulders, her eyes gleamed. He ached to touch the pale flesh beneath her dress – and she seemed to want him to.

'You are married,' he said haltingly.

'My husband has forfeited his right to me.'

'But have I won it?'

She did not answer. Instead, she drew him to her.

Half an hour after leaving The Limes, Richard Davenall was sitting, his shoulders hunched, on a rough backless bench towards the summit of Primrose Hill. Further down the slope, a child played with a hoop whilst her mother read a book. Everywhere, the leaves were falling. He could hear them, if he listened hard enough, fluttering about him where he sat.

Constance would be on her way by now, daring to act where he would have faltered. He could not have explained to her the secret dread that clutched him even if he had wanted to. His compunction, his instinct, his lifelong training, so nearly forbade him to recall it even to his own mind. He had to shut his eyes to prevent the memory causing him to shudder at the shame it inspired.

They had spent the day on the downs and had returned to Cleave Court late in the afternoon. It was the last week of June 1855, its golden endless days wrapping their world in tempting warmth. Sir Lemuel had gone to see his bootmaker in Bath and taken little James with him – or so they supposed. In fact, after their departure, the little chap had complained of feeling sick: a touch of sunstroke, Nanny Pursglove surmised. He had been put to bed, and Sir Lemuel had gone alone.

The house seemed strangely empty, the servants all below stairs or out on errands, the upper quarters silent but for sultry breezes sighing through open windows and stirring the heavy sunshades. It seemed reserved for them – and they for each other.

In Catherine's room, the half-drawn curtains billowed in the soft

120

currents of air. Patches of invading sunlight spread across the carpet and reached the two figures on the bed, warming their flesh where it fell upon it, catching her smile as she took his hand and guided him, heightening the delirium of his abandonment: he was hers, body and soul, and she had seemed to be his.

Then she froze beneath him. Her eyes opened wide. On her face there was a look of such horror as, even now, he could not erase.

She cried out. 'James!'

All he glimpsed, as he twisted his head in the direction of her gaze, was a small scampering figure fleeing through the open door. It slammed behind him like a rifle shot. James had seen them – but not soon enough. She was his for one more moment – and then was lost for ever.

Richard slipped Baverstock's letter from his pocket and read it again. There were more secrets, it seemed, than he had supposed. Something linked September 1846 and June 1855 and the present. And there was only one way to find out what. He would have to see her again, would have to face that stare, that pitiless accusing stare, and wrest from her the truth. He would have to speak to Catherine of all that had lain so long silent between them. He rose from the bench and walked quickly down the hill.

III

Dr Fiveash's consulting-room looked out on to a sloping chestnut-fringed lawn. Beyond, weak sun lit the pale stone of the city-swathed slopes. This very room, Fiveash said, turning back from the view, was where he had told James Davenall the true nature of his illness.

'I little thought', he continued, 'that our conversation would still be causing me sleepless nights eleven years later.' He stood for a moment, lost in thought, then broke off and smiled. 'Well, what brings you here, Trenchard?'

'Your letter,' I replied.

Fiveash sighed. 'I felt you ought to know. I only wish it were more . . . straightforward.'

'Surely your discovery strengthens our case. Miss Whitaker was evidently interested in anything with a bearing on the Davenalls.'

'Oh, yes, that's clear. But a duel fought more than forty years ago? How does that help Norton?'

'I don't know. I thought, by coming, I might be able to find out.'

The Doctor shook his head. 'I fear we've left it too late. It's eight months since Miss Whitaker disappeared.'

'She might have left some clue to her whereabouts – perhaps at her lodgings?'

'You're welcome to try. She lived in Norfolk Buildings, behind Green Park station. Miss Arrow will have the address. I'll ask her to find it.' He lumbered out into the adjoining office.

While he was gone, I took a turn by the window, then caught sight of myself in a mirror mounted on the wall above the examining-couch. The last twenty-four hours had taken their toll, that was clear. I pulled out my watch and flipped it open. Constance would be on her way by now, entertaining Patience with a picture-book whilst the train ran down through Surrey. What would she tell her father? I wondered. What would I tell mine?

Fiveash came back into the room. 'Number thirteen, Norfolk Buildings. She lodged there with the widow Oram.'

'Number thirteen. Thank you.' I made a move towards the door.

'Trenchard.' He stopped me with a touch on the elbow. 'Call it a doctor's impertinence if you like, but you don't look fit to me. Is there anything I can—?'

'I'm quite fit, thank you, Doctor.'

'Is all well at home?'

'To borrow your phrase: as well as can be expected.'

'You mustn't let this wretched business get on top of you, you know.'

'Must I not?'

'Would you care to stop for lunch?'

It was apparent that it was not my company he desired: he was genuinely concerned. The signs of strain were more obvious to him even than to me. Or perhaps it was simply that my mind had steeled itself to disregard them. I brushed aside his solicitations and left.

Norfolk Buildings was a single terrace running down to the riverside in a genteelly decayed reach of Bath. Noise and smoke rose from the nearby goods-yard of Green Park station, but cheery window-boxes and fresh stucco redeemed at least some of the house-fronts. A shabbily dressed girl was playing whip-and-top outside number thirteen, where a bronze plate proclaimed a humble dentist trying to make his way; from an open second-floor window came the plangent strains of a violin.

'I'm looking for Mrs Oram,' I said to the girl.

'Seems 'er be looking for you, too,' she replied, her gaze travelling past me.

I swung round to see a sharp-nosed whey-faced woman with small, twinkling, bead-like eyes staring at me from a ground-floor window. I signalled that I wished to speak to her, but there was no way of judging her reaction from the abrupt tug with which the curtain was flipped back to obscure my view.

Then, quick as a flash, she was standing before me in the doorway, a

122

breathless concoction of pink and sepia. 'You'll have heard the top room's empty,' she trilled, bobbing before me in some travesty of a curtsey. 'It commands a fine prospect. Won't you come in?'

I did not disabuse her until we had reached her trinket-festooned sitting-room. From the corner, a large and ragged parrot, chained to its perch, eyed me suspiciously and fluttered its gaudy wings.

'Fine parrot you have, Mrs Oram.'

'Obadiah is a macaw, dearie.'

Hearing its name, the bird screeched some few word-sounding noises to which Mrs Oram paid rapt head-cocked attention.

'Did you catch what he said, Mr . . .?'

'Trenchard. No, I don't believe I did.' It had been something like 'Misterkin, Sunkysin', but I had paid it scant heed.

'Never mind. You'll have ample opportunity to learn his little phrases. All my PGs do.'

'Perhaps I should explain, Mrs Oram: I've not called about the room.'

Her head was still fixed in the crooked position that seemed to command Obadiah's attention; her eyes swivelled to focus on me. 'Not . . . about the room?' Obadiah loosed another 'Misterkin, Sunkysin', this time with the hint of a triumphant sneer.

'No. But it is about one of your former lodgers. Miss Whitaker. She left you in February, I think. I'm trying to trace her.'

'Miss Whitaker?' She stared intently at me. At close quarters, her pale powdered cheeks could be seen to vibrate with every word. 'You've left it rather late, dearie, rather too late, I should say, wouldn't you, Obadiah?' She shot a glance in the bird's direction, where a downward twitch of the beak seemed to give her the confirmation she sought. 'We had Dr Fiveash looking for her, too, six months back. Quite incorrigible, he was.' She smiled. 'Still, I should say she'd rather be found by you than by him. Not that that'll help you, because I've no idea where she went.'

'It's very important I find her. There might be a reward for anybody who could help me.'

'Hear that, Obadiah?' She turned and grinned at him.

'Misterkin, Sunkysin!'

'I see you have more winning ways than drab Dr Fiveash, dearie, and I'd like to help you, really I would, but Miss Whitaker kept herself very much to herself, I'm afraid. She paid her rent in advance and had spotless habits. I'm not saying anything against her, but she wasn't . . . sociable. And she left without notice. Staid and proper enough, but not . . . considerate. If you know what I mean.'

'She might have mentioned where she'd lived before coming to Bath.'

'Goodness, I was lucky to have two words out of her at a time.' She leaned towards me. 'Some would've called her secretive. I just call her . . . reserved.' She swayed away again. 'What would you call her, Obadiah?'

'Misterkin, Sunkysin!'

123

'Have you mastered his intonation yet, dearie?'

'I can't say I have.'

'It's a phrase my late husband taught him. Something of a card, my Oram, I'm afraid. The vicar called it blasphemous, but he's a terrible sobersides. Quick to preach, slow to laugh. That's always been my—'

'Misterkin, Sunkysin!'

'There! Catch it that time?'

'No.' I smiled and moved towards the door.

'"Mr Quinn, sunk in sin." I thought it was clear enough for a young pair of ears like yours.'

I looked back at her with incomprehension bordering on revelation. 'Quinn?'

'Mr Quinn was a friend of my Oram. They liked a drink together, liked it overmuch in my Oram's case. He made up that silly rhyme and taught it to Obadiah. I don't really know why. But I'm glad to have a reminder of—'

'Quinn was in service with the Davenalls at Cleave Court!'

'That's right, dearie. How did you know?'

'He and your husband drank together?'

'Regular, three times a week at the Red Lion. Never missed till the day he died. It was the drink that killed him. Mind you, my Oram always said water was more likely to kill him than spirits, which turned out true in a sense, if you can count falling in the river blind drunk and drowning. A card to the end, my Oram.'

'What about Quinn?'

'I've not seen him since the day my Oram went on. Seven years ago last Easter. Good Friday, it was. The vicar called it blasphemous—'

'How could I find Quinn?'

'I doubt you could. He was just as tight-lipped as that Miss Whitaker. He left Cleave Court, I do know – but that's the last I heard of him. You might try the Red Lion, I suppose. It's just round the corner, in Monmouth Place. If anybody would know, it would be Wally Fishlock. He was the third member of their drinking school. And I'm told he's still to be found at their table in the tap-room. Isn't that right, Obadiah?'

'Mister Quinn, sunk in sin!' This time, I understood his call.

Fishlock was as good as Mrs Oram's word. A lean, tanned, mournful figure in matted tweeds, stooped over a jug and glass in the musty ochre-lit corner of the Red Lion's back bar, proved, on enquiry, to be the man I wanted. Drink had not loosened his tongue. But money did.

"Course I mind Alfie Quinn. We often supped together. 'Im and Charlie Oram. We 'ad . . . mootual interests. I'd not put it stronger. More'n old Mother Oram ever knew of, though. Least said, see?

'Alf were an old soljer. 'Ard as nails – with more tricks 'n a monkey.

Not what you'd call cut out for valetin'. But 'im and 'is squire – Sir Gervase Davenall, curse 'is memory – 'ad been in the Crimea together. Alf were 'is batman. So they stuck together, seemingly, like fleas and a dog. 'E left Cleave Court three year ago. First I knew of it's when 'e stopped comin' in 'ere. Reckon 'e moved away. Back to London, like as not.'

'Is that where he originated – London?'

'It's where 'e spoke of.'

'And you've not seen him since?'

'Not a once. But Joe 'as.' He nodded towards the stolid figure polishing glasses behind the bar. 'Ain't that right, Joe?'

The landlord was a squarely built, slowly spoken, cautious man who treated me to a penetrating stare. 'I may have done,' he said at last.

I tried to sound nonchalant. 'Recently?'

'February, weren't it?' put in Fishlock.

Joe nodded in confirmation. I moved to the bar. 'You saw him here? In Bath?'

Joe sniffed. 'Maybe. I keep a greyhound, see. I exercise him along the canal bank every morning. One morning last February, I was trotting him along the tow-path where it runs through Sydney Gardens. I noticed a man and a woman on one of the footbridges over the canal. The man looked like Alfie Quinn. I called out, but he moved away. By the time I got up on to the footbridge, he'd vanished.'

'And the woman?'

'She was still there. She said he'd just asked her for directions and that she'd no idea who he was. That may be so. But I knew her. It was that piece who lodged with the widow Oram.'

'Miss Whitaker?'

'I never knew her name. But I'd seen her around. It was her, right enough. As for Quinn . . . well, it was early, I didn't have that good a sight of him – I could have been mistaken. But I don't think I was. Still, it was pretty obvious he didn't want to see me, for all the ale he used to sup in this very room. Took off like a hare who'd seen my hound.'

The place, when I found it later, was as I might have imagined from Joe's description: a quiet shady park bisected by the railway line and the canal. The canal passed under several bridges as it traversed the gardens and, on one of these, he had seen them that cold morning in February. To climb from the tow-path to the level of the bridge he would have had to pass through a gate and skirt round by a winding path, allowing ample time for Quinn to scurry off towards the road and for Miss Whitaker to prepare her excuses.

I sat on a bench by the railway line – where passing trains split the leaf-strewn reverie – and tried to connect the events I had learned of. I

125

no longer doubted that there was a connection. I had only to recall what Fishlock had said of his former boon companion when I had asked him for his assessment.

'Somethin' tied Alfie an' that Sir Gervase. Not a doubt of it. Reckon the other Davenalls put 'im out on 'is ear when Sir Gervase were no longer around to protect 'im. If that's 'ow it was, they made a big mistake. Alfie Quinn weren't a man to cross. If they made 'im their enemy, they'd 'ave needed no other. If that's what they did, like as not 'e'd 'ave made 'em regret it.'

At last I felt certain I had found the chink in Norton's armour. Quinn, the resentful ex-servant – Miss Whitaker delving into Fiveash's records – and Norton's otherwise inexplicable fund of knowledge: I had him. This time, I felt certain, I had found him out.

V

Arthur Baverstock had promised to take his son to Bathampton Downs that afternoon, if the weather held, to fly his kite. He had just tapped his barometer to assure himself that all seemed set fair and begun to clear his desk when Dobson, his clerk, came in with the unwelcome news that he had a visitor.

'A Mr Trenchard, sir. Somewhat excited.'

Baverstock sighed heavily.

'I could say that you had already left.'

'No, no. I'd better see him. Show him in.' What could Trenchard possibly want in Bath? Baverstock wondered as Dobson retreated. More to the point, how long would it take? He looked towards the window and glimpsed the inviting shapes of high mobile clouds: Eric's kite would go well in such conditions, if it went at all.

'Glad to catch you, Mr Baverstock,' came a voice. So here he was, rather shabbier and wilder-eyed than Baverstock recalled. He gritted his teeth, smiled and shook hands.

'I didn't know you were in Bath, Mr Trenchard.'

'A flying visit. But I've turned up some new evidence you might be interested in.'

Baverstock's heart sank. Already, he sensed Lady Davenall would not approve. He wished he had never taken on her affairs and thought ruefully for a moment of the accolade he had first believed her patronage to be.

'What can you tell me about Alfred Quinn?'

'That rather depends on why you ask.'

As Trenchard explained, Baverstock's heart sank still further. Miss Arrow's bicycle – a forty-year-old newspaper-cutting – Mrs Oram's macaw – a sighting in Sydney Gardens: Warburton would laugh at them.

'Quinn, so I'm told, was valet to Sir Gervase Davenall,' Trenchard concluded.

'Yes,' said Baverstock. 'He was. And, later, butler.'

'Was he dismissed?'

'Yes.'

'Can you tell me why?'

There seemed no point in refusing: it would only have encouraged him. 'Lady Davenall reordered her affairs after Sir Gervase's removal to a nursing home. She and Quinn did not . . . see eye to eye. I'm sure I told you—'

'Is that all there was to it?'

'As a matter of fact, no. Some of Sir Gervase's possessions – a gold watch, a silver snuff-box, some cuff-links – went missing. It was suggested Quinn had taken them. The watch cropped up in the hands of a jeweller in Bradford-on-Avon, who confirmed that he had bought the items from Quinn. Quinn claimed Sir Gervase had given them to him prior to his collapse as tokens of his esteem. But selling them told against him. All in all, I should say he was lucky to escape without charges being brought against him.'

'But he *was* turned out without a penny – after more than twenty years' service.'

'Not a moment too soon, some would say.'

'Because he was a shady character?'

'My impression was that he would not have been tolerated in another household. Sir Gervase presumably took him on out of sentiment.'

Trenchard leaned across the desk, a gleam of certainty in his eyes. 'It's my belief that Quinn's plying Norton with all the knowledge he must have accumulated about the Davenalls over the years. It's my belief he put Miss Whitaker up to spy on Dr Fiveash's records. They stand to make a fortune between them, and Quinn would have his revenge on those who turned him out. Doesn't it make sense?'

For all his awareness of how flimsy the evidence would appear in court, Baverstock could not deny that it did indeed make sense. He remembered the occasion, three years before, when he had confronted Quinn in his room at Cleave Court to tell him that he had to go. It was early December 1879, with Sir Gervase but lately removed to his nursing home and Baverstock still flushed with gratitude at Lady Davenall's decision to use his services. It was an occasion, which, until now, had seemed merely a clinical disposal of disagreeable business, an occasion which, he now reflected, might not have been as inconsequential as he had supposed.

'Lady Davenall wants you gone by the morning,' said Baverstock peremptorily.

Quinn turned from the window, where he had been gazing down at the garden, and looked straight at him. It was the first time Baverstock

127

had seen him out of uniform: he was surprised by how muscular the man was, rising fifty but with only flecks of grey in his short-cropped hair to suggest it. Quinn's face was lean and sternly set, the brow somewhat hooded, the eyes darting and penetrative. He had the flattened nose and gnarled hands of a prizefighter, or the old soldier he was known to be. Beneath his respectful manner and featureless accent there had always seemed to be something watchful and threatening, something not quite suppressed. Baverstock shivered: the room was icy cold.

'It's assumed you'll make no trouble.'

Quinn still said nothing.

'Candidly, I think you've got off lightly. Lady Davenall has given you the benefit of very little doubt.'

Quinn put his hands on his hips and stared at Baverstock. Then he cocked one eyebrow and finally spoke. 'Where did she find you?'

'I hardly—'

'Twenty-four years I served her husband. I know more of his secrets than she ever will. Does she really think she can afford to make an enemy of me?'

'That's not the issue, Quinn.'

'Is it not? Be warned, Mr Lawyer. She hounded her son into suicide. She packed her husband off to a nursing home. She hired you to replace her cousin. Now she's easing me off the premises. She's a hard woman. Never forget it.' He turned aside and pulled a carpet-bag from behind a chair; it was already full. 'Tell her I'll be gone by tonight. Bag and baggage.'

'Good. There remains only the question of your outstanding wages. I've brought them with me.' Baverstock drew the prepared envelope from his pocket – and held it out. 'Correct to the end of the month.'

Quinn took the packet and tossed it into his bag. 'I'm obliged.'

'In the circumstances, it's extremely generous.'

'In the circumstances, it's a bloody insult. But don't worry. What this family owes me I'll take – in my own good time.'

The slamming of the office door jolted Baverstock back from his recollections. He looked up, to find himself alone. Trenchard had gone.

V

Nanny Pursglove, in her spick and span cottage by the swollen River Avon, was by some way the most welcoming of my hosts that day. Her only hint of disappointment was when I told her I was alone.

'Mrs Trenchard not with you?' she said, with a downcast look back at me as she led the way into her tiny sitting-room.

'No,' I replied. Then, to forestall further enquiry: 'I was hoping you could tell me something about Alfred Quinn.'

'Bless me, what would you be wanting to know about him?'

'Mr Baverstock tells me he was dismissed.'

'He would know, I'm sure.'

'For thieving.'

'So it was said. Will you take some tea?'

'Was there any other reason suggested?'

'Do sit down, Mr Trenchard. Lupin and I are forgetting ourselves.' She filled a cup from the ever-ready pot and handed it to me. 'I worked with Mr Quinn for more than twenty years. Long enough to judge whether he was a scoundrel, wouldn't you say?'

'Yes, I would. That's why I came to see you.'

'He never fitted in with the rest of the staff. He never seemed suited to a life of service. A scoundrel? Well, so we always thought. But a cunning artful fox of a man. I could have believed he'd steal from his master. He had that in him. But be caught doing it? Not Mr Quinn.' She shook her head vehemently. 'He had Sir Gervase on a string. He had no need to steal from him. Lady Davenall knew that.'

'So she wanted rid of him and any excuse would have done?'

Miss Pursglove looked at me sharply. 'Why do you want to know about Mr Quinn? You never mentioned him when you called before.'

'Something you said then set me thinking. You said that Norton—'

'Mr James, you mean,' she put in.

'You said that he didn't seem surprised when you mentioned that Quinn had left. You said it was as if he already knew.'

'Did I?'

'How could he have known?'

She had grown suddenly defensive. 'Perhaps I had already told him. You know how we old ladies can get confused, Mr Trenchard. I'm being told as much often enough.'

'"Not suited to a life of service," I think you said. What do you suppose led him into it?'

'He was Sir Gervase's batman in the Crimea. Sir Gervase came to rely on him out there and didn't want to lose him when the war ended. It was very generous of him to offer Mr Quinn such a position. Valet to a baronet would be a vast improvement on a common soldier's wages and conditions, I should think.'

'As you say: very generous.'

'I once said as much to Mr Quinn, you know.' She was warming to her theme. '"You fell on your feet with Sir Gervase," I said. And do you know what he replied? "No more than my due." Those were his words and those were all his words. What do you make of that?'

'I don't know.'

129

'No more do I. He wasn't to be drawn on what happened out there. Sir Gervase fell ill: that we did know. Perhaps Mr Quinn nursed him back to health. Either way, there was something between them.'

'But you've no idea what?'

'What Mr Quinn didn't want to tell you, you didn't get told. A man's entitled to his privacy, of course, but he took it further than that. No. He was never one of us. You could see it in his face.'

'I wish I could. Any idea where he is now?'

'Not a one, Mr Trenchard. Not a one where that man is concerned. But as to his face – I can show you that right enough.'

'You intrigue me.'

She needed no encouragement. Already, she was bustling towards a glass-fronted cabinet in the corner of the room. She opened the door, setting the contents quivering, and plucked a silver-framed photograph from behind a porcelain shepherdess. 'Some of we senior staff had our pictures taken . . . oh, it must be twelve years ago. You'll recognize me, no doubt.'

I took the picture from her and held it up to the light. It had evidently been taken in the garden of Cleave Court, with the rear windows of the house in the background. Seated on a bench were two stolid aproned women with a look of the kitchen about them. To one side, Miss Pursglove, indistinguishable from her present self, alert and upright on a chair. Behind the bench, three rigidly posed and uniformed male servants. In the space between the bench and the chair, a waistcoated grizzled man, leaning on a rake, whom I took for Crowcroft the head gardener. Behind the chair, one hand resting on its back, a short, squarely built man in bowler hat and high-buttoned tweed jacket. Towards this last figure Miss Pursglove's wavering finger moved.

'That's Mr Quinn for you. Though it'll not tell you much.'

I peered closer. Was this, I wondered, with a sudden chill in Miss Pursglove's sun-warmed sitting-room, the face of my true enemy? Was this the conspirator for whom Norton was merely acting a part? It scarcely seemed possible. Alfred Quinn, batman, valet and butler to Sir Gervase Davenall, stood, it was true, neither in frozen awe nor in grinning worship of the camera lens. Yet he revealed nothing, by pose or expression, that could hint at his character. A lean, strongly built man whose look was perhaps too proud and piercing for natural servility: that was all.

'When did you say this was taken?' I said at length.

'If my memory serves, as it usually does, it was the summer before Mr James disappeared. 1870, that would have been.'

'How old would Quinn have been then?'

'He came to us as a young man in his twenties. He'd have been about forty when that picture was taken.'

'Any idea where he was born? What he did before joining the Army?'

130

'Not a one. He seemed to know London, but not so well that I could say that's where he came from. He wasn't a man to reminisce – or even answer a civil question about himself if he could avoid it. What I know about him is much what you see there.'

A thought occurred to me. 'Might I borrow this picture, Nanny?'

She frowned. 'Well . . .'

'I promise to return it.'

A lifetime of obedience overcame her reservations. 'Well, be sure you do.'

All the way back to London on the train that afternoon, I thought of Alfred Quinn, the cautious guarded servant who had always been more than that. Where was he now? The question had become my talisman, my token of hope that nothing more sinister than a servant's grudge lay at the heart of the mystery.

VI

Richard Davenall was a man of regular and moderate habits. His few servants, had they not already retired to bed, would have found it inconceivable that their master should still be in his study, the lamps blazing, the fire stoked, the whisky-decanter unstoppered on his desk, as the clock struck midnight and Sunday, 15th October 1882 announced its arrival with a buffet of rain at the uncurtained windows.

It had rained that day, too, Richard recalled. That day in January 1861, of his father's burial at Highgate Cemetery, where half a dozen dutiful employees and grey, dank, bitter chill met to mourn an unloved man. Most members of the family had tendered unconvincing excuses, and the last-minute arrival of cousin Gervase, with the thirteen-year-old James in the carriage beside him, came therefore as a pleasant surprise.

Parsimonious in life, Wolseley Davenall had dismayed his son by his extravagance in death. The purchase of a family vault in the sombrely bowered and ornately wrought Egyptian Avenue, whence the late Mrs Davenall had been transferred from her more humble grave of seventeen years before to join her husband, seemed to Richard an unwarranted and unsuitable piece of ostentation for such a notably puritanical man, rendered all the more grotesque by the paltry turnout of mourners.

As the massive iron door of the vault was ceremonially sealed and the funeral party began to disperse, Gervase, who had turned several disapproving heads by his swaggering gait and lack of uniformly black attire, pulled a hip-flask from beneath his travelling-coat and offered it to Richard.

'No thank you, Gervase.'

'Please yourself.' Gervase took a swig.

Richard winced as Gregory Chubb, his office overseer, glanced back from the knot of lawyers and clerks moving down the avenue ahead of them. 'Glad you could come,' he said to his cousin with an effort.

'Don't mention it, old man. Trust you didn't mind my bringing the boy.' He patted James, walking silently and blank-faced beside him, on the shoulder. 'Felt he ought to pay his last respects to his great-uncle.'

Richard was disconcerted. He had not seen James since his abrupt departure from Cleave Court six years before. Nor, in view of the nature of that departure, had he expected to. Indeed, he had exchanged no more than a few words with the boy's father during that time, banished as he was, at Wolseley's silent bidding, from much of family society.

'Is Catherine well?' he said at last, happy to let his cousin attribute the quaver in his voice to the occasion of their meeting.

'Oh, in the pink. But not much to be stirred from Cleave Court, I'm afraid.'

'Ah, yes. Of course. Do give her my . . . regards.'

'Happy to. Happy to.'

They turned out of the avenue and began to move slowly down the winding path towards the main gate of the cemetery. The rain had become little more than a mist now, a damp veil across the orderly expanse of graves, but the cold had intensified: their breath rose in clouds about them.

'Perhaps I could call on you at the office in a few days,' said Gervase after an interval. 'Make sure everything's in order.'

'I'm not sure I quite follow you.'

Gervase smiled. 'You will be able to take on my legal affairs now, won't you?'

Richard was nonplussed. His father had not encouraged him to think that he would inherit his mantle. 'Oh . . . well, of course. I'd be honoured. But I thought—'

'That cretin Chubb? Not on, old man. Simply not on. Your father told me I was to look on him as his principal assistant – some nonsense about seniority. But I prefer to keep these things in the family. Tell me' – he lowered his voice – 'did you fall out with your father over something? He's treated you pretty damn shabbily in recent years, I must say.'

'I really couldn't . . .'

'I wouldn't blame you. Prickly, I always found him – damned prickly. Still, mustn't speak ill . . . Look round to dinner one night next week, why don't you? I could put you in the picture then. All the ins and outs of my affairs, what?'

Richard found himself smiling. If only Gervase knew. If only his father knew. This meant emancipation from servitude to Chubb and the life of a legal errand-boy. This meant a new beginning, a long-awaited chance to forget the errors of the past.

How long the bell had been jangling Richard had no way of knowing. The moment of its intrusion on his distant thoughts might have been the instant it began or any number of minutes thereafter. He listened: the servants, a sleepy lot even when on duty, had not stirred. The bell rang again. With a sigh, he rose from his desk, took up the lamp and left the room.

Wolseley Davenall, ever a cautious man, had had a spy-hole fitted to the broad front door of his Highgate home. When Richard slid back the cover and peered through, he saw that his late-night visitor was William Trenchard, a sodden and haggard figure in the fitful glow of the porch lamp. He slipped the bolts at once and opened the door.

'Trenchard! What brings—?'

'I got your message.'

'Message? Oh – yes. Come in.' He had, it was true, left word at The Limes that, should Trenchard return there, he would appreciate hearing from him. Now that seemed an age ago. 'I didn't mean to get you out in the middle of the night.'

'Is it so late?' said Trenchard, following him towards the study. 'I've rather lost track of time.'

'I called on you this morning. Constance explained that she is to stay with her family for a while.'

Trenchard did not reply. When they reached the study, Richard helped him off with his drenched coat and ran an appraising eye over him.

'You look all in,' he said, though what he thought was that fatigue and desperation had filled Trenchard with a restless, reckless energy.

'What did you want to tell me?'

'It can wait. Will you have a drink?'

Trenchard nodded and warmed himself by the fire whilst Richard poured him a glass.

'I was sorry to hear that Constance felt the need to . . . go away.'

Trenchard took a gulp from the proffered glass and smiled grimly. 'She's left me.'

'Surely it hasn't—'

'She believes in Norton. My only way to win her back is to prove he's an impostor.'

'I can't believe—'

'I don't have time to waste on pretence and self-delusion any more. I mean to nail Norton's lies, and you can help me.'

'How?'

'He told her that I'd offered him money on Sir Hugo's behalf. That turned her against me. Then he volunteered to withdraw his claim – if

133

she asked him to. He's clever, you see. Damned clever.' Trenchard glared into the fire, where the heat of his hatred seared back at him.

'I'm sorry if my family's troubles have come between you and Constance,' Richard said. 'Truly I am.'

Trenchard looked at him and drained his glass. 'That doesn't matter now. I've been to Bath today – and there I found his weakness. There I found the means to destroy him.'

Richard took the glass from Trenchard's cradled hand and moved to the decanter to refill it. His companion, he realized, was no longer the self-centred well-intentioned husband who had wished only to protect his marriage from a fortune-hunting impostor. In outmanoeuvring him at every turn, Norton had driven Trenchard into the grip of an obsession. And Norton was that obsession.

'What can you tell me about Alfred Quinn?'

'Quinn? Why do you ask?'

As Trenchard explained, Richard grew perturbed. The crazy twisting path that linked Quinn with Norton could only be followed by those compelled to believe in its conclusion. All Trenchard's fevered theorizing would count for nothing if Constance hailed Norton as James Davenall. If that occurred, Trenchard would become a liability to their cause: a jealous, irrational, railing husband. His pursuit of Quinn, however apparently justified, would seem unreasoning folly.

A silence fell after Trenchard had finished, a silence too profound to be ignored. Richard stoked the fire, recharged their glasses and said nothing.

'Well?' said Trenchard at last.

Richard smiled defensively. 'It's a beguiling theory.'

'Is that all?'

'For the moment, yes.'

'But don't you see?'

'I see no connection with Norton – and that is what counts. A dismissed servant bearing a grudge is one thing, hatching a plot like this quite another. What you've found could be nothing more than a misleading mixture of coincidence and circumstance.'

'That's what Baverstock said.'

'He's a sensible man. Why don't you sleep on all this? Stay here, if you like. You might see things differently if—'

'Don't try to fob me off. What can you tell me about Quinn?'

'Nothing you haven't already found out. He was Gervase's batman in the Crimea, later his valet, later still James's valet. Baverstock knows more about the circumstances of his dismissal than I do.'

'Any idea where he is now?'

'None. But, then, I don't make it my business—'

'Any idea where he came from originally?'

'The Army. That's all I know.'

'Did he speak with any kind of accent?'

'Not that I can remember. This is—'

'The surname's Irish. Was he Irish, do you think?'

'No. That is—'

'Your family owns land in Ireland, doesn't it?'

'Yes. But what has—?'

'Wait!' Trenchard clapped his hand to his forehead. 'You told me that Sir Gervase's mother had died only recently. Murdered in the course of a burglary – at her home in Ireland.'

'That's true. But—'

'How much did the burglars get away with?'

'I really don't see—'

'Don't you? Then, you should. Quinn would have known the value of Lady Davenall's property, whether she stored cash and jewellery on the premises, how and when to get into the home.'

'What are you suggesting?'

'That he might have been the burglar – seeking funds for this conspiracy.'

'That's outrageous.'

'Maybe – but it makes more and more sense.'

Richard rose from his chair and grasped Trenchard by the shoulders. 'Listen to me!' he said sharply. 'Listen to me before you go too far. You're tired and overwrought. You're upset about Constance. All that's understandable. But piling together hopeless allegations against Quinn won't help.'

Trenchard looked at him blankly. 'Is that it, then? You won't help?'

'Of course I'll help. We must obviously try to find Quinn. After all, he was James's valet and is therefore a vital witness. If he is behind this, we'll find out. Frankly, I doubt he has the intelligence – or the organizing ability – to have done the things you suspect.'

Trenchard stepped free of Richard's grasp and moved to the window, where rain still spat on the blackened glass. 'I suppose that will have to do,' he murmured.

'For the moment, I'm afraid it will.'

'What did you want to tell me?'

'Nothing that supports your theory, I'm afraid. It concerns the information which Norton used to alarm Prince Napoleon.'

As he related what Baverstock had discovered concerning Vivien Strang and Prince Napoleon's presence at Cleave Court in September 1846, Richard felt his faith in its significance subsiding. Was it, after all, not an even flimsier amalgam of connected coincidences than Trenchard's own suspicions? Another dismissed servant – another treacherous strand of dates and events that led nowhere. Where, in all of this, was their salvation?

'I propose to visit Catherine tomorrow,' he concluded, 'and press her to say what she knows about Miss Strang. It won't be easy.'

'Why not?'

'Because of . . . long-standing differences between us.'

'Another family feud?'

'Not exactly.'

'But another secret that's to be kept from me?'

'I can't repair the damage my family may have done your marriage, Trenchard, but I can seek to limit it. That's why I'm visiting Catherine tomorrow – despite everything. You have my word that the cause of my reluctance is wholly unconnected with our present difficulties.'

'Will you ask her about Quinn?'

'I'll certainly mention him. But I can't guarantee she'll be any more forthcoming where he's concerned than she has been so far about Miss Strang.'

'Why should she keep anything back?'

'I don't know. That's what I hope to find out. Be assured, I'll let you know the outcome.'

'What will you do about Quinn?'

'I'll institute enquiries. That's all I can do.'

With sudden decisiveness, Trenchard plucked his coat from the back of a chair and shrugged it on to his shoulders. 'Very well. I'll await your word. Will you be back within the day?'

'By Monday at the latest.'

'I'll do nothing until then. After that—'

'Trenchard!' Richard looked intently at him. 'Clearly the offer of money to Norton was a mistake. Commissioning you to make the offer compounded that mistake. I'm truly sorry for all the consequences of our misjudgement. But don't make them worse than they already are.'

'How could I?'

'Until this case comes to court, we have a chance to put everything right. Until then, I implore you to trust me. Do nothing without consulting me.'

But there was suspicion now in Trenchard's look: trust was no longer possible. 'I'll do nothing until I hear from you again. After that . . . I don't know.'

Nor did Richard know. He had himself scarcely looked beyond his dreaded encounter with Catherine and all the half-formed doubts that would hover like ghosts about their meeting. When he saw Trenchard off into the wet engulfing night and bolted the door behind him, his mind drew him irresistibly towards the mocking record that time had made of his life. As he retraced his steps along the hall, the light from his lamp flickering and leaping amongst the remembered shapes and furnishings of his father's house, he felt the invisible line tighten and draw him in once more.

'It's settled, then,' said Gervase. 'Meet me at the club, Tuesday at six.'

'I'll be glad to,' said Richard as they emerged into Swain's Lane. The cabs and carriages of the other mourners were already departing, moving at a slightly less solemn pace than when they had arrived. The undertaker was waiting on the other side of the road to transport Richard home, while Gervase's phaeton was drawn up by the cemetery chapel. 'Would you care to step back to the house?'

'Can't tarry, I'm afraid. Have to get Jamie home to pack. Term starts at Eton tomorrow. He's looking forward to it – aren't you, son?'

James looked up bleakly. 'Yes, Papa.'

'Now, say goodbye to your cousin Richard.'

James held up his small gloved hand. As Richard reached down to clasp it, the boy's eyes engaged his own. Before he could prevent himself, Richard gasped. Those eyes – young, intent and staring – that had once seen . . . He snatched back his hand and pressed it to his brow, as if to shield himself from the sudden rush of guilt.

'Something wrong, old man?' said Gervase.

Richard recovered himself. 'It . . . it's nothing. I'm sorry. I felt . . . unsteady for a moment.'

'Strain of the occasion, I expect. Here, do take a sip of this.' He held out the hip-flask.

This time, Richard accepted it and gulped down some of the contents, glad of the burning sensation in his throat with which to lance away the question: Did he remember? When he returned the flask, James was still staring at him, but Richard looked elsewhere.

Gervase touched him on the elbow. 'Well, must be off. Don't forget our appointment.'

'I won't.'

'Come on, Jamie.'

Richard watched them walk the few yards to the phaeton, where the driver was waiting to help them aboard. James looked back once, in what was little more than a glance, and Richard forced himself to smile, but still he did not let their eyes meet.

'Home, Quinn,' said Gervase.

Ignored then, a grey-faced factotum in Inverness cape and dark top-hat, Quinn had eased the horses out into the road, nodded once to Richard and driven the phaeton away. Twenty-one years later, by the light of a dying fire, alone in his Highgate study, Richard could not deny that it was odd Gervase should have preferred Quinn to one of his grooms as driver that day. He had always, he conceded, seemed more a familiar than a servant. What had they known of him, when all was said and done? What trust might Quinn have forged with his master which Catherine was later to break? Could Trenchard be right for all the wrong reasons?

SEVEN

I

It was a bleak and windswept Sunday in Salisbury. Though candlelight could be glimpsed through the cathedral windows and choristers' voices heard, in snatches, on the gusting air, the close beyond its towering walls was empty and silent, save for swirling leaves and the wind's mewling in its ancient eaves.

Not so ten minutes since, when a clutch of gale-blown clerics in billowing cassocks had converged on its north door, one of them a stout, elderly, white-haired figure who had beaten a path across the green from an unassuming red-brick house in one of the remoter corners of the close.

Canon Sumner was an amiably ineffectual priest, who generally bore the most contented of smiles. Yet today his expression, his very appearance, was crumpled and forlorn. He was, self-evidently, a troubled man.

The cause of Canon Sumner's distress, his daughter Constance, sat now to one side of a blazing fire in the cosy if cluttered drawing-room he had just vacated, engaged, though scarcely absorbed, in a game of solitaire. Indeed, though she held one of the marbles in her hand, it had been there for several minutes, whilst her attention had shifted to an oil painting above her on the chimney-breast, a portrait of her mother, ball-gowned and elegant, in the days of her betrothal to a humble chaplain named Sumner.

Constance started in her chair at the sound of the door opening and twisted round. It was her sister Emily, her elder by five years, a confirmed spinster, tireless performer of good works in diocesan circles and, since their mother's death, mistress of the house. Constance had always envied Emily her clarity of thought and placidity of temperament. Emily had always envied Constance her radiant looks and

138

enchanting daughter. The two sisters exchanged warm ungrudging smiles.

'Did I make you jump?' said Emily.

'I'm sorry,' Constance replied. 'These days, I jump at shadows. I thought you were with Patience.'

'I left her with Nanny, whose concepts of child-rearing do not encompass a doting aunt.' Emily gave her sister's hand a squeeze before taking the fireside chair opposite her. 'Besides, I saw Father leaving and thought the time ripe to speak to you alone.'

'I do not know what I can add to all that I said last night.'

'Father would wish you to add a change of heart. Did you not see how he looked at matins?'

'How could I not? You surely don't suppose it gives me any satisfaction to cause him pain?'

'Of course not. I am your staunchest ally in all things. You know that.'

'Bless you, Emily. What would you have me do?'

'I would have you be certain. Can you be?'

'I am certain that James has returned to me. If I were not, I would not be so torn.'

'You married William in good faith.'

'I married William in the belief that James was dead. Only that belief sustained our marriage.'

'Father would say that holy matrimony takes precedence over any emotion, however profound. I would say the same – if anyone other than you asked me.'

'And when *I* ask, Emily? What do you say when *I* ask?'

'I say that William has been a good husband to you. You do not claim otherwise.'

'I only claim that, in my heart, I was a widow when I married William, a widow who now finds that her true husband lives.'

'You know full well that neither the Church nor the Law will acknowledge such a claim.'

'If I am forced to choose between them, I must needs choose solitude.'

'That is a hard choice.'

'All I ask is time to think, time to face myself, time to see the choice for what it is.'

'That you may always have here. This is your home, whatever happens. But tell me: can you honestly maintain that James was justified, first in deserting you, then in reappearing when he knew what distress he would cause you?'

'Oh, yes. That most of all. He has told me the whole truth, you see. I wish I could share it with you, but I cannot yet presume to speak for him. All I can say is that he acted out of love for me. Now I must act out of love for him. When all deny him, I must stand by him.'

'You realize that, if the circumstances of your presence here become known in the close, Father will be severely embarrassed? The Dean may even consider it a disciplinary matter.'

'I will leave before that happens.'

'Then, we must ensure it doesn't. Have you written to William? It would be as well if he did not follow you here.'

'I have the letter here.' She slid the envelope from its resting-place beneath the solitaire board.

'Would you like me to post it for you? The servants might think it odd that you should write so soon after your arrival. They are diligent in everything, but discreet in nothing.'

'Thank you, Emily. Perhaps that would be wise.' She handed her the letter.

'I'll go now. You'd best not come with me. I'll be back in a trice – and Father none the wiser.' Casting a brief glance through the window at the familiar shape of the cathedral, as if to be certain that Canon Sumner's devotions were still in progress, Emily bustled out, happier as ever to be doing than debating.

Left once more by the fireside where she had played as a child, Constance looked again at her mother's portrait and wondered what she would have said of her daughter's actions. Perhaps it was as well that she was not there to witness them.

Constance sighed. Solitude was, as Emily had said, a hard choice. Was she strong enough to make it? William had betrayed her trust: that much was clear. But James? What did he deserve of her? Could she resist his claim? If he came to her, what would she say?

She thought again, as she often did, of their last meeting at the aqueduct in June 1871, of all it had meant beyond what she had known at the time. She remembered sitting in the music room at Cleave Court that morning, remembered Quinn bringing in James's letter for her on a silver tray, remembered reading it and rushing from the room, eager beyond the reach of urgency to see James again and persuade herself that all was well. She could still feel the force of that longing, could still discern the depth of that day's pledged and proven love.

II

Richard Davenall had not visited Cleave Court since Sir Gervase's funeral. That, like all his other visits save one, had been brief and dutiful. It was strange, he reflected, as the carriage moved serenely up the avenue of elms, that he had always presented himself there as a deferential, vaguely apologetic adviser, a man of business, a professional necessity in the life of its family, never as the family member that he truly was.

He smiled to himself. The reason for his enduring humility was not far to seek. There, about him in the park, where the grass was patched with the red and golden spillages of autumn leaves, where all was seasonal pre-ordained decay beneath a grey abiding sky, was every tinge and vestige of his fate, the fate of one who had risked too little and lost too much.

The carriage drew to a halt. Richard climbed out and looked about him. This, he knew, if anywhere could be, was home for the Davenalls, the place they had made, the land they had stamped with their name. Why, then, did he always feel an intruder here – an interloper, one who was not and never would be quite accepted? He shook his head and entered the house.

There had been no answer to his telegram save the carriage waiting for him at the station, nor now was there a clutch of welcoming relatives in the hall; merely Gibbs, the butler, erasing from his expression, as best he could, all hint of embarrassment.

'Trust I'm expected, Gibbs?' Richard said.

'Indeed, sir.'

'Where's Lady Davenall?'

'Presently strolling in the grounds, I believe, sir.'

Richard might have known. He had specified a time, and this was the use Catherine had made of it. 'Then, I'll wait for her to return.'

'Sir Hugo would be grateful if you joined him meanwhile, sir.'

Richard drew up sharply. 'Hugo? He's here?'

'Yes, sir. Since yesterday. Presently in the smoking-room.'

Richard made his way straight there. Already, he felt foreboding closing in on him. He had come to discuss Hugo with Catherine, but Hugo had forestalled him.

The smoking-room was not as he recalled it. Formerly a retreat for Gervase and his more tenacious drinking companions, it was now sparsely and comfortlessly furnished. In the centre of the room, a large wooden chest had been set down with its lid propped open. Seated before it on a low stool was Sir Hugo Davenall.

'Hello, Richard,' said Hugo, without looking up.

'I didn't know you were visiting your mother.'

'I'm not. You might say I'm here on business.'

'May I ask what business?'

'I'm doing what you should already have done, dear cousin.' Now he did look up, grinning sarcastically. 'This chest holds what remains of my late lamented brother. Oddments of clothing, school-books, tie-pins, cuff-links: you know the sort of thing.'

'I didn't realize so much had been kept.'

141

'It doesn't amount to a lot. A cricket cap' – he held it up – 'his college gown' – he plucked out a bundle of black cloth.

'Then, why—?'

'Because we can use this to challenge Norton. Ask him to identify his old possessions. See if, literally, the cap fits.'

'It could be useful, Hugo. I'm glad you've—'

'I've also been speaking to the tenants.' He rose, brushed the dust off his hands and smiled once more. 'Ensuring they understand the importance of being positive in their evidence that Norton is an impostor.'

'You've obviously been busy.'

'I've had to be, in view of your indifference as to whether this man succeeds in stealing my title.'

'Hugo—'

Suddenly, the young man was close to Richard, staring intently into his face. 'If needs be, I'll stand alone against Norton. I'll make him wish he hadn't started this game.'

Richard felt angry and hurt to learn how little Hugo valued his efforts, but he knew it was useless to remonstrate. Instead, he tried to reason with him. 'Regrettably, Hugo, if enough people support Norton, the testimony of tenants and tailors will count for very little.'

'Bah!' Hugo whirled round and stalked to the fireplace. 'What do *you* know?'

'I know what sways a court – a jury if it comes to that. Knowledge Norton could not be expected to possess if he were not James, the recognition of his former fiancée—'

'What?'

'Constance Trenchard told me yesterday that she believes in his story completely. She did not say she would testify for him, but I suspect that, if asked, she would.'

'Curse these women! Nanny Pursglove. Trenchard's wife. They're besotted.'

'She has left Trenchard. Clearly, she does not take this matter lightly.'

Suddenly, Hugo lashed out with his foot at the length of wood which had been used to prop open the lid of the chest. The wood snapped and skidded, in two pieces, across the floor; the lid slammed shut with a crash that set the empty vases rocking on the mantelpiece.

'Believe it or not, Hugo, I am trying to help you.'

'Give me one example of your efforts.'

'It's why I'm here. Your mother must be persuaded to speak.'

'About what?'

'About what happened here in September 1846. About her former governess, Miss Strang. It's what Norton used to intimidate Prince Napoleon. It's what holds the key to all this.'

142

'Then, I wish you well of it. My mother volunteers nothing to me.'

'Very well. I'll see if I can find her.'

'Do that.' Hugo was leaning against the mantelpiece now, his rush of violence ended, his frustration stemmed. He looked at his cousin with an expression drained of anger but not of contempt. 'Do that, Richard.'

Without another word, Richard left. As the door clicked shut behind him, Hugo forced two knuckles of his left hand into his mouth and ground his teeth against them until the pain forced back the sudden flood of tears. Richard, he was determined, would never know. Nobody would ever discover, if he could prevent it, the hideous truth that he had, this day, confirmed.

III

Emily Sumner bustled across Choristers' Green with even more than her usual evident sense of purpose, bound for the pillar box that stood on the corner of North Walk. She was pleased to note the absence of passers-by to observe her errand, for, though she had expressed to Constance the fullest support, and had done so sincerely, she could not deny, now she was alone, that her sister seemed set on an ill-fated course. To fly in the face of so much that was right and respectable was surely madness. Nothing she had been told excused a wife's desertion of her husband.

Yet Emily, for all her spinsterly ways, was at heart a hopeless romantic, a great weeper over sentimental novels, and Constance's plight would have moved her even had they not been related. As it was, James Davenall had been a friend and contemporary of her dead brother Roland and a perfect match for her sister. Whatever good sense dictated, the fact remained that to stand by him, if truly he still lived, was magnificent.

She reached the pillar box. The road was empty as far as St Anne's Gate. The cathedral green was deserted. Thus reassured, she opened her reticule, removed the letter and slipped it into the box. Her mission was accomplished. She turned to go, then pulled up abruptly.

Not more than ten yards away, at the corner of the square, James Norton stood calmly watching her. She knew at once who he was, not merely from her sister's description, but from the evidence of her own memory. Before, she had perceived only Constance's grand illusion, a hopeless if admirable passion for what could never be. Now she knew. She had only met James Davenall a handful of times, all of them many years ago, but there was, in this man's face, that certainty of the immediately familiar that brooked no denial. Instinctively, she knew he was who he said. And Emily Sumner was not one to disobey her instincts.

'I see you know me, Emily,' Norton said, with a touch on his hat. 'I'm glad.'

'You should not have come here,' she said, surprised by her own breathlessness.

'I had to. I must see her.'

'It is impossible.'

'I have respected her wishes by not coming to the house. But I must speak to her. A few minutes, that's all. Anywhere she cares to name, at any time.'

'It cannot be.' She walked hurriedly towards him, intending to pass him and strike out across the square. But he placed his hand on her arm and, though the lightness of his grasp did not oblige her to, she stopped.

'We've not met in eleven years, Emily. Is that all you have to say to me?'

'Mr Norton—'

'Call me James.'

'Don't you think you've caused Constance enough pain already?'

Norton glanced down at the pavement, then looked at her frankly, letting her see the sincerity in his unflinching gaze. 'We love each other. You know that. You once told me we were made for each other. You're not going to deny it now, are you?'

Emily's heart was pounding. A strict upbringing and the expectations of cathedral society contended with the sudden flood of joy she felt. What to do, she wondered, when no course was the right one? 'Whatever Constance does, I will stand by her. But she is a wife and a mother. Those bonds cannot be set aside.'

'Only a word. Only the briefest of words. That's all I ask.'

There was, in the set of her jaw, a sign that she would not refuse him. 'I will tell her that I have seen you.'

Norton smiled. 'The water meadows, tomorrow at ten. We walked there often – as you know. The bench where we used to sit and watch the sun set on the cathedral. It'll be safe and quiet there. Tell her: I'll wait for her.' He touched his hat again. 'Your servant, Emily.' Then he turned and walked smartly away towards the North Gate.

IV

An under-gardener told Richard that he had seen Lady Davenall in the gazebo at the summit of the terraced garden and that, indeed, is where he found her, leaning against the wooden balustrade that fronted the small thatched structure and gazing out with a fixed resolved contentment across the rolling parkland of her home.

Breathless from the climb, Richard paused at the foot of the steps that led up to the gazebo and looked, for a moment, in the direction of Catherine's gaze. Spindly columns of smoke rose from the chimneys of the house beneath them. On all sides, he could hear the gentle patter of bronzed and falling leaves. Here they had come before, at a different season of their lives, and, recalling it now, he silently cursed her for choosing such ground for their meeting.

'Good day, Richard,' she said, without looking down.

He began to climb the steps and risked his first direct glance at her face. They had not met since Sir Gervase's funeral, and he noticed, with a brief sensation of shock, that her appearance – which he had attributed then to mourning – had not changed in the interim. Pale, aloof and beautiful: such was the woman he had once thought he loved.

Her tweed dress was high-collared and fur-trimmed against the chill of the day. Her hair, pinned and plaited beneath the veiled and ribboned hat, was as grey as he had known it would be. None of this gave him pause. What did was the movement of her hands, where they rested on the balustrade. Between her tightly gloved fingers she held the long stem of a single white rose and was turning and twisting it as she looked out across the garden. It was the only sign that she did not feel as calm as her face and expression implied. Richard stared at the rose with growing fascination. The sappy stem had split but not parted. Its thorns were hatching the fine leather of Catherine's gloves. Its dislodged petals, still beaded with dew, were falling to the ground below her. Yet she paid it no heed. Her gaze – and seemingly her attention – remained fixed on a distant horizon.

'Why have you come?' she said suddenly, still without looking in his direction.

'When you would rather I hadn't?' he echoed dismally.

'Precisely.'

'Because I felt obliged to.'

'Such obligations as you had to me lapsed many years ago. I do not wish them to be renewed.' Now she did look at him: a withering sweep of her eyes that shamed him more than any words. 'You are here because of the fortune-hunter.'

He had halted at the top of the steps, six feet from her; it seemed impossible to close the gap. 'Because of Norton, yes, in part. Because of his claim to be your son.'

'You know what I think of his *claim*.'

'Yes. You believe it can be ignored.'

'I disregard it. I employ others to disprove it.' There was no irony in her tone. She was no longer, if she ever had been, the Catherine that Richard had loved. The barriers of autocracy and arrogance behind which she had retreated were impenetrable – to him more than to anyone.

'Norton knows too much to be disregarded – or disproved. Have you once considered that—?'

'He is not my son.'

'Will you say that in court?'

'Yes.'

'Then, you should know the testimony that Norton will give. I cannot predict how forthcoming he will be, but if he says all that he told us at his examination certain painful revelations will be—'

'Save your breath.' She half-turned towards him, letting the shredded rose fall from her grasp as she did so. 'Hugo has already told me . . . the whole sordid account.'

Once more, Richard felt the sharp stab of betrayal: if they could not stand together, what hope was there? 'He had no business—'

'Keeping it from me? I'm so glad you agree. It is best that it should be known to all. Be assured, Richard, I will not faint should this man claim in court – or elsewhere – that Gervase died of syphilis. Is that all you had to tell me?'

He struggled to recover himself. 'No. That is—'

'Perhaps I should acquaint you with what else Hugo has told me. He has concluded, for one thing, that Gervase was not his father.'

Something akin to a moan must have escaped Richard's lips. He found himself leaning heavily against the balustrade, clutching the hand-rail for support.

'It appears that certain things Gervase said shortly before his collapse can now be interpreted to mean that he did not look upon Hugo as his son.'

'Hence his reluctance to have him pronounced his heir,' Richard murmured.

'Presumably.'

'What have you told Hugo?'

'That he is right.'

He looked at her – so icily controlled, so calmly spoken – and realized that he had no idea, not the least glimmering, of what she truly felt. 'Did you' – his voice faltered – 'name the father?'

'I did not need to. Hugo believes he knows already.'

'He said nothing to me.'

'Why should he?'

'Because . . . he's mine, isn't he?'

'Yes, Richard. Hugo is your child, the child of your sundered obligations.'

'Why did you never tell me?'

'Why did you never guess?'

'I suppose I often guessed, or feared, or hoped as much. But there was no way of knowing . . .'

146

'Till now. Till now only I have known. I chose to keep it from you because I did not think you worthy of the knowledge.'

He shook his head, bowed slightly beneath the onslaught of her words. 'You are a hard woman, Catherine.'

'You made me so.'

'I?'

'Yes, Richard, you. Because you were so weak and because I trusted you. You allowed Sir Lemuel to give you your marching orders. You crept quietly away from here twenty-seven years ago and left me to face Gervase alone, left me to face him carrying your child.'

'I didn't know—'

'You didn't care. I would have gone with you, would have fled with you to any hiding-place. But you fled alone.'

'Catherine, I—'

'Be silent!' Her face was a mask of unyielding severity; his obedience, his shame, complete. 'I will tell you now, Richard, for the first and last time, what you left me to endure. When Gervase came home that summer, I already suspected that I was pregnant by you and I also knew you would do nothing to help me. The love you professed was not worth the having. Accordingly, I resolved to hold what little I had: I resolved to preserve my marriage. It was essential that Gervase be given no cause to suspect I had been unfaithful to him. Therefore, on his first night home, I attempted to seduce him.'

Richard's eyes moved to meet her gaze, stared for a moment at the accusation it conveyed, then moved away hastily, furtively, like those of a man unable to face himself.

'I failed. I humiliated and debased myself for nothing. I pleaded with him, begged him, threw myself at him. I would have done anything. But he refused me. My husband was a habitual adulterer. More than one laundrymaid has testified to his lechery. But he rejected me that night and every night thereafter. Why? I thought he must have guessed my motives. I feared that James might have said something to him. We never spoke of it, when my condition became obvious or, later, when Hugo was born: I took his silence for contempt. That, of course, is why he was so reluctant to have James pronounced dead: because we both knew that James was his only son.

'But he hadn't guessed, had he? I know that now. Dr Fiveash had warned him off. I believed he actually preferred prostitutes and other men's wives. Now I know that, somewhere in his hateful soul, there lurked a shred of damnable compunction, a fragment of decency, perhaps a vestige of guilt, that made him cling to the promise he gave Fiveash, if to no other he gave in his life. God curse him, and you, Richard, for what you made of me. Now go. And never speak of it again. For I shall not.'

With an effort, Richard raised his head. He wanted only to do as she

147

asked: creep away and hide from the truth he had done so much to uncover. But he could not. In one respect, at least, Catherine was wrong. His obligations had not ended. They had only just begun. 'Did you tell Hugo all this?' he said at last, in a voice he scarcely recognized as his own.

'I told Hugo nothing. All he knows is what he's guessed. As to the identity of his natural father, he has guessed wrongly. He suspects . . . Prince Napoleon.'

For a crazy moment, Richard thought she might not be in earnest. But her unaltered expression confirmed that she was. 'You let him think that?'

'I neither admitted nor denied it. But any guess, however wild, is better than the truth. He must never know. Do you understand? Never.'

'If that is your wish—'

'It is my command. And I think you will obey.'

'Very well. But there is more to be said. God knows, I wish there were not, but there are certain questions I must put to you.'

'Concerning Miss Strang?'

'Yes.'

'I have already told Baverstock: Miss Strang is irrelevant. I have nothing to say about her.'

'I cannot accept that.'

'You must.'

'Prince Napoleon knew her, didn't he?'

'He met her. There is a difference.'

'When you returned from the Crimea, you implied you had left because of something Prince Napoleon had said or done. Was it connected with Miss Strang?'

'No.'

'Then, what was it?'

'Your questions offend me, Richard. Please leave now.'

'They must be answered.'

'They must not.'

'If you wish to succeed in resisting Norton's claim—'

'I will not look to you for advice. I cannot, of course, prevent Hugo using your services as a lawyer, but I would esteem it a favour if you ceased to handle his affairs.'

'I cannot do that.'

'You can. But, if you will not, I cannot force you. What I *can* do, however, is decline to see you should you call again. Would you not rather spare yourself and the servants such an embarrassment?'

'By God, Catherine—'

'You invoke the Lord's name? Very well, then. In God's name, Richard, remove yourself from my life. You have wronged me

148

sufficiently to owe me that, I think. When we do meet, as no doubt we must, be so good as to remember what we are to each other: strangers, nothing more. Now be gone.'

He turned and, slowly descending the steps, uncertain whether to laugh or cry, he heard her words, all her words, then and twenty-seven years before, as one long siren song in a language he did not understand. The coward's recourse disguised as the right thing to do. The love that was easier to lose than the hatred that followed. The wastrel's life that was, in truth, his son's. Such thoughts pursued him, like the angry chorus of rooks, down through the leaf-drifted borders.

V

Dusk came rapidly that Sunday in the Tuileries Gardens. Only at the last possible moment did the sun appear in the Parisian sky, gilding the gauze of cloud till the western prospect was one vast copper drum, viewed through a filigree of slowly stirring saplings.

Prince Napoleon shifted uncomfortably on a bench beneath a monumental urn and dragged the lapel of his greatcoat across his chest, scattering the ash of a neglected cigar down his front as he did so. He swore and pitched the butt into the dust at his feet, where pigeons pecked for the seed he had brought and distributed earlier in one of the few acts of *largesse* he was still permitted. Quite why he was there, with no brandy on call and only pigeons for courtiers, he was not sure, except that it was a thousand times preferable to inflaming his knees in the bobbing incense-laden company of his pious wife, who would even now be communing with her god and a gabbling priest on the other side of the city.

Ah, women! At once his delight and his despair. What was there, when all was said and done, to choose between the incorruptible Marie Clotilde and the all too corruptible Cora Pearl? Nothing, so his wealth of experience suggested, beyond the different routes they offered to the same desolation. One served on her knees, the other on her back. He smiled. Truth to tell, Cora was prepared to serve on either. Then he winced, as a strained rib muscle reminded him that age no longer forgave his indulgences.

There, he conceded, was the problem. Perhaps both women had taught him too well. Perhaps he had simply lived too long. What could not be denied was that, since his brief *rapprochement* with Cora, his memory had troubled him. A priest – most notably his wife's chaplain – would have called it conscience, but Plon-Plon knew better. He merely felt dogged by the past, pursued by the phantoms of dead friends and departed enemies. Most persistently, since Cora had told him of her meeting with Norton, he had been burdened by recollections of a Scottish governess and a foolish wager for her virtue. That obscure and distant bargain – what did it matter now? He did not know. Yet the thought of it would not leave him.

Perhaps it was to that impetuous excess of their youth – not the greatest or the gravest, to be sure, but somehow the most memorable – that Gervase had meant to refer, on the occasion of what was, in the event, their final meeting. Plon-Plon had been in England for the funeral of the Prince Imperial, the witless youth having contrived to be slain by Zulus while serving in the British army, and had sought refuge from the lachrimose hospitality of the Dowager Empress in Chislehurst by adjourning to Bladeney House, in search of reviving levity. But Gervase had not been at home; Quinn had referred him to the master's club.

July 12th, 1879. A late but far from balmy dusk was settling on London. Though the respectable shops would all now be closed, Plon-Plon chose a circuitous route from Chester Square, for it was not the respectable that he most loved in this city. A Saturday evening in summer would bring the loitering pickpockets and rouge-faced whores out in force. To them and whatever was most scabrously remote from the severity of his own unadmiring kind, Plon-Plon was drawn as is a choking man to air.

In Jermyn Street, he passed the hatter he often patronized, hesitated before rejecting a turning towards Pall Mall and so passed, with an ill-suppressed lightening of his step, into the Haymarket and its rapidly filling streetload of all he found most raw and relishable in the life of the city.

The theatres were rapidly filling, prostitutes gathering in knots by their entrances, pub doors opening on gushes of noise, cabs discharging their fares on to the crowded pavements. Plon-Plon, enjoying here his anonymity as much as his surroundings, ambled through the ruck, shrugging off the ragged-trousered boys who twitched at his sleeve, eyeing but not pausing to engage the blowzy preening whores who winked at him from every doorway. He glanced down alleyways and basement steps wherever music and light beckoned, laughed at the slouching toughs and top-hatted drunkards, leered at the fresh-faced girls whose charms had not yet been sold too many times; he was in his element.

Suddenly, a blundering figure in evening dress lurched from a side-alley and cannoned into him as he walked past. Plon-Plon staggered from the impact, muttered an oath and turned to see the other man clinging for support to a lamp-post. The snarling rebuke died on his lips. It was Gervase.

'I was coming to see you at your club, *mon ami.*'

Gervase pulled himself upright. 'This is my club,' he said, smiling grimly.

'You do not look well.'

The other laughed. 'Did I ever?' Then he swayed perceptibly on his feet and leaned against the wall behind him for support.

Plon-Plon clapped him on the shoulder. 'What is it, Gervase? Too much wine?'

No. He could see that it was not. Unsteady and slurred of speech though his friend was, he was clearly not drunk. He was sweating, though the night was distinctly cool. A muscle in his cheek was twitching with visible rapidity. His eyes were bloodshot. He looked old and pitiably frail. 'Why are you here?' he said, with sudden clarity.

'The Prince Imperial was buried today.'

'Yes, dammit, of course. I read of it. Shouldn't you be consoling the Empress?'

'I left her taking tea with my wife.'

'Tea? Christ, tea!' Gervase's face creased with pain. 'Why do these women want nothing but tea?' He stared wildly at Plon-Plon. 'Remember that tea-party when we were young, old friend? The one where I delivered a message on your behalf. The one where I played the pander for you.'

'I'm not sure—'

'I won the bet, what? I won the bet.'

'*Oui, mon ami.* You won.'

'Do you want to hear a joke, Plon-Plon? I think I was cursed that day. I've never stopped paying . . . for winning that bet.'

'Let me support you . . . as we walk.' So saying, Plon-Plon hoisted Gervase's arm round his shoulders and began to pilot him across the street; clearly, the Haymarket was no place for him in such a state.

'They want to say that James is dead.'

'Is he not?'

'They want to put Hugo in his place.'

They reached the opposite pavement. Plon-Plon headed towards a turning that he knew would take them to Pall Mall. 'Children can be a trial, *mon ami.* A trial – and a sadness.'

Gervase was shivering now and leaning more heavily on his companion. 'I'll show them all,' he whispered. 'She shall not cheat my son.'

'Cheat Hugo?'

'No.' A grinding of the teeth. 'Not Hugo. My son.'

'I do not understand.'

'Nobody does, Plon-Plon. Nobody does.'

'Do you want to go to your club?'

Gervase's voice now was little more than a murmur. 'Home.'

'Then, I must hail a cab. Can you stand alone?'

'Alone? Oh, yes. Always alone.'

Leaving Gervase for a moment, Plon-Plon moved to the edge of the pavement. Empty cabs were readily had on the runs away from theatreland; there was one approaching. It drew to a halt beside him. Asking the driver to wait, he stepped back to his friend.

Gervase was calm now and steady on his feet. He was gazing up at the sky, where the stars were pin-pricked against the night. 'Where is he now, do you suppose?' he muttered.

'Into the cab, *mon ami*. Do you wish me to come with you?'

'No. Quinn is well used to my . . . turns. But you aren't. Dreadfully sorry, old man.'

Gervase climbed aboard, and Plon-Plon closed the door behind him. 'You will feel better tomorrow,' he said with a smile. 'No more talk of cheating.'

'Hah! A fig for their plans.' Gervase snapped his fingers and, as he did so, Plon-Plon saw by the light of the driver's lamp that his friend's face was once more bathed in sweat. 'It is I who will cheat them,' he said, smiling broadly. 'In the end – before the end – I'll tell them.'

'Tell them what?'

'Where he is, of course.' Gervase extended his hand from the cab window and grasped the loose flesh of Plon-Plon's cheek between his finger and thumb. 'A wager without honour is a wager with the Devil. Ain't it so, old friend?'

'Perhaps, *mon ami*. Perhaps.'

Gervase laughed, the laugh of a man in fever, or of a man who has seen what his future holds. Releasing Plon-Plon, he slapped the side of the cab. 'Chester Square, cabby. Go like the Devil!'

The hansom took off at a trot. Gervase waved once to his friend in farewell, then slumped back in his seat and passed, as Plon-Plon watched, away into the night.

'*Votre Majesté! Votre Majesté!*'

Plon-Plon jerked his head upright. What joker dared throw such a redundant title in his face? There was a man stooping over him, an old crooked figure in a frayed and faded coat. The man's face, close to his own, was wizened and drawn, grey flesh stretched to the verge of translucence over sharp white bone. His hair, shaven like a convict's, bristled from the skin of his head and jaw. His eyes, green and gleaming, stared intently at him.

'*Votre Majesté Impériale!*'

'*Citoyen, mon homme, c'est tout.*'

'*Non, non.*' The man tapped the side of his head. '*Je me souviens de vous. Alma. A coté du Commandant en Chef.*'

'*Mais oui.*' Plon-Plon smiled. A derelict old soldier remembered him, riding by at Alma nearly thirty years ago. Now he recognized the coat. It was the greatcoat of a common soldier in the French Imperial Army. He reached up and grasped the man's arm in a fraternal gesture, loosening his grip when he felt how spindly was the limb beneath its sleeve. He took a gold coin from his pocket and pressed it into the veteran's hand. *'Pour vous, mon brave.'*

'Merci, mon général.'

'Merci, mon ancien soldat.'

The man hobbled away. Which had wrecked him, Plon-Plon wondered – the Empire or the Republic? It scarcely mattered. At least he had remembered.

It was growing dark and cold. Time to go home and mortify his wife with some casual blasphemies. Plon-Plon rose. Suddenly, he thought of Gervase again, transformed from the dashing English officer of their Crimean prime into a stumbling, raving old man, abandoned on a London street. What had he meant, with all his wild words? Nothing, in all likelihood, unless, of course, James Norton was the unpaid debt on his wager with the Devil. No, Plon-Plon told himself. Better to believe it was nothing. Better by far. He shook his head and turned for home.

VI

When Dr Fiveash heard that he had a visitor that night, he once more regretted letting Dr Perry slip away for the weekend and descended to his consulting-room prepared to give short shrift to whichever of his junior's patients had been so inconsiderate as to call on him. Accordingly, he did not know whether to be relieved or sorry when he found Richard Davenall waiting there for him.

'Davenall! I'd have received you in the drawing-room if I'd known.'

'No matter, Doctor. This will serve very well. You might say I'm here on a medical matter.'

Fiveash ushered him to a chair and relieved him of his coat. 'I'm not sure I understand you.'

'Trenchard has told me all about Miss Whitaker.'

'Oh, that? I was going to call on Baverstock tomorrow and put him—'

'Did Trenchard explain to you his theory that Miss Whitaker was put up to spy on you by a former servant of Sir Gervase?'

Fiveash frowned. 'No. I gave him Miss Whitaker's old address and that's the last I saw of him.'

'Then, I'll tell you on his behalf.'

Whilst Davenall did so, Fiveash fetched a bottle of whisky from the rear of his medicine cupboard and poured them both drinks. His frown deepened during the account and, by its end, he looked a sorely puzzled man.

'You don't appear to find the theory convincing, Doctor.'

'It's not that.'

'Then, what?'

'This man Quinn. . . .'

'As I say, Lady Davenall had reason to discharge him from her service some three years ago. There's no reason to suppose he remained in this area. Quite the reverse. It's much more likely—'

'That's just the point. I thought Lady Davenall must know.'

'Know what?'

'He visited her husband regularly in the nursing home. I rather think Quinn was the last visitor Sir Gervase had before he died.'

Davenall stared at him in amazement. 'Quinn? A regular visitor?'

'So the nursing staff assured me.'

'But that's not possible. He'd been dismissed by then.'

'That hardly prevents a man visiting his former employer. The first I knew of it, I must admit, was at the very end. March of last year, it would have been. I had stepped up the frequency of my calls because Sir Gervase was manifestly in the final stages of his illness. He had become agitated and spasmodically coherent: the last flare of the candle before it goes out, you might say. I gave it little thought at the time, for obvious reasons, but, looking back, I suppose the circumstances were somewhat strange.'

Dr Fiveash reached Cedar Lodge that morning regretting more than ever its windswept location above the Avon Gorge. It was a spiteful day, greyly bleak and rawly chill, the sort of day, he morbidly reflected, when patients who have endured winter finally abandon hope of spring.

The matron met him in the hallway. 'I think Sir Gervase has made up his mind to go,' she announced. 'He's been very talkative.'

They began an ascent of the winding, echoing stairs. 'H'm. Made any sense?'

'None. Asking for his family, I should judge.'

'Then, he must ask in vain, for I doubt he'll see them again in this world.'

'There's somebody with him now. Not a relative though.'

'Oh? Who, then?'

'He's never given his name. He calls regularly. I think he said he'd served with Sir Gervase in the Army.'

Their routes diverged on the second landing, and Fiveash made his way alone to the room where Sir Gervase Davenall had lately awaited death in merciful oblivion. When he opened the door, he saw the visitor rise hurriedly from a bedside chair and turn towards him. He recognized him at once as Quinn and struggled for a moment to recollect what he had been told about his departure from Cleave Court.

'Quinn, isn't it?' he said, advancing across the room.

'Yes, sir. Just called in to see the old master.'

Fiveash looked down at his patient – gaunt, grey and marked for death. He was drawn up higher than usual on the pillows, one arm flung clear of the covers, the hand cast claw-like on the quilt, its fingers twitching. His eyes, Fiveash noticed, were fixed on Quinn, following him as he slowly moved to the end of the bed.

'I'll be off, then.'

'Very good, very good.' Fiveash deposited his bag on the chair Quinn had just vacated and unstrapped it. A click from the other side of the room told him that he was now alone with his patient: Quinn had gone.

As he looked up from the bag, something on the bedside cabinet caught his eye. For those denied the power of coherent speech, Cedar Lodge supplied a small pad of paper and a pencil to cater for any desire to communicate. Sir Gervase had, in Fiveash's recollection, never displayed any. Yet now he could clearly see that a sheet had been torn from the pad and that the vague imprint of a message had been left on the sheet beneath. Idly, he picked up the pad and peered at it: the imprint was indecipherable. Then he looked at Sir Gervase – the staring eyes, the taloned twitching hand – and shook his head. No, he could not have written anything. He replaced the pad, dismissed the matter from his mind and burrowed in the bag for his stethoscope. When he next looked at Sir Gervase, he saw that he was smiling.

'By the way,' said Fiveash as he showed Richard Davenall to the door, 'what was the medical matter you wanted to discuss?'

'Mmm?'

'You said it was why you'd called.'

'Oh, yes. It was about Trenchard. I'm somewhat concerned about his . . . state of mind. His wife's left him, you know.'

'Good God. He didn't tell me that.'

'I wondered if you would agree with me that, in the circumstances, he might be jumping to outlandish conclusions. Clutching at straws, as it were. Detecting conspiracies where none exists. In short, cracking under the strain.'

'When he came here yesterday, I was certainly struck by the change that had come over him since I'd seen him in London. Now you've told me about his wife, I would probably have to agree with you.'

'That's just it,' said Davenall, pausing on the doorstep. 'In view of what you've told me, I'm not sure you should agree after all. Are *you*? Goodnight, Doctor.'

VII

Two days after returning from Bath, I received a letter from Constance. The postman had arrived just as I was leaving the house. Forestalling Hillier, I had sifted through the letters and come upon the one I had feared as much as hoped would be there. It was postmarked Salisbury and was addressed in Constance's hand. Not daring to open it at once, I set off with it in my pocket.

All the way across Regent's Park, I wondered what she had said. Threading through the crowds in Baker Street, I tried to persuade myself that she was coming home, retracting her mad espousal of Norton's cause, resolving, after all, to stand by me.

Then, alone in my office at Orchard Street, the letter-knife shaking in my grasp, I knew it could not be so. A telegram could have said all I wanted to hear. This envelope, bearing her neat scrupulous hand, contained a different kind of announcement.

> The Little Canonry,
> Cathedral Close,
> SALISBURY,
> Wiltshire.
>
> 15th October 1882
>
> My dear William,
> You will wish to know that we have arrived safely and have settled in well. Patience is enjoying her new surroundings and sends her love.
>
> I have nothing to add to what I said before coming here and I cannot imagine that you have, either. Though I know you will not agree, I am more certain than ever that a parting at this stage is both necessary and wise. I beg you to respect my decision and not to attempt to visit me here until I have been able to settle my mind. You may be assured that I will impose the same conditions on James.
>
> These few words must suffice for the present. I feel too confused to write more.
>
> CONSTANCE

There it was, as bland and as brief as could be. She had sent our daughter's love but not her own. I let the letter fall from my hand and flutter to rest on the desk, then felt for the chair and slumped down into it.

How long I sat there, staring at the single sheet of notepaper, I cannot say. My reverie only ended when the telephone rang.

'Yes?'

'I have a call for you, Mr Trenchard.'

156

'Who is it?' I expected she would say it was my brother, who had insisted on installing the machine and was its most frequent user.

'A Mr Richard Davenall, sir.'

Why should Davenall telephone rather than visit me to report on his findings? Immediately, I grew suspicious. 'Put him through.'

'Trenchard?'

'Yes.'

'I'm sorry to raise you on this thing. I'm rather pressed for time.' Was he really? I wondered. Or could he not face me with what he had to say?

'Have you learned anything?'

'Regrettably, no. Catherine still refuses to discuss Miss Strang.'

'What about Quinn?'

'I . . . I have no more information about him.' Had he been in the same room, I could have judged whether that hesitation implied he did know something but felt unable to trust me with it. 'I'll put my people on to him, of course, but, for the moment, there's nothing else to be done.'

'Nothing?'

'Nothing at all.'

'I see. Well, thank you for telling me.'

'Trenchard—'

'Yes?'

'I'm sorry. Believe me.'

I put the telephone back on the hook and stared again at Constance's letter. She had asked nothing of me, save that I leave her alone and trust in her judgement. Now Richard Davenall, for all his infinite regrets, had asked the same. The message was clear. I encumbered the one and embarrassed the other. Neither would aid me in a search for the truth.

I reached into the inside pocket of my jacket and drew out Nanny Pursglove's photograph. There was Quinn, his blotched and faded image confronting me whenever I chose to look at it, fixed on the sepia-tinted paper as it was fixed nowhere else in the shifts and evasions of the Davenalls' past. I smiled grimly and replaced it in my pocket. Nobody would help me find him. Very well, then. I would find him alone.

VIII

The Salisbury watermeadows form an elongated oval of fertile pasture, criss-crossed by drainage channels and traversed only by the narrow causeway of Town Path. That morning, at the mid-point of the path, seated on a bench, a tall, solitary, elegantly dressed man was smoking a cigarette and savouring, through its drifting smoke, the soaring prospect of the cathedral spire, a grey pinnacle towering above the trees and clustered houses at its base. Most passers-by would have assumed he was merely an admirer of medieval church architecture paying homage to one of its finest creations, yet James Norton had, despite appearances, more pressing reason to be where he was, as might have been construed from his frequent consultations of a pocket-watch and wary glances up and down the path.

At length, he tired of his cigarette and crushed its extravagant butt beneath his shoe. Then, overlooked by no living creature save the retired dray-horse who occupied the field behind the bench, he drew a slim quarter-bound notebook from an inside pocket of his coat, leafed through it to a particular page and began studying the contents closely.

For all the apparent intensity of his concentration, Norton noticed the figure approaching from the southern end of the path almost as soon as it became conspicuous against the straggling wayside hedge. Immediately, without the least sign of haste, he slipped the book back into his pocket. He gazed towards the figure for several minutes until he was certain it was that of a woman: alone, respectably dressed, walking rather quickly and glancing about apprehensively, as if more nervous than anything in the time or place justified. With sudden decisiveness, Norton rose from the bench. As the woman drew closer, he removed his hat and began to smile. Only when she was about thirty yards away did he realize that a sororal resemblance had deceived him. His smile vanished.

'Emily! What does this mean?'

'She isn't coming.'

'May I ask why?'

Emily reached the bench and sat down heavily, as if glad of its support. 'She cannot see you. You must understand that. I came to explain why it is for the best.'

Norton sat beside her and gazed intently into her face. 'I think you will fail.'

'You ask too much of her. She is married to another. Nothing can alter that.'

'Who is this speaking really, Emily? You – or Constance?'

'I am acting as her messenger. I also believe her message is born of wisdom. Only yesterday, she gave her husband a written undertaking that, in return for his forbearance in allowing her this time for reflection, she would not see you. You cannot expect her to breach that undertaking.'

Norton grew reflective. 'No. Naturally not. Is that all that prevents her?'

'What do you mean?'

He looked away, as if regretting the question. 'I'm sorry. I shouldn't

158

ask you to anatomize Constance's motives. They are, as you say, irreproachable.'

'She has prayed for guidance. We all have.'

'This must have been a great strain for your father.'

'I cannot deny it. I know Constance feels terribly guilty for inflicting it upon him.'

'As I do, Emily. As I do.'

'All she asks is time to think.'

'I've had a deal of that myself, over the years. Has Constance told you . . . why I left when I did?'

'No. She said she had no right to speak for you.'

'Ah, I see. Always so just. Well, I'm glad. It's no story for a lady's ears.'

'Yet you told her.'

'Because I love her. There can be no secrets between us.'

Emily's jaw stiffened, as if a moment had come for which she had prepared herself. 'If you truly love my sister, will you not spare her the ordeal of disobeying her husband by testifying for you?'

Norton's head dropped. 'So that's it. That's what you really came to ask me, isn't it?'

Emily spoke hurriedly, her words coming at a pace that left no room for doubt or irresolution. 'She has told me of her undertaking to testify for you at the hearing of your case. She will not go back on that. But I think you ought to know what it will mean for her. A final breach with her husband. The disapproval of respectable society. Public notoriety. Above all, our father's position in the cathedral might well become impossible. I think you ask too much of her and I think you know it.'

Norton looked up. 'You realize that, without Constance's testimony, my case will be immeasurably weakened?'

'Not in my eyes.'

A rueful smile. 'Very well. Take back your message, Emily. There will be no subpoena. There will not even be a polite request. I will not ask Constance to testify.'

'That is generous of you.'

'It is probably very foolish of me. I will also respect her promise to Trenchard. That, too, is probably foolish, but it is at least honourable.'

'Yes, James. It is.'

'And it wins for me the accolade that you address me by name.' He rose suddenly to his feet. 'Farewell, then, Emily.' He stooped to kiss her gloved hand, pausing to look into her eyes before releasing it. 'For the moment.'

She did not watch him as he walked away northwards along the path, nor did she leave the bench to retrace her own steps. Instead, she sat where she was, gazing up at the slender impartial majesty of the cathedral spire. At length, she risked a glance to assure herself that he was out of sight. That done, she felt free at last to draw a handkerchief from her sleeve and dry her tears.

IX

'Thank you, Benson.'

The clerk withdrew, leaving Richard with the file he had requested: a heavily strapped bundle of papers constituting the rent-rolls, tenancy agreements and agents' reports pertaining to Sir Hugo Davenall's Irish property. Richard sifted through them reflectively.

He knew the Carntrassna estate, as did its present owner, by name only. Ten thousand acres remained of the previously vast portion of County Mayo held since the seventeenth century by the Fitzwarren family. These Sir Lemuel Davenall had acquired by his marriage to Mary Fitzwarren, the sole heiress, in 1815, and strangely, despite their long separation, he had bequeathed it to her rather than to their son. Richard remembered his father railing against such a provision. Gervase, on the contrary, had seemed happy to forget not merely Carntrassna but also his mother in her wilful seclusion there.

'Carntrassna?' he had once said. 'Millstone round my father's neck. Glad to be rid of it. A liability, nothing more.'

Liability or not, the diminished acres had reverted to Hugo when nameless intruders had done old Lady Davenall to death in February 1882. Richard had never met her, but acknowledged that to live, for reasons of her own, amidst so much squalor and isolation for so long was an achievement of some kind. He had, like most Englishmen of his age and breeding, a firm opinion of Ireland and the Irish, an opinion based on no personal knowledge whatever but amply reinforced by the notion that a harmless eighty-four-year-old lady should be murdered for no better reason than that she owned a substantial amount of land.

Not that Kennedy, her agent, agreed with such an explanation of the incident. He had written a long letter, Richard recalled, absolving the peasantry of blame and reassuring Sir Hugo of their loyalty. There it was, interleaved with the endless lists of impecunious tenants. Several pages of it, in a firm punctilious hand. Richard pulled it from the bundle and cast his cautious eye over the contents.

Kennedy had been resident in Carntrassna House since February. An absentee owner no doubt suited him very well, hence the stress he laid on the justice and desirability of leaving matters as they were. It was not until the third page that Richard found the passage he sought.

> On the morning of Sunday, 12th February, Lady Davenall was found dead in bed. A pillow had been used to suffocate her. There were plentiful signs that she had resisted, which is remarkable considering her age. Her bedroom window was wide open and a ladder had been placed against the wall outside, having been removed from a nearby store-shed. I know it will be said she was killed by Nationalists or resentful

tenants. (I dare say you will have heard reports of the recent murder of two of Lord Ardilaun's bailiffs in this neighbourhood.) I should therefore like to reassure you that the Carntrassna tenants have always held a warm regard for Lady Davenall and her family. I cannot believe they would have been responsible for such an outrage. Rather, given that some of Lady Davenall's jewellery is missing, this seems to have been a simple case of a thief caught in the act. I am confident that the police will be given every assistance by the tenantry in identifying the culprit and that, when he is apprehended, robbery will be found to have been his motive.

But no culprit had been apprehended. The jewels had never been found. Lady Davenall's murder remained unsolved. Richard had no difficulty imagining what Trenchard would claim: that Quinn was implicated in the murder and that the jewels had been sold in England to realize funds for Norton's case. Yet there was nothing to suggest it was so. The proceeds would surely never have justified such a risk. Like so many other theories, it did not fit the facts. With a sigh, Richard slipped the letter back into the bundle and fastened the straps.

X

Evensong was at an end. Yet Canon Hubert Sumner, who had found in its prayers and hymns little comfort, lingered in his place, kneading the carved wood of the stall end and gazing mournfully at the flagstones beneath his feet. It was not spiritual relief that he sought. For the moment, he had abandoned hope of that. Rather, his delayed departure was intended to spare him the solicitations of fellow-worshippers who could not have missed his downcast looks.

For Canon Sumner was a popular member of the cathedral chapter. His age and geniality, combined with a singular lack of both guile and of ambition, endeared him to all. They would have been saddened to see the stricken expression which, now he was alone, his face had assumed. Gazing into the candlelight and finding there no lessening of the darkness into which Constance's troubles had cast his thoughts, he looked and felt older than his robust spirit had ever admitted. He who had accepted the death of his son as a cruel but pure accident and that of his wife as an inevitable function of nature found it less easy to come to terms with his daughter's plight. For her affliction he could find no healing precept, no consoling text – above all, no right and godly answer.

At length, the echo of the last heavily closing door having long since

161

faded into silence, Sumner rose from the stall, leaning on the prayer-desk to assist him, and turned to take his leave.

A man was standing at the end of the stall. His patient expectant posture suggested to Sumner that he had been there for some time. He was tall, darkly clad and bearded. He held a top-hat in his left hand, whilst his right rested, the fingers extended, across his chest. He was not a priest. That, given his poor eyesight and the gloom gathering within the cathedral as dusk advanced, was all Sumner could make out with certainty. He smiled and peered towards the stranger as he made his way along the stall.

'Good evening, my son. May I assist you in any way?'

'Do you not know me?'

'I . . . don't think I do.'

'It is I. James.'

Sumner pulled up. 'James . . . Norton?'

'Davenall.'

The canon seemed to lose his footing. He swayed sideways, reaching out for support. The rim of the prayer-desk eluded his fingers, and he pitched forward. Then Norton grasped him by either arm and lowered him gently into the stall.

'I'm sorry. I didn't mean to shock you.'

'No, no,' Sumner murmured. 'It is for me to apologize. I must . . . must have tripped. The flagstones are rather . . . uneven.' He adjusted his round gold-rimmed glasses, which had slipped to the end of his nose, and squinted at the other man, who was now seated beside him.

'I felt I had to speak to you. Constance does not wish me to visit the house. That is why I came to you here.'

'Are you . . . James?' The question was put so hesitantly that it almost seemed rhetorical.

'Can you not see that I am?'

'I see that you may be and I know that Constance believes you are. Emily also.'

'Is that not enough?'

'Perhaps.'

'How can I convince you?'

Sumner smiled weakly. 'A priest's conviction, my son, is born of faith. And faith is a gift of God. It cannot be instilled by man.'

'Then, I must hope that God will give you faith in me.'

'I share that hope. Presently, however, I am troubled.'

'By what?'

'The thought that no man who truly loves my daughter would force her to choose between her promises to him, from which she believed his death released her, and her vows to her husband, made in this very cathedral, from which God will not release her.'

162

Norton gazed sorrowfully into the canon's eyes. 'Those whom God hath joined together let no man put asunder.'

'So the Church decrees.'

'And so I believe.'

'You do?'

'Oh, yes. It is what I came to tell you. I will leave Constance to find her own salvation. I love her and will always love her. But love is not enough. You are right. I will not force her to choose. I will not attempt to see her again. I will leave here tonight and will not return.'

For the first time since Constance's arrival in Salisbury, Canon Sumner's face recovered a measure of its former contentment. Some cast of anxiety in his features, which had been growing tauter by the hour, relaxed in that instant. He reached out and laid his hand on Norton's shoulder. 'Bless you, my son. What you are doing is for the best.'

'I wish I could believe that.'

'You will, in time.'

'I doubt it but, if it relieves your mind to think so, I am glad to do the same.'

'Where will you go?'

'Back to London. I intend to continue to fight for what is rightfully mine. But I shall do so without my staunchest ally.'

'Without Constance?'

'You have my word. In return, will you pray for me?'

Sumner suddenly reproached himself for the relief he had displayed. He felt shamed by Norton's self-sacrifice. As a priest, prayer was the very least he owed him. 'Let us do so now, my son. You will need whatever strength my prayers can confer in the trials ahead of you.'

Sumner turned and lowered himself to his knees. He heard Norton drop down beside him. Casting about in his thoughts for a suitable prayer, he alighted upon that laid down for persons troubled in mind or conscience. It seemed, indeed, all too apt. He embarked on it with his own mind freed of its recent burden and included in his words one specific tribute to his companion's sincerity.

'O blessed Lord, the Father of Mercies, and the God of all comforts; we beseech thee, look down in pity and compassion upon this thy afflicted servant, James Davenall. Thou writest bitter things against—'

'Who are you?' Norton uttered the question in a full-throated roar. It filled the choir with sound and reverberated, for moments after, in the vaulting of the roof.

Sumner twisted round in amazement. Norton had fallen back on his haunches. He was clutching the edge of the prayer-desk at arm's length, staring wildly across the aisle at the empty stalls opposite. 'What is it?' the canon said. 'What's wrong?'

163

'Didn't you see him?'

'Who?'

'The man . . . sitting over there.'

'There's nobody there. We're quite alone.'

'I looked up, while you were praying – I don't know why. But when I did there was somebody there in the stalls, exactly opposite me.'

'You must have imagined it. Candlelight, and the shadows beneath those canopies, can play strange tricks.'

Norton seemed to recover himself. He sat back on the bench and passed a hand over his face. 'Yes, of course. As you say. I must have imagined it.'

'Shall we finish the prayer?'

'No!' Norton stood up. 'I must go now. Thank you . . . for all your kind words.' He hurried from the stall and, before Sumner could intervene, was marching smartly towards the nave, his footfalls echoing on the flagstones.

By the time the canon had himself emerged from the choir, Norton was no more than a vanishing shape in the encroaching shadows of the cathedral's western end. He peered vainly into the gloom, till the slamming of the north door told him that Norton had gone. Then, with a puzzled frown and a doleful shake of the head, he returned to his stall. For him at least, there was a prayer to finish.

'Thou writest bitter things against him, and makest him to possess his former iniquities; thy wrath lieth hard upon him, and his soul is full of trouble. . . .'

EIGHT

I

The Times for Saturday, 4th November 1882 carried on its legal pages a short but pregnant article which may be taken to mark the moment when the case of *Norton versus Davenall* became public property.

Affidavits are to be examined on Monday before Mr Justice Wimberley of the Chancery Division to determine whether the suit filed by Mr James Norton against Sir Hugo Davenall, Bt, of Bladeney House, Chester Square, London, makes out a *bona fide* case for ejectment to be referred to the Queen's Bench Division. It is Mr Norton's contention that he is none other than Sir Hugo's elder brother James, who disappeared eleven years ago and was pronounced legally dead in 1880. He is petitioning for the removal of the impediments to his assumption of the property and title of Sir James Davenall. His claim is resisted. Mr Charles Russell, QC, will appear for the plaintiff, whilst the defence will be led by the former Solicitor-General, Sir Hardinge Giffard, QC. A further clash between these famous court-room rivals, together with the sensational features of this case, can hardly fail to render the outcome a source of intense interest and speculation.

II

Richard betrayed not the slightest reaction as he read the article. He had no wish to draw it to the attention of Sir Hugo, who sat beside him in the jolting cab, in view of the black mood in which the young man was already sunk. There were, he knew, extenuating circumstances,

165

not the least being the early hour at which they were due at Giffard's chambers. The fact remained, however, that he had acquired one of the finest advocates money could buy and briefed him as thoroughly as he was able. A little gratitude on Hugo's part would not have gone amiss.

'Giffard has a splendid record,' he remarked conversationally.

'Then I hope to God it hasn't made him over-confident.' Hugo flicked ash from his cigarette through the window. 'He's *your* choice.'

Richard ground his teeth and said nothing. He rather suspected that any other solicitor faced with Hugo's petulant demands over the past three weeks would have withdrawn from the case. For that very reason, he had delayed their meeting with Giffard until the last possible moment.

'Still nothing on Norton?' Hugo's question had become, by force of constant repetition, more of an accusation.'

'Still nothing. Nor on Quinn.'

Hugo snorted derisively. 'He's no loss.'

'As James's valet—'

'As the thief my mother turned out, he'd miss no opportunity to do us down.'

'Perhaps. But Trenchard thinks—'

'To hell with Trenchard! What about his wife?'

'As far as I know, not testifying.'

'Then, why didn't you subpoena her for our side?'

'I've explained that before, Hugo. If you force her into the witness-box, there's no telling what she might say.'

A grudging silence fell. Outside the cab, London was girding itself noisily for the day. Richard closed his eyes for a moment and let the comforting sounds wash over his senses. He had felt so tired these past weeks, chivvying the clerks and Roffey in the search for evidence he did not believe existed, deflecting Hugo's rancorous interventions whilst praying that he had guessed no more of the truth than Catherine supposed, hoping against hope to avert the confrontation awaiting them. But there was no hope. He knew that now. The man beside him must have his support in any folly, his allegiance beyond any other.

For Roffey had found nothing. He was the pick of his dubious profession, yet a month of his tireless enquiries had revealed of James Norton no possibility save one: that he was who he said. The thought beat at Richard's brain whenever he gave it the chance. At such times, as now, it was Gervase he remembered, Gervase insisting against what seemed the overwhelming weight of reason that James was not dead.

Summoned to Bladeney House for dinner one evening in the summer of 1878, Richard was surprised to find himself the solitary guest. Gervase, normally a gregarious host, clearly had something of moment to discuss with him. He was unnaturally subdued, and looked, Richard thought, none too well. His memory betrayed him over a disputed lease, he complained at the closeness of the evening, he had no taste for his food: he was not, in short, at his best. At the conclusion of the meal, he revealed what Richard took to be the cause.

'Catherine wants to have James pronounced legally dead. I said I'd speak to you about it.'

Richard, who had been awaiting this proposal for some time, nevertheless felt surprised that it should be broached whilst Quinn was still in the room. He marshalled his thoughts. 'Seven years having elapsed, such a step is both possible and prudent.'

'Why prudent?'

'Well, your will still nominates James as your heir. I have mentioned—'

'I'll not change it!'

Richard persevered. 'It isn't strictly necessary for you to do so, since Hugo has always been heir in default of James. When the time comes, however, probate will not be granted until and unless James's death has been sworn. To institute presumption-of-death proceedings now would be to avoid complication and delay later.'

Gervase grunted. 'I thought you'd side with her.'

'It's not a question of taking sides.'

'Oh, but it is.' Gervase stared across the table at him. His face was flushed, and a tic was working in his left cheek. 'It's a question of taking sides against my son.'

'I don't understand. James is dead. This is merely a legal—'

The glass Gervase held in his right hand fractured as if pierced by a bullet. Fragments of it scattered across the table, and the port it contained rushed out over the damask cloth in a vivid stain. Richard looked at his cousin in amazement, but Gervase merely dabbed his gashed thumb with a napkin and gazed calmly back. The glass had not fallen or been struck. He had crushed it in his hand.

Before anything could be said, yet with no sign of haste, Quinn had brushed the broken glass away and covered the stain with a mat. For a moment, Richard even questioned whether the incident had really occurred. Then he looked at Gervase again and knew, from the twist of his smile, that it had.

'My son lives,' said Gervase. 'And I will stand by him.'

'Paper Buildings, gentlemen.'

The cabby's cry wrenched Richard's mind back to the present. They had reached their destination.

III

When I reached Orchard Street that morning, Parfitt informed me, with what seemed a disrespectfully knowing smile, that my brother Ernest was waiting for me in my office.

I found him leafing through the wholesalers' catalogues which had accumulated on my desk. 'What brings you here?' I said, hoping to have surprised him by a stealthy entrance.

'You, William,' he replied, with no sign of discomposure.

'Well?'

'This can't go on, you know.'

'What can't?'

'The hours you keep, the way you've spoken to some of our suppliers recently, the disarray' – he flapped a hand at the chaos of my desk – 'in which I find your office.'

In other circumstances, I would have bridled at his insinuations. But I felt weary from the effort of recent weeks. What did I care for Trenchard & Leavis? All my energies had been devoted to the search for Quinn. I had scoured the servants' quarters of half London's private houses, had interrogated the proprietors of every domestic staffing agency, had haunted the old soldiers' drinking clubs, had flourished his crumpled photograph beneath the noses of countless unhelpful publicans. It had all been for nothing – yet it had been all I could do.

'Moreover,' Ernest continued, 'Parfitt tells me you are often the worse for drink.' He reached across the desk and pushed some papers clear of a tumbler in which a residue of whisky was visible.

'What do you want?' I said, too drained to protest.

'I've discussed the situation with Father. He agrees that it cannot continue. Accordingly, I have asked Parfitt to take on your duties – and he has agreed.'

'I dare say he has.'

'We suggest you take indefinite leave of absence.'

'Indefinite?'

'Don't think I'm unsympathetic to your predicament, William.' I had always doubted my brother's capacity for sympathy, but his gift for hypocrisy I had never questioned. 'Constance's behaviour has been inexcusable. Nevertheless, the welfare of the business must be my prime concern. It is clear to me that, until you have put your personal affairs in order, you will not be able to play a useful part here.'

'I'm sure you're right.'

His narrow face assumed the pinched and puzzled frown with which he always greeted irony. 'Candidly, William, I cannot think why you've not taken firmer steps to—'

'Is that all?' I interrupted.

168

'H'm. I see you're not to be reasoned with. Very well. I'll leave you to . . . clear your desk.'

'Thank you.'

As he moved to the door, I noticed the office copy of The Times *lying open amidst the litter of disordered papers. Ernest had obviously been reading it whilst waiting for me. It was folded back on the legal page and there, in the corner, was the article I had read before leaving home, starkly headed* NORTON VERSUS DAVENALL.

'Incidentally,' said Ernest, pausing on the threshold, 'Winifred wonders if you would care to come to church with us tomorrow – and dine afterwards.'

'I don't think so,' I replied. 'I'll be rather busy.'

'If there's anything we can do—'

'There's nothing.'

Nor *was there. The announcement in* The Times *had told me what I already knew: time was fast running out.*

IV

Sir Hardinge Stanley Giffard, Queen's Counsell, Member of Parliament for Launceston and Solicitor-General in the previous Conservative administration, had about him, both actually and metaphorically, many of the attributes of the bull-terrier. Short and stoutly built, with a pugnacious air that age and a succession of legal triumphs had matured into a menacing certainty of manner, he was, in court, wig, gown and meticulous mastery of a complex brief, an awesome spectacle. In his chambers early on a Saturday morning, having consented to name his fee for accepting Sir Hugo Davenall's case, he presented a different image, but one that was no less intimidating.

'You've turned up nothing on who Norton really is, Davenall?' he said to Richard with a disparaging twitch of one eyebrow.

'Nothing.'

'That' – he paused ominously – 'is a pity. Of course' – another pause – 'we don't need to prove who he is, only who he *isn't*.'

'I'd have thought it open and shut,' Hugo put in, a touch too forcibly. 'The family are in no doubt.'

Sir Hardinge fixed him with a stern gaze. 'It would be unwise,' he said slowly, 'to become complacent. To have the better of these proceedings. Norton has only to establish that he has the basis of a case. His counsel will be seeking to win time, hence his task is somewhat easier than mine. It is my belief that his claim will gain strength if it survives the hearing. I therefore intend to ensure that it does not survive. I intend to harry him, gentlemen, to press him, to pursue him, and, in the end, to break him.'

169

Hugo took heart. 'That's the ticket.'

'This dossier on your brother's life, Sir Hugo. . . . ' He nodded to the file beside him. 'I am concerned at the lack of corroboration for many of the particulars.'

'You will appreciate,' said Richard, 'that much of the information relates to events a very long time ago.'

Sir Hardinge's expression did not suggest that he regarded this as a valid excuse. Neveretheless, he let it pass. 'It will have to be improved if the case goes to trial. Let us hope that eventuality does not arise. Your own testimony, Sir Hugo—'

'I'm happy to tell anybody who cares to listen that the man's an impostor.'

'Precisely. A touch more humility would not go amiss. Norton's counsel, Russell, needs watching. It is easy to be caught out by him. He has what is called *flair*. Therefore, do not be too anxious to denounce his client. Confine yourself to the facts. Do not lose your temper.'

'He'll not rattle me.'

'That remains to be seen. Of course, if Norton is routed when he enters the witness-box, the other witnesses will count for nothing. I trust you therefore appreciate the tactics, gentlemen. An all-out frontal assault on his credibility. Frankly, I doubt his capacity to withstand it. Should he do so, however, we will rely on the testimony of close relatives. Your mother, Sir Hugo—'

'Ready to say her piece.'

'Lady Davenall,' Richard said, 'is a match for any barrister.'

'I'm glad to hear it. If she is confronted with the doctor's diagnosis of syphilis in her husband?'

'She is prepared for it.'

'Not *too* prepared, I hope. If Russell uses that evidence, he runs the risk of alienating the judge. Some tears from Lady Davenall would aid the process. All in all, I suspect it would be to our advantage.' He looked at each of them in turn. 'Well, gentlemen, I believe we have the measure of our man. I will see you both on Monday morning.'

He rose, shook their hands and showed them to the door. Farewells were exchanged. Sir Hardinge's smile exuded confidence. Hugo, too, was smiling. All seemed set fair.

'A word before you go, Davenall,' Sir Hardinge said quietly to Richard as he paused on the threshold.

'I'll go ahead,' said Hugo, vanishing down the stairs.

Richard stepped back into the room. Sir Hardinge eased the door to behind him. 'An interesting case,' he said, genially enough.

'I'm glad you find it so.'

'I do – what I know of it.'

'I'm not sure I follow.'

'I have the impression there may be more to it than meets the eye.'

'I assure you—'

'Don't. I merely give you fair notice, Davenall. I'm no gimcrack barrister to be fed half a story. It may be that you've placed all the facts at my disposal. It may be that you haven't. If the latter obtains, that young man' – he pointed to the door – 'will be the loser, not I.'

'I realize that, Sir Hardinge.'

'Very well. So long as you do. Good day, Davenall.'

After Richard had gone, Sir Hardinge returned to his desk and leafed through the file again. Thin, he could not help but feel, decidedly thin. Not for the first time, he regretted taking the case. Russell would be thirsting for vengeance after being worsted by him in *Belt versus Lawes*. Perhaps this was his comeuppance.

Yet how could he have refused? Ten years before, he had been junior counsel to Serjeant Ballantine for the so-called Tichborne claimant, fighting then – and losing – on the opposite side of an exactly comparable case. He had extricated himself before the plaintiff's case had collapsed about his ears, it was true, but the experience had hurt him more than he had ever admitted. Now Davenall had brought him a chance to balance the books, he could not let it pass. What had Ballantine once told him about the Tichborne fiasco? That it should have been crushed at the Chancery hearing, lanced before it grew to the monstrous carbuncle of a hundred-day trial. As ever, the old charlatan had given good advice. The time had come to prove his point.

V

The past three weeks had been trying ones for Emily Sumner. As the unmarried and, in her own mind, unmarriageable daughter of a cathedral prebend, she had learned to lead her emotional life on a vicarious plane. Hence she did not merely sympathize with Constance in her dilemma. She experienced its every pang.

Lately, she had even begun to suspect that her sufferings were worse than her sister's. After all, Constance had Patience to console her. And Constance had not been required to sit impassively on that bench in the watermeadows and watch the finest man she had ever been privileged to know walk bravely away to his fate. And Constance. . . . But such thoughts were unjust, she knew, born of pride, envy and possibly even covetousness: they simply would not do. Constance was subdued to the point of apparent indifference not because she was insensitive but because a prolonged agony of doubt had paralysed her feelings.

A crisis, however, as they both knew, was now at hand. Their father, after breakfast and a perusal of *The Times*, had departed, in pensive vein, to the cathedral. Since he had no business to discharge there, and since his habit was to shun matters ecclesiastical on the day before the sabbath, Emily could only conclude that he had gone there to pray. And Canon Sumner, for all his vulnerability, was not a prayerful man.

He had left *The Times* folded open by his place at the breakfast-table. Emily, being as tidy-minded a daughter as any forgetful father could wish for, dabbed off the spot of marmalade he had left before sorting its crumpled pages into order. That was when she saw the article he had been reading and, with a little cry, bore it upstairs to her sister.

She found Constance in her bay-windowed bedroom at the front of the house, gazing wistfully at the cathedral green. 'There's an article in *The Times* about the hearing,' she announced, flapping the paper in her hand.

'It was only to be expected.'

'What if people remember you were engaged to James?'

'Then, they may seek my opinion.'

'What will you tell them?'

Constance shook her head dolefully. 'I don't know. I simply don't know.'

With a rush of sisterly feeling, Emily sat down beside her on the window-seat and hugged her tightly. 'You must decide soon,' she said.

'I know. It isn't fair on you or Father, or William, or James, to let it go on like this. But what should I do?'

'Attend the hearing?'

'I cannot. If I went, I could not trust myself to remain silent. Yet, if I speak for James, William will feel I have betrayed him.'

'He should not have forced this choice on you. I shall not forgive him for that.'

'Do not be too hard on him. It is difficult not to be jealous of the one you love. I think he knows that he should not have tried to deceive me. Perhaps, by leaving me alone here, he is seeking to make amends.'

'It's more likely he believes this hearing will settle everything.'

'If only it could.' Constance grew thoughtful. 'Emily. . . .'

'Yes?'

'Will you attend the hearing for me?'

'Will *I* attend?'

'Yes. I cannot go, but you can. You would be my eyes and ears. You could tell me all that James says and does. Then, together, we could decide where our duty lies.'

'But . . . that may be too late.'

'Too late for whom?'

'Why, James, of course.'

172

Constance shook her head. 'No, Emily.' She looked back at the window, at the familiar view that must have attended her every thought on her way to this decision. 'You see, if James wins the day, I think I can give him up. But if he loses. . . .'

There was no need for her to finish the sentence. Emily saw at last, with perfect clarity, the resolve to which these past weeks had led her sister. Yes, of course. That was the only way. She embraced it – and Constance – with exultant relief. 'I will go,' she said, struggling to suppress a sob. 'I will be proud to go.'

VI

Richard was secretly relieved when Hugo did not elect to accompany him back to his office after their interview with Sir Hardinge Giffard. He felt the need of solitude in which to contemplate the eminent barrister's parting remarks and ascended the stairs of Davenall & Partners that morning weighed down by the thoughts those remarks had inspired.

He found Benson alone in the outer office, opening the morning mail. 'Good morning, sir,' the clerk said. 'A satisfactory consultation?'

Richard's answer was a non-committal grunt, followed by a change of subject. 'Anything interesting in?'

'A reply from that fellow Kennedy.'

'Oh?' Richard had almost forgotten writing to the Carntrassna agent, requesting further details of his aunt's death, but he was grateful for what scant distraction a reply would offer. 'I'll take it through.'

He closed the door of his office behind him and settled at his desk with Kennedy's letter. It ran to several pages. Really, the man was intolerably wordy. Still he had better see what he had to say.

Carntrassna House,
Carntrassna,
County Mayo.

30th October 1882

Dear Mr Davenall,

I am infinitely obliged to you for your letter of the 17th inst. We who labour here on Sir Hugo's behalf are reassured to know that we are not wholly forgotten. For my own part, my sole thought in moving from the tied house at Murrismoyle was to ensure an efficient management of estate affairs in the absence of a resident landlord. It goes without saying, there-fore, that nothing could give me greater pleasure than. . . .

Unhappily, it did not go without saying. Richard scanned several more paragraphs of defensive prose before he came to what interested him.

As to the circumstances of Lady Davenall's murder, I deeply regret to say that there is nothing I can add to my previous account. The police have made lamentably little progress in their investigation for sheer want of evidence. In response to your specific questions, I can state quite definitely that Lady Davenall, notwithstanding her years, was a most energetic and quick-witted lady to the very end. I had the privilege of serving her as agent for more than twenty years and can therefore fairly claim greater knowledge on the subject than her own family, for I never recall any of her relatives visiting her in that time. I believe the last such visit must have been made during the tenure of my predecessor, Mr Lennox, although this is purely a supposition, since he and his family had emigrated by the time I took up my post here.

Richard tossed the letter aside, with several pages still unread. The fellow's prolixity was unbearable. Not to mention his effrontery. He doubted if Hugo would welcome a lecture on the topic of his grandmother's long-standing ostracism, least of all from a prosy Scotch–Irish land agent. After all, the woman's virtual exile had been her own choice. Richard had that on no less an authority than Sir Lemuel himself. He well recalled the old man telling him on more than one occasion that his wife had gone back to Ireland shortly after Gervase had come of age and had never returned. Sir Lemuel had been damned if he would plead for a reconciliation: she was welcome to stew in the Connaught bog of her choosing. And so she had, for more than forty years, until. . . .

He snatched the letter up from where it had fallen. A chord had sounded in his mind. What was the name? Yes – Lennox, that was it. He had heard it before, not because he had found it recorded obscurely amongst the Carntrassna papers, but because of something else, something infinitely stranger, which his memory told him he ought to recall. But what was it? For an instant, he had seemed to retrieve it, but now it was gone. He leaned back in his chair and passed a hand over his furrowed brow. It was no good. Whatever the name meant lay beyond his recall.

VII

Sunday morning in Paris. A watery sun lit the river, chaffinches sang in the trees along the Quai St-Michel, and Prince Napoleon, manfully seeking to walk off chronic depression and assorted physical reminders of the amount of wine he had consumed at the Russian embassy the night before, paused to lean awhile on the leaf-strewn parapet and glare up-river at the looming bulk of Notre-Dame.

A mood of bilious irony was upon Plon-Plon this contemptibly mild autumn day. How he, a declared democrat and barely concealed atheist, had come to be Bonapartist pretender to the Imperial throne of Catholic France he sometimes failed to understand. It had never given him a gram of satisfaction, nor yet a moment of pleasure that had not been paid for in hours of heartburn and regret. He loosed some phlegm in the general direction of the river, then turned to go.

A few yards down the street stood a news-vendor's kiosk. Plon-Plon trudged towards it, calculating that a packet of *bonbons* might mask, for a while, the bitter taste of failure. But he was out of luck.

'Les journaux seulement.'

Plon-Plon scowled. Casting his eye over the piled newsprint, he observed that the previous day's London *Times* was amongst it. On a whim, he bought a copy and stalked away. Irony, he knew, was everywhere. Twenty-eight years before, his cousin the Emperor had proscribed *The Times* on his account. Decamping from the Crimean front for Constantinople in November 1854, he had only heard later what the impudent 'Thunderer' had said of him. Yet now, as he glared at its innocuous pages, he could still remember the reports that had reached him.

From our correspondent, Paris, Sunday, 19th November, 6p.m.: 'Not less than three different dispatches from the front announce the departure of Prince Napoleon from the Crimea for Constantinople owing to illness. If it be so, it is one of the most unlucky things ever done by him. The effect produced by the mere rumour of his intention to quit the camp . . . has done more injury to him than any previous incident of his life. His chances of the imperial throne, such as they were. . . .'

'I suppose there are more persons than Prince Napoleon who love to strut about in rich uniforms, provided they are not called upon to endure the fatigues of field duty and the perils of war – persons who enter the military service without the remotest intention of ever experiencing its hardships, and who avail themselves of the first plausible pretext to avoid their duty, no matter at what risk of reputation. Unfortunately, in the present instance there is little excuse allowed by the public . . . and I doubt whether the dysentery under which Prince Napoleon is said to suffer. . . .'

Said to suffer? Oh, he had suffered. God alone, if there was one, knew that. The dysentery was exaggerated, of course, but to accuse him of cowardice, to dub him 'Craint-Plomb' in the face of all he had done at the Alma and tried to do at Inkerman: it was too much.

Plon-Plon slumped down on a bench just short of the Petit Pont and wrenched open the newspaper. English journalism, however turgid, would at least save him from having to watch the march-past of worshippers on their way to Notre-Dame.

Here! What was this? 'NORTON VERSUS DAVENALL. Affidavits are to be examined on Monday . . . suit filed by Mr James Norton against Sir Hugo Davenall . . . petitioning for the removal of the impediments to his assumption of the property and title of Sir James Davenall.'

Plon-Plon whistled. So. It had come to that. He should, he supposed, feel some sympathy for his fellow-pretender. But how could he? In recent weeks he had forgotten the name of James Norton. Now it pounced once more into the front of his mind. Who was he really? James Davenall? A worthless fraudster? Or . . . somebody with a different claim on the same title? For even James had known a little of that.

The Great Universal Exhibition of 1867 drew to Paris the industrial and cultural wonders of half Europe. To Plon-Plon it meant six months of mental and physical gourmandizing. There were times, then and more frequently now, when he thought he had never been happier. A morning spent making notes on the fascinating mechanical exhibits, gleaning their intricate mysteries from the attendant experts, expatiating to them on his favourite theme of powered flight; luncheon prepared by a different nation's chef each day; then, those hours of the keenest, most savoured pleasures: the afternoon.

He had commissioned a special closed room for himself at the heart of the exhibition, furnished lavishly with Turkish rugs and divans in a plushly cushioned riot of maroon and gold. It was lit by electricity, with which he never tired of amazing his selected guests. When they had come and gone and his enthusiasm for science had ebbed, when the visiting crowds had dispersed in answer to the call of the *can-can*, when the afternoon had begun to fade into evening, then Cora would come to him to refine his lust with one more variant on harlotry drawn from the expertise of a dozen nations. Life, he was sure, had nothing more to offer.

In July, with the exhibition at its zenith, Sir Gervase Davenall and his son James visited Paris as Plon-Plon's guests. They stayed at his mock Roman villa in the Champs Elysées and enjoyed, to the full, the life of the city. On the third day of their visit, Plon-Plon conferred on James the ultimate privilege: an invitation to take tea in his room at the exhibition. It was, he soon realized, a mistake.

'You are to go to Oxford in the autumn, your father tells me,' he said, a lull having fallen after his demonstration of the light switches.

176

'Yes.' Monosyllables had dominated James's share of the conversation; he seemed unaccountably nervous.

'Are you enjoying Paris? You went to see the Offenbach operetta last night, I believe.'

'Yes.'

'Well? What did you think of it? Did you besiege the stage door for a closer look at Mademoiselle Schneider?'

'No. That is—'

'Mon pauvre garçon. You disappoint me. Why, even the Tsar—'

'We left before the end.'

'Before the end? Mon Dieu. Why?'

'Father recognized somebody in the audience.' James hung his head. He was not nervous at all, Plon-Plon now saw. He was worried – about his father. 'He became anxious. He said we had to leave at once. We didn't even wait for the interval.'

'Whom did he recognize?'

'A woman. Sitting a few rows behind us.'

'Who was she?'

'I'm not sure. Actually, I thought you might know.'

'Moi? How could I? I was not there.'

'No, but Father said her name, under his breath, when he first saw her. He didn't mean me to hear, of course, so I couldn't very well ask him. Besides—'

'What was the name?'

'Vivien Strang. As my father's oldest friend, I thought—'

'Strang?'

'Yes. That was it, I'm sure.'

'L'écossaise! L'écossaise encore.'

'You know her, then?'

Plon-Plon looked up. If only he could take back his words. There was nothing for it but denial. 'No, James. I have never heard of her.'

'But you just said—'

'I was thinking of somebody else. I'm sorry. I know nobody called Strang.'

James looked doubtful. 'If you're sure. It's just that—'

'Nobody!' Plon-Plon rose to emphasize that the subject was closed. He crossed to his desk. There, his eye was suddenly taken by the small tulip-shaped bulb mounted beside the onyx ink-stand: another of his gratifying technological indulgences. It was glowing red, signalling that a visitor had arrived by the private entrance and was awaiting admittance.

James, too, had noticed it. 'What's that?'

Plon-Plon feigned unconcern. 'This? Oh, it is not important. Excuse me for a moment.' He crossed hurriedly to the door and passed out into the vestibule. Ahead lay the main entrance, but he

177

turned right, parted a heavy curtain and stepped into a dimly lit antechamber.

Cora was waiting there patiently, reclining on a divan and smoking a Turkish cigarette. The long black dress she wore would have seemed impeccably modest but for the fact that it was fastened from shoulder to toe by buttons, which happened to be undone from the hip down. 'What are you doing here?' he hissed.

Cora fluttered her henna-tinted eyelids and crossed her legs, displaying the shapeliness of her thigh to maximum effect. 'This is the time you said, my sweet. Don't you remember?'

Then he did remember. Gervase had complained of James's shyness with women and had confided his determination that the boy should receive a thorough sexual education whilst in Paris. Plon-Plon had volunteered Cora's services and agreed to act as go-between. It was, he had felt, the least he could do. But now it was different. Now there were too many echoes, too many reminders of other bargains, other deceptions, long ago.

'The plans have changed, Cora. Go home.'

Cora uttered a mew of protest. 'Plon-Plon! I was looking forward to it! Usually, the young ones cannot afford me.'

Plon-Plon smiled and closed the newspaper. Cora hadn't gone home, of course. A few more buttons had been undone, Plon-Plon had dispatched James on a guided tour of the exhibition and Cora had soothed his troubled conscience for the rest of the afternoon. As for what James had continued to wonder about the mysterious Miss Strang, or what, in due course, he might have discovered about her, he did not know. It was, he acknowledged, better that way. For did he not have his own reasons for wishing he had never heard the name of Vivien Strang?

'The high military grade which the Prince enjoys was not won by valiant services in the field nor after the slow lapse of years. Neither distinguished military talent nor the right of seniority had anything to do with it, and when he was authorized to assume the general's sash and epaulettes it was not solely for the purpose of needless orna-ment. . . . Whatever the cause, unless indeed he was actually dragged, it is said that no man in his position should quit the field who had once entered it.'

They would have had to drag him, too, had he known what awaited him in Constantinople. When the first torrent of his rage subsided, and as soon as was consistent with the progress of his illness, he judged that a diplomatically dutiful call on the military hospitals at Scutari would do something to redeem his reputation. So, accompanied by an aide-de-camp and assorted English and French newspaper correspondents (not including the representative of *The Times*), he descended on the Sisters of Mercy, inspected one of the wards and distributed cigars to a clutch of clamouring amputees.

He had intended to make a swift departure, but the journalists urged him to visit the British hospital as well, where the famous Miss Nightingale had recently established herself, and he did not wish to deny them the chance of describing their encounter.

The British barrack hospital was a vast reeking warren of filthy corridors and cavernous wards. Miss Nightingale regarding the impromptu visits of dignitaries as matters of no importance, they were obliged to seek her out. Before they had penetrated far into the complex, Plon-Plon regretted ever entering it. Row upon row of deathly still or screaming, twitching men, many still in their mud-caked uniforms, patched and clotted with blood. In the gloomy corners of the rooms, on the very bandages of the wounded, insects crawling, infection working, death advancing. Clutching a cinnamon-scented handkerchief to his nose, Plon-Plon blundered through the gore.

Halfway along one of the murky corridors, a nurse hurried out of a side-ward, holding a basin of bloodstained water, and very nearly cannoned into him. Both jumped back a pace. Plon-Plon began to utter a magniloquent apology for the benefit of the journalists. Then his mouth went dry. He could not speak. He was looking directly into the nurse's eyes, and she into his. It was Vivien Strang and it was she who recovered herself first.

'Your Imperial Majesty. This, I confess, I had not expected.' She was older, of course, gaunter, more severe. Her coolness had turned to something bitter, her aloofness to a tried and tested strength. But her eyes? They were the same. They would, he knew, always be the same. In them, for him, there would always be discernible an unanswerable accusation.

'Mademoiselle Strang,' he said at last. 'You . . . you are nursing here?'

'Yes. What of you, Your Imperial Majesty?' Plon-Plon could hear the journalists muttering curiously behind him. 'Are you here, perhaps, to ease your conscience?'

The aide-de-camp stepped forward, but Plon-Plon held him back. '*Un moment*. Mademoiselle, you have nothing to reproach me for, I think.'

'Ask the mothers of the sons who are dying here.'

He had no answer for her. What he did say he instantly regretted. 'Soldiers have their duty to perform. Sadly, death is often a part of that duty. Mothers may find it hard to understand, but—'

'I speak as a mother!' She stared at him with an intensity from which,

179

had he been alone, he would have turned and fled. 'You should know I speak as a mother. You should know, above all people.'

There was nothing else to do but feign ignorance. 'Mademoiselle, I do not know what you are talking about. If you will excuse me—'

The bloody water hit his face before he saw her raise the basin. Its warmth changed to a creeping chill as it flooded down his face and soaked into his general's sash and epaulettes. When he opened his eyes, she had gone. The discarded basin was rattling to rest on the floor. The journalists were laughing. The aide-de-camp was mopping his tunic with a cloth. But Vivien Strang had gone.

Plon-Plon left the newspaper on the bench and headed eastwards, shuffling gloomily through the leaves on the Quai de Montebello. He had never seen her, from that day to this. He had not so much as heard her name mentioned between his discussion with James Davenall in July 1867 and his encounter with James Norton fifteen years later. He had thought she had done her worst, that day in Scutari. But now, if Norton was the man he feared he was, he knew she had not.

VIII

I had been vaguely aware for some days that Hillier wanted to talk to me. For fear that she would ask when Constance would be returning, I had done my best to avoid her. That Sunday afternoon, however, as I was heading out, she intercepted me in the hallway, with such a determined expression on her face that I knew it could no longer be deferred.

'I must speak to you, sir,' she said emphatically.

'I'm really in rather a hurry.'

'It can't wait.'

'Very well.' We stepped into the drawing-room, and she closed the door. 'What is it?'

'I'm givin' you notice, sir.'

'Notice?'

'I . . . have found another position.'

'May I ask where?'

'Mortlake, sir. A very nice 'ouse'old. I think it will suit me . . . very nicely.'

'I don't remember you asking for a reference.'

She blushed. 'I didn't like to bother you, sir, so . . . I asked your mother, bein' as I was with 'er in Blackheath longer 'n I've been 'ere with you.'

It was a minor enough issue, God knows, but somehow, after all the weeks of Constance's absence, this, on top of Ernest closing the doors of Trenchard & Leavis to me, seemed one abandonment too many. 'When do you want to leave?' I said through clenched teeth.

'As soon as . . . it's convenien'.'

'Convenient? Well, Hillier, I think tomorrow will be convenient.'

'Oh! I didn' mean so—'

'Or today, if you prefer.' Her crushed look did not touch me. 'Go whenever you damn well please.'

She burst into a flood of tears, but I did not pause to heal the petty wound I had inflicted. I slammed out of the house, cursing under my breath all the greater and lesser parties to the conspiracy James Norton and the world in general had hatched against me.

I had not realized how thick the fog had become. Its chill, white, swirling presence rose to meet me as I turned into Avenue Road. It was not yet mid-afternoon, but the fog had imposed a night of its own, in which all sounds were muffled, all vision blurred. I blundered down the streets, glad of the moist and cloaking obscurity, happy to be one anonymous figure passing, camouflaged, through a gagged and blinded world.

I had conceived a mad notion to seek out Norton at his hotel, to settle for once and all my contest with him before the courts could make it inviolably public. The fog, I think, gave my fevered plans some eerie form of safe passage to reality. Though it grew thicker as I neared Regent's Park, my steps quickened. I noticed, all at once, that I was panting with the exertion of the pace I had set. My heart was pounding, my lungs were straining. When I put my hand to my brow, it came back damp with sweat. I plunged on through the yellowing, moving curtain of the fog, damning all my lost opportunities to have closed before now with the man who had forced me to see that one of us must be victor and one vanquished.

'Penny for the guy, mister?'

I heard him before I saw him, at the corner of the street: a muffled, under-nourished, saucer-eyed youth holding a tobacco-tin with, propped against the wall beside him, a guy larger than himself, straw protruding from a sack-covered head on which two buttons and a bootlace made a pair of staring eyes and a madly fixed grin.

'Penny for the guy, mister?'

He made to rattle the tin, but no noise came. It was empty. I took half a crown from my pocket and tossed it in. His eyes grew larger still, and his mouth dropped open in a silent gasp. Then I crossed the road and we parted, he, his straw-souled friend and I.

I turned towards the steps that ran down to the Regent's Canal, judging that the towpath would lead me to Paddington more reliably than a maze of fog-choked streets. What made me stop and look back I cannot say, but, when I did, the rimy veil lifted for an instant to show

181

me the boy I had just left on the opposite corner. His trade was looking up. A man and a woman were standing by him. The woman stooped and dropped a coin into the boy's tin. Perhaps she asked him for directions. At all events, as I watched, he turned and pointed straight at me. Then, just as the woman began to turn her head in my direction, the fog reasserted its mastery, closing off the scene with a blank impenetrable wall of white.

Dismissing the stray snatched vision from my mind, I plunged down the steps and started along the path. I must have gone twenty yards before I realized that I had set off in the wrong direction. Muttering an oath at the absurdity of my error, I turned and began to retrace my steps.

The fog was at its thickest here. Its murkiest residue had drained into the cutting of the canal and made of it a phantom world of cotton-wool sound and unseen, barely rippling waters. A dark shape looming ahead of me represented the arch of the bridge from which I had just descended. Reassured of my bearings, I pressed on.

Then, once more, the fog lifted. I looked up at the parapet of the bridge, suddenly disclosed by the fickle plumes of vapour, and saw there a man and a woman, looking down at me.

Her dress was of inky black velvet, ruffled at the collar with white lace. On her breast, as a corsage, she wore a single blood-red rose. She was bare-headed, and her hair, scarcely less black than her dress, fell in thick unbraided tresses to her shoulders. In the set of her jaw, the intensity of her dark eyes, the flicker of an expression about her lips, the way in which she simply stood and gazed down at me in unashamed scrutiny, there was combined the disdain of an empress and the provocation of a whore.

When my eyes shifted to the man beside her, doubt ended and fear began. I knew at once who he was by the flinty grain of his eyes, the lean and grizzled cunning of his face, the square and muscular set of his shoulders. I did not need the photograph to tell me who he was, yet, in that moment, I craved the certainty it seemed to confer, longed for the proof it represented. I drew it from my pocket, glanced down at his captive image and knew there was no room for error. I had found him — or had been found.

I had not taken my eyes from them for more than an instant. Yet, when I looked back, they had vanished. The fog had reclaimed its gift.

I heard my footfalls echo in the brickwork of the arch as I raced beneath it and flung myself up the worn steps three at a time. There seemed so many more than when I had descended. Yet speed made no difference. When I emerged on to the bridge and gaped about me, there was no sound save my own panting breaths, no movement save the wilful ice-cold eddies of the fog. They had gone. And all I could do was shout the name of my quarry at the opaque deriding air.

I walked into the park and cast about hopelessly for a sign of them. There was none. I followed some of the paths I knew, became, for all my familiarity with them hopelessly lost, at length found myself by the boating lake, and eventually traced a route out by Hanover Gate. I was tired now, and the chill of the fog, as dusk aproached, had crept into my bones. I turned for home, refuting in my mind all the reasons why I might simply have imagined what I had seen. Self-doubt, a lack of trust in my own senses and instincts, was gnawing at my confidence.

Then I remembered that they had spoken to the boy begging pennies for his guy. I walked back to where he had been, judging him worthy of another half-crown if he could put my mind at rest.

But he was not there. He, too, had vanished, leaving only his guy to greet me, lolling crookedly at the foot of the wall, straw bristling from his lumpen torso, button eyes still staring, bootlace mouth grinning. I heard a firework begin its invisible flight somewhere above Primrose Hill and remembered that it was Bonfire Night. The straw-stuffed guy had been abandoned. And so had I.

IX

Duty had impelled Richard Davenall to call at The Limes that afternoon. Worried by reports from Roffey that Trenchard had been pursuing an independent search for Quinn, he had telephoned the Orchard Street shop on Saturday, only to be informed that 'Mr William has taken indefinite leave'. The news had left him sorely worried as to the young man's state of mind.

But his journey to St John's Wood had been a fool's errand. The maid, flustered and tearful beyond detailed questioning, had told him only that her master had gone out, destination unknown. The prevailing fog, wispily insignificant in Highgate but blindingly dense hereabouts, rendered further enquiries hopeless. He ordered the cabby to take him home.

When he at last disembarked in North Road, chilled and exasperated by the slowness of the journey, he was aware only of a marked desire for whisky and a warm fire. Yet, as he let himself into the house and felt its familiar reproachful greeting close around him, another sensation, quite unlike those reminders of physical frailty, gripped him and sent a shiver down his spine.

He stood still for a moment, transfixed, whilst the door swung to behind him. It was Braddock's afternoon off, so the upper reaches of the house were deserted. Yet that alone could not explain the atmosphere he detected. In the chilly silence there was something alert, something attentive to his presence, something, as it were, awaiting him.

He made his way towards the study. The tall ceilings and narrow passages of his father's house enclosed and encircled him. He walked straight ahead, needing no light to guide him. At the end of the corridor the study door stood open. He could see it outlined against the faltering glow of the ebbing fire. Then he knew.

It had been an evening such as this, fog-wrapped and deathly cold, in the late autumn of 1859. He had returned from Holborn in bitter mood, wincing at the memory of a series of petty indignities inflicted on him by Gregory Chubb. He had resolved to lodge a complaint with his father, useless though he had known it would be. He had marched boldly in the direction of the old man's study. Then, as now, the door had been half-open, firelight glowing within. Then, as now, in his imagination, an animated conversation had been in progress in the room. It was Gervase, with his father. Realizing that they did not know he was there, he had stopped and listened, as now he stopped and remembered.

'Ten thousand pounds?' Wolseley said disbelievingly. 'If this is a joke, young man, it's in very poor—'

'It's no joke!' Rage was boiling beneath the surface of Gervase's voice. 'I require you to arrange it.'

'As your father's executor, I must—'

'As *my* solicitor, you must do as I say – or I'll find another who will.'

'You have no right to talk to me in those terms.'

'Have I the right to dispose of this money? That's all that matters to me.'

Wolseley's reply came as if through clenched teeth. 'In strict law, it lies within your gift.'

'Then, pay it and have done.'

'I cannot do that. What has he done to earn such a sum? His salary would not amount to this in twenty years.'

'I require no homilies. You have my instructions. There's my signature to them. I want the money paid immediately – and then I want it forgotten. Is that clear?'

'I warned your father that you would squander your inheritance. If he were alive today—'

There was a loud crash, as of Gervase thumping the desk. 'Is it clear, damn you?'

There was an interval, then Wolseley replied in an icy monosyllable. 'Yes.'

'Good. I want him on his way at once. Can I leave you to arrange it?'

'You can.'

'No delays, mind.'

'There will be no . . . delays. Lennox will have his money.'

Richard walked into the study and lit the lamps. Now that he remembered, it seemed even less satisfactory than when he had been unable to call it to mind. Lennox was Kennedy's predecessor, a man who, by all logic, should have meant nothing to Gervase. Yet Gervase had paid him ten thousand pounds. Richard slumped down heavily in his chair and gazed at the desk-top which his cousin had once thumped for emphasis. There was no answer to be found in its varnished surface, no clue to be gleaned from its polished grain. The ghosts had departed. But their secrets remained.

NINE

I

The Vice-Chancellor's Court, Lincoln's Inn, lit by mullioned glass and sizzling gas, furnished in stained oak and buttoned red leather, every table piled with pink-taped bundles and sagging tomes of precedent, every seat taken by wigged advocates and their whispering advisers, every bench filled with a jostling assortment of the idle and the curious, every rafter echoing with the expectant confusion of muttering voices. Such was the arena for the case of *Norton versus Davenall*, and such were its occupants, ranged before the vacant berth, as the appointed hour drew near, that dank November morning.

Those who knew their legal drama and its leading actors had been watching the two senior counsel, Russell and Giffard, preparing themselves on opposite sides of the court, and had looked to them for clues as to what would follow. Russell had been much the less active of the two, exuding his practised air of the casual dilettante. Giffard, by contrast, had been perpetually engaged in murmured consultations with a clutch of juniors, though whether at his instigation or that of his client was unclear. He had been observed to speak testily on one occasion to the bearded grey-haired solicitor whom rumour held to be a cousin of the defendant. Sir Hugo Davenall himself was taken to be the long-limbed tousle-haired young man who was out of his chair, adjusting his collar and fingering his lips, as often as he was in it, drumming his fingers and shooting glances around the court. These often fell, to no obvious purpose, on the elegantly dressed, veiled lady who many assumed was his mother but who had, thus far, neither approached nor spoken to him.

One direction in which Sir Hugo's eyes never moved was that of the plaintiff, the enigmatic Mr Norton. This man, whose claim to be

186

Sir Hugo's brother made him the focus of attention for all sensation-seekers, had held a pose of languid immobility between Russell and the sleek-haired solicitor recognized by the *cognoscenti* as Hector Warburton. He had said no more than a few words to either gentleman and had not so much as glanced at the public gallery. He had conveyed nothing, in short, beyond a quite unreasonable calmness and, whilst some were disappointed, others thought they recognized the hallmarks of a potentially entertaining confidence. Anticipation was running high.

'The court will rise.'

Mr Justice Wimberley had entered the bench from his door behind the throne before the usher had completed his announcement and now squinted querulously around at the rows of awkwardly rising figures. He was a small, orderly, fussy little man with a bobbing, egg-shaped, sharp-nosed head that gave him, in full judicial regalia, something of the appearance of a startled and ill-tempered moorhen. He peered distrustfully at the crowded court, as if to suggest that he had expected – and hoped for – a scantier attendance, then took his seat with a resentful tug at his robe.

Just as the other occupants of the court were about to subside gratefully into their places, the creak of the door serving the public gallery alerted those with acute hearing to the advent of a shame-faced latecomer, a plainly clad lady who crept to a vacant seat with exaggerated stealth, only to have her attention drawn to a Salisbury–Waterloo return railway ticket which she had dropped on her way. Mr Justice Wimberley watched her retrieval of it with piercing censorious eyes but, if tempted to have her ejected, he was evidently dissuaded by her air of flustered sincerity. With a vague slack-wristed flap of the hand to the clerk of the court, he signalled that business might commence.

The case was called and the particulars painstakingly recited, then Mr Charles Russell, QC, rose to address the court. He spoke slowly and softly, implying by his measured composure of tone that his client's claim had every force of sweet, natural, amiable reason. The steel he was known to possess did not glint, the fire he was noted for did not flare. He seemed consciously subdued, as if aware that only one man could win this case for the plaintiff: the plaintiff himself. And, sure enough, sooner than might have been expected, the man known as James Norton was sworn in to testify.

Before his examination could begin, Mr Justice Wimberley made a purse-lipped intervention. 'You give your name as Norton?'

'Yes, my Lord.'

'Then, you admit it is not Davenall?'

'Davenall is the name I was born with. I have not used it for eleven years and shall not do so until my right to it is acknowledged by this court.'

The plaintiff had made a good start. Mr Justice Wimberley seemed appeased, if not impressed. 'You may proceed, Mr Russell,' he said, with a faint nod in the barrister's direction.

'Where and when were you born?'

'I was born at Cleave Court, in the county of Somerset, on the twenty-fifth of February 1848.'

'Who were your parents?'

'Sir Gervase and Lady Davenall.'

'You were their first child?'

'I was.'

'And hence heir to the Davenall baronetcy?'

'Just so.'

'Where were you educated?'

'Eton and Oxford.'

'Which college?'

'Christ Church.'

'In which year did you graduate?'

'1870.'

'How would you describe yourself at that time?'

So. The preliminaries were complete. There was an audible heightening of interest and tension. Many in the gallery leaned forward, eager to hear how he would rise to the challenge. Biographical facts were one thing, convincing self-portrait quite another.

For a moment, Norton hesitated. Was he lost? No. For this was not hesitation. This was deliberation. When he spoke, it was with the dispassionate fluency of one who either did not recognize his twelve-years-younger self or did so all too well.

'I was twenty-two years old. My upbringing had been pampered and privileged. I was the possessor of considerable wealth and the heir to more. The world was at my feet, and I believed it belonged there. At the time, I would have described myself as the exemplar of the English gentleman, deserving of every one of the advantages I enjoyed. Now, looking back, I see that I was a vain and foolish young prig.'

The hush was complete. The court was in his power. For this brief space, they were his to convince. While it lasted, his opportunity was infinite.

'That is admirably frank,' said Russell.

'I object, my Lord,' said Giffard, rising to his feet. 'What my learned friend calls admirably frank I call intolerably offensive to the memory of a fine young man.'

Mr Justice Wimberley compressed his face into a vinegary frown. 'Clearly, Sir Hardinge, it is one thing or the other. But it is too early to say which. You may proceed, Mr Russell.'

'Thank you, my Lord. Let us go forward one year. How would you describe yourself, then, in June 1871?'

Again, a finely judged pause. This time, the court was ready for it

188

and waited patiently. Then Norton resumed. 'I was a year older but no wiser. I had had the good fortune to become engaged to a young lady of excellent character. Had we married, I have no doubt she would have been an improving influence on me. As it was, I was conscious of no need for improvement. The freedom to indulge my every whim – indeed, my every vice – seemed its own reward. My arrogance and my folly had merely increased.'

'Would you care to name your fiancée of those times?'

'I would rather not. She married another, believing me to be dead. I wish to cause her no embarrassment of any kind.'

'I protest, my Lord.' Giffard was once again on his feet. 'The plaintiff's delicacy is the most transparent evasion.'

Mr Justice Wimberley appeared to find these harrying tactics tiresome. 'If so, you may press the point in cross-examination later, Sir Hardinge. Pray proceed, Mr Russell.'

'When were you due to marry . . . this young lady of excellent character?'

'Our wedding was fixed for the twenty-third of June.'

'What prevented it?'

'On the eighteenth of June, I left the country.'

'Under what circumstances?'

'Under circumstances of total anonymity.'

'Please elaborate.'

'I had spent some days in London whilst my fiancée remained with my family in Somerset. I had returned there briefly on the seventeenth. I had met my fiancée and informed her that I could not marry her. I had left a note for my parents indicating that I intended to commit suicide. I had then come back to London and taken a cab to Wapping.'

'With what purpose?'

'The purpose implied in my note: suicide. By drowning.'

'What led you to contemplate such a desperate course?'

The crisis had been reached. All eyes were turned on him, all ears straining for what he would next say. This was the moment when he would either open his heart on a dead secret or pile invention on a nerveless lie. This was either penance or perjury.

'I had been unwell for some months, unmistakably so for some weeks. I had succeeded in concealing the symptoms from those close to me, but they were none the less acute. I had therefore consulted my doctor.'

'The family doctor?'

'Yes. Fiveash. A good man.'

Russell looked up at the judge. 'Dr Fiveash will be testifying later, my Lord.' Then he swung back to the plaintiff. 'What was his diagnosis?'

'Syphilis.'

Somewhere in the gallery there was an ill-suppressed snort of laughter. Mr Justice Wimberley looked up irritably. 'I will clear the court if there is any ribaldry. Proceed, Mr Russell.'

'What treatment did Dr Fiveash suggest?'

'None, beyond palliatives for the immediate symptoms. He said that the disease had progressed beyond his power to halt it and that a slow decline, albeit with many remissions, was inevitable. A decline, that is, unto death.'

'Did he offer you no advice?'

'Only that to marry was unthinkable.'

'Quite. You accepted that?'

'Of course.'

'Tell me, did this diagnosis surprise you?'

The handsome, well-spoken and patently healthy plaintiff gazed into the middle distance. 'Not entirely.' The only movement now was on the defence side. Sir Hugo Davenall and his solicitor exchanged an anxious whispered word. Sir Hardinge Giffard looked round at them, then back at Norton. Mr Justice Wimberley shot a silencing glare in their direction, then up at the public gallery, where ribaldry seemed once more to threaten.

'Why were you not surprised?'

'Because I had been in the habit of consorting with prostitutes.'

Was that a low whistle from the press seats? If so, it was rapidly lost in another intervention by Giffard. 'My Lord, this is the most appalling slander on an eminent and respectable family.'

Mr Justice Wimberley affected not to hear. 'You openly admit to having been grossly immoral, young man?'

'I do, my Lord.'

'Whilst actually engaged to a young lady whom you described as of the finest character?'

'Yes, my Lord.'

The judge shook his head sorrowfully. 'Dreadful, dreadful,' he muttered. 'Proceed, Mr Russell.'

'The diagnosis did not, then, surprise you. How did it affect you?'

'It forced me to recognize the depth of my moral degeneration. It compelled me to realize that I was not merely unable to marry, but also unworthy. It drove me to face the truth: that I had lived such a lie that I had no right to live at all.'

'What did you do?'

'I was in despair, consumed with self-pity and self-loathing in equal measure. To tell the truth seemed worse than simply to end my life without explanation. I resolved to kill myself.'

There was a stifled sob from the public gallery. The woman who had arrived late was crying gently into an embroidered handkerchief. Mr Justice Wimberley looked up, but uttered no word of reproof. Tears seemed almost appropriate.

'And that is what led you to Wapping on the evening of the seventeenth of June 1871?'

'It is.'

'What did you do there?'

'I discharged the cab near a public house. There I sat drinking until the premises closed. I waited in a neighbouring churchyard until the streets had emptied. Around midnight, I descended some stairs that led down from an alley beside the inn to the river. The tide was running high, and it was a moonless night. I could hardly have wished for more favourable circumstances in which to jump in without being seen. I had carried a loose coping-stone from the churchyard and intended to strap it to my person in order to weigh me down. It was whilst engaged in that operation that I was surprised by a police launch moving slowly by. They didn't see me, because I jumped back into the shadows, but they passed by so close that I could hear what was said by the two men on the deck.'

'What was said?'

'The first man said something like "Good night for jumpers, George". I didn't understand what he meant. Then the other man replied: "It is that. I hooked out two myself last night. Fair turns me up to see them laid out on the deck like fish on the monger's slab, half the Thames seeping out of their mouths."'

There were gasps around the court, involuntary expressions of disgust by those for whom Norton's account had become all too vivid. Mr Justice Wimberley glared at the plaintiff. 'This is in the worst possible taste, young man. I must ask you to restrain your language.'

'I am sorry, my Lord, but those were the words used. They had a profound effect on me. After the launch had gone by, I stayed where I was, thinking of how it would be for my family and fiancée if I should be "hooked out". Somebody would have the gruesome task of identifying me. Worse still, I might be rescued alive. Until then, I had not considered what was physically involved in committing suicide. When I did, it was fatal to my resolution.'

'Your nerve failed you?' said Russell.

'Yes.' At a distance of eleven years, some shame still attached itself to his voice. 'Only the coping-stone went into the river. I walked back up the stairs and crept silently away.'

'Where did you go?'

'I walked the streets all night. I hardly knew where I went. By morning, I knew I could not do what I had set out to do. But nor could I return to those who would think me dead and tell them what was even worse than that I had taken my own life. Accordingly, I took a berth in a steamer sailing for Canada. I had hopes of summoning the willpower to jump overboard in mid-ocean. I failed. When the ship reached Halifax, Nova Scotia, I was still aboard.'

'What did you do there?'

'I was aimless, ill and without purpose. I travelled to the United States and took cheap lodgings in New York. Largely in order to buy the alcohol and quinine which gave me some relief from my condition, I found employment as a cab-driver. Several months passed. Then a strange thing happened.'

'What was that?'

'I began to feel better. At first, I assumed it was one of the remissions Dr Fiveash had warned me against. But it wasn't. Time was to show that I did not have syphilis after all. Earlier this year, I obtained a conclusive verdict to that effect from the most eminent of specialists. My exile, you see, had been pointless. I had wasted eleven years of my life in fleeing from the consequences of a disease which I did not have. I had forgone my birthright . . . for no reason at all.'

'And now you wish to reclaim it?'

Norton hung his head. 'In so far as I am worthy of it, yes, I do.'

A silence fell, a silence in which all who had heard his statement, his confessions of failure as well as his claims of title, contemplated the emotional meaning of what he had said. Norton looked solemnly down at the floor, his nobility and his weakness urging his audience to believe him.

'It's a lie. It's all a damned bloody lie!' A dishevelled swaying figure was on his feet in the gallery, bellowing down into the well of the court. He was waving his arms angrily at Norton, as if ordering him to leave. 'Don't believe a word he says! Can't you see?' His voice grew hoarse. He turned towards the gangway, apparently set on descending from his place. He had to pass the latecomer with the embroidered handkerchief as he went, but he succeeded only in cannoning into her. She looked up into his drunken confused face with an unexpected softness of expression.

'William!' she said, with a gasp of astonishment.

II

The usher told me I was lucky to escape being detained overnight for contempt of court. He had hold of my collar at the time and was bundling me out past the gatehouse into Chancery Lane. Fortunately, he took me for a harmless drunk. Had he known the depth of the anger which had seethed within me during Norton's parade of lies, he might have been more inclined to hand me over to the police.

I leaned against some railings a little way up the street, recovering my breath and struggling to rid myself of the dreadful anxiety imposed by what Norton had said. He had changed his story – and I could guess why. The Davenalls would not want him to revert to his original claim

192

to have inherited syphilis from his father, but it was not to oblige them that he had shouldered the blame. When I saw Emily weeping, I realized the depth of his cunning. She was his messenger to Constance. She would persuade her that he was sacrificing his good name to protect those dear to him. And she would urge her to stand by him. His address had not been directed to the court, but to Constance, whose active support, if he could win it, would carry all before it.

A man leaned out beneath the gatehouse arch and stared towards me. Taking his peaked cap for that of a porter who thought I had not moved off smartly enough, I turned and walked away up the street. Strangely enough, though, I could hear footsteps behind me as I went, as if he were following me. At the end of the street, I swung round and there he was, no more than ten yards away.

He was no porter. The cap was grubby and old, the rest of his clothes patched and threadbare. But he was no tramp, either. His handlebar moustache was waxed, and in his left hand he held a smoking cigar. His right hand held nothing, because it was not there. The arm was a mere stump, its sleeve tied beneath it in a flamboyant knot.

'Do I know you?' I said.

'I should say not,' he replied. As he drew closer, I saw that he was a positive rag-bag of contradictions, his smile disclosing a row of rotten teeth for all the affected clip of his voice, his sparse grey hair and pockmarked skin suggesting somebody quite other than the jaunty cigar-smoker with the scarlet cravat who swaggered towards me. 'Saw your . . . display . . . in there,' he said, glancing back towards Lincoln's Inn.

'What of it?'

'Thought I'd congratulate you. . . .'

'There's really no—'

'On one of the most damnable shows of impetuosity it's ever been me misfortune to witness.' He thrust his cigar into his mouth and grinned crookedly.

Norton had drawn all my anger: there seemed none left for anyone else. 'Is that all you have to say?'

'Matter of fact, no. Fancy we might have somethin' in common.'

'I don't think so.' I hailed a passing cab, gave it directions to St John's Wood and climbed in.

'You think wrong, old man.' I looked back at him. 'What we have in common is a grudge against the Davenalls.' He winked and twitched the stump of his right arm. The gesture and his hint of complicity were repulsive but irresistible. I held the door of the cab open and helped him aboard. We set off together.

I had expected him to introduce himself, but instead he said: 'What's your part in this?'

'If you must know, the fiancée he talked about is my wife.'

193

'Aha, an affair of the heart. Might've known.'

'Might you?'

'In my day, we knew how to decide this kind of thing.'

'How would that have been?'

'One of us would've called the other out.'

When I looked at him, I saw that he was smiling. My words began to catch up with my suspicions. 'Who are you?'

'The name's Thompson.'

'How did you lose your arm?'

'Gervase Davenall shot it off in a duel, more than forty years ago.'

'You were Lieutenant Thompson, of the Twenty-Seventh Hussars. You fought a duel with Gervase Davenall in May 1841.'

He frowned. 'You're well informed. Yes, that was me. Broke a couple of teeth chewin' a swagger-stick while they sawed this off for me pains.' He glanced down at his stump. 'Had to leave the Army thanks to Gerry Davenall. Now this and the braid on me cap's all I have to show for servin' Queen and country.'

'You must have known the risks you were running.'

'Risks be damned! I don't regret it. It was a fair fight.'

'Then, why did you say you bore a grudge?'

'Because maimin' me was worse than not killin' a horse with a broken leg. The Army was all I knew, dammit. And he was me friend once. He might at least have made a clean job of it.'

'You were friends?'

He smiled at the recollection and pitched his cigar butt out through the cab window, 'Oh, yes. We were like that.' He crossed the first two fingers of his left hand in a symbol of comradeship. 'Once.' Then he snapped them apart. 'We were chums at Eton. That's why we joined the same regiment.'

'You were at Eton together?'

'Don't look so surprised. I wasn't always a one-armed old beggar. Time was when I was a handsome young rip, with the pick of all the ladies. Just like Gerry.'

'Is that what you fought about – a lady?'

He sniggered. 'Could say, old man. Could say a lady.'

'I've no time for guessing games. Tell me or not, as you please.'

'Don't cut up so rough! I thought you'd be curious.'

'I am. But I'm also impatient.'

'Cards on the table? I need money. You can see that for yourself. It's no fun when your boots let the rain in, nor when your chums won't take your IOUs any more.'

'That's your problem. Why should I pay you to tell me what you quarrelled about with Gervase Davenall all those years ago?'

'Because you want to know who James Norton really is. Don't you?'

The cab swayed violently as it turned into Tottenham Court Road. I *lurched across the seat, collided with Thompson and found my hand resting on the stump of his right arm. He chuckled at the speed with which I recoiled.*

'Saw through him this morning, you see. He did well, but not well enough. He's not James Davenall.'

'I know that.'

'You hope that, you mean. The difference between us is that I don't give a damn, but I know who he is.'

Could it be true? Did he really know? I looked into his lined and ravaged face, the eyes glinting with desperation for all the mocking humour of his smile, and found no answer save my need to believe him. 'How much do you want?'

His smile broadened across the brown and jagged teeth. 'Twenty pounds would get me out of a hole. Shall we say guineas, since we're both gentlemen?'

'I don't have that much on me.'

'Then, give me something . . . on account.'

I drew a five-pound note from my wallet. 'What will you give me . . . on account?'

He grasped the note between his thumb and forefinger, but I did not release it. Then he made a reproachful face. 'That's hard, old man. Damned hard.'

'Earning money this way's bound to be.'

He drew his hand away and slumped back in the cab. 'Fair enough. I'll tell you some of it. He challenged me because I wouldn't take somethin' back. Somethin' I said in the heat of a damn fool argument. I reminded him that I'd caught him out, three years before, at a ball we'd both attended in Norfolk. Country residence of a fellow-officer. It don't matter who. Fancy-dress event, to celebrate the coronation. God, it was a long time ago. Summer of thirty-eight. I was so young then I'm not even sure I was the same person.'

'Come to the point.'

He grimaced. 'Bear with me, old man. We're comin' to it. Champagne, fine cigars, the ladies waltzin' in their provokin' disguises. I don't mind tellin' you . . . Well, point is this. I had me eye on one fetchin' creature who seemed to want more than just a waltz. She told me which room she was sleepin' in, but sleepin' weren't exactly her intention. When I cut along there, in the small hours, I found I'd been . . . forestalled. Gerry had got there before me. There they were, in flagrante delicto. So preoccupied, they didn't even know I was there. Gerry didn't realize, until I told him, three years later. That's why he fought me. That's why he set out to kill me – and damn near did.'

'I don't understand. The way you talk, such liaisons were commonplace.'

He smiled at an agreeable memory. 'Matter of fact they were, old man. We weren't so po-faced in my day.'

'Then, why fight a duel about it?'

He leaned forward and plucked the five-pound note from my hand. 'You hear the rest when you pay the balance.'

He must have been able to detect the straining eagerness in my voice. 'Where and when?'

'The Lamb and Flag, Rose Street, nine o'clock tonight.' He leaned out of the cab and ordered the driver to stop. We were halfway up Albany Street. 'Don't be late,' he concluded, winking. Then he hopped out and crossed the road before I could say another word.

I was still debating whether he was merely leading me by the nose, to pay off some bad debts, when the cab dropped me outside The Limes and I made my way up the drive. Suddenly, without Thompson to distract me, I began to regret my outburst in the court. What, after all, had it gained me but a brief venting of my anger?

Then I pulled up sharply. There was a woman standing by the front door of the house. She turned to look at me as I approached, and I recognized her at once. Her hair was drawn up beneath a narrow-brimmed hat, her dress partially concealed by a short coat, but there was no mistaking the regal tilt of her jaw. Nor the calm dark-eyed severity with which she greeted me. This time, there was no fog to pluck her away. This time, she spoke.

'Good afternoon, Mr Trenchard. I've been waiting for you for a long time.'

III

The luncheon adjournment in the *Norton versus Davenall* hearing found Sir Hugo Davenall, his cousin Richard and Sir Hardinge Giffard patrolling Lincoln's Inn Fields in search of fresh air and inspiration. Neither commodity was, however, in abundant supply.

'He's taken an enormous risk,' Sir Hardinge was saying, 'by changing his story at this stage.'

'Perhaps we should be grateful,' said Richard uncertainly. 'At least your father's name hasn't been dragged into it, Hugo.'

But Hugo looked far from grateful. 'Why's he done it?' he said, drawing heavily on a cigarette. 'What's the bloody man up to?'

'Had you considered,' said Sir Hardinge, 'that he might wish to spare your family's feelings?'

'What the devil do you mean by that?'

Giffard smiled grimly. 'Never mind. Look at it another way. He takes all the blame on himself. He makes a clean breast of past sins. That stands him in good stead with the judge. You follow?'

'Too damn well. You must tear him apart, Sir Hardinge.'

'I'll do my best. There are a good many weaknesses to work on. None of it's central, of course, but it may suffice.'

'I hope to God it does.' Hugo pulled up in his tracks, tossed down the cigarette and ground it beneath his foot. 'You must excuse me now. I said I would speak to Mother before the resumption.'

He walked back towards Lincoln's Inn, and the two men turned to watch him go. As soon as he was out of earshot, Sir Hardinge rounded on Richard with much of his professional reserve abandoned.

'This morning went about as badly as it possibly could, Davenall.'

'I realize that,' Richard said dolefully.

'We must have no more interventions from Trenchard.'

'There's really nothing I can do to influence him.'

'Such incidents only strengthen Norton's hand. They make him seem the injured party.'

'I know, but—'

'The judge is already leaning in his direction. I've never seen Wimberley so partial. And this change of story – it's damnably cunning. If we confronted him with it, it would only reflect well on him. I'd intended to challenge him over the wording of the note, but that hints at his father's responsibility for his illness.'

'You can't use the note now.' Richard's voice was a dull monotone, as if he were orating on a lost cause.

'But the rest won't stretch. Don't you see? To prevent this going to trial, we must break him now.'

'We rely on you for that, Sir Hardinge.'

Giffard looked quizzically at him. 'Sometimes, Davenall, I wonder whether your heart is in this case, I really do. You don't, by any chance, suspect that Norton really is your missing cousin, do you?'

Richard returned his gaze blankly. 'Do you really want me to answer that question?'

'No,' said Sir Hardinge. 'Upon reflection, I don't believe I do.'

IV

I showed her into the house and took her coat. As I eased its fur nap from about her slender shoulders, I saw that she was wearing the same intensely black dress, ruffed at the neck with white lace, gashed at the breast with a corsage of fresh red roses.

'I'm sorry there was nobody to admit you,' I said lamely. Hillier, it seemed, had taken me at my word and gone. 'The household is somewhat reduced at present.'

197

'No matter. It's you I came to see.' Her voice was strangely low-pitched, almost masculine in tone. 'You know who I am?'

'Yes. Dr Fiveash employed you as his secretary earlier this year.'

'I was sorry to deceive the Doctor. He was always very kind to me.'

'I take it Whitaker is not your real name?'

'No. My name is Rossiter, Melanie Rossiter.'

'Miss Rossiter?'

'Yes.'

'And how do I know that isn't another pseudonym?'

'You have my word.'

'But what is that worth, Miss Rossiter?'

Suddenly, she looked up at me with such an anguished expression that I wished I could bite back my words. Her large, deep brown eyes were full of tears. 'I have come to you,' she said falteringly, 'because I have no one else to turn to.'

Whatever I felt, I would not yet admit it. 'You expect me to believe that?'

'I cling to the hope that you will.'

'You admit spying on Fiveash's records concerning James Davenall?'

'Yes.'

'At the instigation of Alfred Quinn?'

'Yes.'

'And James Norton?'

She looked at me with a puzzlement I could not question. 'No. Quinn put me up to it. Until I read of the hearing, I had no idea what he wanted the information for. I've never met Mr Norton.'

'Why have you come to me?'

'Because I want no part of a criminal conspiracy. Because I need your help – to protect me from Quinn.' She looked down and stifled a sob. 'He would kill me if he knew I'd told you even this much.'

'Come, come, Miss Rossiter. I saw you with Quinn yesterday afternoon in Regent's Park. You're his willing accomplice.'

She raised her head and confronted all the accusations I could muster with a courageous sincerity of her own. 'You think that of me? It isn't so, Mr Trenchard. You must believe me.'

'Why did you follow me, then?'

'Because Quinn wanted me to be able to describe you. He wished me to visit your wife in Salisbury and protest. . . . ' She looked away and blushed. 'He wished me to tell her that you had enjoyed my favours but refused to pay for them. He wished me to ask her to pay instead.'

I grasped her arm and pulled her round to face me. The vileness of such a plan had inspired in me shame as well as anger. 'What stopped you?'

'There are limits to what I will do to prevent Quinn ruining me. What he required of me went beyond those limits.' She had spoken *slowly and deliberately, as if to emphasize that, this time, there was no pretence.*

'Why should I believe any of this?' I said at last.

'Because we need each other, Mr Trenchard. Quinn is an enemy to us both. Together, we may yet escape him.'

That, I suppose, was the moment when I began to trust her. I had no reason to, beyond her youth, her beauty and her apparent honesty, but my need to find some proof that Norton and Quinn were conspiring against me overrode my doubts. I showed her into the drawing-room and sat opposite her, wondering how Constance would react when she heard from such a source that she had been misled and I misjudged. Miss Rossiter gazed about at the furnishings of the room, as if over-awed by the setting, though it was humble enough, in all conscience.

'What hold does Quinn have over you?' I said at length.

She flashed a look of startling intensity at me, then dropped her chin and blushed. 'I hardly know how to explain,' *she said, nervously fingering her corsage.* "It's too . . . awful to speak of.' *Her eyes closed for a moment, then opened.*

'You must tell me, if I'm to believe you.'

'I realize that.' *She sighed.* 'So be it. I'm engaged to be married. Have been for over a year. My fiancé comes of an excellent family. His father's a wine merchant in Bristol. A man of means and considerable repute. He has allowed our engagement to go forward, despite my modest standing in the world, because he realizes that his son and I are very much in love. If our engagement were to be ended, I would be heartbroken.'

'Why should it be?'

'Because Quinn has some photographs of me which he's threatened to show my fiancé. The photographs are. . . . ' *She broke off and sobbed, then gave way to tears. Before I had time to question the wisdom of my response, I was beside her on the sofa, one arm round her shoulders, offering what comfort I could.* 'The photographs show me,' *she continued,* 'as only a husband would be entitled to see me.'

'How did Quinn obtain them?'

'He and I were in domestic service together in Bristol two years ago. I was a housemaid, Quinn was a footman, though he claimed to have been a butler in his previous post. That was before I met Clive, you understand. Quinn persuaded me that there was good money to be had modelling for an artist he knew. And there was. It was even better for life modelling, as it was called. Better still if you allowed yourself to be photographed. I was so stupid. I really believed that the photographs were only taken so he could have a likeness to paint by when I wasn't there. Later, Quinn told me what they were really used for.' *She shuddered.* 'It seems he kept some copies for himself. We were no longer

*working together when he came to me, last December, and said that he
would show the pictures to Clive . . . unless I did as he asked.'*

'And what he asked was that you find James Davenall's medical
records amongst Dr Fiveash's papers?'

'Yes. It didn't prove difficult. The Doctor was a trusting employer.'

'Quinn arranged Miss Arrow's accident?'

'Yes.'

'And you lodged with the widow Oram in Norfolk Buildings until
you'd accomplished the task?'

She looked at me in surprise. 'You know that?'

'What did you obtain in return? The photographs?'

'Yes. But they were worthless. As I might have guessed, he has the
negatives as well. They're what he promised me if I would do this further
service. . . .' *She looked away.* 'By disgracing you.'

I patted her hand. 'You have my gratitude, Miss Rossiter.'

'Thank you,' *she murmured. Then, in a stronger voice:* 'Would your
wife have believed such a tale?'

'Possibly. We've been estranged . . . for some weeks. She might have
thought. . . . At all events, the object of the exercise is plainly to win
her over to Norton. No doubt he'd have been on hand to console her
once you'd persuaded her that I wasn't to be trusted.'

'What do you want me to do . . . now I've told you everything?'

*She had placed herself in my power, and when I looked into her frank
imploring eyes I wondered at the bewildering speed with which she had
been transformed from an awesome foe into a winsome ally.* 'I want you
to write down what you've told me. We'll have the Davenalls' solicitor
swear it as a legal statement. Then I want you to tell my wife the truth.'

Her jaw set in a determined line. 'Very well. I'll do as you ask.'

'Unfortunately, I see no way of dispossessing Quinn of the negatives.'

'It doesn't matter,' *she said, shaking her head.* 'He would never have
given them up anyway. I must face Clive with the truth and trust in his
love for me.'

'Where is your fiancé now? In Bristol?'

'No. He's gone to Portugal with his father on business. He knows
nothing of my presence in London.'

'Is there anything I can do to help you?'

'I need your protection above all, Mr Trenchard. I was to have gone
to Salisbury today to see your wife. Quinn was to have met me at
Waterloo off the four o'clock train. What am I to do when he realizes
I've disobeyed him? He knows where I'm staying. I would fear for my life
if I thought he knew I'd betrayed him.'

'You must stay here. I will meet Quinn at Waterloo in your place.'

'No!' *There was a note of desperation on her voice.* 'If he saw you, he
would guess what I've done. Better that he should be left in doubt. He's
a dangerous man, Mr Trenchard. A very dangerous man.'

200

Reluctantly, I conceded the point. 'Very well. I will telegram my wife to return here immediately. Meanwhile, I'd like you to write out your statement, ready for her to see.'

I opened the bureau, found her pen and paper and left her writing while I hurried out of the house and round to the post office in St John's Wood High Street. There I telegrammed Constance in the most emphatic terms I could devise: VITAL YOU RETURN HOME AT ONCE. HAVE PROOF NORTON NOT JAMES. *Miss Rossiter's account did not quite amount to the proof I proclaimed, but I knew it would suffice to shatter Constance's confidence in Norton's honesty. Walking back to The Limes, I felt at last a lifting of the bleak despair which had gripped me for weeks. The coils of Norton's conspiracy with Quinn were not as binding as I had feared. With Miss Rossiter's help, I was about to cut free.*

V

At Lincoln's Inn the hearing had resumed. Mr Russell's concluding questions to the plaintiff had elicited nothing to compare with the sensations of the morning, but, as he sat down, interest heightened. Journalists licked their pencils. Even the least attentive occupants of the public gallery ceased examining their fingernails. For Sir Hardinge Giffard, clearing his throat and hoisting his gown about his shoulders, had risen to confront his prey.

'Mr Norton. . . . ' He had pronounced the name with deliberate emphasis and now paused to judge its effect. 'You are, I take it, serious in your claim to be the late James Davenall?'

Norton's reply was a model of coolness. 'I am more serious in asserting my true identity than in anything I have done in my whole life.'

'It would be as well if you were. Do you realize how severely the Law looks upon perjury?'

'My Lord, I protest!' Mr Russell was on his feet. 'My client is under oath.'

'Indeed he is,' Mr Justice Wimberley replied. 'Sir Hardinge may be seeking to remind the plaintiff, however, that, were he to lose this action, a charge of perjury would almost certainly be brought against him.' He smiled faintly. 'Yet perhaps the plaintiff needs no reminding.'

'I do not, my Lord,' Norton said calmly.

'Very well. Proceed, Sir Hardinge.'

'I questioned your seriousness because, were it not for the distress your claim has already caused the Davenall family, it might seem merely laughable. Has any member of that family even fleetingly acknowledged you?'

Norton replied without hesitation. 'No.'

'What explanation do you offer for their unanimous rejection of you?'

'I cannot speak for them. Their refusal has greatly pained me.'

'Would you agree then, that the most likely explanation is that they simply do not believe you are their late relative?'

'My Lord, I object!' Mr Russell had once more intervened. 'It is absurd for my learned friend to refer to my client as if he were dead.'

Mr Justice Wimberley compressed his lips. 'I gather that Mr James Davenall was prounced legally dead two years ago. Thus Sir Hardinge's appellation of the word "late" to his name is strictly correct.'

Giffard smiled. 'Thank you, my Lord. Well, Mr Norton?'

'I have been forced to conclude that they would rather deny me than face the consequences of my return.'

'You lay that accusation against Sir Hugo Davenall?'

'I do.'

'And his mother, Lady Davenall?'

'Reluctantly, yes.'

'You seriously expect this court to entertain the notion that a mother would refuse to acknowledge her son, a son whom she believed dead, a son whom you claim to be, miraculously restored to her, on grounds of . . . what? Inconvenience?'

'Not inconvenience, no. My mother is a person of fixed and puritanical opinions. To accept me, she would also have to accept the reasons for my original disappearance. They are what she finds so appalling. As for my brother, it is surely obvious what he stands to lose by acknowledging me.'

'Oh, yes. "The reasons for your original disappearance." You claim to have left a note I believe, at the family home in Somerset, hinting at suicide. Remind me of the date.'

'The seventeenth of June 1871.'

'Where did you leave it?'

'In my father's dressing-room.'

'Word-perfect, Mr Norton. I congratulate you. Of course, that much could have been gleaned by studying newspaper reports of the late Mr Davenall's disappearance. What did the note say?'

Norton hesitated. A frown crossed his face. 'I cannot recall the exact words.'

Giffard smiled. 'Because they were not reported. Deprived of a script, we flounder, Mr Norton.'

'It was eleven years ago. You would not expect—'

'Any snatched phrase would suffice!' Giffard's smile broadened.

Norton looked at him with piercing intensity. ' "Dear Mother and Father, This is the last you will ever hear from me. I am determined to end my life this day." Do you wish me to continue?'

The smile drained from Giffard's face. 'That will not be necessary,' he said, after a momentary pause. 'The contents of the note may have been disclosed before now, so we will not pursue the point.'

'My Lord!' exclaimed Mr Russell. 'We dispute that contention. To sustain it, the defence will need to show evidence of the note's publication.'

'As to that,' Giffard replied, 'it would be necessary to study a transcript of the presumption-of-death proceedings, where the note was certainly referred to.'

'Is such a transcript available?' said Russell.

Giffard smiled. 'I fear not.'

'Then the point cannot, as you say, be pursued,' Mr Justice Wimberley put in acidly. 'Proceed with your questions, Sir Hardinge.'

Giffard puffed out his chest, as if to confirm that he had recovered the situation. None the less, a wary tone had entered his voice. 'The touching account of your attempted suicide was lacking in details, Mr Norton. Perhaps you could now supply some. Where in Wapping do you claim to have been dropped on the evening of the seventeenth of June 1871?'

'The swing bridge across the entrance to Wapping Basin.'

'That much was certainly reported. What is the name of the public house where you claim to have spent some hours?'

'Not above two hours, I would think. I don't remember the name. I was in no state to study inn signs.'

'Where, in relation to this nameless public house, was the churchyard from which you claim to have removed a coping-stone?'

'Exactly opposite, on the other side of the street.'

'Doubtless you have reconnoitred the ground. Is that how you come to know of the alley beside the public house and the stairs it leads to? Is that how you settled on the site for your supposed attempt at suicide?'

'No. I've never been there since, though I could take you there easily enough. If, as you suggest, I'd "reconnoitred the ground", wouldn't I have memorized the name of the pub?'

'No, Mr Norton, because you are clever enough to add a little uncertainty here and there for the sake of verisimilitude. Let us turn to your next foray into the events of June 1871. Where did you pick up this putative steamer to Canada?'

'West India Docks.'

'The name of the vessel?'

'*Ptarmigan*.'

'A regular passenger-carrier?'

'No. It was principally a cargo vessel.'

'What cargo?'

'I've really no idea. I never inspected the hold.'

'The name of the captain with whom you negotiated this special berth?'

'I can't remember.'

'What name did you travel under?'

'Smith.'

'Not very original.'

'I didn't feel I needed to be.'

'When did . . . *Ptarmigan* . . . reach Nova Scotia?'

'The voyage lasted about a month.'

'You arrived in mid-July, then?'

'I suppose so. I'm afraid I didn't make a note of the date. No doubt you could unearth a record of it somewhere.'

'No doubt you already have. How long did you remain in Halifax?'

'Less than a week.'

'Then you travelled across the border to New York. Why?'

'It seemed natural to head for a big city. Besides, I was anxious to quit British territory. In the United States, I could hope to lose myself.'

'Have you remained in New York ever since?'

'No. I've moved around the country extensively.'

'Always using the name Norton?'

'Yes.'

'Not Smith?'

'As you said, it wasn't very original.'

'Why a pseudonym at all?'

'Because I wanted my family to go on believing me dead.'

'Weren't you far enough away to escape detection anyway?'

'Possibly, but it wasn't a risk I was prepared to take.'

'In that case, why come forward now?'

'The discovery that I wasn't dying of syphilis altered my view of the world.'

'Tell us where you were, Mr Norton, and what you were doing, when this discovery dawned upon you.'

'It was a suspicion that grew over the years.'

'You spoke earlier of the symptoms of your illness. When did you last experience these symptoms?'

'Some years ago.'

'How many years?'

'Six or seven.'

'Since then, you've been completely fit?'

'Yes.'

'Do you claim, then, to have made a spontaneous recovery from syphilis, or never, in fact, to have suffered from the disease?'

'I suspect the latter, but I'm not qualified to say.'

'What about those who are? This "most eminent of specialists".
Who is he?'

'Dr Fabius, the foremost European venereologist.'

'Where and when did you consult him?'

'In Paris, in February of this year.'

'On whose recommendation?'

'That of my American doctor.'

'Yet you said you had felt completely fit for six or seven years. Why
wait so long to confirm it?'

'There was the prospect of a relapse. Besides. . . . '

Norton's momentary hesitation seemed to galvanize Sir Hardinge.
He turned on him with a swooping gesture, his voice raised accusingly. 'I put it to you, Mr Norton, that the death of Sir Gervase
Davenall last year prompted you to manufacture this preposterous
claim to be his heir. Until then, there was nothing to be gained by it.
Of course Fabius gave you a clean bill of health, because you are not
syphilitic. In point of fact, you are not James Davenall. Are you?'

Norton was unmoved. 'I am.'

'Then, why did you not come forward whilst your father was still
alive?'

'I'm sorry to disappoint you, Sir Hardinge, but the reason is a
prosaic one. Partly, I waited to be certain. Principally, however, I
waited because I was short of money. My upbringing didn't equip me
for lucrative employment. I've had to subsist on modest means for
many years. Dr Fabius's opinion does not come cheap. Travelling to
France to gain his opinion does not come cheap. Engaging lawyers to
prosecute my claim—'

'You anticipated the Davenalls would resist you, then?'

'Sadly, yes.'

'So you've been putting by your cab-driver's tips all these years to
fund this enterprise?'

'In a sense. Actually, I haven't always been a cab-driver. I've worked
in many trades and occupations.'

'Most recently as what?'

'Copy-writer for an advertising agency in Philadelphia.'

Giffard pulled a face. 'A sad fate for an English baronet.'

'As you say.'

'Perhaps you dreamed up this story in a slack hour between carbolic
soap slogans.'

'Not so.'

'Do your former colleagues know what you're about?'

'No.'

'Perhaps that's just as well for their peace of mind.' He paused
rhetorically, then returned to the attack. 'One last question, Mr
Norton. The late James Davenall's fiancée, now married, whom you

205

were too delicate to name: have you met her since announcing your claim?'

'Yes.'

'Did she acknowledge you as her former fiancé?'

'Not publicly.'

'Privately, then?'

'I'd rather not disclose the contents of a private conversation with a lady.'

'How touchingly chivalrous. But it will not do, Mr Norton. I put it to you that this pose of gentlemanly reticence is merely a stratagem by which you hope to imply her support for your claim, without that support being put to the proof.'

'That I absolutely deny.'

'Then, will you admit she has rejected your claim?'

'No.'

'Did she acknowledge you: yes or no?'

'I cannot say.'

'You must.'

Norton looked up at the judge. 'My Lord, I appeal to you. Surely I may decline to answer if I wish?'

Russell was on his feet, suddenly fearful, it seemed, for his client. 'My Lord, I think what the plaintiff means—'

'Thank you, Mr Russell, his meaning is clear.' Mr Justice Wimberley peered down at Norton with an expression of apparently genuine concern. 'Of course you may decline to answer, young man. This is not a criminal action. However, I must warn you that, by not answering, you will leave the court with little alternative but to accept Sir Hardinge's interpretation of your motives. Do you understand the consequences of that?'

'I do.'

'Very well. Will you answer?'

Norton paused. There stood suspended, in the interval of his silence, all the doubts and possibilities raised by his testimony. Many in the court did not understand how this one question had become the ultimate test of his veracity, but they sensed that it had. They knew, intuitively, that his answer would form, for good or ill, the crisis of the case. When he replied, he spoke in an undertone, but his words eluded nobody. 'No,' he said. 'I will not answer.'

Towards the back of the public gallery, Emily Sumner was sobbing gently. It was the only sound in the court.

VI

When I returned to The Limes, it was to find Cook in the hallway.

'Bless me!' she exclaimed. 'There you are, sir.'

I had no time for her chatter. 'Where's Hillier?'

'Took 'er leave, sir, early this mornin'. Said you knew all about it.'

'So I did. Well, what about some tea? I've a guest to entertain.'

'Guest, sir?'

'Yes. She's in the drawing-room. As you'd know, if you'd been here to let her in when she arrived.'

'No one's called, sir. I'd 'ave 'eard the bell from the kitchen. That's where I've been since breakfast.'

Evidently, her hearing was failing. 'Never mind. Tea for two, quick as you like. And some sandwiches. I've an appetite on me.'

'Very good, sir.'

'And make up the guest room. The lady will be staying overnight.' Noting her expression, I added: 'I know it wouldn't normally fall to you, Cook, but, without Hillier . . . well . . . you do understand, don't you?'

'Yes, sir,' she said grudgingly. 'Reckon I do.' With that, she took herself off.

In the drawing-room, Miss Rossiter had evidently completed her statement. She was still sitting at the bureau, but had discarded the pen and was gazing vacantly into space. Her attention must have been elsewhere, for she seemed not to hear me come in.

'Miss Rossiter!'

She looked up with a start. 'Mr Trenchard! I'm sorry.'

'There's no need to be. Have you finished?'

'Yes.' She rose from the bureau and handed me three neatly written pages.

I sat down in an armchair and began to read. Whilst I did so, I was aware of two competing sensations. One was the confidence which grew within me as I studied the document: it said all I needed to prove beyond doubt that Quinn was conspiring against the Davenalls and against me. The other sensation, less intense but no less insidious, was of Melanie Rossiter watching me as she patrolled the carpet by the window. I felt increasingly responsible for her, increasingly moved by all that she was putting at risk to help me. Was she hoping I would protect her from Quinn? Was she praying I would intercede with her fiancé? She must not be disappointed, I knew, on either count.

'I'm most grateful for this,' I said on finishing. 'It's everything you spoke of. It's more that I had a right to ask.' When I saw the pinched line of her mouth and the tight fists into which her hands were screwed, I realized how true my words were. 'You don't have to put your name to it, you know.'

207

'I do. It's the only way to be free of him.'

'In that, I think you may be right.'

I carried the statement back to the bureau and held out the pen. Without hesitating, she took it from me and signed the last page, then initialled each of the others. 'There,' she said. 'It's done.'

The hand with which she held the pen was shaking. Instinctively, I reached out and clasped it in mine. I had meant it to be the merest reassuring squeeze, but found instead my fingers intertwined with hers. 'You can rely on me,' I said thickly.

'Thank you,' she said softly. Then she turned her large dark eyes upon me, searching, as it were, for proof that she could trust me. 'I do so fear for what may happen to me.'

'There's no need to. I'll make sure you come to no harm. I intend to see Quinn behind bars for what he's done.'

'And my fiancé?'

'If he's worthy of you, he'll understand. I'll do all I can to make him understand.'

She turned and looked directly at me, our hands still joined. 'Bless you,' she said, 'for being my friend.' Then she abruptly let go of my hand and jumped back, blushing, for she had seen, as I had not, Cook coming in with the tea.

TEN

I

Richard Davenall left Lincoln's Inn alone that afternoon and in
sombre spirits. Russell had been unable to repair the damage done by
Norton's refusal to answer Giffard's question, and Hugo had reacted
as if the case was already won, clapping Sir Hardinge on the
shoulder, insisting he should meet his mother, even suggesting he
might care to dine at Bladeney House. For all this, however, Richard
had no taste. It was not that he believed Hugo's confidence to be
misplaced; rather that he feared it was all too well founded. There
was the rub. Norton had not merely impressed him more than on
any previous occasion; he had moved him in the most disturbing
way. He had woken in Richard that dormant suspicion that the noble
racked creature he had watched all day in court was none other than
James Davenall himself.

Chill dusk and attendant fog were settling on London as Richard
emerged from Lincoln's Inn. Turning up his collar and buttoning his
gloves, he headed southwards, eager to find solitude in the homeward
rush of the city. He glanced at the new and nearly complete Royal
Courts of Justice, looming to his right behind tarpaulins and
temporary fencing, and reflected for a moment on the sad waste his
profession sowed in the lives of that misguided throng they called
their clients.

He sighed and stepped up his pace, glad, at all events, to have
some task to fulfil which might distract his thoughts from such
morbid paths. Benson had passed him a note during the afternoon
saying that Roffey wanted to see him urgently, so he had decided to
pay the man a rare visit at his place of business. This was a shabby
one-room office above a tobacconist's shop off Ludgate Hill, and
when Richard reached it, through the crowded tangled streets, he was

forcibly reminded of the imperishable necessities which linked such dilapidated premises with the fashionable likes of Chester Square. Only to Richard, who moved in both worlds, was the irony of their connection inescapable.

He found Roffey awaiting him with all the self-effacing patience which was his trademark, and to which he characteristically added an apology. 'Sorry to get you over here, Mr Davenall.'

'Benson said it was urgent.'

'Seeing as the hearing's commenced, I thought you should know straight away. How's it going?'

'So-so. What have you found?'

'Something on Quinn. Not much. Nothing definite. But something.'

'Well?'

'Keep his description, change his name to Flynn and ask a sergeant I know at Scotland Yard: then you get a man the police would very much like to find.'

'Why?'

'They think he's behind a series of burglaries. House break-ins, that is. Houses of the rich and influential, town and country. Safes opened, cash, jewellery and art objects stolen. All done very efficiently, I gather, and not thought possible without inside information. A man who knows servants or ex-servants, or who knows some of the houses and owners himself, is the obvious candidate. They don't know about Quinn, of course. That's my theory, based on rumours circulating in the stolen-goods trade, but it fits the facts. By dismissing him, Lady Davenall may have set him on the road to a more . . . lucrative occupation.'

Richard smiled ruefully. 'This would explain why he's in no hurry to be found by us.'

'Yes, indeed, sir. I should add that a footman was killed in one of these break-ins, so, strictly speaking, there's murder to be considered on top of burglary. If Flynn is Quinn, he wouldn't want anything to do with our enquiries. Unless . . .'

'Unless what?'

'Unless he's already involved. It occurred to me that Mr Trenchard might have a point. Norton needs money as well as information to mount a case. Quinn could be supplying both. There's not a shred of evidence for that, of course, but Norton has gone missing when he's wanted to, perhaps in order to meet his principal. We've no idea where, but—'

'It could be wherever Quinn, or Flynn, feels safe?'

'That was my thought, sir. Does it help?'

'I'm not sure, Roffey. I'm not sure at all.'

Cook's hearing must have failed again, for when the doorbell rang late that afternoon there was no sign of her stirring to answer it. At length, I went myself and found a post-boy on the doorstep, stamping his feet to keep warm in the raw fog-wreathed dusk. He had a telegram for me from Constance. It was a reply to mine of earlier in the day and said simply that she was leaving Salisbury straight away. Before the night was out, she would be back with me, back to hear me vindicated. I tipped the boy and went to rejoin Miss Rossiter in the drawing-room.

'My wife is returning this evening,' I announced.

'I'm glad,' Miss Rossiter replied. 'When will she be arriving?'

'I'm not sure. Late, I imagine. I hope to be back in time.'

'Back?'

'Yes. I have to meet somebody this evening. A man named Thompson, who claims to know who Norton really is. I'm sorry to have to leave you, but . . . ' My words died as a stray thought intruded. Miss Rossiter had removed a forty-year-old newspaper cutting from Fiveash's surgery referring to Harvey Thompson and his long-ago duel with Gervase Davenall. Why had I not remembered before? I could ask her now to explain why she had taken it.

The question never reached my lips. Miss Rossiter was staring past me, her placid expression transformed by terror. With a quivering hand, she pointed towards the window behind me, still uncurtained against the onset of night. 'Quinn!' she cried. 'He's there!'

For a second, I could not take my eyes from her fear-struck face. Then I whirled round, to find only the blank glass of the window-pane waiting to greet me.

'He was there,' Miss Rossiter said from behind me. 'I saw him, his horrid awful face, looking in at us.'

Reasoning that, if he had been there, he might still be in the garden, I raced into the hall and headed for the morning room, where the french windows offered the quickest route out. I fumbled for a moment with the bolts, then flung them open and rushed on to the veranda.

There was nothing. Light from the drawing-room flooded on to the railings and the patch of lawn beyond them. As my eyes adjusted to the darkness, all I could see through the fog was the garden I knew so well. The only sounds to reach my ears were my own panting breath and the derisive hoot of an early owl. I walked to the end of the veranda and waited again for signs of trespass to reach me. But there was none.

Then I saw it. The side-gate was open, no more than a crack, but sufficient to admit a wedge of light from the porch lamp. Burrows always closed and bolted it before going home, but now it was open. I walked across, opened it wide and looked down the empty drive. If Quinn had used that route, he would be long gone by now. I closed the gate and bolted it. It was possible Burrows had forgotten to do so. I remembered him doing as much on a previous occasion, less than two months before, when Norton had first intruded on my world. Or it was possible that Miss Rossiter had truly seen her persecutor.

I went back into the house and found her still sitting on the sofa, staring fixedly at the window. I drew the curtains, then sat down beside her and once more found my arms encircling her shoulders.

'It's all right,' I said. 'If he was there, he's gone now.'

She had been crying. I could see the track of tears on her pale cheeks. She looked at me with undisguised anguish. 'But how far has he gone? For how long? He may just be waiting – for you to leave me alone.'

'Then, I won't leave you alone.' My appointment with Thompson seemed unimportant in that moment, What could I buy from him that compared with Melanie Rossiter's gift of the truth?

'You said—' she began.

'I won't leave you,' I said firmly. 'Trust me.'

'Thank you. You're so kind. After all, I may have imagined it.'

'I don't think so. Either way, you won't be alone.'

III

It was slow going in Fleet Street and the Strand that evening, with a clammy fog descending to add its impenetrable layers to the encroaching darkness, but Richard Davenall did not care. Unlike most of those aboard the swaying trams or hurrying past him on the crowded pavement, he had no certain destination, no object in mind, no purpose to his journey.

Crossing Trafalgar Square, he found himself – if anything, against his inclinations – walking along the north side of Pall Mall, a route which he knew would take him past the club to which he had once belonged and to which Hugo still belonged. He had resolved to disregard the fact, but when he came abreast of it he could not resist glancing across the road at the familiar, mutely lit doorway. What he saw there stopped him in his tracks.

The bay window to the left of the club entrance gave on to what had been known in his day as the Shelburne Bar. Being less private than the other bars, it had always attracted the younger, more ostentatious members. Sure enough, there they still were, lounging beneath the gleaming chandeliers, parading their accents and postures for the admiration of their fellows. Richard looked across at these specimens of the people whose legal affairs he had for so long handled and realized, not for the first time, that the work he had once enjoyed was now, in the truest sense, hateful to him.

Then he looked closer. There, at the centre of the carousing ruck, was Hugo. He might have known. Sir Hugo Davenall, never one to believe that any celebration could be premature, was indulging to the full the victory he had sensed was his at Lincoln's Inn. He would have bought everybody in the room a drink by now, would have crowed to them of his triumph and defied them not to share his pleasure. There was Freddy Cleveland, smiling alongside him, and that fellow Leighton, besides several others whom Richard dimly recognized. Hugo himself, hair awry, cigarette drooping from grinning mouth, champagne-glass in hand, was clearly already drunk, his troubles for the moment forgotten, the remote possibility of failure excluded from his mind.

'Not a pretty sight, is it?'

The voice had come as if from nowhere. When Richard whirled round, it was to find James Norton standing behind him in the mouth of a narrow alley, barely visible in the depth of the shadows.

'Hello, Richard,' he said. 'What brings you here?'

'I . . . I could ask you the same.'

'Put it down to nostalgia. I wanted to take a look at the old place. What should I find but Hugo? Putting on a floor-show.'

'What do you mean?'

'Sorry. It must be an Americanism I picked up along the way. Cigarette?'

'No, thank you.'

'Please yourself. I believe *I* will.'

As Norton pulled his cigarette-case from an inside pocket of his overcoat, lamplight glistened on its silver surface. Richard caught his breath.

'What's the matter?'

'Nothing.'

'Is it this that caught your eye?' He took out a cigarette, then snapped the case shut and tossed it into Richard's awkward grasp. 'Papa gave it me for my twenty-first birthday.' Richard turned it over in his hands. The initials 'J D' were visible, elegantly inscribed at the centre of the design. 'Remember it?'

'I . . . I'm not sure.'

'Even if you were, it wouldn't make any difference. Would it?' Norton lit a match and eyed Richard calmly, then touched it to the cigarette and blew it out. 'Even if I could make you believe me, you wouldn't act on it. Would you?' He reached out and retrieved the case.

'I can't believe what isn't true.'

'You've known me since the day I came to your office. There's no need to pretend now.'

'I'm not pretending.'

'Why do you think I refused to answer Giffard's question?'

213

'I don't know.'

'Yes you do. It's because I love her, Richard. If I didn't, I'd have dragged her into that courtroom and had Russell force her to acknowledge me. But she deserves better of me than that. Which is more than I can say for my family.'

'You've no right—'

'I've every right!' His voice was suddenly bitter. 'Why do you think I lied about how I contracted syphilis? What good did it do me?'

'Perhaps you thought it would win the court's sympathy.'

'That's nonsense, and you know it. I'm trying to save the family's good name, if that means anything to you. I'm giving all of you every chance I can to see reason. But what have you offered me in return?'

'Mr Norton—'

'The name is Davenall! You know that.'

'I know no such thing. Now, if you'll excuse me, I really think—'

'Wait!' Norton's hand touched his shoulder in a placatory gesture. 'Don't turn your back on me, Richard. I may lose tomorrow, for our family's sake.'

Richard paused, a moment longer than he knew he should. The gentle pressure of that hand on his shoulder moved him now he had looked away. More than any words, it begged him for once in his life, to trust the promptings of his soul.

'Look at Hugo,' Norton murmured. In the brightly lit, bay-windowed bar, Sir Hugo Davenall was laughing to drunken excess at his own or another's joke. Freddy Cleveland was slapping him on the back. All his friends were about him, gathering him in the lap of a camaraderie that counted for nothing.

'I don't blame you, Richard. You least of all. I would blame no man – for standing by his son.'

'What did you say?'

'Papa knew all along that Hugo was your child. He told me so himself. Don't worry. He told nobody else. The only person he felt he needed to tell was his only son.'

IV

As the evening stretched towards night, we grew nervous, Miss Rossiter and I. There was nothing more to be done until Constance arrived; and that, I suppose, is what pressed hardest on our minds. All was done now, all was prepared. We had only to wait.

After a dinner of sorts, Miss Rossiter asked if she might go up to her room to rest: she felt drained by the anxieties of the day. I was left alone then, alone to re-read her statement, to swallow a few pegs of whisky and savour the prospect of the victory I felt sure lay within my grasp. I grew easier in my mind, more confident that I could carry off the prize.

When the drawing-room clock struck eight, it roused me from a light doze. I was instantly alert, surprised, almost betrayed, by my own drowsiness. An irrational fear seized me, but was swiftly quelled: there was the statement, where I had left it in the bureau. Nevertheless, the experience worried me. It might be several hours yet before Constance was with us. I folded the statement, slipped it into an envelope, sealed it, then took it up to my study and locked it in the escritoire.

Once it was done, with the key to the lock nestling in my waistcoat pocket, my anxiety faded. I crossed to the window, pushed back the curtains and looked out down the drive into Avenue Road. It was a still, black, fog-wrapped night. I studied the shapes of the trees carefully, comparing each with my memory of what was normal until I was as certain as I could be that nobody, Quinn or anyone else, was lurking near the house.

I drank another Scotch and imagined my reunion to come with Constance: how I would break the news to her, how I would be both more merciful and more masterful than I had ever been. It would not be long now, not long before she saw me in my true light.

Feeling a return of the earlier drowsiness, I stepped out on to the landing and looked down the passage towards the guest room. The door was ajar, but the only light from within was the flickering glow of the fire. I moved towards it, telling myself that a concern for Miss Rossiter's comfort was my only motive.

She was asleep on the bed. I had only to push the door open an inch or so to see her head on the pillows. She had loosened the high collar of her dress and let down her hair from the bun in which it had been tied. Its rich tresses, intensely black against the white counterpane, reached almost to her waist.

I stepped into the doorway and looked at her, at the imperious eyes, closed now but still seeming to command me behind their pale lids, at the full-lipped half-smiling mouth, the faintly jutting chin, the pulse of an artery in her exposed neck, the rise and fall of her bosom beneath the dress, the barely perceptible movement of the petals of her corsage, minutely stirred by the rhythm of her breathing. In that moment, forgetful that I would soon no longer be alone with her, I felt the first rush of a terrible longing. To run my fingers through her hair, to kiss her soft lips, to touch. . . .

I was in the passage again, the door of the guest room closed behind me. I was panting, sweating, grappling to comprehend what I had so nearly done. The monstrous folly even to have thought of it stood compounded by the ease with which I might have succumbed. Within hours, I was to be reunited with my wife. What was I dreaming of? Miss Rossiter had come to me for help, and this is how I had rewarded her.

215

I stumbled back to the study, poured myself another Scotch and swallowed it in two gulps. Calm seemed instantly restored. With Miss Rossiter out of sight, I could dismiss what I had felt as a momentary aberration. I went to the window and looked out once more. All was quiet. I checked the escritoire. It was securely locked.

As I turned back towards the centre of the room, my head swam. I had drunk too much, I was over-tired. Whatever the cause, I felt overwhelmingly heavy of limb and thought. I pulled out my watch. It was nearly nine o'clock, the time when Thompson would be waiting for me at the Lamb and Flag. Or was it so late? The hands and the figures of the watch-face were so blurred when I looked at them that I could be sure of nothing, save that Thompson would wait in vain.

I moved unsteadily to the chaise longue and flung myself down on it. A little rest, I told myself, was all I needed. I would be awake and refreshed long before Constance arrived. But I cannot pretend that my last waking thought was of my wife. It was, in truth, of Melanie Rossiter. It seemed, for an instant, that her face was before me, as it had been when I had watched her sleeping in the guest room. Yet now she was no longer asleep, for her eyes were suddenly open, wide and dark and fathomless, and looking straight at me.

V

Emily Sumner had lodged for the night in a temperance hotel near Charing Cross regularly patronized by the Dean's wife when attending committee meetings of her charity for fallen women of the East End. Whether the Dean's wife would have approved of Emily's mission to the capital is doubtful, but it would certainly not have escaped her attention that Emily had returned to the hotel that evening in a state of unladylike agitation, nor that she had been heard talking to herself in the residents' lounge before retiring to her room with a quite unreasonable request that dinner be served to her there, rather than in the dining-room. In the circumstances, it was as well for Emily's reputation that the Dean's wife was ensconced at the Deanery in Salisbury, blissfully unaware that not one but both of the Sumner sisters had deserted the close.

When there came a knock at the door shortly after nine o'clock that evening, Emily assumed it was the maid, come to collect the dinner-tray. But when she opened the door, tray held ready in her arms, it was to find her sister Constance standing breathless on the threshold.

'Constance!' she exclaimed. 'I never thought—'

'Neither did I. May I come in?'

'Of course, of course.' She set down the tray and ushered her sister in. 'Close the door. Virtually every resident seems to be a friend of the Dean's wife, or at any rate her informant.'

Normally, such a remark would have raised a smile between them, but it was neither said nor greeted humorously.

'I received this telegram from William,' said Constance gravely, handing Emily the crumpled message. 'It left me no choice but to come at once.'

'So I see. But this. . . . It makes no. . . .'

'What is it?'

'William interrupted James's testimony in court today. He accused him of lying. In the end, the judge had to have him removed.'

Constance looked away. 'As I feared. They are at each other's throat.'

'No!' Emily touched her sister's shoulder. 'James did not react at all. He behaved impeccably throughout.'

'Tell me what happened,' Constance replied, facing her once more. 'I must know everything.'

Emily was moved to tears before she had completed her account of the day's proceedings. For her and her sister, Norton's refusal to speak ill of his dead father was obvious evidence that he was indeed the stubbornly loyal son he claimed to be. For them, his refusal to answer Giffard's crucial question was proof they scarcely needed of his nobility and sincerity – above all, of his enduring love for Constance. Without knowing it, he had chosen the one route by which he might still win her, the one route which also ensured the forfeit of his claim.

When Emily had finished, and was drying the last of her tears, Constance, who had remained silent and expressionless throughout, put her hand to the coffee-pot on the dinner-tray and, finding it still warm, poured some for both of them. Only when they had drained the shared cup of black reviving liquid did she speak.

'Do you know what I most loved in James? Do you know what it is that I still love in him?'

'He is a dear good man, Constance.'

'Yes. And so, by his lights, is William. But James, you see, has an inner strength that sets him apart. When he first told me that he was leaving and that our wedding could not take place, I tried every way I could imagine to dissuade him, even. . . . Well, no doubt you can guess the extremity I was driven to. But he was not to be swayed. He could not be tempted. I know now why he felt he had to leave, why he could not, for any sake, marry me: but to have carried through his purpose, to have resisted the need he must have felt to confide in somebody, to have turned his back on the world he knew, to have exiled himself so that his father's shame might remain hidden: that is true courage, that is true goodness.'

'He is still . . . hiding his father's shame.'

'And is prepared to lose this case for the sake of it. I cannot understand what his family are thinking of.'

'Themselves,' said Emily bitterly.

'Yes. I fear it is so.'

'What are we to do, then?'

Constance rose, as if the decision had already been made. 'William would not have made that exhibition of himself in court if he'd had the proof he spoke of in the telegram. It was dispatched at two o'clock this afternoon. When did you say he was removed from Lincoln's Inn?'

'It must have been shortly after noon.'

'So either he came upon the proof in the space of two short hours or. . . .'

'Or what?' Emily could tell by the determined line of her sister's mouth that she favoured the alternative.

'Or his claim to have such proof is as irrational as his outburst in court. I blame myself for leaving him alone these past weeks, alone to brood on his resentments. He has not James's strength of mind, Emily. There's no telling what he may have been reduced to. Come: we must see him at once.'

'You wish me to accompany you?'

'If you will.'

'But he'll be expecting you to be alone.'

'Since William claims to have proof, he cannot complain if I choose to bring a witness.'

Emily was so flattered at being asked to accompany her sister that she scarcely considered what awaited them at The Limes. Constance, however, was already debating in her mind whether William's proof was merely a forgivable device to lure her home or a contemptible bid to add his voice to those already denouncing the man she had secretly loved all her adult life. Whilst Emily busied herself with bonnet and muffler, Constance reconciled herself to facing at last the unthinkable choice between her lawful husband and the only man she had ever truly wanted to marry.

VI

I was lying on the chaise longue, the furniture of the room, its very walls, blurring and shifting around me. I was panting desperately, straining for breath, my heart pounding. My hands, with which I twitched feebly at my collar, were awash with perspiration. Above me, in the very cornicing of the ceiling, plaster serpents uncoiled and hissed their grey probing tongues.

I pulled myself into a sitting position and hung my head, listening to

218

the rasping quest of my throat for air. There were dragons woven in the pattern of the carpet. They had always been there. Yet now they were moving, massing, marching, leering up at me. I dragged my head upright. On the other side of the room, the oil-lamp on my desk pulsed with a golden unnatural energy. Its light was dazzling, its heat tangible.

There came a tapping at the door, scarcely audible yet persistent. When I rose to answer it, my weakness vanished, all its symptoms of a disabling fever transmuted into a certainty of mental and physical strength. I strode to the door and turned the handle. But it was locked. I turned it again and again, to no avail.

The tapping continued, its volume unaltered. 'Who's there?' I shouted. The force of my voice shocked me. It seemed to echo within the confines of the room, bouncing back at me from walls and ceiling and floor. Only when it had faded into absolute silence did I hear the answer, in tones as soft and insistent as the knocking that had gone before.

'Melanie. I've come as you asked.'

I stooped close to the frame and whispered my reply. 'I didn't ask you. Why have you come?'

'Because you wanted me to.'

'No. Go back. Leave me alone.'

'But you wanted me.'

'No, I tell you. No.'

Something akin to a stifled sob reached my ears, then a rustle of fabric.

'Melanie?'

There was no answer. Suddenly I regretted what I had said, regretted it with the ferocity of an immense and sickening remorse. I dropped to my knees and peered through the key-hole. There she was, retreating along the passage, her long dark hair flowing over a white shift. I heard myself shouting her name: 'Melanie! Melanie!' She stopped and turned slowly round. 'Come back! Please come back!' She smiled and ran towards me.

I was on my feet, grappling with the handle. But still it would not yield. I heard her rattling it from the other side, then her voice, raised in distress. 'You said you would let me in.'

'I can't. It's locked.'

'You have the key. You could open it . . . if you truly wanted me.'

Of course. The key. I had it all along. I reached into my waistcoat pocket and drew it out, then stared at the crazily magnified angles and notches of its patterns, stared and tried to comprehend what deception they represented.

'What are you waiting for?'

'There's something wrong. This isn't the right key.'

219

'Of course it is.'

'No. It's . . . for something else. I can't remember what, but. . . .'

'Try it.'

'No. I mustn't. I know I mustn't.'

'Do you want me, William? Do you truly want me?'

'Yes, but—'

'Then, open the door.'

I slipped the key into the lock. It was a perfect fit. I heard the lock slide back as I turned it. Then I pulled the door open, creaking on its hinges.

She had gone. The passage was empty. It was not possible in the time it had taken me to open the door, yet, nevertheless, she had vanished. I felt sick and nervous, inexplicably ashamed. I leaned against the wall as a numbing weakness washed over me and my head whirled.

Then I saw, at the end of the passage, beckoning light in an open doorway. When I moved towards it, my feebleness dropped from me like a mantle. I strode forward, laughing and enjoying the sound of my laughter as it echoed in the fabric of the building. I reached the doorway.

Melanie was standing by the fire, brushing her hair, drawing out the long luxuriant strands of it, then letting each lock fall back to rest against her shoulders. The warm flickering firelight shone through the thin white cloth of her shift, showing me, by the inviting mobile curves it painted, that she was naked beneath.

'Where is he, William?' she said softly.

'Who? Who do you mean?'

'You know who I mean.'

I entered the room and walked to the window, uncurtained against the night. Rain was spitting against the black glass, a sound like her knocking at the door, against glass as raven-dark as her hair.

'Where is he, William?' she said from behind me.

I looked out of the window, down into the driveway at the front of the house. There, at the far end, where the drive met the road, was Thompson. I knew him by the stump of his amputated right arm, close-clad though he was against the beating rain.

'Where is he, William?'

I looked back at her. She had removed the shift. She let me watch the firm pale movements of her body as she took a glass from the mantelpiece and drained it at one gulp. Then she turned to look at me, smiled faintly, shook her head so that her hair shimmered and stirred against her bare shoulders, and said once more: 'Where is he?'

I wrenched my head back to the window. Thompson had advanced a pace and was standing by the right-hand gate-pillar. He was looking up towards me, angling his head as if uncertain of what he saw.

'You must tell me where he is, William.'

220

She was standing by the bed now, facing me in the full glow of an oil-lamp, her pale flesh warmed by its golden light to ripe beguiling perfection. A single red rose stood in a vase on the bedside table. She plucked it from the water and held it against her lips whilst beads of moisture from its stem and petals sprayed across her breasts.

'Where is he, William?' she said breathlessly. 'You know you have to tell me.'

The question had become the only issue between us. If I told her what she wanted, her body would be my reward. I turned once more to the window and saw Thompson's rain-lashed figure in the drive, peering up at me. He raised his left arm in recognition, and I heard myself saying: 'He's there. He's there, waiting for me.' Then a black shape, blacker than the night, moved from its hiding-place behind the pillar of the gate, raised itself above Thompson and, swooping down, engulfed him.

'You had to tell me, William. You know you had to tell me.'

In that moment, I hated her. She had lain on the bed and drawn the sheet up about her, her pale mocking face turned to the pillow, the halo of black hair spread out across the white fabric.

I walked unsteadily towards her. She turned to look at me. 'You may punish me now you've told me,' she murmured. 'If you wish.'

I reached down, tore back the sheet and raised my hand to strike her, then froze in mid-movement. She lay prone and spreadeagled, her wrists and ankles fastened by thick cords to each bed-post. She lay naked, bound and at my mercy.

'You may do,' she whispered, 'whatever you wish.'

I moved to the end of the bed and looked down at her, at her slender ankles chafed by the rope, at the stretched muscles of her calves and thighs, at the parted humps of her buttocks, at the endless black tresses of her hair reaching down her back, at her face, half-turned towards me, and at the smile I could see, flickering on her lips.

'Whatever you wish.'

Suddenly, I, too, was naked, crouching on the bed above her, aroused beyond my power to imagine. As I plunged into her, she screamed. And as she screamed there came another voice, raised in a shriek of agony. It was Thompson, crying for help out in the darkness while I thrust into the black-haired creature of his betrayal, Thompson's and the night's collective screech of withering scorn for what I had done. The vase toppled over and smashed on the bedside table. When I looked towards it, I saw that the rose had vanished and the tide of spilt water advancing towards me was the colour of blood. Then I, too, screamed – and woke.

The ringing was not in my head. It was the doorbell. It had been ringing, I knew, for a long time. There was Cook at last. I could hear her plodding up from the basement, complaining as she went.

I sat up in the bed. What was I doing there? The jolt of a searing headache hit me. Then I looked round and saw Melanie Rossiter, naked and asleep beside me.

There were voices in the hall below. 'I'm expected, Cook. Didn't you know? Where's Hillier?' It was Constance. 'Where's my husband?'

I was in the guest room. The fire had nearly extinguished itself, but the gaslight reaching in from the passage sufficed to show me where I was – and who was there with me. The dream, all its contents in unearthly focus, whirled before me. I looked down at Miss Rossiter and shook her by the shoulder. She moaned but did not stir. Her right arm was flung out across the sheet, but her wrist, which I had seen rubbed raw by the ropes that bound her, was unmarked.

'He must be in his study. We saw the light was on. I'll go up to him.'

I flung myself from the bed and cast about for my clothes. They were not there. I must have left them in the study. All I could find was my dressing-gown, discarded at the foot of the bed. I scrambled into it and lunged towards the door.

It was too late. Already, I could hear Constance's footsteps on the stairs. A board creaked beneath me as I stepped into the passage, and there was Constance, nearly at the top of the stairs, turning towards me and frowning at what she saw.

'William? Why didn't you wait up for me? Didn't you get my telegram? What are you doing in the guest-room?'

She reached the landing and moved along the passage, narrowing her gaze as she approached. I could not move, I could not speak. My mouth opened, but no words came.

'William!' she said. 'What's the matter with you?'

As she neared the doorway, Melanie Rossiter's voice came from the room behind me. At all events, part of it was her voice as I knew it, but part also an expert degraded, ill-bred parody. 'Where you gawn, sir? Won't you come back to bed?'

Constance stopped in her tracks and stared at me. 'Who's that?' she said. 'Who's in there?'

'It's cold 'ere on me own,' Miss Rossiter called. 'Won't you come an' keep a girl warm?'

Constance brushed past me and pushed the door wide open. What she saw was Melanie Rossiter with the covers flung back to her waist, stretching and yawning in the bed, then blinking at the sudden intrusion of light.

At last, I found my voice. 'I . . . I can explain. It's not. . . .'

Constance glared icily back at me. 'Get her out of this house.'

'It's not what it seems. In God's name, believe me.'

She looked me up and down, then glanced into the room, where Miss Rossiter had turned casually to avoid the light. 'How can I believe you? You knew I was coming. You asked me to come. You promised proof.

What is this proof of?' She was quivering from head to toe with the effort of restraining herself.

'Wait,' I said. 'There is proof. Yes. That'll show you the truth of the matter.' I turned and raced along the passage, knowing that, if I could make her read Miss Rossiter's statement, there was some faint hope I might yet persuade her that all was not as it seemed.

I threw the door of the study open and stumbled in. There were my clothes, draped across the chaise longue. Tugging my waistcoat out from the rest, I found the key in its pocket, then lurched across to the escritoire, fumbled with the lock, opened it at the third attempt, reached in and pulled out the envelope from where I had left it.

'Here!' I shouted. 'Here it is!'

Constance was standing in the doorway. I ran back to her and thrust the envelope into her hands. She stared at me uncomprehendingly. 'What is this?'

'Her statement. Hers.' I pointed towards the guest room. 'This is some mad pretence. She's not what she seems. This statement proves it.'

For a moment, Constance hesitated. Then she slid one finger along the seal of the envelope and opened the flap. I watched her face intently as she drew out the contents, hoping against hope to catch some glimmer of a favourable reaction. But all I saw was a squirm of distaste. There had been no time for her to read anything, but, in her expression there was a look of such revulsion and contempt as I had never seen before. My eyes moved to what she held in her hands: not pages filled with Miss Rossiter's neat script, but a batch of photographs. I snatched them from her grasp.

They were all of Melanie, posing nude in some studio disguised as a bedroom. In the first photograph, she stood by a dressing-table, brushing her hair, her head turned away from the camera. In the second, she lay on a pillowed coverlet, sipping from a champagne-glass, the lens trained closely on the pale curves and creases of her proffered flesh. In the third, she was standing, pictured from the waist up, smiling coquettishly and holding a rose in the cleft between her round dark-nippled breasts. In all of them, she had contrived to combine self-possession and blatancy in a way that only seemed to heighten her wantonness.

'Is that the whore?' said Constance slowly.

I looked at the fourth photograph. In it, Melanie lay prone on a bed, her arms and legs stretched wide and roped to the bed-posts. The position of the camera, behind and above her to one side, was instantly familiar to me, as was the glimpse of her face, framed by the dark locks of her hair, turned from the pillow to look back and project from the picture her mocking smile of carnal complicity.

'Is that the whore?' Constance repeated.

I could not answer her. Speech was beyond me. I could only stare in disbelief at what I held in my hands. I could only gape in horror at its final proof that she had destroyed me.

The door of the guest room slammed down the passage. Melanie Rossiter, fully dressed but with her hair still flowing to her waist, strode towards us. Constance's back was turned to her, so she could not see, as I could, the hint of irony in her face.

'Sorry if I've landed you in it, sir,' she said. 'You should'a told me your missus was due back. Don't worry: I'll go quietly. We'll say no more abaht the fee. Keep the pictures as a memento.' She paused at the top of the stairs and let me see in her eyes the relish of the huntress who has slain her quarry. ' 'Ope you enjoyed me,' she added with a smile. Then she turned and began her descent without a backward glance.

My eyes swivelled back to Constance, but found in her face only a depth of loathing I could never hope to erase.

'How could you?' she said at last. 'How could you do this to me?'

My ruin was complete. There was nothing I could say or do to make her think me innocent, nothing to appease or exonerate. All I could do was step back, close the door against her unanswerable accusations and turn the key in the lock.

I pressed my forehead against the cool forbearing wood and felt the tears course down my cheeks. This, I knew, was the end.

VII

Harvey Thompson had been sitting at the end of the Lamb and Flag's crowded bar for an hour, swapping lewd jokes with the barmaid, and had finally despaired of collecting the other sixteen pounds of his bargain with Trenchard. Indeed, he was about to leave when a hard-faced man in a shabby overcoat moved on to the stool next to his and offered gruffly to buy him a drink.

'No, thanks, old man. Must be on me—'

'I'm told you're owed sixteen quid.'

Thompson turned and looked at the newcomer: stockily built, dark hat pulled well down over grey craggy features, short powerful fingers holding the money for his drink. 'Well, since you mention it. . . .'

'I'm from Trenchard. He couldn't get here himself, so he sent me. What'll you have?'

'Me usual, thanks. Maisie knows what it is.'

The barmaid came and served them, raising her eyebrows to Thompson at sight of his unsmiling companion.

When they were alone again, Thompson said: 'I didn't expect a . . . substitute.'

'Why should you care, as long as you're paid?'

'Why indeed? Shall we sit down?'

They moved to a table in a smoky confidential corner. There was something flinty and threatening in the man's gaze that disturbed Thompson. Already, the bargain was beginning to lose its appeal.

'Sixteen was the balance,' he said uncertainly. 'But I'm not sure—'

'Who do you say he is, then?'

'Sorry, old man?'

'Norton. You told Trenchard you knew his true identity. There's the money.' He laid three five-pound notes on the table and weighed them down with a sovereign. 'So let's have it. Who do you think he is?'

'Let's not rush it, old man.'

'Why not? What are you waiting for?'

'Nothin'. It's just that. . . . ' He looked at the stranger's grim unyielding face and did not like what he saw. 'What did you say your name was?'

'I didn't. Does it matter?'

'Suppose not.'

'Well then?'

Thompson's instincts told him to refuse the money, but his creditors were pressing. He could not afford to obey his instincts. He reached towards the piled notes. 'You can tell Trenchard me hunch: Norton's Gerry Davenall's son, all right, but not—'

Suddenly, his questing hand was seized in a vice-like grip. The sovereign gouged painfully into his fingers as they were squeezed in the stranger's ferocious hold. 'Selling information is always a risky business, Thompson. Selling it twice is foolish. Miss Whitaker paid you well to hold your tongue. Didn't she?'

'Yes, dammit, but—'

'I'd like you to come outside with me now. Then we can settle this once and for all.'

'I'd rather not, old man.'

'You'll do as I say.'

But Thompson did not have to. The stranger relaxed his grip just enough to allow him an advantage. Denied a right arm to share the load, his left had grown, over the years, abnormally strong. Now, in one wrenching, twisting movement, he had freed himself and pinioned the other man's forearm to the table. 'I'm known here, old man. You aren't. If I say the word, you'll be leavin' on a pole. Take me meanin'?'

The stranger slowly slid his arm clear of the table, then wiped the palm against his coat. He stared at Thompson, but said nothing, just gathered his money, turned on his heel and walked from the pub.

Pocketing the sovereign still held between his fingers, Thompson picked up his drink and returned to the bar, where he ordered a refill and adjusted his whiskers in the mirror behind the spirit-bottles. 'Nasty piece o' work, 'e looked,' Maisie remarked.

Thompson grinned and suppressed the elation he felt at worsting his opponent. The encounter had raised in his mind complexities too great for him to comprehend. It was six months or more since that enigmatical slip of a girl had approached him. True, he had let her think she had bought his silence, but it was unreasonable for her to think it could be bought permanently and distinctly unpleasant then to set some gimlet-eyed bruiser on him. Besides, how the deuce had they come to know of his negotiations with Trenchard? It made no sense. He had hoped to make capital out of this lawsuit. Now he thought he had better abandon it. Perhaps six pounds was enough. At least it would keep his landlady at bay. If, that is, she ever saw it. He lit a cigar and plucked the sovereign from his pocket, debating how best to use it. Then he caught Maisie's eye and ordered another drink. When she handed him the change, he separated a florin from the other coins, signalled her to lean forward and slipped it into her generous cleavage, laughing as he did so. 'The Davenalls can go hang, Maisie, that's what I say. What the devil do I care, eh? What the devil?' But his words were wasted. Above the screeching from Maisie that accompanied her retrieval of the florin, nobody heard him.

VIII

I was still on my knees at the foot of the door when I remembered Thompson. How much had been dream and how much reality I could not tell, but his part of it could not be erased. She had bewitched me, by means unknown, not simply to disgrace me in Constance's eyes, but for some reason involving Thompson. Her repeated question, 'Where is he?' held a force and a purpose reaching beyond the confines of my entrapment. I remembered the bitter scarifying sense of betrayal with which my answer had left me and then I knew, with a certainty seared into my mind, that he was in danger, in danger because he knew the truth.

I scrambled into my clothes with desperate haste. Suddenly, there was no time to be lost. I pulled out my watch: it was nearly eleven o'clock. How long since I had fallen asleep on the chaise longue? How long since I had slipped unawares into the distorted realm she had shaped for me? Two hours? Or more? I could not be sure. I crossed to the escritoire, opened the right-hand drawer and stared down at the contents: a single-barrelled pistol and a box of ammunition. I kept the gun in the house at my father's insistence, for protection against burglars. Now, in a sense, the burglars had arrived. I thrust the pistol into one of my pockets, the box of ammunition into another. Then I hurried to the door, opened it and stepped out on to the landing.

As I padded down the stairs, I could hear voices in the drawing-room, the hushed intense voices of Constance and her sister. There was nothing to be gained, I knew, by telling them I was leaving. They would know soon enough. In the circumstances, the hideous unspeakable circumstances, they might even expect it. I opened the hall cupboard and took out my hat and overcoat, then crept stealthily to the door.

Outside, the fog had lifted. I stood on the threshold, letting the cold night air goad my senses to life. It was vital I should not think about what had happened, vital I should retain some measure of self-control for a little longer yet. Wait: what was this? Drops of rain against my face. I stretched out my arm and watched as the beads of water gathered in my gloved palm to confirm the fact. It was raining, as it had rained in my dream, as if. . . .

I turned to close the door behind me and saw, at the end of the hall, the drawing-room door open and Constance look out. She was, I think, too dismayed by what met her eyes to let me see what she felt. I, for my part, was too distracted to express any of the remorse even then ravening within me. I slammed the door and ran headlong down the drive.

IX

Emily watched anxiously as Constance returned to the room, her mouth sagging open, her red-rimmed eyes staring, her throat straining to swallow whatever words she might have said.

'What is it, my dear?'

'He's gone. He just . . . walked out. Without so much as. . . .' Then the tears she had so far resisted overwhelmed her and strength deserted her limbs, so that Emily had to help her to a chair and press a handkerchief into her grasp.

'You must tell me what's happened, Constance. That woman, was she really—?'

'A whore? I think so. I truly think so. Her eyes were so . . . so hard and bitter. It was almost as if . . . as if it amused her to be caught out.'

'I . . . I don't understand.'

'Nor I. There was no need to do such a thing. I asked him why he had and he simply slammed the door in my face.'

'But . . . he asked you to come.'

'Yes. He asked me. He wanted me, it seems, to witness this. I thought I knew him, Emily, his vices and his virtues. But this! Never in my wildest imaginings would I have thought. . . . Never.' She shook her head vehemently. 'I'm sorry you should have had to suffer it with me.'

'I'm only glad to be able to offer what comfort I can.'

Constance kissed her sister on the forehead. 'Thank you, Emily,

227

thank you. Such a day – such a night – as this I never thought to see.'
Her voice thickened. 'When James returned, I believed I was acting for
the best. Was it so wrong of me to leave William? Did I drive him to
this?'

'No. A thousand times no.'

'Then, what did?'

'Only he can answer that.'

'But he won't. He won't so much as speak to me.' She buried her
head in her hands and sobbed convulsively. Emily put her arm round
her shoulders and rocked her in a way she had not done since, as a girl
of twelve, she had been charged by their mother to do what she could
to console her seven-year-old sister for the pain of an emergent tooth.

They sat thus, with Constance no longer weeping but still cradled in
Emily's arms, for fully five minutes, until there was a tap at the door
and Cook bustled in with the coffee she had been bidden to prepare.

'Glad to see that baggage 'as been sent packin',' she volunteered as
she set down the tray. 'Reckon she was no better 'n—'

'Thank you, that will be all,' Constance said with sudden firmness.

Emitting only a token grunt of resentment, Cook took her leave.
But, as Emily could see, her sister's self-control had not been assumed
for the servant's benefit. When they were once more alone, she wiped
away the last of her tears and spoke in determined tones.

'There is nothing I can do for William after this. His behaviour
places him beyond my reach and me beyond his.'

'What do you mean?'

'I mean, Emily, that my husband has betrayed me and can no
longer expect me to obey him. He has forfeited my allegiance and
surrendered it to another, to a man worthier of it than he can ever be.'

'To James?'

'Yes. James is prepared to forgo what is rightfully his, to forgo his
very identity, because he feels unable to come between me and my
husband. But that objection ceases to exist as of this night. Henceforth, I will do everything in my power to assist him.'

Emily stared at Constance in silent admiration. The details of William's offence had been withheld from her, though they could not have
exceeded those which she had imagined on seeing the woman in question. The incident, in fact, and William's earlier behaviour in court, were
all of a piece in her picture of him as a weak and wilful man quite
unworthy to be the husband of her sister. Now Constance, too, appeared
to see him in that light and to have decided at last where her loyalty – and
her love – truly lay. Naturally, Emily was shocked by the turn of events:
naturally, she was dismayed. But, naturally also, she thought of James,
noble, handsome, misjudged, maltreated James, left till now to stand
alone against the world. And when she did so the new conviction, the
rediscovered strength, in her sister's eyes gave her cause for joyous hope.

X

The cab dropped me in Long Acre, and I followed the driver's directions to the Lamb and Flag. It was the worst of times to arrive: all the taverns and drinking-dens of Covent Garden were discharging their fuddled patrons on to the streets. Beneath lamp-posts, men pursued bar-rail differences in loud slurred voices. In gutters, drunks who had tripped on the pavement's edge hauled themselves upright, cursing mankind. In dark alleyways, prostitutes struck terms with addled clients.

In the Lamb and Flag, the landlord and two broken-nosed assistants were persuading their last customers that it was time to leave. Of Thompson there was no sign. Behind the bar, a girl was washing her way through stacks of empty tankards. When I approached, she said, without looking up: 'We're closed.'

'I was due to meet somebody here earlier. Perhaps you know him.'

'Doubt it.'

'His name's Thompson. He's lost an arm, so—'

A smile suddenly crossed her face, 'Oh, Cap'n 'Arvey! 'Course I knows 'im. 'E is popler t' night.'

'What do you mean?'

'You're the second bloke bin lookin' for 'im. 'E sent the other one packin'.'

'Thompson has been here, then?'

'Only jus' left. You must'a precious near passed 'im on the doorstep.'

'Which way did he go?'

'Lives Lambeth way, far as I know. Reckon 'e'll be makin' for Waterloo Bridge.'

I hurried into the street. If the barmaid was right, I might yet overhaul him. But, as soon as I struck out, I realized my difficulty. He might have taken any one of a dozen routes to the bridge. At the very first junction, I came to a halt, undecided which way to turn.

Then, as I peered down the narrow street to my left, I thought I saw him. A drunkard and his whore were approaching me, clutching each other as they staggered and swayed along the pavement. But surely . . . yes: beyond them, a one-armed man was flitting silently between the gas-lamps. I was about to shout after him when, suddenly, he vanished. He passed into the shadow between two lamps and did not emerge. Then another figure, whom I had noticed before, did the same. With a jolt of fear, I remembered that I might not be the only one looking for Thompson. I ran towards the space which had consumed them, my footfalls bouncing back at me from the shuttered buildings to right and left.

It was the entrance to a narrow alley. At its far end, I could see the glass roofs of Covent Garden Market. In the alley itself, empty crates and baskets stood in disordered stacks. And there was Thompson, threading his way along the straggling path between them.

'Thompson!'

He stopped and turned round. 'Who's there?' he demanded.

'It's me: Trenchard.' I began to walk towards him.

He raised his arm in recognition. 'Thought you weren't goin' to show up, old man.'

I was running headlong then, frantic to prove I had not foreseen what was about to occur. His hand was still raised, his face creased by a frown of puzzlement. He had started to walk back along the alley, he had passed a doorway to his left, he was no more that twenty yards from me.

It happened so fast I could not even shout a warning. Yet it seemed to happen also with a dreadful dream-like slowness. A man stepped from the shelter of the doorway, little more than a solid shadow in the darkness. In one swooping movement, he swept his left arm across Thompson's throat and, with his right, struck a blow into his back. I heard a gurgling strangled cry. Thompson's eyes widened in a sudden awareness of pain. His hand reached up, too late and too feebly, to pull his assailant off. Then his knees buckled and he pitched to the ground.

I had stopped in my tracks and stood now, looking at Thompson's attacker, a squat, crouching, muscular figure, his breath clouding in the cold moist air, a knife held before him, glinting in a shaft of lamplight. I had seen his grey pitiless face before and recognized him now beyond question, as he must have recognized me.

How long we stood there, staring at each other over Thompson's crumpled body, I cannot say. For me, the instant seemed as measureless as the dream that had gone before it. It only ended when, with one parting rake of his eyes, Quinn turned and retreated into the darkness.

At that moment, I remembered the gun. I reached into my coat and grasped its butt. Then I remembered also that it was not loaded. Quinn had reached the end of the alley by now. I saw him turn into the square beyond, glance back over his shoulder, then vanish from sight. He was gone – and I was powerless to pursue him.

Thompson was lying face down, a dark patch of blood seeping through his coat. When I pulled him on to his side, he looked up through bleary flickering eyes and spat some of the cobble-grit from his mouth to speak.

'Why . . . why d'you send him after me . . . old man?'

I stooped closer, to make sure he could hear me. 'I sent nobody, Thompson. Believe me.'

His voice was hoarse and faltering, all its cock-of-the-walk vigour drained by a knife in the dark. 'Makes no difference . . . who sent him . . . He's done for me. . . . Funny, ain't it?' He grinned through clenched teeth.

'What is?'

'Gerry's . . . finished me off . . . in the end . . . Him . . . or his damned secret.'

I leaned closer still, willing him to live long enough to tell me. 'What is his secret, Thompson? What is it?'

'Wouldn't you . . . like to know?' He winced, squeezing his eyes shut to ward off the pain. When he opened them again, they were filmier than before, focusing weakly on me and the world they were seeing for the last time.

'Tell me. For God's sake, tell me.'

'No cause to worry . . . old man.' I was losing him now, watching him surrender his grip on life, hearing him bid his adieus in stray mumbled words that had no meaning. 'Bit of a joke, what? Bit of a bad God-awful joke. . . . Take it. . . . Take it back, Gerry. . . . We all . . . all make mistakes. . . .'

'Thompson?'

'Go ahead . . . I'm ready. . . .'

I heard the last breath gasp out of him and felt his body sag into oblivion. I closed his staring sightless eyes and lowered his head gently to the ground. He was dead and I, in all but name, had killed him. His blood, staining black the rivulets of rainwater that coursed between the cobblestones, reached its jagged fingers through the filth and fruit-mush of the alley to twitch and clutch at the circle of my guilt.

I stood up. My left hand, with which I had supported his neck, was smeared with blood. Instinctively, I closed my eyes to spare myself the sight of it. But, as I did so, another vision leaped from its hiding-place, another accusation found its voice.

'You may punish me now you've told me.' Her black hair, her pale flesh, her body beneath me on the bed. 'You may do whatever you wish.' I beat my hand against the rain-damp brickwork of the alley wall. 'Whatever you wish.' But all I wished was what I could not have: a dream retrieved, a betrayal rescinded, a temptation resisted.

Harvey Thompson lay dead at my feet, murdered to seal for ever his forty-year-old secret. I looked down at him and wept for the all the evil I had not intended and might not yet avert. There was nothing I could do for him, even in death. The barmaid would say I had come looking for him; the police would take me for his killer.

I pulled some sacking from one of the empty baskets nearby and draped it over him, not to conceal his body but to afford him the only kind of comfort I could. Then I walked away and left him to be found by another.

In the Piazza, the first of the stallholders' carts was arriving. Within a few hours, the Market would be clogged with people and horses, stacked high with barrowloads of produce. Sooner or later, somebody would venture down the alley and discover what lay beneath the sacking. I hurried to the other side of the square and headed south, towards the home Thompson had never reached, towards the river where Norton's conspiracy had found its dark beginning, towards whatever way I might yet find to avenge myself and an old soldier whose blood was on my hands.

231

ELEVEN

I

Richard Davenall sat where duty required him to be, near the front of the court, as the second day of the *Norton versus Davenall* hearing opened at Lincoln's Inn. Nobody could have told from his hunched attentive posture that he was seriously contemplating a course of action which might decide the case more effectively than any legal argument so far presented.

For Richard Davenall was labouring under a burden which no lawyer can support: a call upon his conscience. He faced a stark choice forced upon him by all the flaws of character and failures of nerve which comprised his life. But in the motionless torment of his face there had been reflected so far only an agony of indecision.

Small wonder that Richard could not concentrate on the examination by Dr Russell of the plaintiff's next witness, Dr Duncan Fiveash. The voices of the two men, Fiveash gruff and professional, Russell lilting and interrogative, reached him as if from a great distance. Although he knew the tactical subtleties which lay behind their exchanges, the Doctor's testimony seemed to him almost insignificant, a mere interlude between the vitality of what had gone before and the decisiveness of what would follow. For nearly an hour, while Fiveash discoursed on the characteristics of syphilis and Russell obliged him, time and again, to confirm Norton's account, Richard sat in silent witness to a charade: in all he said, Fiveash never once suggested how James Davenall might have contracted the disease, for the simple reason that Russell never once asked him to do so. Richard wondered how much this most eminent of barristers really knew of his client's case. Was he, perhaps, as much a victim of evasion as its practitioner?

At length, Sir Hardinge Giffard commenced his cross-examination, and the tone of the proceedings altered. There was something blunt and uncompromising about his questions. Russell's dexterity was all very well, they implied, but it was time to come to the heart of the matter.

'How long was the late James Davenall your patient, Doctor?'

'From birth.'

'You were well acquainted with him, then?'

'Yes.'

'Better acquainted than had you known him merely on a social footing?'

'Of course. The relationship between a doctor and his patient is necessarily intimate.'

'You would expect to recognize him without difficulty?'

'Naturally.'

'When you look at the plaintiff, do you recognize him as the late James Davenall?'

'No.'

'When he visited your surgery on the twenty-sixth of September this year, did you have an opportunity to examine him?'

'I did.'

'Did that examination lead you to believe that he was the late James Davenall?'

'No, it did not.'

'In short, then, Doctor, what is your professional opinion as to the likelihood that the plaintiff is your former patient of more than twenty years' standing?'

'My professional opinion, and my personal belief, is that he is not.'

'Thank you, Doctor.'

Richard winced at the clinical efficiency with which Giffard had gone about his business. He had inflicted another wound where there were already too many for comfort. Strive as he might by supplementary questioning to emphasize that only James Davenall could know as much as Norton knew, Russell was helpless to repair the damage done, and a strangled note in his voice seemed to confirm that he knew as much. Richard began to feel sorry for him and sorrier still for himself.

Not that he believed Russell would be found wanting where stamina was concerned: the top barristers seldom were. Sure enough, the next witness brought out the best in him. Miss Esme Pursglove, combining vigour and frailty in her finest tea-time style, inspired in Russell an avuncular fluency that progressively restored his confidence. She, after all, had known James Davenall quite as long as Dr Fiveash and, in her opinion, a good deal better. She was prepared to support Norton's claim just as dogmatically as Fiveash was prepared to deny it. She, in short, was in no doubt. Until, that is, Sir Hardinge Giffard began to cross-examine her.

'How old are you, Miss Pursglove?'

'I beg your pardon?' She had not heard him. It was understandable, considering how softly he had spoken, but Richard recognized the success of a simple ploy.

'I'm sorry. Are you a little hard of hearing?'

This time Miss Pursglove did hear the question. Her reply was indignant. 'Certainly not.'

'It would be perfectly understandable in a lady of your age. What did you say that age was?'

'Eighty-one next birthday.'

'Quite. Permit me to congratulate you on how lightly you wear your years. Of course, a deterioration in some faculties is inevitable, would you not agree?'

Miss Pursglove evidently did not agree. 'I . . . I don't rightly know what you mean.'

'Let us turn to something else, then. The plaintiff visited you at your home during the afternoon of the twenty-sixth of September. Do you happen to remember what day of the week that was?'

The reply came back tartly. 'Tuesday.' A point to Miss Pursglove.

'And you recognized him as your former charge, the late James Davenall?'

'He's my Jamie.' There was a bird-like nod of the head to stress the point.

'What enabled you to recognize him? Was it the sound of his voice? Or have you come to rely more on sight than on hearing?'

'I know my Jamie.' She was not to be moved.

'Let us agree on a combination of the two, then.'

'H'mm. Well . . . if you say so.'

'Incidentally, Miss Pursglove, what time is it?'

'What's that?'

'What time is it? I should be most obliged if you would tell me the time shown on the courtroom clock.'

Miss Pursglove glanced around desperately.

'It's on the wall above the door by which you came in.'   Suddenly, Russell was on his feet. 'My Lord, I protest! What possible relevance—?'

'Yes,' snapped Mr Justice Wimberley. 'What is the relevance of this question, Sir Hardinge?'

'The relevance, my Lord, resides in the poverty of the witness's eyesight and the doubt it casts on her powers of recognition.' Giffard beamed. 'Naturally, I do not wish to press the point.'

Nor did he need to. He had closed with a flourish, leaving Russell to flounder in his wake. When Miss Pursglove eventually left the box, Richard knew, as most in the court did not, that she was Norton's last witness. Her final aggrieved squint towards the clock was, to him, unbearably symbolic. Time had run out for the plaintiff – and for him.

Mr Justice Wimberley chose that moment to adjourn for luncheon. As soon as he had vacated the bench, there welled behind Richard a chair-scraping, coat-gathering murmur of collective departure. But Richard did not move. Giffard jogged his elbow and asked if he would join him outside: he shook his head. He could hear Hugo's braying voice somewhere behind him and felt a flood of relief as it dwindled into the distance. The last of the clerks were gathering their papers now, the swing-doors slamming behind the final stragglers. Richard flattened his hands on the table before him and pushed himself upright. The decision, he knew, could no longer be deferred. He turned to go.

A woman was standing halfway down the aisle between the rows of seats, staring at him with such a wan, pinched intensity as to suggest that necessity, not curiosity, had brought her to Lincoln's Inn. Yet Richard did not recognize her. If she did have an interest in the case, he could not say what it might be.

'Can I help you, madam?' he ventured.

'You are Mr Richard Davenall?'

'Yes.'

'I am Emily Sumner.'

'Sumner?'

'Yes, Constance's sister.'

'Oh, I see. Well, I'm pleased to meet you, Miss Sumner.' They shook hands awkwardly. 'What brings you—?'

'He's going to lose, isn't he?'

'I really don't—'

'James is going to lose this hearing, if nobody else speaks up for him.'

Her very solemnity seemed to rule out prevarication. 'I believe he is, yes.'

'That must please you.'

'No. As a matter of fact, it doesn't.'

'Why not?'

'I'm not sure I can explain.'

'It's because you know he's James, isn't it? Constance has confided in me completely, Mr Davenall. I am here to represent her interests. She has told me that you, of all James's family, may be the one to see reason.'

Her frankness shocked him. Was he so transparent? 'My position . . . is a delicate one.'

'So delicate that you will let him lose?'

'I am Sir Hugo Davenall's solicitor, Miss Sumner. You must appreciate—'

'Will you speak up for him?'

Her vehemence shamed him. Why could he not decide what to do? Why could he not share her certainty?

'Will you?'

Then he heard himself reply: 'Yes.'

She clutched his hand. 'Constance is here, Mr Davenall. She needs your advice, now that we can be sure you will not condone a miscarriage of justice. Will you speak to her?'

'Of course.'

'Then, come with me.'

As Miss Sumner bustled ahead of him out of the court, Richard managed his first weak smile of the day. That anybody should look to him for advice seemed, just then, uniquely absurd. With nobody else to support his claim, however, Norton would lose: Richard was sure of it. His conscience told him he could not permit that to happen. Yet, if he was to prevent it, he must turn his back on his own son. For one reared on the compromises of the Law, the path out of such a thicket seemed impossible to find. Now, in the determination which he remembered Constance Trenchard displaying, and which her sister evidently shared, he believed he might have found the guide he needed.

II

Thoughts of luncheon were far from the mind of Mr Charles Russell, QC, as he sat in Hector Warburton's office at Staple Inn, seeking by every means at his wide command to break the eerily tranquil fatalism which seemed to have gripped his client.

The case of *Norton versus Davenall* was rapidly assuming for Russell a disastrous character. He had accepted it because Warburton was noted for backing winners, because Norton himself was so disarmingly plausible and because such a *coup de théâtre* was exactly what his hopes of political office required. He had not sat in Parliament for the past two and a half years out of love for his constituents; rather, because it rendered him elegible for the post of Attorney-General which he so coveted. To be non-suited at the hearing stage by a former law officer of the opposing party might be tolerated if it were merely embarrassing. But, if, as seemed likely, it would prove fatal to his ambitions, then it was not to be endured.

'I am not sure, Mr Norton,' he said with a determined effort to suppress his anger, 'that you appreciate how perilously we are placed.'

'On the contrary,' Norton replied, 'I appreciate it very clearly.'

'If you had not insisted on deleting all reference to Sir Gervase—'

'Would you have had me drag my father's name through the mire?'

'To save your own from the same fate, yes.'

Norton sat back in his chair and drew on a cigarette. 'Well, I can hardly change my tune at this stage, gentlemen – now, can I?'

'No,' Mr Russell conceded dismally. 'Indeed you cannot.'

Warburton, who had been standing by the window, advanced slowly to his desk and, stooping over it, regarded Norton levelly. 'It is not too late to subpoena Mrs Trenchard. We might request an adjournment for the purpose.'

'I have undertaken to leave her out of this.'

'If forced to testify, would she acknowledge you?'

'I believe she would.'

'Then, I suggest you break your undertaking. It's your only hope.'

'Surely not my only hope, Mr Russell?'

Russell took a deep breath before replying. 'Your refusal to answer Giffard's question is a severe handicap. If there was just one other person besides Miss Pursglove to testify for you, I would entertain hopes of overcoming that handicap. As it is, we will have to rely on breaking down a defence witness. In my view, the possibility is remote.'

'Poor Nanny,' said Norton musingly. 'She was terribly upset afterwards, you know.'

'If I were Giffard,' Russell continued, 'I would reserve the defence and defy the judge to say there is a case to be answered. An hour from now, we may have been non-suited. The defence cannot lose today, Mr Norton. It can only fail to win. For us, on the other hand, there is no second chance.'

Norton smiled. 'For me, you mean. You paint a bleak picture of my prospects, Mr Russell.'

'That is because—'

There had come a sharp rap at the door. Warburton, who had given instructions that they should not be disturbed, looked up irritably at the clerk who entered. 'What is it?'

'There's a gentleman in the outer office, sir, wishing to see Mr Norton as a matter of extreme urgency.'

'Who is he?'

'Mr Richard Davenall, sir.'

Warburton was thunderstruck. What business the defence solicitor had calling on the plaintiff at such a crucial stage he could not imagine. If not unethical, it was certainly unorthodox, and Richard Davenall was neither. What could the fellow be thinking of? 'Tell him—' he began.

'Tell him I'll be out to see him directly,' Norton interrupted.

'That would be unwise. There's no knowing—'

'I'll see him.'

Warburton compressed his lips and nodded curtly to the clerk. 'Put him in Mr Thrower's room for the moment.'

'Very good, sir.'

As soon as the door had closed behind the retreating clerk, Warburton let fly some of the resentment he felt of a client who had

237

rejected his advice once too often. 'You must let me deal with this. It would be quite improper for you to speak to him at this point.'

Norton rose from his chair and smiled blandly. 'Nevertheless, I will speak to him. And I will speak to him *alone*.'

'That would be the height of folly. You have no idea what proposals he may make.'

'My mind is made up. Don't worry, Mr Warburton. I won't blame you if it turns out badly. Now, please excuse me, gentlemen.' With that, he walked swiftly from the room, leaving Warburton and Russell to gape at each other in amazement.

III

Norton followed the clerk's directions to the end of a straggling corridor and opened the door of Mr Thrower's room. It was more cluttered and less businesslike than Warburton's, narrow at the entrance, with a step down to where the vast desk stood piled with pink-bound parchment and an oriel window looked out across the grey censorious roofs of Holborn.

Towards these Richard Davenall had been gazing till, at the sound of Norton closing the door behind him, he turned, nodded a diffident greeting and said: 'You came, then.'

'Of course.' Norton advanced across the room. 'Did you think I wouldn't?'

'I thought Warburton would advise you not to see me at this juncture.'

'He did.' Norton paused on the step and looked down at Richard with no hint of artifice in his open quizzical face.

'He gave you good advice.'

'Why do you say that?'

'Because I might be here to offer you a last-minute compromise, a face-saving formula. I might be here to do a deal.'

'I don't think so.'

'How can you be sure?'

'For two reasons. First, I have no doubt Hugo believes he can defeat me. He wants nothing less than outright victory. He has no need of saving face. Second, even if he had, I don't think you would agree to act as his messenger. Not now.'

Richard stroked his beard. 'You're right. On both counts.'

'Then, what brings you here?'

'I have something to say to you.' Richard rounded the desk and placed himself in front of Norton, gazing up candidly into his face. He swallowed hard, as if plucking up his courage, then said: 'I want you to know that I believe you to be James.' He smiled uncertainly. 'You would say I've known all along and, in a sense, I suppose I have. But you must realize how difficult it's been for the family to come to terms with the fact that you're alive. God knows, like them, I've tried to pretend that you're an impostor, but it hasn't worked. I've spoken to you, I've listened to you, I've heard you testify in court: every day I've grown more and more certain that you are my cousin. And now I can't stand by any longer and let others deny what I know to be true.' He held out his hand. 'Will you forgive me for not acknowledging you from the first?'

'Forgive? Will *I* forgive?' Norton stumbled down from the step and moved unsteadily to the desk. He stooped across it, his hands pressed flat against the surface, breathing heavily and jerking his head aside when Richard touched his shoulder.

'James?'

'It's all right. Give me a moment.' With a tremor, he stepped back, then raised himself upright and let out a long breath of regained composure. 'I'm sorry. Excuse that display. In order to survive, I have inured myself to rejection. Nowadays, only acceptance is too much for me.' He turned, smiling broadly, and shook Richard's hand. 'God bless you, cousin, for accepting me.'

'I could not let the Law denounce you as an impostor, when I know you are not.'

'The Law may still say I am.'

'Not after I've testified for you this afternoon. What I intend to say will ensure you do not lose.'

'You will testify for me?'

'After we parted last night, I came to realize that I had no honourable alternative.'

'My mother and brother will never forgive you.'

'They will, in time.'

'I don't think so. This will split our family irrevocably.'

'I pray not. But, if it does, so be it. I've taken the easy way out too often in my life. Eventually, a man has to face the consequences of his actions. For me, that time has come.'

'I know how much this means to you, Richard. You have my admiration as well as my gratitude.'

'There is nothing admirable in what I'm doing, James. I should have done it weeks ago, when I first knew, in my own mind, that you were who you claimed to be. Even now, I'm not sure I'd have found the courage to come forward if it hadn't been for Constance. She's the one you should be grateful to.'

'Constance?'

'I've just left her. Come and see.' Richard led him to the window. Looking out, they saw below them in the small garden of Staple Inn two women seated on a bench beside the fountain: Emily Sumner, glancing anxiously from side to side and twitching at her bonnet, and her sister Constance, a still, slender figure in grey fur coat and lilac dress gazing pensively into the sprinkling waters of the fountain whilst a stray breeze stirred the feathers on her hat.

Norton frowned. 'I made it clear that I would not involve her. Why is she here?'

'Because she loves you.'

'I love her, too. That's why I wanted to spare her this.'

'She does not wish to be spared. Don't you understand? She wants to prove that she loves you.'

'I require no proof.' He looked at Richard intently. 'Surely, if you will speak for me, that will suffice. There's no need for Constance to do so as well.'

'Her hope is that the effect of she *and* I testifying will be to persuade Hugo to give in without the public agony of a full trial. Her hope is that it will convince him he cannot win.'

'Do you share that hope?'

'Yes, I do.'

'You seriously think he will capitulate?'

'Hugo has no stomach for a losing battle. If his defeat here is comprehensive, I believe he will give it up. Far better that than the ordeal a trial would mean for all concerned.'

Norton grew thoughtful. For several moments, he looked down at the patient expectant figure in the garden. Then he stepped back from the window as if his mind were made up. 'I must go to her.'

'There isn't much time.'

'There's enough. Will you wait here for me?'

Richard nodded his agreement. As Norton hurried from the room, he subsided gently into the chair behind the desk and waited for solitude to remind him of the enormity of what he had agreed to do. If only, for him, it could be as simple as the love those two young people shared. But Richard's motives were obscure even to himself, his every action a confusion of meaning and purpose. Had James appealed to his conscience, or to the self-destructive instinct of a man appalled by his own hypocrisy? Did he want justice for James, or a swift symbolic end to all the shams he had lived?

Richard craned back in the chair and looked out of the window again. Constance was alone now. Emily must have seen James coming, for she was bustling off in the direction of Chancery Lane. And there was James, emerging from the overhang of the building and moving purposefully towards the bench on which Constance sat.

IV

'May I join you?'

'Of course.'

He sat down beside her. 'It's cold out here. I hope you've not been waiting long.'

'Not long.' She looked at him. 'Not nearly so long as you've waited for me.'

'Twenty-five days, since we met beneath Achilles.' He glanced down. 'Every one of those days, I thought of you and wished I could be with you.'

'It was the same for me.'

'I understand why you wouldn't see me in Salisbury. Believe me, I do understand.'

'James—'

There was an explosion of rustling from the next bench. A man who had been throwing crusts to the pigeons screwed up the empty packet, rose and walked away.

'I think we frightened him off,' Constance said, as soon as he was out of earshot.

James smiled grimly. 'If he feeds the pigeons regularly, he should be used to it. Half the park benches in London serve as secret rendezvous for star-crossed lovers.'

'Is that what we are?'

He gave her his answer in the fixed and hopeless longing of his stare. 'Fate has dealt with us cruelly, Connie. With every fibre of my being, I wish we could be man and wife, as we were once destined to be.'

She returned his stare, with all its intensity. 'The longer I have spent trying to forget you, the better I have remembered that destiny.'

Her hand had found its way into his. He seemed about to raise it to his lips, when something stopped him. 'If only we were free to obey our emotions. But we are not. Simply by sitting here and talking, we are in breach of solemn trusts. I promised your father I would not involve you. And you promised your husband you would not see me.'

'William has forfeited the right to hold me to that promise – or to any other.'

'How so?'

She glanced away. 'In time, I will be able to speak of it. For the moment, all I can say is that I no longer regard him as my husband.'

'Do you realize what you're saying?'

She gripped his hand tightly. 'Yes, James. I do.'

'It was never my wish to come between you.'

'Simply by being alive, you come between us. As soon as I knew you had returned, I realized that, in the end, I would have to choose.'

'Between duty . . . and happiness?'

241

Her glance fell. 'If that had been the choice, I could have resolved to sacrifice happiness.' When she looked up again, her eyes were brimming with tears. 'But I will not obey a husband who insults me. And I will not allow your family to deprive you of your birthright.'

Then, at last, he did kiss her hand. He raised it gently to his lips and, as they touched the gloved fingers, he frowned. 'What's this?' he said, tracing with his thumb the protruberance beneath the thin leather of a ring on her third finger. 'You wore only your wedding ring when we last met.'

'I wear it no longer.'

He peeled off the glove and gasped in amazement. On her third finger glistened the fine encrusted diamonds of an engagement ring.

'Don't you recognize it?'

For a moment, he stared at her hand in silent concentration, then looked up into her eyes. 'Of course I recognize it. I gave it to you the night of the hunt ball at Cleave Court, when you said you would be my wife.'

'I am the same person who made that promise, James, and you are the person I made it to. So, at this time of your greatest trial, where would you expect me to be, but by your side, wearing the ring you gave me?'

He leaned forward and kissed her. The touch of his lips on hers bore her back eleven years to a summer-time parting above an aqueduct in Somerset, closing her eyes to everything save the memory-hazed meadow of a lost love restored. But his eyes were open and what they saw, in all its irresistible clarity, was a future he had not till then dared even hope for.

V

The afternoon attendance in the Vice-Chancellor's Court at Lincoln's Inn was disappointing. Some zest seemed to have gone out of the proceedings, some feeling to have gained ground that the case was, after all, too flimsy to deliver the red meat of a long and bitter encounter. It was rumoured, indeed, that the plaintiff had no more witnesses to speak for him and that only a succession of stern-faced friends of the Davenalls could now be expected, wearing down his impertinent claim with the dreary attrition of their denials.

As soon as Mr Justice Wimberley took his seat, however, the mood changed. Something unusual was clearly afoot, for Mr Russell approached the bench and engaged the judge in earnest whispered debate. At length, a vast judicial sleeve was flapped at Sir Hardinge Giffard by way of invitation to join the huddle. Having accepted the

242

invitation, Sir Hardinge began to shrug his shoulders and gesticulate in expressions of dissent. Then Mr Justice Wimberley waved them both away and addressed the court.

'The plaintiff has asked if he may call two additional witnesses from whom sworn affidavits have not yet been obtained. In consideration of the significance which may now attach to their testimonies, I exceptionally grant the request.'

This announcement prompted an outbreak of anxious whispering on the defence side. Slicing through it came Mr Russell's raised voice. 'I call Mrs William Trenchard.'

Trenchard? The name meant nothing to those enjoying such unprecedented elbow room in the public gallery. Its mystery gripped their attention and clamped it on to the slim elegant lady in grey and lilac who now made her way slowly to the box. Her hair was chestnut brown, her face pale: that much could be made out beneath the feather-trimmed hat. The rest, since she looked so resolutely ahead, seemingly unaware of the court from which she had just stepped, was guesswork.

'You are Constance Daphne Trenchard of The Limes, Avenue Road, St John's Wood?'

'I am.' The voice was low but firm, subdued but unwavering.

'How long have you been married, Mrs Trenchard?'

'Seven years.' She had begun massaging what appeared, beneath her glove, to be a ring on the third finger of her left hand.

'Were you engaged to be married eleven years ago to James Davenall?'

'I was.'

'Do you recognize the plaintiff as your fiancé of that period?'

Without hesitation, though strangely without emphasis: 'Yes.'

'Whom you believed, until recently, to have committed suicide in June 1871?'

'Yes.'

'When did you realize that he was, in fact, still alive?'

'When he visited me on Sunday the first of October.'

'That was the first inkling you had of his return?'

'Yes.'

'Did you acknowledge him on that occasion?'

This time, there was a momentary hesitation. 'No.'

'Why not?'

'Because I was unprepared for such a shock and because my husband persuaded me that I might be mistaken.'

'Had your husband ever met James Davenall before?'

'No.'

'Then, how could he know whether you were mistaken or not?'

'It was what he wished to believe.'

243

'My Lord, I object!' Giffard lurched from his seat. 'Witness is being asked to speculate.'

Mr Justice Wimberley frowned. 'May a wife legitimately speculate about her husband's wishes? A moot point, Sir Hardinge. Mrs Trenchard' – he turned to the witness – 'Are you here today with your husband's knowledge and consent?'

'With neither, my Lord.'

The judge raised his eyebrows. 'With neither? Dear, dear. Had I known that. . . . Well, proceed, Mr Russell, but refrain from further questions about Mr Trenchard.'

'As your Lordship pleases. Now then, when next did you meet the plaintiff?'

'In Somerset, six days later.'

'Did you acknowledge him on that occasion?'

'No. But what lingering doubts I had were finally dispelled.'

'How?'

'James – the plaintiff – was able to recall events of which only he or I could possibly know. Lovers' secrets, you might say.'

This indelicate phrase prompted a snigger towards the back of the court. Mr Justice Wimberley reddened and glared threateningly in its direction, then motioned for Russell to continue.

'Your next meeting with the plaintiff?'

'Hyde Park, six days later, by prior arrangement.'

'Did you acknowledge him then?'

'Yes.'

'Yesterday, the plaintiff declined to say whether you had acknowledged him or not. Do you now state unequivocally that you did?'

'Yes. He is James Davenall.'

'Mrs Trenchard,' the judge interposed, 'do I take you to mean that you have been certain of the plaintiff's identity since – if I have it right – the seventh of October?'

'Yes, my Lord.'

'Why have you not come forward before?'

'My husband forbade me to do so.'

'Why have you disobeyed him, then?'

'To prevent a miscarriage of justice.'

'I understand from Mr Russell that no subpoena has been served on you. Am I to conclude that you are here entirely of your own volition?'

'Yes, my Lord.'

'Out of a concern . . . for justice?'

'Yes, my Lord.'

The judge seemed nonplussed. 'Are you aware, Mrs Trenchard, that in the evidence he gave to this court yesterday the plaintiff openly admitted' – he cleared his throat – 'consorting with prostitutes before and during your engagement?'

The answer came without hint of embarrassment. 'Yes, my Lord.'

'And that the plaintiff gave as his reason for disappearing the apparently well-founded belief that he had contracted syphilis as a result of consorting with prostitutes?'

'I am aware of everything he said, my Lord. None of it makes me wish to turn my back on him. Quite the reverse.'

Before the determination, bordering on fervour, that resounded in this last phrase, Mr Justice Wimberley fell back in silent confusion. He nodded feebly to Russell.

'I have no further questions, my Lord.'

Mr Russell sat down and Sir Hardinge Giffard rose, with a brooding crouched reluctance, to take his place. An age seemed to pass before he spoke, but during it the witness's composure, the grave still dignity with which she had confounded the judge, did not falter.

'Mrs Trenchard' – his voice seemed thickened by an ill-suppressed emotion – 'how many times have you met the plaintiff?'

'Since his return?'

'Since his *supposed* return.'

'On four occasions.'

'You have described three of them. When was the fourth?'

'Just before I came into court this afternoon.'

'He sought assurances from you that you would testify on his behalf?'

'No. As a matter of fact, he sought no such assurances.'

A snarl of sarcasm crossed Giffard's face. 'No doubt he pleaded with you *not* to testify.'

'No. He could see that I was determined to do so.'

A snort from Sir Hardinge, a prowl back to the registrar's table, then a switch of attack. 'Mrs Trenchard, are you happily married?'

Russell bobbed to his feet, but Mr Justice Wimberley had already taken the point. 'I have indicated, Sir Hardinge, that I wished no allusions to be made to Mr Trenchard, a gentleman evidently unaware that his marriage is being anatomized here today.'

'I believe it to be germane, my Lord.'

A drumming of judicial fingers, then: 'I will need to be swiftly persuaded of that.'

'Thank you, my Lord. Mrs Trenchard, are you happily married?'

For the first time, the witness's gaze dropped. 'This is not a happy time for my husband and me.'

'How long has it been an unhappy time?'

'I hardly know—'

'Since your former fiancé's magical return from the dead – or longer? I put it to you, Mrs Trenchard, that your sudden conversion to the plaintiff's cause is born not of a concern to see justice done, but of a desire to hurt your husband.'

Stung by Giffard's words, the witness looked up sharply. 'That is unworthy and untrue.'

'Nevertheless—'

'Sir Hardinge!' Mr Justice Wimberley leaned forward. 'I am not persuaded that this *is* germane. You will redirect your questions.'

Giffard bowed before the irresistible. 'As your Lordship pleases. Mrs Trenchard, have you any doubts as to the plaintiff's identity?'

'None.'

'None at all?'

'I am convinced that James Davenall is alive and seated as plaintiff in this court.'

At that, Giffard gave it up. He subsided into his chair with an ill-concealed sigh of resignation. He did not look up as Mrs Trenchard passed him on her way back to her seat, nor when Mr Russell barked out the name of the next witness above the hubbub of whispering.

'I call Mr Richard Davenall.'

The whispering died instantly. This was sensation piled upon sensation. The Davenalls had hitherto held their peace, arrayed anonymously behind a blanket rejection of Norton's claim. Now one of them was to break that silence. All eyes were turned upon him.

'You are Richard Wolseley Davenall of Garth House, North Road, Highgate?'

'I am.' He was a darkly clad, sombre, stooping man with grey hair and beard, watery blue eyes that blinked with tell-tale rapidity and a shifting uncertain stance. Whispering welled in the public gallery: surely he was none other than Sir Hugo Davenall's solicitor.

'What relation are you to James Davenall?'

'He is my first cousin once removed.'

'Do you recognize the plaintiff as your cousin James Davenall?'

'I do.' That said, the witness seemed visibly to relax. He pulled back his shoulders and looked squarely ahead.

'Without question?'

'Without question.'

'How long have you been convinced of his identity?'

'That is not easy to say. The conviction has grown on me steadily since he visited me at my place of work on the morning of the twenty-ninth of September. During the intervening weeks, I have thought long and hard about my memories of James and about the appearance, knowledge and behaviour of the plaintiff. I have now come to the conclusion that he is indeed my cousin James.'

'He looks like your cousin?'

'He looks older, naturally. He also looks . . . well, changed by his experiences. At first, the extent of those changes made me doubt him. Now I believe they are only to be expected in view of all that he has undergone.'

'He is entirely familiar with your family's history?'

'Yes.'

'He knows all that you would expect your cousin to know?'

'Yes.'

'He behaves as you would expect him to behave?'

'Yes.'

'In short, he is the cousin you remember?'

'Yes, I believe he is.'

'Thank you, Mr Davenall.'

When Sir Hardinge Giffard rose to cross-examine the witness, he glared at him from close quarters as if personally affronted by his testimony. 'Mr Davenall, I do not recollect being called upon to question a witness in such extraordinary' – he pronounced each syllable of the word with exaggerated precision – 'in such *bizarre* circumstances in my entire career.'

'The circumstances are not of my making.'

'There I must beg to disagree. Have you been subpoenaed by the plaintiff?'

'No.'

'Then, perhaps you would care to explain why you, Sir Hugo Davenall's solicitor, have volunteered to testify in a manner injurious to his defence and directly contrary to his interests.'

'Because to defend this action is to fly in the face of reason. I *am* serving Sir Hugo's interests, by doing my best to ensure that he takes its defence no further.'

'Ho, ho.' Giffard rolled his eyes and ambled malevolently back to the registrar's table, then turned to stare levelly at the witness. 'How long have you practised as a solicitor, Mr Davenall?'

'Twenty-one years.'

'Have you ever done anything like this before?'

'Anything like what?'

'Like seeking to sabotage a client's case, like leading a client to believe you are his servant and friend, then, without the least hint of a warning, betraying him? Well? How many clients would have come to you, had they known that was your stock-in-trade? How many will come to you, now they do know?'

'My Lord, I object!' cried Mr Russell, rising from his seat. 'Is my learned friend suggesting that the witness should not tell the truth because it may damage his practice?'

'Well, Sir Hardinge?' said the judge. 'Is that what you are suggesting?'

'No, my Lord. I am suggesting that a man who, only this morning, appeared in this court as a convinced and trusted adviser to the defence can hardly now decry that defence without both his character and his testimony being regarded as inherently unreliable.'

The witness looked up at the judge. 'May I answer that accusation, my Lord?'

Mr Justice Wimberley frowned for a moment, then said: 'By all means, Mr Davenall.'

There was nothing hunched and equivocal about the witness now. When he spoke, it was in a firmer, clearer voice than he had used before. 'Sir Hardinge knows I have been unhappy about defending this action from its outset. Indeed, he commented on the fact himself. Well, I do not deny being compromised by my past indecision. I could – perhaps I should – have declined to act as Sir Hugo's solicitor when I realized I could not share his certainty that the plaintiff was an impostor. But I thought it best that he should be advised by a member of his own family, rather than by a stranger. After all, this *is* a family matter. I had the honour to be retained by Sir Hugo's father as his solicitor and hence as guardian of the legal interests of *all* his children. As such, it grieves me more than I can say that one of those children should feel obliged to fight the other in open court. But, if I am forced to choose between them, as I feel forced by these proceedings, then I can, in honour, employ only one criterion: the truth.'

The truth. That one word, pronounced to his evident pain by a member of the Davenall family, swayed the court more than any argument or accusation which Sir Hardinge Giffard could summon. And he seemed to know it, judging by the growl of bitter resignation with which he descended into his seat and waved the witness out of the box.

'That, I believe,' said Mr Justice Wimberley after a moment, 'concludes the case for the plaintiff. Am I correct, Mr Russell?'

'You are, my Lord.'

Mr Justice Wimberley pursed his lips and began sifting through the papers before him. Mr Russell leaned back, smiling, for a word with his client. Sir Hardinge Giffard broodily contemplated some notes passed to him by a junior. Meanwhile, the nearby chair previously occupied by Richard Davenall stood empty. He was seen to have moved to the back of the court, where he was sitting beside Mrs Trenchard, anxiously awaiting, as was the entire rapt throng, the next development.

VI

'The business of this court,' declared Mr Justice Wimberley, 'is to decide whether there is a case to be answered in this action. Questions of identity being notoriously difficult to determine, such claims as the plaintiff's should not be lightly entertained. Nor, however, should they

248

be lightly dismissed. If false, they are contemptible. If genuine, they are deserving of the utmost sympathy. There are no half-measures in such cases. Nevertheless, this court is not required to decide beyond reasonable doubt whether the plaintiff is or is not James Davenall, but to decide whether there exists a sufficient possibility that he may be as to warrant a full trial of his claim. In this respect, the question of acknowledgement becomes vital. If the plaintiff were unable to persuade a single person who knew James Davenall closely that he was James Davenall, then his knowledge of James Davenall's life and doings, however profound, would count for very little. I am therefore struck by the fact that three out of the four witnesses he has called have acknowledged him unequivocally. They were all closely acquainted with James Davenall. None of them has anything to gain by acknowledging somebody they know to be an impostor. Indeed, one might argue that they have a great deal to lose by it. I am therefore minded to conclude that there *is* a case to be answered.' He peered down at Sir Hardinge Giffard. 'Does the defence wish to present evidence at this stage? If so, we shall need to adjourn.'

Giffard half-rose to reply in gloomy tones: 'No, my Lord. My client reserves his defence.'

'Very well.' Mr Justice Wimberley paused for emphasis. 'I am satisfied that the plaintiff, James Norton, has made out a prima facie case for ejectment against the defendant, Sir Hugo Davenall, which case shall be tried before a judge and jury of the Queen's Bench at such time as shall be fixed by the court.'

VII

Richard stood up slowly and waited for the bustle of mass departure to subside. Constance and Emily were standing beside him, strangely awed, like him, by what had just occurred. They had won the qualified victory that justice demanded, but the future it gave them was formidable in its uncertainty.

As the crowd began to thin and the hubbub to fade, they were suddenly aware of James standing in the aisle at the end of their row of seats. He seemed perfectly composed, subdued even, in this moment of his vindication, and said simply: 'It is over, my friends. You have saved me.' Then he added: 'From the bottom of my heart, I thank you.'

At first, they did not respond. Richard, for his part, was acutely aware of Hugo conferring excitedly with Giffard at the front of the court, whilst Constance seemed almost paralysed by the irrevocability of what she had done. It was left to Emily, in fact, to join James in the aisle, grasp his hand, kiss him on the cheek and announce with evident glee: 'I am very happy for you, James. Very happy indeed.'

Then Constance, too, moved towards him, holding out her hand and smiling, but saying nothing, because nothing needed to be said. Seeing this, Richard nodded to James and slipped away down the side of the court. They had, he knew, no need of his company. Duty required him to be elsewhere.

Giffard was stooped over the registrar's table, bundling documents together and pointedly ignoring Hugo, who was pulling at his sleeve and protesting, in a high cracked voice, that he had not hired the most expensive barrister in the Inns of Court to have this humiliation inflicted upon him. Richard was about to intervene, to what effect he could not guess, when Catherine moved into his path and stopped him in his tracks with the force of her glare.

'I asked you to leave Hugo alone,' she said in a steady threatening voice. 'And you refused. I think your conduct here this afternoon gives me the right to *insist* that you leave him alone.'

'I'd hoped you would listen to what I said. Hugo must drop this *now* – for his own good.'

'You are a fool, Richard. Worse than that, you are a gullible fool. I should have known you would be taken in by Norton.'

'Catherine, you are talking about your own son.'

'Perhaps I misjudge you. Perhaps you are merely pretending to believe in him in order to hurt Hugo.'

'That's ridiculous.'

'Is it? I find it more ridiculous to think you could actually believe that man is my son.' She pointed past him towards the door. When he turned to look, he saw that James was just leaving the court, with Constance on his arm. 'He is an impostor, sustained by the credulity of fools and the connivance of knaves. Which are you, Richard? Fool or knave?'

'Catherine—'

'It hardly matters which. Henceforth, you are a party to the conspiracy against my son.'

'There's no conspiracy. This is absurd.'

'You will surrender all papers relating to our family to Baverstock. You will furnish him with all information amassed on Hugo's behalf. You will separate yourself utterly from my son and his affairs. Is that clear?'

'Do you mean to go on with this?'

'That is no concern of yours. Are my requirements clear?'

'Yes.'

'Thank you. This discussion – all our discussions – are at an end.'

The finality of her words was inescapable. He had foreseen this breach as soon as he had decided to speak out on James's behalf. In many ways, he had even looked forward to the relief it might bring him. Yet to experience its reality was a different matter. To live through this moment of bitterest rejection was to understand that where love had once bloomed only hatred could now flourish.

He turned away. As he did so, he saw the doors of the court burst open and Emily Sumner rush into the hall, white-faced and wildly staring. Catching sight of him, she cried: 'Mr Davenall! Come quickly! Something terrible has occurred!'

VIII

I had wandered the streets of London all night and morning until, drawn by fatigue and despair, I had succumbed at last to the lure of a fateful destination.

Late afternoon found me trudging eastwards along the the Strand through a grey world on which winter seemed already to have closed its grip. Around me bustled the ceaseless, pointless turmoil of the largest city on earth, but to me it signified nothing. For reality, if no other companion, had marched with me all the long, sad, dark day, and I had glimpsed in its face a truth I was determined to share: that Norton's was merely a conscious version of all the lies we live.

In Fleet Street, where falsehood is set daily in print and retailed to the masses at a penny a throw, I bought an Evening Standard *and found, recorded amongst its pages, a lie I had helped to write myself.*

MURDER IN COVENT GARDEN

A dead man found early this morning, concealed beneath sacking in an alley adjoining Covent Garden Market, is believed by police to have been stabbed to death late last night. The deceased has not yet been identified, but was distinguishable by having had his right arm amputated. Any person having reason to believe they may know the deceased is asked to contact Bow Street Police Station without delay. The death is being treated as a case of murder.

I threw the newspaper into a bin and headed up Chancery Lane, thinking of Thompson, laid out on a slab in some cold and dripping mortuary, awaiting inspection by anybody who thought they might know a missing, murdered, one-armed man. Then I thought of Quinn – and of Norton, his creature – as I crossed Carey Street and turned into Lincoln's Inn.

The square was empty when I entered it. But, as I made my way along its eastern side, a group of people appeared from the direction of the Vice-Chancellor's Court, talking excitedly amongst themselves. As

I looked towards them, I saw, ambling along at the rear, Sir Hugo Davenall's friend Freddy Cleveland. I rushed through the crowd and seized his arm.

'Cleveland! It's me: Trenchard.'

'Trenchard? Good God. Hardly recognized you, old man. Surprised to see you here, after yesterday's dust-up.'

'Have you been in court?'

'Yes. But, if that's why you're here, you've missed the boat. It's all over – for the moment.'

'What do you mean?'

'The press johnnies are to have the trial they've prayed for. The case has been referred up, so to speak.'

'Norton's won?'

Cleveland smiled. 'Lived to fight another day, at any rate. Hugo looked pretty sick about it. Can't say I blame him. Still, there was never a chance the judge would throw it out once your wife had fluttered her eyelashes at him.'

'My wife?'

'She testified for Norton. Identified him as Jimmy without a qualm. Damned impressive display, I must say. Positively heart-rending. You should keep a tighter rein on her, old man. Otherwise. . . . Well, 'nough said. Must dash.'

He walked on and left me gaping at the grinning invisible faces of my enemies: Melanie, who had deceived me; Quinn, who had defeated me; and Norton, who had displaced me. Their eyes, boring into mine; their voices, rejoicing at my ruin; their hands, clutching at my throat. People were staring and pointing at me as they passed. What they saw was a dishevelled figure standing on the flagstoned path, weeping the tears of a crazed and private despair. But what I saw, when I turned and ran headlong in the direction of the court, was Norton and Constance, walking slowly towards me, arm in arm, my wife and my bitterest foe united in the moment of my destruction.

They halted ten yards away. I saw the colour drain from Constance's face, saw her mouth fall open in dismay. But, on Norton's face, all I saw was the hint of a sneer he could never suppress.

'Move away from her!' I shouted.

'Trenchard,' Norton began, 'we can—'

'Move away from her!' I pulled the gun from my pocket and pointed it straight at him. This time, it was loaded.

'Trenchard, for God's sake—'

'Move away!' I cocked the gun.

He drew his arm from hers and walked as far as the railings bounding the lawn in the centre of the square, then turned to face me. 'This is madness,' he said calmly. 'Don't you understand? You've lost. Give it up, man.'

252

He was right. I had lost – everything. I could see the gun shaking in my hands, could hear the blood rushing in my head. All else was still and silent, a motionless interval in which he confronted and defied me. Then I saw the realization flicker across his face that his success was also his peril. He had said it and he was right. He had taken everything from me. He had left me with nothing to lose. We must have understood each other in the very same instant. For, as he stepped towards me, I pulled the trigger.

William Trenchard's account of the six weeks which transformed him from a contented husband and respected businessman into a desperate outcast from all he had once possessed ends at this point. There can be little doubt that he believed what he had written constituted a complete justification of his murderous assault on Norton. Whether it did or not, however, was for others to decide. And upon their decision his future now depended.

TWELVE

I

The plaster-cast human head on the shelf was disconcertingly close to Richard Davenall's right shoulder. He had glanced furtively in its direction on several occasions, but, until this present lull in the proceedings, had not examined it in detail. Now that he did so, he saw that the skull was criss-crossed by lines cut into the plaster, dividing the surface into a series of irregular shapes, each bearing a tiny labelled number. On the wall above the head hung a framed legend to this atlas of the cranium, equating the numbers to particular instincts or emotions. Richard ran his eye down the list – Veneration, Love of Offspring, Courage, Self-Defence – then stopped abruptly. Number five, a heptangle behind the left ear, was Murder.

'In all the circumstances,' Bucknill said at last, 'I can see no *medical* objection.' He raised himself from a ruminative slouch and looked thoughtfully at each of his guests in turn. 'Indeed, from a strictly *medical* point of view, it is undoubtedly the wisest course.'

Richard wondered for a moment whether this meant yes or no. They had called in Bucknill because he was, beyond question, the most eminent consultant in the admittedly limited specialism of psychiatry, author of the definitive work *Unsoundness of Mind in Relation to Criminal Acts*, founder of *Brain: A Journal of Neurology*, and, until his retirement into private practice, the Lord Chancellor's Medical Visitor of Lunatics. His opinion would undoubtedly outweigh all others. But what *was* his opinion?

With elaborate delicacy, Bucknill removed his steel-rimmed spectacles and placed them on the blotter before him. Without them, his eyes took on a sad, rheumy quality which heightened the lugubrious effect of his full grey beard and dome-shaped head. 'I could say without hesitation,' he continued, 'that when Mr Trenchard committed the

254

offence he was in the grip of strong paranoid delusions, delusions which do not appear to have diminished one whit in the intervening period, as his written account demonstrates.' He turned his bloodhound gaze on Richard. 'I believe you've read that account, Mr Davenall?'

'Yes, I have.'

'Then, you'll have noted the remarkable clarity with which it chronicles Mr Trenchard's mental disintegration. Neither his memory nor his reasoning faculty is at all impaired, only his capacity to distinguish between reality and imagination. Accordingly, he describes genuine and hallucinatory experiences with equal precision, never once doubting the accuracy of his recollections even when those recollections are manifestly fantastic.' A gleam had been restored to Bucknill's eyes, a healthy glow to his features: he was warming to his theme. 'Take, as an example, his unshakeable faith in the absurd explanations he advanced when discovered *in flagrante delicto* with a prostitute. He advanced them, you see, because he believed them to be true. His subconscious mind uses such devices to shield his conscious mind from all that it can no longer bear.'

Richard stirred uneasily in his chair. 'Are you saying, Doctor, that what he wrote was . . . a fantasy?'

'No, Mr Davenall. I am saying that his deluded mind distorts actual experiences in order to accommodate them within his paranoid conviction that the world is conspiring against him.'

'Then he was not responsible for his own actions when he shot my cousin?'

'When he fired the gun, he was firing it at all those whom he genuinely believed to be plotting against him. He was acting, as it were, in self-defence.'

Ernest Trenchard, who had sat till now silent and immobile, suddenly leaned forward in his chair and said: 'What are the prospects of a cure, Doctor?'

Bucknill took a deep breath. 'Not good, Mr Trenchard. Not good at all. Your brother's paranoia is elaborate and deeply rooted. I found him closed to all suggestions that he might be the victim of his own delusions.'

'Then, we would be speaking of a lengthy confinement?'

'Candidly, I could hold out little hope of it being other than permanent.'

Ernest turned to Richard with cautiously raised eyebrows. 'Would that satisfy Norton?' he said softly.

Suppressing a shudder, Richard looked across at Bucknill. 'You should know, Doctor, that, despite the severity of his injuries, Mr Norton has undertaken to prefer no charges so long as Mr Trenchard is placed somewhere where he cannot endanger himself or others. Mrs Trenchard is also of the view—'

'I have her letter.' Bucknill held it up. 'She argues powerfully on her husband's account. She even seeks to take some blame for his state of mind. It is encouraging that so many people wish him well.'

'Then, how should we proceed?' said Richard.

Bucknill smiled. 'I will arrange certification and will notify the magistrates accordingly. When did you say he was next to be brought before them?'

'Wednesday the twenty-second.'

'Well, in view of Mr Norton's accommodating attitude, I have no doubt the Bench will agree to discharge Mr Trenchard into my custody. I can recommend several excellent institutions for dealing with his problems.'

'We want the best for him,' said Ernest.

'The *very* best?'

'Yes.'

'Then I have some brochures which will interest you. You realize, of course, that the very best is . . . very expensive.'

'Money is no object.'

'Would that more of my patients had such enlightened and supportive families.' Bucknill's smile grew broad enough to mask any hint that he knew how much less embarrassing the Trenchards would find an insane relative than a criminal one. 'You may rest assured, gentlemen, that Mr William Trenchard will enjoy every comfort in his confinement. Yes, every comfort.'

It seemed only a matter of minutes later that Richard Davenall and Ernest Trenchard were standing outside Bucknill's Gothically porched doorway, glancing up and down Wimpole Street in the vain hope that a cab might be on hand to part them.

'Well,' said Ernest, 'I suppose that went as well as we'd hoped.'

'Yes,' Richard replied, with a singular lack of conviction. 'I suppose it did.'

'Why your friend Norton—'

'He's my cousin, actually.'

Ernest frowned sceptically. 'If you say so. At all events, why he's being so extemely decent about this business I really don't know.'

'Because he *is* extremely decent.'

'I'm not complaining. A trial would have been bad for business.'

Yes, Richard thought, that was just how this sallow-faced mean-spirited man would regard James's generosity. Saving his brother from a prison cell meant little to him compared with safeguarding the profits of Trenchard & Leavis.

'The fees for the place Bucknill was recommending will run to nearly five hundred a year.' Ernest shook his head at the thought of such extravagance. 'I'm sure somewhere cheaper would do just as well.'

'My cousin wishes to ensure—'

'That William doesn't suffer. Yes, I know. Even so. . . .'

'Since you're contributing nothing to the cost, Mr Trenchard, why should you care?'

Ernest looked at Richard sharply, genuinely perplexed that anybody would spend more than they needed to on his unworthy brother. 'The county asylum would suffice,' he said with an aggrieved air.

'My cousin would not agree.'

'H'm. Well, that's his affair. I dare say it will stand him in good stead where Constance is concerned. Perhaps *that* is the object of the exercise.' Then he added, before Richard had a chance to reply: 'Well, I can't wait for a cab any longer. I must get back to Orchard Street. Somebody has to do the work William abandoned. Good day to you, Davenall.'

Richard watched Ernest walk swiftly away down the street and found himself hoping that he would not need to see him again. The fellow apparently regarded his brother as an encumbrance of which the family was well rid. When asked if he wished to read William's statement, he had declined in the most emphatic terms. He intended, it seemed, to forget his brother, not to try to understand him.

Would that Richard could do the same. But he realized, as he turned up his collar against the chill wind and struck out northwards, that that was something he could never hope to do. He had done his best for Trenchard, of course, but he had owed him nothing less. After all, he had been the one to assure him, all those weeks ago, that Norton was just a nine days' wonder. How wrong he had been, how inexcusably wrong.

Since his release from hospital, James had been convalescing at Richard's house in Highgate, with Constance in perpetual attendance. To watch those two, day after day, tenderly feeling their way towards a rediscovered love, had stilled in Richard the few doubts remaining after his change of heart, had imbued in him a contentment that was no less profound for being based on other people's happiness.

Now all that had changed. Bucknill's patient questioning had drawn from Trenchard a statement which seemed, to all who read it, a graphic proof of his insanity. But, in sealing his own fate, Trenchard had awoken in Richard a dormant suspicion. It might mean nothing, of course. In all probability, it did mean nothing. Yet there it remained, weeviling into the core of his well-being. There it remained and there it would give him no rest.

II

Arthur Baverstock had travelled to Cleave Court that morning in a frame of mind perfectly matched by the damp and dismal greyness which late autumn had brought to the park. The rooks were in rancorous voice amongst the stripped and sorrowful elms. Smoke from simmering leaf-stacks drifted in sluggish skeins across the empty lawns. And the house itself, as Baverstock approached it up the long drive, seemed sunk at the very heart of its family's gathering gloom.

Lady Davenall was waiting for him in the morning room. So much he was told, but so much more he imagined, as he trod the carpeted passages of a house he wished he might never have entered. He brought news which would not please her Ladyship, and she, he felt certain, had instructions which would please him even less.

She was not alone. Sir Hugo Davenall stood by the fireplace, smoking a cigarette and chewing his fingernails. Baverstock's depression deepened: he was to be outnumbered as well as outclassed.

'Mr Baverstock,' Lady Davenall said from her seat near the window. 'Please be seated.'

Baverstock lowered himself on to the upright chair which seemed to have been prepared for him and exchanged the faintest of nodded greetings with Sir Hugo. When he squinted towards Lady Davenall, he could scarcely decipher her expression, so remote did she seem from him in the ill-lit room.

'Do you have any progress to report?' she said, in her quietest, most intimidating tones.

'There is, your Ladyship, news on two counts. First, we have a projected date for the trial: the third of April.'

'Must we wait as long as that?' A pause during which Baverstock nerved himself to remain silent. 'Well, what does Sir Hardinge say about it?'

'That . . . er . . . is the second development, so to speak.'

'What do you mean?'

'Sir Hardinge has . . . ah, indicated that he does not wish to handle the case.'

Sir Hugo kicked the fender violently and seemed about to utter an oath until he remembered his mother's presence. 'Rats and a sinking ship,' he muttered, stubbing out one cigarette and reaching for another.

'What reason does he give?' Lady Davenall asked, in an unaltered voice.

'None . . . your Ladyship.'

Sir Hugo snorted. 'Isn't it obvious?'

A measured pause, then Lady Davenall resumed, 'You will find somebody else, Mr Baverstock. Somebody better.'

'That . . . won't be easy.'

'Nevertheless, I require it to be done. Seek whatever advice you need, but find us a barrister of the highest calibre.'

'I had thought . . . of taking the advice of Lewis and Lewis, the London solicitors who specialize in cases of imposture.'

'Excellent. Do that. It is a pity, Hugo, that your cousin did not employ them. We might then have nipped this matter in the bud.'

'Lewis and Lewis,' Baverstock continued, 'are likely to recommend that exhaustive enquiries be made in the United States to establish Mr Norton's true identity.'

'More money, no doubt,' Sir Hugo put in.

'Money well spent,' his mother averred. 'Arrange a meeting with Lewis and Lewis, Mr Baverstock. There must be no more shilly-shallying.'

Baverstock swallowed hard. 'Very good, your Ladyship.'

'Now, to other matters. There is a tenancy which I wish you to terminate. A minor issue compared with what we have been discussing, but one I want attended to promptly.'

'Which tenancy, your Ladyship?'

'Miss Pursglove's.'

So that was it. He might have known. Indeed, recollecting the low spirits which had dogged him on his journey to Cleave Court, he rather thought he had known. 'Miss Pursglove?'

'Yes, Mr Baverstock, I want Miss Pursglove evicted from Weir Cottage.'

'But . . . it was intended she should enjoy rent-free tenure until her death.'

'I am fully aware of what *was* intended. What was *not* intended was that she should feel free to slander me in court without suffering the consequences. Since she pays no rent, she need be given minimal notice. I want her out by Christmas.'

'But—'

'Is that clear?'

'Er . . . yes. Yes, it's clear.'

Sir Hugo smiled as he tossed his cigarette into the fire. 'Didn't you know, Baverstock? Those who cross my mother are shown no mercy.'

III

When Richard arrived home, Braddock informed him that James was receiving his daily visit from the doctor, so he was not surprised to find Constance in the drawing-room reading a letter by the fire. As she looked up, he noticed the frown of anxiety on her face and could not prevent himself wondering whether she was concerned for Trenchard's welfare or concerned that he should no longer interfere with hers.

'It is agreed,' he announced. 'Bucknill is happy to take William on.'

Was it relief or pleasure that flitted across her gaze? He could not tell. 'I am glad,' she said. 'For William's sake.'

He sat down beside her and squeezed her hand. 'Well, it's for the best, of that I'm certain. Bucknill recommends the Ticehurst Asylum in Sussex. It has a fine reputation.'

'He would be well treated there?'

'He would want for nothing. I've brought a brochure for you to see.'

Constance took the booklet from him and began leafing through it.

'All that remains is for you to sign the necessary form of consent.'

Abruptly, she put the booklet aside and stared at him intently. 'Consent?'

'A mere formality.'

'Yes, of course.' She grew thoughtful. 'We are doing right by William, aren't we, Richard?'

'I believe so. He wasn't responsible for his actions when he attacked James. He needs the help and treatment an asylum can provide.'

'When you say that, naturally I agree. I keep telling myself it's the only solution. Yet I can't help feeling that, in some way, I've betrayed him.'

'Constance, if you were a treacherous wife, or if James were a vindictive man, William might well be on trial for his life. As it is. . . .'

'I know.' With a visible effort, she turned her mind to other matters. 'Emily has written.' She held up the letter. 'She is bringing Patience and my father next week. Are you sure you don't mind them staying here?'

'Not at all. I'll be glad to see Emily again. And to make your father's acquaintance.'

'But we've imposed upon you too much already.'

'It's no imposition.' He smiled. 'This is a cold and lonely house for one, Constance. Having you and James here has been a pleasure. I'm not sure what I'll do when. . . .'

'When we've gone? But gone where, Richard? That, too, troubles me. I am not free to marry the man I love. And that man is not even free to use his own name.'

'Not *yet*.'

She looked down at the engagement ring she wore symbolically on her left hand. 'I wonder,' she said musingly, 'if the uncertainty will ever end.'

Richard, though he vigorously denied it, could not help wondering the same. Nor was he able to dispel any of that uncertainty when, that evening, he paid his customary visit to James in his room after dinner and found him, as was often the case, gazing sleeplessly about, alert but unoccupied. Richard had originally attributed these contemplative phases to the natural lassitude of convalescence and had accordingly expected some change with the passage of time. But none had followed. The condition, he had concluded, was just one of the alterations eleven years had wrought in the character of his cousin.

'The doctor is very pleased with you,' he ventured.

'Yes,' James replied. 'He proposes to cut back his visits to every other day and says I may spend some hours downstairs each afternoon.'

'Splendid.'

'He attributes the speed of my recovery to the excellence of my nurse.'

'Constance has been a tower of strength.'

'I know.'

Richard sat down beside the bed. 'Do you remember what I said to you that day at Staple Inn, James? Do you remember what I said about Constance?'

James smiled. 'You told me that she wanted to prove her love for me. I have not forgotten, Richard.'

'Since you've both been living here, I've grown fond of her – concerned for her happiness.'

'Do you think I'm not?'

'No, of course I don't, but. . . .'

'What are my intentions? Is that it?'

Richard flushed. 'I suppose it is, yes.'

James reached out and patted his forearm. 'Never fear, Richard. We'll find a way. I shall aim as high as Constance permits. Friendship, if that is all she will allow. Ultimately, marriage, if she will have me. Either way, I'll not desert her.'

'What of her husband?'

'I pity Trenchard, I really do, but I don't believe Constance should be shackled to an insane husband. In time, I hope she will come to believe the same.'

'Divorce, then?'

'Eventually, yes, but it must be Constance's decision. And it's one I can't ask her to take until I've won this case. There's no sign of Hugo backing down, you know.'

Richard hung his head. 'I had thought he would see reason. It seems I was wrong.'

'It's my mother who won't see reason. She can't forgive me for coming back – nor you for siding with me.'

'A trial,' Richard mused, 'will be a long dark road for all of us.'

'Yet, at the end of it,' James countered, 'I pray we will emerge into the light.'

Later, alone in the darkness of his bedroom, Richard pondered all that James had said and implied. There had been modification and caution aplenty, but at heart, he was clearly determined to force his claim to its ultimate conclusion: to deprive Hugo of the baronetcy, to force Catherine to accept him as her son, to win Constance as his wife. His brush with death at Trenchard's hands seemed only to have strengthened his resolve. And why not, after all? None of it was any more than his due. Yet, at the thought of it, Richard could find no sleep. At the end of that long dark road down which they must all go, he could see no glimmer of light.

IV

It was a still clear night of unnatural warmth, on which the full moon imposed a strange and colourless day. Plon-Plon was running head-long through the Cleave Court maze, plunging down yew-hedged shafts of moonlight, flinging himself through slashing branches and vast invisible cobwebs. He had heard them before he had seen them: their breathing and his seemed one. As he rounded the last bend, a bat swooped across his face. He flailed with his arm to clear his sight . . . and then he saw. Atop his pillar, Sir Harley Davenall's dead frozen grin. Beneath him, two bodies entwined on the grass, two bodies joined and straining, their bare flesh starkly white in the moonlight. As Plon-Plon stepped from the shadows, Vivien Strang's eyes moved to focus on him. Twisting her head towards him, she opened her mouth, as if to. . . .

Plon-Plon sat upright in bed, panting from the exertion of his nightmare, certain he had screamed at its end even though he had not heard himself do so. He was regaining control now, listening for some sign that others had been disturbed. But there was nothing: dumb silence reigned throughout the house.

It was as well, Plon-Plon reflected, that Marie Clotilde was wintering in Turin. She might have taken his distress for a sign that he had seen the light. As for the servants, even if they had heard him, they would merely have hoped he had died in his sleep.

He hauled himself from the bed and groped his way to the dressing-table. There he poured brandy into a glass, swallowed too much at the first gulp and coughed convulsively. At least it cleared his head. He sat down heavily on the edge of the bed and sipped the rest, waiting for his senses to restore themselves to their normal compla-cency. To find, so late in life, that he had a conscience: it was more than he could stand.

Not that conscience was really the cause, he knew, of this recurrent

262

dream. Three times since he had read of Norton's victory at the hearing in London, this vision of Vivien Strang's betrayal had come to disturb his slumbers. Why? Why now, when it was all so far too late? He swallowed more brandy and felt the warmth of its false courage seep into his soul. He had drunk brandy that night, too, had dosed himself into resentful oblivion when Gervase had not returned by the due time, had masked his sight with insensibility rather than face the truth. But the truth, whatever it was, could no longer be kept at bay. Vivien Strang, whose dreamed scream tasted of the blood she had thrown in his face at Scutari, and James Norton, whose claim encompassed every debt owed to a wronged woman, would allow him no rest.

Plon-Plon raised the glass again, but found it empty. He set it down on the bedside table with a crash, then lowered himself on to the heaped and rumpled pillows. She had warned him, after all. She had warned him, and he could not pretend otherwise. It was not enough, he knew, to have closed his curtains and drowned a frail remorse in floods of brandy. She had warned him and he could not forget.

December 1846, wanting a week to Christmas. A fine frosty night in London, with a sky of deepest velvet cushioning the gemstone stars. Young Plon-Plon felt more than usually pleased with himself as he strolled along King Street, twirling his cane. He had dined with his cousin, Louis Napoleon, and had worsted an opinionated American guest at the table in an argument about slavery. Louis Napoleon had looked quite shocked by his radical remarks. As well he might, Plon-Plon thought. What he was really shocked by was how a true Bonaparte conducts himself.

Plon-Plon paused at the corner of St James's Square to light a cigar. There was nobody near him when he turned aside to cradle the flame and take the first few puffs. Yet, when he turned back to discard the match, she was standing only a few yards away.

Her cheeks were hollowed by hardship, her clothes worn by use. Only in the severity of her piercing gaze was Vivien Strang unaltered. He did not know what to do, whether to ignore her and walk ahead or admit that he recognized her. In the end, she decided for him.

'I have followed you for three days,' she said. 'Since I saw you leaving the theatre.'

He did not ask why, because he knew. They had not met since the night of the ball at Cleave Court. Gervase had boasted of the prize he had won, the night after, in the maze. If nobody else knew why Colonel Webster had dismissed his daughter's governess, Gervase did, and Plon-Plon at least suspected.

'Have you nothing to say, Prince? Nothing to say to the woman you ruined?'

Arrogance found a voice where honour was mute. '*Je ne comprends pas, mademoiselle.*'

'Speak English, Prince. I know you can. You wrote English – in that note to me.'

'I wrote no note—'

'I went to the maze because I thought you would be there. But you deceived me. You were his partner. And I was your dupe.'

'This is not true.'

She stepped closer. 'What did he tell you? That I consented, perhaps? If so, he lied. What I might have given you freely, he took by force.'

'He raped you?'

'He did worse than rape me – he destroyed me. When the Websters threw me out, I still thought, God forgive me, that there had been some mistake, that he had forged the note perhaps, that you did not know what he had done in your name. But when I came to seek your help you had vanished, scuttled away from Bath because you knew all too well what he had done.'

'You exaggerate—'

'No! I exaggerate nothing. The proof of it I carry within me. I am pregnant by your vile friend, *mon prince charmant*. I am pregnant and disgraced, rejected by my family, turned away by my friends. I am destitute – because of you.'

The truth of her words shone in the vehemence of her gaze. But the shame it inspired in him he was young enough to believe he could yet evade. He reached into his pocket and drew out a wad of notes. 'For you,' he said, holding out a handful. 'And for the baby.'

As she reached out to take the money, Plon-Plon saw her expression alter. Every instinct of her pride told her to reject what every experience of her fall compelled her to accept. For this – the making of an offer she could not refuse – she hated him more deeply still.

He made to move past her, but her hand on his sleeve detained him. She was closer now than before, close enough to leave him in no doubt of the sincerity of her words.

'One day, Prince, you will regret how you and your friend treated me.'

'Never.'

'But, by then, it will be too late.'

'*Bonsoir, mademoiselle.*' He shook her arm off and marched away, not daring to look back. He struck out diagonally across the square, bolstering with each step his naïve belief that he could have done with her, outpacing with every yard a hatred he thought too slow to touch him.

Slow, but not slow enough. Thirty-six years later, Plon-Plon raised his stout creaking frame from the bed and shuffled to the window. He parted the curtains and looked out along the empty cobbled length of the Avenue d'Antin. There was nobody there, no figure in the night beckoning in the guise of a forgotten sin. And why should there be? What was Norton to him? What did it matter if Vivien Strang had advanced her son to claim a birthright which, in one sense at least, was truly his? He would stay in Paris, or follow his wife to Italy. He would stop his ears and blind his eyes to their conspiracy. It did not concern him. He would tell himself so until he believed it. Norton had no claim on him. He would cling to the thought until the danger was past.

Plon-Plon returned to the dressing-table and poured some more brandy.

'She shall not cheat my son,' Gervase had said.

'Cheat Hugo?'

'No. Not Hugo. My son.'

'I do not understand.'

'Nobody does, Plon-Plon. Nobody does.'

But that, thought Plon-Plon as he swallowed the brandy, was Gervase's error. Somebody did understand. Somebody whose bulky shape he could see, dimly reflected, in the mirror before him. He understood all too well.

V

The Bow Street magistrates proved as compliant as Bucknill had predicted. On Wednesday 2nd November 1882 they dropped all charges against William Trenchard and consigned him to the care of Ticehurst Asylum. After his brief appearance in court, Trenchard was taken down to the cells, there to await transport to Ticehurst. And there, in the hour or so that he waited, he received a visitor: Richard Davenall.

'How are you, Trenchard?'

'Mad. Didn't they tell you?'

'You must see that this is in your own interests.'

'I see that it's in Norton's interests.'

'You'll find they have every facility at Ticehurst.'

'Except liberty.'

'Bucknill is an excellent man. He believes he can help you.'

'Nobody can help me.'

'You must try to put all this behind you.'

'Why? What have I to look forward to?'

'Listen to me, Trenchard—'

'Listen to *me*! Have you read my statement?'

'Yes.'

'Then you know it's true.'

'At Ticehurst, you will come to see these delusions for what they are.'

'At Ticehurst, I will remember what others wish to forget.'

Richard stood up, exasperated by his inability to refute what Trenchard had said. 'I see you're not to be reasoned with.'

'Tell me, where is Constance?' Suddenly, Trenchard's voice was meek and pleading.

'She is staying with me.'

'And Norton?'

'In the circumstances, I cannot tell you. Constance is well. As is your daughter. Perhaps, in time, they will be able to visit—' He broke off. Trenchard was weeping, his head bowed in shame, his shoulders shaking with each strangled sob. 'I'm sorry,' Richard said. 'Truly sorry.'

Suddenly, Trenchard rose to his feet, the legs of his chair scraping back angrily across the stone floor of the cell. He looked straight at Richard, his face trembling with the effort of self-control. 'Where is she?' he murmured. 'Where is Melanie?'

'Perhaps . . . she never existed.'

'If I'd kept the photographs, I could have asked Fiveash to identify her.'

'But you destroyed them?'

'Yes. I threw them into the river and watched them float away . . . watched her float away.' He paused for a moment, then said: 'Bucknill told me the name Melanie derives from the Greek word *melaina*.'

'So?'

'It means *black*. Black as her hair. Black as her heart.'

'You must forget her.'

His eyes opened wide, reaching past Richard into the mystery which had claimed her. 'I cannot forget her . . . until I see her again.'

Two warders escorted Trenchard to Charing Cross station in a covered van, Bucknill and Richard Davenall following in a cab. During the journey, Richard sought to draw the doctor out on the subject of Trenchard's obsession with Melanie Rossiter.

'In my opinion, Mr Davenall, the connection between Dr Fiveash's sometime secretary, Miss Whitaker, and the prostitute called Melanie exists only in Mr Trenchard's imagination. I doubt Melanie was even her real name.'

'Trenchard imagined that, too?'

'Quite possibly. From a subconscious layer of knowledge, he might have chosen the name to fit his image of the woman he believes to be persecuting him. He could never have found the Miss Whitaker he was looking for. Therefore, he invented her. She appeared out of the fog: by day a damsel in distress, by night a succubine temptress. Until we have cleared the fog from his mind, he cannot be rid of her.'

'And you can clear it?'

'As to that, only time will tell.'

'But you are confident there was no conspiracy against him?'

'Of course. His delusions are classical and unmistakable, Mr Davenall. Rely upon it, that is all they are: delusions.'

But Richard could not rely upon it. Bucknill's diagnosis would have swayed him utterly – had it not been for one stubborn memory. He could not intervene between Trenchard and his fate; indeed, he could only watch helplessly when, half an hour later, the train drew out of Charing Cross and bore Trenchard away into obscure confinement. But he could impose his own test of reality on the memories Bucknill had called delusions. He could impose it – and await the result.

VI

Pale December sunlight, warming the conservatory glass, had lulled Canon Sumner asleep. He sat now, cushioned and cake-crumbed in his wicker chair, dozing gently, whilst on the opposite side of the low table, James and Constance set down their tea-cups in careful silence and exchanged a smile which spoke of the pleasure they took from the old man's drowsy benevolence.

'He is quite reconciled, you know,' Constance murmured.

'*You* could reconcile him to anything.' It was true. Canon Sumner had arrived in Highgate torn between horror at Trenchard's conduct and suspicion of James's motives, but all his scruples had melted away when confronted by his daughter's evident happiness. Faced with that irresistible commodity, he had conferred upon her his old, weak, indulgent blessing.

'Recently,' Constance continued, 'nursing you back to health with my family about us, I've been happier than I've dared to admit.'

'You've made me happy, too,' said James, squeezing her hand.

'I feared Patience might not like you, but it seems I needn't have worried. You've quite won her over.' Patience, whom Emily had taken for a walk into Highgate Village that afternoon, was young enough to have accepted that her father had simply 'gone away' and to have warmed instantly to her 'Uncle' James.

'That's because she takes after you.'

'Perhaps.' Constance looked down. 'But how long can it go on, James – this taste of what we might have enjoyed together all these years?'

'Must it end?'

'Once your recovery is complete, I shall have no excuse to remain here.'

'Nor shall I, but Richard insists he wishes neither of us to leave.'

'Nevertheless—'

'Why not stay? It need only be for as long as this wretched case lasts.'

'But how long will that be?'

'Six months, perhaps. It isn't so very long, compared with eleven years.'

'And then? What when it does end, James?'

Their eyes met. 'When the case is finished,' he said slowly, 'when the law acknowledges me for who I am, then I will feel entitled to come to you and ask—'

'What? What's that you say?' Canon Sumner was awake, blinking and gravel-voiced, struggling to persuade himself that he had never been asleep.

'Nothing, Father,' said Constance. 'Nothing at all.'

'I've been thinking,' the old man continued, pulling himself upright in his chair. 'About that poor soul you said Lady Davenall is evicting.'

'Nanny Pursglove?'

'Yes. It sounds like a deserving case to me. After all, she is a resident of the diocese.'

'What do you have in mind?'

'There are vacancies at the Wilton almshouses. The Archdeacon told me so. Miss Pursglove could live there. Very comfortable, I gather. Would you like me to mention it?'

'Oh, do, Father,' said Constance, smiling. 'I think that is an excellent idea. Don't you agree, James?'

'Yes,' said James. 'I do indeed.' He, too, smiled, reflecting as he did so that perhaps Canon Sumner's interruption had been a blessing in disguise. There was, after all, no need of haste. Indeed, if Constance was to be persuaded to see the future as he did, there was every argument for caution. All, he now felt certain, could be his so long as he continued to tread carefully. All – including Constance – in good time.

VII

Richard Davenall could tell by the apologetic slant to Roffey's expression that he had no progress to report.

'Not a chink of light anywhere, sir. If the woman exists, she's covered her tracks well.'

'Nothing at all?'

'Looking for one prostitute in London is like looking for one stalk in a haystack, if you'll pardon the expression. I've been put the way of several called Melanie, but none of them even remotely fits the bill.'

'What about the Bristol end?'

'I've spoken to the butler of every wine merchant in the city. None of the families boasts a son engaged to a former housemaid. None of them has ever employed Quinn as a footman.'

'And in Bath?'

'Miss Whitaker lodged in Norfolk Buildings, right enough, and Quinn *was* acquainted with her landlady's husband, but that's as far as it goes. I couldn't persuade the landlord of the Red Lion to repeat the story he supposedly told Trenchard; he flatly denied having seen the two together.'

'Do you think he's telling the truth?'

'It's hard to say. Either that or he'd been warned off. He was *very* tight-lipped.'

'Any other news of Quinn?'

'None at all.'

'What about Harvey Thompson?'

'The police think he was murdered by one of the many people he apparently owed money. They seem happy to leave it at that.'

A silence fell, during which Richard stroked his beard and contemplated the barrenness of Roffey's enquiries. Then he said: 'You don't think Miss Whitaker and Melanie Rossiter are one and the same, do you?'

'No, sir. I can't say I do.'

Richard rose and moved to the window. His back was turned to the other man when he said: 'Very well, Roffey. Thank you for your efforts. I rather think we'd better leave it there.'

'As you wish, sir.'

'There's no need to submit a written report. I'd rather there was no record of this.'

Roffey cleared his throat. 'What about Quinn?'

'You'd better drop that as well. Strictly speaking, I no longer have a client on whose behalf to engage you. See Benson with your account. Usual terms.'

'Very good, sir. I'll bid you good day, then.'

'Good day to you, Roffey.'

As soon as the door had closed behind his visitor, Richard returned to his desk and slumped down wearily in his chair. He had as good as known that Roffey would find nothing, but still he had had to put it to the test. Now he had done all he could reasonably be expected to do. Now he had established, seemingly beyond doubt, that there had been no conspiracy against Trenchard. If only he could believe his own conclusion, he might put his mind at rest. But that he could not do. For, unlike Roffey, Richard Davenall had the evidence of his own eyes to tell him that all was not what it seemed.

It was the afternoon of the day following the shooting at Lincoln's Inn: Wednesday, 8th November 1882. The operation to remove the bullet

269

from James's right side had been pronounced a success, and all fears for the state of his lung, close to which the bullet had passed, had been calmed. Richard therefore made his way up the stairs of St Bartholomew's Hospital in better spirits than he had known for some time: he was looking forward to congratulating his cousin on a lucky escape.

It was with some uncertainty that he traced the route Emily had described to James's ward. Indeed, after several wrong turnings, he was obliged to seek directions. These took him, at length, to the correct landing and a lofty anteroom to the ward itself.

At the far end, a nursing sister was in conversation with a lady. As Richard approached them, his shoes squeaking on the polished floor, the lady turned and walked away past him, glancing at him as she went. She was sombrely dressed, in grey overcoat and black turban, her dark hair drawn up beneath it. Richard would have paid her little attention but for the flash of her eyes in his direction as they crossed. It drew his own eyes to her, and he was aware, for a fleeting instant, of a disdainful manner and a startling beauty combined in a presence wholly at odds with the functional disinfected surroundings.

'Can I help you, sir?' the sister said.

'Oh . . . yes. I'm looking for Mr James Norton. I'm his cousin.'

'My, he *is* popular this afternoon.'

'Really?'

'That young lady was asking after him.'

'Isn't Mr Norton well enough to receive visitors, then? I thought—'

'You can see him if you don't stay long. Come with me.'

The sister bustled ahead, and Richard followed, all thoughts of the dark lady who had come to ask but not to visit retreating before concern for his cousin's health. He never thought to ask James who she might have been. Indeed, she soon lapsed altogether from his mind. Then, a week later, he read Trenchard's statement. And there, waiting for him, was the description of Melanie Rossiter that was also a description of the lady he had seen at the hospital. 'There was no mistaking the regal tilt of her jaw, nor the calm dark-eyed severity with which she greeted me.' There was not indeed. Richard knew then that Trenchard's ruthless seductress and the fashionable young lady asking after James were what all logic said they could not be: the same person.

THIRTEEN

I

Richard Davenall was, by breeding and training, a cautious man. He knew, better than most, that suspicion counts for nothing in the absence of evidence. Accordingly, for all the doubts he harboured about his cousin, he continued to behave in every way as a considerate host should. There was nothing he did, as the winter passed, to imply that he had ceased to be the staunchest of James Norton's allies, nothing he said, as the months slipped by, to suggest that he had ceased to trust him. Yet perhaps, when all was said and done, there did not need to be. Perhaps, in the end, intuition was enough to tell James that something had changed between them.

It was not immediate, it was not even consistent. There was nothing overt or hostile about it, yet it was palpable all the same. Some uncertainty entered their relations, some diffidence that grew into the watchful reserve of two men who have lost faith in each other but are not prepared to admit it. Whilst Constance was on hand, it represented nothing worse than a nagging unease, for the confidence she placed in the future was more than sufficient to eclipse their unspoken misgivings about each other. But when, in the middle of February, she decided that James's recovery was complete and that she was free to pay an overdue visit to Salisbury, Richard sensed that, without her, some form of crisis was inevitable. In many ways, he was relieved at the thought, for he had come to crave an end to their pretence of fellow-feeling, however it might be wrought. Perhaps, for all he knew, James had, too.

On the fourth morning of Constance's absence, the two men breakfasted together as usual. Watching James select his food from the hot dishes on the sideboard whilst he pretended to be absorbed in *The Times*, Richard asked himself once more the questions that had dogged him for two months past: Is he really James? If not, does he take me for a fool? Yet, if he truly is my cousin, how much worse than a fool would he think me for doubting him now?

A letter had come for James that morning and lay beside his place at the table. Richard watched as he sat down, opened it and smiled at the contents, a glimpse of which reminded Richard that this was St Valentine's Day, a date when secret love can show its hand. For an instant he toyed with the idea that the sender might be the woman he had seen at the hospital. Then, as if reading his thoughts, James said, 'It's a valentine,' adding, after a significant pause: 'From Constance.'

'Of course,' Richard replied, clearing his throat nervously.

'Did you think it was from somebody else?'

'Certainly not.' Richard tried to smile. There could be no doubt now that James was daring him to go further. Irritated by his own discomposure, he decided to do just that. 'Though I suppose it's not impossible that some young lady lost her heart to you whilst you were in Philadelphia.'

'Perhaps not impossible,' James replied levelly. 'But not, in fact, the case.'

'Still, you must have made some friends over there.'

'None to speak of.'

'No?'

This time James did not answer. He only smiled and promptly changed the subject. 'I believe Prince Napoleon's back in England.'

'Yes. I gather he is.'

'Have you been following the case in the papers?'

'It's been difficult not to.' The Prince's recent maladroit manoeuvres in French politics had indeed been given wide publicity. They had ended with his permanent expulsion from the country. He had taken refuge in London, where Richard suspected nothing short of absolute necessity could have driven him. 'The Prince appears to be as unlucky as he is ill-advised. He has a positive gift for misjudgement.'

'I fear so.'

Suddenly, Richard saw another opening, one which, this time, might give him the advantage. 'He certainly misjudged you – did he not?'

'Did he?'

'You caught him off guard, I remember, with a reference to events at Cleave Court in September 1846.'

'Did I?'

Richard struggled to suppress any hint of over-eagerness in his voice. 'What were they, by the way? You've never said.'

James frowned. 'I'm not sure I understand.'

'I mean what were the events that so embarrassed the Prince?'

James did not reply at once. He returned Richard's gaze calmly, raised his coffee-cup to his lips, took a sip from it, then said: 'I don't know. I must have been bluffing. Poor Plon-Plon's whole life is an embarrassment to him. I must have calculated it was odds on his first visit to Cleave Court being no exception.'

'Yet you specified an exact date.'

'I can't remember being that detailed.'

'You were, believe me.'

'Then, it must have been something Papa told me about. I'm afraid I can't bring it to mind now.' He smiled defiantly. 'But I'll certainly let you know . . . if I remember.'

Richard said nothing. He could not accept for a moment that James had forgotten the information he had used to threaten the Prince, but his reluctance to recall it now proved nothing beyond what Richard had already sensed: that their distrust had become mutual. He stared down intently at his newspaper, silently cursing his outspokenness. He had gained nothing by the exchange: nothing at all. The crisis had been neither confronted nor averted. It had merely been postponed.

II

Plon-Plon had risen late and bathed lengthily. Recent weeks had seen so many of his plans go awry that he was in no haste to stir abroad, in case yet further misfortunes should crash about his head. He sat, gloomily wrapped in a vast velvet dressing-gown, empurpled by invading sunlight, confounded by an unkind destiny and confronted by an English travesty of *petit déjeuner*. At length, he lit a cigar, sipped some coffee and pondered what malevolent working of fate had brought him from the brink of pre-eminence to an ill-aired suite of the Buckingham Palace Hotel.

It had all been Gambetta's fault. If the driving force of French Republican government had not contrived to die so unexpectedly on the last day of 1882, Plon-Plon would not have judged the early weeks of 1883 such a propitious time to reassert his leadership of the Bonapartist movement by publishing a revolutionary manifesto in the pages of *Figaro*. The objective of outflanking his upstart son and the loathsome pack of Royalist pretenders had been achieved, but only at the expense of a month's imprisonment on a preposterous charge of 'endangering the State'. Then, within three days of being acquitted and released, he had been banished from his homeland by decree of the Senate. So it was that he now found himself where he least wanted to be: in London, within walking distance of the court where the case of *Norton versus Davenall* would be tried in seven weeks' time.

Suddenly, there was a commotion in the outer room. Plon-Plon looked up from his brackish English coffee and scowled. An over-zealous chambermaid, perhaps. But no: there were male voices, raised in argument. One was his secretary's, the other . . . not wholly unfamiliar.

The door was flung open and Sir Hugo Davenall strode in, brushing off Brunet's attempts to stop him. 'Good morning . . . Count!'

'*Mon Dieu*! Hugo, what do you mean by—?'

'Call your lap-dog off!'

Plon-Plon restrained himself, for fear of aggravating a grumbling headache. '*Un de mes amis, Brunet. Je lui parlerai.*'

The secretary recovered himself and withdrew.

'Hugo! To what do I owe the pleasure?' In truth, he felt no pleasure; nor, it seemed, did his guest. Hugo looked thinner than when they had last met and somewhat wilder of eye. He was unshaven and perceptibly unsteady on his feet. Had it not been for the cigar-smoke, Plon-Plon suspected he would have been able to detect alcohol in the late-morning air. 'I am not travelling under an alias, *mon ami*. Why did you address me as "Count"?'

Hugo shrugged his overcoat off his shoulders and pitched it over a chair, then leaned against the chair-back, swaying slightly, the muscles of his jaw and forehead working convulsively.

'Is something wrong?'

'I've just come from our new solicitors, Plon-Plon. They're the very best. The most expensive.'

'They are equipped with a bar?'

'All right. I stopped off somewhere. God knows, I needed to.'

'Your solicitor is no longer your cousin Richard?'

'He ran out on us. Didn't you know?'

'I may have read of it. A sad business.'

'Of course you damn well read of it!' Hugo's words came in a rush of bitterness. 'You've been hiding over there in Paris these past four months, *reading* of my misfortunes. I could hardly believe it when I saw in the paper this morning that you were back. But it's only because you had no choice, isn't it? It's only because you had nowhere else to go.'

Plon-Plon bridled. Why should he be interrogated by this impetuous young man? 'I was not in hiding, Hugo! I never hide!'

'Call it what you please: it amounts to the same thing. You were there, hatching your damnable political schemes, while I was left here to face Norton alone.'

'Come, come—'

'Didn't you ever spare a thought for me? Didn't you ever think you should try to help me?'

'*L'imposteur* Norton gave me an uncomfortable half-hour last October. Why would I expose myself to him again?'

274

'For my sake, of course.'

Plon-Plon sighed: this was becoming painful. He rose from the table, walked across to Hugo and clapped him on the shoulder. 'I am sorry for you, *mon jeune ami*, but I am too old for sacrificial gestures. You should know me well enough to realize that.' At such close quarters, he could see the reproachful cast to Hugo's expression and was genuinely puzzled by it. It suggested a naïvety he had never associated with him.

'My mother's told me the truth. There's no point trying to bluff your way out of it.'

'Out of what?'

'I could hardly believe it at first. You, my father's oldest friend. . . .'

'What are you trying to say?'

Hugo's knuckles blanched as his grip on the chair-back tightened. 'That I am the son of Sir Gervase Davenall in law only, of course. I'd suspected it long enough, God knows, but I never thought . . . never guessed. . . .'

'What?'

Hugo looked into Plon-Plon's eyes with undisguised hostility. 'You have the damnable nerve to ask? I can't believe you don't know. You must know. My father was probably still in the Crimea when you bedded my mother; still fighting for his country . . . when I was conceived.'

Plon-Plon stepped back amazed. Among his many conquests, Catherine Davenall had never figured. Nor had he wanted her to. Hugo's accusation was absurd. Yet all he could find to say was: 'This is not true.'

'Are you calling my mother a liar?'

'Did she tell you this fairy story?'

'She admitted you were my natural father.'

'*Incroyable.* Then, yes, *mon ami*. I am calling your mother a liar. When am I alleged to have cuckolded your father?'

'You know well enough. The summer of 1855.'

'Impossible. The Emperor entrusted me with the organization of the International Exhibition that year. I was busy in Paris throughout the summer.'

'You could have found time to visit Cleave Court. For that matter, my mother could have visited Paris.'

'All things are possible, but I think I can prove I did not meet your mother at all during 1855. In other words, I can prove I did not seduce her. I can prove she is a liar.'

All the strength seemed to drain from Hugo. He pulled the chair back, slumped down on to it and put a hand to his forehead. 'Damn,' he muttered. 'Damn it all.'

'I am sorry, but she has misled you.'

275

'For God's sake, why should she?'

Plon-Plon shrugged his shoulders. 'Who knows? Perhaps to protect the true culprit. The strategies of women would elude the finest general.'

Abruptly, Hugo rose to his feet, his face crimson from a mixture of embarrassment at having revealed so much and resentment at having been deceived so completely. 'By heaven, they'll elude me no longer! I'll have the truth out of her if it's the last thing I do.' He grabbed his coat and swept to the door.

'Hugo—'

But it was too late. He was gone, leaving Plon-Plon to stare down into an insipid cupful of English coffee and think of Catherine Davenall. It was true: they had not met during 1855, nor had they wanted to. Their meeting at Constantinople in late November 1854 had left them with a powerful dislike of each other's company. It had been a meeting, indeed, that neither of them was likely to forget – or forgive.

Plon-Plon returned to Constantinople that afternoon in a mood of ill-humoured savagery. The humiliation he had suffered at Scutari still squirmed within him, and he was determined to make somebody pay for it. It could have been anybody – his aide-de-camp, an emissary from the Sultan, an inquisitive journalist – but it was not. Fate decreed, instead, that Catherine Davenall should come calling before he had yet changed out of his blood-stained uniform.

'Prince! What *has* happened to you?'

Catherine was still then the young and winsome creature Gervase had married. She had not yet become the stern inflexible woman of her middle age. But neither her charm nor her vivacity could quench the blinding anger which Plon-Plon felt. '*Un accident, madame.* What do you want with me?'

Pulling up halfway across the room at sight of his thunderous expression, she said: 'Why so gruff? I hoped you might have news of Gervase.'

At another time, Plon-Plon would have recalled Gervase visiting him after the battle of Inkerman and asking him, when he heard that the Prince was about to quit the Crimea, to look up Catherine in Constantinople, whence he had sent her some weeks previously on account of the danger from cholera. He would have recalled his friend's jovial confidences about the advantages of his wife's absence and would have respected them, would have smiled at Catherine and assured her that all was well with her brave and faithful husband. But not now. Not when this dark and boiling fury was upon him. 'I have no news of Gervase, madame, that his wife should hear.'

'What can you mean?'

'I advise you to go home to England. Leave your husband to his . . . consolations.'

Catherine frowned. 'Are you quite well, Prince? You seem out of sorts. It was reported that you had been ill, of course, but—'

'But you did not believe it!' Plon-Plon crossed to the french windows that gave on to the balcony and flung them open to the stagnant late-afternoon air. 'Smell that, madame: the perfume of the Orient. It is the only thing you should believe about the Turks: *l'ordure.*'

'All I meant was that I understood you had recovered.'

'Do you know where I have been today? Scutari. I went to visit your famous Mademoiselle Nightingale. But I did not see her. Instead, I encountered a friend of yours.'

'Of mine? Who was it?'

He swung round from the windows to face her, smiling triumphantly as he did so. 'Vivien Strang.'

'Good heavens.'

'She insulted me before a mob of journalists. She threw a basin of bloody water in my face. She shamed me – on your husband's account.'

Catherine sank into a chair. Her face had lost its colour, her mouth its firmness. 'I do not understand. What is she doing here?'

Plon-Plon had always disliked Catherine for her haughty sanctimonious ways. Now hatred was added to that dislike, a hatred of all the effortlessly disapproving English gentlewomen who had ever come his way, a hatred which convinced him that this one must be made to suffer. 'She is one of the nightingales, madame. She is nursing. Nursing a grievance, you might say.'

'A grievance against Gervase? Why?'

'She lost her position as your governess because of him.'

'No. It had nothing to do with him. She stayed out all one night and refused to say where she had been. Naturally, my father—'

'She was with Gervase!'

'If she says that, she's lying.' Catherine's gloved hands had tightened into tiny fists of determined disbelief.

'*She* does not say it, madame. *I* say it, because I know it to be a fact. Gervase lured her to the maze at Cleave Court that night and raped her.'

'No!'

'He had been obsessed with her for months. That night, the obsession ended.'

'It cannot be.'

'There is more. She had his child, madame.'

Catherine rose to her feet. 'I won't listen to such nonsense. Either she is lying – or you are.'

'She refused to tell you what had happened because she knew she

277

would not be believed. You never liked her, I think. You were glad of the excuse to have her dismissed.'

'None of this is true.'

'Ask Gervase. See if he denies it. Ask Mademoiselle Strang. She is at Scutari now: you could confront her easily enough. You will not, I know. You will not, because you know I speak the truth. You must have realized your husband's taste for . . . variety. That is why he sent you here. So that he could be free to . . . indulge himself.'

Catherine had heard enough. She turned and hurried to the door.

'So there's news of Gervase for you to take away, madame: news of the woman he preferred to you, news of the bastard she bore him!'

The door slammed shut. He was alone. The rage began to drain from him, leaving a dragging emptiness in its place. He went out on to the balcony and watched Catherine's carriage drive away. The sun was beginning to set now, casting its sickly glow on the minarets and mosque-domes of the city. There was a rush of plover-flight across the roof behind him as the muezzins took up their ritual cry. On the Asian shore, beyond the Bosporus, the Barrack Hospital loomed vast and strangely anodyne in the pink declining light. Below him, in a narrow alleyway, a Greek was whipping a thin and overladen donkey. Suddenly, the stench of friendship betrayed filled Plon-Plon's nostrils. He turned and retreated into the room.

'Brunet!' Plon-Plon called when he had finished dressing. 'We shall be leaving London.'

'When, *mon grand seigneur?*'

'Immediately.'

'But . . . to go where?'

Plon-Plon frowned. Where to go indeed? He could neither remain in London nor return to Paris. Turin contained his wife and, which was worse, her family. None of the alternatives appealed, but to one of them he would have to go. 'Anywhere, Brunet,' he said with a sigh. 'Anywhere.'

III

A transitory warmth had come upon Salisbury as the day advanced and now, as Constance and Emily passed through the Harnham Gate, they were struck by how spring-like the close contrived to seem, with tightly wrapped shoots of daffodils sprouting from the grass, doves cooing beyond the walls of the Bishop's Palace and the pale sunlight drawing a golden hue from the cathedral stone.

'It has been like this ever since you arrived,' said Emily, as they walked along, savouring the gentleness of the day.

'Too good to last, you think?' said Constance. 'This whole winter has seemed like that to me, Emily: a taste of pleasures which may not endure.'

'Why should they not?'

'Because, for the moment, I am looked upon charitably by the arbiters of cathedral opinion. Should I follow the prompting of my heart, however, they will not be so understanding.'

'Should you marry James, you mean?'

'You know it is in my mind, then?'

'I know it is bound to be. As does Father. How can it not be—?' She broke off as one of the vergers turned out of the stonemasons' yard and smiled broadly at sight of them. Cordial greetings were exchanged, approval of the weather shared, a longer conversation adroitly avoided. The verger passed on, and Emily resumed. 'Miss Pursglove said as much when I visited her.'

'How is she settling in?'

'Admirably, as you shall see tomorrow. But do not attempt to change the subject.' She smiled at her sister. 'Miss Pursglove said how sorry she was to hear of your troubles but that, in her opinion – trenchant, as you know – they should not stand in your way. James and you are *meant* for each other. Her words, not mine.'

'Very possibly, but words are easier than deeds. I cannot entirely forget William, much as he has hurt me.'

'What do the doctors say?'

'That he is no better. They do not forbid me to visit him, but they do not encourage it. And I hardly seem to have the heart to go.' She looked into the middle distance. 'What could we say to each other after all that has happened?'

'Have you sought . . . legal advice?'

Constance's gaze fell to the ground. 'Richard tells me that, in the circumstances, divorce on grounds of insanity could easily be obtained. As easily, at all events, as such things can ever be obtained.'

'Is that your intention?'

Her reply was scarcely audible. 'Yes.'

'It is what you *must* do.' Emily squeezed her sister's elbow. 'It will set you free – to marry James.'

'He has not asked me to marry him.'

'But he will. The contents of this morning's post did not escape my envious eye.'

Constance blushed and smiled. 'Yes. He will.' Suddenly, a look of alarm crossed her face. 'But what of you and Father? A divorce in the family will scandalize the close.'

Emily looked around at the encircling array of red-bricked canonries and stone-faced deaneries. 'They will revel in it, naturally, but then they will forget it. It's not as if you live here, after all.'

'But you and Father do.'

'Father has grown too deaf to hear gossip. You need not worry on our account.'

'But I do.'

'Then, let me put your mind at rest. We wanted you to marry James twelve years ago – and we want you to marry him now. It won't be the same, of course: it can never be that. But it will be what you both deserve: each other.'

It was the final blessing Constance wanted and needed to hear. As the two sisters passed on towards the Little Canonry, they both knew that the forthcoming trial in London could produce, however gargantuan its efforts, no decision to compare for significance with the one Constance had already taken.

IV

The room was dark, for the sun had gone from this side of Chester Square, and Hugo, curled fully clothed beneath the bedspread, was sleeping deeply. It was a relief and a satisfaction for Catherine to see his boyish head against the pillow, eyes happily closed. She could almost imagine he was a child again, sent to his room for one of his many misdemeanours, only to be found blithely dozing when she looked in to make her peace with him. She eased the door shut and walked softly away down the passage.

Bladeney House held for Catherine no memories that she wished to recall. She glanced at the portraits lining the curving staircase as she descended and silently cursed the serried likenesses of long-dead Davenalls. Still, there was comfort to be had in the way she had cheated them, a comfort only Hugo's loss of the pending lawsuit could erase. For Hugo, she wordlessly told his ancestors, was not a legitimate Davenall at all. He was her victory over them. He was hers alone.

She turned into the music room and crossed to the french windows, shading her eyes to look out into the walled rear garden of the house. There were signs of neglect: she did not allow such slackness at Cleave Court. But here it did not matter. Here was a kingdom she was happy to leave empty, here was her dead husband's hated realm of which she wanted no part. She would be gone in the morning. She would be gone and glad of it.

Catherine had only consented to visit London in order to hear from Mr Lewis (of Lewis & Lewis) what success had attended his enquiries in the United States. With the trial fast approaching, she had looked to him for long-overdue proof of who James Norton really was. But she had been disappointed. She and Hugo had travelled that morning to Mr Lewis's offices in Ely Place. There they had been courteously received, plied with glasses of madeira and assured of industrious detection to come. Yet what had three months of tireless probing into Norton's past produced? Very little, as Mr Lewis had been forced to admit.

'The problem in this case, ma'am, is a subtle one. Mr Norton's account of his life and work in Philadelphia is accurate: that much we have established. But it only takes us back to the summer of 1881, when he successfully applied for a position with the McKitrick Advertising Agency. There are colleagues and acquaintances enough to tell us all we need to know about his activities since then. He visited Paris in January of last year, describing the trip as a holiday. He told nobody that he was going to see a doctor there, but, in the circumstances, that is scarcely surprising. Then, at the end of July, he resigned from his post and left the city, arriving in this country in the middle of September. Nobody in Philadelphia knew of his plans, but, again, in the circumstances, that is only to be expected.

'Where we have experienced great difficulty is in tracing his movements before he arrived in Philadelphia. He applied to the agency from an address in Baltimore, but that, it transpires, was only a lodging-house. So far as we can establish, he spent no more than a few weeks in the city. Where he lived prior to that we have no idea. Nor does Mr Norton seem to want us to find out. All his statements are distinguished by their vagueness on that score.

'If we start from the other end, it is no better. There was certainly a merchant vessel *Ptarmigan* which sailed from the Port of London on the eighteenth of June 1871, bound for Nova Scotia. It docked in Halifax on the twenty-first of July 1871. There is no record of it carrying passengers, but that, of course, is consistent with Mr Norton's claim to have made a private arrangement with the captain. As for the captain, he went down with his ship off Brazil three years later. Mr Norton could have found this out himself, of course. He could have searched the records, as we did – and found a ship and a captain convenient to his purpose.

'What we have to deal with is the cleverest of ploys. Mr Norton did not merely formulate his claim, then step forward to present it. He first sought to distract attention from who he really is by inventing another identity and authenticating it by spending a year in Philadelphia, where he won a reputation as hard-working, sober, respectable, solitary and essentially unremarkable: characteristics ideal for his purpose. He has been both patient and cunning: patient enough to have spent the past two years preparing for this trial, cunning enough to have foreseen all the ways in which we would seek to expose him. Whoever he really is, he is a quite remarkable young man.'

Small thanks Mr Lewis's report had won from Catherine and small thanks it had deserved. She had not needed him to tell her what a menacing opponent Norton was. All she required was a name to put to her enemy, and that Mr Lewis had been unable to provide.

The paucity of the evidence unearthed by their expensive enquiries in America had hit Hugo hard. If Catherine had known where he intended to go after leaving her at the corner of Ely Place, she would have tried to stop him. In a sense, she blamed herself for ever letting him believe his own absurd notion about Prince Napoleon. But she had not known the wretched man was in London again, nor that Hugo would be foolish enough to appeal to him.

So he had returned, red-faced from drink and injured pride, and had demanded to be told the truth. Only that habit of stamping when cross had been lacking to make it a perfect replica of the many tantrums of his childhood. But Catherine was not his mother for nothing. She had been able to call upon wrath enough to eclipse his own. She had crushed his demands as effectively as he should have known she would. He had not been told the truth.

No more of it, at all events, than she judged he could bear. His anger, as ever, had been swiftly spent. Where first Catherine had suborned she had later needed to soothe. For Hugo had cried – tears of wrenching childlike grief – at the threat to his pampered life. He had cried on her bosom, and she had put her arms around him and clasped him tightly, until the sobs had subsided and her son had recovered his peace of mind.

Now he slept, whilst Catherine considered what she must do to protect him. Perhaps Norton did not know how much more deeply she loved Hugo than she could ever have loved the clear-eyed Davenall that Gervase had fathered by her. Perhaps he did not realize that, even had she thought he really was James, she would have fought him for Hugo's sake.

Catherine walked across to the harpsichord in the corner of the room, raised the lid and tried a few experimental notes. In need of tuning, as she might have expected. Yet the sound of the instrument – its high antique tones reaching her ears through the pure silence of the room – reminded her of her music teacher of long ago, a woman she had often thought of recently. It was as well the vile man had not had the nerve to tell Hugo the story of Vivien Strang.

Catherine sat down and began to play, slowly and distractedly but still proficiently, for Miss Strang had taught her well. Their lessons belonged to memories more distant than time alone could justify. They belonged to the forgotten discarded youth of Catherine Webster. They did not matter. Yet could she be so sure? The more she tried and failed to find another explanation, the more the unseen hand of Vivien Strang seemed to hold the answer. Where was she now? Where had she gone, what had she done, since the day of Catherine's petty vengeance?

'My own daughter saw you come in, dammit!' said Colonel Webster, his voice hoarse from pointless railing.

'I have not denied being out all night,' Miss Strang replied with perfect composure. 'I do not dispute the evidence of Catherine's own eyes.'

'Yet you refuse to explain yourself.'

'I have said all that I will say.'

Webster slapped his thigh in baffled despair and turned to Catherine. 'It rests with you, my girl,' he said, with a roll of the eyes.

It was the moment Catherine had been waiting for, the moment when she might cleanse herself of the jealousy that burned within her. She had never liked Miss Strang; she did not believe a young lady's governess should be quite so elegant and learned. And since she had noticed Gervase's interest in the woman she had come to hate her. She hardly dared admit even to herself where she feared Miss Strang had been that night – or with whom. But that did not matter now, for now she had her chance to ensure she need never resent Miss Strang again.

'It is inconceivable that the truth can be other than deeply disgraceful, Papa. Surely her silence confirms it.'

Webster sighed. 'I fear it does. You must leave us, Miss Strang.'

'I only hope,' Catherine went on, 'that other respectable families will be spared her unwholesome influence.'

'That's sure enough, since she'll be leaving here without a reference.'

'May I withdraw now, Papa?'

'Mmm? Why, yes, my girl. Of course.'

She moved towards the door, passing Miss Strang as she went. 'Goodbye Catherine,' the governess said softly. 'I will never forget your exemplary conduct this day.'

Catherine did not reply. With the haughtiest of sidelong glances, she left the room. An hour later, she watched from an upper window as Miss Strang boarded the carriage to be driven to the station. She watched – and celebrated her secret triumph. She was rid of the woman at last, and sure, now, that nothing could distract Gervase from her charms.

Catherine closed the harpsichord and stared into the silence that followed. She had behaved heartlessly, it was true; yet, when told at last by Prince Napoleon what Gervase had done that night, she had not regretted her actions, for regret was not in her nature.

She frowned, scorning the little flare of panic her thoughts had inspired. Was it truly possible? Norton, it seemed, knew of her governess's unjust treatment. He knew what nobody could have told him – except Miss Strang herself. And Catherine did not doubt Plon-Plon's claim that Miss Strang had borne Gervase a child. Therefore, could Norton be that child? Was his claim to be James the wronged governess's long-planned vengeance? 'I will never forget,' she had said. Nor could Catherine forget – that Vivien Strang was a woman of her word.

V

It was late afternoon, but in Richard Davenall's Holborn office evening seemed already to have closed on the crammed bookcases and yellowing stacks of paper, a chill grey herald of darkness that deepened its occupant's mood of self-reproachful indecision. Three months before, he had staked his professional reputation on acknowledging James Norton as his cousin. Now, he admitted to himself if to no other living soul, he wished he had not done so. It was not that he disbelieved James's claim: he could find no cause to do that. It was simply that, for whatever reason, certainty had left him. There was so much he did not understand, so much that remained hidden or unexplained, so much – his father would no doubt have said – to which he was not equal.

Glancing up at Wolseley Davenall's faded photograph on the wall behind his desk – the lean, set, familiar features with their preserved hint of disapproval – Richard thought once more of the argument he had overheard between his father and Gervase in the autumn of 1859. 'Lennox will have his money.' But why? What had he been paid for? What, for that matter, would poor mad Trenchard have made of it – had he but known?

When Richard looked back from the photograph, he was no longer alone. He felt every muscle in his body tense at the sight of James Norton standing before him. There had been no sound, no warning of his arrival. But he was there none the less. And he was not a ghost.

'Good afternoon, Richard,' James said with a smile. 'I'm sorry if I surprised you.'

'No, no. Not at all.'

'Benson told me to come straight in.'

Benson, Richard knew, would have told James nothing of the kind. Nevertheless, he might well have been persuaded to let him enter unannounced. The question was why James should have wanted to take Richard unawares. To surprise him in just the mood which had indeed been upon him? To steal some glimpse of what he truly thought? With an effort that may have been apparent, Richard retreated towards an inexpressive professional manner. 'What brings you here?'

'I thought I'd look in on my way back from Warburton's.'

'A satisfactory consultation?'

'Warburton remains confident, certainly.'

'I'm glad to hear it.'

James took three slow casual steps across to a bookcase and leaned back against it, his elbows propped on one of the shelves. 'Actually,' he said, smiling amiably, 'my visit does have a particular purpose.'

'Oh, yes?'

'I wondered if you would do me the favour of accompanying me on a journey this afternoon.' He paused. 'A journey, you might say, into the past.'

'What exactly do you mean?' Richard told himself to be cautious, but already he could feel the curiosity stirring within him.

James pushed himself away from the bookcase and moved to the window. 'I've been thinking of undertaking the journey for some time, as a matter of fact.' He put his hand to his mouth and patted his lips nervously, as if missing a cigarette. 'I should not care to have to go alone.'

Was this a devious ploy or a cry from the heart? As ever, Richard could not be sure. 'If it's so important, I'll happily go with you. But what's our destination?'

'Wapping, Richard. The spot where I thought to end my life twelve years ago. I feel I must go back – to exorcize the memory.'

So that was it: a risk too great, surely, for any impostor to run. With a rush of remorse, Richard wondered if it really was a memory James was seeking to exorcize – rather than the distrust that had grown between them. Either way, this promised to be the crisis he had sought that very morning to engineer. 'Very well,' he said. 'We'll go.'

James looked back at him. 'I wouldn't want Constance to hear of it. She would think it morbid. That's why. . . .'

'You waited until she'd gone away?'

'Yes.'

It was as good an excuse as any, Richard reflected, if an excuse were needed. But pretext and reality had fused too often in his mind to be separable now. 'I'll say nothing to Constance. When do we go?'

'At once, if you will.' James glanced out of the window. 'It'll be dark in an hour. There's no time to lose.'

They took a cab to the Tower and walked from there, through St Katharine Docks and on towards Wapping, threading their way along the confused and crowded thoroughfare of wharfs and warehouses, struggling to make themselves heard above the clattering hoofs and grating wheels.

'It's kind of you to come with me, Richard,' James said. 'I do appreciate it.'

'It's the least I can do.'

'I worry that you feel excluded from the family because of this wretched business.'

'I fear that's inevitable.'

'When it's over, I hope you'll agree to handle all my affairs.'

'If you wish it.'

'I do, I do.' Ambiguity and suspicion had infected all their exchanges. Richard was not sure now what his own words meant, let alone James's.

The light was fading and the neighbourhood coarsening as they pressed on eastwards. Shambling beggars and gaping barefoot children were beginning to outnumber tradesmen. The Thames glinted at them and tracked their steps from the far ends of sloping bale-hung alleyways. For Richard this was a disconcerting alien world, where trust and treachery threatened to become indistinguishable, where he had fewer ways than ever of knowing how much his companion remembered – or how much he had merely imagined.

'There'll be so much I don't know,' James went on, 'so much that's changed in twelve years. I intend to be a model landlord, but I'll need your help and advice.'

'Then, you shall have it.' For an instant, the prospect was one to savour. This man would be so much worthier a client than Hugo, so much more deserving of Richard's advice. Then they passed over the swingbridge across Wapping Basin and entered, or re-entered, the miniature world James had recalled at the hearing: Wapping High Street, with a neglected graveyard on one side and the Town of Ramsgate public house on the other. 'This is the place, isn't it?'

'Yes,' James replied. 'This is it.' He led the way up the next street on the left, to where rusty creaking gates gave on to the burial-ground. He pushed them open and Richard followed him in.

'This is where you waited? This is where you chose the stone to weigh you down?'

'Yes.'

Richard looked around at the cluster of crooked gravestones and mould-draped mausolea, his breath clouding in the frosting air. It was possible, yes, all too possible. On this frozen patch of funeral-planted land, between the drab crammed vastness of the slums and the grinding ceaseless commerce of the river, a man might truly have sought an end to misery. In that moment, though only for that moment, Richard was convinced. 'I'm glad your nerve failed you,' he said, resting his hand on James's shoulder. 'You deserved better than to be brought to this.'

'Did I?' James glanced round at him, his expression indecipherable in the gathering gloom. Then, abruptly, he stepped away towards the gates. 'Shall we take a look at the stairs I followed down to the river?'

'By all means.' But James's movement had been too quick for Richard's liking. It was as if he had recoiled from sympathy, as if he had found either the memory or the deception too painful to bear. As they walked back in the direction of Wapping High Street, Richard sensed that his companion was at his most vulnerable in this place and at this time. If he were ever to drop his guard, this would be the moment. 'You meant what you said about being a model landlord?'

'Certainly.'

'You'll have much to consider. The Irish property, for instance. It's been entirely in the agent's hands since your grandmother's death. You went there once, I think.'

'To Carntrassna? Yes, when I was a boy.'

'With your father?'

'Yes.'

'What year? Do you remember?'

'1859. Soon after Grandpapa's death.' And shortly before, Richard calculated, Gervase paid the Carntrassna agent ten thousand pounds for no known reason. 'Papa felt that, as his heir, I ought to meet his mother.'

'Did you enjoy the visit?'

'Hardly. I found County Mayo raw and forbidding.'

'And your grandmother?'

'Not one to suffer fools – or children – gladly. She was rather . . . intimidating.'

'Do you remember the agent there? A man named Lennox?'

'No. I can't say I do.'

They entered the alley that cut down between the Town of Ramsgate and the walls of neighbouring buildings towards the river. Light and warmth were fleeing from the day, with mist rising ahead of them from the brown and turbid mass of the Thames. At the end of the alley, a flight of steps ran down and vanished into the water. They halted at the top of them and looked around at the soaring weed-fringed faces of brick that the warehouses showed to the river, at the distant slime-hazed wharfs of the Surrey shore, at the lapping murky infinity where the Thames passed on towards the sea.

'A dismal spot,' said Richard, after a lengthy silence.

'A dismal spot for a dismal deed. It is strange to return here – after all these years.'

'Does it feel as you expected?'

'I don't know. I'm glad to have come, though – as I'll be glad to leave.'

The tone of James's voice swayed Richard more than the words he spoke. Such a tone could not, he sensed, have been assumed for his benefit. It conveyed the memories this spot held for him more poignantly than any word-perfect courtroom testimony. It carried the unmistakable ring of truth.

'Shall we go now?' said James, after another wordless interval.

'If you've seen enough.'

'I believe I have.' A violent shudder ran through him then, more violent than the encroaching chill could explain. 'Quite enough.'

Richard nodded and set off back along the alley. Before he had covered ten yards, he realized that James was not following. Pulling up in puzzlement, he turned and saw his companion still standing at the top of the steps – rooted to the spot, it seemed – staring down into the river. He called his name, but there was no response, no sound or movement to indicate that he had heard. Richard walked back to him and reached out to touch his shoulder. Then, at sight of the expression on James's face, he stopped.

Previously, it had been too dark in the alley to make out a man's features, but now a lamp had been lit in one of the lofty warehouses to their left, casting a sallow distorted rectangle of light down on to the steps and a portion of the river beyond. Pallid and flickering though it was, it sufficed to show Richard that James was in the grip of a disabling terror.

'What's wrong?'

Still there was no answer. Following the direction of James's gaze, Richard looked down at the base of the steps, where the lamplight showed grey opaque water and a floating litter of matchwood slapping idly at the lower treads.

'For God's sake, man, what's the matter?'

At last, James spoke, in a husky quavering travesty of his former confident tone. 'Don't you see it?'

'See what?'

'In the water.'

'I see nothing.'

'Nothing?' James stared at him incredulously.

'Nothing at all.'

'Then . . . Then it must be . . .' he looked back down the steps, and his voice trailed into silence.

'Must be what?'

At first, James did not reply. He took several deep breaths and squared his shoulders, as if preparing to exert some enormous effort. Then he turned towards Richard, his expression clear and self-controlled. 'Nothing,' he said, in a voice to which calm and rigour had been restored. 'It's as you say, Richard. Nothing at all.' And with that, quickly yet without the least sign of haste, he strode away along the alley.

He had turned into Wapping High Street and vanished from sight before Richard began to follow, bemused by what had happened, cheated of the crisis he had anticipated yet sensing that a different kind of crisis might nevertheless have occurred. But what kind he did not know, for he had seen nothing, on the steps or in the river. And whatever James had thought he had seen was invisible now beneath the fog that rose from the water like the final exhalation of countless drowning men.

FOURTEEN

I

During the lengthy interlude between hearing and trial, the outside world had succeeded in entirely forgetting the case of *Norton versus Davenall*. A five-month truce had sufficed to blank out all awareness of even its most sensational aspects. To the public mind, it seemed as if it had never happened.

The law, by contrast, had not forgotten. It had merely bided its limitless time until, with neither haste nor hesitation, the appointed day drew near. The truce was about to end.

On the very last afternoon before its expiry, James Norton and Constance Trenchard were walking arm in arm across the grassy slopes of Parliament Hill, breathing the clear air with the desperate pleasure of two who knew such idle freedom would soon no longer be theirs to enjoy.

'Russell thinks it may last two months or more,' said James, with a heavy sigh. 'I wish it could be over quicker. I wish I could just snap my fingers and have done with it.'

'But you can't,' said Constance.

'No,' James replied, shaking his head. 'It seems it must be endured – if I'm to be accepted for who I am. A heavy penance for such a modest privilege: to use my real name. Sometimes I wonder why we shouldn't simply run away together and forget the whole thing. If Hugo wants the baronetcy that badly, why not let him keep it? I've done without it so long I'm not sure I care one way or the other.'

Constance looked at him uncertainly. 'You don't really mean that?'

'Part of me does, yes. The part that made me stay away all those years.'

'And the other part?'

'It tells me not to run away a second time. Besides. . . .'

'Yes?'

'I don't have the right to ask you to do such a thing. For your sake, if for nobody else's, I'm determined to see this through.'

She leaned up to kiss him. 'We'll see it through *together.*'

He smiled. 'It's not too late to change your mind.'

'Oh, but it is. This very day, Richard has instituted divorce proceedings on my behalf.' She stepped back. 'You look surprised.'

'I didn't think you'd feel able to consider such a move until the case was over.'

'The case doesn't make any difference, James. That's what I want you to understand. It doesn't matter to me who the world says you are. I already know. You're the man I'd gladly marry tomorrow if I were free. . . .' She blushed. 'And if I were asked.' Then she shrieked, for he suddenly clasped her about the waist and whirled her in a circle.

'As soon as you're free,' he cried, 'you will be asked.' He kissed her, and they laughed breathlessly, turning to look down in smiling private triumph at the grey and smoking city. 'James Davenall and Constance Sumner will marry – after a twelve-year engagement. You have my word on it.'

Just as Constance was about to reply, there came a shout from behind them. 'Davenall! Is that you, Davenall?' They turned to see two smartly dressed men of about James's own age walking towards them. One was thin, sallow-faced and lugubriously moustached, the other portly, ruddy-complexioned and smiling broadly: it was evidently he who had called out. About ten yards to the rear, a third man stood watching them with little apparent interest, although the two had seemingly just left his company. 'It's Jimmy Davenall, isn't it?' said the red-faced man as they drew nearer.

'Yes,' said James cautiously. 'I don't believe —'

'Don't you remember me? Mulholland. Reggie Mulholland.' He pointed to his companion. 'And Charlie Borthwick.'

James stroked his chin and looked from one to the other of them. 'Mulholland and Borthwick,' he said thoughtfully. 'Yes, of course. You were in the same year as me at Christ Church.'

'Spot on, old man. You've placed us. I've put on a bit of weight since then, admittedly, but I'd have known you anywhere. Good to see you again, ain't it, Charlie?'

'Certainly is. How are you, Davenall?'

'Very well, thank you.' He smiled at each of them in turn.

'Won't you introduce me to your friends, James?' Constance put in.

'Why, yes, of course,' said James. 'But perhaps I should first explain what notorious pranksters these two fellows were at Oxford. It will help you appreciate their little practical joke on this occasion.'

'Joke?' said Mulholland, frowning. 'I don't quite take your meaning, old man.'

'You see, Constance, this is Reggie Mulholland' – he pointed to the one introduced as Borthwick – 'and this is Charlie Borthwick.' He pointed to the other. 'Not, as they would have you believe, the opposite way about.' The two men stared at him dumbfounded. 'And the fellow loitering down the slope behind them is, I strongly suspect, a clerk in the employment of Lewis and Lewis, come to witness our reunion. Isn't that so, Charlie– old man?'

'This is preposterous,' Borthwick spluttered. 'I—'

'Have they paid you to enact this charade? Or are you doing it for old time's sake?'

Mulholland plucked at Borthwick's sleeve. 'Best give it up, Charlie. He's seen through us.'

'He's just guessing, dammit!'

'No. Reggie's quite right. I have seen through you. You're as transparent as you always were.'

'Let's cut along,' Mulholland muttered. 'This game's not worth the candle.'

Borthwick seemed about to contest the point, then all his bluster suddenly deserted him. With a puff of the chest, he turned and retreated, Mulholland following. The third man fell in between them and they marched away down the slope amid sufficient head-tossing and arm-waving to suggest a lively exchange of recriminations.

'I don't understand,' said Constance as they faded from view. 'What were they trying to do?'

'They were trying to trick me into providing them with evidence to use in court. It's clearly been made worth their while to testify against me. Think how much more damaging their testimony would be if I'd been taken in by their exchange of identities.'

'But how could they think you would be?'

'I knew them only slightly at Oxford. And it's thirteen years since I last saw either of them. They must have thought there was a good chance of bringing it off.'

'Who could have put them up to it?'

'Who do you think?'

Constance frowned. 'You mean Hugo?'

'Or my mother. It hardly matters which. I dare say one of their lawyers actually suggested it – but evidently they didn't object.'

'But . . . to try to trick you like that: it's shameful.'

James put his arm round her shoulders and held her tightly. 'It's only the start, Connie, only the first shot in the campaign. From now on, it'll be open conflict – with no holds barred.'

II

Proceedings in the case of *Norton versus Davenall* commenced *nisi prius* at the Royal Courts of Justice on 3rd April 1883, with the Lord Chief Justice, Lord Coleridge, presiding. Under his direction, a retinue of QCs and juniors took issue, backed by pensive solicitors and anxious clerks, attended by officious registrars and obsequious ushers, observed by twelve solemn-faced jurors, a scribbling pack of journalists and a varying, ever mobile mass of spectators.

To those closely involved in the case it seemed strange, later, how little they could remember of the days and weeks they were destined to spend in that lofty fan-lit courtroom, as the argument ebbed and flowed about them. At the time, their attention was undivided, their concentration ferocious; but, in retrospect, the phases of its long convoluted drama fused into one indistinct parade of question and answer, accusation and denial, claim and counter-claim.

What can be said with certainty is that it was on the tenth day of the trial that James Norton entered the witness-box. Russell, in his lengthy preamble, had prepared the ground well; but this, everyone knew, was the ultimate test. At the hearing, a single day had seen Norton's testimony completed, but points which had then been established within minutes were now pored over and analysed for hours at a stretch. It took a week for him to reach the events of 17th June 1871 and another week to bring his story to the present day.

Then came his cross-examination by the defence. Sir Hugo Davenall's new senior counsel, Mr Aubrey Gilchrist, proved only a marginally less acute inquisitor than his predecessor, Sir Hardinge Giffard. For days on end, he and Norton fenced and parried over the same ground. Sometimes Gilchrist gave place to one of his juniors, but only, it seemed, in the hope of lulling Norton into unwise relaxation. The plaintiff was given no quarter, allowed no rest. The search for an opening was tireless, his exertions to prevent one ceaseless.

In the event, Gilchrist was as unsuccessful in challenging Norton's account of himself as he was incapable of discrediting his recollection of distant events. The colour of the nursery wallpaper at Cleave Court, the name of the dog one of the gamekeepers had accidentally shot in 1857, his academic and sporting career at Eton and Oxford, his friendship with Roland Sumner, his courtship of Constance Sumner, his consultations with Dr Fiveash, his flight from the country in 1871, his subsequent movements and occupations through a dozen cities of Canada and the United States: all this and more was sifted through, and never once did he falter.

Late in the seventh week of the trial, Norton's cross-examination ended. There was neither fanfare of triumph nor admission of defeat, but it was clear none the less that, thus far even if no further, he had had the better of it.

III

The Times, London, 21st May 1883: 'Prince Napoleon has been in England during the last few days on private business; it has been surmised that he would like to obtain from the Empress Eugénie a more explicit recognition of his position as political chief of the Bonapartists than has been vouchsafed to him as yet.'

Plon-Plon flung down the newspaper in disgust and began an ill-tempered patrol of the Chinese rug by the window. It was a mistake to have come to Farnborough Hill, he concluded. The fourth anniversary of the Prince Imperial's death did not fall until 1st June, but Eugénie was already in a preparatory trance of black-crêped debility: a useful discussion of politics was entirely out of the question.

She had never liked him, he reflected as he gazed gloomily out of the window at the vast and ugly building taking shape in the grounds. A mausoleum, he gathered, for the accomodation of her husband, her son, and in due course, herself. An abbey alongside was also planned, for the comfort and convenience of the flock of refugee monks whose bat-like presence threatened to blot out spring in this corner of Hampshire. Not that any of it surprised him, stemming as it did from the perversely pious nature that had made her reject his sexual advances in Madrid in 1843, when she was seventeen and he was in his prime. Forty years later, it was painfully clear that her taste had not improved.

There was a knock at the door, and Brunet came in, but Plon-Plon's hopes that Eugénie at last felt able to see him were swiftly dashed.

'A lady wishes to see you, *mon grand seigneur*.'

'Who is it?'

'Catherine Davenall.'

'*Merde!*' This was bad news indeed. If Eugénie came to hear of his involvement in the Davenall case, he could bid adieu to any hopes of a pact with her. 'Where is she?'

'In the red drawing room.'

'I will speak to her.' He hurried to the door. 'But listen to me, I absolutely forbid any interruptions, do you understand?'

'Yes, *mon grand seigneur*, absolutely.'

*   *   *

She was standing on the far side of the room when he entered, gazing up at a large oil painting of Eugénie with the Prince Imperial. In the instant it took her to turn round he wondered if they had ever been alone together since her visit to his apartment in Constantinople nearly thirty years ago; on balance, he rather thought not.

She had changed. He could see it in her set and regal bearing, her pale indomitable face. Where once there had been vanity, ignorance and a trusting nature, there was now a hard-won tempered resolve. She had left the errors of youth behind and attained a flawless sense of purpose, whilst for Plon-Plon, alas, the fallibilities of the past remained the snares of the present. 'Madame,' he said, pressing the door shut behind him and inclining his head in the faintest of bows. 'A *votre service*.'

Catherine made no move towards him. Across the carpeted gap of the drawing-room, their glances joined, acknowledged their differences, and parted. 'I have come to ask for your help,' she said abruptly.

Plon-Plon frowned. For one who had long shown him nothing but the coldest contempt now to seek his assistance, with neither apology nor explanation, was incomprehensible. '*My* help, madame?'

'There is nobody else I can ask.' Her expression implied, though she did not say, that he was, in truth, the very last person she would turn to. 'You have followed Hugo's lawsuit?'

'*Avec l'imposteur*? of course.'

'*L'imposteur*, as you correctly term him, has made an excellent impression on the court.'

'So the newspapers tell me.'

'In the opinion of my lawyers, Norton will win the case.'

'They have said that?'

'No. I observe that they think it. What they tell me is quite different.'

'Have you no witnesses to speak against him?'

'A positive regiment, I believe. But they will not prevail.'

'You are certain?'

'Yes. If I were not James's mother, I would be taken in by this man. The jury believe him, and the judge is inclined to. The case has many weeks to run, but its outcome is already decided.'

'Then, you have my sympathy.'

'That, Prince, is of no use to me. What I require is your help.'

Plon-Plon walked slowly across the room towards her, until they were standing at either end of the painting she had been inspecting. He glanced up at it and curled his lip: Eugénie looked matronly and prematurely old in her widow's weeds, the Prince Imperial callow and faintly ridiculous in his Woolwich cadet's uniform. 'This house,' he remarked, 'is full of memorials to the Empress's late son, as you may have observed. A mausoleum-in-waiting, you might say, until the genuine article is complete.'

'I had noticed.'

'Eugénie carries her bereavement with her like a pack on her back, like a ball and chain about her feet.' He looked directly at Catherine and continued: 'But you, madame, never mention your dead son, as distinct from his impersonator. Why is that?'

'James is dead. He belongs to the past. I do not.'

Plon-Plon shook his head in puzzlement. 'So frank, so decisive, so . . . detached. You were not always so.'

'I dare say neither of us, Prince, wishes to be reminded of what we *were.*'

'*Touché, madame. C'est vrai.*'

A flicker of impatience passed across Catherine's face, as if the discomfort of their encounter was one she wished to foreshorten. 'I have come to speak to you about Vivien Strang,' she said suddenly.

Plon-Plon stepped back in amazement. 'Vivien Strang?'

'You were eager enough to speak to me about her in Constantinople, were you not?'

'A long time ago, madame.' He struggled to recover his dignity. 'You said yourself that such reminders were unwelcome.'

'I simply wish to know where she is.'

'You think *I* can tell you?'

'You know more of her life since she left my father's house in 1846 than I do. You knew she was pregnant – and by whom. You knew she was nursing in the Crimea. I hoped, therefore, that you might still know something of her.'

'No, madame. I know nothing of her.'

'Yet you have guessed, as I have, that she is behind this conspiracy against my family.'

So. He was not alone in his suspicions. 'I have . . . guessed that. Yes.'

'But you have done nothing about it.'

'What should I have done? It is not evidence. It is not proof. And why should I have done anything even if I could? Since we are being so very candid, madame, pray tell me what I could possibly gain from becoming involved in this . . . *cause célèbre.*'

She shook her head. 'Nothing, Prince. Nothing at all.' She turned and moved slowly to the window, where she gazed out for what seemed an age before looking back at him. 'Gervase raped her, I ruined her – and you deceived her. What we have done to her is unforgivable.'

'You admit these things?'

'I admit them to you because you and I alone know the truth. To have it known to the world would be only marginally less awful than for Norton to win his case. I have told nobody that I suspect he is my husband's son by my former governess, that his resemblance to James

296

is that of a half-brother, that his motivaton is his mother's desire for revenge. I have told nobody – because nobody must know. But you and I already share the secret, do we not? So there is nothing to be lost by telling you.'

'But what is it that you want me to do?'

'It was you who deceived her. I thought you might now be able to dissuade her.'

'*Moi?*'

'I gather what drew her to the maze that night was the prospect of meeting you. Perhaps, therefore, she might be prepared to meet you again – and to call off her son.'

'*C'est absurde.* She would do nothing for me, even supposing I could find her.'

'What she would never accept from me she might accept from you. A compromise. A settlement out of court.'

'It would not work, madame. If you are right – if *we* are right . . . she has planned this too long to be deflected now.'

But Catherine was unmoved. Her certainty was unarguable, her implication clear that, by this one service, Plon-Plon could win back her respect. 'If we share what we know of her, Prince, I believe we can find her. The question is therefore a simple one. Will you help me?'

An hour had passed since Catherine's departure. Plon-Plon peered from the window once more and winced at sight of the scaffolded shell of the mausoleum. Was this domed and crenellated monument to a redundant dynasty so much worthier a life's work than his own random brilliances? He thought not. But he, as ever, was in the minority.

Forty years ago, in Madrid, Eugénie had flirted with the bullfighters and ridden bareback through the streets; she had smoked his cigars and dressed like a gypsy. Now she wore dresses that looked like shrouds and sat in darkened rooms studying plans of the mausoleum with its architect. If he were to win her over, his only reward would be the offer of a shelf for his own coffin.

So why not? Why not quit Farnborough and embark on the grandest folly of his life? Not because his dead friend's proud and pitiless widow had abased herself to plead with him. Nor yet because the sheer impudence of Norton's fraudulent claim irked him by the envy it inspired. Not even because he wished to look on Vivien Strang's face once more and win from her some form of absolution. No. He would not seek her out for any of those reasons. He would seek her out because he wanted to. He would find her in order to prove that he could.

IV

Nanny Pursglove's testimony was more effective than it had been at the hearing. Clearly, she still resented the suggestions made then that her memory and eyesight were suspect. Accordingly, she set about proving that they were not by a display of unflagging vigour during two days in the witness-box. Gilchrist was unable to make the slightest impact, and her eviction from Weir Cottage, skilfully introduced into her evidence by Russell, at once ensured her of the jury's sympathy.

As for Dr Fiveash, equivocal though he might be, he could say little that did not strengthen the plaintiff's case. There were times when he seemed to be pinned on the horns of several dilemmas, uncertain how much or how little to reveal. At one point, indeed, he seemed inclined to claim that his records had been spied upon, but Russell succeeded in strangling the idea at birth.

'Who do you suggest could have done such a thing, Doctor?'

'A temporary secretary whom I employed in January of last year.'

'Interesting. Why did you take her on?'

'My permanent secretary was injured in a cycling accident.'

'How could this *spy* have known such a vacancy would arise?'

'I can only think the accident was . . . contrived. The bicycle may have been . . . tampered with.'

'Did you have cause to think so at the time?'

'Ah . . . no.'

'And why should such a . . . *spy* . . . have thought there was anything to be found in your records, given that, according to your previous testimony, nobody knew James Davenall had even consulted you?'

'I . . . cannot acount for that.'

'I see. Well, thank you, Doctor, for raising this interesting, if remote, possibility. I feel sure the jury will know how to regard it.'

Dr Fabius, being so much more eminent than Fiveash and possessed of an altogether more confident manner, rounded off the medical evidence in a way which, from the plaintiff's point of view, could hardly have been bettered. Fiveash had asserted that the symptoms of syphilis were unmistakable and that a spontaneous recovery from the disease was impossible, but Fabius refuted both contentions.

'Even with my specialist experience, I would not be confident of correctly diagnosing syphilis on every occasion. It often appears in disguise. Similarly, it may vanish altogether for no apparent reason. It is *le feu follet* of diseases. It is deceptive, misleading, unpredictable. There is nothing certain about it.'

'You cannot say, then, Doctor, whether my client has recovered from syphilis or has never suffered from it at all?'

'I cannot. All I can say is that he does not suffer from it now.'

'How did he react when you told him this?'

'Like a man reprieved from a prison sentence. Like a man told he may live again.'

'Not like a man who knew what you would say before you said it?'

'I hardly think so.'

As the eighth week of the trial ended, the defence had still to make an impression. Norton was riding high.

V

The slats at Plon-Plon's end of the bench reacted with a discomforting jerk to the arrival of a second waiting passenger. He, too, was large and lugubrious in appearance and, like Plon-Plon, anxious to be on his way.

'She's late,' he said irritably.

Plon-Plon did not respond. His companion had already aroused his suspicions by the expensive but tasteless cut of his overcoat. Now the coarse but swaggering tone of his voice convinced him that he was dealing with an example of one of the types he most detested: the *nouveau riche*.

'What brought you tae Dumfries, then?' An answer, had Plon-Plon cared to give one, would not have been easy to frame. The only sure facts known to Catherine Davenall about the origins of Vivien Strang were that she had been born in Dumfries, the daughter of a local draper. Now, gazing across the railway line at the grey roofs of this grudging little town, Plon-Plon reflected without pleasure on the attempt he had made that day to explore those origins.

Broom Bank, the house where Vivien Strang had been born, was tall, angular, raw-stoned and dour, comfortlessly perched in bedraggled gardens high about the River Nith. Plon-Plon had to wait for a long time in the sunless porch before the doorbell was answered.

'Moncalieri,' he announced, doffing his hat to the moon-faced maid. 'Jerome Moncalieri.'

'Goodness!'

He pondered for a rueful moment the mystery of why only the commonest women seemed impressed by him, then said: 'I would very much like to speak to your mistress.'

'Which one?' came the gape-mouthed question. Plon-Plon was at a loss for an answer. Fortunately, the maid went on: 'There's only Miss Effie – Mistress Euphemia, that is – at home.'

'Then, Mistress Euphemia it is.'

'Well . . . I don't know . . . I shall have tae ask. . . . What . . . what shall I say your business is?'

'Personal – and urgent. I have come a long way.'

That, he reflected during the slow-moving minutes for which he was left in the porch, was no word of a lie. A long way, a long time . . . and perhaps he should never have come at all.

The maid returned, marginally less flustered than before, and showed him in. Soon he was alone again, in a high-ceilinged drawing-room at the back of the house, furnished after the fashion of a crowded junk shop he had passed on his way from the station, smelling of camphor, hassock-covers and new bread.

The door opened to admit a tiny, slight, panting creature clad all in quivering pink. 'I am Euphemia Strang,' she said, mincing towards him. 'I believe you wanted to see me.' She gazed up at him with huge dormouse eyes and extended a delicate trembling hand. '*Signor* Moncalieri?'

According to Catherine, Vivien Strang had spoken of having two sisters: this, he concluded, must be one of them. He stooped, kissed her shrivelled knuckles and looked up to find her blushing a deeper pink that her dress. 'Charmed, Mademoiselle, to make your acquaintance.'

'You are not . . . Italian?'

He smiled. 'French.'

'Oh.' Her eyes widened. 'Well . . . would you . . . care for some tea?'

'That would be delightful.'

Tea was duly served, whilst Plon-Plon engaged his hostess in conversation. This was not difficult, for, whatever he said, Miss Strang merely cocked her head and stared at him in rapt awestruck attention, never once pressing him to explain his visit, apparently for fear that it might be cut short. Midway through his second cup of tea and his third slice of Dundee cake, he decided he could prevaricate no longer.

'I fear I must turn, mademoiselle, to the reason I called here this afternoon.'

'Oh . . . yes?'

'It concerns your sister.'

'Lydia?'

'Your *other* sister.' Euphemia Strang's eyes extended still further their phenomenal circumference. 'Vivien.'

'You know . . . Vivien?'

'I knew her many years ago. Alas, we have since lost contact. I hoped you might be able to put me in touch with her.'

'How many . . . years ago, Monsieur?'

'More than thirty.'

'1846 perhaps?'

'As a matter of fact—'

'Euphemia!' The voice was harsh and censorious. It came from a tall, stiff-backed, lean-faced woman in grey who had entered the room without their noticing and stood now by the door, glaring across at them. 'What is the meaning of this?'

Plon-Plon rose and essayed a charming smile. 'Mademoiselle Lydia, I presume?'

'Correct. Who are you, sir?'

'Moncalieri. Jerome Moncalieri. Your sister has made me—'

'Leave us, Euphemia! I will speak to this gentleman alone.'

Her tone left no scope for protest and reduced Euphemia to a state of mute trembling obedience. She had scuttled from the room before Plon-Plon was properly aware she had gone.

'Kindly state your business, sir.'

It was at once obvious to Plon-Plon that Lydia Strang lacked all her sister's susceptability to charm. 'I came to enquire about your sister Vivien.'

'I have only one sister. She has just left this room.'

'Come, come. Vivien Strang—'

'I know nobody by that name.'

'You grew up with her. It is absurd to deny it.'

Lydia Strang's narrow mouth tightened. 'I must ask you to leave this house, sir. At once.'

'All I want to know is where she is.'

'I told you. She does not exist.'

'She bore a child out of wedlock. Is that why you disown her?'

A searching intensity came into Lydia's hostile eyes. 'Did Euphemia tell you so?'

'No. I knew it already.'

At that, her resolve faltered, though only slightly and only for an instant. 'You will be so good as to explain yourself, sir.'

'I am anxious to locate your sister Vivien. I am not interested in old scandals. I do not wish to cause you any embarrassment. I merely wish to know Vivien's current whereabouts.'

A curl came to Lydia's thin lips that could have denoted satisfaction. 'It scarcely matters. We do not know where she is. We do not know whether she is alive or dead. We do not care. Our father, may the Lord preserve his memory, expelled her from this house and this family thirty-seven years ago. He sent her away, a harlot, to seek her Babylon. From that day forth, she ceased to be our sister.'

'She was found to be pregnant and she was turned out. Is that how it was?'

'You may phrase it so if you wish. Now, please leave.'

'Very well, madame. I will leave. But you would do well to remember: every harlot was a virgin once.'

301

'So. Were you here for business – or pleasure?'

Plon-Plon's companion on the railway station bench was not to be deterred.

'Could'nae be pleasure, though. Not in this town. Business, then. Successful?'

'No,' said Plon-Plon, relenting at last. 'Not successful.'

'A wasted journey, then?'

'Yes. A wasted journey.'

VI

The dignity which Constance Trenchard brought to her testimony inspired respect on all sides. She endured Gilchrist's sarcastic and often offensive cross-examination with nobility and restraint. Perhaps because of this, Gilchrist's attempt to impugn her honour proved his greatest error.

'I put it to you, Mrs Trenchard, that you acknowledged the plaintiff as James Davenall because you saw, in doing so, a way of extricating yourself from an uncongenial marriage.'

'I acknowledged him because not to have done so would have been false, deceitful . . . and wrong.'

'But is it not true that you have recently instituted divorce proceedings?'

'Yes. I have.'

'And is it not also true that, should you succeed in those proceedings, you will marry the plaintiff?'

'I cannot say.'

'But there is an understanding between you to that effect?'

'Objection, My Lord! My learned friend is encouraging the witness to incriminate herself in an unrelated action.'

'Objection sustained.'

'As your Lordship pleases. Mrs Trenchard, is your *present* husband a wealthy man?'

'We are comfortably placed.'

'But you would be more comfortably placed as the wife of *Sir* James Davenall?'

'How can I say?'

'It must have crossed your mind.'

'It has not. This has nothing to do with money. If it had, I would have awaited the outcome of this case before suing my husband for divorce, would I not?'

Gilchrist ignored the question but, by doing so, rendered it all the more effective. English juries do not enjoy the spectacle of well-bred young ladies being bullied by venal barristers. Their displeasure at this would quite eclipse, it was thought, any prejudice on the subject of divorce. It would ensure that their sympathy was reserved for Mrs Trenchard – and hence for Norton.

VII

The morning did spring full justice, which was rare in Plon-Plon's experience of London, but its perfection failed to lift his spirits. Walking through Hyde Park, he had taken some brief pleasure from the riot of birdsong and blossom, but after crossing Park Lane and starting along South Street he had remembered his destination and all his false, vicarious good cheer had vanished.

He had not wanted to meet Florence Nightingale in 1854 and he did not want to meet her now, but Vivien Strang had been one of her nurses all those years ago and might still be known to her today. Thus, though a selfless young heroine who had grown into an idolized old maid was the last person whose acquaintance he wanted to make, he found himself ascending the steps of the famous Miss Nightingale's house and knocking at the door.

It was opened by a commissionaire, a tall lantern-jawed old man with a crumpled cock-eyed expression which could have been either kindly or forbidding.

'Is Miss Nightingale at home?' Plon-Plon asked.

'To whom?' said the commissionaire in a deep tolling voice.

'Prince Napoleon Bonaparte.'

'Have you an appointment?'

'No, but—'

'Then, Miss Nightingale is *not* at home.'

Plon-Plon glowered at the fellow in his most intimidating fashion. 'This is a matter of some importance, my good man.'

'Not to Miss Nightingale.'

Plon-Plon took a deep breath. 'Will you at least ask her if she will see me?'

'It'll do no good. Mr Gladstone called last week without an appointment. She wouldn't see him, either.'

'Nevertheless—'

'If you insist, I'll *ask*.'

'I do insist.'

'She'll want to know the purpose of your visit.'

'Say it concerns a nurse who worked under her in the Crimea. Miss Vivien Strang.'

With a grunt, the commissionaire retreated, leaving Plon-Plon to shift uncomfortably from foot to foot. He turned, locked eyes with a woman walking her dog on the other side of the street, and turned back. At length, the commissionaire reappeared.

'Miss Nightingale is prepared to see you,' the fellow announced, with no change in his expression. Plon-Plon was about to step into the house when he added: 'Tuesday of next week. Three o'clock.'

'What?'

'If you'll take my advice, you won't be late. She doesn't like to be kept waiting.'

VIII

For two men who lived under the same roof, Richard Davenall and James Norton had seen remarkably little of each other in recent months. Whether by accident or by design, they had only conversed at any length in the presence of others. Since visiting Wapping together on 14th February (an occasion to which neither of them ever now referred), they had moved inexorably apart, maintaining all the outward courtesies but secretly awaiting the moment when their charade of fellowship could be ended.

That moment, as both knew, would be when the protracted legal action in which they shared a common cause was successfully concluded. Until then, neither could risk the consequences of open disagreement. Whatever he truly thought, Richard had to testify on James's behalf and he had to do so without revealing one shred of doubt for the defence to seize upon. He was, after all, the only member of the Davenall family who had acknowledged the plaintiff. The part he had to play was crucial.

Inevitably, therefore, the weekend before Richard's testimony was due to begin provided a stern examination of the two men's nerves. By Sunday evening, they were both, it seemed, eager to break the silence that had reigned so long between them. When Constance retired to bed, they did not, as had been their custom, retreat to separate rooms. Instead they sat by the drawing-room fire, with brandy and cigars, calmly discussing the progress of the trial as if their unity of purpose had never been questioned. Not that, in the legal sense, it had been. Richard's doubts centred less on James's claim than on his methods of advancing it, and these were not referred to, even obliquely, until, towards midnight, Richard suddenly and significantly changed the subject.

'Constance's divorce is likely to be heard during the second week of June,' he said abruptly.

'She will be glad to have it settled,' James replied.

'As will you?'

'I will be glad for her sake.'

'Has she said much to you about it?'

'I gather there should be no difficulty. She speaks highly of your handling of the matter.'

Richard smiled drily: it was evident he took no pleasure from the compliment. 'It has been remarkably straightforward. Of course, Trenchard is in no position to defend the action. Indeed, Bucknill will be happy to tell the court how beneficial he feels a clean break will be to his patient's condition. Accordingly, it should go through very much on the nod.'

James said nothing. They contemplated each other in the wavering firelight, listened to the spatter of passing rain at the back of the chimney and drew on their cigars with all the practised composure that had become the measure of their distrust.

'As to Trenchard's condition, would you like to know what Bucknill told me?'

'*Is* there anything to know?'

'There has been no change, certainly. Trenchard is said to be subdued amd uncommunicative, still very much in the grip of the delusions which Bucknill first identified.'

'No doubt that was to be expected.'

'No doubt.' Another stealthy searching pause. 'He is permitted visitors, you know.'

'Really?'

'But I gather he has received none.'

'That, too, does not surprise me.'

'No?'

'We both met his brother. A dry dog. There's little feeling there, I suspect. As for Constance, I know she believes it will be easier for them to meet *after* this is settled.'

'And you?'

James frowned. 'The fellow tried to kill me, Richard. Whilst I realize he wasn't responsible for his actions at the time, you can hardly expect me to pretend it didn't happen.'

'Yet you pay his asylum fees. You pay to ensure he has the best treatment available.'

James's frown became irritable. 'When that was agreed, I asked that it be treated as strictly confidential. I asked, as I recall, that it never be mentioned.'

Richard inclined his head in a gesture of apology. 'You did indeed. I'm sorry. It's simply that I never properly understood your reasons.'

'I didn't want Constance to have any cause to reproach herself for agreeing to his confinement. At the same time, I didn't want her to feel beholden to me. Hence Ticehurst. Hence the secrecy.'

'Ah, yes,' Richard said slowly, leaning forward to look at him more closely. 'Of course.'

305

James drained his glass. 'What other reason could there possibly have been?'

Richard delayed his reply long enough to leave no doubt of its insincerity. 'None at all, of course.' There was a moment of level-eyed scrutiny, then he added: 'It's really very generous of you. Very generous indeed.' But generosity was not the motive he was imputing to James. Clearer than any words could explain, he was telling him that he did not believe James was seeking to protect Constance's conscience by his provision for Trenchard. He believed he was seeking to protect his own.

IX

Plon-Plon had expected Florence Nightingale to be the slim and saintly figure of Crimean myth. He had not expected a stout, red-faced, rudely healthy old lady with absurd pretensions to invalidity. But such was the woman who received him in her South Street drawing-room promptly at three on the appointed afternoon. Clad in the most shapeless black dress, shawled and scarfed against imaginary draughts and reclining on a couch with supplies of sal volatile on hand, she irresistibly reminded him of the wolf disguised as Little Red Riding-Hood.

'It is many years,' she announced, in tones which suggested she began many sentences with the words, 'since I was fit to receive visitors standing – or even sitting.'

'No matter, madame,' Plon-Plon relied. 'The honour of meeting you eclipses all niceties.'

'It is also many years since I had time for idle flattery.' Clearly, nothing ailed her sense of purpose. 'I agreed to see you because you spoke of Nurse Strang. For no other reason.'

'You remember her, then?'

'Of course. I am surprised, however, that you should wish to recall her to my mind – or to your own.'

'Why?'

'Because she offended you when you visited Scutari in November 1854. And she embarrassed me by so doing.'

'Ah. Our contretemps on that occasion came to your attention? Well, it was a long time ago. There is no need to apolo—'

'I was not about to,' Miss Nightingale cut in. 'As an uninvited visitor to a busy hospital, you had only yourself to blame.'

Plon-Plon took a deep breath. 'I must have misunderstood you, madame. You did speak of your *embarrassment*.'

'I refer to the profound disapproval which, as Superintendent of the

Female Nursing Establishment at Scutari, I was bound to express when one of my staff needlessly demeaned her calling.'

'Ah. I see.'

'What is it you wish to discuss with me about Nurse Strang?'

'I am trying to find her. I hoped you might be able to assist me.'

Miss Nightingale transferred her gaze to Plon-Plon from the window whence it had, till now, been directed. 'Why should you wish to find her?'

Plon-Plon smiled grimly. 'Let me not intrude upon your valuable time with lengthy explanatons.'

'Very well. At all events, I fear I cannot help you. Nurse Strang's whereabouts are unknown to me. Following her encounter with you, I dismissed her and sent her back to England.'

'You dismissed her?'

'Certainly. I could not allow such conduct to go unpunished. *"Pour décourager les autres"*, you understand.'

'Have you no idea where she went?'

'As I say, back to England, by the first available boat, third class, on salt rations.' Plon-Plon winced. 'What she did once she was home I really cannot say. She may have continued nursing, she may not. I have neither seen nor heard of her since then.'

'I thought you might have . . . an address.'

'She was recruited from one of the London hospitals to join the nursing party I took to Constantinople in October 1854. She was one of the more reliable members, as I recall. Until, of course, the lapse which led to her dismissal. That is all I can tell you.' She glanced sharply at Plon-Plon's disappointed face. 'If you have no further questions, I should like to return to my paper on Indian sanitation. The Viceroy has urgent need of my conclusions.'

'Of course, of course.' Much good may he have of them, Plon-Plon thought as he rose to his feet. Then, as Miss Nightingale reached for the bell with which to summon the commissionaire, he added: '*Pardon, madame.* I do have one last question.'

'Yes?' Miss Nightingale sounded impatient.

'Do you know what provision Miss Strang made for her child during her absence from the country?'

'Child?'

'Did you not know she had one?'

The cowled red face darkened with indignaton. 'Nurse Strang was a spinster. A *child*' – the stress she laid on the word made it sound like a disfiguring disease – 'would have disbarred her from nursing in any hospital I had charge of.'

'You did not know, then?'

'I most certainly did not.' She rang the bell and shuddered at the suggestion he had just made. 'Good afternoon, Prince.'

X

On the first day of June, and the forty-fourth day of the trial, Russell informed Lord Coleridge that the plaintiff's case was complete. It was evident from the tone of his voice that he believed it was not simply complete, but impregnable. Richard Davenall had been the last witness he had called and in some ways the most effective: not merely a member of the Davenall family firmly convinced of Norton's identity, but a lawyer, whose cautious, meticulous, unsensational testimony was of the stuff to impress a judge as well as a jury. Russell's whole manner suggested that he could not imagine the defence being able to make good the damage such evidence had done. Whether he would have remained so confident had he overheard a whispered conversation between his client and his solicitor as the court dispersed that afternoon is, of course, impossible to say.

'Lechlade has completed his enquiries into that other matter,' Warburton said to Norton as they were filing out.

'Oh, yes?'

'Concerning Trenchard.'

'It is as I supposed?'

'Yes. Five visits since the middle of February. All by the same person.'

'And that person is?'

'Richard Davenall.'

Norton nodded.

'You don't look surprised.'

'That, Mr Warburton, is because I'm not.'

FIFTEEN

I

When Gilchrist opened for the defence, there was no doubting the efficiency with which he marshalled the evidence against the plaintiff: a mother who claimed not to know him, discrepancies in handwriting and differences in appearance which it was doubtful an absence of twelve years could alone explain, the mystery of his recovery from syphilis, the assorted friends and acquaintances who remained unconvinced of his identity, the occasional vaguenesses in the account he had given of his life in exile. But efficiency, it had become clear, would not be enough. Gilchrist would need to appeal to the jury's hearts as well as to their heads.

To do this, it was generally agreed, he would have to call upon more than cool argument and a battery of expert witnesses. The real source of the defence's strength was the Davenall family. Richard, it was true, had gone over to the other side, but neither Sir Hugo nor Lady Davenall had spoken at the hearing, although, if the plaintiff was to be believed, they were his closest relatives. In what they would say, therefore, lay Gilchrist's best chance and Norton's greatest peril.

In Sir Hugo's case, the peril was short-lived. Even under Gilchrist's sympathetic questioning, he contrived to seem graspingly self-centred. He was given ample opportunity to protest that Norton's claim insulted the memory of his dead brother, but he seemed unable to sustain the theme. At every step, with every ill-humoured answer, he revealed the true state of his feelings: his wealth and his status were threatened, and he would not surrender them to any man, even, by implication, the brother to whom they rightfully belonged.

This air of sulky petulance proved Sir Hugo's undoing during his cross-examination. Russell succeeded, without seeming to try, in portraying him to the jury of solid, hard-working, middle-class men as a feckless, dissolute young wastrel, given to high living and free spending, whose reaction to Norton's arrival on the scene was that of a spoilt child to the realization that he can no longer have his way.

'Is it not true', said Russell at one point, 'that your father refused to have James pronounced legally dead?'

'Who told you that?' Sir Hugo's response was typically peevish.

'Is it not true that *you* initiated the presumption-of-death proceedings – after your father had suffered a stroke and was no longer able to prevent it?'

Sir Hugo seemed to think he had seen a way out. 'I was advised my father would not live long. The question of his succession *had* to be sorted out.'

'But why did your father not take the necessary steps as soon as James had been missing for the statutory seven years – in June 1878? He did not fall ill until November 1879.'

'I . . . I don't know. He hadn't been himself for some years.'

'Can you suggest any reason for his inaction other than a belief that James was not dead?'

Sir Hugo thought for a moment. 'We didn't get on,' he said, tossing back his head. 'I took it the old boy wanted to spite me.'

If obliged to, then, Sir Hugo would portray his father as petty and vindictive, whereas Norton had never spoken of him – nor, indeed, of any of the family – less than respectfully. The contrast was not lost on the jury: Russell made sure of that.

Later, another element emerged in Sir Hugo's determination to resist the plaintiff's claim. Russell had asked him when he had become convinced that Norton was an impostor; his answer made it clear that he had never considered any other possibility.

'My mother forewarned me.'

'She told you that a man claiming to be James had called on her?'

'Yes, and —'

'And you accepted at once her claim that he was *not* James?'

'Of course.'

'The plaintiff called on you at your London home on the thirtieth of September last. Did this give you an opportunity to verify your mother's conclusion?'

'Well . . . yes. Yes, it did.'

'But, Sir Hugo, do you dispute the plaintiff's account of that visit? He testified that he was removed from the premises by your servants before he could so much as engage you in conversation.'

'I *saw* him.'

'For a few moments – before the door was slammed in his face.'

'I saw enough.'

'Have you spoken to him since?'

'Of course. There was a meeting – at his solicitor's.'

'Ah, yes. The examination of the eleventh of October. Since then?'

'I've been forced to sit in the same courtroom as him for ten damnable weeks. Isn't that enough?'

'Not for my purpose, Sir Hugo. Have you met him other than at the bidding of the law since he was refused admittance to your home on the thirtieth of September?'

'No. Of course I haven't.'

'Then, when have you had an opportunity to satisfy yourself that he cannot be your brother?'

Sir Hugo's lip trembled, his face coloured. His answer was to fall back on the stubborn denials which had already betrayed him. 'The man is an impostor. He is *not* my brother.' Then his eyes moved towards the plaintiff and, for what must have been the first time in all the weeks that they had sat together in the court, they looked at each other. In Sir Hugo's face, in that instant of confrontation, many saw what he truly feared: not that his opponent would win the case, but that he deserved to; not that Norton would defeat him, but that Norton was his brother.

II

Plon-Plon was overdressed for the warmth of the day in top-hat and frock-coat and had been reduced to using one of his gloves as a fan. A figure less likely to be taking his ease in a deck-chair in Green Park in the middle of an airless June morning would have been hard to imagine, but the strangeness of the phenomenon was shortly to be explained: he was not there for the good of his health.

A lady in grey was approaching from the direction of Constitution Hill. She moved slowly but with perfect elegance and, as she drew closer, the pin-stripes of pink in her dress and the gossamer white of the scarf about her hat suggested an immunity to the heat in stark contrast to Plon-Plon's discomfort. She was by no means young, but there was about her bearing that rare facility to combine dignity and insouciance which can render age irrelevant.

Plon-Plon did not rise to greet Catherine Davenall: he was too depressed to make the effort. The two, indeed, exchanged no word or smile of recognition. Catherine merely sat in the adjacent deck-chair, waited for the attendant to come, be paid and go, waited a moment longer in measured silence, and then said: 'You have not found her, have you?'

'No, madame,' Plon-Plon replied.

'I am to testify next week. Hugo has already done so. Time is fast running out.'

'I fear no amount of time would make any difference.'

311

'Have you learned nothing?'

'I have learned much, madame. Perhaps too much.'

'What do you mean by that?'

'You were correct. She returned to Dumfries after your father dismissed her. But, as soon as her own father discovered she was pregnant, he threw her out. The family disowned her. She came to London and bore Gervase's child. At some point, she became a nurse. She was one of the party Florence Nightingale took to Constantinople in 1854. Following my encounter with her at Scutari, she was dismissed for indiscipline and sent back to England. Then – *rien.*'

'Nothing?'

'I sent Brunet on a tour of all the hospitals, nursing homes and governesses' agencies in London. None of them has any record of her.'

'She might no longer be a nurse – or a governess.'

'She might indeed. But to find her? One may as well look for a needle in a haystack. It is impossible.'

Catherine cast him a withering look. 'You mean *you* find it impossible.'

'Have it how you will, madame. I have done what I can. I can do no more.'

'You're abandoning the search?'

'I have no alternative.'

'I looked to you to help me, Prince. As ever, you disappoint me.'

Plon-Plon bowed his head. 'It was bound to be so. *Quelque part, nulle part.* She cannot be found, she does not wish to be found: in the end, it makes no difference. I cannot help you, madame. If Vivien Strang is your enemy, she does not mean you to know it.'

For a moment longer, Catherine sat gazing into the heat-shimmered distance. Then, with an air of decisiveness, she rose to her feet. 'You were my last hope,' she said, with the merest hint of irony.

He looked up at her. 'I am sorry. Truly sorry.'

In Catherine's cold responding stare there was no gratitude for the sorrow he had expressed or the efforts he had made, merely a disdainful recognition of predicted failure. Without another word, she turned and walked away across the park.

III

Sir Hugo Davenall had been his own worst enemy: his fear of Norton had revealed to the court an unreasoning avarice that tainted all he said. Catherine, Lady Davenall, was plainly, however, somebody who knew no fear. There was, therefore, never any likelihood that she would betray herself.

And so it proved. With no need of Gilchrist's prompting, she laid before the court a simple inflexible belief: the plaintiff was not her son. To bear a child, to feed, nurse, clothe, cherish and protect him through all the years of his youth, was to know that child better, to know him more certainly, than anyone else could ever do. She defied the jury to doubt a mother's word. She pitted against them the forces of nature and tradition. She did not plead, she did not cajole. She merely insisted that, whatever had been said, whatever might be said, her rejection of Norton's claim was absolute.

It was clear, therefore, that Russell's cross-examination of Lady Davenall would be the most delicate passage of the case. If he tried to browbeat her, he might make the same mistake Gilchrist had made in questioning Mrs Trenchard. Yet, if he were too gentle, it would smack of capitulation. Small wonder, then, that he approached his task cautiously. A full day passed in which he pressed for little more than reiteration and emphasis. Then, on the second day of cross-examination, he showed his hand.

'Lady Davenall, do you take issue with anything the plaintiff has told the court about his childhood?'

'I take issue with his claim to be my son.'

'Of course. But do you dispute his version of events? Do you dispute that any of the events he described actually took place?'

'No.'

'You would agree, then, that the plaintiff's knowledge is very close to what you would expect of your son James?'

'He has been coached well, certainly.'

'*Coached*, Lady Davenall? You are suggesting the plaintiff has been provided with this information by somebody else?'

'I am.'

'By whom, pray?'

'I do not know. Somebody with a grudge. A former servant, perhaps.'

'Do you have one in mind?'

'There was . . . Quinn.'

Russell looked up at the judge. 'Mentioned earlier, my Lord. James Davenall's valet. Efforts have been made to trace him, without success.' He returned to the witness. 'Is there some reason why this man should bear a grudge, Lady Davenall?'

'He was dismissed . . . for stealing.'

'I see. How long was he with you?'

'Twenty-three years.'

'Let us agree that he would know a good deal about your family. Enough, do you think, to coach the plaintiff?'

'Yes.'

'But what of events before he joined you? What of James's

313

schooldays, his time at university? What would such a man know of all that?'

'James may have told him.'

'And Quinn remembered? Why should he have paid so much attention, unless you are suggesting he foresaw his master's disappearance?'

'I am not suggesting that.'

'Do you have any evidence, in fact, that the plaintiff has been in recent communication with Quinn?'

'No.'

'Or that Quinn even knows these proceedings are taking place?'

'No.'

'So Quinn's part in this is merely a flight of fancy.' Russell smiled. 'Let us turn to other fancies, Lady Davenall. I refer to your late husband's reluctance to have James pronounced legally dead. Sir Hugo attributed it to spite. Is that how you regarded it?'

'My husband was certainly a spiteful man, but I believe he would have agreed to take the necessary steps eventually. He was also a vain man. He wanted Hugo to plead with him. But my son pleads with nobody.'

She had said too much. Her dignified assertion of the rights of a mother stood confounded by the revelation of a loveless marriage. Russell pounced. 'So your husband was vain and spiteful. You would not say the same of yourself?'

'No. I would not.' There was no way of telling from her voice that she recognized the mistake she had made, nor the danger to which it exposed her.

'Then, how *would* you characterize your decision to evict Miss Pursglove from Weir Cottage?'

'I don't understand you.'

'Miss Pursglove worked for the Davenall family for more than sixty years. I take it you were offended by her acknowledgement of the plaintiff as your son. Would you not agree that to retaliate by expelling her from her home was just that: vain and spiteful?'

'I object, my Lord.' Gilchrist had intervened. 'The circumstances of Miss Pursglove's eviction from Weir Cottage have no bearing on this case.'

'The objection is sustained.'

Russell conceded with good grace, as well he might, for the point he had succeeded in making was worth any number of rebukes from the Bench. 'How many conversations have you had with the plaintiff since he visited Cleave Court on the twenty-sixth of September last, Lady Davenall?'

'None.'

'Once was enough to make up your mind?'

'Once was more than enough. I looked at him. I listened to him. But hearing him out only confirmed my immediate reaction. He was sufficiently close to James in looks and voice to deceive some, but not to deceive me. I would know my own son at once. I did not know the plaintiff.'

'You have never had cause to doubt your conclusion?'

'Never.'

Russell had been rewarded. Lady Davenall's strength of mind – her composure that bordered on arrogance, her conviction that verged on intransigence – had told against her. The certainty of a mother was one thing, the ruthlessness of a matriach quite another. Her rejection of Norton was bound to carry weight, but the cruelty of which she had shown herself capable was a telling counter. It made it possible for the jury to believe that she might, just might, deny her son to his face.

IV

Having paid a necessary but far from reassuring visit to his stockbroker in Lombard Street, Plon-Plon had set off back towards the leisured west of the city by cab, only to find that the close of the working day and a brief but violent thunderstorm had combined to snag and clog the streets. He gazed out morosely at the slow-moving knots and straggling threads of homeward-bound humanity, shading his eyes against the dazzling reflections of sunlight and brooding on his many misfortunes.

As the cab entered St Paul's Churchyard and began to edge through the ruck towards Ludgate Hill, Plon-Plon's wayward attention was suddenly seized by two people standing near the south door of the cathedral. One of them was James Norton; his humiliation at the fellow's hands eight months before remained etched in his memory, and he had no difficulty in recognizing him. Norton's companion was a lady, simply but startingly clad in black. Her dress moulded itself to an enticing figure: Plon-Plon let his eyes follow its curves for a satisfying instant. Her face had a taunting beauty he could believe he had dreamed of, flushed red with anger or anguish (he could not tell which). Norton was talking to her, half-turned away from the road and a little stooped, as if anxious not to be overheard. The lady was breathing hard and looking directly ahead, turning and twisting in her gloved hands a folded newspaper.

The cab jolted forward through an opening in the traffic: the vision was gone. Plon-Plon sat back for a moment, wondering what it could mean. Catherine had linked Norton with Trenchard's wife, but the lady he had just seen was too young to be her, not to mention too exotically magnificent ever to have married a dullard like Trenchard. Yet, if not her, then who? Suddenly, an impulse seized him. Perhaps he could yet pay back Norton and vindicate himself in Catherine's eyes. He leaned out and ordered the driver to stop.

As soon as he had climbed out and paid the fare, he began glancing across the crowded thoroughfare to check if the pair were still where he had seen them. They were. Then, as he struggled to find a safe route to the other side, they separated, Norton marching smartly away westwards whilst the lady began walking slowly in the opposite direction.

By the time Plon-Plon had reached the south door of the cathedral, Norton had vanished and the lady was thirty yards or so away. He began to follow her. She cast the newspaper she had been carrying into a wayside bin and quickened her pace, so that Plon-Plon had difficulty keeping up. Then, as she reached the corner of the street ahead, she stepped into a cab that must have been waiting for her. The traffic was lighter here than on the other side of St Paul's, and the cab made off northwards at a clip. Plon-Plon pulled up and swore under his breath.

Then he noticed the newspaper, protruding from the bin alongside him. He plucked it out and ran his eye over the page at which it had been folded open, finding there the normal diet of accidents, inquests and burglaries. It was an evening paper, dating from several days before. He was about to discard it when he saw the headline over one article: TRENCHARD DIVORCE.

Mr William Trenchard, whose father Lionel is chairman of the Trenchard & Leavis retail stores company, has been divorced. His wife Constance, of The Limes, Avenue Road, St John's Wood, was today granted a decree nisi in the Admiralty, Probate and Divorce Division by reason of her husband's insanity; she was also granted custody of their five-year-old daughter.

It will be recalled that Mr Trenchard was implicated in a murderous assault on 7th November last on Mr James Norton, the so-called Davenall Claimant. Charges against Mr Trenchard were subsequently waived in exchange for undertakings that he be confined to a lunatic asylum. Dr John Bucknill, the eminent psychiater, stated at this morning's hearing that his patient—

'Good afternoon, Prince.'

Plon-Plon swung round to find Norton standing only a few feet away, smiling gently and drawing on a cigarette. His smile had less the appearance of a greeting than of amusement at a private joke.

'Rooting in dustbins? Scarcely an imperial trait, if you don't mind my saying so.'

316

Plon-Plon could feel his face colouring with irritation. 'Who is she?' he snapped.

'I don't know who you mean.'

'*La belle jeune fille.* You were talking to her a few moments ago by the door of the cathedral.'

'Not I.'

'I saw you.'

'You were mistaken.'

'What is she to you? You were discussing the Trenchard divorce, weren't you?' He held up the newspaper. 'Why?'

Norton stepped closer; his eyes narrowed. 'I thought we agreed when we last met, Prince, that you would do well to steer clear of my affairs.'

Plon-Plon tossed back his head and squared his shoulders. 'You seek to frighten me with an old scandal? It will not work a second time, monsieur.'

'It is a sad and sordid tale. You do not emerge from it with credit.'

'Yours, monsieur, is the greater danger. You are Vivien Strang's son, are you not?'

Momentarily, Norton seemed taken aback. 'You think that?' Then his composure returned and, with it, the goading smile. 'You may harbour a whole fleet of suspicions if you wish, Prince. But what can you prove? Nothing.'

'You are *not* James Davenall.'

'How is Cora these days? Have you seen her recently? I take it she has not come to share this latest of your many exiles. Do you remember when you both stayed at Bladeney House in November 1870? I do. I remember it very well indeed. One night, when Papa had taken you to the club, Cora offered . . . Well, perhaps it is best that you should not know what she offered.'

'You think you are very clever, monsieur. You think you can deceive everyone. Maybe you are right. But be warned: no man is infallible. Sooner or later, you will make a mistake. Just one is all that is necessary. When you make it, the world will know you for who you really are.'

With that, Plon-Plon thrust the newspaper back into the bin and walked quickly away, reassembling as he went the fragments of his dignity. Norton *le menteur*, Norton *l'imposteur*: what did it matter to him? Forget the man, he told himself, forget the Davenalls and all you know of them. It should not be difficult: a Mediterranean cruise might do the trick. He hurried on, his determination growing with every tread to leave England and, this time, never to return.

Norton finished his cigarette and watched Plon-Plon's bulky shape vanish into the crowd beyond St Paul's. He was alone now, with nobody to see him pluck the newspaper from the bin, glance at the article headed TRENCHARD DIVORCE, then toss it back amongst the rubbish. Nor was there anybody to hear what he murmured to himself as he crushed out the cigarette beneath his foot. 'Just one mistake, eh, Prince? Just one. Perhaps you're right.' He exhaled the last of the smoke. 'Perhaps I've already made it.'

V

The later defence witnesses were pure anticlimax. Fiveash was recalled, in order to emphasize that he did not recognize Norton as his former patient. Once again, however, an equivocal vein in all that he said told against him. Emery, his Harley Street friend, completed the medical evidence. Under cross-examination, he was obliged to admit the truth of what Fabius had said: that nobody could tell for certain whether the plaintiff had suffered from syphilis or not.

Whether Freddy Cleveland intended to introduce a comic note into the proceedings was not clear, but, by seeming to change his mind from minute to minute as to whether Norton was James Davenall or an impostor, he weakened the defence case still further. Borthwick and Mulholland appeared on cue: both insisted the plaintiff could not be James Davenall, both denied trying to trick him when they had met on Parliament Hill.

Assorted artists, photographers and physiognomists expressed the considered opinion that the plaintiff was not the James Davenall who had posed for the camera in Christ Church cricket teams and graduation robes, but Russell forced all of them to concede that they could equally well be wrong. A graphologist argued that the plaintiff's handwriting, though similar to examples of James Davenall's that he had studied, was not identical. Russell extracted from him an admission that handwriting could feasibly change in the course of time and altered employment.

After the scientists came the tradesmen: hatters, shirtmakers, tailors, glovers and bootmakers. Few had kept written records. Thus their fallible memories of collar sizes and leg measurements, in so far as they were at issue with the plaintiff's, scarcely comprised an effective challenge.

At last, in the fourteenth week of the trial, the defence concluded its case. Russell's closing speech followed – a brilliantly effective appeal to the jury to disregard the trifling points made against his client and to concentrate on one issue and one issue only: did they believe the plaintiff was James Davenall or not?

VI

A Sunday evening in Chester Square, the mellow rays of the setting sun contriving, as they glinted through the drawing-room windows of Bladeney House, to deepen Catherine Davenall's trance of melancholy. She had stayed with Hugo since Easter, forgoing all the pleasures of spring and summer at Cleave Court so that he might have her presence to fall back upon whenever his courage failed. She had attended the court every day, had scarcely missed an hour of its proceedings, had sat passively but a few yards from her son's tormentor, had bided her time and held her peace. Now, with the moment of decision finally at hand, she felt weary of the whole dispute, drained by the exertions her determination had driven her to. Tomorrow, the judge would commence his summing-up. Tomorrow, or the next day, he would send the jury out to consider whether James Norton could henceforth call himself her son, evict her from her home, seize her property, appropriate all the wealth and status that she and Hugo had hitherto enjoyed. It was too much – for a jury to decide or for a mother to face.

There was a tap at the door, and Greenwood came in. Normally the calmest and most self-effacing of men, he appeared now red about the cheeks and flustered in his bearing.

'A gentleman, ma'am . . . desires to see you.'

'Who is he?'

Greenwood seemed to have difficulty in answering. 'Mr . . . Norton, ma'am.'

For a moment, Catherine said nothing. It was nearly ten months since Norton had called on her at Cleave Court. What could he want now? Hugo was at his club, bolstering his spirits in Freddy Cleveland's fatuous company. Did Norton know that she was alone, on this last evening before whatever end lay in store for both of them? Is that why he had come? She looked up at Greenwood, taking care he should catch no glimpse of her secret turmoil. 'Show Mr Norton in.'

As soon as the door had closed, she rose and moved to the window. She must appear perfectly composed, grave to the point of severity. Standing just so, with the light behind her, regally self-possessed, was how she would receive him. She forced herself to stop winding her finger in the locket chain about her neck, breathed deeply and imposed the authority to which her emotions had always given best.

Greenwood reappeared, announced Norton and was gone again, leaving them to face one another in absolute silence. He would be unable to see her expression clearly, Catherine reminded herself, yet one might be forgiven for inferring, from that clear-eyed confident stare of his, that he saw her more clearly than she would ever have wished. She broke the silence.

'Why have you come here?'

He smiled faintly. 'No fonder words than those, Mother, for your long-lost son?'

She spread her hand across the antimacassared back of a chair and paused long enough to quench any anger his words had inspired. 'We are quite alone, Mr Norton. There are no witnesses, no spies, no eavesdroppers. There is no need to continue the pretence for my benefit.'

'Then, why continue your own pretence? You know who I am. You knew from the moment you set eyes on me.'

'You are *not* James.'

'The court will say differently.'

'That remains to be seen.'

He took a few steps into the room, glancing about at the pictures and furnishings. 'Fewer alterations here than you've made at Cleave Court,' he said musingly. 'I remember it all so well.'

'Spare me your well-rehearsed performance, Mr Norton. Why have you come?'

He stopped and looked directly at her. 'Because it's not too late, Mother, to—'

'Don't call me that.'

He dipped his head in a gesture of obedience. 'Very well, though the world will soon call you so on my behalf. I came here this evening to appeal to you. Why not give it up? Why not concede my claim before the court forces you to do so? There's still time. Tomorrow, at a word from you, our lawyers could meet to agree terms.'

'Terms?' She looked at him disbelievingly. 'What terms could there possibly be, short of abject surrender by one side or the other?'

'There could be . . . an accommodation. I demand my rights, naturally, but I've no wish to be vindictive. I don't want to put Hugo in the poorhouse or you out of Cleave Court. After what's happened, it's hard to imagine we could live together as one happy family, but there are ways and means. . . .'

'Those are the terms of which you speak?'

'Yes. You may find the alternatives . . . less pleasant.'

'What alternatives?'

'You have the money Papa settled on you, of course, but it'll not keep you and Hugo in the manner to which you're both accustomed. I mention Hugo because he'll be wholly dependent on you. All that he has will be mine before the week is out. All of mine that he has already spent he will be required to repay. He will have nothing left. And I don't see my brother as the self-sufficient type. Do you?'

'It isn't any of that you wish to avert, Mr Norton. You simply want to be let off the hook. When this case ends in your defeat, you will face a charge of perjury. All you will have gained, before the week is out, is a cell in Newgate Prison.'

He smiled. 'I rather think I might be granted bail.' Then he grew serious again. 'As you say, the stakes are high for all concerned. I knew that, of course, when I decided not to blacken Papa's name in court. Believe it or not, I did so for the sake of our family. It's in the same spirit that I'm appealing to you not to fight me, all the way, to what can only be a bitter end.'

'Then, you are appealing in vain, Mr Norton. There will be no surrender, no compromise of any kind. Even if the court is mad enough to uphold your claim, I will still find some way to defeat you.'

'There is no way, Mother.' He took a deep breath. 'I'm sorry to have offended you by using that name again, but there it is: in a few days, you will have to accept me as your son, *Sir* James Davenall.'

'Never.'

'Is that your final word?'

'No. My final word is for your mother, Mr Norton. Your real mother, that is: Vivien Strang.'

Norton frowned. 'I don't know what you mean.'

'Tell her this. I admit I wronged her. But she'll find revenge brings a poor reward. The price of forcing you on me is that she can never claim you. She'll have to stay forever hidden, forever apart. If she should once try to see you, be assured I will know of it. Then I will find her. And, when I do, I will show her no mercy.'

'You speak in riddles, Mother. Vivien Strang is nothing to me, nothing but a distant figure from a discreditable past. She has no bearing on the present. She has no part in what you have forced me to do.'

'You have your answer, Mr Norton. Is that all you came for?'

'If you change your mind—'

'I won't.'

He bowed his head in courteous acknowledgement of her decision. 'Very well. I will bid you good night. We will meet again soon – on my terms.'

She watched him leave the room and listened to the front door close behind him. So he was gone, not with what he had come for but with more than she should have let him have. She had said too much, revealed too great a hatred. Yet why not? What difference, now, could it possibly make? Norton was right in one thing if in nothing else. Before the week was out, the struggle would be over and with it, perhaps, the life she had lived till now. It could not be altered. It could not be prevented. It must run its course and find her ready, dignified and waiting. Norton might win his case, but never her admission of defeat. He might be called her son, but never by her.

VII

Before his elevation to the Bench, Lord Coleridge had served his turn at the Bar with great distinction. One of his many triumphs was to have defended a celebrated action superficially similar to the one he was currently presiding over: that of the so-called Tichborne Claimant. Perhaps aware that this had given him something of a reputation as an exposer of imposture, he went to considerable lengths to ensure that his summing-up in this case should be a model of impartiality. If Lord Coleridge had made up his mind for or against the plaintiff, nobody could have gleaned as much from the day and a half during which he analysed and summarized the evidence for the benefit of the jury. At length, he sent them out to consider their verdict with less in the way of specific direction than those familiar with his career could ever recollect him conferring.

In the late afternoon, the court was recalled, but only to hear that the jury wished to continue their deliberations overnight. They were dispatched to a hotel, whilst those anxiously awaiting their verdict were left to pass the night with what patience they could muster.

VIII

The night was of that clammy oppressiveness only an English midsummer can conjure up. In the garden of Richard Davenall's Highgate home, there was neither breath of wind nor shaft of light to break the dark and humid spell. Nor, now midnight had passed, was there any sound to distract James Norton from thoughts of the morrow as he sat in the rose-clad arbour, smoking cigarette after cigarette as the hours of his vigil drew slowly on. No sound, that is, till a footfall on the gravel path alerted him to the presence of another member of the household for whom sleep had proved elusive.

'Good evening, Richard,' James said quietly, as the familiar figure of his host came into shadowy view. 'Or should I say good morning?'

'I couldn't seem to rest,' Richard replied. 'The heat, you know.'

'Cigarette?'

'I believe I will. Thank you.' Richard normally smoked nothing beyond an after-dinner cigar. He stood by the arbour for several minutes, smoking in silence, then said: 'We have come a long way, have we not, James, since you presented yourself at my offices last Michaelmas?'

'I could not have come so far without your help.' In the shadow of the arbour there was no way of telling what expression accompanied James's words.

'Be that as it may, you have been proved right and I wrong.'

'In what way?'

'I thought Hugo would see reason, but he has not.'

'Ah, I see. In that way.'

'Tomorrow, I think he will have to.'

James drew on his cigarette, the tip brightening in the darkness as he did so, then said: 'You ought to know that, on Sunday, I visited Mother and appealed to her to call the case off.' He paused, as if waiting for Richard to react. Then, when Richard said nothing, he added: 'I didn't expect her to agree there and then, but I felt I had to make the effort. In the event, I'm not sure it didn't do more harm than good.'

'She refused outright?'

'Yes.'

'Was Hugo present?'

'No. I called at a time when I thought he would be at the club. I felt what chance there was lay in seeing Mother alone.'

'Did she speak about Hugo at all?'

'No.'

'I ask because I bumped into Freddy Cleveland in Piccadilly one day last week. He *did* speak about Hugo. And what he said I found rather disturbing.'

'In what way?'

'Cleveland's not one to take anything too seriously, as you know. But he seemed genuinely worried by Hugo's state of mind, concerned at the effect the trial's had on him. He commented on how depressed Hugo's been since his spell in the witness-box.'

'It's scarcely to be wondered at, Richard. The trial's been an enormous strain for all of us.'

'But you are strong and resilient. Hugo isn't. You know how weak he really is. How do you think he will react to losing the case? Everything – his money, his title, his property – will be gone. How will he cope?'

James said nothing. There was indeed every reason to doubt Hugo's capacity to bear the loss he might be about to suffer, and Richard, more than anyone, was bound to worry about the consequences, but both men knew the only way James could spare Hugo was to sacrifice himself. And that he was not about to do.

'What I'm saying, I suppose, is that I'd like to think you won't be hard on him because of his foolish conduct towards you. You have it in your power to destroy him. What I'd like to think is that you'll be generous in victory.'

'You have my word on it. Whatever his faults, Hugo remains my brother. If I win, he will be provided for.'

'I'm glad to hear you say so.'

'But you're assuming the jury will find in my favour. What if they find for Hugo? Would he be . . . generous in victory?'

323

There was a lengthy silence, during which both men contemplated the question in the blankness of the night. Then, when the need to give an answer had almost passed, Richard said solemnly: 'No. He would not.'

IX

The Royal Courts of Justice: Wednesday, 18th July 1883. The seventy-seventh and final day of the trial of *Norton versus Davenall*. Nothing in the courtroom or its occupants signalled that the day was different from all the tortuous others through which the case had wound its length. Nothing in the wigged and stooping practitioners of the Law or their crammed and craning audience denoted that this was the end. Yet so it was. *Norton versus Davenall* had run its course.

The jury entered and took their seats. Beyond the normal level of fidgeting and shuffling, they and all their observers detected a shocked and faintly ill-prepared dimension to the proceedings. Even though the issue had been carefully debated for more than three months, its enormity seemed only now to have been borne in upon them. One man, the plaintiff, would, in a matter of minutes, be transformed from the calmly polite figure to be seen whispering to his counsel into one of two things: a wealthy and vindicated aristocrat or a vile and contemptible impostor. In the same space, another man, the defendant, presently darting back to his seat with a tousled look of nervous anticipation, would either be restored to a life of untroubled ease or prised loose from his very name.

The jury settled. None of them had the look of a wild romantic or crazed anarchist. On the contrary, all were made of dull and stolid stuff. Yet what they were about to do was inescapably dramatic. The foreman, a tubby, bespectacled, tweed-suited fellow, adjusted his glasses and consulted some notes with which he must already have been well familiar.

Lord Coleridge entered. The court rose and then subsided, with his Lordship, into its place. The judge, at least, seemed unmoved by the occasion. He nodded to the clerk to proceed. As if on wires, the foreman of the jury bobbed up from his seat.

'Gentlemen of the jury, are you agreed upon your verdict?'

'We are.'

'And is it the verdict of you all?'

'It is.'

'How say you, then, in this case? Do you find for the plaintiff or the defendant?'

'We find for the plaintiff.'

SIXTEEN

I

Shortly before eleven o'clock on the morning of Wednesday, 18th July 1883, James Norton ceased to exist and James Davenall resumed a life suspended. The cheer that went up in the court when the jury found in his favour was almost as much one of astonishment as of acclamation. His victory had been predicted by many, but, now the moment of its announcement had arrived, the meaning of what he had achieved burst on their minds with the force of a revelation. The so-called Davenall Claimant had become Sir James Davenall in truth and in law. Against all odds, despite all doubts, in the face of all opposition, he had won. Everything he had ventured he had gained. Everything he had claimed he had been granted.

No sooner had the judge confirmed the jury's verdict and closed the case with a few formal words than the well of the court exploded in a confused and jostling mass of figures. Within seconds, the plaintiff was mobbed by more supporters than he can have been aware of having. Strangers were slapping his back and shaking his hand, journalists were shouting questions in his ear. Sir James himself, however, as if overwhelmed by the significance of what had occurred, said nothing in reply to the flood of congratulations. He seemed bemused, ill-prepared, uncertain how to react.

Then, at sight of Constance Trenchard threading a path to his side, his expression changed. As he reached out to clasp her hand, a smile came to his lips that left no room for doubt: she was the one person with whom he wished to share his triumph. Taking her arm in his, he led her calmly towards the exit, looking neither to right nor to left. This, his bearing implied, was the richest of all the prizes he had won that day: this was what made it all worth while.

Later, during the brief privacy of a cab-ride from the Courts to

Staple Inn, where Warburton was to host a celebration for those who had contributed to the victory, Sir James asked Constance Trenchard to marry him as soon as she was free to do so. She accepted without hesitation and he, for his part, promised never to desert her again. In the rapture of a re-discovered love, they spoke only of the future they would spend together. The past – and those in it who might still have calls upon them – they were happy to forget. For the past, they felt sure, they had escaped for ever.

The welter of publicity which attended the sensational conclusion of the case of *Norton versus Davenall* faded with surprising speed. The newspapers tired of the new baronet once he had made it clear that he would neither give interviews nor sign articles trumpeting his victory for the entertainment of their readers. Within a few weeks, the world went a long way towards doing what it seemed he wanted them to do: forget him.

Not that it was hard to understand Sir James's desire for privacy. Overnight, he had become the owner of a fine London residence, a large country house, a lucrative portion of the Somerset coalfield and a sizeable estate in the west of Ireland. The Council of the Baronetage had formally welcomed him to their ranks, the Davenall family banker to his doors. He had become a wealthy man. All his problems were behind him. Of publicity he had no need.

Perhaps this also explains why Sir James showed himself to be such a magnanimous victor. He made no swift or unreasonable demands on those of his family who had opposed him. He refrained from any move that might smack of vengeance. It was not, indeed, until early August that he asked his cousin Richard to convene a meeting with Warburton, Baverstock and Lewis in order to arrive at a final settlement of the dispute. Even then, the terms he proposed were more generous than they needed to be. When he visited Richard at his Holborn office to hear the outcome, he could reasonably have expected to hear that his offer had been gratefully accepted.

'As far as litigation goes,' Richard announced, 'it's certainly over. The judge stipulated, you may remember, that an appeal could only be considered if there were new evidence. Lewis candidly admits there is none.'

'Good. What of the rest?' Here, however, the surprises began.

'Your mother rejects the idea of remaining at Cleave Court, just as she rejects the proposed allowance. She wishes to be beholden to you for nothing. She intends to move out immediately.'

'To go where?'

'Baverstock said she plans to rent a smaller property somewhere. Anywhere, I gather, so long as it isn't on land you own.'

Lady Davenall's refusal to compromise, even in defeat, was, in its own way, admirable. The conduct of the case had evidently ensured there could be no reconciliation between them. 'So it's come to that,' said Sir James, sounding more disappointed than surprised.

'I fear so.'

'And Hugo?' His brother's response to generosity was less predictable. Greed and weakness might have induced him to accept what jealousy and his mother's disapproval should have forbidden him to consider.

'He will be out of Bladeney House by the end of this month.'

'But the allowance?'

'I don't know. Baverstock hedged. But the first payment's been made. Either Hugo hasn't noticed – or he grudgingly accepts. One thing is certain, however. There can be no healing of the breach. Neither Catherine nor Hugo wishes to see either of us, under any circumstances.'

'I'm sorry for your sake, Richard. I know you hoped the end of the case would be the end of the feud, but there was never any real chance it would be. Mother went too far in denying me to turn back now. And Hugo went with her.'

Richard sighed. 'So it seems.' Then he sighed again, in a different vein: the vein of a man settling for the best there was to be had. 'One thing the meeting did achieve. There are no longer any obstacles or objections to your control of the property and investments Gervase willed to you. From this day forth, they are yours to dispose of as you see fit.'

It was strangely subdued, this final conferral, this last word of ratification. Less than a year before, James Norton had stepped off the boat from America as a penniless stranger. Now, as Sir James Davenall, he stood high amongst the moneyed and well-born of the land. 'I remain more grateful than I can say, Richard, for your efforts on my behalf. I hope I can continue to rely upon you.'

Richard smiled. 'I have done no more than duty obliged me to do. I know you spoke of asking me to assume administration of your financial affairs, but—'

'It is what I earnestly wish.'

'Then, I would be honoured to do so. There is much to be attended to.'

'For the present, I must leave it all in your hands.'

A crestfallen look crossed Richard's face. 'You don't intend to play an active part?'

'Eventually, yes. But the trial, as you predicted, has been a draining experience. I feel the need of a long rest. Constance has agreed to accompany me on a Continental tour: it is the change of scene we both need. We will take Emily with us' – he smiled – 'by way of chaperone.'

'How long will you be away?'

327

'Three months or so. By the time we return, there will only be a short while to wait before we can marry. At that point, with Constance beside me as my wife, I will feel able to discharge my responsibilities as I would wish.'

After all that had happened, Sir James's need of a period of recuperation was understandable, and Richard was the obvious choice to oversee his affairs whilst he was away. It was strange, therefore, that when they fell to discussing the details of what would be involved a hint arose that rather more than mere stewardship was at issue. Nothing specific was said on either side but, somehow, it did not need to be. Their understanding of each other was sufficient for the implication to be clear and the inference obvious. Once Richard accepted responsibility for Sir James's interests, any doubts he still harboured about him would either have to be set aside for good or brought into the open at last. And accept he did. The unspoken challenge was taken up.

II

In one of the dining-boxes of a luridly decorated casino-cum-supperhouse near Leicester Square, Hugo Davenall was seeking to cauterize the wound his pride had recently suffered with an excess of food, drink and raucous company.

Cheers, whistles and stamps greeted the newest arrival on the small stage at the centre of the throng: a scantily dressed song-girl constituting the most daring act yet on the ever racier programme. Behind and above her, flaring gas-jets and bottle-plug candle-flames danced in banks of cheap crystal, while smoke swirled in the cavernous mouths of gilt-framed mirrors.

Hugo glanced contemptuously at the snoring figure beside him of Toby Leighton, then looked across the table at Freddy Cleveland, who drained another glass, replaced the cigar in his mouth, and smiled crookedly back.

'You look horribly sober, Hugo,' Cleveland remarked.

'I've drunk the same as you, bottle for bottle.'

'You wouldn't know it. Still thinkin' about the case?'

'How can I forget it? I can't go home tonight without remembering *he* owns the bed I sleep in. I can't put my name to a cheque without remembering it's *his* money I'll be drawing on. God damn it, Freddy' – he crashed his glass down on the table – 'the bastard's taken everything from me! You expect me to forget that?'

'You're goin' to have to, old man. What choice d'you have?'

Hugo gazed into the darkness beyond their table. 'That fellow Trenchard had the right idea. It's a pity he didn't finish the job.'

'Maybe, but look where it got him: the madhouse.'

'In my father's day, I could have called Norton out. That would have settled his hash.'

'Or yours, old man. With your marksmanship, you'd be lucky to hit a tart's arse at five paces.'

But Hugo was proof against humour and reason alike. His eyes narrowed as he contemplated, for a brief moment, the possibility of revenge. 'If Norton was in my sights, I'd hit the target, believe me.'

'That's the champagne talkin'.'

'Then what would you have me do?'

'Make your peace with the fellow. The world calls him your brother: go along with 'em. If you don't . . .'

'He'll cut me off without a penny.' Hugo nodded bleakly.

'Reckon so, old man. Reckon that's just what he'll do.'

Hugo ground his teeth. 'Damn the man, Freddy,' he muttered. 'Damn the bloody man.'

At that, Cleveland plucked the cigar from his mouth and struggled to adopt a serious expression. 'Take my advice: swallow your pride and make it up with him. D'you know what Bullington said to me last week?'

Bullington was generally held to be the power behind the chair of their club committee. Hugo looked at his friend with a stirring of curiosity. 'What did he say?'

'That the committee's thinkin' of invitin' James to resume his membership. After all, he never formally resigned.'

'They wouldn't do that to me!'

'They would. They *will*. If you go on opposin' him, you'll be floggin' a dead horse. It'll put you distinctly out of favour. Maybe *out* altogether.'

Hugo's mouth sagged open, but he said nothing. He stared at the green distorted reflection of himself in the champagne-bottle. Behind him, through gusts of music and laughter, came a high-pitched whine only he could detect, a mosquito-buzz of ridicule that threatened to grow into the deafening roar of his destruction.

III

Richard Davenall, Canon Sumner and little Patience, with her nanny, were at Victoria station to see James, Constance and Emily off on the boat-train. Barely three weeks had passed since the end of the trial, but, despite many last-minute panics, all the necessary preparations had been completed, mainly thanks to Emily, who had organized her maiden venture abroad with the precision of a seasoned traveller.

Canon Sumner had failed to comprehend the need for such a hasty

329

departure, but nobody had seen fit to enlighten him. Patience, of course, being too young to appreciate how long her mother would be away, was likewise in ignorance. And Emily was so flattered to be asked and excited to be going that she had not quibbled about the timing.

As a slamming of doors and gathering of steam signalled the imminence of departure, Richard stepped back to let Canon Sumner impress upon James some last concerns for his daughters' welfare, whilst Constance and Emily made a farewell fuss of Patience.

Richard was happy, in truth, to stand a little aloof from the sentiment of the scene, relieved not to have to wish James a platitudinous *bon voyage*. He let his gaze wander along the platform, where many a fond adieu was being exchanged. He saw the guard at the back of the train clamp a whistle between his teeth and raise the green flag. Then, just as he was about to look back at his friends, he noticed a porter hurrying a latecomer past the guard's disapproving glare: a woman, slim, elegant and darkly clad, seemingly without luggage. She stepped aboard, and the door closed behind her. As it did so, Richard caught a glimpse of her face, turned momentarily to look in his direction. He knew her. As the guard unfurled his flag and blew his whistle, Richard realized who she was: the woman at the hospital who had been asking after James, the woman whose appearance was so uncannily close to Trenchard's description of Melanie Rossiter.

For a second, he was too dumbstruck to act. Then it was too late. The train was moving. Patience was being held up by her nanny to wave goodbye through the piston steam. Constance and Emily were waving back. James, standing behind them, had raised his hand to Canon Sumner. The train was slowly accelerating. Richard's companions were walking after it along the platform to delay the last exchange of blown kisses. But Richard stood where he was, staring straight ahead as the row of lowered windows and smiling occupants slid past him.

One window was empty. The compartment he had seen her enter flashed by too quickly for him to see if she was sitting in it, but, even had she not been, he could not have doubted the evidence of his own eyes. Once might have been a coincidence, a misapprehension founded on a chance resemblance. But now there could be no mistake. She existed. She was real. And she was following James Davenall.

IV

From the spacious precincts of Cleave Court, Catherine Davenall had moved to a rented house in Brock Street, Bath. Despite the loss of most of her servants and all of her much-loved gardens, however, her spirit was undimmed. Undeterred by the ostracism of those who thought her conduct disgraceful and the restrictions imposed by her reduced circumstances, she remained as proud and as self-possessed as ever.

Nor had she, whatever Richard Davenall might have been told to the contrary, abandoned her struggle with the man the world now called her son. When Arthur Baverstock called on her one afternoon in late August, it was on no trivial errand: he had come to report the progress of continuing enquiries into the mysterious past of James Norton.

Alas for Baverstock, he had little to report. 'Mr Lewis is of the opinion', he explained, 'that we shall make no headway whilst we continue to deal through intermediaries. He feels we should send a member of his staff to the United States to conduct a thorough investigation.'

'Tell him to go ahead, Mr Baverstock. I wish for no half-measures.'

He had feared she would say as much. It obliged him to express his own unflattering reservations. 'Such a course of action would commit you to substantial expenditure, your Ladyship.'

'That is no matter.'

Baverstock squirmed. 'But, as Mr Lewis points out, your resources are not as considerable as they were. He fears—'

'Let me be the judge of what my resources are or are not equal to.' Her glare had lost none of its power to intimidate him. 'I wish no stone to be left unturned and I will pay whatever that costs. Tell Mr Lewis he may have his money in advance if he wishes.'

'I'm sure that won't be necessary.'

'I hope it will not be. I am enduring this modest standard of accommodation, Mr Baverstock, in order to ensure that the search for the truth about this man can continue to the end.'

Baverstock, who secretly believed the truth was already known, nodded in agreement. 'Of course, of course.'

'He believes he has beaten me. That will make him complacent. Complacency breeds carelessness. The longer it goes on, the likelier it becomes that he will make a fatal mistake. It is all I ask of him.'

'Yes, your Ladyship.'

'I know you and Mr Lewis believe I am pursuing a pointless vendetta. Don't trouble to deny it. But its results will surprise you – rely upon that. We are taking steps to monitor his movements on the Continent, I trust?'

'Yes, indeed. Mr Lewis has one of his best people on it.'

'Good. His eagerness to quit the country interests me. It may be an elaborate method of contacting his principals. If there are any developments, however trivial, I wish to be informed at once.'

'You will be, your Ladyship.'

'Be sure I am. He thinks he is safe now, Mr Baverstock, so very

331

safe. But it is not so. In truth, his peril is greater than before. Whilst there is breath in my body, he will not want for an enemy.'

This last Baverstock did not doubt. Lady Davenall's objective was clear. Only in the possibility of its fulfilment did he have no faith.

V

It was the last day of August, grey and crushingly hot. Richard Davenall sat in his office, gazing out at the weary ferment of Holborn, trying and failing to apply his mind to the work he had on hand.

The weather, or something more insidious, had sapped him of energy. Why, he wondered, was he still pursuing doubts his rational mind ought to shed? Only a few days before, he had received a letter from Constance in Salzburg proclaiming that all was well. There had been nothing in anything she wrote to sustain his belief that Melanie Rossiter was following them. Maybe he had not seen her after all. Maybe he had imagined doing so. Maybe he was simply losing his grip.

When Benson put his head round the door, Richard assumed it was to report nothing more spectacular than the arrival of the afternoon post. Instead, he said: 'There's a man wanting to see you, sir. Without an appointment.'

'Who is he?'

'He says he's Alfred Quinn.'

Suddenly, after all the efforts Roffey had made to find him, suddenly, when it was too late to matter, Quinn had come.

He had changed little with the years. A short muscular figure in tweeds, holding a bowler hat by his side. The short-cropped hair was rather greyer than before and extended now to a beard, but otherwise he was much the same: stiff-backed and square-shouldered, with a pugnacious bearing, steely-eyed and expressionless, his whole uncompromising demeanour hinting at sides to his character he was too cautious to reveal.

Richard stood up and rounded the desk, holding out his hand and smiling, concealing shock and curiosity behind the insincerity of his greeting. 'It *is* Quinn, isn't it?'

'Yes, sir.' His handshake was that of a strong man, his smile that of a grim one. 'I heard you were looking for me.'

'We *were*, yes. Did you not know about the case?'

'Not while it was going on. I've been in New Zealand for the past two years. Only got back last week. That's when I heard that James – *Sir* James, I should say – had reappeared.'

'You've been in New Zealand?'

'That's right. My uncle emigrated there in the forties and took to sheep-farming. Twenty years ago, they found gold on his land. He became a wealthy man. The first I knew of it was when I heard he'd died – and left it all to me. Seems I was his only living relative. So I've been over there, settling my inheritance, you might say.'

'What brought you back?'

'I'd sooner end my days in England than in Otago, sir. I sold up – for a good price. I've come home to enjoy my retirement. Hearing about Sir James . . . well, that *was* a turn-up for the books. I thought I'd come and pay my respects to him.'

'He's abroad at present, on holiday.'

'I'm sorry to have missed him. Perhaps there'll be an opportunity when he returns.'

'I'm sure he'll be glad to hear of your good fortune.'

'I'm sure of that, too, sir.'

The pace of Richard's unspoken thoughts had drained his remarks of originality. Could it be true? Had Roffey been mistaken all along? A windfall inheritance in New Zealand explained Quinn's absence and his evident prosperity just as well as a life of crime in London. If he was to be believed, Trenchard could never have encountered him. And, if Trenchard had imagined that, perhaps he had imagined Melanie Rossiter as well. 'What are your plans, then?' he said lamely.

'I've a yen to try my hand in the racehorse game, sir. I'm negotiating the purchase of some stables near Newmarket. Working with horses was what I most enjoyed in the Army. It'll be good to be involved with them again.'

'An expensive pursuit, I believe.'

Quinn nodded. 'It is that, sir. But now I have the money there's nothing to prevent me indulging myself.'

'I suppose not.' So Quinn, too, had fallen on his feet. The whims of fate, thought Richard, were strange indeed. The dismissed servant of four years before had stepped off the boat from New Zealand with more money to his name than his former employer. He took his pick of Newmarket stables, whilst she paid rent on a terraced house in Bath. 'You must be sure to let me have your address, Quinn, so that Sir James can look you up.'

'I'll do that, sir. Will he be moving into Bladeney House when he comes back?'

'I expect so. Why do you ask?'

'It's just that I called there first, thinking he might be at home. But Sir Hugo – *Mr* Hugo, that is – is still in residence.'

'Ah, yes, he would be. Did you speak to Hugo?'

'Yes, sir, I did. If you don't mind my saying so, he's taken events very hard. Very hard indeed.'

'What makes you say that?' Richard was far from sure that he wanted Quinn's opinion on his former master's state of mind.

'I've known Mr Hugo a long time.' The sharpening of Quinn's tone indicated that he had read Richard's thoughts. 'He was always a man for ups and downs. But if he was angry you knew it: he was never mopish.'

'You found him so on this occasion?'

'Yes, sir, I'd have to say I did. All the spirit seemed to have gone out of him. Quite saddened me to see it.'

'It's been a difficult time for all the family,' said Richard, assuming an unconcerned expression. 'I'm sure Hugo will pull round.'

The truth, of course, was otherwise. After Quinn had gone, Richard felt more beset than ever by the bitterness and enmity that had flowed from James's return. Who of all the people touched by the event would not, in their heart of hearts, prefer to turn back the clock and restore the assumptions and conventions by which their lives had been governed till he had come to change them? It was not James's fault. It was not anybody's fault. Yet many must have wished he had stayed away, or truly drowned in Wapping twelve years before.

Richard rose and moved to the window, from where he could see down into the street. As he watched, Quinn emerged on to the pavement and walked quickly away, an obscure, private citizen dwindling into the London crowds. There was no reason to disbelieve anything he had said. It made perfect sense. It proved what Richard should all along have accepted: that Quinn was neither master-criminal nor arch-conspirator, merely an old soldier whose luck had turned.

VI

Constance opened the french windows and stepped out on to the balcony of her hotel room. There was a cooling breeze this high above street-level, but already the day held presentiments of burning heat. Gazing at the clock-towers and neatly tiled roofs around her, she felt glad that today they would be heading south into Italy, for Zurich's air of industry and discipline had disappointed her after the gaiety of Salzburg.

She looked down into the tiny square beneath her, no more than a pocket handkerchief of raked gravel around a fountain when viewed from her fourth-floor eyrie. The little café opposite the hotel had few customers at this hour: the merest smattering of glum-faced Zurichers immersed in newspapers. There was also, she noticed, a single woman among them, sitting at one of the outermost tables facing the hotel. A slim creature in a cream dress, with long dark hair beneath a straw hat: such was all Constance could see of her.

Suddenly, she heard behind her a knock at the door of the room. She called 'Come in' and was delighted to see that her visitor was James, already dressed for travelling. He crossed the room, smiling, and joined her on the balcony.

'All packed?' he asked.

'I believe Emily has everything in hand.'

'As ever.' They exchanged a kiss. 'I have news from England. A letter from Richard.' He patted his jacket pocket.

'Is he well?'

'Oh, yes. But an interesting thing's happened. It seems Quinn has turned up at last.'

'Quinn?'

'My old valet. His testimony would have helped the case along, but he couldn't be found at the time. Apparently, he's just returned from New Zealand, unaware of all the efforts that were made to locate him.'

'How strange.'

'Isn't it? Richard says he's come into some money, though I doubt it's changed him.' He stepped to the edge of the balcony and leaned out from the railings to sample the air. 'Another hot day, I fancy.'

'I fear so.'

'In which case, the sooner we start the better. We've a long journey to—' His words were cut off in mid-sentence. When Constance looked at him, she saw that his face had gone quite white. He was gazing down fixedly into the square, at the placid scene of fountain and tables in which she had found so little of interest. But in James the view seemed to have inspired a sudden irrational terror. Alarmed, she stepped towards him, but the movement seemed to break whatever trance had briefly held him. He pushed himself back from the railings and smiled at her, the colour rapidly returning to his cheeks. 'It's all right. No cause for concern.'

She took his hand in hers and found his grip reassuringly firm. 'For a moment, you looked dreadfully ill.'

'A touch of vertigo, I think. Nothing more.'

'It's so unlike you.'

'Yes. I'm sorry. But, honestly, I feel perfectly well again now.'

'Shall we go in?'

'Yes, let's. Breakfast might complete my recovery.'

As they turned towards the room, Constance glanced down into the square, still wondering what had upset James: she had never known him to suffer from vertigo before. She saw, however, nothing that could have inspired such a reaction. All was quiet and orderly in the square. Nothing had changed in the past few minutes, except that the solitary female customer at the café had left her table and was walking away down the street.

VII

Richard walked past Bladeney House several times before summoning sufficient courage to ring the bell. It was absurd, he thought, as he waited for the door to open, that his heart should be racing like this, his hand shaking, merely at the prospect of seeing Hugo for the first time since the end of the trial. Hugo did not know, after all, what they truly were to each other. He must never know.

'Good afternoon, sir,' said Greenwood. There was no inflexion in his voice or twitch of his eyebrows to indicate surprise that Richard should have called again after so long an absence.

'Is Hugo in?'

'Yes, sir. You'll find him in one of the top-floor rooms, I think.'

Richard's misgivings grew as he ascended the stairs. The top floor of Bladeney House had been given over to servants' quarters in Gervase's day. Reductions in the household had followed and, so far as Richard knew, it was mostly storage space now. He could not imagine what would have drawn Hugo there.

Silence reigned on the topmost landing. Richard paused and looked around. Then came a sound from the far end of the passage, towards the back of the house, as of a heavy object being moved in stages. He hurried in its direction.

An open doorway led him into a small box-room, probably a parlourmaid's bedroom once, now stacked high with packing-cases and tea-chests. Hugo was stooped in a corner, loosening the leather straps round a scratched and dented metal trunk. He looked up in surprise when Richard called his name, his face flushed from his exertions, or perhaps, it struck Richard later, from guilt.

'What brings you here, cousin?' Hugo stood upright, brushing the dust from his hands. The glare of hostility in his eyes was unmistakable.

Richard stepped into the room, lowering his head where the ceiling sloped beneath the eaves. 'How are you, Hugo?' he said, ignoring the question he had been asked.

'Wonderful. Never felt better. How did you expect me to be?'

'The trial ended nearly two months ago. I hoped I might find you . . . reconciled to the verdict.'

'I am. As you see. Happy as a sand-boy. Can't think why I didn't renounce my title and give away all my money long ago. It's been the making of me.'

'Hugo—'

'Don't say anything, Richard!' Suddenly, the veil of sarcasm had dropped. 'You think two months can make good what you did to me? Nothing can. Nothing ever will.'

'James has been as generous as—'

'He's made me crawl, you mean. To his banker for money to live. To his solicitor to plead for a roof over my head. He took the bread out of my mouth, and you helped him do it. What in hell's name made you think I could be *reconciled* to his theft of everything I owned?'

Richard swallowed hard to mask the anguish he felt; he must be calm and tolerant – above all, loyal to his own actions if to nothing else. 'I helped James assert his natural and legal rights: that is all. I advised you against contesting his claim, but you paid no heed. Now I can only hope you will pay heed. Admit you were wrong, Hugo. Acknowledge James as your brother, the rightful holder of the baronetcy and the rightful owner of this house.' Irony crowded in upon Richard as soon as he had finished speaking. If only he could be sure that what he had said was really true. If only he could believe that Hugo, not he, had been the fool.

'This house! Is that why you're here? To make sure I clear out before he returns from gallivanting around Europe with another man's wife? My God, he's the only man I know who believes in taking the honeymoon before the wedding!'

'There's no point—'

'Well, don't worry! I'll be out soon enough. Freddy's recommended me some rooms in Duke Street that I should be able to afford on my so-called brother's so-called allowance.'

'You don't have to take his money.'

Hugo crashed his hand down against the lid of the trunk. The noise of the blow echoed in the tiny room. 'God damn it, what else can I do?' With a despairing sigh, he lowered himself on to an upturned orange-box, and stared up at Richard with bloodshot reproachful eyes. 'There'd be the devil to pay if Mother ever found out I was taking his money. But I have no choice.'

'There is always a choice.' Richard remembered excusing his desertion of Catherine all those years before on just the grounds Hugo had now advanced. Yet he knew the futility of pretending a choice could truly be said to exist for a son as weak as his father.

'It's easy for you to say that. It's easy for you to stand there and tell me what I should and shouldn't do.'

'Believe me, I'm only trying to help you.'

In Hugo's expression as he glared up at Richard, hurt pride had conquered self-loathing. 'I don't need your help – or your advice. What the hell does it matter to you whether I choose to take his money or not?'

It was one question Richard dared not answer. It was too late, far too late, to explain why he should feel so shamed and diminished by Hugo's humiliation. He could only stare back blankly.

'Get out, Richard. Get out and leave me to lead the life you and Norton have forced on me in whatever way I see fit.'

'I'll be going away on business soon. I thought—'

'I expect I'll be out of here by the time you return. I shan't burden you with my new address, because I shan't expect you to call.'

'If you don't want me to—'

'I don't.'

Hugo's bleak broken-spirited look confirmed that there was nothing more to be said. With the faintest of farewell nods, Richard turned and left the room.

'On business, you say?' Hugo called after him. '*Sir* James's business, no doubt. Much good may you have of running errands for him.'

Richard walked away slowly down the passage. It was strange, he reflected, that Hugo should throw that last insult at his back, for he was not going away at James's bidding. In a sense, he was going for Hugo's sake. He was going to seek the truth on his son's account.

Hugo waited until Richard's footsteps had faded away down the stairs. He was alone once more, rid of his cousin's pious solicitude, out of the sickening sight of his prying eyes. He turned to the trunk, threw back the straps and raised the lid.

Inside were all the surviving remnants of Sir Gervase Davenall's military career: his sabre in its scabbard, items of uniform neatly folded, a pair of binoculars, map-tubes and assorted charts, a bundle of saddle-bags and harnessing, a portable chess-set, a small folding card-table and the dismantled legs, struts and castors of an old camp-bed.

Carefully, almost reverentially, Hugo delved through the piles of distinctive Hussar pelisses, tunics, sashes and trousers. He found what he was looking for, concealed at the base of the trunk: a shallow rectangular wooden box, measuring about thirty inches by fifteen. With some difficulty, for it was deceptively heavy, he lifted it out and laid it on the floor, then drew a bunch of keys from his pocket and began looking through them for the one that would fit the tiny lock that held the box shut. He did not hurry, for he knew what was in the box and would recognize the right key as soon as he saw it. He knew because he had seen it opened before.

When Hugo returned to Bladeney House that night in September 1876, Quinn told him his father was waiting for him in his study. It was past midnight, but no excuse would be acceptable. His presence was required.

It was immediately obvious that Sir Gervase was slightly drunk and very angry. 'Have you anything to say for yourself?' he demanded as soon as Hugo entered the room.

'I don't understand, sir.'

'Don't prevaricate with me. Wigram spoke to me at the club this evening.'

'About what?'

'About your dispute with his son.'

'Ah, that.' Young Wigram had accused Hugo of cheating during a late-night game of faro. And Hugo had indeed been cheating, though he had denied it strenuously; the two had parted on the worst of terms.

'Well may you say *that*. Have you any idea of the embarrassment you've caused me? To be told that my own son cheats at cards – on club premises. Damn your eyes, Hugo, have you nothing to say to me?'

'I didn't cheat, sir. Harry Wigram was mistaken.'

'His father said you'd denied it – then walked out.'

'What else could I do?'

'What else?' Sir Gervase stared at his son incredulously. 'Good God, can you be serious? Your action was virtually an admission of guilt.'

'I wasn't prepared to sit there and be insulted.'

'Then, you should have called him out.'

Hugo frowned. Now it was his father's seriousness that was in doubt. Surely he must know that duelling, once the *sine qua non* of a gentleman, was looked upon nowadays as the refuge of romantics and the indulgence of idiots. 'Well, sir, we do things rather differently these—'

Sir Gervase thumped the desk and eyed Hugo with revulsion. 'You mean you haven't the backbone for it. Dammit, boy, you sicken me. I've given you the finest education money can buy, but you understand the value of nothing, not even the good name of this family.'

'I could hardly have—'

'Last year you were in hock to that Jew. Now this. Where will it end? When will I ever stop wishing you, rather than James, had had the damned decency to drown himself?'

Never. Hugo knew that well enough. There would never come a time when his father would cease reminding him of all the ways in which he was his dead brother's inferior. 'I think James would have done the same as me,' he muttered resentfully.

'He would never have cheated at cards, you mean. But if anyone had ever accused him of such a squalid stupid thing he would have known what to do.' Stooping over his desk, Sir Gervase pulled open one of the lower drawers and lifted out a large flat wooden box. He laid it on the desk-top and glared at Hugo with undisguised contempt. 'He would have demanded satisfaction. As I would have done. As I have done, in the past.' He drew a small key from his waistcoat pocket and, leaning forward, unlocked the box. Then he raised the lid and looked back at Hugo. 'James would have asked me

339

to let him use these. And I would have been proud to let him. Proud of him – as I can never be proud of you.' At that, he turned the box round to face his son.

Hugo opened the box and gazed in at a pair of Purdey percussion duelling pistols. The octagonal barrels were finely patterned, the locks and mounts elegantly engraved, the butts saw-handled and deftly carved. About the sleek opposing lines of the two weapons nestling in their green-baize compartments there hovered still, more than forty years after their last fateful outing, a strange, seductive aura that was a grudging love for the means and methods of vengeful death.

Hugo lifted one of the pistols out and weighed it in his hand, feeling the crafted balance of it, sensing the treacherous perfection of its purpose. Then he held it at arm's length, pulled back the cock with his thumb, imagined James Norton standing in front of him, squeezed the trigger, heard the lock strike – and found his target.

VIII

Emily Sumner had concluded an exhausting awestruck tour of the Cathedral of Santa Maria del Fiore in Florence in great need of sunlight and fresh air. Emerging by the south door of the cathedral into the open dazzling expanse of the Piazza del Duomo, she paused for a moment to let her eyes adjust to the sudden brightness. As she stood there, she was surprised to see, a short distance away, the retreating figure of Sir James Davenall, whom she had believed to be enjoying a late breakfast with Constance at their hotel, the pair having long since professed an inability to keep pace with Emily's arduous schedule of sight-seeing.

Before she could call out, James had reached the doorway at the foot of the campanile, near the western end of the cathedral. Stepping in, he tossed a coin to the attendant and disappeared up the stairs. Emily had not intended to ascend the tower until later in the day, but, seeing her friend, she changed her mind and decided to follow him.

The stairs were steep and ill-lit, the treads shallow and worn in places. Accordingly, Emily made slow progress. At every bend, she looked ahead for a sight of James, but to no avail. Eventually, on the third flight, she observed that some relief was in prospect: the stairs led up to what appeared to be an open floor about a quarter of the way up the tower. She pressed on towards it.

It was as she neared the doorway at the top of the stairs that she heard James's voice, raised and lacking its usual gentle tone. 'I intend to marry her. Is that clear enough?'

Emily pulled up. What could it mean? James had entered the campanile alone, yet now he was talking to somebody, apparently about Constance. From the step where she had halted, she could see the flagged floor beyond the stairs, glaringly bright in the daylight that reached it through tall windows set between the pillars and buttresses of the tower. Nobody was visible, but James must be close by, so well had his voice carried. Emily was about to venture further when she heard James speak again.

'You are entitled to reproach me. Of course you are. But I have come to love her and she to love me. I cannot betray her.'

Emily had to thrust her hands against the stone wall either side of the stairs to steady herself. Breathless now from more than the climb, she craned her head and listened.

'I admit that. But I must weigh her needs against yours.'

Emily realized that she could hear only James's share of the conversation. She edged closer and, this time, caught the other's words. 'Have you forgotten all that I did for you?' It was a woman's voice, young and almost certainly English.

'I have forgotten nothing. But, sometimes, what I remember seems like another life, not my own.'

'You promised me a share of all you gained.'

'You may have it. As much as you want. Regularly, via the bank in Zurich.'

'It's not money I want. I want to be what you said you would make me: the wife of Sir James Davenall.'

Emily clapped her hand to her mouth to prevent herself crying out. What was this? She had come to trust if not to love James as much as Constance. Who was he talking to? What was she to him? 'I cannot help it,' James replied as she listened. 'You will survive without me. Constance would not.'

'Have you any idea what I have done to help you?'

'Don't think I'm not grateful, but—'

'I won't let you marry her!' The voice was suddenly harsh and insistent.

A brief silence fell, during which Emily could hear no sound but the pounding of her own heart, then James replied: 'You can't stop me. Not now. Follow me as long as you like. Dog my every footstep. It won't make any difference. I'm sorry. So very, very sorry. Our love is dead, and nothing you can say or do will bring it back to life.'

'I won't let you marry her.'

'For God's sake, be reasonable.'

'Why should I be? So that you can have all and more than your due? Be warned: I know more about you than you do yourself. If you go through with this, if you marry that woman—'

'I will, believe me.'

341

'Very well. You will. But, when you do, remember that you bring the consequences on your own head.'

'What do you mean by that? What consequences?'

'You'll find out. I'll make sure you do.'

'This is foolishness. We—'

'I won't follow you any more. But I will wait for you. Not long, but long enough, should you see reason. If not. . . .'

Silence was re-imposed. Emily felt trapped, physically as well as mentally, between flight and confrontation, between complicity and accusation. She could not turn and run, nor could she go on. She could not guess what looks or meanings were passing between James and his companion now they were not speaking, nor could she make sense of all that she had heard.

'I love you,' the woman said abruptly.

'I love another,' James replied.

'Then, goodbye. And God help you.'

Suddenly, in a flurry of skirts and a scattering of powdered stone, a figure burst on to the staircase, blotting out the light behind her and plunging down the steps. She hardly seemed to notice Emily as she brushed past her in the darkness and rushed on towards the turning and the next flight beyond.

James did not follow. When Emily looked up at the doorway, there was no sign of him. Perhaps he had gone on up the tower. Perhaps he had stayed where he was. Unable to bear the uncertainty any longer, Emily took several deep breaths, composed herself as best she could and climbed the steps into the daylight.

James was standing on the far side of the tower, leaning against the parapet and smoking a cigarette as he gazed out across the city. He could hardly have looked, in his panama and cream linen suit, a more perfectly composed or untroubled figure. It was scarcely possible to believe that he had just been involved even in the mildest of disagreements.

Some movement caught his eye as Emily approached. He whirled round – and smiled broadly. 'Emily! What a surprise!' She could detect no tension or unease in his voice as he added: 'How long have you been there?'

This was the moment, if there would ever be a moment. This was her chance, the only one she would ever have, to challenge him on her sister's behalf, to call him to account for whatever he had kept from them. Yet, even as she began to frame the words, she began to see and fear the consequences. Constance was so happy at last, so perfectly contented, and James had said nothing disloyal to her: if what she had witnessed was what it seemed to be – a secret quietus with a woman from his past – why not leave it at that? What could anybody gain by dragging it into the open?

342

'Is there something wrong?'

'No,' Emily replied hastily. 'Somebody coming down as I was coming up nearly bowled me over, that's all. And I didn't expect to find you here.'

James smiled sheepishly. 'Felt the need of a stroll before breakfast. Would you care to accompany me to the top?'

'Yes. That would be delightful.'

And so they went on, neither giving the other the slightest hint that anything was amiss. From the summit of the tower, they admired the dome of the cathedral, identified Florentine landmarks and gazed about at the hazy rim of the surrounding hills. James was, as ever, charming and solicitous, the ideal guide, the perfect companion, the considerate friend. When Emily glanced at him, she still saw the man whom she regarded as her sister's rightful husband, but she also heard, above his genial commonplace remarks, the voice in which he had denied the love of another. Then she realized, with the shock of a brutally shattered illusion, that she did not really know him at all. He had become what she had refused to believe he was: a stranger.

IX

Davenall & Partners,
4 Bellows Court,
High Holborn,
LONDON WC.

24th September 1883

Dear James,

I have today received your cable from Rome indicating that you will be returning to this country around the middle of next month. I trust your decision to come home earlier than planned does not mean there is something amiss.

I thought it best to write this letter now for you to read upon your arrival, since there is every likelihood that I will not be on hand to welcome you in person. I have arranged to visit Carntrassna early next month in order to satisfy myself that Kennedy's management of the estate serves your best interests. I have, of course, no way of knowing how long I will need to spend there, nor, indeed, what I may learn in the process.

Until we meet again, I remain

Ever Yours,
RICHARD

SEVENTEEN

I

The steamer in which Constance had travelled with James and Emily from Naples docked in London on a still grey October morning. Constance suspected that she would have found her first sight of London's drab relentless skyline depressing enough, after the warmth and colour of Italy, even without the added sadness of knowing that it meant she and James must soon be parted. It was small wonder, then, that her heart sank as the dockside approached.

Curiously, she could not escape the impression that her two companions were relieved to be home. The proximity imposed by shipboard life had reinforced a suspicion she had first felt in Florence: that James and Emily were, in some strange way, at odds with each other. They had done their best to keep it from her, but she had guessed it all the same. It explained why they had argued in favour of cutting short their holiday, which she had hoped to extend to Greece, and why, now, they did not seem to share her sorrow that the voyage was over.

Constance had not expected her father to bring Patience up from Salisbury to meet them. In her present mood, indeed, she preferred that reunion to be postponed. She had, however, assumed that Richard Davenall would be on hand to greet them. Instead, when they left the tender, only Richard's clerk, Benson, was there to welcome them. Benson had a letter for James from Richard, which James read to her during the cab-ride away from the docks. Richard, it seemed, had gone to Ireland on estate business, news which James appeared to take amiss.

Such, at least, was Constance's fleeting impression, though, in her distracted state, she paid it little heed. Her thoughts centred now on how best to tolerate the brief separation which she and James were

344

obliged to endure before they could marry. Compared with that, even the coolness she had detected between James and Emily faded into insignificance. As for what Richard might be doing in Ireland, it was the last question likely to occupy her mind. So far as she was concerned, it had no bearing on her future, no bearing at all.

II

It had rained heavily during the night. Richard had been woken several times by gusts rattling against the windows of his room. But now, when he parted the curtains and looked out across the rank lawns of Carntrassna House, it was hard to believe, so blue and untroubled was the sky, so calm the distant waters of Lough Mask. He wrenched up the sash and breathed in the sweet mild air, wondering how long the serenity would last before some engulfing storm rushed down from the mountains behind the house. It would not be long, he felt sure. If he had learned little else in his three days at Carntrassna, it was that nothing there could be relied upon.

He turned back to the wash-stand, poured some water into the bowl and immersed his face in it to goad his sluggish brain into alertness. He was growing too old for such far-flung journeys as this, he told himself, too reliant on the orderly predictable ways of London. Carntrassna, with its vistas of dark peat and brooding mountains, its vivid, ever changing weather and inky-black impenetrable nights, had unnerved him.

Dabbing his face with a towel, Richard remembered his arrival at Westport station and the ride from there to the house in Kennedy's dog-cart as if they had happened an age ago. He had got the measure of the man since and knew now that he had been anxious to impress Richard with both his diligence and his difficulties.

'That's where they found Lord Ardilaun's bailiffs last year,' Kennedy had said, pointing out across the lough as they caught their first sight of it from the muddy rutted track. 'Trussed up in sacks and drowned like runts in a litter.'

'It seems hard to believe such violent acts could be committed amidst all this natural beauty,' Richard had lamely replied.

'Don't let the look of the land deceive you, sir. It's a treacherous place, particularly for those of us doing our duty. You never know when Captain Moonlight may come calling.'

It was true enough, Richard did not doubt. Yet, if so, why had Kennedy – and the local constabulary – been so certain Mary Davenall's murder had not been politically motivated? The journey to Carntrassna had passed the neglected Church of Ireland chapel where

345

generations of Fitzwarrens, Mary amongst them, had been buried; and there, pausing to pay his respects at the graveside, Richard had challenged Kennedy on the point.

'You're sure the Fenians had no hand in this?'

'Sure as I can be, sir. Lady Davenall was well liked and respected. Many of the older tenants still speak gratefully of her kindness to them during the famine years.'

'Even so. . . .'

'And Fenians wouldn't steal jewellery. No, sir, it's my belief the old lady disturbed a burglar.'

Richard had stooped to inspect the inscription on the stone: MARY ROSALIE FITZWARREN, 1798–1882. It had seemed as pointedly stark to him then as it seemed perversely inaccurate now. 'Why is only her maiden name used?' he had asked.

'That was her wish, sir. She was most insistent on the point. I suppose. . . .'

'Yes?'

'I suppose she regarded herself as more of a Fitzwarren than a Davenall. That's all I can think.'

Patently, it was so. Richard had never met the old lady, but her determination to exile herself from the Davenalls was mirrored in the overgrown forgotten setting she had chosen for her final resting-place. Even their name, in the end, she had discarded.

Richard returned to the window and gazed down the drive. There was Kennedy, in the dog-cart, starting early for an appointment in Castlebar. He would be likeable enough, Richard conceded, if he were not so anxious to please. As it was, this would be the first day when he would not be obliged to accompany the man on his endless rounds of the estate, when he would be free to begin the task he had come to Carntrassna to perform.

Small thanks to Kennedy, even so. It had been left, in fact, to the man's wife to give Richard the clue he needed. She had talked more willingly than her husband of their predecessors, the Lennoxes, and Richard had asked her what memories she had of them.

'None at all, sir. They were gone by the time we arrived in these parts.'

'Did Lady Davenall speak well of them?'

'She hardly mentioned them, sir.'

'Do you know why they left?'

'To emigrate, we were told.'

'Not a step you've ever considered?'

'No, sir. Of course, we don't have a child to think of. The prospects here for—'

'The Lennoxes had a child?'

'A son, sir, yes. A bright boy, apparently. They must have been looking to his future when they decided to try their luck in Canada.'

Canada. And a son. More than twenty years ago. A short step from Richard's room took him to the landing, where an oil painting of Mary Davenall hung high on an ill-lit wall. He had stared at it several times since his arrival and now did so again, puzzling over the secretive, reclusive, hidden personality of its subject. A handsome woman, he could not deny, somewhere in her mid-forties when the portrait was made, to judge by her appearance and the style of her dress, red-haired and fiery-eyed, confident and domineering, not at all the sort to hide herself from the world. Why had she done so? Why had she been killed?

'How do you know the Lennoxes had a son?' Richard had asked Mrs Kennedy. 'Did Lady Davenall mention him?'

'No, sir. Not that I can recollect. But, shortly after we'd moved into Murrismoyle, a gentleman from Galway came calling, under the impression that the Lennoxes still lived there. Evidently, he was tutor to their son. He seemed quite taken aback that they hadn't told him of their plans.'

'A gentleman, you say?'

'A very learned gentleman, sir. That I know, because he still writes articles in the *Connaught Tribune* from time to time. Mr Kennedy often reads them to me. They're very edifying pieces.'

The more Richard learned, the less he understood. As agent for the estate, Lennox would have been little better than a glorified servant. What business had he engaging a tutor for his son? What business had he being paid ten thousand pounds by Sir Gervase Davenall? Perhaps the one man who had known the Lennoxes and could still be found might give him the answer.

'Can one of the men drive me to Claremorris, Mrs Kennedy? I wish to take the train to Galway.'

'To Galway, sir?'

'Yes. I may spend the night there before returning.'

Waiting on the front steps of the house for the gig to be hitched and brought round from the stables, Richard felt himself shivering, for all the mildness of the morning. Carntrassna, with its peeling stucco and clinging shanks of ivy, its weed-clogged gardens and gaunt shuttered remoteness, had eaten into his reserves of self-discipline. But that was not all. Something else was clawing at his resolution, something more potent by far than the air of resentful dereliction Mary Davenall had conferred on her family home.

'I've never understood my wife and I never will,' Sir Lemuel had once said. 'I served with her brother in the Peninsula: a fine man. Killed at Vittoria. I knew him better than I ever knew Mary, for all that we lived together for more than twenty years.'

'Might I ask, sir,' Richard had said, 'what took her back to Ireland?'

'God knows, my boy. She gave me neither warning nor reason. And

347

I've not cared to beg for an explanation. She packed her bags and left, one summer's day in 1838, while I was in London. Since then, she's never so much as written me a letter.'

The gig set off down the drive between the dank ill-kept lawns and the straggling hedges of fuchsia. The sun was shining on Richard's back now, but still he felt cold, chilled beyond the reach of any warmth by the sudden realization that the truth was close at hand.

III

If Freddy Cleveland ever admitted to feeling the pangs of a genuine emotion, it was only in the privacy of his unspoken thoughts. No gentleman, he believed, should display anything but the most studied indifference to the dramas of life. He would, therefore, have been hard put to explain why, on calling at Hugo Davenall's new residence in Duke Street only to learn that his friend was spending the afternoon at Lazenby's Gymnasium in Hammersmith, he had not simply strolled towards Pall Mall and a few quiet hours at the billiards table.

Instead, he found himself ascending a rickety staircase beside one of the least salubrious of Hammersmith's alehouses and enquiring, of a short, broken-nosed, bald-headed man in a tiny office festooned with programme cards for recent boxing bouts, whether his friend was truly to be found in such improbable surroundings.

'You mean *Sir* 'Ugo Davenall?'

So. Hugo was still making free with the title he had forfeited: it was worrying. 'Yes. That's right.'

'There's a shootin' gallery aht the back o' the gym. You'll find 'im there, like as not.'

Freddy followed a narrow corridor, partitioned off from the gymnasium so that he could hear, but not see, the exertions of assorted weightlifters. It led him into a high-ceilinged brick-walled range, where the reports of rapid gunfire pounded at his eardrums. In one of the cubicles, he found Hugo, whose attention, after much shouting, he managed to attract.

'What the devil are you doin' here, Hugo?'

'What does it look like?'

'Shootin', of course, but. . . .'

'I'm no marksman. Isn't that what you said? Watch this.'

Hugo raised the old-fashioned gun he held in his hand and trained it on the target at the end of the range, about thirty feet away. As he pulled back the cock and took aim, Freddy glanced at the target and saw that it was the two-dimensional wooden likeness of a man, carved as if the man were standing side-on. There were circles marked in red on the head and chest, circles within which small jagged holes had already been torn in the wood. Hugo fired.

When the noise of the shot had faded and Freddy had unclenched his eyes, he saw that another hole had been added to the topmost circle. Hugo had scored a direct hit. 'Not bad, eh?' he said, smiling back at Freddy.

'You've been practisin' this?'

'Of course. Practice makes perfect, after all.'

'But . . . why?'

'Why do you think?'

Freddy could hardly believe what he was forced to conclude: that Hugo was still indulging his fantasy of challenging Sir James Davenall to a duel. 'Can we talk somewhere, old man? I don't think well under fire.'

They adjourned to the alehouse downstairs, where the landlord was induced to open the snug for their use. Hugo looked better than he had all year, fitter, harder, unnaturally self-assured.

'I've not seen you at the club lately,' Freddy remarked, sipping at his whisky and soda.

'Didn't Bullington tell you? I've resigned.'

'Resigned? Why?'

'Because they've gone ahead with their invitation to Norton. And he's accepted. Bullington told me so.'

'Good God, old man, there was no need to—'

'But that's neither here nor there. He won't have long to enjoy his membership.'

'What d'you mean by that?'

'As soon as he sets foot in London, I intend to challenge him.'

Anywhere else, at any other time, Freddy would have laughed in Hugo's face. Duelling had long been regarded by their generation as the most absurd of anachronisms. But the intensity of his friend's expression forbade such a reaction. Instead, he said, in sober responsible tones he scarcely recognized as his own: 'It's not on, Hugo. You must forget the very idea.'

But Hugo merely smiled blithely back. 'I wasn't going to leave you out of it, Freddy. In fact I'm glad you're here. It gives me the opportunity to ask if you'll do me the honour of acting as my second.'

'You are jokin', aren't you?'

But Freddy was wasting his breath. It was obvious Hugo had never been more serious. 'Will you do it? Grass before breakfast, old man. It was a common enough way to settle differences in our fathers' day.'

'But this isn't our fathers' day. You'll make a laughin'-stock of yourself.'

'I don't think so. If Norton accepts the challenge, I'll be ready for him. If not, I'll have exposed him as a coward.'

349

'He'll never accept. Dammit, why should he?'

'Because, if he were really James, he'd do the decent thing. Wouldn't he?'

'I don't know. Twelve years ago, a chap might still sneak off to France and take a pot-shot at a rival without bein' called a ninny by all and sundry. Jimmy might have done it then, yes. But not now.'

Hugo drained his glass and stared levelly across the table. 'Will you act for me, Freddy?'

'It's a tomfool idea, Hugo. You must—'

'Yes or no?'

It was strange, thought Freddy, to discover, so far advanced in his feckless existence, that there was a genuine fund of loyalty his friends could call upon at direst need. The amoral code he claimed to live by should have led him to desert Hugo in short order. But that, he now realized, he could not do. 'Yes,' he said through gritted teeth. 'I'll act for you.' He, too, drained his glass. 'Damn it all.'

IV

Denzil O'Shaughnessy, self-appointed spokesman of the thinking classes of Connaught, stepped sprightly from the platform of the Salthill tram as it turned into Eyre Square, Galway, plucked a sheaf of papers from the inside pocket of his coat and struck out towards the offices of the Connaught Tribune Printing and Publishing Company.

His progress across the square was impressive in its own right. A tall, heavily-bearded, broad-shouldered man wearing a dashing if dented top-hat, and a flapping overcoat in the fashion of a cloak, he flourished the papers in his hand like a swagger-stick, glanced about to right and left with his head tossed haughtily back and flipped coins to the beggars huddled beneath the Dunkellin monument as if throwing handfuls of seed to birds at his feet.

If any observer had judged O'Shaughnessy, by this display, to be some arrogant local magnate indulging in a piece of tastelessly conspicuous expenditure, they would have been sorely mistaken. He could, in fact, ill afford to give even loose change away. His clothes, though stylish and well made, were threadbare, his stout boots painfully thin-soled. For an educated man nearing sixty, he was scandalously ill-prepared for the privations of old age, and the air he exuded of leisured contentment owed nothing to the cramped lodging he had set out from not half an hour since.

Denzil O'Shaughnessy's finances were, in truth, ransomed to his integrity. His forays into journalism had so often betrayed a contempt for the landed and Protestant gentry of Ireland that his more remunerative occupation – tutoring the same gentry's children – had lately been in short supply. Not that he felt restrained by this from continuing to inveigh in print against the tide of violence sweeping his homeland or the reasons for it, for he was a man who always acted according to the promptings of his conscience: a rare phenomenon indeed.

Breezing into the *Tribune* offices, his face wreathed in the broadest of smiles, O'Shaughnessy was already preparing some artful rejoinder to the misgivings of his editor when he noticed a well-dressed grey-bearded man leaning against the counter, to whom the clerk, young Curran, said as he entered: 'You're in luck, sir. Here's Mr O'Shaughnessy in the flesh.'

The stranger turned towards him. Middle-aged and rather weary-looking, O'Shaughnessy thought. Probably English. Too watery-eyed for any kind of commerce, too doleful to be a tourist. Not, whatever else, a happy man.

'This gentleman was enquiring where he might find you, Denzil,' Curran put in. 'I was just after giving him directions.'

'I'm Richard Davenall,' the stranger said, holding out his hand. 'Perhaps you recognize the name.'

O'Shaughnessy did. 'Your family owns the Carntrassna estate,' he said, shaking the man's hand.

'Yes. Sir James Davenall is my cousin. I represent his interests.'

'I'm pleased to meet you, Mr Davenall. What can I do for you?'

'I wonder if we might have a private word somewhere?'

'I was thinking of stepping over to the Great Southern for a glass and a bite to eat.' He caught Curran's eye: the lad clearly knew he had formed no such intention until confronted by a man who might willingly pay hotel-bar prices on his behalf. O'Shaughnessy's generosity of spirit, it will be understood, had never excluded himself. 'You'd be welcome to join me.'

'It would be my pleasure.'

O'Shaughnessy grinned triumphantly at Curran and slapped his article down on the counter. 'See this reaches Mr McNamara with my compliments, Liam. It's for the Friday edition. Explain I couldn't linger.' With that, he turned to his English visitor and led the way.

'You've still not told me why you sought me out, Mr Davenall,' O'Shaughnessy said, half an hour later, relaxing in the afterglow of a meal which his companion had already paid for. 'It can't be on account of my scribblings in the *Tribune*. They ruffle no feathers in Dublin, leave alone London.'

'Mrs Kennedy spoke highly of your work.'

'You amaze me. I should hardly have thought the Kennedys shared my views.'

'You're acquainted with them, then?'

'Slightly.'

'Kennedy's sure my aunt's murder last year had nothing to do with politics. Do you agree?'

'As a matter of fact, I do.'

'May I ask why?'

'Because she was the last of the Fitzwarrens, a well-liked family. And, even as absentees, the Davenalls haven't been bad landlords. Besides, there'd be no sense in the Fenians committing a murder and then not claiming the credit for it. There have been enough political killings in Connaught these past few years – more than enough – for their hallmarks to become well known. In your aunt's case, they were entirely lacking. But I'm sure the police have already told you that.'

'Yes. They have.'

'So in what other respect do Sir James Davenall's interests concern me?'

'You followed the court case?'

'Naturally. Who could resist such a romantic tale? Even here, amidst all the feuds and vendettas, it had them by the ears.'

'Have you ever met Sir James, Mr O'Shaughnessy?'

'No.'

'Or Sir Gervase before him?'

'No. I haven't been to Carntrassna for more than thirty years.'

'What took you there then, might I ask?'

'My work.'

'As a journalist?'

'No. As a teacher.'

'Mrs Kennedy said you were tutor for some time to the son of their predecessors as agents – the Lennoxes.'

'That's right, I was. The Lennoxes educated their boy Stephen at home. They engaged me as his tutor.'

'A bright boy?'

'Stephen Lennox was my star pupil, Mr Davenall. I think you could say he had a gift for scholarship. I wish I could have done more to cultivate it. The wilds of Mayo were no place for him, that's certain. I wanted him to put in for Trinity College, Dublin. He'd have walked it. But his family decided to emigrate instead.'

'Did that surprise you?'

'I had no warning, if that's what you mean. I saw the boy up to Christmas of fifty-nine. Then, without a word, they left.' It was strange, he reflected, how keenly he still remembered the disappointment of Stephen Lennox being plucked away from him, so near the culmination of eight years of tuition. He had harboured a genuine affection for the boy and felt it still, despite all the years that had passed since. 'It came as a bolt from the blue.'

'How old was Stephen Lennox at that time, Mr O'Shaughnessy?'
'Oh, sixteen.'
'He would have been born when?'
'1843.'
'And would be, what, forty now?'
'Yes. I suppose he would. Still in Canada, presumably.'
'Where did your classes with him take place?'
O'Shaughnessy frowned. What the devil was the man driving at?
'The Lennoxes' home at Murrismoyle, of course.'
'Not Carntrassna House?'
'No.'
'Yet you said your work took you there.'
'It did on one occasion, when I was first appointed. 1851, that would
have been. Lady Davenall interviewed me for the post.'
'Did that not strike you as odd? After all, strictly speaking, the Len-
noxes were your employers, not my aunt. In fact, did it not strike you as
odd that the Lennoxes were able to afford a tutor for their son at all?'
'I was in no position to look a gift-horse in the mouth, Mr Davenall.
Andrew Lennox was scarcely the man to bother overmuch about educa-
tion, it's true, but he must have made an exception in his son's case. I
was well and regularly paid. I wish I could find such clients now – and
such pupils.'
'You missed the boy when he'd gone?'
'I confess I did, even more than I missed my fee. He was growing into
a fine young man.'
'What do you remember about him?'
'He was the model pupil, Mr Davenall. Quick, perceptive, studious,
witty. A voracious reader. A considerable intelligence in the making.
And courteous to boot. It was a pleasure to teach him. A real pleasure.'
He smiled and cast back his throughts to the hours he had spent with
young Stephen in the attic-cum-schoolroom at Murrismoyle. Much of
the best of his own learning he had left there, in the ever eager, absor-
bent mind of that boy. Would that Stephen could have followed him to
Trinity College and then made more of his life than he ever had. He
remembered their explorations of the classics, their literary sparrings,
their historical debates, their nature rambles by the shores of Lough
Mask.
'Would you still recognize him?'
'I should hope so.'
Richard Davenall reached into his jacket pocket and took out a crumpled photograph which he laid on the table between them. It was a
head-and-shoulders portrait of a young man, well groomed and faintly
smiling, in ermine-trimmed graduation robes. 'Could that have been
Stephen Lennox at twenty-one?'
O'Shaughnessy looked at the picture in amazement. 'It could well be.

He'd have changed a good deal from the sixteen-year-old I knew, but it has the look of him. In fact I could almost swear it is him. Where did you—?'

'This is a photograph of my cousin, James Davenall.'

'The devil it is!'

'You look surprised.'

'I am. It's almost as if. . . .'

'As if there's a family resemblance?'

'Yes. But . . . there can't be. Can there?'

V

Since returning to England and moving into Bladeney House, Sir James Davenall had taken up a solitary style of life. Constance, it had been agreed, should remain in Salisbury until her divorce became absolute. In the interim, James did not appear to desire much company of any kind. Such invitations as he received to balls and soirées were declined. Those who called at his home were turned away. The successor he appointed to Greenwood (who had insisted on following Hugo to Duke Street) became a specialist in polite refusal.

The one exception James made to this shunning of society was to resume his membership of the Corinthian Club. There, two or three times a week, he would spend a few hours at the bar, in the affable if scarcely intimate company of assorted idlers, loungers and men-about-town who had, he did not doubt, been as sympathetic to Hugo in the past as they were to him in the present.

It is possible that James chose the club as a refuge because it was the one place where he could be sure of not meeting Hugo, his brother having resigned his own membership in a fit of pique. If so, he can have been ill-prepared for the encounter which awaited him there one mid-week evening at the end of October. Hugo, it was to transpire, could not be avoided for ever.

Standing at the bar, swapping improbable solutions to the Sudanese problem with a clutch of fellow-members, James could have been forgiven for failing to notice Freddy Cleveland put his head round the door, then hastily withdraw. Nor, when Freddy returned a short while later and slipped away to a corner, looking furtively unlike his normal gregarious self, did James have cause to pay much heed. After all, if Freddy wished to avoid him, so much the worse for Freddy.

There was, however, more to it than that. After a few minutes, something quite startling occurred. Hugo walked into the room. Without looking at Freddy or anyone else, he stared straight at James and began threading his way towards him through the knots of people, jogging elbows and spilling drinks as he went. By the time he had reached the edge of the group James was standing with, he had caused quite a commotion. Several people had recognized him and called out, several others had protested at his clumsy progress. But Hugo ignored them. His face was gaunt and drawn, his gaze unflinching, his concentration absolute.

'A stranger in the camp,' somebody said.

'Yes,' said James, hiding any surprise that he may have felt. 'It's good to see you, Hugo, though somewhat unexpected.'

Everyone else had fallen silent by now. Their attention was fixed on Hugo as he stared unblinkingly at James and said levelly: 'You bastard, Norton. You lying, scheming bastard.'

Breaths were sharply drawn, worried looks exchanged, disapprovals muttered. The people between James and Hugo must all have stepped back, because, suddenly, they were standing face to face, their eyes contesting the narrow space separating them.

'I think', James said calmly, 'that you're rather out of order, brother.'

'The only brother you have is the devil,' Hugo snapped back. 'Stand there smiling as long as you like. Delude my friends as much as you can. Say whatever you please. I know you to be a worthless impostor and I've come here tonight to prove it.'

'I advise you to go home and sleep it off, Hugo. I really do.'

'Will you withdraw your claim to be my brother? Will you give back all that you've stolen from me?'

'Don't be absurd. Gentlemen' – James turned and smiled at those around them – 'I must apologize on my brother's behalf. He's clearly overwrought.'

'I take it you refuse.' Hugo seemed oblivious to the touches on his shoulder, the gestures towards the door. 'If so, I must ask that you give me satisfaction.'

'What?'

'You heard. I challenge you to meet me, at a time and place of your choosing, so that we may settle our differences once and for all.'

'This is preposterous.'

'I demand it – as of right.'

A silence fell. For an instant, the company stood in awe of his assertion of an ancient code. Then the nonsense that time and changing values had made of that code were borne in upon them. Somebody laughed – a snorting bray of derision. It voiced the contempt which one generation always reserves for the standards of another quite as much as it ridiculed Hugo, but to his cause it was fatal. All around him, the vain and vapid friends who had deserted him chorused their verdict in the sniggers and cackles of a brutal mirth.

Hugo's face began to twitch, his lower lip to tremble. This was the one issue he had not foreseen. He had thought James would either give him what he demanded or be denounced by the world as a coward. But no. That had never been the choice at all. The world had grown too falsely wise for such indulgences.

'Go home, Hugo,' James said mildly. 'Let us forget this act of folly.'

'Never.'

'You must.'

Pettigrew, the steward, had appeared from somewhere and now took Hugo by the arm. 'Excuse me, Mr Davenall,' he said. 'I believe you're no longer a member of this club. Might I ask you to leave?'

'Go to the devil!'

'Be a sensible fellow, Mr Davenall. I must insist you come with me.'

'Be a sensible fellow.' Perhaps those were the words which finally laid waste his resolve. The laughter around him, the taunts and mocking gestures – above all, James's unforgiving stare – lanced into his fragile confidence. With an inaudible sighing curse, a crumpling of the face and a sudden stooping frailty, he turned and let Pettigrew lead him swiftly from the room.

VI

Amongst the callers whom he might have expected on a quiet Friday afternoon at his offices in Cheap Street, Bath, Arthur Baverstock would never have numbered Richard Davenall. Such business as they had been required to conduct in the aftermath of the trial was long since concluded and that, he had assumed, would be the unregretted end of their association.

'What brings you here, Davenall?' he said cautiously. 'You look rather tired.'

He had not exaggerated. Richard Davenall sank into a chair beside the desk with a weary sigh. His clothes were more travel-stained than a journey from London would justify, his features more lined and preoccupied than professional necessity could explain. 'I'm sorry to call on you unannounced, Baverstock. It's a matter of some urgency.'

'You could have telephoned.' He would, in truth, much have preferred him to.

Davenall shook his head. 'No, no. I'm here in transit, you see. I arrived in Holyhead by ferry from Dublin this morning and decided to make a detour here on my way to London.'

'It *is* urgent, then.'

'Yes. It is.'

'What took you to Ireland? The Carntrassna estate?'

'You could say so.' Davenall's thoughts seemed to drift for a moment, then he passed a hand across his face, sat up alertly and said: 'Can I take it Catherine – Lady Davenall – is still pursuing her enquiries into Sir James's American past?'

Baverstock was thunderstruck. Assurances had been given that such enquiries had ceased. The fact that such assurances were false scarcely warranted, to his mind, Davenall's scandalous suggestion. 'You can take nothing of the sort. May I remind you—?'

'She is, isn't she?' The fellow's drained dogged insistence seemed strangely powerful. 'I know her well enough to realize she wouldn't abandon the struggle, whatever you felt obliged to tell me on her behalf.'

'Well, I—'

'Let me reassure you. I'm not here at Sir James's bidding. I'm not here to cause you any trouble at all.'

'Then . . . why?'

Davenall leaned forward in his chair. 'To point you in the right direction.'

'What do you mean by that?'

'You're still using Lewis and Lewis?'

'I can't possibly. . . .' Then the look in Davenall's eyes overcame his reservations. 'Yes.'

'Tell Mr Lewis this. A former agent for the Carntrassna estate, Andrew Lennox, emigrated to Canada in the winter or spring of 1859 to 1860. Sir Gervase paid Lennox ten thousand pounds shortly before they left. Mr Lewis's investigator will be looking for the real James Norton. Suggest he look for the Lennoxes instead. Especially their son Stephen. Born 1843, about the time Sir Gervase spent a year or so living at Carntrassna. Able and well educated. Strikingly similar in appearance to my cousin James.'

Baverstock did not know how to react. More remarkable than what Davenall was saying was the fact that he was saying it at all.

'I've been unable to establish exactly when they left or where they arrived. Probably Quebec. I have no idea whether they remained in Canada or went on into the United States. But Lennox would have had more than enough money to set himself up in some style and to send his son to a good school to finish his education. Perhaps to a university. It should be possible to trace them.'

Still Baverstock said nothing. Certainly he would pass the information to Lewis, even though he did not fully understand its implications, but why should Richard Davenall choose to aid enquiries which previously he had resolutely denounced? Before he had a chance to ask, Davenall rose from his chair.

'We'll leave it there. I'll bid you good day, Baverstock.'

'One moment. . . .'

'Yes?'

'Are you suggesting that the boy, Stephen Lennox, might be James Norton?'

'I'm not sure.' He looked away. 'It's possible. Just possible.'

'If anything comes of it, do you want Lady Davenall to know of your part in it?'

Davenall smiled grimly. 'No,' he said, shaking his head. 'Tell her what you please. But don't mention me.'

VII

Lake Geneva was at its most urbanely placid, stretching away before the boat towards the mountains of Savoy. So late in the season, with the snow-line edging down from the peaks, this hour of early-afternoon perfection could prove deceptive, but Plon-Plon, a morose and muffled figure in the stern of the vessel, was armoured against its charms. He watched the irksome shroud of the Swiss national flag billow and deflate in the weak and fitful breeze behind him, squinted back towards Nyon and the mansards of his home, then cast a cigar butt into the frothing wake and turned to face the shores of France.

In a few minutes, the boat would stop at Yvoire to pick up and set down passengers, then set off back across the lake towards Switzerland. All who came and went would do so with perfect freedom; all, that is, save Plon-Plon, who knew he had only to disembark at Yvoire to provoke a diplomatic incident. Since leaving England in June, he had confined himself in fretful ease at Prangins, the Swiss villa he had bought more than twenty years before as a refuge in troubled times. He had paced its lawns and glanced all too often, these past months, at the tantalizing proximity of France. But now his long forbearance seemed about to reap its reward. There was every reason to hope he would soon be allowed to end his exile.

This fact he had chosen to suppress upon hearing from his discarded but persistent mistress, Cora Pearl, that she wished to see him; nothing daunted, Cora had announced her determination to visit him in his retreat. 'The madame', as she had tastelessly put it, 'must come to the mountain.' To receive her at Prangins was unthinkable, his latest consolation of the flesh, the marquise de Canisy, being blowzily and none too benignly in residence. Accordingly, under severe protest, he had consented to a lacustrine rendezvous. He would not, in truth, have gone even this far had it not been for a tone in Cora's letters which implied some form of threat; he felt curious to know what it might portend.

The boat tied up at the Yvoire jetty, and Plon-Plon craned his neck to observe the boarding passengers. At once, he saw that Cora was among them. He could not help feeling, indeed, that she would be obvious to anyone in her strawberry-striped dress and extravagant millinery, swaying up the gangway in what she clearly believed to be the style of Queen Elizabeth joining a royal barge on the Thames. Only a gratuitous display of fishnet-stockinged calf to the goggle-eyed sailor who helped her aboard marred the regal effect.

'I see that you are well,' Plon-Plon remarked, as Cora settled herself beside him in a flurry of petticoats.

'Not at all,' Cora replied, projecting a sparkling smile towards a distant purser. 'I am merely keeping up appearances. Perhaps you should devote more effort to doing so yourself.'

'Appearances count for little in politics.'

'Really? That was not my impression. But a man with your record of glittering successes would know better than I.'

Plon-Plon took a deep breath, reflecting that one of the few benefits of old age was that it made sarcasm easier to bear. 'Will you forgive me, Cora, if I urge you to explain the purpose of our meeting?'

'Possibly. What I will not forgive is your heartless neglect of me. It is more than a year since we last . . . came together, shall we say?'

Plon-Plon found Cora's bedroom badinage strangely unpalatable in the opalescent air of Lake Geneva. He turned towards her with the weakest of smiles. 'How can one be heartless to somebody who has no heart? Come to the point, Cora, please.'

She pouted and flounced her dress. 'For shame, Plon-Plon. There was a time when you enjoyed the prelude as well as the climax.'

'Cora—'

'I am short of money.' She raised her plucked eyebrows and stared at him. 'Beneath the frills and powders, I am growing old. Not for a politician, perhaps, but old for one of my calling. I need capital to sustain my. . . .' She glanced down, with the hint of a blush. 'My declining years.'

Plon-Plon's first instinct was to be flattered that she had come so far on a begging mission; she could just as well have importuned him by letter. Either way, he was not likely to begrudge her a modest contribution. Then suspicion tainted his generosity. Why *had* she come so far? 'I sympathize with your plight, Cora. For that matter, it is one I share.'

She looked at him sharply. 'You expect me to believe that?'

'Alas, it is true.'

'Madame de Canisy stays with you out of a sense of charity, I suppose.'

Plon-Plon began to feel angry; they were both too old for shows of jealousy. 'Let us not quarrel, Cora. You know I am not a mean man. I will see if I cannot spare you a little something.'

She tossed her chin sulkily. 'There was a time when you paid me twelve thousand francs a month.'

'And there was a time when the State paid me a million francs a year. But such times are past.'

'You could re-create them for me.'

He frowned. What could have deluded her into thinking he could, or would, do any such thing? 'What do you want of me, Cora?' he asked, with sudden impatience.

'I want', she replied in measured tones, 'fifty thousand francs.'

'Hah!' He slapped his thigh and stared at her in amazement. 'Your wits must be fading with your charms. I have neither the desire nor the ability to give you such a sum.'

'It would not be a gift. It would be a payment for a service.'

'What service?'

'The omission of all that I know about you from my forthcoming memoirs.'

'Memoirs? You?'

'Monsieur Lévy has commissioned me to—'

'Lévy the publisher? *Ce crapaud juif.* He would never dare.'

'He would and he will.'

It was intolerable. She had come here to blackmail him. He rose to his feet and looked down at her indignantly. 'I will not pay you a penny. Is that clear?'

'Be reasonable, Plon-Plon.' She gazed up at him through fluttering eyelashes. 'You will regret it if you reject my offer.'

'A fig for your offer.'

'I have been jotting down various recollections of what we did together over the years. The public will find it all very entertaining, I feel sure.'

'A Bonaparte cannot be threatened in this way.'

'Except by what he has actually done. What he did the night his daughter was born. How he wore a gag when making love, so as not to disturb his wife in the next room. The use he made of a horse-whip on afternoons when it was too wet to go riding. Oh, I remember it all – in loving detail.'

'You go too far!'

'We both went too far, Plon-Plon, as my readers will learn. I fear they will have to learn of your other dalliances as well. Rachel, for instance. The Emperor told me all about what you and she did in that train when you thought he was asleep.'

'The devil he did!'

'Your fling with the Empress. You boasted of it often enough.'

'*Mon Dieu—*'

'And let us not forget Vivien Strang.'

'Vivien Strang?' Suddenly, he had stooped and seized her by the

360

chin, the better to see whatever meaning her expression might reveal. 'Who told you, *ma perle émoussée*, about Vivien Strang?'

'She told me herself.'

'What?'

'We met, Plon-Plon. We found we had a great deal in common. Ill-treatment at your hands, for one thing. Did you think she was your little secret? I'm afraid not. I know all about her. Why, I'd even considered asking her to contribute a chapter to my book.'

He released her. His hand moved slowly to his watch-chain and began winding its links in his fingers. Slowly, he stood upright and gazed out across the lake. His eyes had narrowed, his lips compressed, in a sudden potent concentration divorced from the moment. To think of all the time and effort he had wasted in looking for Vivien Strang. It was absurd, it was laughable. Cora knew her all along. Cora, who had come to blackmail him, could lead him to his quarry.

VIII

Richard Davenall's arrival in Salisbury, *en route* from Ireland to London, was as surprising to Canon Sumner and his daughters as it was welcome. He was urged to remain for the weekend and did so, but the pleasure Constance and Emily took in his company seemed strangely one-sided. Richard's efforts to express interest in their accounts of European travel were unconvincing and his enquiries after James's health half-hearted. The origins of his distracted downcast mood did not become apparent to Constance until she found herself alone with him in the drawing-room on Saturday afternoon.

'Did you find all in good order at Carntrassna?' she asked conversationally. 'I know James will wish to take an active interest in his Irish property.'

'You think so?' Richard looked inexplicably doubtful.

'Of course,' Constance replied, dismayed to find herself nettled by his tone. 'As will I.'

'Has he spoken of taking you there?'

'Not in so many words, but I presume—'

'I wouldn't, if I were you. I doubt very much if James will ever visit Carntrassna.' Abruptly, as if regretting the harshness of his words, Richard left the sofa and walked to the window, where he gazed out into the close.

Constance felt bemused and not a little upset. Why was Richard, James's staunchest ally for the past difficult year, talking in such unsympathetic terms? In a hasty effort at conciliation, she smiled and said: 'Well, it's no great matter, after all.'

But Richard did not respond. Only a pressing of his hand to his forehead revealed that he knew what pain he was causing her.

'Is something wrong?' she asked in mounting alarm.

His reply was barely audible. 'No. Nothing is wrong.'

Suddenly, she thought what it might be. 'Is there some difficulty over the divorce?'

Richard spun round. 'The divorce?' The expression on his face was a confusion of doubt and pity. 'No. No difficulty. It will go through straightforwardly – if you wish it.'

'Of course I wish it. James and I hope to be married by Christmas.'

Richard seemed about to say something, then regretted it. His jaw set in a grim determined line.

'Is anything likely to prevent us doing so?'

'No.'

'Then, shall we have your blessing?'

His gaze fell to the carpet. His lips shaped themselves to trial words. But he did not speak.

'Richard?'

'Had you . . . considered postponing the wedding . . . until the New Year?'

'No. Why should we?'

Again, he seemed at a loss for an answer. There was an interval of strained silence, then he said: 'You must excuse me, Constance.' He walked quickly towards the door.

'Richard!' It would have been easier to let him go, but Constance's strength of character deterred her from such a course. He stopped in his tracks and turned to face her. 'Shall we have your blessing?'

In the turmoil of his expression and the furtive darting of his eyes to avoid her gaze, she had an answer. It was the exact opposite of what he said, in the hoarse voice of one ashamed by his own words. 'Yes. Of course you will.'

IX

Plon-Plon glanced up from the desk in his study at Prangins to confront the plaster-cast likeness of his famous uncle. What would the first and greatest Napoleon have done in his shoes? Much the same, he suspected. After all, sexual propriety had never been his strong suit, either.

'Pay Miss Cora Pearl the sum of twenty thousand francs.' It was more than he would have wanted to pay and less than she had hoped to receive. Still, compromise was the essence of diplomacy. He raised his pen to sign, nodding his head in silent affirmation as he did so. On balance, he thought it a fair price to pay for suppressing some of her more lurid reminiscences, among them the one story she had to tell which he had never heard before.

France's defeat by Prussia in the war of 1870, and the consequent disintegration of the Second Empire, had forced Plon-Plon and Cora to decamp to England. Following a humiliating expulsion from the Grosvenor Hotel, London, when the manager discovered who the 'Countess of Moncalieri' really was, they embarked on a tour of the West Country, passing Cora off as Marie Clotilde – so successfully, in fact, that they were handsomely entertained wherever they went.

Early October found them installed at the Imperial Hotel, Torquay, a fact swiftly blazoned across the pages of the local evening newspaper. On the third day of their stay, Plon-Plon accepted an invitation from the commodore of the Torquay Yacht Club to join him on a cruise round the Devon coast, leaving Cora to amuse herself at the hotel.

The day proved more amusing than Cora had anticipated. Breakfasting on her first-floor balcony, she had the distinct impression that she was being stared at by a woman in the hotel garden. Later, taking tea in the sun-lounge overlooking Torbay, she felt certain that the occupant of a palm-screened corner table was the very same woman, who, this time, had the effrontery to walk across and sit down at her table, uninvited and unabashed.

'I don't believe I know you, madame,' Cora said, reminding herself forcefully that, as Marie Clotilde, she could hardly utter the coarse dismissal that was on her lips.

'But I know you,' the woman replied. She was tall and middle-aged, inclining to gauntness and grey hair, yet possessed of an austere beauty which Cora judged some men might find attractive. There was, in her voice, the hint of a Scottish accent. 'I read of your arrival in the newspaper.'

'Really?'

'It reported that Prince Napoleon had brought his pretty young wife, the Princess Clotilde of Savoy, to enjoy the English Riviera.'

'As you see—'

'But you are not the Princess Clotilde.'

'I beg your pardon?'

'You are Cora Pearl, most notorious of all the whores in Paris.'

'This is outrageous!'

'Outrageous, but true. Do you deny it?'

'Certainly.'

'Then, feel free to break into the Princess's native Italian by way of proof.'

Cora pursed her lips. The last thing she wanted was a repetition of the Grosvenor Hotel fiasco, something which this disagreeably know-ledgeable woman seemed well capable of arranging. She leaned across the table and whispered: 'Who are you and what do you want?'

'My name is Vivien Ratcliffe. And I want you and your so-called husband out of Torquay.'

The strangest part of it all was that they had so much in common. Adjourning to Plon-Plon's suite to continue their discussion, they discovered, much to their mutual astonishment, that they actually quite liked each other. Neither had anything to hide, except from other people. Vivien certainly had no wish to hound Cora, for she, too, had been a prostitute once. What she could not risk, however, was her doting and well-heeled husband discovering any of the truth about the Miss Strang he had married from Plon-Plon, whom they would inevitably meet at the ball Sir Lawrence Palk was planning in his honour. Cora had been pointed out to her in a box at the *Théâtre des Bouffes-Parisiens* during her honeymoon in Paris three years before. Thus had she been able to confirm her suspicion that the last woman Plon-Plon would be likely to bring to Torquay was his wife. Thus had she hit upon the means by which a catastrophic encounter might be averted.

Pleased to know more about Plon-Plon than he thought she did, and finding Torquay too restful by half, Cora was happy to do as she was asked. That very evening she created such a fuss that Plon-Plon meekly agreed to their immediate departure: the banquet was cancelled. Nor was Cora's service forgotten. When reduced to auctioning the contents of her house in the rue de Chaillot in May 1877, she was surprised to receive a gift of money from 'Mrs Ratcliffe of Torquay, now a wealthy widow'. Vivien Strang's sympathy for a fellow-victim of Plon-Plon's treachery was greater than Cora had ever deserved.

A trite, insistent tinkling reached Plon-Plon's ears through the study window. He sighed. That would be the Marquise, back from her tricycling expedition. Really, the woman was straining his tolerance. If this went on, she would have to go.

He sealed the letter to Cora and dropped it into the post-bag, sniggering at the thought of what the Marquise would say if she knew how much more he was paying a former mistress than he had ever paid his present one. But, then, Cora had rendered him a service more valuable than any bedroom favour. She had given him the means of finding Vivien Strang. She had handed him a chance of exoneration.

X

When Constance complained to her of Richard's begrudging attitude towards her forthcoming remarriage, Emily expressed more sympathy and puzzlement than she genuinely felt. Dearly though she loved her sister, she had begun, quite irrationally, to resent her peace of mind. By telling her nothing of what she had witnessed in Florence, of course, Emily only sustained that which she resented, but what else, she often asked herself, could she do, on the basis of her ill-gotten solitary suspicions? The news of Richard's outburst suggested an answer: she might share the burden of doubt she had borne so long alone.

The first opportunity to do so came early on Sunday morning, when, by pleading a headache, Emily was able to excuse herself from joining Constance and her father at matins in the cathedral. Instead, she sought out Richard, whom she found packing in his room.

'Are you leaving us so soon?' she asked in some alarm, for the thought that he could be her ally had made her hope he might prolong his stay.

'I fear I must return to London at once,' he replied. The lack of conviction in his voice was not lost on Emily: both knew he could scarcely have urgent business in London on a Sunday morning.

In one sense, the need of haste was a relief to her. 'Are you going because of what you said to Constance yesterday?' she asked, glad, now it had come to it, to blurt out the question without prevarication.

'She told you?' Richard seemed surprised by this evidence of their closeness.

'Yes. It's why I wanted to speak to you this morning – alone.'

'I'm not sure I understand.'

'Why did you urge her to postpone the wedding?'

His expression suggested that he thought she meant to rebuke him. 'I don't know,' he said cautiously. 'I should not have done so. It was stupid of me.'

'Was it? Would it surprise you to learn that I've wanted to do the same myself for many weeks past?'

He stared at her in amazement. 'You? But why?'

She told him then, in a rush of revelation, all that she had seen and heard at the campanile in Florence and all that she feared it might portend. She had hoped Richard might be able to assure her that all was well, but not so. He believed he had seen the same woman as Emily had: at St Bartholomew's Hospital a year ago and at Victoria station in August. Clearly, she had followed them to Florence. As to her reasons, however, Richard harboured a suspicion more dreadful than anything Emily could have imagined.

'I saw her more clearly than you had a chance of doing,' he said.

'She reminded me of somebody who's already been described to me in unforgettable detail.'

'Who?'

'Melanie Rossiter. I know it must seem incredible, but the likeness was unmistakable. On both occasions, I felt uncannily certain that the woman I'd seen was the woman whom Trenchard claimed to have been deceived by.'

'But that's not possible. She was—'

'A whore? So Trenchard's doctors assured me. According to them, Melanie Rossiter only existed in his imagination.'

Words deserted Emily. Could the common prostitute she had seen leaving The Limes that dreadful night in November 1882 be the well-spoken young woman she had heard Sir James Davenall pleading with in Florence eleven months later? Richard clearly believed she was. But how could it be so? For if she was. . . .

'I have visited him regularly since the spring, Emily. In the end, they may persuade him that he was the victim of his own delusions, but they will not persuade me. I have listened to his account too often now to doubt that it contains more of the truth than we ever thought possible.'

Emily looked out of the window into the close. The cathedral wore its Sunday raiment of pious industry: within its walls Constance might even now be praying for confirmation that she was right to end one marriage and begin another. She could have no idea with what stealing dread others now viewed her future. 'What must I do?' Emily said, turning back to face Richard.

'For the moment, nothing.'

'But they are due to marry in a month!'

'I have instituted enquiries which I can only hope will bear fruit before then.'

'If they do not?'

'I'm not sure. I'm not sure of anything, in fact, except this: that I will not allow James to marry Constance until this matter is settled – one way or another, for good or ill.'

EIGHTEEN

I

The Times, Tuesday, 18th December 1883:

It was announced yesterday, five months after the victorious conclusion of his celebrated legal action, that Sir James Davenall will marry the former Mrs Constance Trenchard in a civil ceremony at Kensington Register Office on the 24th of this month. Last week, Mrs Trenchard was granted a decree absolute in the Admiralty, Probate and Divorce Division, thus bringing to a close proceedings for her divorce from Mr William Trenchard, who has been confined for the past year to a lunatic asylum.

II

'Candidly,' said Mr George Lewis of Lewis & Lewis, fixing an anything but candid stare on his guest, 'I was puzzled to hear of your part in this.'

'I dare say you were,' Richard Davenall replied, in a tone that gave nothing away.

'I can only assume', Mr Lewis continued, 'that this morning's announcement in *The Times*' – he flapped a hand at the copy folded open on his desk – 'explains your desire for a hasty conclusion.'

'It does indeed. I realize it cannot be of concern to your client, but I wish, if at all possible, to uncover the truth *before* Mrs Trenchard marries Sir James.'

'Quite so.'

'So is there anything you can tell me?'

Mr Lewis sighed. 'I am far from sure that I am free to tell you the results of our enquiries. After all, they have been undertaken on Lady Davenall's behalf, not yours.'

'But at my instigation.'

'This aspect of them, yes. We are grateful for your assistance. Nevertheless. . . .'

'Have you proof that he's Stephen Lennox? That's all I want to know.'

Lewis pondered the point silently. Then he said: 'No. We have not.'

'Then, what have you found?'

'Perhaps, after all, there is no harm in your knowing.' He pulled open a drawer, lifted out a file of papers and began leafing through them as he spoke. 'The Lennoxes evidently moved at an early date from Canada to the United States. Andrew Lennox bought a substantial property on Long Island in July 1860. Stephen Lennox attended Yale Law School during 1860 and 1861, then abandoned his studies to enlist in the Union army at the outbreak of the Civil War. He rose to the rank of captain in the cavalry. When the war ended, however, there is no sign of him returning to the law or to his parents' home. We simply don't know what he may have done. What we do know is that Andrew Lennox's finances were by then in a chaotic state, owing to a series of unwise investments. By 1866, the family had moved to rented property in Boston. There followed a steady decline in their fortunes. Andrew Lennox died – very largely of drink, it seems – in 1869. His widow lived obscurely, in genteel poverty, in Worcester, Massachusetts, until her death in 1880.'

'And her son?'

'We don't know. Mrs Lennox's neighbours were told of a son living in California, who sent her money but never visited. That is all.'

'All? Surely there must be contemporaries at Yale or in the Army who could identify him?'

'That is our hope. But tracing them twenty years later has not been easy. When we do, we will need to bring them here to confront Sir James. We are, alas, a long way from being in a position to do that.'

'I see.'

'You had hoped for more?'

'I had hoped, I suppose, that the hateful task could be accomplished without my part in it becoming known. I see now that it cannot be.'

'What will you do?'

'I will take appropriate action, Mr Lewis. Action I have tried – till now – to avoid. Action that will bring this case to a close, once and for all.'

III

It was early evening, and Sir James Davenall was on the point of setting out from Bladeney House to spend a few hours at his club, when his cousin Richard was shown in. It was immediately apparent that this was not a social call. Curtly declining to accompany James to the club, Richard said bluntly: 'I must speak to you at once – in private.'

At first, James appeared unruffled by such brusqueness. 'It has become unusual', he said when they were alone, 'for you to speak to me at all, Richard. I could be forgiven for thinking that you had been trying to avoid me.'

'Perhaps I have.' Richard had made no effort to contact Sir James since returning from Ireland several weeks before. He had been, in fact, deliberately evasive. But it was clear now that he had done with such tactics. The doubts he had long harboured about Sir James were about to emerge into the light.

'Why, may I ask?'

'Because I no longer believe you to be my cousin James.'

They faced each other across the hearth-rug, shocked into silence by the realization that their uneasy truce was over. In a show of composure, James lit a cigarette, then said: 'You can't be serious.'

'Deadly serious.' The tempered bleakness in Richard's gaze confirmed as much. He needed no reminding of all the lies he now believed he had played a part in.

'Then I must tell you that you're making a very grave mistake.'

'My mistake was ever to be taken in by you.'

James paused, as if still prepared to give Richard a chance to reconsider. 'I don't need to prove who I am any more,' he said slowly. 'The world knows me to be Sir James Davenall.'

'The world is mistaken.' There was an interval then, though it lasted no more than an instant, when the two men stood upon the brink of Richard's accusation, each knowing and accepting that it might carry them beyond recall. 'You are Stephen Lennox of Murrismoyle, County Mayo. Your mother was the wife of the Carntrassna agent, Andrew Lennox. Your father was Sir Gervase Davenall.'

'That is an absurd suggestion.'

'I believe Sir Gervase only learned you were his son when he visited Carntrassna in the autumn of 1859. Out of guilt, or alarm at your resemblance to his legitimate son James, he paid the Lennoxes to emigrate to Canada and to take you with them. Much later, you met Quinn and conspired with him to steal Hugo's title and property on the basis of your physical similarity to James and Quinn's knowledge of the family's affairs. Quinn's reward is to be set up as a country gentleman, yours to lead a life of false title and stolen wealth.'

'Extraordinary.'

'You deny it?'

James stepped away and lowered himself slowly into an armchair. His voice remained calm, his self-control unshaken. 'I must urge you, Richard, to tell nobody else what you have just told me, because, if you do, they will think you a fool. You changed your mind about me once before. If you do so again, you will be totally discredited.'

But Richard showed no sign of weakening. 'I cannot allow Constance to marry you under the illusion that you are James.'

'You cannot prevent her marrying me. She will not entertain your preposterous allegations for an instant.'

'I have proof.'

James smiled. 'That I doubt.'

'Your former tutor, Denzil O'Shaughnessy, is prepared to come to London and identify you.'

'O'Shaughnessy?' James said thoughtfully. 'I'm afraid I don't know the name.'

'He taught you for eight years, long enough for him to be sure, when he meets you, that you are Stephen Lennox.'

'We are to meet?'

'He will be in London by the end of the week. I insist you meet him, in front of witnesses and in Constance's presence, before the wedding takes place.'

'If I refuse?'

'I shall go to law. You may meet him in private or in court, as you please, but meet him you must.'

'Those are your terms?'

'They are.'

James rose from the chair and faced Richard, still unmoved, it seemed, by what he had said. 'Let it be in private, then. I have no wish to embarrass you in court. Will you notify me of the time and place?'

'I will.'

'Then, perhaps we had better say no more until you do. Except. . . .'

'Yes?'

James smiled in a hint of conciliation. 'If your allegations went no further, Richard, we could dismiss them as mere aberrations. For that matter, we could agree to forget them altogether. If you persist in them, however, you will alienate yourself from me – and from Constance. Since you've already alienated yourself from Hugo and my mother, don't you think you're going to feel rather lonely?'

Momentarily, Richard seemed to waver. 'It's too late to turn back now.'

'Surely not. I never saw you as the boat-burning type.'

'What do you mean by that?'

'I mean why force a crisis? My claim has been settled. Why rake over it again when you stand to lose more than anyone by doing so?'

'You have forced a crisis, not I,' Richard replied, with renewed conviction. 'You have been a party to much worse than fraud and imposture. You let Quinn arrange, or carry out, the murder of my aunt, because she alone of the family could identify you. You put up your mistress – for I take it that is what she is – to spy on Dr Fiveash's records and to trap Trenchard into seeming to behave so badly that Constance would desert him. Because you needed her to testify for you at the hearing, Trenchard had to be disgraced in the foulest manner possible. By trying to kill you, he only made it easier for you to conquer Constance's affections. That, I suppose, is why you volunteered to pay his asylum fees: to ensure he was so well treated that Constance would have nothing to reproach herself for. But there is one thing I cannot understand.'

'No doubt you're about to tell me what that is?'

There was a trace now of something close to horror in Richard's voice. 'Why do you mean to marry her? Your deception of her has served its purpose. And your mistress, I gather, is waiting in the wings. So why prolong the charade?'

'Because it is not a charade, Richard. I am your cousin James. I love Constance as I have always loved her. There has been no fraud, no imposture, no murder plot, no conspiracy. I am who I am – and you are wrong.'

When Richard had gone, James remained as calm as ever, his composure unwavering, his movements unhurried. He finished his cigarette and poured himself a large whisky. Then he carried the glass out with him to the hall and walked slowly up the stairs to where an oil painting of Sir Gervase Davenall hung proudly amongst his ancestors. There, sipping the whisky and staring at the handsome painted likeness of his father – the likeness, that is, of what he had been before disease came to twist his arrogant features – James reflected on what had occurred. Whether Richard's allegations had angered or frightened him, whether he proposed to face O'Shaughnessy or flee, whether he had been moved to sorrow or to contempt, there was no way of telling from his guarded ironical expression. Even in solitude, it seemed, he was not about to betray himself.

IV

Plon-Plon peered through the thicket of cream-jugs and sugar-sprinklers at the marquise de Canisy, who was in the act of pouring treacle into a bowl of grapefruit segments. She had become, he believed, even more disgusting at the breakfast-table than in the bedroom. Indeed, she had nearly succeeded in the impossible: making him think nostalgically of his wife. On the whole, he could not imagine why he allowed her to remain at Prangins.

Then the padding approach of a servant, followed by the discreet placement of a newly pressed copy of yesterday's *Times* of London by his elbow, reminded him of the reason: he simply had more important things to think about.

'*Merci, Théodule,*' he said, positioning a monocle in his right eye and picking up the newspaper. He turned at once to the court and social page, noting with relief that no member of the British royal family had recently visited Farnborough Hill. Then he shuddered at a nauseating sound from the end of the table: something midway between a suck and a swallow. He opened the paper wider.

There, staring at him out of the columns of newsprint, was a name he recognized. 'It was announced yesterday . . . that Sir James Davenall will marry . . . on the 24th of this month.' He folded the page back in a rustling burst of energy.

A month of time-consuming and expensive enquiries by private detectives had only confirmed what Cora had told Plon-Plon: that Vivien Strang now lived in Torquay, wealthily widowed, under the name of Ratcliffe. Of any connection with Sir James Davenall – indeed, of the existence of a son at all – there had been no sign. Plon-Plon had debated with himself at length what to do next, but had come to no conclusion. Whilst to do nothing seemed craven, his enthusiasm for a confrontation with Vivien Strang had waned since his humiliations of the spring. Now, however, with this news of Sir James Davenall's impending marriage, it was suddenly rekindled. He would show the detectives how to do their job. He would prove to Catherine that he was more resourceful than she supposed. He would pay back Norton for making a fool of him. And he would wring the truth from Vivien Strang.

There was, besides, another aspect to consider. In France, the addlepate Bonapartists were increasingly looking to his ingrate son Victor for leadership. To reassert his supremacy, Plon-Plon would have to return to Paris, unite the party and sweep the board at the elections due in 1885. This, however, was easier contemplated than achieved. As the fiasco of his manifesto last January illustrated, he needed pet newspapers and tame candidates to serve as his mouth-piece. Above all, he needed money: the commodity he had hoped to gain by becoming involved in the Davenall case in the first place. On that score, Hugo had let him down badly. But, if he could be restored to the baronetcy thanks to Plon-Plon's intervention, his generosity might know no bounds.

'Plon-Plon,' said the Marquise, slurping down the last of her grapefruit, '*où est-ce que nous allons pour Noël?*'

'*Noël, madame?*'

'*Oui. Nous partons?*'

'*Je pars, oui. En l'Angleterre.*'

'*En Angleterre? Merveilleux!*'

'*Mais non—*'

But it was too late. Already, like a smartly steered pirate galleon, the marquise had billowed up from her seat, rounded the table and smacked a kiss on his flinching forehead. '*J'aimerai l'Angleterre,*' she announced, with a treacly grin.

'*Vous comprenez mal, madame,*' he snapped back. '*J'irai en Angleterre seul.*'

V

Not till the second day of his re-engagement to monitor Sir James Davenall's movements were there any movements for Roffey to monitor. Throughout Wednesday 19th December there had been neither comings nor goings at Bladeney House beyond the normal round of activities at the tradesmen's entrance: Sir James had not stirred. Nor, accordingly, had Roffey, who, stamping and shivering in his tree-screened corner of Chester Square, could only think enviously of the toe-toasting fires his quarry must be enjoying.

At last, shortly before ten o'clock on Thursday, 20th December, his patience was rewarded. Sir James emerged, warmly clad in overcoat and top-hat, twirling his silver-topped cane and drawing on a cigarette in just the manner Roffey could believe he had patented. After pausing to sample the chill morning air, he set off briskly toward Grosvenor Place.

Roffey followed at a discreet distance. Sir James, he noted with relief, carried no bag and disdained to hail any of the cabs that passed. A daylight flit therefore seemed unlikely: this had more the flavour of a gentlemanly promenade. Not that Roffey was surprised. For all Mr Davenall's nervousness, he did not believe Sir James was one to cut and run. He had come, indeed, to respect the style and subtlety of the man, which was why he would never have entrusted to a subordinate the demanding task of following him.

At Hyde Park Corner, Sir James turned into Piccadilly. Roffey began guessing at his destination. The club? A little early perhaps. His tailor? Always a possibility. But no. He reached Piccadilly Circus without turning off, then diverted into the narrower byways of Soho. Roffey eyed with distaste the louche eating-houses and dingy theatre-backs that lay on their route. It seemed that the acquisition of a baronetcy had not reduced one whit James Norton's enthusiasm for such districts: Roffey well recalled losing his trail in these parts early on in their strangely intimate relationship.

But not so this morning: Sir James's erect striding figure remained in his sights all the way. They emerged, at length, in St Giles Circus and headed on eastwards. Holborn was not far off now. Perhaps he was going to visit Mr Davenall: that would be a turn-up for the books. Even as the thought formed in Roffey's mind, however, Sir James contra-dicted it by a turn towards Bloomsbury.

The British Museum: that was their destination. Roffey smiled to himself as he walked through the gates. This smacked of an assigna-tion. Parks in summer, museums in winter: his innumerable divorce cases always adhered to the formula. Sir James took the stairs to the upper floor, and Roffey followed, restraining his steps so as not to get too close now the end was in sight.

Sir James moved swiftly through several rooms, ignoring both the exhibits and their admirers. Then his pace slowed, as if the agreed meeting-place was drawing near. And, sure enough, rising from a bench halfway along one of the Egyptian galleries, was the woman Mr Davenall had described: Melanie Rossiter. Roffey caught his breath, stepped aside from his route and took a slow wheeling course between the sarcophagi, head bowed towards the mummified contents whilst his agile practised eyes remained fixed on the target.

Sir James had joined Miss Rossiter on the bench, and they had at once begun talking in low and urgent tones. A mule-voiced teacher instructing a pack of schoolchildren in embalming techniques on the other side of the room dashed Roffey's hopes of hearing what they were saying. He would have to edge perilously close.

She was beautiful: there was no doubting that. The fur collar of her coat caressed a delectable chin. Sloe-dark eyes scanned Sir James's face as he spoke. And her lips, as they shaped themselves to some passionate entreaty, were such as to make any man forget his duty, whatever his duty was.

Roffey was standing now by a mould-stained casket which he feared might contain a mummified crocodile. Not that it mattered, for its position was all he cared about. He had only to take one rapt and studious step back, he judged, to catch a few words. And so it proved.

'I thought you had agreed to meet me because you had changed your mind,' said Miss Rossiter.

'I came here to warn you,' Sir James replied. 'That is all.'

'Surely you exaggerate the threat this man poses?'

'No. If O'Shaughnessy identifies me, how can I prove he's wrong?'

'And you think—'

Roffey cursed silently. He had moved an inch too close, or lingered a moment too long. Whichever was the case, he had aroused their suspicion. Keeping his eyes fixed on the casket before him so as not to compound his error, he heard them rise from the bench and walk away down the gallery. When he dared to look round, it was only to catch a glimpse of them passing on into the next room. Though naturally he would follow, he knew he could not now afford to draw the slightest attention to himself without risking a disastrous confrontation.

He need not have worried. When next he saw them, they were on the point of separating. They were standing on the high and echoing landing at the head of the stairs, exchanging a parting word, when his glance through the wide doorway of the adjoining gallery alighted upon them. There was no kiss, no squeeze of the hand; not even, as far as Roffey could see, an eloquent meeting of the eyes. Sir James merely set off down the stairs without a backward glance, whilst Miss Rossiter watched him go. Then she circled the stairwell and walked slowly away towards the next set of galleries.

Sir James would go back now to Bladeney House: Roffey felt sure of it. Yet he would have to follow him for safety's sake. Thus his instinct, which was to follow Miss Rossiter, had to be ignored. So little was known of her that he would have liked to find out more. But his instructions were clear, and Roffey was not a man to disobey those who employed him. Glancing regretfully after Miss Rossiter's retreating figure, he started down the stairs.

VI

The Little Canonry,
Cathedral Close,
SALISBURY,
Wiltshire.

20th December 1883

My dear Richard,

I write these few lines in haste and with a troubled conscience. Constance continues eagerly to anticipate her wedding in merciful ignorance of what we know may well prevent it taking place. The fact that I am sure we are right to intervene in this way makes it no easier for me to bear the thought of the anguish we will cause her.

So far as the practical aspect of your proposals is concerned, you need have no fear. We shall travel up by the first train on Saturday morning and will therefore be in Highgate by eleven o'clock. Father does not propose to come up until Monday morning, and Patience will remain here with her nanny. It affords me some slight consolation to think that they will not witness what takes place.

There has been no word of any kind from James. Thus your suspicion that he might try to forewarn Constance appears to be unfounded. She is full of nothing but plans for spending Christmas at Cleave Court as Lady Davenall, plans which make her happier than I believe I have ever known her. What suffering it causes me to make an outward show of sharing her joy, whilst inwardly knowing the grief that awaits, I shall leave you to imagine. Be assured, however, that I shall not falter. I have prayed long and hard enough to be certain that what we are doing is right, for what is right is seldom easy.

May God be with you.

Affectionately yours,
EMILY

VII

Sir James Davenall left home early on the morning of Friday 21th December, took a cab to Liverpool Street station and there caught a train to Newmarket. To Roffey, trailing the cab in one of his own hiring, standing a few places behind in the ticket queue and sitting a few compartments away on the train, Sir James seemed as unaware of being followed as he was careless of the possibility. But Roffey remained suspicious, for previous experience had taught him that this man was at his most elusive when he seemed most transparent.

It was mid-morning, and numbingly cold, when they reached Newmarket. Roffey left the train without hurrying and lingered in the ticket office until Sir James had negotiated the hire of a trap and set off in it. There was, at this stage, no doubt of his destination. He could have business in Newmarket with only one man: the recently installed owner of Maxton Grange, Alfred Quinn.

On hearing from Mr Davenall of Quinn's reappearance at the end of August, Roffey had made some desultory enquiries on the strength of a reward being offered in connection with a spate of housebreakings supposedly organized by a man named Flynn. He had found nothing to disprove Quinn's account of himself, but he was too old a hand to believe that a windfall inheritance in far-off New Zealand was anything other than a convenient excuse.

At length, Roffey purchased a map of the area, hired a bicycle and made a start. Maxton Grange lay some way south of the town, out along a straight road between fir-fringed paddocks. A bitter wind was blowing across the flat featureless landscape; such horses as he could see in the fields were jacketed against the chill. From a long way off, the grandiose brick-arched lodge-gates of the Grange were clearly visible, but of the house, which the map told him was set among trees some distance from the road, there was no sign. A chain was stretched across the entrance to the drive and a newly painted notice proclaimed STRICTLY PRIVATE – KEEP OUT. Roffey rode by without even slowing.

About a quarter of a mile further on, he stopped, leaned his bicycle against the fence and climbed over a nearby stile. A narrow path ran away arrow-straight between high but patchy hedges. The map showed it as a public footpath to the village of Cheveley, its appeal to Roffey being that it passed Maxton Grange closer than any road. He started walking, glancing to his left every few yards for a sign of the house.

This vast, open, wind-scoured country made Roffey nervous. He would have preferred the seamiest reach of London to such exposed terrain. That, it occurred to him, might be why Quinn had chosen the place: so that unwelcome visitors could be seen long before they arrived.

Abruptly, the Grange emerged into view through its shroud of trees. It was indeed well camouflaged. If the trees had been in leaf, they would completely have obscured it. Roffey shouldered his way through a thin stretch of hedge for a clearer view. It stood three fields away – recently built, he surmised, elegantly proportioned and well set up with bays, wings and gables, but somehow raw of outline, not yet rooted amongst its lawns and paddocks. Be that as it may, Quin had done well for himself. Very well indeed.

Roffey slipped a pair of binoculars out from beneath his coat and trained them on the house. Smoke was rising from the chimneys. A servant was raking a gravel path. Everything else seemed quiet. Then, when he moved round to focus on the low line of what he took to be stables away to the right, he saw them: Quinn and Sir James, walking out slowly from the stable-yard towards the paddocks.

Quinn did not fool him, even at that distance. A heavy tweed suit, riding-boots, a switch flicking rhythmically in his right hand, a gold watch-chain glinting on his waistcoat: none of it lessened Roffey's impression of a hard, low-born, ruthless man, cunning and brutal by turns. Sir James was doing most of the talking, and nothing on Quinn's lined grey face betrayed a reaction.

They reached a double line of fencing and paused. Then Quinn began talking, his mouth barely moving, his eyes fixed on Sir James.

377

There was one swift expansive gesture of the arm, as if to emphasize the extent of his property. Otherwise he was all unsmiling economy.

What were they talking about? Roffey wondered. Had Sir James come here to warn an accomplice that the game was up? Or to congratulate a former servant on his good fortune? From what little he could see, there was no way of telling.

Suddenly, the conversation became animated. Quinn brought his hand down on the fence-rail so hard that it shook visibly. Then he raised the switch in his hand and jabbed it at Sir James as he spoke. There was an aggression now in his gestures and a curl to the harsh line of the mouth that suggested contempt as well as anger. If the display was meant to cow or provoke, however, it was in vain. Sir James did not so much as flinch.

When Quinn had finished, turned on his heel and stalked away towards the house, Sir James made no move to follow. He merely lit a cigarette and smoked it slowly through, leaning on the fence and gazing thoughtfully into the distance. A horse came across to him from the middle of the field and nuzzled his arm, but he scarcely seemed to notice. Whatever far and secret stretch of the past or future his mind had fled to, there it stayed and, as Roffey knew, there it could not be followed.

An hour later, both he and Sir James were aboard the London train.

VIII

Richard Davenall's house in Highgate was where Constance had nursed her beloved James back to health in the autumn of 1882. It held for her happy memories of their slow second courtship. Accordingly, she could not have imagined a more fitting or agreeable location in which to spend the two days immediately prior to their wedding. She arrived there with her sister Emily on the morning of Saturday 22nd December in the best of spirits; in that radiant mood, in fact, which only the imminence of a long-denied fulfilment can confer.

This alone, she thought later, must have accounted for her failure to notice any of the many omens there were to detect: Emily's pensive reticent mood on the journey from Salisbury, her consultation of the clock at every station, her increasingly fretful state as they crossed London; Braddock's stilted formality on their arrival at Garth House, his direction of them to Richard's study rather than to their usual rooms.

All these signs should have alerted her, but, as it was, only when they entered the study to find Richard standing grim-faced by the fire, with, alongside him, a large, bearded man whom Constance did not recognize, did she realize that something was amiss. She crossed the room, kissed Richard on the cheek and knew at once, by the way he shrank from her and looked elsewhere, that his reservations of a month before – his hints of disloyalty to James – were about to bear their bitter fruit.

'This is Mr O'Shaughnessy,' he said hurriedly, turning to the other man. 'From Galway.'

'Your servant, ma'am.' O'Shaughnessy stooped to kiss her gloved hand.

'I am pleased to meet you, Mr O'Shaughnessy. What brings you to London?'

'Duty, ma'am.'

Constance turned to introduce her sister. As she did so, she caught in Emily's expression a flush of something close to guilt. Though she might not know this man, she did know why he was there.

'Would you care to sit down?' said Richard.

Constance did not care to sit down, not whilst her companions were shifting awkwardly from foot to foot and exchanging complicitous glances. But nor did she see why she should have to plead for an explanation. She stared straight at Richard, defying him to look away a second time.

'I'm sure we'd all be more comfortable—'

'Tell her!' Emily interrupted, in an anguished voice. 'Tell her and have done with it.'

They were all in it. Richard, the Irishman, her own sister: she saw that now. They had joined forces to some purpose she could not guess at. 'Tell me what?' she said at last, struggling to retain her composure.

Richard pursed his lips and glanced at the clock on the mantelpiece; it showed ten minutes to noon. 'It might be best . . . if we waited.'

'Waited for what?'

'Tell her now,' Emily pleaded.

'Very well.' Richard faced Constance, this time without flinching. 'This gives none of us any pleasure, my dear, but it has to be done.' He sighed. 'Your eyes, I fear, must be opened. Opened, that is, to the truth. If you had agreed to postpone the wedding. . . . But let that pass. I am sorry. Truly sorry. But I cannot let you marry James . . . in ignorance of his real identity.'

She glanced from one to the other of them. Richard pained. O'Shaughnessy embarrassed. And Emily torn between fidelity to her sister and to whatever higher truth she thought she was serving. 'What do you mean, "his real identity"?'

'He is not who you – who *we* – thought he was. He is not James.'

They were mad. They had to be. How could Richard – or Emily – believe such a notion? After all that she and they had suffered for the

379

sake of acknowledging James, how could they doubt him now? It made no sense. Yet, when she looked into her sister's eyes, she saw that it was so. They had deserted him. They had deserted her.

'His real name is Stephen Lennox, a half-brother of James. Astonishingly similar, as we know, but not James.'

'You believe James to be an impostor?'

'Yes.'

'You've changed your mind about him?'

'Yes.'

'As have you, Emily?'

Tears were flowing down Emily's face. But they were not the tears of indecision. 'He is not what he seems, Constance. He is not true to you.'

'And you, Mr O'Shaughnessy? What is your part in this?'

O'Shaughnessy cleared his throat as if to answer, but Richard did so for him. 'Mr O'Shaughnessy was Stephen Lennox's tutor for eight years. He will be able to identify him.'

'Identify him? I cannot believe you mean this, Richard.'

'I fear I do, my dear.'

There was a tap at the door and Braddock looked in. 'Sir James has arrived, sir.'

'Show him in,' said Richard. 'And ask Benson to join us. Then come in yourself.'

'Very good, sir.'

'It would be as well if we had as many witnesses as possible,' Richard explained when Braddock had gone. 'There must be no room for doubt.'

Constance could not speak. Her faith in James was intact, but around it lay the ruins of her faith in Richard and in Emily. From the horror of what they believed she could only recoil. When James entered the room, she flew to his side and found, in the strength of his clasp and the confidence of his gaze, the comfort she craved.

'There's nothing to worry about, Connie,' he said, holding her close and staring across the room at the other three. 'I'm here now.'

'Do you know what they've been saying?'

'Oh, yes. I know. Surprised to see me, Richard? Perhaps you thought I wouldn't show up.' With the gentlest of touches, he disengaged himself from Constance. 'This gentleman, I take it, is the celebrated Mr O'Shaughnessy.'

'You know who he is,' snapped Richard.

'Do I? Perhaps we should let Mr O'Shaughnessy be the judge of that.' The door clicked shut behind them. He glanced back at Braddock and Benson, who stood side by side, solemnly attentive. 'The party appears to be complete. Well, gentlemen' – he smiled at Richard and O'Shaughnessy in turn – 'shall we proceed?'

IX

After all the difficulties he had experienced earlier in the year, Plon-Plon felt bemused by the absurd ease with which he had now accomplished his task. There he stood, in Vivien Ratcliffe's large and comfortably furnished drawing-room, a December gale rattling the window beside him and buffeting the rhododendrons in the long and sloping garden beyond the glass. And there she stood, a tall grey-haired woman, more wizened than he had expected, yet also more gracious of bearing: the one Strang sister to break free, or be cast out, of her father's house.

Behind her, the fire roared and crackled in the grate and the wind moaned in the chimney. She did not speak, but her eyes – the only part of her that had not grown old – searched his face with all their proud preserved intensity. He wondered what Gervase would say if he could see her now, frail and elderly, but as defiantly haughty as ever. Would he still think the wager had been worth the prize?

'You do not seem surprised to see me, madame,' Plon-Plon said, determined to break the silence. 'I might almost believe you had been expecting me to call.'

'After all this time, Prince? I hardly think so. Indeed, I cannot imagine a single good reason why you should wish to seek me out. But, then, your reasons were seldom good.'

Plon-Plon permitted himself the faintest of smiles, then said: 'I think you know why I am here.'

'I have told you. I cannot imagine.'

'You covered your tracks well, I must say. Even your sisters know nothing of you.'

'You have seen *them*?' A note of incredulity had crept into her otherwise guarded voice.

'There was no other trail to follow, madame.'

'How did you know where to find them?'

'Catherine – Lady Davenall, that is—'

'*Her!*' Vivien's eyes narrowed. 'So. You are here at *her* bidding, are you?'

But Plon-Plon did not care to be taken for any woman's errand-boy. 'Largely, madame, on my own account.' It struck him then how alike Catherine and Vivien had grown, how sourly elegant, how icily untouchable. Just as Catherine declined to grieve for a dead son, so Vivien wasted no curiosity on the sisters who had disowned her. 'You will not pretend, I trust, to be unaware of recent events affecting the Davenall family?'

'Of course not.' Her lips flirted with a smile, then dismissed it from their presence. 'It has afforded me considerable satisfaction.'

'You admit that?'

381

'Why should I not? You of all people, Prince, should know what I suffered at their hands.'

'Quite so, madame. Quite so.'

She stared at him for several moments, then said: 'What are you implying?'

'As I said, I believe you know why I am here.'

'No. I do not.'

Yet she *had* expected him: he was sure of it. The ease of his admission, the gravity of his reception, the calmness of her manner: they all smacked of prepared defences. 'Where is your son, madame?'

'My son?'

'Let us prevaricate no longer. The man calling himself Sir James Davenall is an impostor. You know that. I believe him to be your son by Sir Gervase Davenall. I believe him to be your revenge for all the wrongs inflicted upon you by Sir Gervase and his wife.'

She was laughing. He had never heard her laugh before, but now the sound of it rose mockingly to his ears. Yet there was no joy in it. When her face relaxed back into its sombre lines, no pleasure was to be seen in her eyes or remembered in her gaze. 'Is this what Catherine believes, too?' she asked, with sudden flashing venom.

'Yes.'

Her scrutiny of him intensified. 'Truly?'

'Why else do you think I am here?'

'To offer me your overdue repentance, Prince. I thought old age might have elevated your soul. I see that I was wrong. Well, no matter. I have no need of revenge, but, if I had, this delusion of yours would supply as good a form of it as any.'

'Does this amount to a denial, madame?'

'What you allege, Prince, is too absurd to warrant a denial.'

'Then, tell me: where is your son? Where is the son you bore Gervase? Or do you propose to deny bearing his child?'

Vivien walked slowly across to the window where Plon-Plon stood and stared at him with frank hostility. 'I once threw blood in your face for daring to remind me of that. I was once so dazzled by you that I went to meet you, by night, when I knew I should not. What was my reward, Prince? Do tell me. Was it just? Was it fitting? Was it fair?'

'No, madame. It was none of those things. For the follies of my youth, I can offer no reparation, to you or to myself. Your reward for being Gervase's victim was to be turned out by Catherine, turned away by your family—'

'And forgotten by you?'

It was as well, he thought in some separate dispassionate part of his mind, that he had waited this long, waited till he was old enough to bear the shame of what he was about to admit. 'Yes, forgotten. Until I was forced to remember.'

'Forced by whom?'

'By your son, madame. When Monsieur Norton, as he was then called, revealed that he knew what had occurred at Cleave Court, what crime had been committed in the maze that night, thirty-seven years ago, I knew who he must be, though I tried to close my mind to the possibility. For how could he know what happened, unless he had heard it from his mother's lips?'

Vivien looked away, out through the window, into the garden and beyond, to where heaving surf crashed across the crumbling rocks of Torbay. In her wistful gaze Plon-Plon thought he saw the first sign of the weakness he had hoped to exploit.

'He should not have confronted me with it, although it served his purpose at the time. Ultimately, it has proved a fatal mistake.'

'Fatal?' she said in an undertone, her eyes still fixed on the distant foaming sea.

'To your cause, madame. To your conspiracy.'

'There is no conspiracy.'

'Why deny it? In one sense, you have merely given him what is rightfully his: his birthright. Do not think I blame you. I see the justice of it. Truly, I do. But I cannot allow it to continue.'

Then, at last, she looked back at him. 'You cannot allow it?'

'For all our sakes, madame, the pretence must be ended.'

'Very well.' She nodded gravely. 'I must ask you to wait here for a few minutes, Prince, whilst I fetch something. Something which will indeed end the pretence.' And, with that, she walked slowly from the room.

X

Absolute silence reigned. Denzil O'Shaughnessy walked steadily forward, until he was standing but a foot or so from Sir James. They were about the same height, and their eyes, meeting naturally, held one another in a timeless interval of piercing scrutiny. Only when O'Shaughnessy stepped to one side, as if to examine Sir James's profile, did their gazes part, and then only for a moment, because O'Shaughnessy swiftly resumed his place in front of Sir James and, as soon as he did so, their unblinking stares were rejoined.

'Well?' said Richard impatiently.

But neither man seemed to pay him any heed. They were remote from those looking on, alone in a realm where their confrontation was all that mattered, where nothing could be heard but their own unspoken exchanges.

O'Shaughnessy cleared his throat and, reaching out, took Sir

James's right hand in his. Both men remained expressionless as O'Shaughnessy held the hand out flat, looked down at it, then released it once more. He took a deep breath and, turning back to Richard, said: 'I am satisfied.'

'You recognize him as Stephen Lennox?'

O'Shaughnessy shook his head. 'No.'

'What?'

'I am satisfied that this man is *not* Stephen Lennox. The absence of a scar on his right hand confirms it. He is not my former pupil.'

A note of desperation entered Richard's voice. 'But he must be. For God's sake, man, think again.'

'When he first came into the room, I thought he might be Stephen, but I see now that he is not. I am more certain of that than of anything in this world.'

'But, if he isn't Lennox, then who . . .?' Richard's voice faded into silence as his gaze moved from the stubborn insistence of O'Shaughnessy's face to the slowly emerging smile on the face of Sir James Davenall.

XI

Plon-Plon had been alone for no more than a few minutes when Vivien returned. If she had been to fetch something, it was small enough to be slipped into a pocket, for she carried nothing in her hands.

'I expected you to call, Prince, it is true,' she said, rejoining him by the window. 'But not for the reason you suspect.'

'Then, why?'

'Because Cora warned me you would.'

'*La traîtresse!*'

'Do not be too hard on her. It made no difference. Nothing could.'

'What do you mean, madame?'

'Read this.' She slid a single sheet of paper from a pocket of her dress and handed it to him. Plon-Plon held it up to the light and clamped a monocle in his eye. It took him no more than a few seconds to see what the document was and to scan its contents. 'It is true I bore a son to Sir Gervase Davenall,' Vivien said. 'That is his death certificate.'

Plon-Plon had been as certain as he had been mistaken. There, before him, in crabbed thirty-year-old clerical handwriting, was the proof of his error. 'Oliver Strang, died 2nd August 1854, aged seven years. Cause of death: cholera.'

'You cannot imagine the poverty and degradation I endured for Oliver's sake. And it was all for nothing. Even after his death, I went on believing that it was not only right, but possible, to lead a noble life. Not until the saintly Miss Nightingale sent me home in disgrace from Scutari, and every hospital in the land closed its doors against me, did I understand the depth of my folly. From that moment on, I did whatever was necessary to obtain the wealth and privileges my son had been denied. As you see, I succeeded. I am no longer a good woman, but I am a happy one. That, Prince, is the only kind of revenge I desire.'

Plon-Plon looked at her in blank astonishment. 'But, if he is not your son, madame, then who . . .?' His words trailed into silence. He knew the answer to his unfinished question. But he did not dare to voice it.

XII

Sir James Davenall and Constance Sumner were married that afternoon. After what had happened, neither had any wish to wait another two days; Constance could hardly remain in Richard's house under such circumstances, and James, now he had been vindicated, was eager that they should at once commence their life together.

Richard did not attend the wedding, shocked by his own misjudgement into believing that a further reconciliation was impossible. Emily, however, amid floods of tears, was forgiven by her sister and her new brother-in-law, though not, it seemed, by herself. She it was who saw them off after the ceremony at Paddington station at the start of their journey to Cleave Court, where they were to begin a new life, at last unfettered, as Sir James and Lady Davenall. For all the anguish that day's work had caused, it had at least sealed their future happiness as man and wife. They who had believed themselves lost to each other were joined now for all time.

NINETEEN

I

Constance woke slowly, the contentment of slumber giving place gradually to the pleasure of awareness. The touch of the starched sheets against her chin, the sight of the corniced ceiling above her head, the flickering of the fire in the corner, the dull grey light of a winter's dawn seeping between half-parted curtains: these were her first, drowsily reassuring perceptions of Boxing Day 1883, the fourth morning of her marriage to Sir James Davenall and of their life together at Cleave Court, a home she was coming to love nearly as much as she loved her husband.

Turning on to her side, she reached out instinctively for James's hand, only to find that his half of the bed was unoccupied. Propping herself up on one elbow, she peered round the room. He was not there. But the sight of the fire at once put her mind at rest. He must have stoked it up to ensure she did not wake to a cold room, then taken himself off to the bath. It was strange, though, that no sounds of running water or singing pipes reached her ears. Perhaps he had gone downstairs to summon breakfast. She lay back on the pillow, wondering if he were planning some surprise for her; then, deciding she could wait no longer, rose, slipped on the silk *peignoir* that had been one of his wedding gifts to her and walked across to the window. She pulled back the curtains, smiled at the prettiness of the frost on the lawn, then retreated to the dressing-table and began combing her hair.

A gilt-framed photograph by the mirror caught her eye. It was her favourite picture of Patience, taken on her fourth birthday eighteen months before. For an instant, the enormity of all the changes that had occurred since then rushed into Constance's mind, but, as quickly as the thought had come, it wilted before the joy that the recent past had brought her. Emily and her father were due to arrive with Patience

386

later that day. It would not only be delightful to see them again and to be reunited with her daughter. It would also be the final confirmation that Constance's family approved of what she had done, that Emily had forgotten the doubts Richard Davenall had planted in her mind.

Suddenly, there was a tap at the door. Constance started, so absorbed had she been in her thoughts that she had not heard anyone approaching. Before she could say anything, the door opened and Dorothy, the maid, came in, cradling a breakfast-tray in her arms and smiling nervously.

'Good mornin', ma'am.'

Constance frowned. 'Good morning, Dorothy. I had assumed we were breakfasting downstairs. Has Sir James given you no instructions?'

Dorothy looked nonplussed. 'No, ma'am, for 'e ain't . . . That is . . .' She gazed perplexedly around the room. 'I dain't think 'e were up yet.'

'Never mind. Perhaps he's taking the morning air. Put the tray over there.'

After Dorothy had gone, Constance looked into her husband's adjoining dressing-room. Sure enough, his cigarette-case was missing from its normal place and the Norfolk jacket was absent from its hook on the back of the door. It must have been as she had said: he had gone for an early stroll, probably believing he would be back before she woke; he had donned boots and overcoat downstairs and taken a swift circuit of the grounds; he would be back any moment.

Constance returned to the bedroom and to the window, where she could have a clear view of the drive and the deer park. He would probably come back that way and, if he did, she would be there to wave down at him. She would not start breakfast yet. It could only be a short while before he rejoined her: better to breakfast together than alone. She felt faintly disappointed that he was not already in sight, but consoled herself with the thought that, this way, she could be sure of seeing him before he saw her. Soon, she did not doubt, he would emerge from the woodland path beside the house or come into view along the drive. Very soon, her husband would be restored to her side.

An hour later, the coffee had gone cold in its pot and the bacon fat had congealed on its plate. Constance still sat on the window-seat, gazing out into the park, her pleasurable anticipation become an anxious vigil. Sir James Davenall had not returned.

II

Religious festivals generally plunged Plon-Plon into fits of curmudgeonly atheism. It may therefore have been a kindness to all those who knew him that he was obliged to spend Christmas 1883 in saturnine solitude at the Imperial Hotel, Torquay, barking at waiters, leering at chambermaids and scowling from his window at the scudding clouds and slanting rain of the Devon seaside in winter.

Not that Christmas was the sole contributor to his mood. He was also weighed down by the memory of his humiliation at the hands of Vivien Ratcliffe and the prospect of even greater humiliation at the hands of Cathcrine Davenall. The proud and foolish sense of duty which had brought him to gale-lashed Torquay also impelled him to proceed next to Bath and report the failure of his enquiries to their merciless investigator. The very thought of doing so reduced him to quivering despair.

By Boxing Day, however, he had decided that his pride should be spared further suffering. Concluding that misogyny was the better part of valour, he penned the briefest of notes to Catherine and posted it at the railway station before catching the nine o'clock train to London, proposing to spend the journey in pleasing contemplation of expelling the marquise de Canisy from Prangins by the New Year.

Three hours later, when the train drew into Westbury station, with another three still to go before it reached London, Plon-Plon had succeeded in putting the bravest, if not the smuggest, of faces on his lamentable part in *l'affaire Davenall*. His perfunctory letter to Catherine had acquired, in his own esteem, the status of a valedictory address. He had washed his hands of the whole disagreeable business. If he had owed them anything on account of the errors of his youth, the debt had been discharged. Glancing out of the window of his compartment at the drearily clad passengers on the platform, he felt buoyed up by an awareness of his own superiority. It was good to be alive and it was splendid to be himself.

Suddenly, in the midst of a euphoria which the dwindling contents of his hip-flask did much to explain, a woman caught his eye amongst those stepping forward to join the train. At first, he could not believe what he saw, but a swift adjustment of his monocle confirmed that he was not mistaken.

It was the woman he had seen at St Paul's six months ago in urgent conversation with James Norton: Sir James Davenall, as he was now reluctantly compelled to think of him. She wore a long grey caped coat, with the hem and ruffed neck of a black dress visible beneath; her gloves and veiled hat were also black. Such a plain and modest outfit would not normally have attracted Plon-Plon's attention, but her face, now as before, drew his gaze magnetically. In all his vast and varied experience of womankind, he could not recall a more haunting, hopelessly tempting beauty. What she was, or had been, to Sir James, Plon-Plon neither knew nor cared. It seemed to him, in that moment of rencounter, that she was a woman who, had he been but a few years younger, he could happily have followed to the ends of the earth.

A moment later, she was out of sight aboard the train, several carriages along. Another moment, and the train had begun to pull out of the station. Plon-Plon pressed his head back against the seat and chewed pensively at the monocle cord. Who was she? Where was she going? If he did not try to find out before they reached London, the chance would be gone for ever. Yet, if he took the chance, he might live to regret it.

Yielding to impulse, he plucked a sovereign from his waistcoat pocket and spun it in the air, catching it as it fell and pressing it flat on the back of his hand. 'Luck is all,' he murmured to himself, uncovering the coin. Then he sighed with disappointment, for there was Queen Victoria's severe averted face to tell him what he must do. And that, as he might have expected of so staid and proper a source, was nothing at all.

Plon-Plon grimaced. Well, so be it. Perhaps, after all, it was for the best. He slipped the coin back into his waistcoat pocket and reached for the hip-flask.

III

A second dawn found the owner of Cleave Court still absent, his whereabouts unknown. Emily Sumner, who had slept scarcely at all during the night, sat by the window of her guest room, watching she hardly knew for what, but watching anyway, for some sign that the dreadful suspense of waiting might be about to end.

As she gazed out across the mist-cloaked parkland, Emily reflected on how all the fears she had entertained when setting out from Salisbury the day before, and which had seemed then all-important, had been banished utterly by the turn events had taken. Would she be restored to her sister's confidence following the O'Shaughnessy episode? Could James overlook the doubts she had harboured about him? Should she confess her errors and ask forgiveness, or pretend, for all their sakes, that such errors had never been made? These concerns seemed trivial and self-indulgent now, compared with the vital issue of what had become of Sir James Davenall.

Emily had reached Cleave Court with Canon Sumner, Patience and Patience's nanny the previous afternoon, to find Constance distraught and the household in confusion. The grounds had been

389

searched, neighbours questioned, villagers alerted – all to no avail. Sir James Davenall was missing. He had quit the house some time around dawn, before any of the servants was up, wearing (so far as could be established) an Inverness cape and carrying a walking-stick. He had left no note or message of any kind. Constance had assumed he would be back within the hour. Since then, she had expected him with every minute that had passed. But he had not come.

The village policeman had been sympathetic but unable to offer much help. He had suggested waiting until morning before raising the alarm. Now, as Emily saw by the slow grey advance of it across the still and frozen park, morning had indeed come, but with it, no sign of James.

It was a comfort to her that Constance, at least, would have passed a restful night. The previous evening, Dr Fiveash had been summoned from Bath to administer a sleeping draught. He had not departed without implying to Emily that Sir James's disappearance in some way confirmed his opinion that the man was an impostor. Emily had rejected the implication as both unfounded and unworthy, but later, in the lonely reaches of the night, she had begun to wonder what else could possibly explain his conduct. If some accident had befallen him, surely they would have heard. If not, where was he – and with whom?

Suddenly, a sound reached her ears: rapid hoof-falls on the drive. She rose from the window-seat and craned forward for a better view, but nothing was visible. Then she caught sight of a closed carriage, drawn by a pair of horses, flitting between the elms. The horses were being driven hard on what could only be, given such speed at such an hour, an urgent errand. She thought at once of James.

As she watched, the carriage turned off the drive and pulled up sharply in front of the house. At once, the nearside door was flung open and a tall thin man in flapping coat, straggling scarf and pulled-down hat emerged. He headed straight for the front steps. From the other side of the carriage, the burly figure of a policeman appeared, hurrying to catch up. The sight of his uniform was final confirmation for Emily that they had news of James. She rushed at once from the room.

By the time she had reached the stairs, a regular hammering had started at the front door and Escott, the butler, had made his way along the hall and commenced sliding back the bolts. As soon as he opened the door, the tall thin man stepped over the threshold, flapped some form of identification in his hand and said: 'I am Inspector Gow; this is Sergeant Harris. We wish to see Sir James Davenall at once.'

'He's not at home, sir,' Escott replied.

'Then, where is he?' At that point, Gow noticed Emily coming down the stairs.

'Lady Davenall?' he asked, glancing at her sharply.

390

'No, Inspector. I am Lady Davenall's sister. You have news of Sir James?'

'Far from it, ma'am. It's news of him I seek.'

'But . . . have you not spoken to the constable in Freshford?'

'We've had no time for that, ma'am.'

'He would have told you Sir James has been missing from home since early yesterday morning. When I saw you arrive, I thought –'

'Early yesterday morning, you say?'

'Yes. We have no idea where he may be.'

'Is that so?' He raised one eyebrow and glanced meaningfully at the sergeant.

'May I ask what you want with him?'

Gow looked back at her. 'I wish to speak to Sir James on a matter of extreme urgency, ma'am: the murder last night of Mr Alfred Quinn of Maxton Grange, Newmarket.'

IV

Eight hours had passed and now, with identical words, grave-faced Inspector Gow of the Suffolk Constabulary stated his business to Richard Davenall in his Holborn office as advancing dusk beyond its windows announced the close of the second day of Sir James Davenall's disappearance.

'I wish to speak to Sir James on a matter of extreme urgency, sir: the murder last night of Mr Alfred Quinn of Maxton Grange, Newmarket.'

'Quinn murdered?' said Richard in amazement. 'How?'

'All in good time, sir. First, do you know where Sir James is? I gather you *are* his solicitor.'

'Indeed I am, but . . . well, I assume you will find him at his country residence, Cleave Court, in Somerset.'

Gow smiled grimly. 'No, sir. I was there this morning. Sir James has been missing from home since dawn yesterday.'

'Missing?'

'Apparently so. Nobody has any idea where he is.'

'You spoke to his wife?'

'Briefly. Lady Davenall is very upset, as you might expect. I gather she and Sir James are only five days married.'

'That is so, but –'

'Where do you think he might be, sir?'

'I . . .' Richard reflected for a moment on the irony that, only a week before, Roffey had been monitoring James's movements and finding little enough in them to substantiate Richard's suspicions.

Now Roffey had been called off, James had vanished and Quinn was dead. 'I cannot imagine, Inspector. I have neither seen nor heard from Sir James since he left London last Saturday.'

Gow's mouth twitched inscrutably beneath his walrus moustache. 'Do you recognize this, sir?' He took a cigarette-case from his pocket and laid it on the desk between them. It was silver, engraved with the initials 'JD'. Richard recognized it at once.

'It belongs to Sir James.'

'So his wife said.'

'How did you come by it?'

Gow held him with a cold-eyed stare as he replied. 'Clutched in Alfred Quinn's hand, sir, when he was found. It was the devil of a job to prise it loose.'

Richard took a deep breath. 'How did Quinn meet his death, Inspector?'

'It seems he was in the habit of walking round his property each night before retiring, though whether to take the air or to check that all was secure I'm not clear. At all events, he was waylaid in the stable-yard and done to death in pretty horrible fashion. His head was held underwater in a horse-trough until he'd drowned – or suffocated, however you care to look at it. There was a hell of a struggle, as you might expect, but, by the time the servants had been roused by the commotion and come to investigate, Quinn was dead, with Sir James Davenall's cigarette-case clasped in his hand. I assume the murderer hadn't time to remove it before beating a retreat. The alarm was raised, of course, but it would have been easy enough for him to make good his escape across the fields.'

Richard said nothing, his mind racing to keep pace with the consequences of what Gow had told him. Roffey had followed James to Newmarket the previous Friday and seen him argue with Quinn. But murder? It tallied with none of the possible explanations of their relationship. And James, if he was nothing else, was a careful intelligent man. He would surely not leave such glaring evidence at the scene of a crime, however pressing the need of haste. Yet, if he had not left Cleave Court and gone to Newmarket, where had he gone and what had he done?

'I gather Sir James visited Maxton Grange on the twenty-first of this month,' Gow continued, 'and that he and Quinn fell out about something. We don't know what. Do you?'

'No,' said Richard emphatically. It had suddenly occurred to him that Gow might jump to all manner of outlandish conclusions if he knew Richard had employed Roffey to follow James.

'Aren't you going to leap to your cousin's defence, sir?' Gow asked, with what appeared to be a grin. 'Aren't you going to tell me it's inconceivable he could have murdered his former valet?'

'It *is* inconceivable, Inspector. But you don't need me to tell you that this cigarette-case proves nothing.'

'As to that, sir, I must disagree. We know Quinn was acquainted with his attacker. There was ash from his cigar near the trough, suggesting he'd stood there smoking for some time. There were also two cigarette ends from the same brand as those in the case: one of Sullivan's most expensive – Sir James's favourite, by his wife's admission. So we know Quinn and his attacker must have stood talking before their differences took a violent turn. We also know Quinn can't have anticipated what would happen. He carried a knife in his jacket, but never had a chance to use it. I make that a pretty strong case against Sir James. Don't you?'

'I . . . I'm not sure.' Of anything, he might accurately have gone on to say. O'Shaughnessy's failure to identify James had hit Richard hard. He had passed a depressed and lonely Christmas counting the probable cost of his grotesque misjudgement. Now he sensed, with the coming of this latest news, that vindication was at hand. But it was vindication in a form he did not recognize and at a price he did not care to pay.

'Tell me, sir,' Gow said, leaning across the desk, 'how did Quinn come by the money to set himself up as a country gent?'

'An inheritance, I believe. An uncle in New Zealand left him a tract of gold-bearing land.'

Gow nodded. 'They peddled me that one, too. I'm having it checked. Frankly, I don't expect to find there's any truth in it.'

'Then, what do you suggest?'

'I spoke to Sir James's mother earlier, sir. She told me Quinn was dismissed from the family's service for stealing. Also, it appears my colleagues from the Metropolitan Constabulary had their eye on Quinn in connection with a series of housebreakings. Did you know that?'

'No.' As he said it, Richard knew he was taking a risk. It was possible, albeit barely so, that Roffey's informant at Scotland Yard had told Gow of his interest in Quinn.

'Did Sir James ever express dislike of Quinn?'

'Not that I can remember.'

'Did he mention him at all in recent months?'

'Not to me.'

Suddenly, Gow rose to his feet. 'Well, we'll leave it at that for the present, sir.' He smiled. 'Unless you can suggest why Sir James should have murdered Quinn?'

'I don't believe he did, Inspector.'

'No. Naturally not. You'll be sure to let us know if Sir James contacts you, won't you?'

'Of course.'

'Good.' He moved towards the door, only to stop halfway as if he had just remembered something. 'By the way, sir, where do *you* stand over Sir James's identity?'

'I beg your pardon?'

'I followed the case like everybody else. It was plain to me this morning that the dowager Lady Davenall regards Sir James as an impostor, despite the verdict of the court. You testified on Sir James's behalf, didn't you?'

'Yes.'

'So may I take it that you have no doubts that the court's decision was correct?'

'None at all, Inspector.' What was the man driving at? Richard wondered during the silence that followed. What warped recondite theory was he forming to explain the inexplicable?

'Thank you, sir,' Gow said after a pause. 'I'll be in touch.' And, with that, he left Richard to the company of his own unavailing thoughts.

V

That evening, at Cleave Court, Constance retired early to bed, ostensibly so worn out by anxiety that she proposed to take another dose of Dr Fiveash's sleeping draught in the hope of a restful night. The truth, however, as became apparent once she had locked the bedroom door behind her, was otherwise.

The news of Quinn's murder had, in a curious way, relieved her mind. She had feared, until then, that James had met with a fatal accident. Now, in the suspicions of Inspector Gow, another possibility had taken shape, a possibility which implied that James was very much alive and well. If so, he would be relying on her to remain loyal to him in his absence, and she was determined not to let him down. Knowing that Gow proposed to return on the morrow and that he might well wish to search her husband's possessions, she had decided that, if he did, he would find nothing to strengthen his case.

Late on Christmas afternoon, Escott had brought in a letter for James whilst he and Constance had been having tea. James had opened the letter, read it, then tucked it away in his pocket. He had made no comment on it, nor had he told Constance who it was from. She, for her part, had expressed no interest in it. A trifling note from the estate manager, she had assumed, in so far as she had assumed anything. Now, however, the incident had acquired a sinister colour.

Stepping into James's dressing-room, Constance opened the wardrobe and ran her eye along the racks of coats and blazers. There it was: the burgundy smoking-jacket he had been wearing on Christmas afternoon. She reached into the nearest pocket – and felt the letter, folded at its base.

The envelope bore only James's name, with neither address nor postage stamp. This was as she would have expected, for there had been no deliveries on Christmas Day. The letter must have been dropped in by hand.

James had opened the envelope with his thumb: the flap was torn jaggedly across. Inside was a single sheet of paper, folded once. Constance noticed how much her hand was shaking as she held the note up to read.

Be at the Dundas aqueduct at half-past eight tomorrow morning.
Do not fail me this last time. M.

There could be no doubt. It was to keep this rendezvous that James had left the house so early on Boxing Day. The handwriting suggested what Constance least wished to believe: that 'M' was a woman. Yet, if this were a secret assignation, why leave the evidence there for her to discover? And why was this to be the *last* time?

Returning to her bedroom, folding and refolding the letter in her hands, Constance rehearsed the possibilities in her mind. Perhaps James knew 'M' from his years in America: he had always been reticent about the friends he had made there. Perhaps he had jilted her, or she him. Perhaps she had heard of his new-found wealth and status and come to England to exploit their former intimacy. All this, however dreadful, was infinitely preferable to any other explanation she could think of. James would have met 'M' in secret rather than have her berate him in public. He would have done so to spare Constance, not to spite her. The choice of a meeting-place which meant so much to both of them would merely have been an unfortunate coincidence.

Yet, if this was true, why had James not returned? Had 'M' some way of forcing him to accompany her? Surely not, for 'M' herself had called it 'this last time'. It smacked more of a farewell than of a confrontation.

Constance took a deep breath. She must be brave, she must be resolute: she must stand by James until he could stand before her in person and explain himself. Everyone else would place the worst possible construction on such a note. Therefore, they must never see it. Tearing the envelope and its contents into four, Constance cast the pieces into the fire and finished with the poker the work that the flames began.

VI

As Richard Davenall descended the stairs of Garth House, Highgate, on the morning of Friday, 28th December, he wondered with bleak foreboding, what the newspapers would have to say about the murder of Alfred Quinn and the disappearance of Sir James Davenall. He himself no longer doubted what the two events in some way signified –

that James was not who he claimed to be – but, if only for Constance's sake, he hoped that the outside world had not yet reached the same conclusion.

Richard, like many an ageing bachelor, was a creature of habit. He therefore restrained his curiosity about the newspapers long enough to tap the barometer, which told him the cold spell was set to continue, and leaf through the morning mail, left by Braddock on the small table halfway along the hall. It was as well that he did so, for otherwise he would not have seen the third letter in the pile as soon as he did. It caused him to catch his breath and stand for a moment utterly bewildered, for it was addressed to him in what he instantly recognized as James's handwriting.

Richard's desire to open the letter at once was overwhelmed by his highly developed faculty of caution. Only several minutes later, in the privacy of his study, did he dare to read what James had written.

My dear Richard,
By the time you receive this letter, I will be out of the country. It is quite possible, given the purpose of my journey, that I will not return alive. Since I would not wish to die with a lie on my conscience, I propose to lay before you certain facts which I know I can trust you to act upon when and if the time comes.

In view of the doubts which you have recently entertained concerning my identity, you may wish to know that, in pursuing my claim to the baronetcy, I merely pursued what was rightfully mine. In seeking to alienate Constance from her husband, however, I pursued what was rightfully another's. At first, I freely admit, I did so in order to win Constance's public support of my claim. There seemed no one else to turn to in view of my family's refusal to acknowledge me. Later, however, I came to love her and to believe I could win her for my wife.

I knew Constance would stand by her husband, whatever her feelings for me, unless he behaved so outrageously that she felt compelled to desert him. Yet Trenchard was, by his lights, a decent and faithful man. To lure him into self-destruction, it was necessary to make him believe I was an impostor, whose elaborate conspiracy he alone could unravel.

So, Richard, I am telling you what I suspect you have already concluded from those many visits to Trenchard of which you thought me unaware: he is as sane as you or I. He followed a trail I laid for him. He behaved as I hoped he would. He was indeed the victim of delusions, but delusions I devised for him.

Of my accomplices and their methods I will say nothing.

They must answer for themselves. But I would not wish Trenchard to languish for ever in an asylum because I had died without confessing my part in his downfall. As my cousin and my friend, as a man of the law and a man of honour, I call upon you to bring these facts to the attention of the authorities. William Trenchard is no madman. Nor, in trying to kill me, did he do more than I can readily excuse. He should be given back his liberty.

Trenchard's deception is the only part of all this I regret. For the rest I make no apology. It has been as it was bound to be. And it will end the same way.

Ever Yours,
JAMES

'It is quite possible . . . that I will not return alive.' What was he going to do? 'For the rest I make no apology.' What, for that matter, had he already done? There was no address or date on the unheaded notepaper, no hint in its wording of where it had been written or when.

Richard picked up the envelope and peered at the postmark. Tonbridge, Kent, 8 p.m., 27 December. So he could only have left the country the night before. But why Tonbridge? What could have taken him there?

Richard moved unsteadily to the bookcase and pulled down a copy of the South Eastern & Chatham Railway timetable. At the back was a route map and what it showed him added another contradiction to James's letter. If he had been heading for Dover by train, in order to leave the country by the quickest route, he might well have passed through Tonbridge, but he would scarcely have stopped there long enough to post a letter.

Then it came to him. Five stops down the Hastings line from Tonbridge was Ticehurst Road. That is what had taken James there. He had been to see Trenchard. He had travelled to Ticehurst, returned as far as Tonbridge and there caught a train to Dover and a night sailing for the continent. And, at the last possible moment, he had entrusted Richard with the means to put right a long-standing injustice.

VII

When Escott told her that Miss Pursglove had called to see Constance, Emily felt more irritated than she knew she conscientiously should. After all, Sir James had restored the dear soul to Weir Cottage and it was therefore understandable that she should wish to express her concern

397

about his disappearance. Emily feared, however, that the old lady's twittering solicitude could only distress her sister in the present circumstances and she therefore went to speak to her with every intention of bustling her, gently but quickly, off the premises.

'Constance is resting and cannot be disturbed, Nanny,' she began, stating the simple truth. 'I'm sure you understand.'

'This is not a social call,' Miss Pursglove replied, her insistent tone seeming to confirm as much. 'It concerns Sir James.'

Emily smiled indulgently. 'I'm sure you're just as worried as –'

'I saw him, Miss Sumner! I saw him *after* he left Cleave Court on Boxing Day morning.'

In a trice, Miss Pursglove's presence had been transformed from inconsequence into momentousness. Emily ushered her into a chair and implored her to explain.

'I only had the news from Constable Binns yesterday, my dear. Until then, I'd have thought . . . well, as you shall hear, I'd have thought Sir James was here with his wife, as providence intended. It only goes to show –'

'When did you see him, Nanny?'

'Boxing Day morning, my dear, as I said. It must have been some time between eight o'clock and half-past, because it was only just light. I was at my gate, calling for Lupin, when Sir James came walking along the lane from the railway bridge. He bade me a cheerful good morning and said he had a mind to take a stroll along the towpath as far as the aqueduct. He seemed in handsome good spirits. I asked him in for a cup of tea and a bite of breakfast, and he said he'd be happy to accept but must have his stroll first. He said I should expect him back in half an hour. Then he walked on up the lane towards the canal. I felt sure he'd return as he said, but he didn't. After an hour or so, I supposed he'd forgotten all about me and gone straight home. Well, it would have been understandable enough. It was only yesterday I learned that that's not how it was at all. Where did he go, Miss Sumner? That's what I want to know. Whatever became of him?'

'I don't know, Nanny,' Emily replied, helpless to explain to her own satisfaction, never mind Miss Pursglove's, why James Davenall should have vanished for the second time in his life. 'Nobody knows.'

VIII

'So your cousin has a conscience after all,' Trenchard said, handing the letter back to Richard. 'I suppose I should be grateful.'

It was not the reaction Richard had expected. He had sat often enough with Trenchard, comfortably confined in his private suite of rooms at Ticehurst Asylum, to know the frustrated longing for justice and retribution which consumed him and had shown, in over a year, no sign of abating. So why, when handed the means by which he might be vindicated, had he responded in so subdued a fashion? Why, for that matter had he referred to James as Richard's cousin, something he would normally have refused to do?

'It seems', Trenchard continued, 'that I was wrong, but not in the way everybody thought. Well, I'm glad it's to come out at last.'

'You're taking this very calmly, I must say.'

'I've learned patience here if I've learned nothing else. By losing my head now, I'd only spoil my chances of release.'

'Did you know he would write this letter?' That, Richard had begun to think, must explain Trenchard's composure: James had visited him in order to forewarn him.

'No. I had no idea.'

'Did he not mention it to you yesterday?'

'Yesterday?'

'When he visited you.'

Trenchard frowned. 'He hasn't been here, Richard. I haven't set eyes on him since that day last year at Lincoln's Inn.'

Could it be true? Richard had felt so certain, so positive that James had been to Ticehurst. Recovering the envelope, he held it out for Trenchard to see. 'It was posted in Tonbridge yesterday evening, not fifteen miles from here. I assumed –'

'I don't know why he should be in Tonbridge, but he wasn't on his way here.'

Suddenly, Richard felt uneasy. If James's letter had come as a bolt from the blue to Trenchard, his calmness was inexplicable. Every month for the past ten, Richard had visited him in this famously well-appointed repository for the wealthily insane and had sat with him in his room, listening to him rail against his plight. Despite all the honeyed words and well-meant promptings of his attendants, Trenchard had kept fresh in his mind every one of his grievances against those who thought him mad. He had refused either to forget or to forgive. But now, without warning or reason, he had seemingly done both.

'You will do as he asks, won't you, Richard? You will bring this to the attention of the authorities?'

'Of course I will. But what of James? I'd hoped you might know where he'd gone.'

'Abroad, by his own admission. To avoid facing Constance, I suppose, with all that he did to win her from me.'

'He doesn't say that.'

'No, but why else should he go? Why else should he flee when he had nothing to lose by staying?'

399

Richard hardly felt he knew Trenchard any longer. Angry, baffled, foolish: he had been all of those. But never guarded or knowing or subtle: never as he was now. Nor had thirteen months in a lunatic asylum made him so. This was a transformation of the recent past. This, Richard could not help but feel, was the transformation of one who knew what was about to happen.

IX

'I fear I must ask you some further questions, ma'am,' said Inspector Gow, in a voice which suggested he wished to convey more regret than he actually felt.

'Of course, Inspector,' Constance replied. 'I do understand. Please proceed.'

'Has your sister told you of Miss Pursglove's statement?'

'She has.'

'From it we know that Sir James was heading north along the canal bank that morning. Where do you suppose he was going?'

'To the aqueduct and back, presumably.'

Gow sighed. 'That, ma'am, is what he told Miss Pursglove. We know it is not what he did. I'm advised that a man wishing to catch the first train to London and setting off from here on foot might well find it quicker, and certainly less conspicuous, to walk up the canal to Bathampton, rather than go over the hill into Bath. From Bathampton, he could catch a stopper to Chippenham and connect there with the fast train to London.'

'I'm afraid I couldn't say, Inspector.'

'Take my word for it, ma'am, it is so. He could have been on his way to Newmarket before you were even awake.'

'Or on his way virtually anywhere else.'

'Quite so. But we do have evidence of rather closer links between Quinn and your husband than you had cause to suspect.'

'Such as?'

'Quinn had in his possession documents relating to a bank account in Zurich: an account held jointly in three names, of which Quinn's was one and your husband's another. Did you know of the existence of such an account?'

'No, I did not.'

'The balance is a very healthy one, to judge by the statements we found in Quinn's safe: tens of thousands of pounds, in fact, with more being deposited regularly. Can you suggest where the money might be coming from?'

'No.'

'Not, I'll warrant, from a gold mine in New Zealand. I think the source is rather closer to home, don't you?'

'I've really no idea.'

'But your husband was one of the depositors, ma'am.'

'My husband does not discuss his financial affairs with me, Inspector.'

'I daresay, but the date the account was opened is interesting: the fifth of September this year. I gather from your sister that Sir James was in Zurich around that time. Can you confirm that?'

'The three of us were there around then, yes.'

'So your husband would have had the opportunity to open such an account in person?'

'I really –'

'But he never discusses his financial affairs with you.' Gow smiled.

'I'm sorry. It quite slipped my mind. Of course he doesn't. What about his other affairs?'

'I beg your pardon?'

'The third name in which the Zurich account is held is that of a woman, ma'am: Miss M. Devereux. Do you know the lady?'

'No.'

'The name means nothing to you?'

Constance's mouth set in a determined line. 'Nothing at all, Inspector.' But the colour that had come to her face suggested a different answer.

X.

The first snowfall of winter had come to the grounds of Ticehurst Asylum in its sheltered fold of the Sussex Weald. No bird sang in the powdered privets, nor wind stirred the festooned firs. Even the ivy-clad façade of Ticehurst House wore a beard of white to complete the scene of frozen strangeness.

Down a long straight path leading away from the house towards the distant roof of an ornamental pagoda, two men walked at a sombre pace, hats pulled well down over their ears, greatcoat collars turned up round their chins, the snow crunching beneath their feet in time with their strides. One was William Trenchard, an inmate of the asylum. The other was Abel Kitson, his attendant. To the untrained eye, however, they would have appeared like two friends of similar backgrounds and tastes discussing the ways of the world during an afternoon stroll. Kitson himself, had he been asked, would readily have admitted that Trenchard was neither well-bred nor addle-brained enough to fit readily into the bizarre but ordered society of Ticehurst.

Nor would he have needed to look far for examples of the type of inmate Trenchard clearly was not. Beyond the rhododendron hedge that lined the path, the Reverend Sturgess Phelps and Lord Tristram Benbow were currently engaged in a snowballing contest, the Reverend Phelps having temporarily forgotten his oft-voiced conviction that he had been unfrocked as a result of an Anglo-Catholic conspiracy (affecting the highest reaches of Church and State) in order to indulge the forty-eight-year-old Lord Tristram's unshakeable belief that he was still a boy of twelve.

'Do I take it, Mr T,' Kitson said, smiling as a stray snowball arced across their path, 'that you're shortly to be leaving us?'

'What makes you think so, Abel?'

'Well, you've been looking around the grounds this afternoon with what I can only describe as an expectation of nostalgia.'

'Hah!' Trenchard clapped Kitson on the shoulder. 'Why the devil does Newington employ doctors in this place when you could give him all the psychological insights he needs?'

'Because, Mr T, I'm too busy playing the double bass at his musical teas to play the doctor as well.'

'You're wasted, Abel, believe me.'

'You admit the diagnosis is correct, then?'

'Perhaps. I have hopes, as you know.'

'More than hopes, I should say.'

'I assure you –'

'Two visitors in as many days, one a solicitor? The signs are clear, Mr T, crystal clear.'

'Richard Davenall comes every month. As for my brother – '

'Brother?' Now it was Kitson's turn to laugh aloud. 'That man was no brother of yours.'

'How would you know?'

'Call it a psychological insight.'

Suddenly, bursting on to the path between the rhododendrons in a scatter of snow and a cloud of frosting breath, came the crouched and black-clad figure of the Reverend Sturgess Phelps. 'You two!' he cried at sight of them. 'Which way did he go?'

'If you mean Lord Tristram . . .,' Kitson began.

'Not Lord Tristram, you dolt,' Phelps screeched. 'The stranger!'

'I'm afraid we haven't –'

'He's a Puseyite spy, not a doubt of it! But never fear: he won't escape me!' With that, Phelps lurched away through the bushes.

Kitson watched the troubled priest describe a purposeful zig-zag away across the snow-covered lawns, before deciding, on balance, that he would come to no harm. When he looked back along the path, he saw that Trenchard had gone ahead and was standing now on the wooden verandah of the pagoda, gazing out to the south across the white-wreathed countryside.

402

'Looking for something, Mr T?' Kitson said, on catching him up.

'Waiting more than looking, Abel. Tomorrow is the twenty-ninth, isn't it?'

'I believe it is.'

'What time do you think it'll get light?'

'Between eight and half-past, I should say.'

Trenchard nodded thoughtfully. 'A little over sixteen hours, then.'

'Who was he, Mr T, your mysterious visitor? Not your brother: you've described him to me before, and that fellow who came here yesterday didn't match him by a mile. So who was he? He spent nearly all day with you. You must have had a lot to talk about.'

'We did, Abel. We did.'

'But you're not going to tell me what, are you?'

Trenchard smiled ruefully. 'No, I'm not.'

Kitson clicked his tongue in mock disappointment. 'After all you've confided in me.'

'Don't take it to heart, Abel. What he told me I can't tell another living soul.'

Trenchard did not exaggerate. He was bound to silence by the most solemn of promises. Two days before, he would have dismissed the idea of keeping a secret for Sir James Davenall as absurd, yet he had since agreed to do just that. For now he knew the truth – and knew also that it could never be told.

'What do you want with me?' he remembered demanding, when he had seen who was waiting for him in the empty visiting-room: not his brother, as he had been informed, but the tall, slim, irksomely elegant, infernally cool figure of Sir James Davenall. 'Come to gloat, have you?'

'Far from it.'

'Then, why have you come?'

'Because I want to tell you freely what I've tried till now to prevent you finding out at all costs: the truth. I want to confess, you might say.'

It was a trick, Trenchard had felt certain, some vile twisted scheme to increase his agony of mind. 'Confess that you're not James Davenall, you mean?'

'Exactly.'

Still Trenchard had believed Norton was taunting him. 'You want to provoke me into making accusations which will be taken as further proof of my insanity. That's it, isn't it?'

'No. It isn't.'

'It must be. Constance has married you, hasn't she?'

'Yes. Five days ago.'

'Believing you to be James?'

'Yes.'

'Then, what do you mean by coming here now and admitting you're

403

not? Is it because we're alone, without witnesses, because I'm a certified lunatic whose word counts for less than nothing? Is that why you feel free to torment me? Damn you, Norton, you've taken my wife and my liberty – isn't that enough?'

'Yes. It's enough. Enough to make you the one man entitled to hear the truth from my own lips. You're not mad. We both know that. And now I'm prepared to tell the world so. To end your confinement here. On one condition.'

Trenchard had not dared to believe release was possible. Yet he could not have denied that, if any man could bring it about, it was Norton. 'What condition?'

'Hear me out. That's all I ask. Listen to what I have to say. As to witnesses, when I've finished I think you'll be glad there aren't any.'

And so Trenchard had been. Now, as he heard again in his mind Norton's long and calmly told story, the story he had heard in silence as they sat together in that dismal room, he was more certain than ever that Norton was right: it must remain secret for ever.

'My real name is Stephen Alexander Lennox. I was born at Murris-moyle, County Mayo, on the twenty-eighth of July 1843. My father, Andrew Lennox, was agent for the Carntrassna estate of Sir Lemuel Davenall, whose estranged wife Mary lived in Carntrassna House whilst he remained in England. My parents were both Scottish by birth. They had married, and kept a farm, in Scotland before moving to Ireland in 1840.

'Although my earliest memories of Mayo date from the famine years, when the peasantry died in their thousands and most of those who survived fled across the Atlantic, I can only recollect a carefree, not to say cosseted, childhood, insulated in my nursery at Murris-moyle from the tragedy unfolding about me. Not until Denzil O'Shaughnessy became my tutor and shared with me his knowledge of the world and its ways, did I begin to understand how privileged my upbringing was.

'Privilege, however, did not extend to warmth. My father was a cold remote figure to me, and my mother, though affectionate at times, could as often lapse into timid tight-lipped reserve. They gave me every comfort and advantage, yet seemed to take no pleasure in doing so. It was strange indeed to see the tenants on the estate raising large and happy broods of children in turf-hutted squalor whilst I grew up in pampered joyless solitude.

'Only when I had grown to manhood did the contradictions of my early life become apparent to me. At the time, I did not wonder why I should be educated at home rather than banished to a distant school. Nor did it ever occur to my mind that my father treated me more as a dutiful guardian would than a loving parent.

'I was told of my father's decision to emigrate, like all of his decisions, without warning. I was sixteen at the time and hopeful of winning a place at Trinity College, Dublin. Our sudden removal to Canada, and thence to the United States, came as a complete and far from welcome surprise. Nor was I given any explanation of the move. There had been no disagreement with Lady Davenall – that I could discover. It was simply that my father had somehow acquired sufficient money to warrant our making a new and independent life elsewhere.

'And a new life it certainly was. We moved to New York, where my father bought a vineyard on the north shore of Long Island and an elegant house near Port Jefferson. How he financed or conceived his transition into the wine trade I did not understand, but, at first, he prospered and was able to send me to Yale to complete my education. A year there converted me into an arrogantly well-educated young man happy to forget his obscure Irish origins.

'I think I would have qualified as an attorney and gone on to practise the law with some success had the Civil War not broken out in 1861 and the Union Army claimed me for the duration. I emerged after four years altered for ever by the experience, as were so many of my fellow-recruits, grown harder in some ways, more vulnerable in others, wiser as I thought, yet more fallible as I later discovered.

'My father urged me to join him in business, where he was greatly in need of help, the war having disrupted the wine trade to a ruinous extent. But I would have none of it. An army friend, Casey Garnham, had gone back to Oregon to run his father's newspaper, the Portland *Packet*, and had invited me to join him as a partner. Imagining my father's plight to be exaggerated, I accepted Casey's offer with alacrity.

'The challenge and excitement of the years that followed are hard now to recall. Neither Casey nor I realized that we were to preside over the *Packet*'s decline and ultimate demise. We truly believed it could survive and prosper. By the time events had shown that we were wrong, it was too late to turn to my father for help. He had gone bankrupt in 1866 and had died three years later, leaving my mother to live alone in a rented house in Worcester, Massachusetts. Nor was there much I could do to relieve her situation, my commercial inadequacies being by then as obvious as my father's.

'After the final collapse of the *Packet* in 1872, I remained in journalism, for it was the only work I knew, but the days of my editorial pretensions were gone. I had to learn the craft of a reporter over again on the staff of half a dozen newspapers from Portland to San Francisco. It was a hard and humbling life, but not an unworthy one. Indeed, I believe it is a life I would have led to this day had I not been so unfortunate as to meet and fall in love with Miss Madeleine Devereux.

'You know her, of course, by other names. Marion Whitaker.

405

Melanie Rossiter. You know her by all the dreamed and half-formed tempting visions she cared to plant in your receptive mind. And so, for that matter, do I. She was beautiful, yes. She was young and desirable, certainly. She had a quick and subtle mind gifted in all the arts of fascination, it is true. Yet you may set all of that on one scale and still it will not outweigh what rests on the other: the dark enfolding mystery of what, in her, could always conquer reason.

'I met her in San Francisco in 1878. She was barely twenty-one and already a rising politician's mistress. He was Howard Ingleby, a candidate for the state governorship. I was working for the Sacramento *Star*, whose editor was running an energetic anti-Ingleby campaign and had instructed me to seek out anything that might discredit the man. When I learned that he spent less time with his wife and family in Sacramento than he did with an expensive mistress in San Francisco, I felt certain that the story would be the breaking of Ingleby and the making of me.

'I confronted Madeleine at her apartment overlooking San Francisco Bay about a week before the elections. I had learned that she was a pretty, quick-witted actress who might have been called a whore had it not been for the eminence and respectability of her clients. I had visions of persuading or paying her to confess for the benefit of the *Star*'s readers, thus blasting Ingleby's prospects.

'But to be with her, as you now know, is to forget every resolution, however firm. To be with her is to begin a dream which only she can complete. Thus no exposé of her life with Howard Ingleby was ever written, and he, though he lost the election, did not have me to blame for his defeat. Madeleine won my silence by the same method she has always used to achieve her aims: a brief taste of her pleasures and a distant promise of more.

'For the next three years, Madeleine Devereux obsessed me. She had deluded me into believing she would one day be mine, but only the force of my infatuation with her sustained such a hope. It was cruelly obvious to me, in rational moments, that, without money and position, I could no more possess her than I could the stars in the sky.

'I have spoken of being in love with Madeleine, and so I thought I was, but now I see that love was strangely absent from the many ways in which she drew me to her. The ruthless edge to her carnality inspired not adoration but a form of worship, in which jealousy and self-loathing were more often felt than mere desire. What made her as she was I never discovered, for she was as silent about her past as she was expansive about her future. She came to look upon me, I suspect, as somebody with whom she could relax because she owed me nothing: amusing company for an idle hour.

'By the spring of 1881, I was living and working in San Francisco, the Sacramento *Star* and I having long since parted company.

Madeleine had discarded Ingleby about a year before and now divided her attentions between a wealthy hotelier and a shipping magnate. On the few occasions when she consented to see me, she tormented me. When she refused to see me, it was worse. I knew that to go on pursuing her was futile and foolish. Nevertheless, I went on. To you, at least, I need not explain why.

'One day, as I was leaving the newspaper offices, I was approached by a stranger who identified himself as Alfred Quinn and asked me to give him a few minutes of my time. Thinking he might have a story to sell, I went with him to a nearby bar and heard him out.

'I did not recognize Quinn, but he recognized me. He had been in the service of the Davenall family for more than twenty years and had accompanied Sir Gervase to Carntrassna in 1859; it was from that visit that he remembered me. He had expended much time and effort in finding me, my mother having died the previous year and having maintained, besides, no connections with Carntrassna that I knew of. Quinn refused to say how he had traced me, and I could not imagine any reason why he should have wanted to do so, until, that is, he outlined the plan he had devised.

'You know what Quinn's plan was. You suspected something of the kind from the first. He showed me photographs of James Davenall, missing heir to the baronetcy, and I was taken aback by the similarity: they might have been photographs of me. Quinn explained that the resemblance was not so very surprising, since I was James Davenall's half-brother. My mother had succumbed to Sir Gervase's charms during a visit to Carntrassna in 1842 and I was the issue of their brief liaison. My father had been persuaded to raise me as his own by Lady Davenall, who had known how matters stood from the first. She it was who had insisted I should have a good education and she it was who had paid for it. Sir Gervase had remained ignorant of my existence until his next visit to Carntrassna, in 1859. Horrified by my resemblance to his legitimate son and fearful that the relationship might become generally known, he had paid my father a great deal of money to emigrate, taking me with him.

'So at last did many things become clear to me: my father's lack of paternal feeling; the care he nevertheless lavished on me; the source of the money with which he had set himself up in America; my mother's nervous guilt-ridden silences. Not that any of it seemed to matter much any more. The people involved were all dead, their secrets and their sins long forgotten. So why had Quinn come halfway round the world to seek me out? Not to square the account for his dead master, that was certain. His reason, it emerged, was rooted very much in the present and in our mutual profit.

'The James Davenall I so closely resembled had been missing, presumed dead, since 1871. Were he to reappear, he could claim the wealth, property and title recently inherited by his younger brother. Quinn's proposal was that, armed with his considerable knowledge of the family, I should pass myself off as James Davenall and thus make both of us rich men. Sir Gervase and my parents were dead. So, Quinn told me, was old Lady Davenall. Nobody but he and I knew the truth of the matter. We stood to gain a fortune. In his judgement, we could scarcely fail.

'My first inclination was to reject the idea as madness. A striking physical resemblance was one thing, but even Quinn could not know all that I would need to know in order to carry it off. Besides, was not the so-called Tichborne Claimant even then rotting in an English gaol for attempting a similar fraud? Quinn conceded that he was, but insisted we might learn from his mistakes. I would spend a year constructing a new life far from San Francisco under an assumed name. Quinn, for his part, would find out why James Davenall might have wanted to commit suicide. We would prepare for every eventuality, guard against every challenge, research every aspect of the dead man's life. Only when absolutely certain of our ground would we act. And then we would be sure to win.

'It was when I asked for time to think that Quinn must have sensed he had me. Indeed, I cannot rid myself of the suspicion that he knew all along the most compelling reason why I might accept. It was not merely that I had little to lose and much to gain. It was that I finally had something to tempt Madeleine away from her tame politicians and fawning businessmen. It was a prize to eclipse anything she might hope to attain in California. I could offer to make her the wife of an English baronet.

'The longer I delayed giving Quinn my final answer, the likelier it became that he would have the answer he wanted. Whatever the cause – my emotionally starved childhood, the disorientating effects of the war, Madeleine's morbid influence – the fact remained that I was drifting towards a lonely and penurious middle age. Quinn's plan, however hazardous, offered the only chance I was ever likely to have of a new and better life.

'Even so, I hesitated. It was not that my conscience deterred me from entering upon a criminal conspiracy. After all, I *was* Sir Gervase Davenall's eldest son. In that sense, I would only be claiming what was rightfully mine. What held me back was the fear of failure, a dread not so much of arrest and imprisonment as of discovering that I was neither brave enough nor clever enough to sustain the pretence.

'Accordingly, I let Madeleine make up my mind for me. Before meeting Quinn again, I went to her and told her everything. I invited her to join the conspiracy. I asked her if she would agree to become my wife in the event that I succeeded in obtaining the baronetcy and the wealth that went with it.

'Had Madeleine turned me down, I would have rejected Quinn's proposal. Then none of what has followed would ever have happened. I wish now, with all my heart, that she had done so. But she did not. She swept aside my every scruple and reservation. She granted me what I thought I wanted more than anything in the world: the promise that she would become my wife if I could become Sir James Davenall. In that moment, I realized for the first time that I would go through with it. In that moment, the conspiracy was truly born.

'To my surprise, Quinn raised no objections to Madeleine's involvement. I had expected him to be reluctant to take a third party into his confidence, especially when that third party was a woman, but instead the two of them established an immediate affinity which I found utterly baffling. Recently, I have come to realize that they recognized in each other the same streak of ruthless remorseless cunning that marked them both out from the rest of weaker-willed humanity. At the time, I merely resented the ease with which Quinn convinced Madeleine that he could provide all the information we would need.

'Not that there was any doubt of his thoroughness. He had brought a dozen different photographs of James Davenall with him, innumerable samples of his handwriting on letters, cheques and bills, tie-pins and cufflinks he had owned, even a silver cigarette-case monogrammed with his initials. There were photographs also of every living member of the Davenall family. There were several pictures of Constance, as well as of her brother, sister and parents. There were notes of James's measurements, the sizes he took in hats, shirts, trousers and shoes, significant dates in his life, his academic and sporting record at school and university, group photographs of classes, clubs, teams and societies to which he had belonged, together with the names of fellow-members. There was even a copy of the suicide note he had written on the seventeenth of June 1871. Nothing was left to chance.

'Quinn was not prepared to say how he had amassed such a wealth of detailed information. It was apparent, however, that he must have been assembling it prior to his dismissal by Lady Davenall, so resentment of the way she had treated him could not have prompted his approach to me.

'For the present, though, I had more to think about than what Quinn's motives really were. I had to practise James Davenall's handwriting and signature for hours on end. I had to be coached by Quinn in the way his former master walked and talked, his favourite expressions, his commonest mannerisms. I had to persuade a dentist to remove a healthy tooth from my mouth to match James's loss of one. I had to grow a beard and take up cigarette-smoking. All these characteristics, added to my existing similarity to James in weight, height and appearance, made the match as near perfect as could be.

'There was ample time in which to grow accustomed to my new identity during the year I spent working for an advertising agency in Philadelphia. To do so was to make a virtue of necessity, since it was essential to establish a plausible background from which I could in due course emerge as James Davenall, alias Norton. I saw little of Quinn and Madeleine during this time. For safety's sake, we communicated mostly by letter. They spent six months in England, gathering material, notably regarding James Davenall's health, which Quinn felt sure held the clue to his reasons for killing himself. By manoeuvring Madeleine into Dr Fiveash's employment, they were able to discover the truth of the matter. It was then that we hit upon a spontaneous recovery from syphilis as a satisfactory explanation for my reappearance. I was accordingly dispatched to Paris to procure a clean bill of health.

'By the summer of 1882, Quinn had decided we were ready to act. When his message reached me that my year of suspended animation was over, I felt less alarm than relief at the prospect of attempting at last what I had so long planned. There never was a time when I wanted to return to the life I had led in San Francisco. Indeed, I had rehearsed my performance as James Davenall so exhaustively that it no longer seemed a performance at all. In the guise of James Norton and through the months of his cautious painstaking life in Philadelphia, my dead unmet half-brother and I acquired a strange and potent unity. At first only fleetingly, but later for hours at a stretch, I could blank from my mind all awareness of my true past and my real identity. I could become the man I would shortly claim to be.

'I booked my passage from New York in the name of James Norton of Philadelphia and arrived in Liverpool on the sixteenth of September 1882, feeling as ready as I possibly could for the challenge ahead. From now on, every step had to be taken carefully. Madeleine met me in Birkenhead and we travelled to Chester, where we stayed for three days in a hotel as Mr and Mrs Brown, reviving our American accents in order to mislead the staff whilst rehearsing in private the details of my claim.

'I had not seen Madeleine in months, and those few days in Chester were, in fact, the longest time I had ever spent with her. I had looked forward to our reunion as would a hungry man to the end of a fast; but, strangely, when it came to it, I realized that our enforced separation had in some way broken her spell over me. She remained as beautiful and entrancing as ever, but her body and her mind retained for me too few secrets to reassert their former hold. Whether Madeleine sensed as much I cannot say, for, if she had, she would have taken every care to ensure she did not reveal it, but certain it was that something had changed – or been changed – between us.

'From Chester, we went our separate ways. I travelled to London and booked into the Great Western Hotel, feeling on arrival much as I imagined James Davenall would had he truly been returning. I made no attempt to contact Quinn, even though Madeleine had told me how to do so, for we had agreed that I should henceforth proceed as far as possible alone. The money she had passed on to me from him was ample for my immediate purposes and remained so, later, even in the face of enormous legal costs. Quinn knew, of course, that he would be repaid several times over if we succeeded, but how he amassed the capital to finance my claim I was never told.

'It had been agreed that I would first show my hand by visiting Cleave Court on the twenty-sixth of September, ten days after my arrival in England. That allowed me a week of solitude in London, passed mainly in my hotel room, ingraining the personality that I was about to assume into my very soul. I stood endlessly in front of the mirror, mouthing and practising what I would say and how I would say it. I sat at the desk filling page after page with my altered style of writing, repeating over and again the signature of James Davenall. I visited Wapping and constructed to my own satisfaction a detailed version of what had happened there on the last night in the life of the man I was about to become. Under cover of darkness, I walked to Chester Square and looked at Bladeney House, matching windows to the layout of rooms Quinn had described and listing in my mind the paintings that had hung on the staircase, and still hung, in the order James Davenall would remember.

'Then, just before midnight on the twenty-fifth of September, I burned all my notes and lists and records: everything, in short, that an impostor would have about him. The following morning, I left the hotel, caught a train to Bath and recommenced a dead man's life. On the twenty-sixth of September 1882, James Davenall was reborn.

'At first, all my painstaking preparations seemed to have been in vain. The Davenall family set their faces against me and I had always known that, without the acknowledgement of at least one person who had been close to James Davenall, my physical resemblance to him and my knowledge of his affairs would count, in the end, for nothing. There seemed nothing else for it then but to try my luck with Constance. Had just one of the Davenalls accepted me, I like to think I would have left her in peace. But it was not to be.

'Quinn had surmised all along that Constance would be susceptible and he was proved correct. He had told me of her secret meeting with James at the aqueduct, information which I used to make an immediate impression on her. Knowing why James could not explain his reasons gave me a crucial advantage, but, from the moment I set eyes on her, I saw there was more to it than that. She wanted to believe I was James badly enough to overcome any reservations. And why? Because she had passed seven years of sedate and uneventful married life wondering what might have been if only James had not killed himself. Desire, you see, is at the root of all conviction. The Davenalls wanted James to be dead. Constance wanted him to be alive.

'From the first, I must tell you, there was also something uncanny about Constance's belief in me, something that stemmed as much from me as from her. A sympathy for James's plight when he had to abandon the woman he loved for her own sake became something more when I saw how poignant Constance still found memories of those times. Initially, I kept the emotion within strict bounds, knowing that to feel affection for her would only be to hamper my efforts to deceive her. But the portents of a stronger bond persisted. How did I guess the means by which she had sought to persuade James not to run away? There is no sure answer save in the strange pervading confidence I felt in all my dealings with her; no answer, that is, but for the intuition that often grows with love.

'Still and all, it was certain that Constance would not testify for me in court if you forbade her to do so and, without her testimony, my prospects were bleak. Her withdrawal to Salisbury gave me some hope, but it proved groundless. The only course open to me appeared to be to subpoena her, but to have done so would have been to break a promise and something else, along with it, of even greater value. There had to be another way, and I was determined to find it.

'A few days before the hearing, I met Quinn at his hideaway in Deptford and put to him my plan: that if we could discredit you in Constance's eyes she might be persuaded to speak up for me. I had expected Quinn to favour subpoenaing her, but it transpired that he was worried by your attempts to trace him and was therefore keen to move against you. Your eagerness to prove a connection between him and Marion Whitaker was what prompted him to suggest that Madeleine would be ideally placed to spring the trap.

'I deliberately refrained from enquiring into the methods Madeleine chose, but, when I read your account of how Melanie Rossiter had deceived you, it became clear just how effective those methods were.

'Quinn knew Sir Gervase was slowly dying of syphilis long before his family. He had it, as he had much else that was later of use to him, from his master's own mouth. To relieve the symptoms, Sir Gervase became a regular user of laudanum. Later, when the dosage had become heavy as well as regular and recourse to it an addiction no longer strictly related to his ills, Quinn became his accomplice, buying and frequently administering the drug. Thus he became familiar with its effects not only on the senses but also on the imagination. And Madeleine became his willing pupil.

'It was opium, not madness, that deceived you that night, Trenchard. Madeleine slipped some either into the food you ate or the whisky you drank. She came to you while you were asleep and under the drug's influence. She planted ideas in your mind, which, in the receptive state of your imagination, expanded into the visions which later seemed to confirm your insanity. She lured you to her bed so that, when Constance came in answer to your telegram, she would find you there.

'I wish I could let you off as lightly as that, for all that you tried to kill me, but I fear you cannot be rid of the experience so easily. Opium cannot create desires, it can only expand them. In other words, what the drug made you believe you were doing was what you secretly wanted to do. She is still in your mind, is she not? She is still, in some world of wishes you can neither confess nor fulfil, all and more than she was that night.

'At the time, of course, all I wanted to know was that the plan had succeeded. Horrified by your apparent betrayal of her, Constance came to me and volunteered to testify on my behalf. The gamble had paid off. Only when I saw you pointing that gun at me in the hour of my triumph did I realize that it had paid off too well.

'But I survived. Call it luck if you will, but reflect as you do how fickle an ally luck can be. It preserved me that day, yes, but only to make of me its perpetual plaything. And you, Trenchard? Did you think I was your enemy? I have never been that. I bore you no ill will for what you did. I would have done the same. Perhaps, indeed, I may be about to emulate you. It was not merely to spare Constance's feelings that I had you sent here rather than to prison or some squalid institution for the criminally insane. It was also to spare my own.

'As I slowly recovered my health under Constance's devoted care, I came to see the ultimate contradiction in the method I had chosen by which to win her to my cause. I had supplanted you in her affections so completely that she now wanted what I had implied could be hers without reservation: a future as the wife of James Davenall, her first and only true love. To pile complication on contradiction, I realized that she, too, had supplanted another. Madeleine's hold over me had withered in the face of what I had come to feel for Constance. For she had given me something Madeleine never could: happiness.

'To make matters worse, I had time aplenty in which to indulge my new-found state. Madeleine expected me to sustain Constance's belief that I would marry her until my claim had finally been upheld. Only then would she require me to abandon Constance and make her my wife instead. This, I knew, would be an unalterable condition. She might be piqued that I no longer cared for her, but no more than that. What she would not accept was my refusal to give her the social status she craved. That would be the sticking-point. For months to come, I could delay the choice; but, sooner or later, it would have to be made.

'Not that there was ever any real doubt as to what my choice would

413

be. Even had I not grown to love Constance, I would still have felt incapable of abandoning her. To inspire love in another is to breed it in oneself; to betray it becomes unthinkable. Therefore my vows to Constance were always bound to take precedence over my promises to Madeleine.

'As soon after the trial as it could decently be arranged, I took Constance and Emily on a European tour. I dare say Richard told you of it. To Constance it seemed an agreeable way of passing the months until we could marry. To me it was a way of delaying still further the confrontation with Madeleine. Not that it achieved its purpose, for she followed us wherever we went, never showing herself openly but ensuring I knew she was close at hand, waiting impatiently for me to honour our bargain. At last, in Florence, we met and there I told her that I could not marry her.

'I knew she would be angry. I could hardly blame her, after all, when I who had gained the baronetcy denied her the share of it she had been promised. She tried every argument she knew to sway me. She even offered me the affection of which I knew her to be incapable. But I, as I believed, held the trump card. Now that the world recognized me as Sir James Davenall, I was beyond her reach. I no longer needed her help. Now that I was a wealthy man, she was welcome to as much money as she wanted, but her claim against me ended there.

'Or so I thought. When Madeleine threatened me with dread but unnamed consequences if I married Constance, I thought she was bluffing. I truly believed she could no longer touch me. But I was wrong. Madeleine Devereux's threats are never empty. The consequences she spoke of were real enough and more dreadful than I could ever have imagined.

'Meanwhile, however, there was peril from a different quarter. The steps we had taken to cover my tracks in the United States ensured that nobody could connect James Norton of Philadelphia with Stephen Lennox of San Francisco unless I let slip that I knew something of Lennox's life. To guard against this, I took advantage of Hugo's decision to involve Prince Napoleon by reminding him of a scandalous episode in his past. Quinn had learned from Sir Gervase in a moment of opium-induced candour that he had fathered a child by his wife's governess. What better false clue to plant in my opponents' minds, therefore, than information which might imply I was that child? Only Richard seemed to see through it. What first made him suspect that he had been wrong to change his mind about me I do not know, but certain it is that by February of this year he had begun to harbour serious doubts about my identity and to connect them with events at Carntrassna. He returned to the subject over and again, like a dog to his bone, seemingly with even greater energy after the trial than before.

'It was Richard who inadvertently acquainted me with a disturbing truth: Quinn had lied. In the spring of 1881, he had told me that Mary Davenall was already dead, but from Richard I learned that she had not actually died until February 1882, whilst I was in Philadelphia, and even then not of natural causes. To the obvious conclusion – that Quinn had murdered her – I did not care to devote too much attention. I would never have embarked upon the conspiracy had I known she was still alive, as Quinn must have realized, but it was too late to turn back now. What struck me most forcefully was that her killing constituted the one flaw in a plan I had thought till then was genuinely flawless. It was what finally persuaded Richard that the truth was to be found in Ireland. Had Mary Davenall died in her sleep at the age of eighty, he would never have insisted on visiting Carntrassna. And, if he had not gone there, he would never have found Denzil O'Shaughnessy.

'I was helpless to intervene in Richard's enquiries and could only hope he would return empty-handed. Instead, my worst fears were confirmed. He came back to tell me that he would not permit me to marry Constance until I had faced O'Shaughnessy.

'There seemed nothing for it but to try to brazen it out. I had no cause to think O'Shaughnessy would fail to recognize me, but I knew that to refuse to meet him would mean certain ruin. Nor could I flee without admitting my guilt. Therefore, hoping against hope that I could in some way retain Constance's love, I stood my ground.

'Before the meeting took place, I warned both of my co-conspirators that the game was almost certainly up. Quinn neither admitted nor denied that he had murdered Mary Davenall, but he did make it clear that he believed he could survive my fall well enough. He had drawn sufficient capital from the Davenall estate since I had gained control of it to ensure a comfortable future and was confident our connection could never be proved. My exposure had become a loss he could afford to bear.

'So, alone and, as I thought, deserted, I faced O'Shaughnessy in Richard's study last Saturday and nerved myself to bear the inevitable. Unaccountably, however, O'Shaughnessy spared me. It was clear from the first that he knew me, yet he lied about a scar I had never had in order to prove to the satisfation of all that I was not Stephen Lennox.

'Why he took mercy on me I could not guess and, in the circumstances, could scarcely ask. The effect of his doing so, however, was unmistakable. It cut the ground from beneath my accusers' feet. What they had thought would prove I was not Sir James Davenall proved the exact opposite beyond further doubt. My new identity was not merely intact, when I had feared it would lie in ruins about me. It had become impregnable.'

'A friend of yours, was he?' said Abel, after they had stood beneath the eaves of the pagoda for some while in silence.

Trenchard looked at him as if he had not heard the question, as if his

415

thoughts had been so firmly fixed elsewhere that they had difficulty in adjusting to the present.

'Your visitor. The one you can't tell me anything about. I should have thought you could at least say whether he was a friend or not.'

'I didn't think he was. Now I'm not so sure.'

'Why? What's changed?'

'Nothing. Nothing at all.' Trenchard gazed into the distance. 'But it soon will. Tomorrow, to be exact. Tomorrow, everything will change.'

XI

It was late afternoon when Richard Davenall arrived back in London, but he felt tired enough for it to have been midnight. Every turn in his pursuit of James, from the moment he had begun it more than a year before, had led him down a twisting road to nowhere. Was everybody lying to him? Or were they as helpless as he was himself?

Sure of nothing any more, save that, as ever, James was several steps ahead of him, Richard headed for Highgate. Already, night was threatening, the third night of Sir James Davenall's disappearance, and Richard felt weary to the very fibre of his being. In the solitude of his home, he might hope at least to find some rest.

But it was not to be. Braddock greeted him with surprising news. 'Lady Davenall is waiting for you in the drawing-room, sir.'

'Constance is here?'

'No, sir. The elder Lady Davenall.'

Catherine had come to see him. She who was famous for her inflexibility had broken her own embargo. Perhaps James had written to her as well, Richard thought, as he hurried down the hall.

'Where is my son, Richard?' Nothing had changed. He could tell that by her expression. She had called because she wanted to know what he knew and for no other reason. The segment of the past they had shared would remain as distant as ever.

'Surely Inspector Gow told you that James –'

'My real son, Richard, not the man whom some are foolish enough to believe is my son. I am not remotely interested in *his* whereabouts. I am concerned about Hugo.'

'Hugo?'

'He has gone abroad. Do you know where – or for how long?'

'I've no idea. I didn't even know he was going.' He had, in truth, largely forgotten Hugo's doings since his visit to Carntrassna. The foolish young man was, he had dolefully assumed, drinking his days away in Duke Street.

416

'When did you last see him?'

'It must be several months ago.'

Catherine stepped closer and revealed a little of her hatred of him in her gaze. 'So much for your concern on his behalf. When his need was greatest, you turned your back on him.'

'That's not true.'

'Did you know he'd resigned from his club because that man Norton had been admitted?'

'No.'

'Have you visited him since he vacated Bladeney House?'

'No.'

'Then, how can you deny it? You deserted him – like everybody else.'

With this jibe, Catherine achieved what few ever had: she angered Richard, and he, too drained by all that he had endured to cling to appeasement, flung back a jibe of his own. 'You told me to leave him alone. If I *have* deserted him, it's been at your insistence.'

To that, Catherine had no answer. In the nearest she could come to an acknowledgement of guilt, she stepped back and looked away.

'Why did you think I would know where he'd gone?'

There was a strain now of weakness in her voice. 'I hoped you would, that's all. I'm worried about him, Richard. Worried about what he means to do.'

'What do you think he means to do?'

'I don't know. I came to London to talk to him about Norton's disappearance and what it might mean, only to find that he, too, had disappeared. Greenwood said he left early this morning, with Freddy Cleveland, bound for the Continent.'

'A long weekend in Paris: that's probably what they have in mind.'

'No. Greenwood told me that Norton visited Hugo late on Wednesday night.'

'He visited Hugo? On Wednesday?'

'Exactly. After his disappearance from Cleave Court. Greenwood can't be sure of the time, because he was in bed asleep, but he thinks it must have been in the small hours – two or three o'clock yesterday morning. He was woken by the sound of Hugo letting a visitor out of the front door. When he looked out of his window, he saw the visitor walking away down the street: he feels sure it was Norton. Hugo wasn't in when Greenwood went to bed, so he can't say whether they came in together or not. At all events, Hugo told him in the morning to pack a bag for him: sufficient for a few days. He was out for the rest of yesterday, then Freddy Cleveland collected him this morning and off they went.'

Richard put his hand on Catherine's arm, neither of them remarking or regretting the consoling gesture. 'With Freddy along, it can only be a holiday.'

'No. It's too much of a coincidence. They've gone to meet Norton, I

417

know it. Greenwood told me something else. Hugo's been practising target shooting for the past three months.'

'What?'

'Using Gervase's old duelling pistols. He's had them restored to working order, Richard. And when Greenwood showed me where he keeps them . . . they weren't there. Now do you understand?'

XII

Toby Leighton was seldom at his best before eight o'clock in the evening, especially when woken abruptly from a pre-dinner doze to be informed that a brusque-mannered relative of Hugo Davenall insisted on seeing him.

'Couldn't this have waited?' he plaintively enquired, on finding Richard Davenall pacing the carpet in his father's drawing-room.

'No, it could not. Where is Freddy Cleveland?'

'Freddy? Out of the country, I –'

'They told me at the club that you might know where he's gone.'

'Oh, yes.' Toby scratched his head. 'He did say something about it when I bumped into him last night.'

'Well?'

'Ostend, I think. Or was it Austria? No. Ostend, I'm sure of it.'

'Did he say when he would be back?'

'Tomorrow night, as far as I can remember. I suppose that proves it can't have been Aust –'

'Did he say why he was going?'

Toby frowned; the effort of recollection was painful. 'No. But, then, he –'

'Or who with?'

'No. Matter of fact, all he said was that he had to go. Duty called. Some such tomfool nonsense. I didn't pay much attention. But he wasn't happy about it, that I do remember. I've never seen him so damned po-faced about anything.'

Already, Richard Davenall was heading for the door, without so much as a thank-you.

'What's the hurry?' Toby called after him. 'Anyone would think it was a matter of life and death.'

TWENTY

I

Dawn came late to the Belgian coast on Saturday, 29th December 1883 and later still where the sea-mist was at its thickest, on the long, flat, dune-lagged shore that stretches north-east from Ostend to the Dutch border.

On the narrow coast road halfway between Ostend and Blankenberg, only one vehicle was visible at this early hour: a fly, occupied by a driver and two passengers, rattling along at such a pace as to suggest they were already late for an appointment. The passengers were Hugo Davenall and Freddy Cleveland, their only luggage a slender but weighty box presently shrouded beneath Freddy's cloak.

As the fly topped a minor eminence between the dunes, Hugo pulled a watch from his waistcoat pocket and squinted at its face. Then he glanced reproachfully at Freddy and said: 'We're going to be late.'

'It can't be helped, old man,' Freddy replied. 'This fellow's goin' hell for leather as it is. Besides, I thought you said Norton would wait until we arrived.'

'Oh, he'll wait.' Hugo's eyes narrowed. 'I just don't want him to think I've lost my nerve.'

The wonder, to Freddy's mind, was that Hugo's nerve had remained as steady as it had. More than twenty-four hours had passed since Norton's unexpected acceptance of his challenge, but Hugo's determination to go through with what Freddy viewed as an act of lunacy had shown no sign of faltering. Freddy had hoped Hugo might take fright even if he remained blind to reason, but not so. Throughout the previous day, he had been unnaturally calm in the face of what he proposed to do. Nor had a ferry trip from Dover and a night in an Ostend hotel dented his resolve. He would meet Norton, and there was an end of it.

This dawn journey along the eerily empty, mist-wrapped shore accordingly found Freddy the more nervous of the two. He should never have agreed to act as a second in the first place, never mind accompany Hugo to Belgium. He should have gone to a member of the Davenall family and had them intervene. Failing that, he should have gone to the police. But, at every stage, he had told himself nothing so very terrible could come of a duel. Hugo would call it off. Or Norton would. If the worst came to the worst, they would merely exchange shots at a safe distance with no harm done and call it quits. Their honour, whatever that was, would be satisfied and Freddy's mind relieved.

Now, gazing past Hugo at the grey sand beach beyond the dunes, lapped in slow and silent rhythm by the windless tide, Freddy felt nothing but a growing dread of the meeting which would shortly occur. When he looked back at Hugo, he scarcely felt he recognized his friend. Hugo's expression reminded him of the words which had dogged his thoughts during a sleepless night in Ostend, a fragment of Tennyson's *Idylls of the King,* forgotten since his days at Oxford but brought now irresistibly to mind.

' . . . there, that day when the great light of heaven
  Burn'd at his lowest in the rolling year,
  On the waste sand by the waste sea they closed.'

'What's that?' snapped Hugo.

Freddy started in his seat. He must have spoken the last words aloud. 'Nothin',' he replied. 'Nothin' at all, old man.'

Suddenly, Hugo's attention was diverted to a milestone at the side of the road. As they sped past it, he leaned out of the fly to read what it said. When he looked back at Freddy, he was smiling. 'Seven kilometres to Blankenberg,' he announced. 'So only five to the meeting-place.'

Freddy shuddered. In the flushed and twisted eagerness on his friend's face, he recognized at last what it truly was that he dreaded. Yesterday, in London, it had seemed the most absurd of fleeting suspicions. Now, as their fly jolted on towards its destination through the shifting salt-tanged fog, it had become a certainty he could no longer resist. There would be no compromise, no withdrawal of the challenge, no patching-up of the dispute, no token firing in the air. Hugo would ensure that this duel was fought to a finish.

II

A solitary cab sped past the shuttered houses lining Ostend's Kapelle-straat, the hoof-falls of its horse and the rattling of its wheels on the cobbles magnified in the grey twilight by the vestigial silence of night.

Inside the swaying, jolting cab sat Richard and Catherine Davenall, their pale drawn faces revealing the anxious hours they had both endured since discovering the reckless course their son had embarked upon. Less than an hour ago, the ferry that had brought them from Dover had docked. They had at once commenced an urgent tour of Ostend's hotels in search of the one where Hugo and Freddy were staying. At the third attempt, they had been successful, only for a bleary-eyed night porter to tell them that they were too late: the two young men had set off an hour since by hired fly towards Blankenberg.

'The porter said Freddy was carrying a small case,' Catherine murmured, in her first remark since leaving the hotel.

'I know,' Richard replied, 'and Blankenberg is a quiet spot among the sand dunes. But the journey will take them a good hour by fly. We can be there in half the time.' He had calculated that, if they could catch the train due to leave for Bruges in five minutes and connect there with a service to Blankenberg, they might yet forestall whatever madness Hugo was contemplating. He did not need to add that they had no way of knowing Hugo's precise destination, nor that dawn, the traditional hour for duels, was already upon them. He and Catherine were both well aware of how unlikely it really was that they would arrive in time.

'Poor Hugo,' Catherine said, as much, it seemed, to herself as to Richard. 'I had no idea he would feel driven to do such a thing as this.'

'Nor I,' came Richard's doleful reply. 'From what I was told at the club, he issued the challenge more than a month ago.'

'Why did Norton accept? What has he to gain by it? Surely he doesn't want to kill Hugo.'

'He may see it as a way of finally proving that he *is* James.'

'Nothing can prove that.'

'Not even risking his life for the sake of his brother's recognition?'

An expression flitted then across Catherine's face which suggested that, for the very first time, her certainty that Sir James Davenall was not her son had ceased to be absolute. But, as quickly as it had come, it was gone. 'No,' she said sternly. 'Not even that.'

'Then, we must hope and pray neither of them comes to any harm.'

'I am concerned only for Hugo.'

'You should not be. Consider what would happen . . . if either of them . . . ' Richard's voice petered into silence, as if he did not dare to tempt providence by saying what was in his mind. Ever since leaving London, he had been unable to dismiss from his thoughts the question of what the world would say if blood were shed in a fratricidal duel. And he had realized what had clearly not occurred to Catherine. To fight such a duel at all was to invite scorn. But to win was to court ruin.

III

On the tussocky summit of the last dune before a plain of Belgian sand reached towards the North Sea, Sir James Davenall sat smoking a cigarette and gazing into the mist-shrouded distance. Apart from a periodic motion of his arm as he raised the cigarette to his lips, he was perfectly still; immune, it seemed, to the bitter chill, content to wait calmly till the dawn brought him what he knew it must.

Striding back and forth across the sand at the foot of the dune was a second man: tall, black-caped and top-hatted, with a habit of tossing his head and sniffing loudly as he gazed impatiently around. A black goatee beard and harshly aquiline nose would have suggested a brutally autocratic nature even without the long scar running down one side of his face, which had snagged the right eyebrow in permanent semi-closure and showed now, in the ice-cold air, as a livid red against his white and wasted cheek.

Looking up at Sir James, the man drew the neck of a flask from an inner pocket and raised his unscarred left eyebrow. Several seconds passed, then Sir James shook his head. The man shrugged his shoulders and let the flask fall back into his pocket. Then he tossed his head, sniffed and said, in a heavily Germanic accent: 'A drink might steady your hand, Sir James.'

In answer, Sir James held his right arm out straight. The cigarette was rigid between his fingers, a length of ash undisturbed on its tip, the thin plume of its smoke unwavering in the windless air.

'The tide is coming in,' the other man continued. 'Do you think your brother will be very late?'

The hint of anxiety in his voice did not escape Sir James, who smiled faintly, as if to signal that he knew what had prompted it.

'Perhaps –'

Some upward dart of Sir James's gaze silenced him. He turned and saw, emerging from a rough track between the dunes on to the beach about fifty yards away, two men, one of whom was carrying something beneath his arm: a slender wooden case.

'Ah,' the man said, in unmistakable relief. 'So he has come after all.'

'Yes,' Sir James responded, breaking his long silence. 'He has come. So please remember what we agreed, Herr Major. I want no mistakes.'

'There will be no mistakes, Sir James, believe me. Everything will go according to plan.' At that, he smiled, though perhaps it was as well for Sir James's peace of mind that he could not see him do so, nor perceive therefore how much worse than a scowl a smile is on such a face.

IV

As the clock in his sitting-room at Ticehurst Asylum struck the half-hour, Trenchard rose from the chair where he had passed a sleepless night and moved towards the window. It was the same dull metallic note that had recorded all the many thousand other intervals of his confinement, but this time its accuracy was not wasted. This time, it did not remind him how little had changed; rather, how much was about to.

He threw open the curtains and stared out at the slowly waking world. No birds were soaring across the threatening sky, no figures moving on the cleared gravel of the drive. All was silent and immobile, imprisoned by the tensions of the night, held captive by his fore-knowledge of the day.

He glanced back at the clock. Another minute had passed, another fragment of Saturday 29th December 1883 had faded from its face. It was happening, he knew, even as he stood there in remote and unprotesting witness. On a beach, on the other side of the Channel . . . He knew, because Norton had told him.

'I did not expect to hear from Madeleine again. I assumed that my marriage to Constance would end her pursuit of me, that she would see the futility of further harassment, take what she thought she was due from the bank account I had opened in Zurich and so vanish from my life.

'On Christmas Day, however, three days after Constance and I had arrived at Cleave Court as Sir James and Lady Davenall, a letter was delivered to the house by unseen hand and brought in to me during tea. I recognized Madeleine's writing on the envelope at once, but opened it casually enough to persuade Constance that nothing was amiss.

'"Be at the Dundas aqueduct", it read, "at half-past eight tomorrow morning. Do not fail me this last time. M."

'What had prompted her to make such a demand of me I could not guess. My first inclination was not to go, if only because her choice of meeting-place seemed so needlessly pointed. Then I reflected that, if I did not meet her as she asked, she might come to the house. Though I could scarcely believe she would expose herself to the danger such a visit would entail, it was not a risk I could afford to take. Besides, she referred to it as a "last" meeting, and I could not help feeling that I owed her that much in view of my refusal to make her Lady Davenall.

'So, next morning, before dawn, I rose and slipped from the house, leaving Constance asleep. I intended to tell her later that I had gone for a walk, which would have seemed innocent enough. Certainly I had no doubt as I hurried down the drive that I would soon be back to calm

423

any fears that might have arisen in my absence. I even stopped for a word with Nanny Pursglove and told her that I would look in on my way back. I would be, I assured her, no more than half an hour.

'Then, as I strode north along the towpath, eager to reach the aqueduct and have done with the encounter, I saw him. It was a still, cold, misty morning, with neither sound nor movement on the canal to break the lifeless grip of winter. The water was a flat and unrelenting grey, the reeds along the bank sagging and forlorn, the trees beside the path stark and bare. There were no leaping fish or dabbling moorhens to flit across the edge of my vision. When I saw him, albeit at the margins of my sight, there could be no mistake. He was there.

'I had seen him twice before. In Salisbury Cathedral, when Canon Sumner had offered to pray for me, he had appeared opposite me in the choir-stalls. At Wapping Old Stairs, when I had retraced too well his final steps in this world, his body, drowned then as before, had floated into view. Now he had come again. A glimpsed figure on the opposite bank of the canal, keeping pace with me as I strode purposefully on, seeming not to hurry yet never falling back even when I accelerated.

'When I stopped, he stopped. When I went on, so did he. Whatever hope I had contrived to retain that he was not who I thought was dashed when I summoned my courage to turn and look directly across at him. For then the opposite bank was empty. Yet, when I turned away, he reappeared. He would not leave me, yet he would not let me face him.

'No, Trenchard, I am not mad. What do you or I know of him? What do we care about the man whose place in this world we both tried, in different ways, to take? Was he the man I portrayed for the benefit of a gullible jury? Or someone else, someone nobler and finer than I had any right to claim to be?

'When I first learned of what had driven him to suicide, do you know what I felt? I have told nobody till now. They would have thought it absurd. I felt proud of him. Perhaps it *is* absurd, but I felt proud of my brother James. What spurred me on, of course, was envy and ambition, but somewhere, buried deep, there was a wish to give some solemn form of meaning to his life – and to his death.

'I do not expect you to understand. But I think he understands. At first, I feared his visitations. Now I see the truth. They were his own fraternal gesture. He did not come to threaten me. He came to warn me.

'That is why he vanished when I turned the bend in the canal and saw Madeleine waiting for me on the aqueduct. Because then he knew that the warning was in vain. I would hear what she had to say.'

424

V

Freddy Cleveland glanced from one Davenall to the other. Hugo stood like a graven image, staring straight ahead, only the sound of his rapid shallow breaths betraying the turmoil he felt. James's responding stare, by contrast, was almost too casual to warrant the description, the only movement on his face being an occasional twitch at the side of his mouth that might have denoted a smile he would not permit to appear.

As for James's second, whom he had introduced as Major Reinhardt Bauer of the Austrian Imperial Army, Freddy had seldom set eyes on anyone he so instinctively distrusted. Scar-faced and sour-mouthed like some croaking bird of prey, he was here, Freddy wondered, for what? Amusement? Money? Or the satisfaction of a depraved taste for vicarious bloodshed?

Whatever the reason, Freddy knew it was one he could neither share nor respect. Wrenching his thoughts back to what seemed to be growing more inevitable with every moment, he struggled to recollect how he would normally have laughed aloud to see four gravely dressed and sombre-faced men standing on a remote and empty beach with the serious intention of observing a redundant code of honour. It could only be, he concluded, something in the time and place – this hour so grudgingly yielded by a cold grey winter's morning, this shoreline of limitless sea-rippled sand where infinity seemed almost tangible – that compelled him to play his obedient part. When he spoke, it was not to demand that his companions come to their senses, but to utter the only appeal to reason that the canons of duelling would allow.

'Major Bauer, does Sir James feel able to say anythin' that would placate my friend? I'm sure you agree it's not too late to patch up the quarrel.' But his words were sustained by the most unreasonable of hopes. Compromise was a drum to whose beat Major Bauer had never marched.

'Sir James, Herr Cleveland, has nothing to say. Naturally, if Herr Davenall were to make an unconditional apology and withdraw his slander against Sir James, we could –'

'Never!' Hugo put in sharply. 'I won't withdraw a damn thing.' Then he added, staring at James: 'This man is an impostor. Is that clear enough?'

'Clear enough', Bauer responded, 'to render further discussion useless, would you not agree, Herr Cleveland?' Then, taking Freddy's silence for affirmation, he went on: 'Perhaps, therefore, you would be so good as to open the case and let Sir James choose his weapon.'

VI

'Madeleine stood against the parapet, gazing down at the river where it wound through the mist-layered fields. She knew I had met Constance there fifteen months before. She knew because we had planned the meeting together. What we had not planned was how much the occasion would come to mean to me. So now, I suppose, she had chosen the place again, when winter had squeezed all colour and warmth from the setting, to remind me of how I had betrayed her.

'I leaned against the parapet and tried to look into her face, but she kept it averted, kept it trained on the river and the frosted meadows below. What seemed an age passed, though it cannot have been more than a minute, then she said softly: "So you came."

'"I came because your note called it 'this last time'."

'"Oh, it will be that, you may be sure."

'"If it's an apology you want –"

'"An apology?" Suddenly, she turned and stared straight at me. "You think you can apologize for marrying that woman in secret, when you had promised to marry me?"

'"You've known for months that I intended to marry Constance. The wedding wasn't brought forward to deceive you."

'"You expect me to believe that?"

'"It happens to be the truth."

'"I gave you till Sunday to be rid of her. Then I went to Bladeney House and was told by a *servant* that you had married her the previous afternoon."

'The simmering rage in her look was beginning to trouble me. I had expected contempt, not anger; threats, not recriminations. "I've explained as best I can that I love Constance and can never love you. What could possibly make you think I wanted to be rid of her?"

'"Honour. Honour among thieves, if you like."

'"What are you talking about?"

'"I'm talking about what you owed me – what you still owe me – for saving you from O'Shaughnessy."

'"Saving me? What do you mean?"

'"Why do you think he spared you? Why do you think he let you off the hook?"

'Amongst all the possible explanations that had occured to me for O'Shaughnessy's conduct, intervention by Madeleine had never featured – till now. Suddenly, I realized what I should have realized before: that if anybody could have brought about what had seemed so improbable, it was she. "Are you saying you're the reason he didn't identify me?"

'"Yes. When we met in the British Museum, you seemed convinced there was nothing to be done. Well, you were wrong."

426

'"How? How did you do it?"

'"I went to Holyhead and waited for him to arrive from Ireland. With the description you'd given me, it wasn't difficult to pick him out from the crowd. I travelled on the same train with him to London last Friday. During the journey, I made his acquaintance. He was surprised when I revealed that I knew the nature of his business in London. And even more surprised when I explained the compelling reason why he should say you were *not* Stephen Lennox."

'I did not understand. For all his Bohemian airs and epicurean ways, O'Shaughnessy was a man of honour and principle, to whom truth was the noblest of callings. Not even Madeleine's formidable wiles could have induced him to stray from it.

'"I thought you would realize that you had me to thank for what he did. I thought it would bring you to your senses and make you keep your promise to me."

'"How did you do it?" I gripped her arm and pulled her towards me. "How did you persuade him to lie?"

'She looked down at my hand clasping her arm, then back up into my face, ensuring by our proximity that I would recognize the meaning in her gaze when she said, in a measured undertone: "Take your hand off me."

'In San Francisco, that very first time, when she had given herself to me for what had seemed the most transparent of purposes, she had used those same words, married to the same look, to warn me of what about her was least transparent of all: her strange ability, not to command obedience, but to plant it within those who pursued her, so that, to them, it seemed not a voluntary act, but an instinctive reaction.

'I let go of her arm. Several seconds passed in silence, then she said: "You were right about O'Shaughnessy. He is a man of rare fidelity to the truth. Had you offered to marry me after all, I would have told you he'd succumbed to my usual charms, but I see now you would never have believed that."

'"Then, what did he succumb to?"

'"The only weapon I had left to use: the truth."

'"What do you mean?"

'"I told him the truth about you, Stephen. The whole truth – which you've never known. And, when he'd heard it, he agreed you should be left to live in peace as Sir James Davenall. As you would have done, if you'd married me. Instead, you chose to defy me. Well, you wouldn't expect me to share O'Shaughnessy's spirit of mercy, would you? Least of all when it's failed to bring me what I'd hoped for. Accordingly, I see no reason why you should be left in happy ignorance of who you really are."'

VII

Freddy had watched in a horror-struck trance the selection and loading of the guns. He could not understand why James and Hugo were both so unflustered in their handling of the weapons, so unhurried in their every movement. What he had hitherto refused to believe could ever happen was now, beyond question, about to occur. James and Hugo must have known that as well as he did. Why, then, were their preparations so calm and fluent, so damnably poised, whilst all he felt was churning anxiety and a paralysis of nerve? It was almost as if they were acting out a scene they had rehearsed together, staging for the benefit of others a charade whose end they already knew.

'Herr Cleveland,' snapped Major Bauer, 'is Herr Davenall ready to proceed?'

'What?' Freddy glanced at Hugo, who nodded curtly in confirmation. 'Well, yes. That is –'

'Good. Sir James tells me that he has accepted Herr Davenall's challenge to a duel *au signal*. You agree that is to be the method?'

'*Au* . . . what?'

'As Herr Davenall's second, I assume you are familiar with the procedure?'

'No, dammit, I'm not.'

Major Bauer tossed his head, sniffed and glared at Freddy. 'To avoid misunderstanding, Herr Cleveland, I will explain the rules to you. The duellists take up position twelve paces apart, cock their guns and hold them pointing to the ground. At the first signal, they commence walking towards each other. At the second, they raise their guns and take aim. At the third, they fire. The timing of the signals is, of course, at the discretion of the signaller.'

Freddy stared back at Bauer in stupefaction. He had clung till now to the thought that inexperienced marksmen separated by the length of a cricket pitch were unlikely to do each other serious harm. Now even this consolation had been snatched away from him. The meaning of Bauer's brutal sneering expression was clear: blood was certain to be shed.

In desperation, Freddy turned to Hugo. 'There must be some mistake here, old man. You can't have –'

'Major Bauer is quite right,' Hugo interrupted. 'That is how I wish the duel to be fought.'

'And I also,' added James.

'Were you not forewarned, Herr Cleveland?' Bauer sarcastically enquired.

'No,' Freddy replied, searching Hugo's face for some flicker of explanation but finding only a set impenetrable blankness. 'I damn well wasn't forewarned.'

VIII

'Madeleine's eyes never left mine as she spoke. "You have always been more gullible than me, Stephen," she said. "That's why you accepted Quinn's story at face value. And that's why I didn't – not for a moment. I could never believe, you see, that Sir Gervase would have paid Andrew Lennox to take you to America simply because you looked like James. After all, what would it have mattered to him if the relationship *had* become known – to his wife, say? You had no claim on him. And, from what we know, he did not much care what his wife thought of him. He made no attempt to buy Vivien Strang's silence. So why go to such lengths to buy Lennox's?

'"Amongst Dr Fiveash's records, I found a newspaper article about the duel which had led to Sir Gervase's banishment to Carntrassna in 1841. It was while he was there, living down the disgrace, that he fathered you. But why had he fought the duel in the first place? The article did not say. It occurred to me that the reason might explain his subsequent actions. So I traced the man Gervase had wounded in the duel: Harvey Thompson. At first, he didn't want to talk about it, but eventually I charmed him into telling me why they'd fought. Then everything became clear to me and I understood why Gervase should have wanted you out of the country – at whatever cost. Because you reminded him of something far worse than merely seducing another man's wife. You reminded him that he had seduced his own mother.

'"Thompson had caught them in bed together after a coronation ball in 1838. He'd never intended to let Gervase know that he'd seen them, but he blurted it out in the heat of an argument three years later. That's why Gervase challenged him and tried so hard to kill him: because Thompson had confronted him with evidence of something he wanted to pretend had never happened.

'"I went to Quinn and demanded that he tell me the truth. Seeing that I had learned too much to be deflected, he did so.

'"A beautiful young wife whose husband is too old to satisfy her is often driven to take a lover, of course, but Mary Davenall found herself drawn to a handsome and daring young man who happened to be her own son. Gervase escorted her to a country house weekend in Norfolk in June 1838, when he was twenty-one and she was not quite forty. He was jealous of her fortune-hunting suitors, she of his witless young admirers. Such an opportunity, under such intoxicating circumstances, had never occurred before. They succumbed to temptation.

'"Horrified by what had happened, Mary Davenall fled to Ireland, hoping to ensure by exiling herself there that there would be no repetition of the incident. No doubt Gervase hoped the same. Then came his foolish duel with Thompson and his father's decision – irony

429

of ironies – that he should live with his mother until the dust had settled.

'"Is it hard to imagine what inevitably followed? Thrown together in a remote part of Ireland with few distractions from their own company, how could they not remember what they had once been to each other? How could they not re-enact their crime?

'"When he left Ireland to return to England in the autumn of 1842, Gervase must have believed it was the final break. His mother would remain at Carntrassna, mortifying her soul for what she had let him do. He would rejoin his regiment, find some sweet young heiress to marry and bed sufficient whores and serving-girls to purge his memory of all recollections of incest. The only fact he had overlooked was that his mother was not past child-bearing age. He had left her pregnant, and you, Stephen, were the son she was carrying."'

IX

Freddy was still staring at Hugo, hoping in vain that he had somehow misunderstood his friend's intentions and quite oblivious to what Major Bauer was saying, when Sir James stepped between them, raised Freddy's right hand and slipped a coin into his palm.

'Do as the Major asks, Freddy, there's a good fellow.'

'What?'

'You have to toss for the right to signal.' James smiled in reassurance, as if, for all the world, Freddy, not he, were the one about to risk his life.

'Yes, Herr Cleveland,' Bauer put in. 'What are you waiting for?'

It was the strange, bizarrely solicitous expression on James's face that still dominated Freddy's attention as he looked at the coin in his hand. At last, with a sigh of resignation, he balanced it between thumb and forefinger, flipped it into the air and watched it climb above his head before falling towards the ground. A second before it hit the sand, Bauer called.

'Heads!'

Freddy stepped forward. Until now, he had not noticed that the coin was a gold Austrian schilling. But now the fact could hardly escape him. For it was the head of the Austrian Emperor which glinted up to greet his stooping gaze.

'Heads it is,' said Bauer from close behind. 'I win the toss.'

X

'Worse than it seemed possible for the worst to be, harsher than any truth yet told, surely this retribution, alone of them all, was undeserved. Yes, I was the first-born son of Sir Gervase Davenall. Yet I was also his brother, child and companion of the one sin his conscience would never let him forget. This was one revelation too many. Since hearing it, I have felt sickened by the very thought of it, sullied by the knowledge of it beyond any power of cleansing, revolted by what I find, after all, that I am.

'Every time I glimpse my face in a mirror, or hear my own voice, or see my hand reach out in front of me, I shudder and shrink away. Can you imagine what it is really like to be disgusted by what your own existence signifies? An abomination. An unspeakable sin. A horror in the eyes of God and man. It is all that and worse. And something else as well. It is what James must have felt when he took his own life. It is, irony of ironies, just what he suffered, too. Neither of us deserved what our father left us to remember him by. Yet we must either bear it or end it, as James chose to do.

'I hardly know how, or with what words, I left Madeleine at the aqueduct. I remember running, as James must have run that summer's day in 1871, north along the empty towpath. There was only one face I wanted to see now, only one confession I needed to hear. If nemesis had truly found me, then I was determined to lead it also to Alfred Quinn. For he had made me an accomplice in my own mother's murder.

'My mother. She who was also my grandmother, the remote forbidding mistress of Carntrassna House, whom I had spoken to perhaps a dozen times in my whole life. Now I knew why she had ensured I had a good education, why she had been willing to give Andrew Lennox whatever he demanded in return for raising me as his son. No doubt she harboured some maternal affection for me that even her shame could not erase. As for my real father, he must have been horrified to learn that I had ever been born. Simply by existing, I reminded him of what he most loathed about himself. Small wonder, then, that he was prepared to pay Lennox ten thousand pounds to remove me from his sight and his knowledge. It did not work, of course. What they tried so hard to destroy every record and memory of outlived them all – and survives in me.

'The proof of it is that, but for me, Harvey Thompson would be alive today. Madeleine had paid him well to tell nobody else why he and Gervase had fought their duel. But, when the hearing brought my name into the newspapers, he guessed what she had already guessed and tried to capitalize on it. The poor fellow can have had no idea what he was meddling in. When you told Madeleine that you were to

431

meet him, and why, his fate was sealed. She alerted Quinn whilst you were asleep, so that he could keep your appointment for you – and kill Thompson before he could tell anybody what he knew.

'What I tried to do was wrong through and through, but never as rotten and cankered as Quinn had forced it to become. Your incarceration was enough for my conscience to bear, but Quinn had added two murders to that, plus a host of lies which screamed in my ears for justice. Yet I was powerless to put right the wrongs I had set in train. My only excuse rang still with Madeleine's scorn. Gullible? Yes, I had been that. Greedy? Foolish? Vain? All of those, too. But I had not intended, not planned, not foreseen the smallest fraction of what Quinn had willed upon me.

'All thoughts of maintaining the pretence were gone in the wake of what I had learned, all hope of returning to Constance shattered. I had only one end left in view, only one intention to sustain me through the hideous eternity Madeleine had made of my every empty hour. I would have the truth from Alfred Quinn. And then I would make him pay for it.'

XI

Major Bauer had produced a tin whistle from his pocket and given a demonstration blast on it sufficient to rouse Freddy from his reverie and force him to attend to the Major's words.

'That, gentlemen, will be the signal. Let me remind you that there will be three such signals. At the first, you will commence walking towards each other, guns cocked but held pointing to the ground. At the second, you will raise your guns and take aim. At the third, you will fire. Should either of you pre-empt one of the signals, you will be required to stand your ground whilst the other has a free shot. Is that clearly understood?'

James and Hugo nodded in confirmation.

'Very well. You will kindly stand back to back and take twelve paces each, then turn to face one another. Herr Cleveland and I will then withdraw to the top of the dunes, where I will signal that the duel may commence.'

XII

'It was dark when I reached Newmarket, but I waited several hours before walking out to Maxton Grange. Quinn had told me the time of his regular evening patrol, and that, I knew, would be the best opportunity I would have to speak to him alone.

'I reached the stable-yard shortly before ten o'clock. Within a few minutes, Quinn appeared. He did not seem surprised to find me waiting for him. For once, indeed, he looked almost pleased to see me. Since establishing himself at Newmarket, he had acquired a proprietorial air and a cock-of-the-walk confidence which lent a superficial joviality to his manner. But the transformation had come too late to deceive me.

'"Sir James," he said, smiling and drawing on a cigar. "What a relief it is to know you're still a free man."

'"No thanks to you," I replied levelly.

'"How did you get away with it?"

'"O'Shaughnessy decided he didn't recognize me after all."

'"That was fortunate. Very fortunate."

'It was as I stepped towards him and entered the pool of light cast by the lamp above the stable-clock that he saw the expression on my face for the first time. Then his tone altered.

'"What brings you here, Sir James?"

'"The truth, Quinn. I will have it now, if you please."

'"The truth? What do you mean by that?"

'I told him then what I had learned from Madeleine. Though he went on smoking his cigar calmly enough as I spoke, leaning against the paddock rail as if my words meant nothing to him, I noticed his eyes narrowing in steely concentration. By the time I had finished, he must have realized I could no longer be deceived.

'"Hell hath no fury, eh?" he said. "I see you've found that out in the end. You should never have crossed her, you know."

'"Forget Madeleine. Just tell me whether what she told me was true."

'"As far as it goes, yes."

'"What do you mean – 'as far as it goes'?"

'"She doesn't know everything. She only thinks she does."

'"But you did murder Thompson?"

'"I killed him, yes. To protect our interests."

'"And my mother?"

'"Is that what you'd call her? Your 'mother'?"

'"What would you call her?"

'"I'd call her an obstacle . . . which I removed."

'"When you came to me in San Francisco, you said she was already dead."

'"I lied. I took you for the squeamish type and I reckon I judged you right. What difference does it make whether she died with or without a little assistance?"

'"The difference is that she was my mother."

'"That may matter to you, Sir James, but not to me."

'I restrained a rush of anger and continued talking in the steadiest tone I could manage. "You were planning this for years before you approached me, weren't you?"

'"Yes."

'"How could you be so confident I'd agree to play my part?"

'"It was an offer too good to refuse. Don't try to blame your own greed on me."

'"I might have been rich in my own right. I might have been happy and successful. Then I'd have wanted no part of it."

'"But you were none of those things, were you?"

'"How did you know I wasn't?"

'He chuckled. "Because Andrew Lennox's widow wrote to Sir Gervase from America two years before she died, hoping he would agree to help you. She told him all about the life you were leading, the kind of man you'd become. She even sent a recent photograph of you. It proved that your resemblance to James hadn't dimmed with the years. Of course, what she didn't know was that James was no longer on the scene."

'"And that's what planted the idea in your mind?"

'"Not exactly. Sir Gervase planted it in my mind. It was his idea. His last, mad, syphilitic scheme. He hated his wife for bearing a son by his cousin. And what he hated even more was the thought of that son succeeding him as baronet."

'Deceived in turn by every false conclusion, I saw him now for the first time. I was within reach of him at last, within a faltering grasp of his shrinking shoulder, and I no longer doubted what I would see when he turned to meet me. His face, rotted through, eaten away by the death he had brought upon himself and his son, sustained by nothing but the mocking grin Quinn had preserved for him: the life he had made for me was the lie he had borne laughing to the grave.

'"How did you think I came by all that information, Sir James? The dates, the times, the places, the people. The photographs, the letters, the proofs, the means. Who could have given me a copy of James Davenall's suicide note but the man he sent it to? Who could have equipped me to make you a replica of James Davenall but his own father?"

'Richard told me once of a dinner he had had at Bladeney House in the summer of 1878, when he had tried and failed to persuade Gervase to have James pronounced legally dead. Gervase's final reason for refusing had seemed to Richard incomprehensible. "My son lives," he had said. "And I will stand by him." Now I knew what his words had meant.

'"Sir Gervase knew he only had a few years left to him. He made me promise I would track you down after his death and inveigle you into impersonating James. Then he gave me all the evidence he could lay hands on and told me everything about his son that he could remember. At first, I went along with it just to humour him. After his collapse, I dismissed the idea from my mind. I even went so far as to sell some of the things he'd given me. That was the pretext his bitch of a wife used to have me dismissed. And that's when I started thinking. Why not do it after all? Why not see if the old man's scheme might not actually work?"

'It had worked. God knows, it had worked better than he could have imagined. I had supplanted Hugo. I had taken what would have been James's. I had dispossessed Gervase's hated wife. But victory had exacted a heavy price. There was blood on my hands and murder on my conscience.

'"To do the old man justice, I must tell you he didn't expect me to act while either he or his mother was still alive. I was happy to wait the short time he had left, but she was a different matter. On my last visit to him, in the nursing home, I told him she'd died and that nothing any longer stood in our way. He must have died a happy man, thinking of the havoc I'd make you wreak in his family."

'"You don't regret any of it, do you?" I said at last.

'"Why should I? It's made me a wealthy man. Sir Gervase's scheme has given me what his wife tried to deny me: a comfortable retirement."

'"But what about me, Quinn? What's it given me?"

'He reached out and ran his finger and thumb along the hem of my shoulder-cape. "It's given you a gentleman's coat to your back, Sir James." He slapped me on the chest. "It's put money in your wallet."

'"And for that you expect me to forget two murders?"

'"I don't care how you square your conscience, Sir James. That's your problem, not mine. It was you who insisted on knowing the truth, not me on telling you. I don't really know what you're complaining about. The death of a senile old woman and a decrepit old soldier? A small price to pay, I'd have thought, for title, wealth, property – and another man's wife."

'He was right, of course. I had benefited as much as he had, if not more, by Mary Davenall's death and, whilst I had never condoned her murder, I had been prepared to ignore it. But now it was different. Now she was my mother, who had done her poor best to ensure I did not suffer for the perversion of my birth. She was my mother, whose only reward for trying to protect me from the truth was to be murdered in my name so that a lie might flourish.

'"You should be grateful to me, Sir James. After all, where would you be without me?"

'Where indeed? Quinn, I did not doubt, had learned early – and never forgotten – that he who cares least survives longest. But therein lay his mistake. For, though I shared his crime, I did not share his ruthlessness. "What would you say, Quinn," I asked, "if I told you I wasn't going on with it?"

435

'At that, he snatched the cigar from his mouth and stared at me intently. "What do you mean – 'not going on with it'?"

'"I mean I'm throwing in my hand. Admitting that I'm an impostor. Making a clean breast of the whole damnable business."

'"You can't be serious."

'"Never more so."

'He laughed. "You're mad."

'"Yes. Perhaps I am. But I mean to do it." With that, I made to turn away, but he seized me by the shoulder with sufficient force to stop me in my tracks. When I looked back at him, the lamplight casting shadows across his face, I could not see his eyes clearly nor tell from the shape of his mouth whether he was smiling or in earnest, but still I guessed, before he said it, what his parting taunt would be.

'"Confess now, Sir James, and you're more likely to end up in a lunatic asylum, like Trenchard, than a prison cell; but, either way, I won't be there with you. What evidence there is to link us can be destroyed. And evidence that I murdered Thompson and the old woman just doesn't exist. So make a fool of yourself, or not, as you please. But don't think you can take me with you."

'Everything he had said was true, and this last was truest of all. By confessing, I could destroy myself and others besides, including the woman I had come to love, but Quinn would do what he had always done: survive. It was the sure and certain knowledge that he would escape whatever fate I willed upon myself that provoked me, as much as the pressure of his hand on my shoulder, as much as the sudden realization that, with the same hand, he had ended my mother's life. From some deep rebellion within me against the lie he had forced me to live came a surge of violent anger, so engulfing that what happened next is still only a hazy recollection – a glimpse, it seems, of the actions of another man. Perhaps, indeed, they were the actions of another. Perhaps it was James Davenall's strength, added to mine, that enabled me to overpower Quinn. Perhaps I was his vengeance for the telling of his secret.

'All I can say with certainty is what I felt in that instant. I wanted to rid my sight of Quinn's face, my ears of his words, my mind of the knowledge that he would survive me. I wanted him dead. And I had my way. The spasm of violence, the convulsive struggle as I held his head beneath the water, the spluttering and choking, the reaching, clutching, straining hands: they form now no ordered picture in my memory. But the silent seconds after – the body sagging in the trough, the pools of spilt water at my feet, the slowing percussion of drips from the rim, the yellow and black pattern that the lamplight made of what I had done – seem more real than wherever the present finds me. They recur whenever my mind's determination to resist them slackens. They spring forth if I merely close my eyes for an instant, to paint themselves upon the darkness.'

436

XIII

Freddy Cleveland was slumped at the top of the dune-bank, staring incredulously at the two figures who had measured out their paces and turned to face each other across a chain of Belgian sand. Only the meticulous, impassively observed formalities which had culminated in this moment could explain the transfixed immobility with which he awaited and thus condoned the final act. He knew he should either try to prevent it or at least deny them the sanction of his presence. But still he sat and watched, aware that Major Bauer, standing beside him, was about to raise the whistle to his lips.

Were those two slim, erect, implacable figures whose coats lay beside them on the sand really Sir James and Hugo Davenall? At this distance, in this strange, stark, unearthly border-zone between sea and land and sky, they could have been two strangers, two characters posed on an unfinished canvas, whose future an unseen hand was about to paint upon the mist that framed and rolled about them.

'Attention!' roared Major Bauer. At the word, the two figures cocked their guns and held them towards the ground.

Something was paining Freddy's right hand, something he had held too long in a grip whose ferocity he had not noticed till now. Opening his hand, he glanced down and saw that the object was the coin he had tossed earlier with Bauer. There was the Austrian Emperor's head to prove it. As his grip slackened, the coin fell away from the mound of his thumb and settled the other way up in his palm. And there still was the Austrian Emperor's head – embossed on the other side of the coin.

James had given it to him. And Bauer had called. And it was double-headed. And Bauer was to time the signals. The significance began to hammer at the doors of his brain. And then he understood. But, as he did so, there was a shrill blast on the whistle. And the two figures started walking.

XIV

'Quinn was dead. There was nothing to regret in that. But his death was as irrevocable for me as it was for him. It ensured that my stolen life as Sir James Davenall must end. As if to declare that it was so, I took from my pocket the cigarette-case Quinn had given me – the silver monogrammed case that had belonged to the real James Davenall – and pressed it into his lifeless hand before fleeing across the fields.

'I reached Newmarket station in time to catch the last train to London. During the journey, I measured the consequences of Quinn's death for those I loved and those I had wronged. It was not the charge of murdering him I feared, but what it would lead to. The winding entrails of our whole conspiracy would be dragged into view. Constance, whom I loved and whom I was sworn to protect, who had trusted me when others had called me a liar, who had loved me when she did not need to, would suffer more than I would and would go on suffering, long after my punishment was past. Wherever justice lay, it did not lie down that road.

'Then it came to me. I could not go on with the pretence, but neither could I rescind it. I could not continue as Sir James Davenall, but I could be remembered as such, for a dead man can neither lie nor tell the truth. Only that way could the justice I desired be served, for only that way could Constance's trust in me be saved.'

XV

'Give that whistle to me!' Freddy shouted, scrambling to his feet. 'God damn it, Bauer, you've played us false!'

The whistle was clenched firmly between Bauer's teeth, but still he managed a ghastly mocking smile before closing his lips around the mouthpiece and blowing the second signal. As Freddy lunged towards him, he feinted to one side, then thrust his right foot between Freddy's sand-logged stride and swung both arms hard against his shoulder. Freddy was sent toppling, sliding helplessly down the soft and sucking wall of the dune, swinging his head back as he went to glimpse the inverted image of two black-clad figures closing on the white expanse of beach.

There could only be a few yards between them, yet still the third signal had not come. They were homing on each other in the upside-down, double-headed, looking-glass convergence of a treachery he could not understand. No man could miss another at such range. No man, indeed, could fail to kill.

At the foot of the dune, Freddy rolled over and raised himself on all fours. The two figures had stopped walking. There was no space between them, no gap of yards or chance of error. He filled his lungs to shout some warning or protest, but it was too late. The third signal rang out – and was swallowed by the roar of a single gunshot.

XVI

'Hugo agreed readily to play the part I had prepared for him. He, too, knows the truth now, but he will never be able to tell it, because to do so will be to confess to a murder. He had to be told, because otherwise he would never have trusted me to do what I said I would. But never fear. The secret is safe with him.

'It seems strange to say it, but I am grateful to Hugo. Had he not challenged me to a duel in the first place, I would never have realized how well such an end would serve my purposes. Well, for what I owe him, he will have his reward. He will have back all that I took from him: the money, the title, the property, the name. He will be restored to his inheritance. And he will be welcome to it.

'Hugo means to bring Freddy with him as his second. Poor Freddy. He will be the only one of us ignorant of the true purpose of our meeting. To him, and the world when it is told, it will merely seem that the Davenall feud has claimed its final victim. And so it will have, in its way. We cannot know which of the two guns Gervase used in that other duel to seal the secret, more than forty years ago, but I hope, for what it is worth, that it is the one I carry. This time, you see, only one gun will be fired. And it will not be mine.'

XVII

Freddy was running across the beach. It was too late, far too late, but still he ran, the only moving figure on the whole frozen reach of tide-encroaching sand.

Hugo had dropped the gun. It lay at his feet, its barrel buried by the force of its fall. He was breathing hard, mouthing words he could not say aloud and staring down at the lifeless body of Sir James Davenall, whose right arm, stretched out in the moment of death, had cast his own weapon to where the swift and silent rim of the advancing sea had claimed now another yard of sand.

Freddy pulled up. He hardly dared to step closer. He should have known the bloody wreckage the shot of a duelling pistol at point-blank range would make of a man's face. But the reality was worse, far worse than his racing mind had guessed as he had run from the dune. Nor was even the sight of torn flesh and smashed bone the worst of all his realizations. For that he had to look not at the face of a dead man but at the face of one living.

Hugo said nothing. He did not need to. The furtive twitching of his lips, the anxious wiping of his hands, the guilt-shot darting of his eyes: they all proclaimed it loudly enough. Freddy had not watched a duel. He had witnessed a murder.

XVIII

'I have no doubt I shall be able to find someone desperate enough to act as my second – at a price. And I feel sure we can rely on Hugo. The only question that remains, therefore, is whether you, too, will agreed to stand by me, Trenchard.

'You have read the letter I mean to send to Richard. It will suffice, I think, to win you your liberty. And, whatever Richard suspects, neither he nor anyone else will feel able to disbelieve the last words of one about to die. Though some may continue to doubt my identity, they will not prevent me being buried as Sir James Davenall. Constance will never understand why I agreed to fight Hugo, but at least she will never have cause to doubt that she is Sir James Davenall's widow.

'I have come to you for her sake. At first, she may be too grief-stricken to face you but, as time passes, she will have need of your support. Who else can I ask to help her but the father of her child, the man who was once her husband – and may be once again?

'This is neither bravery nor madness. If I stay, I am a dead man and Constance is a ruined woman. If I flee, I only spare myself by making her suffer more. So what choice do I really have? This way, Hugo gets what he wants and so do I. This way, nobody will ever be able to prove that I was not James Davenall. It is a strange thought, is it not? The impersonation will be complete – in the living and the dying.'

As the ninth strike of the hour faded into silence, and with it his recollection of everything that Norton had told him, Trenchard stepped back from the window. He took a deep breath and passed one hand across his face. It would be over now, there could be no doubt of that. For Norton, the pretence would have ended at last. Whereas, for Trenchard, it was just about to begin.

XIX

Some spreading limb of the rising tide had slid in across the sand until, reaching the dead man who lay in its path, it spread the dark stain of his blood with bewildering speed into every bubbling pool and runnel of the shore.

With a groan of horror, Freddy started back from the red and rippling line of water, but Hugo seemed not to notice as it lapped accusingly at his feet. Then Major Bauer stepped between them, oblivious to the spectacle. Like some buzzard come down from his branch to pluck the carrion clean, he stooped over the body, reached into one of the waistcoat pockets, pulled out a tightly folded wad of bank-notes and turned back to Freddy, smiling grimly.

'What the . . .?' Freddy stammered. 'What the devil . . . are you doing?'

Bauer slipped the wad into his coat. 'My fee, Herr Cleveland, for services rendered.'

'Your . . . fee?'

'I have done all that he asked of me. We agreed the fee in advance.'

'Good God.'

'Accept my apologies for the double-headed schilling. Its use is normally limited to the casino. Keep it as a memento.' Then he tossed his head, sniffed and glared past Freddy towards the dunes. 'You must excuse me, gentlemen. I see that we have company, which I suspect I shall find uncongenial. You will forgive me if I leave *you* to explain what has happened.'

With that, Bauer strode off across the beach. Freddy watched him for only a few seconds before looking in the opposite direction. Two people, a man and a woman, had emerged from the track between the dunes and were hurrying towards them. Freddy recognized them at once, even in this place where he would least have expected to see them: Richard and Catherine Davenall.

'Do you know what he did, Freddy?' Hugo said suddenly. 'Do you know what he did, the instant before I pulled the trigger? He smiled. God curse him, he smiled.'

Freddy looked down at the body on the sand. The bloodstained water was rising around his stretched and lifeless limbs. Soon he would be afloat. If his smile had existed other than in Hugo's imagination, it was no longer visible. But the cause was, as Freddy could clearly see. The bullet had done more than kill Sir James Davenall. It had changed his features beyond recognition. No man could say now with certainty who he really was.

EPILOGUE

I

It was seven years, almost to the day, since William Trenchard had looked up from the croquet bench in his St John's Wood garden and caught his first glimpse of the man the world now remembered as Sir James Davenall; nearly six since a duel on the Belgian coast had ended, yet also preserved, the most daring imposture ever to deceive an English court of law. What posterity said of Sir James Davenall remained, for all this lapse of time, a fiction. But of that, as of much else, posterity was unaware.

It was five years since William Trenchard, restored to the family firm following his release from Ticehurst Asylum, had opened a newspaper one morning on the jolting top deck of an omnibus and read with dismay of the collision in a fog-bound London street which had claimed the life of Sir Hugo Davenall and extinguished for good and all a bitterly contested title. The subsequent inquest had returned a verdict of accidental death, though whether the jury would have opted for suicide had they known the odium and ostracism which had been Sir Hugo's reward for killing his brother in a duel is impossible to say. For of that, as of much else, the jury was unaware.

It was three years since the death of his father had made William Trenchard a wealthy man in his own right, able to abandon Trenchard & Leavis to his brother's keeping and fulfil an old pledge by seeking out Sir James Davenall's widow at the villa in Provence where she lived in secluded mourning. Ernest Trenchard, for one, had viewed William's determination to visit his former wife as the sheerest folly. But of William's real motives, as of much else, Ernest was unaware.

It was just over a year since Emily Sumner had been taken aback by the news that her sister had agreed to remarry her former husband and become Mrs William Trenchard once more. Constance's explanation

442

– that she did not wish Patience to grow up as the daughter of divorced parents – had seemed to Emily's mind scarcely adequate in the face of William's proven infidelity. But of the true nature of William's infidelity, as of much else, Emily was unaware.

It was six months since William and Constance Trenchard had been rejoined in matrimony, before a handful of guests, in a civil ceremony at Aix-en-Provence. Richard Davenall had served as William's best man, which might have seemed an odd choice in view of their previous differences. But of those differences, as of much else, there had been a healing of which all but they were unaware.

It was a fortnight since William and Constance Trenchard, having installed Patience at her new boarding school near Lucerne, had embarked on a leisurely tour of Switzerland which was the nearest they had come to a second honeymoon. What better way, they had thought, to lay to rest the sadnesses of seven years? What indeed? They could hardly be blamed for their error. For of the risk it exposed them to, if of nothing else, they were unaware.

It was only an hour since William Trenchard had left Constance resting in their hotel room in Lugano and taken a stroll along the lakeside into the town. There he had bought a drink at a quay-front café, lit his pipe and admired the view of the lake and its enfolding mountains, bathed in mellow late-afternoon light. It was the last day of September 1889, but there seemed no other endings than that to detect in the mild Swiss sanative air. Nor had William Trenchard cause to suspect that there might be any. Of the strange timings of fate he, like everyone else, was unaware. He did not know, nor could he, that seven years sufficed for the mischief of a moment to run its course. He did not know, but, in less than an hour, he would.

II

A tall bulky figure was standing with his back to me at a nearby confectionery-kiosk. Something in the way he carried himself, some haughty jerk of the head as he turned away with his purchase, struck me as familiar and made me watch as he ambled to a lakeside bench, subsided into it and began unwrapping his chocolate.

It was many years later, in circumstances he should have foreseen, that William Trenchard completed a written account of the events which reached their quietus that seemingly unportentous Sunday afternoon in Lugano. His reason for writing such an account was as understandable as its effect is appropriate, for it ensures that to him belongs that which once seemed so conclusively to have been denied him: the last word.

For several minutes, I went on watching him, waiting to be certain that he was who I thought. Seven years older, certainly, but outwardly not much altered: a large fleshy figure clad in cream linen, breaking off squares of chocolate and swallowing them greedily whilst squinting out across the lake from beneath the brim of a straw hat. Sunlight glinted at me from a signet ring on his left hand and flashed on his watch-chain as he reached down to check the time. His lower lip protruded in a significant gesture when he saw what it was, and then I was certain. He was Prince Napoleon Bonaparte.

I doubt he would have recognized me without being prompted, and I wish now I had refrained from jogging his memory. But there seemed no good reason to let the chance pass. Neither of us had profited by the circumstances of our last meeting: a little commiseration seemed suddenly in order. I finished my drink, rose from the table and walked across to him.

'Good afternoon, Prince. Do you remember me?'

He looked up with a petulant frown. His eyes narrowed. Then he smiled faintly, though whether in greeting or in recognition of a pleasing irony I could not tell. 'William Trenchard. Quelle coïncidence.'

'May I join you?'

'By all means.'

I sat down beside him. 'It's been a long time. We've not met since —'

'Spare us both the recollection, mon ami. What brings you to Lugano?'

'Mere pleasure. And you?'

'The same . . . you might say.'

'You're staying here?'

'I have a friend who owns a villa on the other side of the lake. I expect to be collected in my friend's launch . . . ' He peered into the distance. 'Very shortly.'

'It's a beautiful place.'

'Do you think so?' He looked at me in brief but piercing scrutiny. 'When you live in this country because your own will not have you, mon ami, its charms fade rapidly.'

'Even so —'

'Even so, there are compensations?' He nodded. 'Yes, it is true. There are.' Once more, he stared out across the lake. This time, his eyes seemed to find what they sought: the wake of a small steam-launch, approaching diagonally from the opposite shore. At sight of it, his mouth set in some crooked amalgam of a frown and a smile, as if he were uncertain whether to be pleased or disappointed.

'Your friend?' I asked, gesturing with my eyebrows towards the distant craft.

'Yes.' Abruptly, he rose from the bench, filled his lungs with air and smiled down at me. 'Will you walk with me to the landing-stage, Trenchard? It is not far.'

I agreed and we started southwards down the long avenue of lime trees which followed the shore of the lake. The Prince kept glancing to his left as we went, checking, I assumed, the progress of the launch, whose engine I could hear growing steadily closer.

'Tell me,' he said, after we had covered several yards in silence, 'do you ever hear news of Catherine Davenall?'

'Never. As far as I know, she still lives at Cleave Court, but as privately as ever.'

'No doubt she took Hugo's death badly.'

'No doubt she did.'

'The newspapers implied it was suicide.'

'Did they? I understood from reports of the inquest that he strayed into the cab's path because of thick fog.'

'Do you believe that?'

'I've an open mind on the subject.'

'Vraiment? Come, come, mon ami. The irony cannot have escaped you. All that you and I and others suffered on account of the Davenall baronetcy was for nothing.' He snapped his fingers. 'The title is extinct. And both its claimants are dead. By the same means, I suspect.'

Suddenly, I felt uneasy, not because of what he was implying, but because of what he must know in order to imply it. 'What do you mean by that, Prince?'

'Of their own volition, Trenchard, isn't that how it was? Sir James, in a so-called duel. Sir Hugo, in a so-called accident.'

'There's no evidence –'

'I require no evidence!' He pulled up sharply. By the time I had done the same and turned to face him, I found that he was staring at me with an expression of seemingly genuine sympathy. 'I read that you remarried your wife,' he said, smiling slowly.

'Yes. I did.' But our wedding had received virtually no publicity. How could he have read of it?

'She is here with you?'

'Yes.'

'Then, take my advice.' He touched me on the shoulder. 'Leave Lugano.'

'Why?'

'Because, Trenchard, if you and I share anything, it is . . . irresolution. That is why, for your own sake, and for you wife's, you should leave this place.'

'I don't understand. What are you trying to say?'

His smile became lop-sided, his gaze less intense. 'No matter,' he said after a moment. Then, glancing over his shoulder: 'I must go. My friend

445

is waiting.' It was true; I had not noticed. The gap between the next set of trees in the avenue gave access to a landing-stage, at the foot of which the launch we had seen earlier was tied up, its gangplank extended to receive its guest. 'Farewell, Trenchard,' the Prince said. 'And good luck.'

'You think I'll need it?'

'We all do, mon ami. Luck is all.'

With that, he turned on his heel and strode down the sloping landing-stage towards the launch. A crewman helped him aboard, then made ready to depart. I watched the Prince move to the stern of the vessel as it eased away from the jetty, exchange a word with somebody obscured from me by the angle of the wheel-house, then go below.

As the launch manoeuvred out into the lake, it swung round parallel to the shore, and so it was, standing at the edge of the lime avenue puzzling over what the Prince had said to me, that I saw the person he had spoken to: a woman, dressed in black, her dark hair blowing free of her shoulders in the gathering breeze. I knew at once that she was his friend from the other side of the lake, because she was also the woman I had dreamed of seeing a hundred times, but never had, since a single night in St John's Wood seven years before. She was Madeleine Devereux.

The launch was gaining speed, froth churning in its wake. The gap between us was only a few yards, but soon it would be more. Soon, she would be out of sight. For that instant, but for no longer, she would look at me and I at her. Then, I knew, she would be gone.

She was unaltered: the pale, hauntingly beautiful face; the dark searching eyes; the imperious tilt of her chin; the hard but perfect line of her mouth. She recognized me, but her recognition betrayed neither malice nor mercy. We both knew what she had done to me – and to one other, who was six years dead – but the knowledge inspired neither forgiveness nor defiance. What had drawn us together, now and for ever, would hold us apart.

Yet still I went on watching her. Till her face was no more than a pale speck on the black receding shape of the launch, I watched, and hoped to see what I knew I never would: some hint that she regretted the part she had played in the past. But there was none. Then, and always, there was none.